HAMMER
OF
GOD

HAMMER OF GOD

The Dark Ages Saga of Tristan de Saint-Germain

BOOK TWO

Robert E. Hirsch

OPEN ROAD
INTEGRATED MEDIA
NEW YORK

ISBN: 978-1-5040-7922-8

This edition published in 2023 by Open Road Integrated Media, Inc.
180 Maiden Lane
New York, NY 10038
www.openroadmedia.com

This book is dedicated to my beloved paternal grandparents, Tressie and Leo Hirsch of Medford, Wisconsin. Despite having never set eyes on me other than in pictures, despite their humble status as county dairy farmers, and despite impossible governmental red tape exacerbated by war, they struggled tirelessly to see that I was able to escape war-torn Korea in 1953 and establish a new future in America. This they accomplished only through unwavering perseverance, their own innate, deeply engrained goodness, their inviolable love of family, and the generous assistance of United States Representative from Wisconsin, Alvin Edward O'Konski (1904–1987).

HAMMER
OF
GOD

CHAPTER ONE

ASSASSINATION IN THE YEAR 1085

It is often said that man drives his own destiny and is the master of his fate. In truth, and despite the grandiose, hope-driven rhetoric of civilization's greatest poets and orators, there is no such possibility. Each of us, without exception, is caught in the raging currents of forces that far outweigh our feeble capacity to fight the sweeping tides of time and circumstance. That we may be able for a brief moment to steer our own destiny merely encourages self-deception, and self-deception leads into an even more perilous backwash than simple fate alone. Best, then, to place our faith in God rather than in ourselves.

The graveyards of history are filled with those who have ignored this simple principle. Indeed, as certain men through calculation and intrigue have managed to manipulate the theatrical stage of their own ambitions, they have lost consciousness of the grand drama, which encompasses the entire world. Nevertheless, every generation spawns a handful of self-appointed visionaries who attempt to drive the compass. When these miscreants encounter other miscreants of the same thread, but of opposing visions, they manage to unleash an apocalyptic maelstrom that washes over the innocents and the landscape, leaving a wake of destruction that lingers for millennia. There is no better example, perhaps, than what occurred in Europe during the end of the Eleventh Century.

As the Year of our Lord 1085 dawned on the continent of Europe, the city of Rome had been captured by the Germans under the military hammer of King Heinrich IV of Germany who had two times been excommunicated by his Holiness, Pope Gregory VII. King Heinrich had for years been conducting a bloody war against Pope Gregory, having declared him dethroned as Pope on two different occasions while accusing him of being a False Monk. After three attempts King Heinrich finally defeated Pope Gregory by capturing Rome in the year 1084 and proclaiming his Archbishop, Guibert of Ravenna, as the new Pope under the title of Clement III. Immediately following this maneuver, Heinrich then arranged to have Clement III consecrate and crown him Holy Roman Emperor. This forced the elderly Pope Gregory VII into exile in Lower Italy under the protection of the Normans where he shortly thereafter died a bitter and broken man on May 25th of 1085. Lying in death's grip, with his final breath, he uttered, "I have loved righteousness and hated iniquity; therefore, I die in exile."

Italian adherents of Pope Gregory VII, as well as Catholics in Spain, France, and England, refused to recognize Emperor Heinrich's installation of Archbishop

Guibert of Ravenna as Pope Clement III, and referred to Heinrich's pope as the anti-pope. So it was on the night of September 20th in the year 1085 that young Brother Tristan de Saint-Germain met with his superior, Brother Dieter Muehler, within the secret underground tunnels of Monte Cassino Monastery, a Benedictine stronghold in Lower Italy.

"I congratulate you on your recent ordination into the Benedictine Order, Tristan," Brother Muehler rasped, fighting the damage done unmercifully to his throat and larynx by a heartless jailer during a previous imprisonment in England. "We are in the midst of dark days for the true Church since the death of our Holy Father Gregory four months past. We are a rudderless ship without a Pope. The College of Cardinals, the Normans of Lower Italy, and Countess Mathilda of Tuscany all plead with Cardinal Desiderius of this very monastery to accept the Pope's tiara as requested by our deceased Gregory. Thus far, Desiderius continues to decline the position." He paused then and his voice dropped low, as in prayer. "If we don't acquire a leader soon, the true Church will dissolve, I fear."

Tristan nodded, staring hard across the table at Brother Muehler through the meager light afforded by the candle sitting between them, its flame a-flitter in a weak dance throwing odd, distorted shadows across the wall of the dank underground space. "This mission to Rome, Brother Muehler," he said, "I am a bit apprehensive." Tristan tried hard to make out Muehler's face saying this, knowing well that his superior would be displeased, but Muehler's monk's cowl obscured his features, and this obscurity was compounded by the veil he wore that covered all but his eyes to conceal the hideous burn scars and pock marks that disfigured his entire face.

"Apprehensive?" said Muehler, his eyes gazing inward. "You've been here in training with our best Papal agents for months. They claim that you'll be one of the best to ever come out of Monte Cassino. Realize, lad, there is a price to pay at times for doing God's labor. Is it the fear of being caught that has you slinking backwards?"

Tristan shook his head. "No, not that, Brother."

"Well, what is it then?" Muehler insisted, impatience seeping into his tone.

"It's the possibility of violence. I have never in my life injured anyone, except one time when I struck a boy at Cluny while a student there. I mean, they tell me that at times we must even *kill* the adversary."

"Ah, *that*. I *s-see* . . ." sighed Muehler, his voice growing serpentine. "Perhaps then you would rather die than dispatch the life of another, eh?" Then he leaned into the candlelight and raised a hand, tearing the veil from his face. "Or perhaps it's just that you fear ending up like *this*!" he hissed, pointing a trembling finger at his face.

Tristan recoiled with repugnance as a chill washed up the run of his spine and culminated in a gasp as Muehler appeared subhuman, like some dark and ungodly creature crawled up from some black chasm beneath the earth's crust, having smoldered for eons in the very fires of Hell itself. "No, not even that!" Tristan objected, wincing. "It's just that I don't wish to harm others. I became a Black Monk to raise others up, not to place them in their graves."

Muehler's smoldering eyes focused bitterly on the handsome young monk across the table, wanting to hate his fine features, his startling grey eyes. Then he closed his eyes for a length of time and slumped as he slowly placed his palm to his forehead, as though something had viciously cut him open there, carving out bitter memories. The grizzly details of his encounter with the unforgiving jailer in England had subsided little, and due to its lingering horror, a shadow of disquiet now ruled Muehler's existence. Finally he sat erect, and when his eyes opened again, they had returned to a cold, expressionless state. "I've seen the bloody work of the Church's enemies," he said, "and that ugly sight moves me forward. All I need do is look at my own face each morning, or visit the Benedictine graveyards, and each night as I struggle to find sleep, I lay awake wondering what evil they are hatching." Then his brows drew together and he nodded. "When I first became a monk I hoped to be doing good labors on behalf of the poor and infirm, but have since learned we live in a world of scaffolds and executioners. I've left a young man's innocence behind me many years passed and found that cold deliberation and craftiness are the only effective instruments for dealing with the ugliness of this world . . . and at times that includes murder. You are young yet, a word of caution; the Benedictine underground does not tolerate hesitancy. Then, too, it was *you* who came to us claiming you wished to follow my path and that of Brother Handel rather than remain cloistered behind monastery walls. You didn't want to spend your life on your knees praying the Book of Hours or sitting day after day in the scriptorium copying manuscripts. We took you in, and our fraternity is the most difficult of all to enter within the Benedictine order. If you balk at taking this mission, then I'll write Cardinal Odo de Lagery and it'll be back to the Cluny monastery with the other Black Monks."

This response was severe, and cut with the precision of a razor. Furthermore, Tristan knew Muehler meant what he had just said; his grave eyes betrayed no emotion. Swallowing hard, Tristan placed both palms on the table, then clasping his fingers, he exhaled heavily. "Brother Muehler, did you never hesitate at the beginning of your underground career? I mean, after learning the truth of what this particular vocation entails?"

At this, Muehler issued a slow rasp and sat back, slipping his veil back into place. "That was a long time ago. I don't remember. It may have been that way." With the raised eyebrows of the fiercely virtuous, he said, "The Church is deteriorating now, slipping into the morass, perhaps never to rise. The anti-pope Clement holds the Vatican and we must get it back. So what is the price, lad, to save Mother Church and regain Rome? A little blood? Do we simply bow to the enemy because they are violent? Do we remain on our knees while they slaughter our ranks? Do we surrender our cause because they lack conscience? There is only one way to fight a bear, and that . . ."

"And that is with a bear," interrupted Tristan, completing Muehler's thought.

"Indeed, in the wise words of Cardinal Odo de Lagery," Muehler said, a near smile lighting his dark sockets, "there is only one way to fight a bear, and that is with a bear!"

"Very well, Brother Muehler," Tristan sighed. "I will do as the Lord directs."

That next morning before sunrise Tristan busied himself within his quarters packing his saddlebags. Standing thoughtfully beside his bed within the meager circle of light afforded by a horn lantern, he unfolded a small kerchief of Ypres linen and examined the small ring tucked there for safekeeping. It held little monetary value, being made of low-grade Moorish silver, but it was the only remaining remnant of Tristan's childhood, so he treasured it above any other possession he owned. It was given to him at age seven by a Romani girl named Mala who was only ten, and on its tiny flat surface was engraved a crescent moon with a star sitting within its arc. He rolled it about between his fingers, thinking back to the night she had given it to him beside a campfire along the Seine. Then, finally, he folded the ring within the linen with ceremonial reverence and tucked it into his pocket. It would be going to Rome with him. Since receiving it from the Romani girl, it had never left his immediate possession.

An hour later Tristan was leaving the safety of Monte Cassino Monastery and guiding his mount north toward Rome, dressed as a young aristocrat in the casual, fine style of a young Norman noblemen from Lower Italy. His thick blond curls and striking grey eyes fit the role perfectly as his appearance was characteristic of the Normans who had come south from France to conquer Sicily and Lower Italy decades earlier. The Normans were originally Danish Vikings who had first conquered England, then frightened the French King, Charles the Simple, into ceding them Normandy along the western coast of France as a bribe to keep other Vikings from attacking France.

Tristan wore his hair in the Norman style, cut somewhat short and shaved on the sides.

Due to his clandestine designation and secretive duties for the Benedictines, he was one of those rare Black Monks not required to wear the traditional tonsure of monks where the crown was shaved except for a strip of hair around the head, which was a monk's declaration of abandoning worldly fashion and esteem.

Reaching Rome, he reported to a designated location along the Tiber River and met there a certain Brother Domingo as instructed. Domingo had taken up residence in Rome four years earlier and now possessed a small, elegant villa along the river. To Tristan's surprise, despite the Benedictine reform movement that espoused chastity and prohibited concubinage and marriage of clergy, he quickly discovered that Brother Domingo kept three women within his villa, all of whom apparently bestowed sexual favors on him in exchange for shelter, provisioning, and spiritual guidance.

"Aha, what a fine, strutting peacock you are!" said Domingo, a man in his middle forties. "So a bit of good news to welcome you to Rome, young man.

You'll be pleased to know that I share the flesh of these buxom beauties with my guests. Then, too, they have an appetite for young roosters like you!"

Looking about the villa and observing these women who moved about in various states of dress and undress, Tristan nodded saying, "I appreciate your generosity, Brother, I sleep alone."

"Eh?" said Domingo, his joviality dissolving as he fired a sharp glance at his young guest. *You think you're better than me*, the glance said. Then he stepped back and pointed a finger at Tristan. "Be warned then, lad, I neither tolerate nor appreciate *preaching* about sins of the flesh from those who enter my doors. When I became a monk years ago, concubinage was acceptable . . . though I'm Benedictine, I don't swallow all this reform that's been shoved down our gullets this past decade!"

An awkward silence then fell between them then until finally Tristan offered a humble reply. "Yes, certainly, Brother Domingo, I understand."

Domingo and Tristan then got to the business at hand and began discussing the Benedictine situation in Rome. "The anti-pope's agents have recently uncovered three of our men and separated them from their heads," said Domingo. "A rash of treachery, we think, brought on by one person in particular who works directly for that bastard Archbishop of Heinrich's."

"You mean Pope Clement?"

Domingo looked at Tristan and his eyes drew down to slits. "Never call that damned pretender a pope in my presence! If ever there was a false monk, it's Guibert of Ravenna, lapdog of Germany's thieving king. Oh, he may parade about the avenues of Rome in his papal garb and fake the celebration of mass within the Basilica of Saint Peter, but he's an imposter and will burn in Hell upon leaving this woeful world!"

Tristan shrugged with apology, having had no intention whatsoever of inflaming Brother Domingo. He understood well the Benedictine bitterness directed against the Germans.

"So," he said, "I was told that Brother Jurgen Handel is overseeing our work here in Rome. Am I to meet with him at some point?"

"No, probably not. He's working in concealment with a Brother LeDoux of Dijon, France. They're posing as Carthusian monks."

"Oh?"

"Yes, the climate's too unfriendly for us Benedictines. Besides, our black robes attract too much notice from the German crowd. Now, as for you, your task is quite simple. Since you're new to the game and this is your first outing, you'll only be doing surveillance, nothing extraordinary. Handel's not positive yet. He believes he may have sniffed out who's responsible for uncovering our agents. He and Brother LeDoux will carry out the assassination of this person. We need you to keep an eye on two ancillary characters we've been watching in case Handel's hunch is wrong."

"Assassination?" said Tristan.

"Ay. This enemy spy Handel's after has already undone three of our agents, all good monks of Christ from Monte Cassino. We're hemorrhaging here in Rome, lad. If we don't put an end to this individual, who knows who'll be next? Shit, maybe even me! Anyway, don't worry, you'll just be working the Byzantine piers, that's all . . . keeping an eye to two dockmen that wear identical blue striped stocking caps. We thought these caps were regular Byzantine shipmen's gear at first, although last month we learned that these particular caps are only worn by Byzantine agents so they can identify each other coming in and out of port. Anyway, you won't be able to miss these two fellows . . . they're the biggest hulks on the Byzantine Pier."

"That's comforting," said Tristan, masking sudden concern. "So what exactly am I watching for?"

"Well, this agent Handel's after might be Byzantine. As you know, Emperor Heinrich of Germany has recently allied himself with Emperor Alexius of the Byzantine Eastern Christians. So now Germans and Byzantine spies are cooperating in an effort to root the Benedictine underground out of Rome, knowing that we intend to retake it as soon as we elect our new Pope." Then he gave Tristan an unexpected look of empathy. "Yeah, I remember well my first trip out. Was jumpy as a damn snared rabbit. So really, how're you doing, lad?"

"Fine, Brother," Tristan lied.

"Well," Domingo chuckled, dismissing Tristan's placid countenance. "A man's first assignment can be like a man's first diddle, good, but a little worrisome." Then a smile slipped onto the corner of his mouth and he winked. "Sure you don't want a woman tonight? You know, to settle your nerves a bit before morning? Nothing more settling than plying the ripe thighs of a young Roman wench, you know."

"No, my nerves are fine," Tristan replied. Then he stood, crossing himself, and went to his bed.

That next morning Tristan donned a different outfit of the southern style, then sought Domingo, but could not find him anywhere. Finally, peering into Domingo's sleeping chamber, he spied Domingo's women lying about naked upon three different bedding palettes. Two quickly smiled while the third stood and came to Tristan's side, beckoning him with the pull of a finger toward her palette. "I'm looking for Domingo," Tristan offered weakly, setting the woman's hand aside. Then he bolted from the room, appalled that a Benedictine monk such as Domingo could live so awash in sin yet claim to be God's servant.

Within the hour he came to the piers and soon identified the Byzantine section. And just as he had been told, he identified two burly dockmen standing on one of the piers wearing the very caps described by Domingo. Keeping an eye to them all morning, Tristan moved back and forth from the pier several times pretending to inspect goods coming off the various vessels and striking up meaningless conversations with various individuals moving to and from the docks. By noon, Tristan took up a seated position away from the Byzantine zone, still within eyesight of it. The two men in question gave no appearance what-so-ever of covert activity and seemed to be, in actuality, going about legitimate chores. So, as dusk arrived and he had seen nothing of interest, he stood and turned to return to Domingo's villa.

At that very moment, he heard a loud commotion arise a short distance off that appeared to be moving in his direction through the approaching darkness. Then a man broke from the gathering crowd, staggering about, followed by several other individuals who appeared to be trying to assist him in one way or another. The man was pushing them away, moving desperately forward and away from them with great effort. His eyes widened seeing Tristan and he raised a weak arm as though gesturing to him.

And that was when Tristan saw the blood. The entire front of the man's tunic was dripping with rivers of blood emanating from an especially dark stain on his abdomen. The man had been stabbed and was gasping for breath, and motioned once more to Tristan before collapsing facedown onto the pavers. In that single instant, just as he was falling, Tristan recognized the victim and saw his mouth purse open. "Tristan!" the man cried.

It was Domingo.

CHAPTER TWO

INN OF THE SPARROW

Jolted into action, Tristan ran to him and quickly turned him over, scooping his shoulders into his arms. "Domingo!" he cried. "What hap...?"

"G-get to Handel!" Domingo gasped, his eyes rolling about in their sockets like eggs cast into a bowl. He clutched at his abdomen with blood-crusted fingers and wheezed, desperate to breathe. "L-LeDoux was supposed to help him assassinate the Byzantine, but LeDoux's been killed in the Square! Th-they caught us together!"

"The Byzantine?" cried Tristan, knowing that Domingo's time was short.

"Y-yes, Handel's confirmed that the spy we're hunting is a . . . Byzantine from Contantino . . ."

At this Domingo's eyes bugged and his mouth gaped open, then closed. His palms turned up, fingers slack, and his face grew bloodless and vacant. Then his face slipped sideways and Tristan felt Domingo's torso shudder three times as his throat issued the slow rattle of death.

And at that moment, just as he looked up to utter a prayer, he saw the two Byzantine dockmen approaching from the piers. They had spotted Domingo staggering toward the docks, and Tristan could tell from the damnation in their eyes and their accelerated pace that they were coming for him. They had by now surmised that he was connected to Domingo.

Rising, Tristan fled down the avenue, shoving his way through the evening throngs on their way home from their workplaces. He could hear the two men giving chase behind him, yelling at him to stop, exhorting others to block his path. "Thief!" they shouted. "Stop him, he's a pickpocket!"

After twisting his way around four or five corners, Tristan ducked into a vendor's booth and quickly slithered beneath a huge mound of picking baskets, quickly dragging several over his frame to cover himself. Moments later the two dockmen then appeared just paces from where he lay prostrate and motionless, barely daring to breathe. The two men stood there a while, peering here and there into the darkness and exchanging suppositions; all of this within three or four seconds. Then Tristan felt one of the men kick at the pile of baskets. At this Tristan sagged, dispirited, certain that he was about to be discovered. He then braced himself, certain also that once these men got their hands around him, they would kill him. Wincing, Tristan thought back on Domingo's bloody end, and determined that a life of prayer cloistered behind monastery walls might have, indeed, been a wiser choice of vocations than spying on the enemies of the true Church. He heard the shuffle of feet and the dissipation of footsteps; the men had left.

He waited a full minute or so more, then shoved the baskets aside. Remembering Domingo's last words, he moved briskly toward Saint Peter's Basilica, which was not far away from the piers, to seek the Inn of the Sparrow. Moments later he located it, two blocks west of the Basilica of Saint Peter just as Domingo had instructed. Pausing to scan the streets to ensure that he was not being followed or watched, Tristan then entered the inn.

Despite a good number of candles and several crude horn lanterns hanging from the rafters, the interior of the inn was dim and shadowy. The crowd within was sparse and comprised of a handful of guests sitting about engaged in conversation and spirits. In the far corner sat a solitary monk, his form stooped, his face obscured by his cowl. Through the dim light Tristan could ascertain that the monk's habit was made of the white serge characteristic of the Carthusian Order of France. The monk's scapular, worn over the shoulders of the Carthusian robe, was joined by bands at the side and had the hood attached to it, unlike the black robe of the Benedictines whose habits were of single fabrication. Tristan took a seat at the monk's table, his back to the door, and strained to see his face. "Handel?" he whispered. "Is that you?"

No reply.

"Handel? It's Tristan. I'm here in place of LeDoux."

Recognizing Tristan's voice, the monk nodded without raising his head. "Tristan?" he whispered. "What are you doing here? Where the hell's LeDoux?"

"Dead. Stabbed in the square just a short while ago. Domingo's been killed, too, but he managed to get to me in time to warn you. You may be in danger. We best leave quickly!"

The cowl of Handel's white robe slowly shook *no*. "Not a chance," Handel hissed. "I'm waiting on the Byzantine. No damned wonder we've had such a foul time uncovering this agent, the Byzantine is . . ."

At that very moment the door to the inn creaked open and two people walked in: a nun dressed in Eastern Orthodox garb followed by a tall, imposing nobleman who carried both sword and dagger attached to his belt and wore the Byzantine fashion. The two did not appear to be together.

"*That's* the target LeDoux and I've been trying to root out these last months," whispered Handel, motioning toward the door.

The nun passed through the room in silence, head bowed, then moved immediately up the stairs. Tristan and Handel followed the sound of her light footfalls, then heard a door creak open and closed as a lock fell into place and she secured herself for the night. As Handel slowly raised his head and appeared as though he was about to make a move, the large nobleman gestured to two men sitting together at the next table and sat down with them.

After only a comment or two, he stood, then himself moved toward the stairs. Tristan and Handel listened to his heavy footsteps tramp down the upper hallway, then heard the groan of rusty hinges opening, then closing.

"Quickly, up the stairs!" said Handel.

Tristan complied, wondering about the sizable man who had just mounted the stairs. He had learned at Monte Cassino that anyone, even an over-sized opponent, could be overcome by using the element of surprise. Failure to be swift and accurate with such a stout target could be fatal. Consequently, as he followed Handel up the stairs, Tristan's nerve began to dissolve a bit and his stomach began to knot. By coming to the Inn of the Sparrow to warn Handel of the murder of LeDoux and Domingo, Tristan had hoped that Handel would realize the danger and abandon this effort. Proceeding down the hall, Tristan realized that he had actually thrown himself into the position of participating in Handel's assassination of the enemy spy. His hands tremoring, Tristan reached down and patted the dagger tucked in his boot, even though he had no intention whatsoever of using it. No, he would leave the bladework to Handel, who was practiced in this craft and also did not struggle with breaking God's commandment about killing others.

"Fourth door to the left," Handel whispered, pulling a dagger from his billowing Carthusian sleeve. "When I kick in the door, move quick or we're *done for*. Go high for the arms and cover the face, I'll go for the belly straightaway and take care of the rest." When they slipped up to the fourth door, Handel put his finger to his lips, then stepped back and raised his foot to kick the door. "Ready, lad?" he whispered.

Tristan nodded though his heart was full of dread. Then, too, his head was pounding with his blood running so fast and thick that he could feel his temple arteries pulsing. Before he could blink, Handel kicked in the door and rushed the room. Tristan followed; a hammer blow to the head could not have unsettled him more than what he encountered. Standing there within the room was the nun who had entered the inn just minutes before. She was facing the door and had already removed her wimple from her head, chin, and neck. Furthermore, she was disrobing, and at the moment of their forced entry, had just dropped the top of her habit to her waist and was standing there bare-breasted, her eyes agape, staring at the intruders who had burst into her room.

Awkwardly, Tristan halted mid-step, seized by one of those moments of utter confusion that forces one into both mental and physical paralysis. He then muttered something foolish in an attempt to excuse himself and Handel for breaking into the wrong room. Not hesitating, Handel continued his blind charge forward, tackling her about the waist and throwing her back onto the small bed just behind where she stood. This further unhinged Tristan; the scene before his eyes unraveling so quickly that he had no time to deliberate. So he stood there mute and frozen.

As the nun reeled backward onto the bed, furiously thrust there by the full weight of Handel's charge, she reached below her bare abdomen down into the bottom of her habit and withdrew a dagger. Looking up at that same moment,

Handel saw the blade coming at him but was unable to stop its swift arc over his shoulder and into his upper back. "Aiee!" he cried.

Tristan was already backing his way out of the room. He had been expecting the large Byzantine man who had strode into the inn, not a half-naked nun. Furthermore, the sight of Handel's continued assault despite this error was more than Tristan could reasonably process, and already had him so confounded that he doubted whether what he was seeing was actually real.

"Tristan!" Handel bellowed as the woman stuck him between the shoulder blades a second time.

Hearing Handel's scream and fathoming that the nun was stabbing him, reality finally registered in Tristan's brain and he gathered his senses. Charging forward, he propelled himself onto Handel's back, which drove Handel down hard onto the nun, knocking his forehead into hers. Tristan then scrambled to secure her flailing arm, pinning it and the knife to the bed. "I've got her!" he cried.

"Kill her, dammit!" Handel howled, stuck between Tristan and the nun, blood now seeping profusely through the white serge of his Carthusian robe.

The nun was struggling with such ferocity against Tristan's grip that he was afraid to let go of her arm lest she stab Handel yet again, or himself.

"Goddammit!" Handel swore. "Your dagger, you fool!"

Tristan forced her knife arm down with one hand and fumbled down into his boot with the other, trying to retrieve his dagger. He felt their intertwined bodies heave and roll to the side, and in that instant Handel was able to free his own hand. He came over his shoulder with the blade of his own dagger and plunged it straight down into the nun's throat. Tristan heard the sickening puncture of steel into flesh, then the deep gurgle of blood bubbling from the nun's throat as she gasped for air. Then everything grew still, until he began to vomit.

"G-get off me, dammit!" howled Handel, grabbing at his shoulder. "And get me the hell out of here!"

Tristan swiped vomit from his lips with a brush of his sleeve and pushed himself off Handel. Reaching down, he pulled Handel off the murdered nun, his hands trembling uncontrollably. He couldn't find his voice. The nun's dead eyes were staring directly at him from her tomb there on the bed, as though accusing him of the most ungodly of crimes. Struggling, Handel stuck his hand over his shoulder, placing pressure on his wounds to close the hemorrhaging. "I'll live if I can stop this goddamn bleeding!" he said. "Come on, let's go!"

A large shadow filled the doorway. It was the Byzantine nobleman, rousted from his room across the hall from all the commotion. He stood there, sword in hand. "What in God's Hell's going on in here!" he thundered, a look of confusion washing over his face as he tried to assess what he had witnessed. Then, flicking his sword back and forth at knee level, he cried, "My God, you bastards have just murdered a bride of Christ!"

Tristan tried to object, but only managed to utter a series of unintelligible sounds. Handel, sensing that escape was blocked, slowly backed toward the dead nun, never taking his eyes off the Byzantine. Stealing a hand behind him, he fumbled about blindly for the handle of his dagger. Then, pulling it from the nun's gullet, in one swift under-handed sling he fired it across the room straight into the Byzantine's heart. Unaware that he had been struck, the man's eyes frogged shut and open with a single blink, and his jaw dropped. Confused, he looked down and saw the hilt of the dagger handle protruding from his chest. In that moment, he glanced up at Tristan with a singular focus and shrugged, as if to ask . . . *why?* Then his knees dissolved and he collapsed to the floor in a heap.

Tristan needed no instructions at this point. He quickly grabbed Handel by the shoulders and an arm and led him out of the room and down the stairs. The people downstairs had also heard the ruckus. Spotting the blood-soaked back of Handel's white monk's robe, they shrank back, not daring to rise or interfere. Accepting this, Tristan and Handel managed to hobble out of the Inn of the Sparrow and hasten their way down the street, then disappear into the darkness.

Handel's hideaway was just five blocks from the inn, but his condition made the short journey arduous and required that they stop every thirty paces or so. Finally arriving there, Handel flung himself belly-down covering his lone table. "W-water's in the basin," he stammered. "Get me bandaged up before I bleed to death!"

His nerves still jangling, Tristan hurriedly tended to Handel's wounds which, fortunately, proved not deep enough to be crippling. Though the nun had managed two strikes, she hadn't been able to apply full leverage because of her awkward position on the bed with Handel's weight restraining her from above. "I . . . I'm sorry, Handel," Tristan stammered. "I went into a panic back there. It's just that, I was expecting a man in that room! You know, the Byzantine you killed in the doorway!"

Sitting up, Handel shook his head with agitation. "Dammit, you nearly got us killed," he winced. "You said Domingo told you to come to the Inn of the Sparrow, that I'd uncovered the anti-pope's agent. Didn't he tell you his spy was a Byzantine nun?"

Tristan shook his head. "No, he was dying and just said a Byzantine. And when that big fellow walked through the inn, I thought it was him."

"No, you didn't think, you assumed! And when we busted in the door, you assumed again, that we had the wrong room. Then when I attacked the nun, you assumed yet again, this time that I'd lost my mind for attacking a nun. Finally, when the big Byzantine showed up at the door, I guess you just assumed that old Handel here would save our asses! You just stood there like a goddamn stump!"

"I'm sorry, Brother Handel," said Tristan. "I just . . ."

Handel looked at him with irritation. Appreciating Tristan's remorse, he softened a measure. "Some lessons to learn here, lad," he grunted. "First, *never* pity anyone who chooses this line of work, eh? That bitch tonight was the cause of three dead Benedictines. She only "turned them in," but she may as well have dropped the ax on their necks herself. Second, don't *ever* think the anti-pope's people won't use women. Hell, they've even put children in the field! Christ, think about it. Didn't Abbot Hugh and Cardinal Odo use you a time or two as a damn boy to gather information before the war broke out?"

Tristan nodded.

"Third," Handel continued, "you better get over this hesitation shit, lad, or you'll be dead before the month's over, and you'll end up taking some of us with you. Do you understand?"

"Yes," Tristan said, feeling Handel's callous years of experience as an underground agent beating at him.

"And fourth, you better wake up. That nun came into the Inn of the Sparrow and had her own room. Think about it. When have you ever heard of a nun staying at a goddamn inn? Christ, lad, what Christian order in this world allows that? Especially alone! She was dressed as a Greek Orthodox nun, and even though the Byzantine Catholics follow a different rite than we Roman Catholics, they are nevertheless still Catholic and their nuns follow the same practices as ours."

"My God, we killed a nun," said Tristan, his voice trailing off, fathoming the horror of what had actually transpired at the Inn of the Sparrow. "The thought of killing a nun gives me the horrors, even if she *is* the enemy, and that man that walked in on us, he did nothing to deserve death!"

"No, nothing! Only show up with a sword in his damned hand which might have ended up in our bellies! Hell, that conscience of yours is going to get you skewered," Handel sighed. "As for the woman, don't ever think for one second that nuns don't work the shadows just like us. Christ, all you have to do is take one look at Brother Muehler's goddamn face! Remember that Norman bitch that tracked him in Paris and had him arrested after he came ashore in England?"

"Yes," Tristan replied, "a certain Madame Madeleine."

"Ha! *Madame,* my *ass!* We've since learned she's the abbess of the Convent of Rouen in Normandy, in the immediate employ of William the Bastard! So let that be a lesson to you. Dieter Muehler's my best friend on this earth and now he can't even bare his face since it gives people the frights. A *nun* did that. Listen, you better think long and hard about tonight. If you're going to let your conscience get you killed, then maybe you better get yourself back to Cluny, eh? And I don't say that to throw mud, lad. I just wouldn't want to see you get hurt. Besides, you're just too damn valuable to the Black Monks to be led to the slaughter by your own hands."

At this Tristan dropped his forehead into his palm as defeat began to etch itself over his face. After a long silence his face filled with resolve and he looked at Handel. "Handel, forgive me," he said. "I'll do better next time out."

Tristan did not sleep well that night. When it finally did come, it was furtive, troubled, suspending him somewhere between consciousness and the nether world; in that place where one is forced to return to the pillories of self-flagellation and atonement for violating the laws of both man and God . . . in this case, murder. But when Tristan awoke that next morning, though he did not suspect it, he was no longer the same person. In the Inn of the Sparrow night before, he'd passed through the decisive hour of his destiny.

CHAPTER THREE

KUKU PETER

After returning to Monte Cassino Tristan descended into a period of melancholia brought on by his shoddy performance in Rome. He was unaccustomed to failure, and his hesitancy in Rome could well have been fatal if not for the quick-thinking Handel. Furthermore, he knew that Brother Muehler was displeased with him over the near debacle in Rome. As often occurs when one sinks into self-defeat, Tristan was overcome by a sudden sense of isolation. This, in turn, unexpectedly caused him to instantly realize that he had little in life in terms of personal relationships other than his mother, his brother, and Cardinal Odo de Lagery, all three of whom he seldom saw anymore due to distance and circumstance.

His upbringing in the monastery might have been fertile ground to develop lifelong friendships among classmates, but Tristan's time had been spent with Odo, who was serving as Grand Prior in those days, and with Abbot Hugh or the other monks due to his phenomenal academic abilities . . . which they had immediately put to use in adult monastic endeavors. He had, therefore, missed out on boyhood and neither engaged in the frivolities of youth nor cultivated the camaraderies that typically arise among schoolmates. And now, due to his current clandestine status within the Benedictine underground, he again was trapped in isolation.

This had never bothered him before, thus he had a difficult time comprehending this sudden onslaught of introspection and profound loneliness that now buried him. After enduring this self-pity for several days, memories of the young Romani girl began to occupy his thoughts. Her name was Mala and he had met her when he was but a boy. That incidental encounter had led her to visit him several times over the years at the monastery, and from the youthful innocence of childhood, a strange and complex attraction had somehow blossomed between the two; strange in that he and Mala were of such different thread and complex in that each of their encounters had been brief, then was punctuated by a three or four year separation. He had last seen her a year ago at his ordination ceremony. She had wished him well, but as she uttered these words, Tristan had not missed the shadow of regret that darkened her eyes caused by his entry into monasticism.

Seven days after his return to Monte Cassino, the dark emotional shroud that blanketed Tristan was lifted when Brother Muehler called him to his chambers. "I'm sending you to France," Muehler said, adjusting his veil higher to cover his cheeks. "I need you to go to Dijon to inform Brother LeDoux's family of his fate at the hands of the anti-pope's assassins in Rome. While in France you may visit Cluny Monastery where you were brought up by Odo de Lagery and the Black Monks. At some point with a little good fortune, you might even cross paths with Cardinal Odo. He, too, is on his way to Cluny this next month." Muehler paused then and closed his eyes as a hand stole towards his face, touching it. When he reopened his eyes, it was as if he had returned from a distant place, and despite the cover of the veil that shrouded his face, a glimmer appeared in the depths of his eyes. "Then, too," he said, "you may visit your mother at the Convent of Marcigny which is not far away. She has recently completed her novitiate, I hear. Please convey to her my eternal gratitude. At great peril to herself and several others, she stood firm in my hour of need and saved me from certain death in England."

Tristan nodded. "And it is *you* she credits, Brother Muehler, for saving her from England as well."

Though Tristan suspected that being sent to France to deliver Brother LeDoux's death notice was a deliberate maneuver by Muehler to give him a menial assignment, Tristan was nevertheless pleased to be returning to his native France and began packing immediately. He did one other thing also. In the privacy of his room he wrote three notes, then quietly had each dispatched by the monastery courier to a different city in France, giving Cluny monastery as the point of return communication.

Several days later he was standing aboard a westbound vessel crossing both the Tyrrhenian and Mediterranean seas. Reaching Cluny, he spent his first entire day in the audience of the great Abbot Hugh of Semur, revisiting and sharing tales of his arrival at the monastery as a seven-year-old boy with his younger brother, Guillaume.

"Aha, good days those were, Tristan," smiled the abbot, "even though your mother's actions created a great deal of sadness and confusion in you at the time, you took the yoke and bore it, arose to the challenge, and became our academic wonder of Cluny! We're extremely proud of you, lad."

While at the monastary, Tristan also took time to visit his childhood mentor, the kindly old Brother Damien, warrior monk in youth and now Chief Infirmarian of the monastery at the end of his career. In addition he stopped in to see the ingenious Brother Loiseaux, headmaster of the academic cohorts which were comprised of noblemen's sons from across France who had come to Cluny to seek the highest education available on the continent. He was most pleased when he ran into one of his former classmates, the stubby dwarf named Scule who had, upon completion of his studies, entered the novitiate of the Cluny monastery and was now a Black Monk himself.

"Ha," cried Scule spying Tristan, "the boy who never wished to become a monk! And still handsome as ever, I see."

The two gave each other a comfortable embrace. "And you look fabulous also, Scule!" replied Tristan. "It appears they are feeding you well, my friend. You have grown like a weed since my departure. Looks like you've gained perhaps a full *tenth* of a millimeter!"

"Ay," Scule grinned, "and if you think *that's* impressive, then you'll want to take a look at my root before you leave!" Then he pointed to his crotch. "A veritable oak trunk!" he exclaimed.

"Ha, more like a veritable oak stump, I wager!" said Tristan, feigning a frown.

At this both broke into laughter, then Scule settled. "Where is your brother now, Tristan?"

"In Italy, fighting alongside members of my mother's former Danish Guard on behalf of la Gran Contessa Mathilda of Tuscany against King Heinrich and the Germans," said Tristan, his face shining with pride at the mention of his younger brother, Guillaume.

"Ha, the luck of you two! Mathilda is the richest, most famous woman on the continent. To think that she adopted you two out of pity years back for being disgraced by your father, abandoned by your mother and sent here to Cluny as children! You're reunited with your mother somehow, yet continue to have the Countess as your sponsor. Oh, how kind was the backswing of fortune's pendulum! Nevertheless, I am told things are bloody in Tuscany and that King Heinrich has put Mathilda on the run. I suppose Guillaume faces danger daily, eh?"

Tristan nodded. "Ay, it is always ebb and flow in Italy against Heinrich, but Mathilda continues to frustrate the Germans. As for Guillaume, despite the great flow of blood in those parts, he is doing well as a Tuscan Knight and establishing a reputation as a fierce warrior. It is reported that despite him attaining only the age of seventeen, Mathilda has already placed him in charge of a small, elite cavalry unit that harries the Germans mercilessly."

"Ha, we all knew he would become a formidable man-at-arms, it was inevitable!" Scule laughed. "Oh, and some news about our former classmates. Young Letellier is about to be knighted by his father in your birthplace of Saint-Germainen-Laye even though father and son, by all accounts, despise each other."

"Indeed?"

"Ay, Lord Letellier is a lout as we all know, which is why he is referred to behind his back as Letellier the Liar, while his son is becoming a budding gentleman of the highest degree. So another inevitability, father and son fight though they share the same blood! Oh, and you remember Hébert of the same Stable Cohort as your brother and Letellier? He, too, is about to be knighted, in Flanders. And because of his father's recent slaying in the border dispute between the Flemish and the Normans, young Hébert is about to become one of the wealthiest nobles of northern France!"

"Ah, good for both Letellier and Hébert!" said Tristan. "And you, Scule, how are you faring here at Cluny?"

"Things couldn't be better. I work as a circutor already for the new Claustral Prior, and after that I aspire to one day become the Grand Prior and manage the Treasury Tower. So it appears our old class of Cluny is doing quite well on all fronts. Given time, one day we might yet rule the continent!"

Tristan shook his head with this statement. "May Heaven help us," he grinned, "and the continent!"

Several days later Tristan appeared at the gates of the Convent of Marcigny. There lacked any presence of guards, yet the walls of the convent gave the appearance of a heavily fortified stronghold, as did the massive iron gates that cloistered the convent from the outside world. He dismounted and rang the greeting bell three times before anyone appeared. "I am here to see my mother," Tristan announced, presenting his Monte Cassino documents.

"Papers or no papers, we adhere to strict rules here," said the ancient nun who limped to the gate. "Those within cannot receive visitors unless designated as a sister of means. Is your mother in that class?"

"Indeed, she is a sister of means," said Tristan, knowing that the poorer nuns lived under a different code than did the wealthy who had delivered a hefty dowry to gain access to the cloistered walls of the Marcigny Convent. "She is known here as Sister Asta of the Norman Danes."

"Oh, *Asta*," said the old nun, a tone of deference entering her voice. "Yes, I'll go fetch her. Come in, come in. Do not venture beyond the Visitation Parlor. No men are permitted beyond that point."

Tristan took a seat in the parlor, and shortly there after his mother appeared from the other side of the heavily-timbered doors that separated the parlor from the actual convent itself. She was dressed in the full habit of the Benedictine Sisterhood, but at the age of only thirty-two, her stunning beauty remained undeniable, even beneath the wimple that covered her head. She blushed, recognizing her son, then went to him and softly kissed his cheeks, one after the other. Then she embraced him, and her eyes grew moist.

"Oh, son, my son," she whispered, embracing him. "How good to see you."

Tristan's face also began to take on the flush of emotion, as happened every time since their reunion after an eleven year absence from each other.

"Mother!" he exclaimed.

They had been conversing comfortably for half an hour or so, relating the newest developments in their respective lives when Tristan looked at her with reticence and said, "Mother, I have recently entered the underground service of the Benedictine Brotherhood. I am required to do questionable things at times, and am having certain difficulty with it."

Asta looked at her son, and nodded with unmistakable empathy. "You were born with a gentle heart, Tristan, so I would expect no less. You were also born a man, and as much as I have despised the violence of men, it is inevitable that blood will stain your hands . . . even as a monk. Your brother, Guillaume, now a Christian warrior who defends the true Church against Heinrich and his anti-pope, will see even more blood than you; bathe in it even. He was born the fearless one, you the thinker. Thinking, unfortunately, leads one to the edge of the precipice time and time again. So tell me, what is it that disturbs you, Tristan?"

"I assisted in the assassination of an Eastern Byzantine spy just a month ago. A nun of the Eastern rite. It shames me to the bone. First that we killed at all, secondly that we killed a *woman*. Then, too, an innocent man became ensnared and lost his life as well."

Asta looked at Tristan, feeling her son's disquiet as only could a mother, and clasped his hands in hers. "There is division between the Byzantine Christians and we Roman Christians, Tristan, and even now our Roman Church itself has fractured into two warring camps, and in war there is little mercy. Did this nun earn her death?"

Tristan thought a moment. "She was the root of three executed Benedictines, then contributed to the death of two more in the Square of Rome, Mother, who knows how many others before that."

Asta sat back a moment, and looked deep into her son's eyes. "Very well then, Tristan," she said, her voice barely audible, "this woman *chose* her profession, and her *profession* chose her fate, not you. You were defending the true Church against Emperor Heinrich and his wicked anti-pope, the Archbishop Guibert. Sleep well from tonight on, then, and may God guide your dagger, keeping it righteous as opposed to cruel and purposeless."

Tristan was not expecting such affirmation from his mother, now a Benedictine Sister of Marcigny. There existed no one else on this earth whose words could have thus assuaged the bitter personal angst that had been shadowing him since Rome.

"Thank you, Mother," he said, kissing her hand, "you have cleared my confusion, and cleansed my heart. Brother Muehler said much the same, but it carries more weight coming from you."

"Ah, and how is my dear Brother Muehler?"

Tristan smiled. "I believe that he is in love with you, Mother. Every time he mentions or even hears your name, his eyes catch fire. It's the only time I see him forget his venom."

Asta smiled at this, and her cheeks grew pink. "Oh, if you had only known him before," she chided. "He was the most forgiving and compassionate of men. Virtuous and courageous. These wars and the politics that have followed have turned him, I fear, just as they have turned others." Then she reached over and softly curved a palm about the back of Tristan's neck, her eyes unable to mask a slight gleam of dread. "Just as they are turning *you*, Tristan. Sadly, *no* man can stand against the weight of war. I fear there no longer exists a middle course even for you."

Then, as if nothing had passed between them, she retrieved her hand and began to describe the new garden plot that the nuns were cultivating to feed the poor.

They spoke for another hour more, then Tristan left, well convinced that his mother had finally found the sanctuary of her dreams, away from the violence of the world, and far from men.

He then made his way toward Dijon where this particular year the fields appeared uncharacteristically parched and depthless, reminding Tristan of great sores littering the landscape. He wandered about for some time, and after a bit of difficulty, finally managed to locate the parents of Brother LeDoux. They were living in a bleak shanty two miles before Dijon, scrabbling a meager living from a small patch of dusty earth they called home.

"I regret to inform you that your son, Brother Bernard LeDoux of these parts, has passed on to the next life," said Tristan to the two elderly, decrepit peasants who had brought LeDoux into this life and raised him. "Also, please know that your son met his end while actively serving his Lord, who he is now with. Be it known also that he surrendered his life in the service of the true Church against Emperor Heinrich and his papal pretender, anti-pope Clement III."

At this, tears began to stream down the old woman's rugged face, slipping into the deep and crooked furrows that creased her cheeks. The old man passed his hand across his forehead, as if to dispel a cloud, then slightly shook his head and crossed himself. Watching this, Tristan wished to offer something more meaningful than the scripted recitation he had just delivered to these two pitiful souls. Reaching out, he touched the old woman's shoulder lightly. His heart began to swell and he could muster no words, so he withdrew his hand. *Any words I offer at this point are meaningless to these people,* he thought, *for I am a stranger, and they have lost their only offspring, the only trace of their existence on this earth after their own passing.*

An hour later he entered Dijon, intending to stay the night at the Benedictine monastery before returning south again to Cluny, then sailing east back to Italy. When he got to the town square, he saw two men shackled to a post being heckled by a small gathering of onlookers. The two military guards who flanked the post were also heckling the prisoners, and seemed to be thoroughly amused by their own abuse of the captives. Curious, Tristan approached, dismounted, and made an inquiry to a man standing at the back of the crowd. "What have we here?" Tristan asked, pointing toward the two shackled men in the distance.

"Ha!" said the burgher, "We have a drama being played out," he said, "and a good one at that!"

"Oh?"

"Indeed. These two travelers there, one a late teen and the other in his thirties, perhaps, came to the region and stopped at Lord Truffault's manor asking for water and sustenance. Even though hospitality is not at all in his nature,

Truffault agreed, knowing that the older man was a monk and Dijon's feast day is approaching. Truffault left the manor, once he returned that evening, he discovered his nubile young wife, the Lady Agnes, in a state of complete undress within her chambers with the monk!"

"With the *monk*?" said Tristan, straining to better see the two prisoners. The younger man was handsome in face, figure, and dress, but the monk was disheveled, wore a simple hair-shirt, and had no shoes upon his feet. Furthermore, he appeared filthy and wild-eyed. "That makes no sense," Tristan said. "Is the lord's wife blind, then, to pick the monk over the young dandy there?"

"Ha, not blind at all, and quite a little blossom to boot . . . which is why this drama is so amusing!"

Just then a nobleman in the company of three heavily armed riders stormed onto the square from nowhere, followed by two wagons loaded with laborers and timber.

"Ah, here's Lord Thierry Truffault the cuckhold, himself," said the burgher with a grin.

Truffault rode up to the prisoners and spat on the monk. "You bastard!" he shrieked. "Oh, you'll hang in the morning as soon as my men finish building your perch! And for good measure, your sniveling young nephew will hang beside you. That'll teach you not to diddle in another man's plot!" Then he began barking instructions to his laborers as they piled out of the wagon and began laying out timber for the future scaffold.

Tristan shrugged, looking at the burgher. "Is Lord Truffault not angry at his wife? Why is she not here with the two prisoners?"

"Oh no, the moment she was caught Lady Agnes Truffault claimed innocence!" the burgher laughed. "She insists that the monk accosted her, though she had no bodily marks, nor ripped clothing and she was lying bare ass naked on her bed while the monk stood just a few feet away, also unscathed! Lord Truffault's vanity forces him to accept the story though we all in Dijon know well that his wenchy little wife has been poked by many a knight and merchant of the region!"

Suddenly a voice burst out, a commanding voice ringing with passion and fire. "Hark! You sinners standing about out there! Yea though you may burden yourself with today, your true future lies in the forever of Heaven where the righteous will enjoy spending eternity beside the Lord God, our Father!" It was the monk shouting, and the more he spoke the more he moved, straining to free his arms and legs from the iron pull of his shackles. Soon he became so animated that he was gyrating wildly and frightening the children of the sparse crowd.

"Damndest thing," chortled the burgher, "instead of begging for mercy, this crazy little monk will remain silent for an hour or so, then erupt into preaching for no apparent reason, and fascinating preaching at that. However, he has yet to beg for leniency, or even once deny his crime or implicate the guilt of Truffault's wife."

"Odd indeed," said Tristan. "Does anyone know who this monk might be?"

"He's a stranger to us, yet a pilgrim passing through this morning identified the monk as a hermit from Amiens. A madman called KuKu Peter."

"KuKu Peter!" exclaimed Tristan, now completely dismayed. Taking several steps forward, he peered closely at the prisoner, and perceived that the wild-eyed, filthy monk shackled to the post was indeed Peter the Hermit, a bizarre but disturbingly charismatic monk that he had twice met during boyhood. Realizing then that it was Peter the Hermit who would be hung in the morning, Tristan quickly shouldered his way through the onlookers and made his way to the prisoners. "Peter?" Tristan said.

As soon as the monk heard his name, he halted his spastic movements, then leaned forward to blow the strands of matted hair from his eyes and gaze at the man who had stepped forward to address him.

"Tristan?" he cried, his eyes dilating even more than during his evangelical diatribe. "When I saw you last they had shaved your crown in the Benedictine tonsure and ordained you as a Black Monk! Now your hair is grown back and you wear layman's garb. Surely you've not abandoned God's calling, lad?"

"Oh, Peter," sighed Tristan, distraught at the sight of the Hermit in such circumstances. "How distressing to see you here like this!"

"Lad, don't avoid my question. Have you left the Brotherhood? Oh, you'll be damned to Hell forever!"

To divulge details about his status would have been a severe violation of the Benedictine underground, so Tristan said, "No, no, I am still a Black Monk, Peter. I have been awarded a temporary dispensation from the robe and the tonsure. It is *you* that we must worry about. I have been told of your crime and I—"

"Crime?" interrupted Peter, squatting on his haunches, resting his shackles across his knees. "Aha! There is no crime here from Peter! I was merely on my way to Cluny, having heard that Cardinal Odo de Lagery himself is expected there shortly from Ostia."

"Yes, I hope to see him when I return to Cluny. Peter, tell me about the charges against you."

The Hermit shrugged and with great fanfare pointed to the other man. "Look at my nephew there, *he* is the offender!"

At this, the nephew's throat lumped and he began to bawl like a baby.

"Peter," said Tristan, "did Lord Truffault not catch you in his lady's chambers?"

"Ay, he did, and she was naked as a goat's ass, her legs spread wide and her bush exposed!" exclaimed Peter, his eyes rolling about in a circular manner, glancing from Tristan to the crowd then back to Tristan. "Indeed, this fine young rooster next to me was pounding her pelt like a mad little March hare and I caught them together. In a fury I took my rod to his back and he fled like the coward he was born. Then I laid into the Lady Agnes with preaching, telling her she ought to be ashamed luring such a virginal young lad into her she-wolf's lair. Rather than listen, she taunted me by displaying her crack, stroking her bush, and making other lurid gestures! And then, much to Beelzebub's glee, the lord of the manor walks in from nowhere." Then he pointed to his nephew again. "Of course, young Innocenzo here, named after my own grandfather of Amiens, was hiding and 'twas *me* that was caught with the bird feathers in my mouth. Bah!" Then he began to kick at his nephew.

"'Tis true! 'Tis true!" wailed the young man, his face growing more twisted than a briar root. "Oh, uncle, forgive me!"

"Did you not explain to Lord Truffault the truth of things?" said Tristan, perplexed.

"What?" cried Peter, standing erect and launching his face to Tristan's nose. "And send poor Innocenzo here to his Maker alone after rutting around like a little hedgehog between that damnable wench's thighs as his last act before facing his judgment at the Gates of Saint Peter? Oh, nay, nay. I must be there at his side to explain this boy's sheer naivety."

"I will remain here with you until morning then," Tristan said woefully. "Let me tend to my horse and report to the monastery, then I will return shortly."

It was dusk when Tristan returned to the square, about the same time that craftsmen, merchants, and field hands were returning home in droves for the evening. As Tristan approached Peter's position at the post, he could see that many of these people had stopped to listen to KuKu Peter. Noticing the sudden appearance of heavy traffic, he had broken into another animated seizure of the Holy Spirit, moving back and forth, dropping to his knees, then rising up with great drama, rolling his eyes to the Heavens with pontifical certainty.

"God's watching you, each and every one of you this very moment!" he cried, pointing to the east, toward Jerusalem. "He's right there, do you not see him, just there? He tells me He's angry because you just stand idly by awaiting the execution of two innocent pilgrims, one being his own man of the cloth!"

At this, the swell of onlookers laughed, an uncomfortable laugh, one that caused them to sling sideways glances at each other, or look down at their feet with discomfort. Gradually, this first commotion of ridicule and hilarity gave way to a sudden sepulchral silence, broken only by the monk's charismatic pronouncements of eternal damnation. Soon the burgeoning crowd was listening, open-mouthed, with a sense of entrancement mingled with admiration and surprise that a man could speak so well.

"Lord Truffault is going to hang a monk!" an old woman standing in the midst of the assembly whispered aloud. "Dijon will then be damned and cursed by the Almighty for allowing such a heinous thing!" Then she clapped a palm to her forehead and abruptly collapsed to the ground.

This caused a stirring among those within earshot and more whispering commenced, spreading lizard-like, growing louder. KuKu Peter perceived this and immediately raised his shackles skyward. "Oh, Lord, I plead that you forgive these innocent people of Dijon who willingly witness my martyrdom along with that of my pure young nephew, Innocenzo, named after your very own innocence upon the cross at Golgotha! Do not curse this wicked city of Dijon though they allow the butchery of your own innocent sheep, I pray! Do not hurl hellfire down to envelope this town from the Heavens, nor open the earth and swallow them into the fires of Hell itself!"

At this, people began to glance at the ground and move aside, as though expecting the very earth beneath their feet to yawn open and devour them. The sudden appearance of God himself could not have created more of a stir than that which rippled through the crowd. "Bless the innocent!" someone cried from the back of the crowd. This caused yet another stirring within the crowd, and was followed by someone else from the opposite direction yelling, "Protect the innocent! 'Tis God's law!"

This great ruckus and noise began to alert others in the town and the mob continued to swell until, by dark, more than a thousand angry citizens stood within the square raising torches and farm implements, chanting, "Lord Truffault! No, no, no! Lord Truffault! No, no, no!"

Tristan watched KuKu Peter's rousing of the crowd, awed by the manner in which the filthy little man was able to puppeteer the small crowd, who had initially mocked him, into a swollen mob of fury-filled citizens who were ready to defend him. Then, too, the two guards flanking the post and the laborers who had been constructing the scaffold had by now grown fearful. One of the guards gave the other a terrified look and cried, "This riotous horde is about to attack and will take their anger out on us and those poor fellows building the hangman's platform!"

At that very moment, as if a signal were passed, a cry went up from the mob and people surged forward in a swarming mass, screaming like banshees and pointing at the laborers and guards who turned to flee; the crowd was upon them before they could escape. Taking the shackle keys from the guards, the mob commenced to beat them to a bloody pulp. They also assaulted the scaffold laborers, burying them in a sea of fists, kicking feet, and swinging implements. Tristan tried to quell the crowd, but was swept aside by their sheer mass.

Then, in the midst of this outbreak of madness, a trumpet sounded in the darkness. It was Lord Truffault and his men-at-arms returning to inspect progress on the scaffold building. "Ho there!" he thundered, sitting rigid and rooted astride his great speckled horse as though posing for a portrait. "What goes on here? Release those guards immediately, I say!"

Surprised, the mob fell silent and began to retreat as Truffault and his armed men moved their horses into the crowd, parting them like the prow of a ship halving the raging waters ahead. Truffault unsheathed his sword and swung it about in demonstrative arcs as if to magnify his presence and force penance from the disrespectful townspeople, which was a grand miscalculation. Unlike Truffault's serfs who lived in virtual slavery under his thumb, this bastard class of town burghers and craftsmen possessed the nerve and the will to defy Truffault. Furthermore, like many nobles who lived a life of entitlement founded on the backs of the poor and unfortunate, Truffault did not believe that sheep could ever turn into lions although this is exactly what was occurring.

A voice rang out from the crowd. "Get Truffault! Get his men! They will cause the destruction of Dijon through God's fury!!"

As though a match had been lit, the mob resumed their rampage, shouting, screaming, and pointing at the hapless Truffault who had unsuspectedly marched right into a hornet nest. The crowd closed in about Lord Truffault and his escorts, pulling them from their mounts, taking them to the ground, and pummeling them without mercy.

Horrified, Tristan watched for a moment until feeling a tug at his sleeve. It was KuKu Peter, now free of shackles.

"Shit!" he cried grabbing Tristan's arm. "Let's be gone from this place before order gets restored!" Then he signaled to his terrified nephew and the three of them fled.

CHAPTER FOUR

BLESSED CARDINAL DESIDERIUS

By the year 1085, Cardinal Desiderius, Abbot of Monte Cassino Monastery, had developed both a strong reputation and a firm base of power within the Catholic Church through his relationship with the conquering Normans in the realms of Lower Italy. In particular, he had served as intermediary between the former Pope Gregory throughout his stormy relationship with the violent Norman warlord, Duke Robert Guiscard, also known as Robert the Wily. Indeed, it was Cardinal Desiderius who convinced the tempestuous Guiscard to march north and rescue Pope Gregory at the final hour just as he was about to be captured by King Heinrich in 1084.

Now, as Emperor Heinrich and his anti-pope, Clement III, controlled Rome and the Vatican, the faithful adherents of the ousted and deceased Pope Gregory looked to Cardinal Desiderius to lead the movement against Heinrich and restore rightful authority to the Vatican. This was due in great part to the fact that as Pope Gregory lay dying in exile at Salerno, he proclaimed Desiderius as his first choice of successor. Desiderius was reluctant to accept this mantle, far preferring to maintain his role as the unchallenged Church power broker in Lower Italy under the safe shadow cast by the Normans. Nevertheless, there was another issue that he kept hidden from all but intimate acquaintances: his health. Men somehow sense when the sands of the hourglass are about to run short, and somewhere in the back of his brain Desiderius had already begun to imagine that the angel of death was beginning to stir.

Born in 1027 under the name of Dauphar, he was the only son of Prince Landulf V of Benevento. After expressing at an early age his interest in becoming a monk, both of his parents violently opposed the possibility. At age twenty, his father was killed in battle in 1047, and at this same time, he fled from a marriage that had been arranged for him by his family.

Though he was dragged back by force, he fled once again and obtained permission to enter the monastery of Saint Sophia at Benevento where he received the name Desiderius. Finding that Saint Sophia was not strict enough to suit his designs, he first moved to the island monastery of Tremite San Nicolo in the Adriatic, then joined a colony of hermits in 1053 at Majella in the Abruzzi.

On Easter Day of 1058, he was installed as Abbot of Monte Cassino and immediately set about rebuilding the cathedral and conventual buildings, established schools of art, and raised interest and enrollment in the Benedictine community of Monte Cassino. On October 1st of 1071, he had the magnificent Basilica of Monte Cassino consecrated by Pope Alexander II, which established his reputation and brought to the abbey many gifts, foundations, and exemptions.

At a time when the Church was rife with power thirsting and corrupt clergymen from one end of the continent to the other, Desiderius was a shining beacon of piety and devotion to the Lord. Though he had never contrived a single design toward ascending to the Papacy, he now found himself being thrust forward as the next Pope by Gregorian papists.

And so it was on the morning of September 5, 1085 that a stable boy rushed into the office of the Abbot of Monte Cassino and threw himself at the feet of Cardinal Desiderius. "Oh, Abbot!" the boy wailed. "Duke Borsa has entered the monastery with armed troops, and he's in foul humor! He's already pummeled two monks who humbly asked him to state his business here and—"

At that moment the door was flung open and Duke Roger Borsa stormed into the chamber. He was an imposing figure, tall and thick, and long accustomed to shouldering out others as had his fearsome father, the notorious Duke Robert Guiscard the Wily. As he entered the room looking about, he possessed that keen look about his eyes and nostrils common to predators nosing the trail for scent. "You! Get out!" he bellowed, pointing to the stable hand.

The boy's nervous little eyes darted from Borsa to the Cardinal, then back again before he clumsily gained his feet, bowed, and fled.

"Quite an entrance, Lord Borsa," said Desiderius dryly, remaining seated at his desk. "Reminds me of your father. Truly, Sir, was it quite necessary to beat my monks coming through the gates? This is a monastery, after all, not a gauntlet run."

Borsa rolled his shoulders about for a moment, then, unclenching his hands which had turned to fists, he pawed at the neck veins convulsing up and down the length of his muscled neck. "Desiderius, I've about had it with you! I'll no longer tolerate this hesitancy that's overtaken you on accepting the Pope's tiara. Italy burns, your supporters wait, and the Church dissolves while Heinrich's pretender rules the Vatican. Christ, man, what in hell's name is wrong with you?"

Having schooled himself against the pressing of others, Desiderius ignored Borsa's fury, passing it off as nothing extraordinary. "Indeed, Italy burns," he said, "but Italy has been afire for five years now, ever since King Heinrich and Pope Gregory, bless his departed soul, began their dance of death denouncing and dethroning each other. Those who fight are not my supporters. I have no wish to be Pope. They are, in reality, Pope *Gregory's* supporters and *your* supporters."

"Dammit, Cardinal, they are the supporters of the true Church! How can you of all clerics turn your back on Mother Church? Step up, man. *Jesus Christ Almighty*, what goddamn clergyman doesn't dream of attaining the papacy for God's sake? My army just last month escorted you to Rome as soon as they put the anti-pope to flight, but then you refused to enter the city for the election of our next Pope, which has now caused us to put off the goddamn election for Christ only knows how long!"

Desiderius shook his head with disapproval. "Careful, Duke, how you use the Lord's name," he said in the tone of a benediction. "I refused to enter the city because I have learned of your plot with the Cardinals to force the tiara upon my head. I've told you a thousand times just as I told your father; I have no wish to be Pope. I continue to support all political and spiritual efforts to reclaim the Vatican, and as you well know, have harnessed Monte Cassino's Benedictine wealth and resources to help finance this campaign."

"Desiderius," Borsa snorted, scowling like a dog about to snap. "We need someone to represent this effort, a figurehead! The loyal Cardinals want you in the Vatican, Countess Mathilda wants you in the Vatican, Lower Italy wants you in the Vatican, as do France, Spain, and England. It's your *duty*, dammit!"

Desiderius sat back, and though his eyes remained patient, lines of strain began to form across his forehead. "Though I hold you, Mathilda, and the Cardinals in high stead, the bunch of you will *not* force the red cope upon me."

"Goddammit, the hell we won't!" snapped Borsa, his dark eyes igniting to embers.

Desiderius abruptly stood, as the patience he had held in check to this point dissolved. "Borsa, I'm beginning to tire of your brooding and your bluster! I'll have no more of it! Furthermore, selection of the Pope is none of your affair. It's Church business, not military business!"

Caught off guard by this unexpected burst of passion from the placid Desiderius, Borsa paused, but only for a moment. "Ha! Was it not *you* who implored that my father rescue Pope Gregory from Heinrich just a year ago, thereby prompting us to move our Norman armies north against Rome to save Gregory? What was *that* if not military business mixed with Church business?"

"Ay, it was," acknowledged Desiderius with a sigh, struggling to reclaim his calm. "When the Roman people protested Norman entry into the city, in a fit of anger your father unleashed your Norman hooligans and Saracen allies on the Roman populace to pillage and rape, leaving the city a heap of ashes! And those disgraceful actions turned the entire population of Rome against Gregory. Humiliated by this Norman ravaging of a Christian city, Gregory left the city in shame and went into self-exile. So much for you and your father's expertise in *Church* matters, my dear Borsa! And as a result of his uncontrollable temper, it now appears the Romans prefer Heinrich's false pope over a legitimate Gregorian pope!"

Had any other man voiced such words, Borsa would have assaulted him where he stood, but Borsa fell silent, his spirit raw from the verbal flagellation just delivered by Desiderius, the revered clergyman who had baptized him as a child. In actuality, Borsa admired and respected the old Cardinal. Desiderius had more than once pulled his family from the quagmire of their own intemperance. In fact, when Pope Gregory had excommunicated Borsa's father for attacking Papal territories years earlier, it had been Cardinal Desiderius who pleaded the case to allow him back into the Church.

"Very well," grunted Borsa contritely. "Tell me, Cardinal, just how many more times shall you flog my family over that business of sacking Rome, eh? We've confessed our sins on this matter, then accepted and performed the penance that you yourself administered to us, harsh as it was."

"Indeed you did," replied Desiderius, feeling a prick of compunction at the charges he had just flung. "I'll not bring it up again, Duke Borsa, but while you're here, tell me, why this sudden feuding that has broken out between you and your elder brother, Bohemud."

"Bohemud is but my *half* brother, Cardinal."

"Well? What have you to say about this feuding?"

"My father named me as successor as he lay dying in Cephalonia, and Bohemud went into a rage claiming that he was the eldest son. But his mother was Alberada the Norman, and as you know her marriage to my father was dissolved by the Church for political reasons years before he married my mother, Sichelgaita of Lombardy. Bohemud is a bastard son then as far as my mother and I are concerned, and as far as the Church is concerned for that matter. Therefore, despite being the eldest, he deserves nothing! Besides, father was displeased with Bohemud's military incompetence against the Byzantines in Greece and further east."

"I have long been arbiter on behalf of the Normans here in Lower Italy, Duke Borsa, so I pray this bitterness does not turn to war."

"As I do, Cardinal," Borsa nodded. "That depends on whether Bohemud stands down or not. Well then, I've said my peace so I'll take my leave. But know this, I'll be back." Then he added, "with others."

"Oh?" said Desiderius. "So then, my friend, just who is it that you think might persuade me into changing my stance on accepting the papacy?"

"Two people," Guiscard replied. "First, the most passionate supporter of the true Papacy who ever lived, la Gran Contessa Mathilda of Tuscany, and second, the greatest spiritual figure in all Christendom next to yourself, the Cardinal-Bishop of Ostia, Odo de Lagery."

Acknowledging these names, Desiderius' brows drew together and a quiet look slipped over him then, as when one contemplates a riddle. Then he looked at Borsa and said, "You know, Duke, so appropriate that you should mention Cardinal Odo de Lagery. Do you not see a simple solution here?"

"Huh?" said Borsa, casting about for meaning in the Cardinal's question.

"Yes, on his deathbed Pope Gregory recommended me as his successor, which is why I am now hounded about the papacy. It was Cardinal Odo de Lagery who Gregory mentioned next. Why does no one bring forward the name of Cardinal Odo de Lagery for Pope? Has anyone even asked him?"

This confused Borsa a bit, and although he knew that Cardinal Odo had been cited by the dying Gregory just as Desiderius had mentioned, he did not care for the idea; he had no personal ties with the Cardinal-Bishop of Ostia.

"No one has asked," said Borsa, "because the Holy Father Gregory chose you first, Cardinal Desiderius, not Cardinal Odo de Lagery. It was his dying wish, and as God's direct representative on this earth, Gregory's wish was *God's* wish."

CHAPTER FIVE

THE HAG

Fleeing the Dijon square, Tristan, Peter the Hermit, and Innocenzo hastily secured their mounts and fled south as the pale moon slipped in and out of dark banks of clouds so that they rode in darkness for a moment, then in light the next. Because of the chaos they had just left in their wake at Dijon, Tristan would have preferred a faster pace, but he held his horse to a canter so his two companions, who quietly trotted alongside, riding their mangy donkeys, could keep up.

Having originally been headed to Cluny in hopes of meeting Cardinal Odo de Lagery, the Hermit was delighted to learn that Tristan himself possessed the same intention of going to see the Cardinal.

"Aha!" he cried, his voice ringing out for no apparent reason, shattering the silence of their flight. "Once again God has redeemed the righteous of this world! And once again I am saved from the scaffold!"

As he said this Tristan saw the whites of Peter's eye illuminate and flare into that wary, unblinking stare that reminded Tristan of a frog gazing across the surface of the pond that stretches before him. Had the circumstances not been so dire, Tristan would have laughed at this image; there was much about the Hermit's exaggerated mannerisms that was utterly comical. Instead, Tristan kept his eye to the road ahead and his ear to the road behind them.

"Will Lord Truffault and his men pursue us, do you think?" he said.

"Most definitely," Peter replied, shaking his head vigorously. "If they manage to break free of the mob they'll be upon us in a hurry, but fear not, God will protect us, lad. He told me so, even as I was shackled to the post watching the gallows being constructed."

"Yes," interjected Innocenzo, nodding to Tristan through the milky light, "my uncle converses with the Almighty, you know."

I know because he has told everyone so incessantly, Tristan wanted to say, but he remained silent, content that Peter had escaped yet another brush with disaster of his own devise. Yet he wondered about this strange misfit of a monk who flaunted his own poverty, inflamed others, and subscribed to the theory that he was a chosen prophet of God Almighty himself. Indeed, despite his blighted appearance and demonstrative manner, he had prophesized just enough events to make himself arguably credible. And though this credibility was most gener-ally refuted by both the hierarchy of the Church and the nobility, it was hungrily embraced by the poor, the ignorant, and the superstitious.

Several hours later Peter finally guided his donkey from the road into the brush. "We'll sleep here in hiding," he said.

Tristan and Innocenzo found sleep quickly, but in the middle of the night Tristan stirred in a dream and his hand stole out, pointing in a symbolic gesture. He thought he heard a loud diatribe being rattled off by the Hermit. Still, a part of Tristan yet dangled in sleep and the Hermit's voice sounded distant. Momentarily raising his head in a half conscious state, Tristan thought he witnessed Peter the Hermit pacing amongst the shadows addressing the night sky as though engaged in an active conversation, at times asking questions, at times objecting, and at times shaking his head in agreement. "Aye, I understand!" he cried at one point. "I shall do as you instruct, and none shall bar my way nor silence my tongue!" Then, after a few additional words, Peter made the sign of the cross and laid prostrate to the ground next to his nephew.

"Is s-someone there?" mumbled Tristan, still lingering somewhere between the nether world and reality. "Who are you speaking to, Peter?"

Then his head dropped and he fell back into a deep sleep just as the Hermit muttered, "To the Father, of course! He's been instructing me for weeks to spread word throughout France of Cardinal Odo's impending papacy, because shortly he'll be wearing the Pope's crown. Indeed, that's why I was traveling to Cluny in the first place."

That next morning, the three travelers arose and continued south toward Cluny, keeping an eye to the road behind them. By noon they came to a small village embroiled in commotion and quickly forgot the threat of pursuit by Lord Truffault. An angry band of town folk was shouting and cursing at an old woman who lay bleeding on the ground before them, wounded by stones they were hurling at her. "Die, sorceress!" cried the man who appeared to be leading this assault upon the helpless oldster. "Witch!" cried another as he flung a stone at her, striking her squarely on her already bleeding forehead.

The old woman cried out, then raised a trembling forearm to shield her face. "Be damned, you merciless cowards!" she wailed, her voice tinged with a foreign accent. "And woe to every one of you in this village who raises your hand to this pitiful old soul."

Incensed by what he saw, Tristan kicked his mount and rode between the woman and those tormenting her. "Ho, there!" he shouted, pointing at the man orchestrating the attack. "What has this woman done to be treated so?"

At this Peter quickly prodded his donkey forward, taking a position beside Tristan before the man could respond. "Tristan," he warned, "don't interfere. I've encountered this woman before during my travels and she's the harbinger of misfortune."

Tristan looked at Peter, surprised by his lack of compassion. Then a woman in the crowd hurled another stone at the old hag and struck her on the arm, which infuriated Tristan, causing him to turn his attention away from the Hermit. Without thinking, he charged his mount forward into the midst of the villagers, scattering them like chickens. "Stop, I say! I'll ride right over the next one who raises a hand against this poor woman!"

Considering this, the old hag dropped the arm that shielded her face and tried to look up to determine who was interceding on her behalf, but the sun was positioned in such a manner as to throw a blinding glare behind Tristan's head and shoulders so she saw no face. "These people mean to kill me," she rasped nevertheless, gasping for air, "and they will succeed unless you get me quickly from this place!"

"No, Tristan, let her be!" the Hermit said, maneuvering his donkey in front of Tristan's horse.

"Ay," agreed Innocenzo, "this woman is cursed. We saw her in Orléans this past year where she foretold the arrival of disaster, and two days after her departure a fire broke out and gutted much of the town, burning and killing many!"

"Indeed," interjected Peter, "and a similar thing happened six months later in Tours, in the form of a flood. I tell you, Tristan, this hag carries the devil in her teats!"

Tristan looked speculatively at Peter, then nodded. "Of course . . . and I suppose that God has informed you of this?"

"Indeed," he said, crossing both arms across his chest with finality, having missed the lilt of mockery in Tristan's tone. "And His word is final. No mercy for this old foreign hag; she carries Satan with her wherever she appears."

The old woman glared up at the Hermit, and it seemed her fear of the villagers turned into contempt for him. "Ha, I know who you are!" she cackled, her voice shrill with belittlement. "And you are no different than me, Hermit. God shows me what's to come and I warn others of impending punishment brought on by their own sins, yet I am hounded and called the scourge of France . . . yet you do the same and hail yourself as a prophet! What hypocrisy, I say!"

"You are the Devil's whore," snapped Peter, "and news of your very approach runs ahead of you!" Then a furrow formed between his brows as a raw and surly expression overtook his face. "Aye, God talks to me, and he has warned me about you, woman." Then he looked at Tristan and said, "As is common among those who possess only a single idea, this old bitch has become obsessed. Her obsession is delivering bad news, and this dark cloud now follows her every step."

"Oh, you charlatan!" the woman hissed, her voice dripping venom. Then she raised a bony finger toward the Hermit and cried, "Behold everyone! Kuku Peter, farce of the Catholic Church, clown of Christianity!"

This angered the Hermit beyond words and he was about to leap from his donkey and assail the old hag with his prodding whip when Tristan dismounted, scooped the old woman from the dirt and balanced her sidesaddle upon his horse. "I'll take her from here," he said, directing his words to the aroused villagers. "She'll bother you no more."

This caused a rash of grumbling from the crowd, then several of the villagers nodded and within moments the assembly turned their backs to return to their labors, but the Hermit remained displeased.

"Surely you don't intend to bring her along with us," he complained.

Mounting his horse, Tristan carefully secured the old woman on the saddle in front of his own position. "I intend to bring her with me, and get her a good distance from this town at least. Whether you choose to continue at my side is up to you, but I refuse to leave her in this snare. God in Heaven, Peter, both you and Innocenzo just last night barely escaped such a situation! I would think you would see that. Besides, as this woman says, there in essence may be little difference between the two of you."

The Hermit bristled at this. "No similarity!" he barked, his eyes flaring with anger. "Indeed, she claims that God whispers to her, but it's all an act to frighten others and empower herself."

At this the old hag directed a smoldering gaze towards the Hermit that sent chills down Innocenzo's spine, and he cringed. Yet she held her tongue and contented herself with the knowledge that she had escaped the mob.

"Very well, then," the Hermit grumbled, "Innocenzo and I will continue to accompany you to Cluny, Tristan. I say that we leave this woman along the road as soon as we distance ourselves from this village."

Tristan was about to respond, but the old woman spoke first. "I have no wish to travel far with the Hermit," she grunted, staring coldly ahead without turning to address Tristan. "If you will just get me to the next town, I'll be on my way."

"Very well," said Tristan, puzzled by the bitter relationship that existed between these two people who appeared to be of such similar grain. Then, urging his horse forward, he took the lead and directed the small contingent south.

An immediate wall of silence arose the moment they moved forward as the Hermit simmered with tight-lipped resentment over the woman's presence. As for Innocenzo, he dared not even look at the old hag, feeling it best not to draw her attention in any manner. Therefore he, too, fell mute. The old woman, injured and spent, blankly stared at the road ahead as her chest heaved with labored breathing and the streams of drying blood running down her face and through her hair began to crust over in scabrous roots. So as they moved down the rutted path, the only sound to be heard was the creak of saddle leather and the plodding rhythm of hooves clattering against hardscrabble terrain.

CHAPTER SIX

THE HAG'S TALE

After several hours of riding, Tristan found the self-induced silence forced upon the group by the Hermit and the old woman awkward, and finally spoke. "Do you have a name, Madame?" he said to the old woman.

Her stooped frame remained motionless. Then finally, not deigning even to turn her head from her perch in front of Tristan, she muttered, "Duxia de Falaise." Then she said nothing more.

Looking down at the top of her grey head which was already filthy, now also matted with dried blood, Tristan pitied the old soul. "There is a spring ahead not far from here," he said. "I stopped there on my way to Dijon. We will rest there a moment; perhaps you can wash and clean some of your wounds. My name is Tristan de Saint-Germain." He felt her stiffen as he said his name, as though prodded by something, but dismissed it knowing that he often made much of what others did not even notice. "What has passed between you and the Hermit, Madame?" he continued. "It seems a poisonous dance that you two perform."

"We hate each other, 'tis all you need know. That and the fact that he is dangerous."

Dangerous? thought Tristan. *The Hermit? Unusual perhaps, but dangerous?* Her words fired his mind into the past, to that time he had first encountered the Hermit. Tristan had been a boy of ten under the care of Odo de Lagery who was at that time the Grand Prior of Cluny Monastery. Peter the Hermit, not of the Benedictine Brotherhood, had descended on the monastery from nowhere in a tempest of rhetoric and motion, and had even brought the ever patient Odo de Lagery to the brink of fury, something Tristan had never seen any other person come close to doing.

The Hermit had publicly been proclaiming throughout Burgundy prior to that visit that Odo de Lagery would soon be Pope, that it was the will of God and that God was passing this direct word down to the populace through the Hermit himself. This had alarmed Odo, so he could neither quell the Hermit's passionate insistence on this matter nor curb his public preaching on the subject, which in the end infuriated Odo. During that initial encounter, the Hermit had also pulled Tristan aside one day in the stables of Cluny, and throwing himself into a transcendental trance that frightened the boy, the Hermit had predicted Tristan's fate and claimed that the boy was '*dangerous and would sow the seeds of war*' as his ultimate destiny. This had profoundly disturbed Tristan at the time. Even though he had attained his nineteenth year, there still remained in him a faint trace of disquiet that he carried about due to the Hermit's prophecy that day.

This disquiet went unspoken, yet festered occasionally in a hidden corner of his heart, feeding silently on Tristan's own uncertainties about himself, the world, and his faith. Indeed, he had always felt that something extraordinary awaited him in the future. It was a sense of unwelcome expectancy that had been stalking him since birth, then followed him from childhood into adolescence, only to continue pursuing him from adolescence into manhood.

It is one of the strange foibles of man that he might know a thing for certain yet deny it, chasing it away with effort and vigor, which is exactly what Tristan had been doing for some time now. What disturbed Tristan most about whatever awaited him was the uncertainty of the course it would run. Oh, this secret, inevitable thing would be extraordinary, yes, but extraordinarily *glorious*, or extraordinarily *disastrous?*

Such is the burden, then, of those who are gifted with exceptional intelligence and perception. They become victims of their own wandering imagination, which in turn creates complexity and confusion in their own future decisions. Like the lost sailor cast overboard into a raging sea, clinging desperately to a floating spar for life itself, these gifted souls find little peace.

Having thus lost himself in such thought riding his horse as it ambled down the road, Tristan reached within himself and closed the doors to the past, forcing himself back to the present. "And so, Duxia de Falaise," he said, his own voice sounding like a distant drone that belonged to another, "you claim the Hermit is dangerous. You might be interested to know that when I was a boy, he claimed that I was dangerous. Now you claim that *he* is dangerous, yet the villagers who nearly killed you believe *you* to be dangerous. Are we, then, each and every one of us on this earth dangerous? If that be the case, then there is nothing extraordinary about being dangerous, which is also to say that there consequently would be nothing dangerous about being dangerous."

"I do not engage in riddles, and find no amusement in your words," the old woman snapped. "I can already tell that you suppose me to be ignorant." Then she spat toward the Hermit who only stared glumly ahead, unaware of the conversation going on beside him. "Just as does that jackass, Kuku Peter. But know this, God does not reserve his gifts for men. He gave me little in this life, but he did give me the simple gift of "sight." Just because you and others are blind doesn't mean that Duxia de Falaise, too, must be blind. It is a simple thing, to *see*, one need only look about and take notice. Must I be cast aside as a pariah purely because I notice the obvious and others don't? Wherein, then, lies the difference between sorcery and prophecy? Ha! 'Tis simply that I am a *woman*."

These words struck Tristan, as did her lucid delivery of them and the conviction with which she spoke. The combination of these things spawned in him several suppositions.

"Well stated," he said. "It is an extremely rare thing to meet a woman in your apparent state of helplessness who communicates so clearly." Then he paused a moment before probing further. "Your accent, it is Finnish, yet you carry a French name. I detect also that you have been educated somehow along the way. You read and write, I would suppose?"

This question quickly moved the old woman into silence again. Despite Tristan's urging to answer yet another question or two, the old hag refused all communication, which Tristan found perplexing.

So silence fell upon the small troupe once again as the hot sun fell to their backs, casting long shadows that ran ahead of them on the road. Finally, after several hours they came to a wide bend in the road that was framed on one side by a stony outcrop that protruded from a tangle of brush smothered by wild roses. A small spring bubbled from a rupture in this outcrop, and the burbling lure of cool water finally brought words to the travelers.

"Come, Innocenzo," said the Hermit, "let's drink quickly before this witch taints the spring, which she will surely do when she touches the water."

Believing his uncle's words to be gospel, Innocenzo immediately scrambled off his donkey and ran to the spring. Keeping an eye to the old woman, he then cupped his palms, taking in long, deep gulps from the cold water cascading from the rock's crevice, as would a thirst-crazed horse.

Tristan dismounted and reached up, setting Duxia on the ground. He then slipped a hand up his sleeve and retrieved a slip of cloth. "Here," he said, offering it to her, "cleanse your wounds."

She took the cloth without acknowledgement and stamped about in place for a moment to limber her taught joints. Then, while attempting to straighten her horribly stooped spine, she raised her head and gave Tristan a furtive glance, as though thinking to unearth something in his striking features. But in that fleeting glance upward, something flicked her as the cold went out of her eyes and a feeble convulsiveness took over her body, for just an instant, then disappeared like a glimmer. She then cast her eyes to the ground, her eyebrows blinking in reflection as the past stirred in her, which in turn gave rise to ancient impulses that even she did not understand . . . impulses she had acquired at birth and then had driven her forward in life toward hardship and ruination.

"Hey, Boy," she said, "was your mother by chance a beautiful Danish girl? A mere *child* who did not even attain her thirteenth year until a month after your birth?"

This surprised Tristan, and he stared at her a moment, struck by the trace of trepidation that had slipped from her tongue. Then, as he peered closer, it appeared that she had taken on a strange, wistful gaze, like that of the executioner as he gazes at his victim just before dropping the ax; that gaze that says, *What I am about to do to you is not my wish, but my duty.* And this caused him to feel that an unwanted change of balance was about to occur if he replied to her question. Nevertheless, he advanced.

"Indeed, that describes my mother when I was born. Her name is Asta, of the Norman Danes."

At this Duxia shriveled back, like a leaf afire, and she uttered a faint cry as her shoulders began to shake. Confounded, Tristan stepped forward and came close enough that deep within each of her pupils he saw his own reflection, and imagined for an instant that he somehow looked dead in those ancient, sunken sockets.

"Do you know me?" he whispered, as if not wishing the world to hear her reply.

"What are you two talking about over there?" cried the Hermit who had been watching their exchange with displeasure. "Tristan, heed my warnings. She's a walking disease!"

Ignoring this, Duxia scratched at the wart protruding just above her left brow as her brows drew down and she nodded. "Oh yes, boy, I know you. Indeed, I delivered you into this world, and also your baby brother, Guillaume. When you mentioned your name earlier, it gave me a start, but I wasn't certain it was the same family I knew in Saint-Germain-en-Laye many years ago. Now, looking at your pale eyes, I *know*."

"But I have never seen you in my . . ."

"I worked for your grandfather's people back then. His name was Guntar the Mace and he was executed before your birth by his overlord, William the Bastard of Normandy, for opposing the marriage of his twelve-year-old daughter into the French Saint-Germain clan. It was all part of a greater political arrangement for treaty purposes to keep peace between the Bastard of Normandy and Philippe, King of France. Indeed, know also that I delivered your mother, Asta, into this world as well, and raised her up. She was like a daughter to me and I loved her more than anyone on this earth." Then she paused, and her face twisted with bile. "And I followed her household into that accursed marriage to Lord Roger de Saint-Germain, a man thirty years her senior. What a wicked breed of Frenchmen was that entire Saint-Germain bunch! Taking your mother as his twelve-year-old child bride, Roger de Saint-Germain filled her full of his foul semen though she was but a babe herself; thus *you* were born. Oh, that union was frowned upon by God above, and *still is*, boy! Yes, I continued to serve your mother, and cared for you, too, until shortly after your brother was born. Of course you would not remember me, you were three when I left. But from the moment you were born, I could never forget those frightening pale-grey eyes you possess, nor your fair hair and fine skin."

Tristan shook his head with doubt though he knew somehow that the old woman's words were true. "But I have never once heard mention of you, not from my mother, nor from the members of my mother's Danish Guard who—"

"Oh yes, the Danish Guard. I knew them well. They were like her family, charged with protecting Asta by her father upon her birth. As I recall there was Orla the Ox, Ivar Crowbones, Sigurd Fairhair, and many others." Then the wrinkled furrows creasing her forehead deepened. "Four years after I left your mother's household, I received word of your father's execution for treason, also at the hands of the Bastard of Normandy."

"You know about that?"

"Indeed, *predicted* it years before."

"Eh?"

"'Twas nothing extraordinary, boy. Disloyalty was in his blood. I basically *spoke* the predictable while others kept silent. After learning of his beheading, I wasn't unhappy to hear that my words had come true. But I *was* happy for your mother, though losing his wealth and being dishonored created hardship for her. It only lasted a short while, I heard, huh? I was told she remarried your father's brother, Desmond DuLac, to extract herself from those difficulties . . . and also heard that she abandoned you and your brother, sending you off to a monastery as part of that bartering process with her new husband who *refused* you. Oh, I could scarcely believe my ears. Asta did truly love you boys beyond description."

At this Tristan bridled and shook his head. "It was more complicated than all that, I assure you. It was not until later that I came to understand the details and complexity of her decision to send me and Guillaume to the Black Monks. She was well justified in her actions under the circumstances. Tell me then, how is it that you came to *leave* my mother's service?"

Duxia retreated a step at this question, and ran her tongue over cracked lips as a bitter expression slipped over the crags of her face. "I was *driven* away," she said.

"By my father?"

"No. By your mother."

"What? I don't believe you. My mother, Asta, is the gentlest soul God ever placed upon this earth, and is even now a Bride of Christ at the convent of Marcigny. She would never deprive anyone of their work nor drive them from her home, especially someone who raised her and loved her as family."

"Do you think I *lie* then?" Duxia's tiny mouth spewed in a burst of anger that startled Tristan. Then she snapped it shut as though realizing she had over-spoken, and he could see her working her tongue and lips with agitation in tight little convulsions.

"What's going on over there?" came a voice from the spring. It was the Hermit. "I advise that you not converse with that old bitch. She's trouble, lad!"

Tristan dismissed the comment with a flap of the hand and turned back to Duxia. "Very well then," he said, "knowing my mother's infinite kindness for others, there must have been a good reason she drove you off, eh?"

"Yes, there was a reason, although not a good one." Here she paused a moment, and threw Tristan a look of defeat. "'Twas *you*, the reason."

"Me? Oh come now! Ridiculous. How is that possible if I was three years old?"

"Oh, only three perhaps, boy, but you came into this world with a burden attached to your black soul. And though you were the most beautiful infant France has ever birthed until the arrival of your baby brother, as I was pulling you from your mother's loins you looked up at me with those cold grey eyes and I nearly fainted with dread; knew from that moment you were marked and would be a curse to all who embraced you!"

"You saw and determined this at the moment of my birth?" said Tristan, unable to disguise condescension. "I noticed earlier that your accent is Finnish. My mother's people, the Danes, have long claimed the women of Finland possess a gift for foretelling the future, especially as they attain old age. That pouch about your neck, I suspect it contains the desiccated bones of a small bird, and that you *read* those bones. One of the Danes who protected my mother was named Ivar Crowbones, and he learned to roll bird bones from his Finnish grandmother. He used this skill to some advantage, they say, before each battle in which he and the Danish Guard engaged."

"Oh, you're a clever one, seeing and hearing so very much with a single gaze or turn of the ear. Ay, you're correct, as I already said, what is about to arrive is nothing extraordinary. The future is at times obvious to any who possess the gift of perception. That was the only gift God gave me, but as with all things sublime, it has also been bittersweet, and served as a stone about my neck. Oh, I tried to warn your mother from the moment you sucked in your first breath of air that fortune and prosperity would wilt at your feet upon your very approach! In the blood that she shed birthing you there were black lines of goo that spelled misfortune. I told her that death would be your message, and beauty would be your lure; drawing others in, beguiling and disarming them just before the strike. She shunned my warnings despite our tightly woven relationship. Oh, she was like my blood and we spent every day together. Indeed, it was Asta who taught me to read and write. It was the only good time of my life."

Tristan stood motionless, his eyes silently refuting every charge she had set out concerning any curse he might have carried from birth. Even this acute denial could not disguise the malaise which had begun to slip up his spine. "Regardless of what you believe, I am not a serpent, Duxia," he said with cool deliberation.

"Ha, oh how you deceive yourself, young Tristan de Saint-Germain!" she sneered. Then she spat at his feet. "Death shines all about you, boy, like distant starlight perhaps, but it will one day be a close and raging fire that shall spread over the land, devouring all it encounters. This I even told your mother and the Danish Guard years ago who dismissed me as a crank." Here she paused again, thinking it perhaps best to say no more, but Tristan's expression of disdain pressed her forward. "So then," she continued, her eyes narrowing, "on the day of your Brother's first birthday while bathing you, I tried to drown you, but the silent Dane they called Guthroth the Quiet saw me, snatched you from the water, and then nearly choked the life out of me. He then told your mother, and though she had patiently endured three years of my pleas and warnings about you, she could not abide by this act. She immediately drove me from the Saint-Germain family manor though I loved her more than life itself."

Tristan stood gazing at her in mute wonder, so appalled by the old woman's tale that he could find no words, nor even summon anger at what the old hag had just revealed.

"Since that day," she continued, gazing inward, "I have wandered the roads begging, depending on the kindness of those I encounter and the generosity of monasteries along the way." Then, raising her crooked finger at Tristan, her eyes flicked involuntarily and she began nodding her head up and down with affirmation. "But through this all," she said, her face shining with prophecy, "I was right from the moment your startling grey eyes shone upon me from between your mother's bloody thighs, and I am right to this very day." There was no triumph in her voice, only resignation.

"You make a great commotion about my grey eyes at birth, old woman," Tristan said, his tolerance beginning to erode, "yet they are no different than those of my mother, Asta, nor of my brother, Guillaume. Are they cursed also, then?"

"No!" Then the old hag turned and moved toward the spring. "Leave me here at this juncture in the road for I no longer wish to see your face, nor be within reach of your long, pallid shadow." Then, as she limped away, Tristan heard her mumble, "Oh, I wonder what it is that you want, boy . . . and how many men shall die as you strive to seek it?"

CHAPTER SEVEN

BLESSED CARDINAL ODO DE LAGERY

Peter the Hermit and Innocenzo were quite content to abandon Duxia de Falaise at the spring despite Tristan's hesitancy to leave her there alone. The old woman's tale had perturbed him, yet he pitied her also, wondering how she had managed to survive so long in a world that had rejected her. Then too, his mind was aswirl with refutations to the things she had said about him. *She is insane*, he thought at first. *No, far too coherent to be mad*, he then decided. *But the look in her eyes, and the insistence of her voice.*

And so with each step forward of his horse he wrestled with himself until finally the Hermit, observing that Tristan was greatly distracted, spoke up. "Aha," he snorted smugly, "she has fired her poison straight to your brain, eh, lad? Ha! I tried to warn you, but oh no, you never listen to old Peter, huh? She has a dead spirit and everywhere she goes she stirs the muck of misery. By the thorns upon Christ's own bristling crown of thorns, did you not hear the earth whisper beneath her very feet? She is the Dark Prince's witch, that one!"

Tristan nodded though he was barely listening. His mind was beginning to slip into the backwaters of dread, where men conceal their unspoken fears in black, scumcovered pools of uncertainty and doubt. And even as he ventured there, unwillingly, gray threatening clouds arose ahead, heavy with ominous rain and thunder. Then from the north he felt a restless wind arise, lifting at his hair, raising it in errant tufts. *A storm is coming*, he thought. This disturbed him even more. Though he knew it to be foolish, he could not help but attribute the darkening skies to the old hag left at the spring.

It has always been common for the powerful and the educated to convey dread to the weak and the ignorant. But when this trick is reversed, which is rare, the powerful and educated often begin to unravel, and this is exactly what was transpiring in Tristan's brain as his horse ambled south toward Cluny. Tristan began to summarize the events of his life and began to draw connections he had never before considered. This is when it began to dawn on him that there had, indeed, been a wake of misfortune amongst many whose existence had touched his.

To begin, his father had been denounced and executed. Soon afterwards, his mother had been forced into a miserable marriage for twelve years to the malicious Lord DuLac, and his brother had been forced into the Cluny Monastery at age four along with Tristan. Then, too, he thought back on the merciless ravaging of the Roman populace he had witnessed just a year before by Duke

Robert Guiscard's violent troops. Thousands had been slaughtered, women and children had been raped, and much of the city had been reduced to ash. *Is it possible that I brought this upon the innocent people of Rome*, Tristan wondered, recalling that he had prayed within the Vatican itself for three days and nights that Duke Robert Guiscard's Norman army would come to the rescue of Pope Gregory who was besieged in Rome by the Germans. Indeed, Duke Guiscard's forces had arrived at the final hour just as Tristan had prayed, but then the volatile Guiscard unexpectedly unleashed his forces upon the civilian population of the city, and they set the city to waste, mercilessly butchering and mutilating the innocent by the thousands.

And more recently, Brother Domingo had been killed in Rome as was Brother LeDoux of Dijon, as was the Byzantine nun, as was the innocent Byzantine nobleman who unluckily appeared at the nun's door as Tristan and Handel had ended her life. Even though each incident in Tristan's recalled litany of horrors distinctly involved outlying factors and individuals, Tristan began to imagine a common thread within the sum of these misfortunes, *himself.*

"She'll have you blaming yourself for Adam's loss of Eden, lad," laughed the Hermit, amused by Tristan's glum demeanor, "as well as for the fall of the Roman Empire and the great barbarian invasions that ensued! She knows nothing but misery, and therefore spreads it everywhere she may go. Forget the old bitch, I say, or you'll devour yourself from within! Were I not a monk, I'd happily end her vile poisoning of the human spirit with a hammer blow to the head, but God forbids such things. In any case, she'll encounter justice when God rewards her with His final punishment, the fires of Hell."

Finally arriving at Cluny, Tristan immediately inquired about Cardinal Odo de Lagery.

"Ay," said the gatekeeper, "he arrived from Ostia with a small entourage just yesterday. You'll find him in Abbot Hugh's quarters. And good news he bears. It's said that la Gran Contessa Mathilda is holding against the German onslaught in northern Italy."

"Eh?" said the Hermit. "Oh, what glorious tidings Odo brings then! If only Mathilda could put them on the run and then move south and take Rome back from the false pope. Then we could reclaim the Vatican and set Cardinal Odo upon the Pope's throne! Oh, what good would it do for we true Catholics to see that archbishop's head lopped off and tossed into a picking basket!"

"Take Rome back from Guibert of Ravenna?" said the guard. "Have you not heard? The citizens of Rome have themselves chased the anti-pope from the city."

"What?" cried the Hermit. "Oh, God be praised!"

Tristan was pleased to hear this news, but something else was pulling at him so he left the Hermit and quickly made his way to the priory where Benedictine couriers picked up and delivered correspondence to the monastery. "Has anything arrived for Tristan de Saint-Germain?" he asked.

The young monk seated at the work table looked up at Tristan with interest. "Indeed," he said. "*Three* messages. One from Paris, one from Avignon, and . . ."

"Yes, yes," Tristan said, trying not to sound impatient.

The monk reached beneath the table to a hidden compartment and withdrew the letters, each stamped with a black wax seal indicating that it was of the highest confidential order, not to be discussed, never to be left in the open.

"Thank you," said Tristan, slipping the letters down into the front of his trousers. Then he made his way to Abbot Hugh's chambers and soon located Cardinal Odo. Seeing him, Tristan dropped to a knee and bowed reverently.

The Cardinal immediately pulled him to his feet and wrapped his arms about him in a hearty embrace. "Ho, Tristan, lad," he laughed, "off your knees! You embarrass me with such formality!"

Standing, Tristan returned the hug, then stepped back, his face aglow being in the company of the great Cardinal once more. He loved this tall, commanding man who had been his de facto father since the age of seven when he and Guillaume had first arrived at the Cluny monastery. "I have worried about you in Ostia, Cardinal Odo," Tristan said. "Being just an arm's reach from the anti-pope, I have always feared that he might turn on you at any moment. I just heard that he has been run out of Rome by the citizenry, so I'll worry less now."

"Yes, but he will be back, for serpents never retreat for long. Even when he ruled Rome he could do little more than keep an eye to me. The balance there is so fragile, so delicate, that it would take just a spark to ignite a bloodbath. The Imperial Prefect and half of the population supports Heinrich and have never forgiven Duke Guiscard's rape of the city when he rescued Pope Gregory, but the Roman consuls and the other half of the city support *our* cause. Therefore, any act of retribution by him against me would have stirred an uprising of our faithful, and the anti-pope could ill afford that, especially with King Heinrich back in Germany and Mathilda still on the loose in Tuscany."

"Yes, I have already heard that my aunt continues to harry the Germans in north central Italy."

"She is pushing back against Heinrich's occupation militia there, and you'll be proud to hear that your brother carries his own banner for her. They say Guillaume presses the attack with unparalleled courage. But then, you and I know what he's made of, eh?"

"Guillaume has been fearless since birth, and blessed in physical skills and panache. Yet, I fear for him at times, Cardinal. His courage invites peril."

"Your old friends, the Danish Guard, now serve in Guillaume's cavalry contingent though he is slightly past seventeen, and they remain as ferocious as ever I am told."

Mention of the Danish Guard precipitated a sudden flood of memories in Tristan as the faces of Orla the Ox, Ivar Crowbones and Guthroth the Quiet came to mind. These men had been like family to him prior to his being sent to the monastery, and had been by his mother's side since her birth. These men had remained at Asta's side after taking Tristan and Guillaume to Cluny, and stayed with her even when she moved to England to marry the loathsome Lord DuLac. Then, after nearly twelve years of misery, the Danish Guard turned on DuLac's French forces and helped Asta escape England in a daring gambit that nearly brought all of them to annihilation. But the Danes had prevailed, and had established a new life in Italy in the military service of Countess Mathilda of Tuscany.

"Yes, they are masters of the ax and hammer," said Tristan. Then he paused and looked to the floor.

"Well, what is it, Tristan?" said Odo. "I know that look."

"It . . . well, you need to know that Peter the Hermit has accompanied me to Cluny."

"He's here? *Now*?"

"Yes, he heard you were coming from Italy and has made his way here to meet you."

Odo clapped an open palm to his forehead and closed his eyes. "Of all men, KuKu Peter," he muttered, dropping his head and crossing himself. "Lord in Heaven," he whispered, "please help me remain calm."

Tristan was about to explain how he had found the Hermit. Before he could utter the first word, the door burst open and the Hermit entered the room, both hands raised, flagging about in jubilation. "Aha! Our next Pope!!" he cried with that revelatory boisterousness that startled others, but only served to agitate the Cardinal. He approached Odo, then began pacing in circles around him for no apparent reason other than to gawk blankly at Odo's feet, his back, and his face. "Oh, I foretold this development," he exclaimed between his pacing, "and you did nothing but berate me, Odo! And though my timing might have been a bit premature, the truth is the truth, I say!"

"Premature?" said Odo with derision. "Really, Peter? Ha, that was nearly ten years ago when you began this silliness about me becoming Pope! I told you then to stop it, and I tell you now the same. I had no plans to be Pope then, nor do I now . . . and respectfully request that you not start up such talk again."

"Oh, you may *respectfully* request anything you like, Odo," the Hermit proclaimed, his eyes widening to impossible dimensions, "but God's will shall not be silenced! Nor shall his messenger!" Then he stopped moving about and plopped his arms across his chest. "Uh, and God's messenger," he added, lowering his voice, "that would be me, of course, Odo."

"Of course, but has God not informed you, Peter, that Pope Gregory announced the faithful Cardinal Desiderius as his choice of successor on his deathbed?"

"Details, details! Of course He did! God also mentioned to me that Pope Gregory was an old and broken man, feeble of mind at the time. Gregory simply misspoke! Yes, he *said* Desiderius, but he actually *meant* to say Odo de Lagery!"

"That's ridiculous," Odo replied. "Once you get something in your head, Peter, you surpass the obstinacy of your own donkey! Cease this talk. I want no more of it. Furthermore I have communicated my support of Desiderius to both Countess Mathilda and Duke Robert Borsa of Lower Italy. We all three stand together in pressing Desiderius to accept the Pope's tiara just as Pope Gregory requested."

"Aha! He balks! He refuses the position, we hear in France. He understands God's will, I say. Besides, he's tepid and soft. In these dire times we need a strong leader to reclaim the Vatican and restore the true Church, and there's none stronger than you, Odo!"

Tristan and the Cardinal exchanged a glance. Tristan could see that Odo had not made even the tiniest impression on the Hermit, and he also began to see that lines of strain were beginning to crease Odo's face. "Peter," he interjected, "the Cardinal has spoken. Out of respect for his position, perhaps you should for once heed his counsel, eh?"

"Heed his counsel" you say? What? The Church is crumbling at the foundation, King Heinrich of Germany and his lapdog Guibert of Ravenna control the Vatican, and the entirety of Christendom hangs by a thread, and you say *heed Odo's counsel*? Ho, this is not the time to wither! Indeed, 'tis time to blast the trumpets and hail our new and legitimate Pope, Odo de Lagery!"

Seeing that he had only further inflamed the Hermit, Tristan shrugged and looked helplessly at Odo, who had by now raised both hands to his face in exasperation. "Have you already begun spreading your prophecy, Peter?" said Odo, already certain of the answer.

"Indeed, from Paris east to Dijon! And I would have spread the word from Dijon south to Cluny were we not fleeing from Satan's grip in the form of a French lord named Truffault who tried to have me hanged, but I raised the angry mob up against him in the nick of time."

"Hanged?" said Odo. "Yet again? Must you always embroil yourself in the impossible? Must you always create an uproar and inflame the masses? Could you not just once, Peter, behave like a normal monk?"

At this a look of indignation flooded the Hermit's face. Then he threw both hands to his hips and his voice elevated even higher than its normal, permanently boisterous timbre. "What, you say? And deny my calling? Disobey my Lord and Savior? I am what I am, Odo, because I faithfully do God's bidding. Nay, nay, never will I hold my tongue when God orders me to wag it! Not even for you!"

"Very well then, Peter, but know this: I shall do everything possible to see that Cardinal Desiderius becomes Pope. Now, if you please, I have endured all the haranguing that I can bear in a single session. Go to the stables and make arrangements to stay the night."

"The stables?" said the Hermit.

"Indeed, Peter. You are still banned from the Cluny Guest Hall due to your last stunt."

"Stunt? Oh, sir, I was merely preaching the word and . . ."

"No, you claimed that half the noblemen within the Hall were going straight to Hell upon their final judgment, which resulted in an armed riot and the destruction of half the refectory."

"But they *are* going to Hell, Odo. God told me."

"Peter, go to the stable! And do not leave those premises until the morning or I shall have you booted by the Burgundian Guard. Do you understand? And furthermore, do not even speak to the horses or the oxen for I have neither the time nor the energy to quell an uprising of the livestock!"

At this Tristan burst into laughter. In detecting that Cardinal Odo's expression was devoid of humor, he quickly stifled it. "Oh, Peter," Tristan then added, "do not terrorize the stable boys as you did me years ago. I still carry the burden of your frightful words in my dreams."

It was not Peter the Hermit who was on Tristan's mind, but the old hag, Duxia de Falaise, whom they had abandoned at the spring. Just as the Hermit closed the door behind himself, Tristan envisioned the ancient woman trying to hold his head beneath the water to drown him as a baby, and as this dark image unveiled itself in his imagination, this time she succeeded.

CHAPTER EIGHT

WINDS OF UNCERTAINTY

At day's end Tristan retired to his room, and after closing the door behind him, pulled the three letters from his trousers and set them on his bed. After opening the first, he shook his head with disappointment, then leaned over and set the edge of the letter to the candle flame until it shriveled into black curls of ash, finally disintegrating into specks of nothing. He then opened the second, shrugged, and set it afire also. After reading the third, which was routed from Paris, his mood lightened as he read, "*The Romani party you seek has established a camp along the Loire River just north of the city of Orléans. There are about twenty people in this group which is headed by a young woman by the name of Mala. Though they claim to be an entertainment troupe, it has been reported that while in Paris this past year, they made their fortune through theft and deception. Take caution when approaching them.*"

Tristan read the message twice more, then placed it to the candle just as he had the others. As he watched the flame devour it, he tried to envision the beautiful and mysterious Romani girl named Mala who had migrated north out of Spain as a child to escape the Moslem incursions. He wasn't sure why she had so recently resurfaced in his thoughts of late, especially during moments of solitude and reflection. He secretly hoped that he might encounter her again.

Nonetheless, these letters indicated something stronger than the vagueness of idle hope. Indeed, he had deliberately sent out three inquiries to three different parts of France prior to leaving Italy using the Benedictine's underground network of informers and spies, knowing that such action for personal purposes was a violation of conduct. Nevertheless, he still carried the horror of his recent venture in Rome with him, and the confusion caused by that experience had begun to erode many things Tristan had once imagined carved in stone. Surely, he rationalized, such an indiscretion as acquiring personal information was insignificant as compared to the killings he had been complicit with through Handel in Rome. Thus, bolstered by his own reasoning, Tristan went about his business, satisfied that he had not sinned, and even more content that he at least now knew of Mala's whereabouts.

Meanwhile, Cardinal Odo de Lagery had spent two vociferous days disputing with Peter the Hermit on the subject of who should ascend to the papacy once the anti-pope, Guibert of Ravenna, was removed. "Cardinal Desiderius!" Odo would insist over and over, but he may as well have been talking to the wall.

"Nay! Never!" the Hermit would counter bitterly. "He's not willing, nor is he worthy! Any cleric who stands idly by and does not accept the challenge of retaking the Vatican while the true Church dissolves in the hands of the Germans does not even *deserve* consideration for the papacy. Besides, such a thing would end poorly!"

"End poorly?"

"Ay, God himself would be displeased by such a selection, and would see to it that it ended quickly! Then we'd be right back in the same fix. Best that you step forward right now and save us all time, effort, and blood!"

"Oh, and I suppose *God* has relayed this message to you, Peter?"

"Of course he has."

Tristan was present during many of these arguments. So, on the third morning he called Cardinal Odo aside. "The Hermit is a solitary man on a donkey. Why do you allow him so much familiarity, or even so much of your valuable time? We both know that he never gives ground because he believes that God speaks to him directly, although we know better. Would it not be simpler to just send him on his way?"

Odo looked at Tristan a moment. "You speak bluntly, my boy. That is not like you."

"There is no possibility of swaying the Hermit. He will do what he wishes, even in the threat of death. He is a fanatic."

"Yes, of course he is. He creates damage by throwing my name about for Pope, as well as confusion. We need unity now, not division."

"His damage will be slight, because his influence is slight. Besides, everyone of significance believes him to be mad. His words will have little weight in the end."

Odo was struck by the straightforwardness of Tristan's counsel. "You are absolutely right," he said. "The man has an uncanny way of getting under my skin, but you are on the mark so I will not waste another moment arguing with him!" Then he looked at Tristan. "Such counsel coming from you? What happened to the wide-eyed, thoughtful little boy who landed in my lap some twelve years ago?"

Tristan shook his head, and nearly smiled. "*You*, Cardinal. You took me in, saved me from ignorance and dishonor; educated me. You advised me, showed me how the Church and men think. To me, as a boy, you were the most magnificent, intelligent man alive, and still are. You opened the world to a lost boy. Too, this past year has been a different journey for me. I, well, I have begun to see things differently. Though we attempt to drive others this way or that, we barely manage to drive ourselves; *that* only if either fortune or God allow it. It is more difficult to drag a single mule than to lead a thousand sheep; the Hermit being the mule, of course."

"Of course," laughed Odo. "Oh, I've missed you this past year. Must I now worry about this new journey of yours? Let us hope it doesn't hone too hard an edge upon you, eh?" As he said this, Tristan thought he perceived in Odo's glimpse a knowing acknowledgement of some sort, as a parent might issue gazing at their maturing offspring.

That very afternoon Odo ordered the Hermit and his nephew to depart Cluny. "Oh, you shun me now," the Hermit cried with agitation at Odo, looking over his back as he and Innocenzo were led out the monastery gate by the guards, "but heed my words!" Then his eyes narrowed and he pointed skyward, as if probing the future. "Desiderius as Pope will end poorly, Odo! God has ordained it, and I have *twice* passed this message along to you, so watch now and regret!"

Odo and Tristan watched the Hermit and Innocenzo disappear out the gate on their donkeys, the Hermit flapping his arms about with obvious ire and his nephew nodding with vigorous agreement to every gesture his uncle made. "Now he threatens a poor end to the Papacy of Desiderius since you refuse to agree with him," said Tristan, shaking his head. "Indeed, the Hermit *does* operate on frightening others, just as he accuses the hag that he so bitterly despises."

They separated then and Odo made his way back to Abbot Hugh's private chambers. Prior to Odo's appointment as Cardinal-Bishop of Ostia, Abbot Hugh had been Odo's superior at Cluny. Theirs had been an extremely intimate relationship, and the two high clerics greatly respected each other.

Abbot Hugh was among the most revered clerics in all Europe, and his position at Cluny had long placed at his disposal political clout and wealth that eclipsed even the Vatican itself. For Abbott Hugh, little had changed over the years. The monk, Odo de Lagery, who once served under Abbot Hugh had also risen to the extreme heights of the Church. As Cardinal-Bishop of Ostia, he had served as chief counsel to Pope Gregory and as de facto spokesman for the College of Cardinals. Furthermore, Pope Gregory had appointed him Papal Legate to both France and Germany, which had even further expanded his authority and range of influence.

Following the loss of Rome to King Heinrich and the loss of the papacy to anti-pope Clement, Cardinal Odo found himself in a most unusual position. On the one hand, as a passionate supporter of the ousted Pope Gregory, he was thrown into a tenuous political position on the heels of the German takeover of Rome. On the other hand, King Heinrich and his anti-pope could not imprison or execute Cardinal Odo without enraging the remainder of Europe and many within Rome. An uneasy truce ensued, then, as Heinrich and anti-pope Clement contented themselves with keeping Odo under close scrutiny in Rome, knowing well that he remained loyal to the Gregorian papists.

Interestingly, as the most powerful and highly respected Gregorian in all of Italy other than Cardinal Desiderius of Monte Cassino, he found himself in an even greater position of power than before within the Gregorian party of Europe. Simply put, Odo was located in Rome whereas Desiderius was located in Lower

Italy. In essence, it was Odo then who managed the ongoing business of the true Church in Rome during this perplexing period of schism and war. All those who hoped for the defeat of the Germans looked to Odo to hold the Church together until the legitimate papacy could be restored.

This was a heavy burden, then, in terms of expectations and responsibility that Odo de Lagery carried upon his shoulders. Being a deeply pious and devout monk of traditional Catholic roots, Odo de Lagery was driven by a singular mission: to restore the Vatican to its rightful shepherds and drive the usurpers back to Germany for good.

"And so," said Abbot Hugh welcoming Odo into his chambers, "whereas the news of the anti-pope fleeing Rome is good, what is this unfortunate schism developing amongst the Normans in Lower Italy? They have always been our strongest allies against Heinrich, so division bodes ill for our cause."

"Yes. As you know our Norman champion, Duke Robert Guiscard, died of fever in July along with five hundred Norman knights during the siege of Cephalonia in Greece. He had taken a hundred and fifty ships east to reclaim territories lost by his eldest son, Bohemud, last year to the Byzantines. In death he left four sons and the eldest, Bohemud, is furious that his father named the second son as his successor in Lower Italy."

"What? The old Duke named the younger Roger Borsa as successor? Why?"

"Bohemud was born of an earlier Norman wife, and Roger was born of Sichelgaita whom Duke Guiscard adored. Furthermore, Guiscard was unhappy with Bohemud for losing all the Byzantine territories Guiscard had fought so hard to take from Emperor Alexius. I shall try to sort things out between the two brothers since the Normans of Lower Italy along with Countess Mathilda of Tuscany are our backbone in the fight against the Germans."

"What of the two younger sons?"

"The third son is Guy of Amalfi and the fourth is Robert Scalio. Fortunately for us and Lower Italy, they have both steadfastly refused to become entangled in their older brothers' dispute."

"I pray you succeed in preventing a civil war between Borsa and Bohemud then, Odo. Tell me about Rome now that the anti-pope has fled."

"The year is coming to a close in several months, and with the sudden retreat of anti-pope Clement, we think it wise to make ready for a new Papal election in Rome, hopefully by Easter."

"We should have had our Pope months ago, right after Pope Gregory's passing. Pope Gregory proposed Cardinal Desiderius as his successor, and the College of Cardinals was in agreement!"

"Yes, but Cardinal Desiderius refused the office."

"Ah, Desiderius, dear Desiderius. Such a deserving man. He receives much criticism for not accepting the office, but he has privately shared with both of us his concerns about his health. I wonder, though. Perhaps he makes too much of this business with his health."

Odo shook his head. "Desiderius is seen by others as a strong, unshakable Gregorian Catholic, yet there is a frailty about him that even he recognizes. His greatest fear is that he is at the limits of his endurance and that the papacy would break him. And as he told me, a broken Pope is not what is needed if we ever hope to reclaim the Vatican."

Abbot Hugh agreed. "You know, Odo, if Desiderius continues to refuse the position, there is only *one* other name."

"Yes, Abbot."

"And if this occurs, are you ready to shoulder such weight, my friend, in these times of blood-letting and hatred? Such things can crush the strongest of men."

"I have prayed on it, Abbot. That is to say, I have prayed that it doesn't come down to me as Pope. In the end, I believe Desiderius will see that he is the key to resolving our current dilemma. If we pray, God will strengthen him."

"If not, Odo, there still remains no other name but yours. Funny thing, you know, I spoke to the Hermit just before you ousted him from the monastery today. He has long said that *you* would be Pope one day, well before all this mess with King Heinrich. They say out there in the hinterlands that this shoeless tramp on the donkey does truly possess the gift of prophecy."

Odo nodded. "I know what they say, Abbot. I also know that the Hermit thrives on his own puffery, and is convinced of his own miraculous powers and private connection to God. Let's hope and pray, the *Hermit* is *not* the one that God has truly chosen to communicate through, eh?"

This forced Abbott Hugh to smile a bit. "Ah, remember, Odo, God sees no more value in kings and Popes than in children or fools. In any case, I stand with you regardless of the pendulum's swing. Then he stood and crossed Odo with a blessing. "Dieu nous dirigera," he said. "God will direct us."

CHAPTER NINE

A SUDDEN TWIST

Two days prior to Cardinal Odo's departure from Cluny, he summoned Tristan and handed him a bundle of documents. "Review these carefully," he said, "then you are off to Paris to the court of King Philippe."

"Paris? My instructions were to return to Monte Cassino upon completing my affairs here in France. Brother Muehler is expecting me and . . ."

"Sit a moment, Tristan," said Odo, ushering Tristan into a chair. "It is time that you know something." He paused thoughtfully a moment then before continuing. "Tristan," he finally said, "Brother Muehler works for *me*. I manage the underground, and I have decided to change your calendar."

A slap to the face could not have confounded Tristan more. "What?" he said. "I thought Cardinal Desiderius managed the underground through Muehler at Monte Cassino."

"No. I run the underground from Rome, *through* Muehler at Monte Cassino. Desiderius is far too fragile and altruistic to be associated with such dirty activities. During his papacy Pope Gregory ran the underground from the Vatican. When he was exiled, he placed me in the position."

Tristan was speechless, chasing one wild thought after another until finally his face colored and he looked down. "You know then about the business in Rome? Our murder of the Byzantine nun and the nobleman who innocently wandered into . . ."

"Yes," Odo interrupted, "and that your hesitancy nearly got Handel and you both killed; also that this bitter lesson has stirred confusion and shame in you. Oh, Tristan, that is how I tried to raise you, isn't it? Fortunately, the lesson in Rome also hardened you a bit, and thick skin is a necessity if one is to survive the underground."

Still unable to digest this sudden revelation about his adored mentor and father figure running the Benedictine spy network, Tristan stared mutely at the tabletop. Finally he looked up. "The underground is such a violent business. I could never have imagined that you could be involved in it, Cardinal Odo. I . . ."

"Oh, nor could I at first. In view of what the Germans were doing with impunity to our own ranks, I embraced the responsibility, and do to this very day. There is something else. Your request to join the underground, I blocked it at first, knowing that such work might turn you on your head. I also knew you had no wish to spend your life cloistered away in some monastery copying manuscripts. Besides, to lock such gifts as God has given you within the confines of monastery walls would have been a sin. Shelter exists behind such walls, but you have chosen to expose yourself to the wilds of men. You are learning that it is a bloody domain where parasites feed on the corpses of others, seeking God-only-knows-what during their short existence here in this life."

"And *us*, Cardinal?" said Tristan, treading lightly. "Are we any different?"

Odo shot Tristan an unsettling gaze, one more severe than Tristan was accustomed to experiencing from Odo. "Yes, we are *very* different, lad. We do not seek gold or power, only to save souls, for eternity. We labor not for ourselves, but for others, and for God. When you come to this realization, Tristan, your hesitancy will dissolve as did my own. Judging from your own hard words about the Hermit the other day, I believe you have already taken the first steps along that path."

Tristan nodded with uncertainty. "Perhaps. I doubt I will ever be as hard as Muehler or Handel. Then he opened the packet Odo had handed him. "So, the court of King Philippe, the Amorous in Paris then?"

"Yes. As we prepare for the papal election, we must know where the French King stands. The anti-pope is still poised to counterattack Rome at any point. We don't anticipate receiving Philippe's active support in the form of troops or money, but then we must also ensure that he is not carrying on secret negotiations with King Heinrich or the Roman imperialists who back him."

"A French alliance with the Germans? King Philippe?"

"Philippe is not pleased with the Church at the moment, nor are we pleased with him. He has since a tender age had a weakness for female flesh and openly allows his scrotum to be his compass. Queen Bertha has tolerated his wandering erection for years now. Our patience with his open promiscuity dwindles, and he knows it. The bigger issue is his practice of simony and investiture. We hear rumors that King Philippe continues to sell the offices of bishop and archbishop to the highest bidder, an act that flies in the face of all that we reformists stand for. It is a festering sore that continues to grow within his realm, therefore we must keep an eye to him."

Even though Tristan heard every word that Odo said, a part of him was also elsewhere, secretly calculating the proximity of Orléans to Paris. *The Loire Valley, south of Paris, is a bit off the track, but not completely out of my way to the king's court.*

"Anyway," Odo continued, "I have decided you would be the perfect guest of the French court, and will appear there posing as a Papal diplomat under the name Lucien Broussard. The bundle there contains your letters of introduction and finances. We have had a member of the underground in Philippe's court for years now, old Brother Augustine. He will brief you when you arrive and hand over the documentation we seek concerning the French king's violations of selling clerical office. As for any potential alliance with Germany against us, that is for you to root out."

"When I finish, do I report back to you here in Cluny then?"

"No, I leave shortly for Lower Italy. Bad blood has effused between Roger Borsa and Bohemud over the succession of their father's territories. From there I go to Rome. After your visit with King Philippe, you will eventually bring everything back to me in Rome. Besides, I want you there for the Papal election. Hear this word of caution, Tristan: The French court may not be as bloody as the streets of Rome, but it is treacherous none the less. Be on guard, especially for the women of the court. They spin intrigue skillfully, and devour their prey. Someone like you will quickly attract their attention, and their intentions. Do you understand?"

"Yes, Cardinal, of course," Tristan replied, already plotting a course in his head for some unknown spot along the Loire River just north of the city of Orléans.

"When you leave Paris, before meeting me in Rome you will return first to Cluny and spend time with Abbot Hugh, continuing your role as the diplomat, Lucien Broussard."

"Oh?"

"Yes, Abbot Hugh is entering into negotiations with a delegation of Moors from North Africa in six weeks or so and will need your expertise with the Arabic tongue and customs. We are on the edge of war down there also, but prefer to settle things peacefully since we already have our hands full with King Heinrich and the Germans. Oh, and one other thing, during your month or so in Cluny, I want you to grow a beard."

"A beard?" said Tristan, who had been clean shaven since puberty.

"Yes, and a mustache. When you join me in Rome for the election of the Pope, it is best that you not be recognized by anyone. There may be more underground work for you in Rome in the future, and between your previous years in Rome and this recent episode concerning the assassination of the Byzantine nun, it is best that we set your true identity aside lest someone makes the connection. When you meet me there for the Papal election, you will arrive incognito."

"No longer Tristan, nor the Norman dandy, nor the Papal diplomat, then?"

"No, you will arrive as a mercenary, a French officer from Burgundy by the name of Captain Stephane Broussard."

"Broussard? That's the name you've given me for the Court of King Philippe."

"Yes, same last name, but different first name; two different people as far as the world is concerned. From now on you will always use the last name of Broussard. This way the other Benedictine agents can more easily keep track of your whereabouts and activities. Go now and see Abbot Hugh's tailors. They will have you measured and fit with various diplomatic outfits, and upon your return will have completed a Burgundian captain's uniform which you will start wearing the moment you leave Cluny. You will also wear an eye dressing over your left eye with the military uniform, as though covering a battle wound."

"Eye dressing? Do you mean like a bandana?"

"Yes, to conceal even more of your face in addition to the beard and mustache when arriving in Rome where you were well known by many as an adolescent.

Oh, one final thing. Muehler was not especially pleased with your performance in Rome with Handel. I have just placed you at the very center of three significant missions: the court of King Philippe, negotiations with the Moors, and a return to Rome for the selection of the new Pope. Be careful, be smart, and do not disappoint me. Understood?"

Tristan looked at Odo a moment, then bowed with deference. "Yes, Cardinal," he said, "I clearly understand, and I thank you for placing so much trust in me."

CHAPTER TEN

MALA

It was nearly dusk when Tristan arrived in Orléans and he thought it opportune to stop for the night at the Benedictine monastery within the city. Not quite yet dark, his puzzling over where Mala the Romani girl stood in his existence drove him forward. Finding the road that led north out of the city, he followed its meandering course along the banks of the Loire. Shortly beyond the city darkness fell quickly and Tristan soon found himself urging his horse forward through heavy thickets of forest broken only by occasional patches of farmland. Fortunately the moon was full and it cast enough of a ghostly luminescence through the branches above to allow him to follow the pale outline of the road winding ahead. As he approached an especially dense section of forest whose overhanging branches shrouded all but the faintest trace of moonlight, he thought, *What an ideal place this would be for the execution of some dark deed*, urging his horse to a brisker pace.

The next moment, he heard a furtive sound in the nearby brush. His horse heard it, too, and whinnied nervously with a start. Then came a shout, and another, and someone vaulted into him from the darkness, quickly taking him to the ground. Breaking free, Tristan sprang up with a lurch and a stagger, grasping for the dagger hidden within his boot. Before he could get at it, another figure came at him from the opposite direction, tackled him, then held him fast as he raged and struggled. The first man then joined in the effort, and Tristan lay gasping for air, pinned firmly to the ground. Then Tristan heard some quick Romani speech that he did not understand pass between the two.

"I seek Mala and her Romani troupe!" Tristan cried out, eyeing the glint of a steel blade pointed at him in the pale moonlight.

At this, the two men loosened their grip on him, then fell still a moment. "Who are you?" the bigger man then said with an accent. "And how do you know Mala?"

"I'm her friend!" Tristan exclaimed, still unsure of the men's intentions. "I've known her since childhood."

The large man waved the other off and brusquely pulled Tristan to his feet. "We'll see," he growled. Then putting his blade to Tristan's throat, he added, "Any quick move and you're *dead*. Now follow me."

The big man led Tristan into the brush, dragging his foot a little like a bear drags his paw, while his partner walked behind them, dagger in hand, and after a lengthy trek through briar and bramble, they drew close to a campsite.

Nine wagons were circled about a campfire, its pale flames lazily licking at the charred, leaning remnants of three logs that had been positioned in a tripod. Several people sat or stood about the fire watching a young, long-haired girl dancing lithely to music provided by an old man dragging his bow across the strings of his lyre and a younger man plucking at a Moorish rebab. As the girl danced, the jangle of zills upon her fingers created a lively percussion that complemented the efforts of the two musicians and filled the air with whimsical rhythms whose roots lay in the Far East amongst the original Romani tribes and their Arabic counterparts.

As the figures of Tristan and his two captors emerged from the shadows, everything within the camp came to an abrupt halt. The girl who had been dancing stepped forward. "So, Fernando," she said, "what have you found in the forest there?"

Tristan recognized the voice immediately and was about to call out Mala's name, but the large man cuffed him in the mouth. "Be still!" he snarled. Then he turned to the girl. "A visitor," he said. "And a *wealthy* one," he then added, holding out Tristan's document packet for all to see. "He's only alive because he cried out your name."

"Eh?" asked the girl, stepping closer.

"Yes, it's *me*, Mala!" Tristan blurted, when the man, Fernando, had stepped away from him. "It's Tristan!"

Recognizing his voice first, and then his face in the firelight, she at first fell motionless, as happens when one sees a close acquaintance in the most unexpected of places. She squealed and ran to him, embracing his neck with a surge of tenderness. "Oh, Tristan! Tristan!" she cried with delight, which brought smiles to all in the camp except Fernando who stood glowering at Tristan with a fixed, unblinking stare. "Bring wine for the monk!" Mala shouted with a clap.

"Monk?" said Fernando. "He doesn't carry a monk's robe, Mala. He appears to be a merchant!"

At this Mala stopped in her tracks and examined Tristan a moment. His unlikely arrival had so stirred her that she had not taken notice of the absence of the black robe of his ordination a year earlier. "Well, then, Brother Tristan de Saint-Germain," she said with curiosity, "and what do you have to say about *that*?"

"Later, please," Tristan whispered.

Seeing that concern had swept over his face, Mala shoved her question aside, then playfully dragged him to a log beside the fire and pulled him down to her side. "I can't believe it," she whispered, nudging her cheek against his while clasping his hands in her own. "Every time we've met, 'twas *me* seeking you. Now, you've come to find me here on the edge of the Loire in the middle of nowhere! How is that possible? Tristan, how did you know I was here of all places?"

"A chance piece of information I happened to hear in Orléans while on my way to Paris," Tristan said, evading the truth. "I have not seen you since the night of my ordination, and I thought it would do my soul good to see a friendly face. *Your* face."

"Oh, and a sad night that was for me, smart boy, your ordination," Mala sniffed.

"Ha! Smart boy!" Tristan laughed. "Mala, must you forever call me that?"

"Yes, of course! You were seven when we first met. I remember you speaking Danish, and French, and Spanish that night your people rescued us from the kidnappers there on the Seine River. Then those times I saw you again at the monastery, you kept getting smarter and smarter. You are the most intelligent creature on this earth, Tristan, and the most certain!"

"Not so any more," Tristan sighed. "I fear that, if anything, confusion has become my friend of late."

"Not possible!" She looked at him with sudden realization, and whispered, "You don't look a bit monkish now. Your hair, your black robe? Tell me, has something come between you and the Benedictines?"

"Ah, no," Tristan replied, his voice barely audible so the others could not hear. "A temporary dispensation of tonsure and garb, that's all," he said, again evading details. "What brings you to the Loire Valley from Paris, Mala, and why is your troupe so secluded here in the forest rather than in town?"

"Because of the prejudices and fancies of your fellow Frenchmen, Tristan," she replied, her voice turning bitter. "Because of our skin, many think us to be Arabs, therefore Saracens. Others consider us foreigners, therefore we are not welcome in town."

"I didn't know things had been so difficult for you."

"Tristan, I remember leaving Spain as a young girl for my mother's dreams of a better life in France. You saw her just before I took her back to Spain four years ago; what France did to her. She and her sister became slaves and whores so we could camp on the edge of some nobleman's property and have bread on the table. Then they were raped by that nobleman's son. Surely you haven't forgotten that I am still declared a murderess and hunted to this day in Normandy for killing the LeBrun boy after he raped my mother and cut her face to ribbons for resisting his advances?"

"Yes, LeBrun, my wretched former classmate," said Tristan, remembering Mala's fiery temper. She kept it under control most of the time, but when it ignited, she burst into flames.

"Your fine Frenchmen, they cling to every scrap of their own greed and corruption on the grand scale yet chased us Romanis from Paris for the petty thievery some of our men committed while there. Imagine that."

"Thievery?" said Tristan. "Mala, surely you do not approve of such a thing."

"No, of course not. Do you not see the sheer hypocrisy? They call us thieves for scrabbling about to survive while they feast off their own extortionate demands upon the peasants and the helpless, stealing not only their possessions, but also their lives! Smart boy, you've been living the sheltered, prosperous life provided by high clerics such as the one who dragged you off to Rome. I will tell you this, your Church is little better than the nobles. Let me not annoy you with reality. In any case, my camp will be splitting in two within the month because I refuse to allow those who thieved in Paris to remain part of my troupe. The ones caught thieving are thinking it best to return to Spain since life is hard here in France for the Romani."

"And you, Mala, you are staying here in the Loire then?"

She shook her head. "Only for a while longer. Fernando tells us that things are better along the Mediterranean coast. He says the weather and the people there are more pleasant. I like his suggestion so I'm thinking of moving the troupe to Toulon perhaps, or Marseilles. I hate Normandy, I despise Paris, and I begin to tire of these people of the Loire. They treat us no better than did those in Paris."

Tristan shrugged, and began to fidget with the strings of his mantle. He had never heard such talk from Mala, but then most of their acquaintance was as youngsters. "You sound angry, Mala, and with reason, I suppose. I hope that I, being French, have not contributed to your difficulties."

Mala shook her head, as though to dispel her anger, then smiled. "Oh no, not you, my little handsome! You are the one thing that has fueled my hope over the years, even though nothing came of us." Then she laughed a bit as she wandered into a reminiscent vein, recalling the last time they had seen each other. "You know, the night of your ordination, I came several days early all the way from Paris hoping you might yet change your mind about donning the black robe. I was madly in love with you then, you know. You meant every thing to me. Four years before that, I was about to move to Cluny so I could be near you while you studied at the monastery, then you moved to Rome with that Cardinal who raised you."

At these words a shadow seemed to fall between them, and Tristan stared hard into the darkness that lay beyond the wagons while Mala stared into the fire. This was not the conversation he had longed for when he set into motion his quest to locate her. He had hoped that finding her, he might unburden his own sore heart.

Sighing heavily, Mala shook her head. "There's something I've never told you, Tristan. After you left for Italy I *did* come back to Cluny. I lived there for nearly three years alone, scraping a living as a seamstress, dancing on occasion along the street for tips . . . thinking and hoping you might come back one day."

"*What?*" said Tristan.

"Ah, a young, lost girl's dreams," Mala muttered. "So *foolish*. Yes, I kept an eye on the north road day after day, *certain* that God would bring you back to me." She smiled then, chortling a bit. "It was a naïve girl's fancy. I've long since left such things behind, though it's difficult at times to let the past be dead. But life demands it if we're to survive. Besides, I refuse to end like my mother—broken, penniless, helpless. There's a future out there for me and I intend to find it."

Shifting a bit on the log, Tristan reached into his pocket and fished out a linen kerchief. "The ring you gave me that night we first met," said Tristan. "I carry it with me always, and will take it to the grave."

Mala gazed at the ring in wonder. "Oh, my God," she whispered, "you still have my ring?"

"Yes," Tristan replied, hypnotized by the silhouette of her striking face as its caramel complexion reflected like amber against the red embers of the campfire. She was more beautiful than ever; her fine facial features, delicate neck, stunning smile. As the evening breeze stirred her cascading raven tresses, sending fine wisps streaming about her eyes and mouth, her hair shimmered more brightly than polished anthracite. Her large almond eyes captivated him, too, and then he noticed her ample breasts, their exposed cleavage heaving against the tight confines of her tunic top with every breath she took.

Indeed, without even uttering a word, Mala's beautiful form sitting beside him was now weaving a witch's spell over him. He remained lost there for a long while, content to be in her presence. Something she had said pricked him and he spoke. "Mala, you and I, are we nothing more than part of a dead past?"

The question quickly pulled her attention from the ring, and she looked at him, puzzled. "I pursued you over the years, never heard from you between my visits to come see you, you then chose the Church and I have not seen or heard from you for yet another year, then you appear from nowhere, for no reason. What am I to think, smart boy?"

Tristan nodded apologetically. "Mala, everything you say is true, except that I didn't appear here for *no reason. You* are the reason. Just as you sought me out in the past, it was I who came looking for you this time."

"I see," Mala nodded, looking nearly amused. "And could you then explain how it is I drew you here?"

Having no answer, Tristan resorted to the truth. "I have no idea, Mala. All I know is that your face appears to me at times, when I least expect it. In moments of solitude, or distress. Why? I have no ideas about that either. God threw us together as children under most unusual circumstances for *some* reason. There must be something to that, do you not agree?"

"Yes, I agree that ours has been an oddly twisted road. I think of you also from time to time, at unexpected moments. As to God throwing us together, I'll leave that to your monkish fantasies." At this she playfully jabbed him in the ribs. "I now declare the dead past revived then! Agreed?"

"Agreed," Tristan smiled.

"Come then, it's late and you shall sleep in my wagon," she said, taking him by the hand as she stood. Tristan balked a moment, and Mala, feeling this tug of indecision, pulled harder at him. "I'll not deflower the purest of black monks in my own wagon, smart boy!" she laughed. "At least not on *this* night. You can sleep on the ground over there with Fernando, if you prefer, eh?"

Tristan glanced over at Fernando who was sitting across the fire and had never once taken his scowling eyes from Tristan. *I should have finished you off in the woods . . . kept your money and said nothing to her or the others,* the scowl said.

"I'll sleep in the wagon, Mala," Tristan replied, quickly swayed by Fernando's saturnine glare.

As they settled into the wagon, they spoke for another hour or so, joking and tittering as would adolescent siblings poking fun at each other. And though such proximity to the beautiful Mala was exhilarating for Tristan, he finally fell asleep, wondering whether his presence in the wagon was a sin, or an indiscretion since no carnal violation had been committed.

He moaned and shivered in his sleep, troubled by disturbing dreams. Mala, sitting wide awake, watched this until nearly dawn, wondering what it was that made him so restless. "What has become of you, smart boy?" she whispered, purring gently, then stretching her hand over his bare belly as would a lazy cat stretching her paws in contentment. "Whatever it is, I'm glad it brought you back to me."

CHAPTER ELEVEN

THE VATICAN WARS

Pope Gregory VII was both revered and despised during his Papacy of 1073–1084, depending on one's position in favor of or opposing reform within an abusive and corrupt Catholic Church. It is often forgotten that until Gregory's tenure as Pope, it was the emperors of Europe who controlled the politics of God . . . and they twisted them to their fancy. Consequently the papacy itself was a most unstable proposition, popes generally being appointed by the most powerful reigning nobility of Italy. Many of these puppet popes were unqualified, impious, and some even insane. They were with frequency deposed, imprisoned, or assassinated by the power brokers of Europe according to their political whims. Indeed, between the short years of 872–904 there were twenty-four popes, and from the brief period of 896–904 there were nine popes.

One of the greatest illustrations of such political outrage took place in the year 897 when Pope Formosus was placed on trial by Pope Stephen VII on the orders of the Duchess Agiltrude who was still furious at Pope Formosus over past political conflict. Incredibly, when this trial occurred, Pope Formosus had been dead already for nine months. Pope Stephen and the Duchess, not to be deterred, had Formosus' rotting corpse dug up, dressed in pope's garments, and propped in the defendant's stand at the trial that became known as the Synodus Horrenda. Formosus' corpse was found guilty on all charges, of course. Furthermore, all the dead pope's acts and ordinations were declared null and void, his corpse was stripped of papal vestments and reclothed in ordinary garb, the three fingers of his right hand which he had used to issue his papal blessings were cut off, and his corpse was then deposited in an ordinary grave. Interestingly, Pope Stephen VII was deposed only eight months after this lurid mockery of a trial, stripped of his own papal vestments, and thrown into prison where he was soon thereafter strangled to death.

Having assended to the papacy in the year 1073, Pope Gregory VII began to issue a series of reforms considered radical and unacceptable by those prospering under Church corruption. These reforms included the prohibition of concubinage among clergy, prohibition of simony which permitted the sale of religious objects and office, and mandatory celibacy of priests and monks. His most controversial move was his resolute stand against investiture, the established practice in which kings and nobles could appoint priests and bishops to high Church office, thereby controlling them and the vast power and property that accompanied such positions.

This action by Pope Gregory outraged King Heinrich IV of Germany, the most powerful emperor of continental Europe, and war quickly ensued. This Investiture War was not a war over territory, but a war over *principles*, which is the very deadliest form of conflict, and far more visceral than other forms of war. As a result, a bitter schism occurred within the Roman Catholic Church as clerics in support of reform sided with Gregory, and clerics who opposed change sided with Heinrich. The nobility of Germany and Italy also divided, those thinking that Gregory had stripped them of power siding with Heinrich, and those who opposed Heinrich politically, siding with Gregory. In other words, the feud between pope and king resulted in a bloody and hopelessly complex civil war that pitted clergy against clergy, nobles against nobles, Germans against Germans, and Italians against Italians . . . all in the name of God.

After multiple unsuccessful attempts, Heinrich finally defeated Pope Gregory and captured Rome in 1084, which resulted in Gregory's escape and self-exile into Lower Italy which was controlled by King Heinrich's violent enemy, Duke Robert Guiscard the Wily.

After Heinrich's victory in Rome, his first maneuver was to install his political Archbishop, Guibert of Ravenna, as his newly appointed Pope under the title of Pope Clement III. This, of course, created a new outrage amongst the supporters of Pope Gregory who became known as Gregorians. The infuriated Gregorians immediately denounced Heinrich's puppet pope and referred to him as the false "anti-pope."

Though Heinrich had succeeded in capturing most of Upper Italy and Rome, his German forces had never been able to defeat Pope Gregory's most ardent supporter, Countess Mathilda of Tuscany in west-central Italy who also happened to be King Heinrich's first cousin. By the year 1085 the two cousins were engaged in their fourth year of war, and though the Germans were winning, they had been unable to completely subdue the iron countess. Nevertheless, the war had taken a great toll on her wealth, resources, and vast territorial holdings, and for the most part her fate and the fortunes of her armies had been hanging by a thread as she struggled to hold back the invasive Germans year after year.

Mathilda, known as la Gran Contessa of Tuscany, was one of the most unusual and fascinating figures of her era. Her childhood included noble birth of the highest order, the early death of her father, and kidnapping of herself, mother, and brother by her German uncle, King Heinrich III, father of her cousin and current enemy, King Heinrich IV. This kidnapping was a terrible ordeal in which she was held hostage for several years, and resulted also in the death of her mother and brother. When she was released and returned to Italy as a young woman, she found herself inheriting her deceased father's lands and vast riches in Tuscany, and thus immediately became the wealthiest, most powerful woman on the continent. She was also by this time an educated woman of letters who spoke five languages, which was unusual for a woman of this era. Even more extraordinary was the fact that when she was released from captivity, she immediately began training in warfare and military strategy under the celebrated arms tutor, Arduino della Padule, and soon became adept at riding, carrying a lance and pike, and wielding a sword.

She had come to know her younger cousin Heinrich while being held hostage by Heinrich's father, the German king, and the two actually shared an affectionate relationship during childhood. A devout Catholic and supporter of Pope Gregory, Mathilda severed all ties with Heinrich following the outbreak of the Investiture War, and the two quickly became bitter enemies.

And so it was one evening during Mathilda's bleak period of this war that her adopted nephew, Guillaume de Saint-Germain, came to her camp with three men-at-arms, his armor stained with German blood, his pale grey eyes afire with passion despite having led two exhausting cavalry sorties against the Germans that very day. The men at his side were his kinsmen and members of the small, highly mobile cavalry unit Mathilda had placed in his charge even at seventeen years of age. This unit was referred to as the Dane Wing by Mathilda's Italian troops because it was comprised of an odd collection of Normans who had refused to abandon the old traditions of their ancestors, Vikings from Denmark. Although other Normans had long since abandoned their Danish heritage and adopted French language and culture, this curious, tightly-knit little clan of throw-backs still spoke Danish amongst themselves and refuted the dress of the southern Europeans in favor of their own ancestral attire.

"Contessa, it's been a good day!" Guillaume cried to Mathilda. "A bit of news. We've detected a developing pattern in the German strategy, one they're starting to use on a small scale now, but that we suspect will soon be put into play against your main forces."

Mathilda, a stout woman of thirty-nine years, had herself returned from the front and was sitting on a camp stool removing her hauberk while in discussion with General Arduino della Padule, her former arms tutor when she was younger, who she had since elevated to commander of her military. Weary as she was, but upon hearing Guillaume's voice, she sat erect and smiled with undeniable affection. "Be seated, Guillaume," she said, "and tell me, where do you find such strength? Do you never tire?"

"Not when I fight the Germans." Then he pointed to the men who had accompanied him to camp. "Nor do the Danes. They sent a score of Germans to their graves today."

"Eccellente!" said General Padule, who had known and mentored Guillaume since the boy first appeared under Mathilda's wing. "It's been a good week for Tuscany, Guillaume, and your light horse contingent has made a fine showing, lad!"

"Indeed," added Mathilda. Then pointing to his kinsmen, she added, "And the Danes, such fearsome warriors."

The three large men nodded respectfully. Had they been from Tuscany they would have bowed subserviently to the Countess and her general, but these rough-hewn men were formerly of Lady Asta's private Danish Guard, and were not yet familiar with the etiquette of the Italian military, thereby lacked their graces.

"Yes," Mathilda continued, "it's my good fortune to have their services since their flight from England with your mother, Guillaume." Then she motioned for them to be seated about the camp table.

"So, Guillaume," said General Padule, "you say you've found out something?"

"Yes. Actually it was Guthroth the Quiet here who brought it to my attention. Guthroth, would you like to explain it, or shall I?"

"N-n-no," Guthroth stammered, shaking his head vigorously. "Y-you do the t-talking." Guthroth was the victim of a severe speech impediment at birth. This and merciless ridicule by his father over his stuttering had caused him to turn inward as a child. He shunned attention, and seldom spoke unless necessary. Nonetheless, he was extremely perceptive and far cleverer than others imagined, and absolutely ferocious in battle.

Guillaume continued. "As instructed, General, we of the Dane Wing have been harrying the German flanks with fight and flight tactics. This last week the Germans have twice come at us with small contingents, taking great care to make themselves appear vulnerable and isolated so we'll think them an easy mark and attack with our light cavalry. We took the bait, but both times we attacked these easy marks, a concealed reserve appeared from nowhere and tried to encircle us. We managed to slip out of their snare due only to our swift horses. A larger force of heavy cavalry could not have escaped as handily."

"A good thing then that I've given the Dane Wing my finest horseflesh," said Mathilda. "Go on."

"Guthroth seems to think it's something they're experimenting with on a small scale now," said Guillaume, "but soon intend to spring into play against your main force. He also believes that we can reverse this tactic by appearing to take their bait, then when the German reserve unit springs their trap, we'll unleash our *own* hidden reserve, thereby trumping *their* surprise with our own surprise."

"I see," said General Padule, cupping his chin thoughtfully, giving Guillaume's words a moment of grave regard. "But the massing of a large reserve is a difficult thing to conceal. It might slow us down or betray our position. Mobility and concealment have been our strongest suits against the Germans. Guillaume, it's a good concept you suggest here, but risky, and we can't afford to gamble."

At this, the largest of three Danes stepped to the camp table and poked at the terrain map with three distinct taps of his index finger. His name was Orla Bloodaxe, in reference to his skill with the war ax and in accordance with the Nordic tradition of awarding colorful monikers to all males. "*Our* reserves, General," he said, "will not be massed in one location, but will be concealed in three smaller groups to maintain stealth and mobility. Each would be in a different location, allowing us to spring our attack from different flanks. This will cause confusion to the Germans, thereby spreading panic."

"Ay," said Ivar Crowbones, Orla's younger brother. Slightly less massive than Orla, he was often mistaken as Orla's twin. They possessed identical features, but his left arm had been severed in England by an enemy broadax during a vicious battle known as the Gamekeeper's Revolt. "Unlike the Germans," he continued, "when we hide our reserves we'll not pitch tents and set up house, but sleep on the ground in our mantles and light no fires to avoid detection." Then he drew his hand across his throat as though holding a razor. "If we do this thing right, we'll enjoy a spring butchering just like on the old farm."

Mathilda and Padule looked at the two brothers, then looked at Guthroth as light began to dawn between their brows. "Very clever," said Padule.

"My compliments, Guthroth," nodded Mathilda.

Guillaume pointed to the map and said, "We've already identified several potential holding areas, and I'd like to set the trap when next it appears that they are hiding a large reserve, which we suspect will be very soon. General, we'll need to deploy three of your Tuscan units from the main force as our hidden reserve while you lead the main force. Do we have your blessing?"

"Yes, yes. We'll put the wheel in motion as soon as you deem appropriate. It's best that we not speak of it outside this table until such time arrives."

Guillaume acknowledged Padule's reply, but his eyes rested on Mathilda and narrowed in a look of reflection. *There's more,* the look said.

"Yes, what is it?" said Mathilda, familiar with that expression.

"I wish to be placed in command of the three reserve units. Not permanently, of course, but just for this particular maneuver. Countess, I know that some of your Tuscan commanders resent me, especially Commander Balducci, but this plan is intricate and one person alone must coordinate and implement it, and I think that should be me." Then he glanced at Padule and said, "I can make it work, General."

Mathilda nodded, but Padule was less certain. His other commanders had grumbled amongst themselves about Guillaume: first that he was not Tuscan, then about his age, and finally of his status as Countess Mathilda's adopted nephew. Padule knew this criticism to be unwarranted. Guillaume had been trained from the age of eight in weaponry, horsemanship, and strategy by Padule himself. Furthermore Guillaume possessed uncanny battle instincts as well as phenomenal physical prowess. More importantly, he was a natural leader and possessed no fear, yet remained judicious in making decisions. Nevertheless, the general was not enthusiastic about inflaming his commanders by making them subordinate to young Guillaume.

After an awkward silence, it was Mathilda who replied to Guillaume's request. "Yes," she said, looking at Padule, "if the Germans put together such a ploy as Guillaume suspects, then place him in command of the three hidden reserves." Having said that, she then gazed at Guillaume and added, "It will only be temporary. Understood?"

"Yes, Countess."

"Guillaume," she continued, "Balducci will not be pleased, of course, and it's Balducci who speaks for many of the Tuscan Knights. Best that we keep him under General Padule's wing with the main force rather than place him under your temporary command. The maggot of vainglory has eaten into his brain and he would not easily abide by you telling him what to do."

"But Countess," Guillaume objected, "we'll need our swiftest riders for the reserve, and he's the best we have, or at least his horsemen are."

"True, Countess," said Padule, "his wealth has outfitted his contingent with fine horse and weaponry. For such a ploy as the Danes suggest, Balducci's horses would be essential."

"Very well," Mathilda sighed. "Padule, you know how Balducci can be at times."

"Indeed," said Padule, "but he's a soldier, so he'll have to do as he's told."

CHAPTER TWELVE

LIEUTENANT GUILLAUME DE SAINT-GERMAIN

It was late when Guillaume and the Danes returned from their meeting with Mathilda to their own small encampment nearly a mile and a half further east, which was also a mile and a half closer to the Germans. Due to the small size of Guillaume's light horse troop and their capacity for swift movement, this high ridge site was ideal for purposes of serving as advance guard for Mathilda's main force as well as for keeping an eye on the Germans and their allies, the Lombards, northern Italians who had sided with King Heinrich against Mathilda and the Gregorian Church.

There were twenty-two men remaining in the actual Dane Wing, not counting the handful of their own sons who were brought along to tend camp, care for the horses, and fill other duties as needed. These former members of Asta's Guard were seasoned veterans of war and had already during their short tenure with the Tuscan army established themselves as an elite and formidable fighting force. Although Guillaume was actually far less experienced, new to their ranks, and did not actually consider himself a Dane but a Frenchman, the Dane Wing had accepted his youthful leadership out of loyalty and devotion for Lady Asta who was not only Guillaume and Tristan's mother, but their former Mistress. Mathilda's Tuscan knights found it curious, of course, that such violent and aggressive warriors as the Danes could be managed by one as young as Guillaume. Yet, in the end, shrugged it off as the absurdity of foreigners.

"So what do you think?" Guillaume said to Orla as they dismounted near the campfire where other members of the Dane Wing were gathered, some conversing lowly or sleeping on the ground beneath their mantles while others filed weapons.

Before Orla could reply, a young boy ran into their midst, afire with anticipation as Guillaume returned to camp. The seven-year-old was Orla's son, Hrok Fivehands, Fivehands coming from his habit as a child of quickly getting into absolutely everything. "Sir Guy!" he shouted, "Here, let me take your horse! I have your meal awaiting!"

The look of idolatry upon his young face was unmistakable, and this made his father and the others laugh. "Ha, and what about *me*, FiveHands?" Orla shrugged, feigning dismay. "What about *my* horse and where is *my* meal, Hrok? Must your poor old father go unattended while Guillaume here is treated like royalty?"

This caused the boy to brake mid-step, nearly stumbling into Guillaume. Then, after flushing red, Hrok recognized the humor in his father's great blue eyes and took the reins of Guillaume's mount. "I'll get yours next," he grinned, appeasing his father with vigorous shakes of the head.

"No, I'll take your horse, Father," said Knud, Orla's fourteen-year-old son. His moniker was Knud the Curious, Knud meaning *kind* in Danish, and Curious derived from the questioning expression of his soft eyes that fell thoughtfully upon everything he observed, as though dissecting it from every angle. He had none of the burley, muscular traits of his father or uncle, and was slight of build like his mother had been, and because of his lack of impressive physical presence, he had always felt somewhat lacking. Even his little brother Hroc was large boned and aggressive for his age. "And I should like to speak to you afterwards," Knud said, leading the horse away.

Orla's eyes were fondly following Hroc pulling Guillaume's horse away from the fire.

"Ja, Guillaume," he chortled, "young FiveHands thinks you are the King of Italy. A good thing to be a child and have a hero."

"Ho!" shouted Croswbones who happened to be listening. "And a greater thing yet to have a son, brother. My wife gave me four daughters!"

"Oh, only because you earned them!" Orla fired back, grinning.

"H-Ha!" cried Guthroth the Quiet, amused by the brotherly banter, wishing to join it. "Only because y-you errearned th . . ." he stuttered, then abruptly broke off, embarrassed by the hopeless entanglement of his own tongue.

"Well, what do you think, Orla?" repeated Guillaume, ignoring Guthroth's vexation. "You know, about the prospects of our strategy and my proposal to the Countess?"

Orla did not reply immediately. Finally he looked at his young lieutenant and said, "We know our plan holds water. Furthermore, Crowbones has three times rolled his bird bones and the omens are certain, he says, but I'm not sure your final request was wise. 'Tis a lot you ask of Mathilda and Padule, about being in charge of the reserves, I mean. The Tuscan knights won't like it, and these Italians can be a brooding, girlish lot when feeling slighted. Might have been better to recommend one of their senior commanders for the lead."

"Like Balducci?"

Orla nodded, which caused Guillaume to look at Orla's brother. "And *you*, Crowbones?"

"Ja. No need to shit in the nest, lad. These Tuscans are peacocks, and ruffled feathers will do us no good, eh? They already resent us a little, *you* in particular."

Guillaume then looked at Guthroth. Still embarrassed by his ill attempted effort at banter, Guthroth averted his eyes, not wishing to speak. His expression said it all. *Orla and Crowbones are right,* the expression said, *no need to stack more wood on the fire.*

"Very well," said Guillaume, "I'll retract the suggestion then, and recommend Balducci."

Orla and Crowbones signaled mutual approval. "A sensible conclusion," said Orla. "That's one of your strengths, lad. You don't let your head carry you away in the end. That'll save your ass one day, and the asses of those behind you."

"Ja, Guillaume," laughed Crowbones, "like *us!*"

"J-j-ja, like us," Guthroth uttered in a low voice.

For any subordinate to converse with their military superior with such familiarity would have ended in severe punishment in most military circles of the day, perhaps even execution. But it was a rare and unspoken relationship that tethered Guillaume and the Danes. They had been his mother's protectors her entire life until her recent cloistering behind the walls of Marcigny with the Benedictine Sisterhood . . . which meant they had been like his uncles until age four when he and Tristan had been sent to Cluny. So there existed between Guillaume and the Danes a familial connection that overplayed military decorum. The Danes clearly understood that Guillaume had been designated as their lieutenant and would direct their destiny, and Guillaume clearly understood that his role involved far more than superior rank. His mother would expect him to treat the Danes as his kinsmen, with respect and stewardship. And for that matter, his older brother, Tristan, who had spent more years among the Danes as a child than himself, would expect the same.

As the men began to settle into their sleeping spots, Orla's older son approached. "Ho there, Knud!" cried Crowbones, calling to his nephew. "I happened to see your stunts upon the horse yesterday, lad. Very nicely done. Keep that up and you'll be a cavalry captain one day!" Crowbones adored his nephew, and though the boy was quiet, Crowbones admired his intelligence and called him the "Thinker." "Don't do as I did and lose an arm," he laughed, waggling the stub of his severed arm about the air. "It makes staying on a horse a hell of a lot harder!"

Knud grinned, pleased by his uncle's attention. Then he turned to Orla. "Father, have you given more thought to my request?"

Orla placed his huge paw across the boy's shoulder. "You're too young yet, Knud," he said. "The answer remains no."

Knud's eyes dropped and he scratched at the ground with his foot, his hoard of boyish dreams sadly dissolving. "You've told me many times that you and Uncle Crowbones went to war at age twelve, and I'm two years beyond that."

"Knud, it was different time back then, and our village was constantly under siege . . . we had no choice. Besides, we were twice your girth at twelve, son, and you have neither gambeson nor hauberk for protection, and these Germans are a bestial lot, big and devilish. Be content with riding surveillance as we've had you doing. It's an important task, keeping an eye to the valley. Your time with a sword will come."

Knud gave that shrug of the disappointed and said, "Were I not so small you'd let me fight." Then he turned and disappeared into the darkness.

Guillaume had been talking to one of the other Danes. As he finished, he started to walk back to the fire to settle for the night, but young Hrok FiveHands ran up carrying a trencher of boiled meat covered with grease drippings. "Here, Sir Guy," he said, "it's still hot." Though Guillaume was only seventeen, to Hroc he was a grand figure of influence and sophistication. He was handsome and fearless, strong and wise. Furthermore, as the nephew of la Gran Contessa Mathilda, he was high nobility.

Guillaume looked down at Hroc and accepted the trencher as he continued to walk. "You know," he said, "I don't speak Danish as does my brother and all your people, because until the Danish Guard came to Italy, I had not heard the tongue spoken since I was four. I know why they call you FiveHands, but tell me, what does the name Hroc mean in Danish?"

The boy looked up, shadowing each of Guillaume's steps with two stutter-steps of his own. "It means brave warrior or hero," he said, scarcely able to quell the swell of pride that rapidly filled his chest. "And *that's* just what I shall become," he said. "Just like *you*, Sir Guy!"

CHAPTER THIRTEEN

COMMANDER VINCENTO BALDUCCI

Strangely, and to the surprise of Mathilda's army, an abrupt lull followed in the fighting as it seemed the German troops had disappeared from the small valley that had just recently been so hotly contested. General Padule directed Guillaume's Danish Wing to probe about, even sending them into the valley beyond to the east which the Germans had successfully secured two weeks earlier, but they found nothing. "We explored as far as the River Serchio and just beyond, but they've vanished," Guillaume reported after four days of scouring the gorges and lowlands.

The Tuscan commanders sensed a German retreat and soon Commander Balducci appeared with several of them at Mathilda's camp. "We implore you to move the main force quickly to the east and reclaim the ground that we've lost to the Germans these last months, Countess," said Balducci, his tone edged with controlled arrogance. "God's spine! Let's not lose an opportunity here."

Mathilda looked at him with deliberation. *He believes himself to be second in command after Padule,* she thought, *though I have given no such designation.* She did not care for Balducci. He was one of those narcissistic aristocrats who trampled over the peasants, craftsmen, and merchants as though they were placed on this earth only to appease his needs. Furthermore, Balducci had been raised as an only son among two whiny sisters by an absurdly doting mother who he now abused because he thought all women to be inferior to himself. These attitudes infuriated Mathilda who was an independent woman and also a champion of the city communes that had begun developing in Tuscany, often granting them free charters such as she had done in Florence, to establish their own governmental processes. In her estimation Balducci's only accomplishment was to have had the good fortune of being born into wealth, yet he seemed to credit himself for being a man of great vision and inspiration to others. Though life had readily dropped family prestige and territorial holdings into his pampered lap, Balducci hungered for more. So, Mathilda thought him a ravening swine. Moreover, she was convinced that his only motivation for being involved in this war was the fact that the Germans had overrun and confiscated his vast holdings in northeastern Tuscany, thus his only hopes of regaining them rode on the backs of herself and General Padule.

As Mathilda had not deigned to reply to Balducci, General Padule spoke. "The Countess hesitates to advance, Balducci, because we're not certain what the Germans are up to. They may be devising a counterattack. She doesn't wish to commit the main force until things become clearer."

Balducci glanced a moment at the other four Tuscan commanders who had accompanied him, then said, "And what do you believe, General?"

Padule weighed the question. "Don't be impertinent, Balducci. The *Countess* issues the commands for this army, you know that. I enforce her commands, and you, Commander, *follow* them."

Balducci felt the reproach, yet continued. "We've inflicted a bloody cost onto the recent German advance," he insisted, "and they're depleted. Now is the time to attack, I say."

This brought a chorus of agreement from the other Tuscans, but Mathilda's sudden dark gaze quickly stilled their tongues. "I'm no novice to the battlefield, Vincento," she said, settling her cold eyes upon her impertinent commander who knew immediately that he was about to be scalded because Mathilda rarely called him by his first name except when angry. "And have led more armies into battle than you can count. This is your first war, so I find it odd that you've so quickly mastered the art of strategy and impertinently question my leadership. Is it because you are a man and I am a *woman*?" The glint in her eye as she emphasized the last word would have curled a serpent, and Balducci sensed himself on tender ground.

"Of course not, Contessa," he insisted quickly. "It's just that we have finally made headway against the enemy and it seems a shame not to capitalize on circumstances."

"Vincento," she continued, "it's no wonder you are forty-years-of-age and still wifeless! No woman would have you save the limp-wristed Lady Marianna Bertucci of Genoa to whom you've promised yourself only for purposes of her dowry. It certainly couldn't be for her looks. She's as homely as a mule. And oh yes, I've heard how poorly you treat your mother and sisters. Never, *never* confuse me with women of such weak constitution!"

"Si, Contessa. Of course, my Lady."

Then she pointed to Guillaume who was watching Balducci's sudden dance for survival with amusement. "Lieutenant Saint-Germain and the Dane Wing came to me and General Padule some time ago and informed us of a developing German strategy that they believe will be put into play soon. For this reason I feel it prudent not to rush to judgment."

"Yes," Padule interjected, "and the Danes have been scouting this valley and the next for Germans all week."

Averting his eyes from the Countess, Balducci regained his erect posture and said, "And General, did they find them?"

"No, not a trace."

"I, and the other commanders, believe that's because they have retreated, General."

Guillaume had heard enough. "Just because we didn't find them doesn't mean they aren't out there, Commander. The valleys are broad and forested, rife with hiding places. You and the others are anxious to get back at the

Germans, I know, but something's abnormal here. The Germans are up to something."

Swallowing Guillaume's words, Balducci blenched, making it evident he had little regard for any military counsel a seventeen-year-old might offer. "And so now, lad, you offer war counsel to the Tuscan Knights?" Then he glanced at the other captains and General Padule, as though he had just fired a dart that had hit its mark. With a condescending headshake he continued. "And surely, General, you don't value young Saint-Germain's recommendation over that of your commanders, eh?"

"His men are seasoned warriors who have fought Germans, Saxons, Scotts and even the French," countered Padule. "The recommendation comes from *them*. Guillaume has merely passed it up the chain on their behalf."

"Yes, Commander," added Guillaume. "My lead scout, Guthroth the Quiet, was the first to observe the German tactics and . . ."

"Guthroth the Quiet?" shrugged Balducci, his voice riddled with mockery. "Isn't he that blathering fool who can barely get a word out of his mouth without choking on his own tongue? Surely to God you're not listening to him!"

It was Mathilda who spoke. Whereas she may have been a woman stuck in a man's world, she was manlier than most men, including Balducci. She went to her feet, and as the chain links of her hauberk jingled and she placed her palm upon the pommel of her sword, she summoned her height and pointed a finger at Balducci as her eyes drew down to slits. "Balducci, if you persist with this coy little round of cat and mouse, I will personally snip off your furry little balls and feed them to my hounds. Then I'll have a pike run up your ass and mount you for display before my tent! Capisci?"

Her words rattled the other commanders and they retreated a step, quickly creating distance between themselves and Balducci, the target of her ire. Balducci, stung, gathered his wits and found the wherewithal to snap to attention and issue a salute. "Si! Clearly understood, Contessa!" he exclaimed. Then he offered a bow while arcing his hand forward in a demonstrative sweep of deference. He knew well that Mathilda possessed fangs, and though she did not bare them frequently, they were deadly. Gesturing to the others to follow as he turned and briskly tramped out of Mathilda's camp, he silently simmered until out of view. Then, seething in impotent fury, he let loose a burst of profanity and angrily slapped his gloves against his thigh. "Goddammit! Can you believe that bastard nephew of hers is now directing strategy!" he chafed. "He's barely got whiskers and she listens to him on how to conduct war!"

CHAPTER FOURTEEN

A SPY'S REVELATION

Knud ambled his horse along the crown of the ridge, keeping an eye to the valley below, but his mind was not on the Germans. As with most boys stuck between the immaturity of boyhood and visions of manhood, he was daydreaming, imagining himself charging into battle against the German foe, pressing furiously ahead, his galloping mount beside his father, Uncle Crowbones, and Guthroth. He had listened since infancy, saucer-eyed, to their harrowing tales of war and narrow escapes from death, and longed to be part of it. His mother had been slain the year before during the escape from England, and Orla had been since then raising him and Hrok within the company of the Dane Wing. And though Knud had sorely missed his mother at first, he seldom thought of her anymore. He was now more focused on following the path of the Dane warriors.

Lost in these thoughts, he was jolted from his reverie by a sudden stir on the road below the ridge. Dismounting, he left the trail and parted the brush before him, peering down, and spotted Commander Balducci and several of his men wrestling a man to the ground and beating him. Not understanding Italian well, he could not tell exactly what Balducci was shouting or what precisely was occurring, but saw enough to conclude that they had somehow captured and subdued a German. Gathering his horse, he quickly rode back to camp to inform his father.

"Father," he said as he arrived, "The Tuscans have captured a prisoner!"

"Eh?" said Orla.

"Ja, they had him on the ground beating him, trying to get a confession I think, but the man wasn't cooperating. Sir Guillaume would want to know such a thing, huh?"

"Ja, absolutely," Orla nodded, turning to fetch his lieutenant.

"Wait, Father," Knud said. "I wanted to let you know that Guthroth has been helping me handle the sword and ax these past months, and how to brake, swivel, and heel my horse. He and Uncle Crowbones both say I'm getting good at it and . . ."

"Stop, Knud! We've been through this a dozen times and I don't wish to go through it again!" Orla said, beginning to feel his irritation rise. "Upon your mother's dying breath, the last vow I made was to keep you and Hrok safe. When the time arrives, I'll outfit you with hauberk, helmet, and shield. Until then, you'll wait. You dream of fighting, but know nothing of the horror of killing a man, or of a man coming at you with the sole purpose of ending your existence! Besides, you're not yet strong enough."

Knud began to object, then broke off, dropping his head with dejection. "Very well, Father," he mumbled.

Finding out from Orla what had transpired on the trail, Guillaume immediately hastened to Mathilda's camp knowing that Balducci would eventually bring any prisoner there. By the time he got there, Balducci had already arrived with several of his knights, dragging a badly beaten prisoner in tow. "We captured this fellow in plain sight this morning coming down the road, Contessa!" Balducci said, his chest swollen with bravado, having already forgotten Mathilda's agitation from their previous encounter. "He claimed he was seeking you, of all things! Such nonsense! From his accent it's obvious he's a German though he had no weapons, merely a dagger. A spy, no doubt. He even had maps of Canossa on his person."

Mathilda was seated at her camp table with General Padule studying maps and gave the man only a perfunctory glance at first. Looking again beyond his bruised cheeks and the blood weeping from his forehead, she gave a start. "Indeed he's German, from *Bavaria*!" she said, alarmed. "He's also a spy, Balducci, but a *papal* spy working with the Benedictines!" She quickly stood and moved toward the man, cradling his head. "Oh, my poor Handel, what have they done to you?"

"B-beat me, Contessa, and tried to force a confession that was not possible," the man groaned, struggling to speak coherently.

"You know this man, Contessa?" asked Padule.

"Yes, his name is Jurgen Handel, and he's on *our* side."

"I tried to tell this lout," Handel said, pointing at Balducci, "but he wouldn't hear of it though I cited names and codes."

"Bah!" snorted Balducci, crossing his arms with agitation. "I have no knowledge of codes. What was I to do? I thought he was scouting our positions!"

"Come sit, Handel," Mathilda said, ushering the maimed Handel to a camp stool.

Handel slumped onto a stool. Regarding Guillaume, an expression of curiosity came over him. "Say there, do you have a brother by chance?" he said, struck by Guillaume's appearance. "A Benedictine by the name of Saint-Germain?"

"Yes," Guillaume replied. "Tristan de Saint-Germain."

"Ah, it struck me so," he said, rubbing his cheek that was still tender from Balducci's pummeling. "You bear an uncanny resemblance to him." Then, pulling at tiny clots of blood that had dried onto his lashes and brow, he added, "I've known him since he was a boy working with Odo de Lagery when he was Grand Prior of Cluny. I may have even come across you a time or two there."

"God's spine! Enough blathering about old times!" exclaimed Balducci. "What the hell were you doing in the valley and why are you looking for the Contessa?"

"To pass along information, just as I told you ten times on the way here between beatings, you blockhead!" Handel retorted, his demeanor promptly gathering heat again.

"Information?" asked Guillaume, his interest pricked.

"Yes, I was returning north from business in Rome," he said, careful not to mention that he had encountered Tristan there a month earlier. The Monte Cassino code required silence concerning the whereabouts of fellow travelers. "The anti-pope and the Germans were chased from Rome just last week when a revolt of sorts broke out within the city. The anti-pope's army moved north to wait in Lombardy for more German reinforcements to arrive from Germany so he can again reclaim Rome. In addition to Heinrich sending reinforcements to the anti-pope for another go at Rome, one of our Lombard agents informed Cardinal Odo that King Heinrich has been quietly slipping reinforcements in from Germany for a final offensive against you here in Tuscany, thinking to finally overwhelm you with numbers. The Cardinal sent me to locate their positions and warn you."

"Ha, numbers," sniffed Balducci. "Heinrich can send in the whole of Germany, but we Tuscan Knights will outmaneuver them as always."

Ignoring Balducci's boastfulness, General Padule looked at Handel with concern. "You say German reinforcements have been sent, yet earlier this week we couldn't find a German within the next two valleys."

"That's because they're in the *third* valley," Handel replied. "They're massing and moving this way. Have you not heard that Heinrich has been flooding troops down from Germany to Verona through the Brenner Pas along the Via Raetia?"

"The Via Raetia? No, that damned road's too far to the east for us to keep an eye on."

"Well," continued Handel, "I was there three weeks back running ridge tops, and I tell you the Germans are coming at you, and soon! Strange thing, though." Here he paused and shook his head. "When an army comes at you en masse, they generally stay together in a tight formation for deployment and communication purposes. Two days ago they began to break up into an advance camp while the main army remains well to the rear."

At this, Guillaume slapped the table and stood. "I knew it!" he exclaimed, looking at Mathilda and Padule. "They're not coming en masse! If they do you'll simply melt away just like you've been doing for four years now, which is why they haven't been able to corner you. It's a trap they're devising. The very one that Guthroth the Quiet sniffed out."

"What the hell are you talking about?" said Balducci.

"I tried to tell you the other day," answered Guillaume, "but you chose to mock my lead scout rather than listen."

"They wish to catch us on an open battlefield, Balducci," Mathilda said, "so we can't continue to capitalize on the mountains. We believe they mean to lure our main force in by presenting a sacrifice . . . a German unit that appears vulnerable and unprotected. Then, once we commit a large force to wipe it out, they'll spring hidden reserves on us."

"Hmm . . . you sound like you might have a plan to counter the German buildup, then," said Handel, who then began to survey the map spread out on the table. "In that case I'll need to mark the German positions on your map, Countessa." Then he looked at Balducci. "Uh, my *maps*, if you don't mind, Commander?"

Balducci signaled one of his knights, and the knight produced the two maps that they had confiscated earlier while interrogating Handel.

"Guillaume," said Mathilda, "when Handel completes his markings, finish laying out the plan you and the Danes have been discussing and be prepared to show it to our entire leadership. Balducci, summon the Tuscan Captains for war council immediately. Tell them we attack!"

CHAPTER FIFTEEN

DOGS OF WAR

War, since its inception, has always been a brutal proposition. During the Eleventh Century it was especially visceral and gruesome because battle was conducted face-to-face, man bludgeoning man, no quarter given and none expected. Unfortunately, for the common man, the quality of weaponry, protection, and horseflesh depended solely on one's degree of riches. Only the wealthy could afford to outfit themselves or the men serving beneath their banner with horse, saddle, lance, sword, shield, and armor, which in those days before the advent of plate armor consisted of a chain mail garment called a hauberk that covered the torso and reached down to the knees. Beneath this was worn a padded wool blouse called a gambeson which added protection and prevented chafing caused by the hauberk. Helmets came in the form of the single piece conical steel helmet outfitted with a nasal guard which was popularized by the Normans, or the traditional Spangenhelm which was welded from several pieces of steel. Finally, beneath the helmet was worn a chain mail hood called the coif. Such was the war gear of eleventh century knights.

Lesser men, the infantry, were left with ax, hammer, bludgeon, pike, or falling star. As very few of these soldiers could afford chain mail, their body protection was leather or padded clothing accompanied by a lesser grade shield, often made of wood, and a poorer quality of sword. The most dangerous combination was bow and archer through distance, accuracy, and rate of fire, though the bow was less effective in forested terrain, against flanking movements, or in close quarters. The crossbow was in its infancy, and though deadly, a crossbowman of the time could only fire two bolts a minute while a seasoned archer could fire ten to fifteen arrows a minute.

And so it was, with grim and gritty determination, that Mathilda's forces began their final preparations for battle in that somber pall that descends upon all armies just before the final judgment so mercilessly meted out by the fortunes of war. In this case, after having been informed by Mathilda's war council that they would be vastly outnumbered and could only count on surprise for victory, the camps were especially quiet, except for prayer.

Guillaume, having surrendered his initial request to be in charge of the hidden reserves, presented the entire strategy for what he referred to as *Guthroth's Snare* to the Tuscan captains. Balducci, despite his shortcomings, was still an able warrior and had somehow garnered the support of the other Tuscan commanders. Padule, therefore, placed him in charge of the three hidden reserve units of cavalry that would descend upon the Germans when alerted by trumpet code: single blast-pause, single blast-pause would alert the first reserve unit to attack; double blast-pause, double-blast-pause would alert the second to attack; triple blast-pause, triple blast-pause would signal the third. Prior to that, Guillaume would assault the German bait unit with the Dane Wing and two other cavalry units assigned for the purpose, and this action would shortly be reinforced by Mathilda's main cavalry and infantry force.

Two days later the Germans appeared. Just before daybreak, a moderate force of five hundred footmen and a hundred horsemen began crossing the knee-deep stream that spanned the mouth of the valley and marched noisily forward. Making their way across the shallow river, they immediately began pitching camp and lighting fires in the meager light of pre-dawn.

Watching from a ridge knoll that Orla's son, Knud, had located weeks before as an observation post, Guillaume poked Guthroth. "Just as you said, they set a trap. We were correct to assume they would set the bait in that vast meadow just on this side of the stream. All the better to catch us on an open field, eh?"

Gazing down at the enemy through the dim light, Guthroth merely grunted.

"Ja," said Orla who was seated astride his horse beside Guthroth, "and they make no secret of their arrival."

"Ja!" echoed Knud who was riding with the Danes that morning as a scout. "Even the deaf and blind would sense their presence!"

"Well, they undoubtedly believe that by making enough ruckus and lighting fires they'll gain our attention within a day or so," said Guillaume. "Little do they suspect that we've already anticipated their ploy and will attack at sunrise today."

Knud looked at his father, wanting to ask again about taking part in the upcoming battle. Orla looked back at him and shook his head no, already anticipating what the boy was about to say.

Crowbones waved the stub of his severed arm to the east, pointing it beyond the wide, shallow stream that was barely visible in the valley below. "According to that spy, Handel, their main force is hidden on the other side of the river within the forest."

"I hope he's right," said Orla. "The Countess claims she'd bet her life on the man. We'll find out soon enough, eh?" Then he looked over at his son. "Good work bringing us here, Knud. It's the perfect perch for observing the entire valley."

Knud, though still disappointed about Orla's refusal about fighting, smiled, feeling warm in this rare praise just issued by his father, even though he at times often felt that his father favored his younger brother, Hroc.

Certain by now that they had correctly surmised the Germans' intent, the Danes quickly reported back to Mathilda and General Padule, who were waiting for word to deploy. "Balducci placed all three of his units in position last night where you recommended," Padule said, "one on each ridge running parallel along the meadow, and one in the wooded stretch along the river to the east. As our main force engages the Germans, his two units across the ridges will come in at them from the sides, then the unit along the river will come in from behind them."

Guillaume nodded, glancing at Mathilda. "Good. Hopefully Balducci followed instructions and set no fires and pitched no tents last night. If we're to spring our final surprise successfully, it's essential that the Germans have no idea we already have men positioned at their flanks."

Mathilda looked at Guillaume as he said this, her eyes edged with concerned affection. "I'm proud of you, Guillaume," she said in a low voice. "This will be a bloody day. It may even spell our end. I know you are fearless, but don't make yourself a target for the Germans. In the name of Christ our Lord, be safe. God speed."

Guillaume leaned toward her from his saddle, and grasped her hand. "I thank you for everything, Auntie. My life would mean little without your shelter and your guidance these past years. I owe you everything, and you are as a mother to me. God speed to you, also."

Then he spurred his mount and galloped to the head of the Tuscan army where the Danish Wing and two Tuscan cavalry contingents awaited him to lead the advance into the German trap. His heart was thumping like a drum by then, and adrenalin was surging like a thrashing, runaway river through every vein of his body as he looked about; his three hundred horsemen in full battle regalia, blood on the rise and fire upon the brow. Even the horses were stamping and pawing at the ground, nostrils flared, braying with impatience, sensing somehow through their riders that something was about . . . and once sprung, could never be retracted.

Guillaume raised his lance, its head marked with a red pennon for all behind him to see, and as he tipped it forward to signal the advance, his hand began to tremble the slightest bit. It was not fear. It was thirst for German blood and zeal to oust King Heinrich's anti-pope, the false monk, which spurred on. Moving forward, he turned his head over his shoulder to take a final look at the great army of la Gran Contessa Mathilda of Tuscany. It marched forward, slithering behind him like the serpent's endless train, bristling with razored instruments of war, heralded by bright gonfalons and pennons streaming in the dawn breeze. Moving as one, hooves and boots began to tramp out a desolate rhythm upon the landscape, warning that a scything rain of blood would shortly erupt just over the rise, in a pastoral valley where the sun was just beginning to break.

As Guillaume gazed at this spectacle behind him, awed by its terrible splendor, he saw knights, footmen, and archers, all trudging forward looking neither right nor left, only straight ahead where awaited the enemy, and either glory or death. Inspired by what he saw, he swiveled forward then, spurred his horse, and couched his lance into his armpit. Had he waited just a moment longer, he would have seen a lone rider, a boy, hurry his way down from the forested slope and slip in behind the last rank of fighting men, the archers.

CHAPTER SIXTEEN

GUTHROTH'S SNARE

The six hundred Germans who entered the valley before dawn that morning knew well that their role was somewhat sacrificial in that their objective was to lure the Tuscans into open-field combat. They had been assured by their commanders that upon attracting the attention of Mathilda's army within a matter of a day or two and inducing them to attack, all they had to do was bear the initial brunt of the Tuscan assault. They would then blast the bugle code for reinforcements, and the massive German reserve would flood across the shallow river from their hidden position within the gorge, separate into two wings, and close around the enemy in a pincer movement, thereby eliminating any hope of a Tuscan retreat. It was with great confidence, then, that the German advance unit began setting camp.

They had barely completed pitching their tents when the perimeter guards perceived a low, rumbling sound in the distance, approaching the meadow. Unsure from which direction the sound was coming due to the confusing echo caused by the steep surrounding mountainsides, they gazed about in all directions, exchanging looks as alarm began to etch itself into their faces. Then, within seconds, the low rumbling sound erupted into the thundering clatter of heavy-laden hooves pounding hell-bent against the rocky terrain of the valley floor as three hundred knights washed forward through the dawn mist, driving their war horses at full gallop, shields at the ready, lances on point.

Guillaume led the charge, surrounded by the Dane Wing, as they drove the weight of their horses over the first wave of hapless guards who had already turned to flee, crushing them to a bloody pulp. Without slowing a single measure despite having ridden over and razed more than a hundred of the enemy, Guillaume and the Tuscans then lowered their lances, impaling all who then stood in their path. Many lances were lost in this effort, having pierced their victims clean through and broken off or having shattered against enemy armor. Knights finding themselves without lances then immediately withdrew swords and rode the enemy down, stabbing and hacking at them as they ran for arms or cover.

Having never fought with lances prior to arriving in Italy, the Dane Wing was not fond of them and kept to their hammers, axes, and falling stars. Many of them had developed the ability to stand high in their stirrups while simultaneously spurring and turning their mounts, thereby turning half a ton of horse-flesh into lethal battering rams that delivered murderous blows to the enemy.

This technique also freed both hands, enabling them to hold their favored bludgeoning weapon in the left hand while wielding a sword in their right, especially in tangled frays where the horses could not easily advance. Unlike the Tuscan knights, the Danes preferred weapons in both hands as opposed to lance or sword in one hand, shield in the other.

Of the hundred German horsemen who had come into the valley that morning, only a handful of them had even time to place a bit in their horse's mouth or throw a saddle on. The German archers were, of course, next to useless in such confined combat so it fell upon the German infantrymen to hold the Tuscan assault. Against cavalry, their effort was doomed. Cursing their fortune and the commanders who had put them forward as bait, they began to flee toward the knee-deep stream.

"It's a rout!" cried Guillaume to Orla.

Orla's horse had just brought a footman down with raised, steel-shod hooves and was trampling him as he tried desperately to escape. Leaning over, Orla swept his hammer down in a deadly arc, crushing the man's skull in such a manner that his brains splattered about like an egg crushed in the hand. "Pursue them to the river!" Orla cried. "No time to lose! We've got to kill as many as we can before the German reserve comes across."

"Ja!" shouted Crowbones who was nearby. "Cause then it'll be *us* on the run!"

Even as Crowbones spoke, the Germans were crossing the stream, having first heard the commotion of the Tuscan attack, then the blast of the German bugle calling for reinforcements. First came the cavalry, wave after wave, three thousand strong. They were ill-equipped and neither in their designated units nor in any type of formation because the entire German reserve had not been prepared for battle when the Tuscans struck. They, like the bait unit, had not anticipated a Tuscan attack coming so quickly.

Guillaume led his three hundred horsemen into the disorganized crush of German cavalry flooding across the stream, and the Tuscans were able to inflict many casualties at first. The sheer weight of numbers quickly turned the tide and Guillaume wrenched his horse back nearly to his haunches and spun him around as the Germans washed forward. "Blow the retreat!" he cried to his bugler. "Back to the meadow to meet Mathilda's main force!"

The first objective of Guillaume's cavalry charge was to wreak havoc on the advance German force, which was accomplished brilliantly though the enemy outnumbered his force two to one. His great advantages had been surprise and horse against footmen. His next objective was to harry the German reserve force as it crossed the stream, inflicting more casualties, then retreat to meet Mathilda and Padule as their main force entered the battle. This he also accomplished, and as his contingent retreated and the main Tuscan army rushed forward to meet the Germans, several things occurred. First, the cavalry charge for both sides was eliminated as the battle evolved into a giant, knotted scrum of horse and humanity locked in close quarter combat as the Tuscan force of five thousand pushed against the on-rushing force of fourteen thousand Germans. Next, the Germans had been caught off guard, their initial plan of deploying a pincer cavalry maneuver to surround the Tuscans fell apart because of disorganization and haste in trying to rescue their advance unit. Then, despite valiant and ferocious fighting, Mathilda's main Tuscan force began to lose ground due to the massive crush of German numbers.

This was forseen, and at the moment Mathilda and Padule sensed this shift of momentum, their bugler gave a single blast of the horn, paused, then another single blast, then paused. This pattern he repeated several times, and as the signal echoed through the valley, four hundred Tuscan horsemen charged down from the tree covered slope that ran parallel to the German' left flank and drove furiously into the German mass, their horses plunging through and over German footmen as they tried to press forward. This charge inflicted severe damage to all on the outside of the German flank and caused surprise and confusion within the remaining German ranks. Nevertheless, the impact of four hundred horsemen against fourteen thousand enemy troops was not able to break the German scrum. Fifteen minutes later, the Tuscan bugler issued a double blast of the bugle, paused, gave another double blast, paused, and continued this series for several minutes. Identifying this call, another four hundred Tuscan horsemen descended from the opposite slopes and threw their horses into the enemy's right flank, crushing or driving lances through hundreds of Germans where they stood, locked in place trying to break through their own forward ranks in order to get at Mathilda and the main Tuscan force. The sheer force of this jarring onslaught shocked the German scrum, pushing men on the inside of the scrum to their feet, knocking weapons from their hands, and causing general confusion. The German mass soon righted itself as again the effect of four hundred Tuscan horsemen against a massive knot of fourteen thousand Germans began to wane.

Padule and Mathilda were fighting on horseback side by side at the very center of the Tuscan front, and Guillaume and the Dane Wing had also joined them there after retreating from the stream. "Bugler, call the third reserve! Call the third reserve!" Mathilda cried, fighting off a swarm of footmen trying to pull her and Padule from their mounts.

Spotting this, Guillaume drove his horse into them, flailing his sword in every direction and cursing, like a man in the grips of some obsession. "Orla! Crowbones!" he shouted, barely even able to hear himself above the furious clamor of steel on steel, horses braying wildly, and men screaming in agony. "To arms! We need you here!"

More Germans charged into the circle swinging swords and axes and jabbing with pikes, many now going after the horses. Padule's horse went down on front legs with a crushing hammer blow to the leg, and Padule was slung to the ground. Three Germans rushed him, but Orla and Crowbones appeared simultaneously. Wildly slinging his falling star about his head with his only hand, Crowbones smashed the faces of two of the Germans, one after the other with the same swing, collapsing their teeth, eyes, and noses into a fountain of blood and gore as they fell to the ground writhing in blind agony. Orla dispatched the other with his ax, decapitating him mid-step just as the footman swung his sword at Padule. The man's sword and head dropped in unison as the trunk of his body fell to its knees, wobbled, then collapsed awkwardly in a heap to the ground.

Just as this occurred, the Tuscan bugler was blindsided by an oncoming German knight.

As the German knight's lance punctured his belly and exited his back, obliterating his entire spine, the bugler tried to raise his horn to his lips, but then his head dropped like a stone and his terrified horse went up on its hind legs, flinging its dead rider to the ground. Mathilda and Padule watched this, and a hammer blow to the head could not have left them more aghast. Their entire plan hinged on the bugle call to the final Tuscan reserve. "God in Heaven!" cried Mathilda. "We are lost!"

The words had no more than escaped her lips when Commander Balducci's five hundred horses boldly appeared from the wooded thicket near the river and swarmed the Germans from behind. He had not heard a bugle call, of course, and knew nothing of the slain bugler. Watching the battle impatiently from his position in the tree line, it dawned on him that he might miss an opportunity for glory. His impatience and unequaled narcissism therefore, led him to disregard instructions and attack early.

And this charge was so brutal and so violent, that even though the first two Tuscan flanking moves had only unsettled the Germans and not dislodged them, the entire German force became unnerved with Balducci's onslaught as terror began to spread like wildfire. "They've unleashed yet a third cavalry attack!" the ground troops wailed. "We're surrounded and outnumbered!"

When pandemonium strikes, there is no stopping it. The German commanders knew from intelligence reports that they could not possibly be outnumbered, and were confident they could still carry the day through their own numerical superiority. Irregardless, as panic spread amongst their troops, the commanders were unable to quell it. The rear and center portion of the German force began to flee the field on foot and horseback in droves. Furious commanders struck at them with their swords, cursing hoarsely and threatening them with death, to no avail. Then three Tuscan cavalry units that had entered the fray from hidden reserve began to charge about in an orgy of butchery, riding down and slicing Germans to ribbons as they tried to escape.

The Germans at the head of the force could neither see nor hear what was occurring behind them so they fought on. Furthermore, they had been steadily pushing the main Tuscan force backward since first engaging them, and were confident that victory would soon be theirs. It appeared they were correct to all who were fighting on the front line, whether Tuscan or German, as men hacked and hewed at each other in the midst of frantic horses plunging savagely here and there, their heaving flanks lathered in sweat and their legs trembling from exhaustion. Indeed, it was a wild and vicious melee with men striking, shouting, and milling about in a tight pack, decimating the sea of changing enemy faces that kept coming at them, as from some endless fountain devised by Hell itself. The wounded staggered about in confusion, often stumbling blindly right into the enemy while wailing over horrendous wounds and severed limbs. As the slain began to litter the field like stacked cordwood, the earth began to flow and saturate with blood, matching the bloodred sun that had by now settled upon the eastern crest of the mountain tops.

Not knowing that Balducci was carving the Germans from behind or that the two Tuscan Calvary reserves on each flank had made inroads and were doing the same from their respective positions, panic began to set in amongst the Tuscan footmen who supported Mathilda's front line of cavalry. These men had been taking atrocious casualties and it appeared to them that the German advance had succeeded in inflicting a severe Tuscan defeat. Without any indication, they lost heart and began to flee the field also, leaving Mathilda, Padule, and the Dane Wing precariously isolated. One of the German commanders took advantage of this and pressed forward on his horse, rallying his troops. "Kill the head of the snake!" he cried, pointing at Mathilda as she and the surviving Danes furiously fought back swell after swell of Germans. "There stands Mathilda the Beast, Pope Gregory's whore! Slay the Tuscan Bitch and we'll own Italy!"

This precipitated a wild rush forward by scores of Germans, most on foot carrying pikes and bludgeons. Tearing into Mathilda's circle with a singular urge, they knew they could end this hellish morning by doing exactly as their commander had just said. "Kill Matilda!" they cried. "Slay Pope Gregory's Whore!"

Now fighting for their lives, their horses crippled or slain, the surviving fourteen members of the Dane Wing formed a circle around Mathilda as the now severely wounded Padule lashed out at the attackers in that crazed fury brought on only by the immediacy of annihilation. Crowbones swung his falling star, Orla his ax, Guthroth his hammer, and Guillaume his sword. And with each rush, the Germans fell like leaves shaken from a dormant tree as the Danes slaughtered all who came near. But the Germans kept coming, and the Danes, lathered in sweat, their arms numb with weariness, finally began to falter. Several more dropped from mortal wounds as the Dane defense began to dissolve.

Guillaume took a sword blow to the left arm, and though his chain mail prevented severing, the blow broke his arm. Guthroth fell to the ground, struck unconscious by a bludgeon strike to his helmet. Then Crowbones went down, his right thigh sliced by an ax and his good arm jabbed through with a pike. Only Orla and Mathilda remained intact, and though he was so exhausted he could barely stand, he cursed at the Germans, scything his ax back and forth, creating a swath of death for any that advanced. This he did in a state of near blindness; streams of his own salty perspiration had begun to blur his vision and flecks of German blood had begun to cake over his eyes. Mathilda's sword was also laboring feverishly as she swung it about in a fit of fury, swearing at the oncoming Germans, felling several as she slowly retreated one step after the other.

The Germans rushed forward in mass, trying to separate the two. One grabbed Mathilda and pulled at her, but Guillaume rushed in, and despite his broken arm, he raised his sword in agony and dropped it into the opening between the man's helmet and his mail hauberk, crushing his collarbone and killing him instantly. The Germans did manage to subdue Orla, falling upon him as a pack of wolves would a wounded bear. His ax still in hand, he swung it about wildly while kicking and biting. Finally, one of the enemy managed a hammer strike to his helmet, and he fell as his eyes lost focus and his body went limp. The Germans then dragged him aside and stretched him out. And as Orla lay there in a haze, he sensed a big German straddled over his waist, broadax held over his shoulders, ready to drop it into his skull. *And so, this is how I shall die*, he thought groggily, everything before him a thick a fog. "Cr-Crow-bones!" he then uttered, as a man drunk with wine, "Brother, can you hear me?"

Crowbones was wounded on the ground, watching, unable to move. "Orla!" he bellowed, desperately trying to drag himself toward his brother. "I am here, Brother!" As he cried out, time froze for him, and he sensed neither sound nor movement, as if caught in a dream. Then the big German set his feet, went to his toes raising the ax high over his shoulders, and began the motion of descent. "Orla!" screamed Crossbones, his throat shredding in a final salutation to his beloved brother.

In that very instant, as the ax began its deadly descent, the ground shook and a horse thundered in from nowhere, its massive weight driving through the big German, shattering every bone of his body, hurtling his corpse aside. It happened so quickly and unexpectedly that Orla and Crowbones both blinked with confusion, unable to fathom what had just taken place. Then Orla's eyes widened in utter shock. "Son! Knud!"

Turning his horse to acknowledge his father, two Germans pulled him from his horse and wrestled him to the ground. One of them severed the boy's arm with an ax while the other buried the point of a pike into his chest. Witnessing this, Mathilda charged forward and dispatched both men from behind as they mutilated Knud's body. Several other Germans in turn began to rush Mathilda then, but Balducci and a platoon of Tuscan horsemen swarmed onto the scene and slaughtered every German there. "Contessa!" he crowed. "Vittoria! We carry the day!"

Aghast, Orla stumbled toward his son, lifting his shoulders up into his massive arms. "Knud," he whispered, trembling, his heart dissolving. "What have you done?"

The boy, barely clinging to life, gazed up at his father and gasped, "B-battle, Father. I-I've been f-fighting the Germans . . . so y-you would be pr-proud of me . . ." Then his head fell to the side, his eyes frozen open; his heart still.

Crowbones, dragging himself along the ground, began to snuffle with the grief of a bereaved hound. Then, kneeling near Orla, he threw his hands up, grasping at Knud. "Oh, Knud!" he cried. "My poor, gentle little nephew!"

Mathilda and Guillaume then knelt by Orla's side with heartfelt deference as he held his son's upper torso in his lap, staring at his face, trembling with every breath. "I t-told you no, Knud," he mumbled repeatedly in that muttering tone of those too stunned to do anything but repeat themselves. "I t-told you no, Knud. I told you n-no."

CHAPTER SEVENTEEN

THE COURT OF KING PHILIPPE

Tristan spent several days with Mala and her Romani troupe along the Loire River before departing for Paris. It was the first time in his entire existence that he had experienced unadulterated freedom, and it was intoxicating. No expectations, no decorum, no pretensions. He wandered the forest with Mala in the mornings, accompanied her and the musicians into Orléans during the day where Mala danced for money, then settled in at night by the fire. They slept together for four nights in her wagon, and though they engaged in much hand holding, playfulness, and tender talk, the nights were actually rather chaste. He spoke much of the beauty of Italy and Rome though he never mentioned his work there, and she spoke of the troupe's travels throughout France. Then they would fall asleep in each other's arms, holding onto each other as two lost children facing the terrors of the world. And thus they each, in the other, somehow recovered a tiny fragment of the childhood they had both been denied.

It was a sad parting, then, when Tristan mounted his horse for Paris. Mala begged him to stay for just one more day, but Tristan was already overdue in the Court of King Philippe. "When I have finished my work there, I will come back through the Loire before returning to Italy. I have been instructed to spend time in Cluny before reporting back to Cardinal Odo, so I will cut a few days from that stop and spend them with you here."

Considering this, Mala's angst dissolved and she smiled. "I haven't been this happy in years, Tristan," she said. "In this world I have always felt a little alone. Since that very first time we met as children, every time I see you that emptiness vanishes. It's strange and I don't really understand it, but it's true." Then she dropped her eyes, as though perhaps she had misspoken. "There now, I've said it aloud, so now you know."

"I understand, Mala," Tristan said, flushing at the collar. "I have felt a strange abandonment in life also. You change that in me, too." Then he leaned from his saddle to kiss Mala on the cheek, but she grasped his head and gently pressed her lips against his. The kiss was chaste enough, yet in it they both felt a sudden stirring.

Realizing what she had done, Mala retreated a step; not that she regretted her action, but she could see that the pink creep that had appeared at Tristan's collar moments before had now turned scarlet. She, too, then flushed red, laughing. "Goodbye, smart boy! You think about that kiss while you're at court!"

* * *

In Paris several days later, he presented his ambassadorial documents from Cardinal Odo and was immediately admitted to court. He then located Brother Augustine as instructed. The old man was laboring within the royal scriptorium under the pseudo-name of one Stephane LeBeau, a layman and professional calligrapher of the highest capability. Despite his advanced years, Brother Augustine's eyes possessed a youthful glint, and he often winked impishly whenever making a point during conversation.

"Ah, ha," whispered Brother Augustine after their initial exchange of code words, "I was wondering when Odo would finally send someone my way. Since the death of Pope Gregory, King Philippe has become even more blatant than before about ignoring Church law. He sells bishoprics as though they were plums falling from his royal orchard! He's filled the royal treasury to brimming with such chicanery. I'll bring you my documentation in a week or so upon completing my latest entries."

Two days later Tristan was formally presented to King Philippe and his wife, Queen Bertha, as Monsieur Lucien Broussard, papal ambassador under the direction and employ of Cardinal Odo de Lagery, Cardinal-Bishop of Ostia. Since so much of his time over the last years had been engaged in the struggle against King Heinrich in Italy, Tristan was not especially versed on the royal affairs of his native France, nor was he recognized by a single soul of the French court. His fresh face in the king's court proved to be an immediate advantage.

"Finally someone young with some personality and life about them," King Philippe commented to Tristan. "I've grown so weary of these old curmudgeons Rome has been sending to check on me these past decades!"

Philippe was the son of Henri I and Anne of Kiev, and had been crowned king at the age of seven in 1060 upon the death of his father, after which his mother and Count Baldwin V served as co-regents until Philippe reached the mature age of fourteen. His name, unusual and exotic for Western Europe, was given to him by his Eastern European mother from the Greek "Philippos" which meant "lover of horses." If names were a true reflection of character, she should have named him "lover of women."

Queen Bertha was the daughter of Floris I, Count of Holland, and Gertrude of Saxony. She married Philippe in 1072, a marriage that came about only as a treaty arrangement to resolve a bloody feud that had developed between Holland and France. Whereas her husband was a lustful lout, Bertha herself was a devout Christian. Unable to produce a child for the first nine years of the marriage, she finally gave birth to a son and heir to the throne of France. Interestingly, she claimed that her fertility had been restored only due to the earnest prayers of a certain hermit, Arnoul, who also bestowed the child with the name of Louis.

Tristan found Queen Bertha to be an engaging soul, and she in turn appeared to be very pleased by Tristan's arrival at court. Struck by his fine appearance and unusual intelligence, she quickly adopted him as her court pet and began taking him everywhere she went when not performing queenly duties. She found his conversation scintillating and his wit entertaining. She especially took delight in watching the envious reaction of other women at court as she strolled hither and yon with Tristan tightly attached to her arm.

"Ah, Ambassador Broussard, you are a welcome sight to a shunned woman such as myself," she sighed one afternoon with no regret in her tone. "I suppose coming from Rome you already know that my husband ignores me in favor of more "youthful" thighs?"

"I cannot imagine why," Tristan replied graciously. "Yet, yes, I have heard that the king is fondly referred to as Philippe the Amorous."

"Fondly?" the queen snickered, grasping Tristan and pulling him close so others would not hear. "Ha! 'Tis a name of derision. Were he not king, he could not even talk a whore into his chambers with that disgusting little grub stuck between his legs!" Then she laughed. "Do not pity me, Ambassador, for I am quite content to be queen, and more content yet that Philippe no longer violates my chambers. We were thrown together only to end a war and seal a treaty. I do not care for him, and he certainly feels no attraction toward me. Lately he has begun to complain that I am gaining too much weight, though he himself is now too fat to mount a horse!"

Tristan found such comments difficult to grasp at first, but within days learned that the French king was truly shameless in his pursuit of other women at court, often rubbing them on the rump or even fondling their breasts in public, indifferent even to the presence of husbands. Whenever this occurred, everyone, including husbands, turned away as though the king was blowing his nose.

Aside from the queen, Tristan's presence at court managed to create a bit of a stir amongst the other women at court, whether single and married, or he often found himself fending off their flirtatious advances. Several women, of course, went well beyond the realm of flirtation and openly offered themselves to him . . . in the garden, in the stables, or in secluded nooks and crannies of the palace. One overly eager matron even tried to physically drag him into her chambers during the brief absence of her husband with the assistance of her two chambermaids. Though flattered by this unexpected attention from the ladies of King Philippe's court, Tristan thought them all shallow and insincere compared to Mala who ceaselessly seemed to come to mind, especially at night.

"Ah, ha, you now begin to see the decadence of the French court!" winked Brother Augustine as he slipped into Tristan's chambers at the end of his third week at court. Then Augustine handed Tristan several encoded documents. "Here" he said, "my documented list of religious offices sold by the French crown . . . dates, locations, names of recipients, names of parishes and dioceses."

Tristan leafed through the papers a moment. "Saint of Heaven," he whistled, clapping his forehead with disbelief. "There must be over a hundred names on these lists!"

"One hundred and twenty-one to be exact. Some are even convicted criminals."

"No, not possible! Serving as priests and bishops?"

"Ay, representing the Church and stealing their parishes and dioceses blind! Philippe's whoring of Church office is far worse even than King Heinrich's investiture violations, but Pope Gregory couldn't take on both of them at the same time. Heinrich being the greater threat, the Pope turned a blind eye to France."

"I never had any idea this was going on here in France, nor that Pope Gregory would allow such a thing. So disappointing! I always admired the integrity of Pope Gregory, but this is shameful and . . ."

"Whoa, lad, don't be so harsh. Gregory did what he could. No other Pope would have taken on Heinrich as Gregory did. A double war with Germany and France holding hands against the Vatican? Be sensible. Even now with all this documentation I've gathered, we can't do a damned thing about it."

"What's the purpose of all you've done, and at such great risk?"

Augustine offered a smug smile. "At times it's good to know things, even if you can't change them. Ignorance, after all, is lethal. Perhaps the new Pope will be able to address this, or the one after that, who knows? But my work's not in vain. Now we have the facts, and they'll come into play one day, mark my words."

Tristan shook his head with disgust. "To think that the king of France is selling Church office, or that people out there in the parishes have no idea that many of the clerics leading them in prayer are filling their pockets while preaching virtue without believing in it!"

"That's why we are Benedictines, boy . . . to reform such things, and save the world." Then Augustine crossed himself and placed a hand on Tristan's shoulder. "Dieu vous bénit, mon frère. God bless you, 'tis good work you do, too."

"Thank you, Brother, but I have not uncovered a single trace of communication between King Philippe and King Heinrich. It seems that Philippe's primary diplomatic activity is filling his treasury by selling his neutrality in wars amongst powerful nobles, or making alliances against William the Bastard of Normandy. I've found no interest in the war in Italy."

"Very well then, you have your answer. Where there're no tracks, there's no game, eh? Despite our concerns about King Philippe, an alliance with Heinrich is apparently not one of them. And it begins to make sense. A war in Italy would not benefit him, especially if he can continue to do as he pleases with impunity. Go then and let Cardinal Odo know that France will not be coming to Heinrich's aid as long as we continue to leave King Philippe to his whoring of crown, Church, and wenches of the court. Your work here is done."

"Very well then, upon your judgment I shall pack my things and return immediately to Cluny, then be on my way back to Italy."

Tristan did not go immediately to Cluny. Instead, he made haste for the Loire Valley to see Mala again, knowing that his work might well not provide such an opportunity again. And though he knew he was violating orders as well as the trust of Cardinal Odo, his urge to share time with her outweighed the inevitable guilt that kept creeping into his brain despite his efforts to blot it out. He began to feel in his heart that cowardice when men take something but do not want it known.

"I've thought of nothing but you these past weeks!" Mala cried, running to embrace him as he rode into the Romani camp. "I wasn't sure whether you'd be back or not."

"I have only a few days, Mala," he said, returning her embrace. "Then I must report to Cluny."

The few days turned into a week, and for Tristan this week was even more intoxicating than his first visit as he and Mala shared conversation, laughter, and at night, affection within the wagon as they fell asleep holding onto each other as two lost souls overwhelmed by a world of turbulence and complexity. And though there was no actual exchange of carnal pleasure, these sheltering nights in each other's arms seemed to somehow nullify the despair and hurt that each had experienced in their respective lives.

With each passing day, the other Romani grew more and more concerned because they looked to Mala, despite her youth, as their mother figure. They had also determined that Tristan, whatever else he was, was transient and would not be making contributions to their already meager existence. He was, therefore, somewhat of a threat to their dependent existence with Mala. Yet they tolerated him knowing that to do otherwise would displease Mala . . . and Mala's temper, which rarely showed its face, once ignited, knew no bounds. They contented themselves, then, with hoping he would depart soon.

Fernando felt a deeper threat than the others. As he watched Mala's and Tristan's heartfelt daily exchanges of affection, he sensed that something more profound was developing between the two. This created in him a simmering jealousy that began to devour him; in his dreams, Mala was his. He struggled desperately to contain this jealousy, but within a matter of days he could scarcely bear to look at Tristan without wishing him dead. Tristan was perceptive enough to be aware of Fernando's resentment and did his best to deflect this hostility, but his efforts did little to assuage the brooding Fernando. As for Mala, she had never thought of Fernando as anything but a fellow Romani traveler, therefore she had little sense of the actual depth of feelings Fernando possessed for her.

Had Tristan remained much longer in camp this situation would have undoubtedly come to a head sooner or later. Fernando's agitation abated watching his nemesis pack his horse to return to Cluny, even though it pained him deeply to watch Mala kiss Tristan goodbye, then cling longingly to his leg as he settled into the saddle.

"And so," she said, on the edge of tears, "yet another farewell . . . and no idea whatsoever where you'll be or when I'll see you next."

"Indeed. You will be in my thoughts always, and I, hopefully, in yours. In any case, if the troupe moves to Marseilles or Toulon along the coast as you have been discussing this week, you will be much closer to Italy where I will most probably be."

"We made the final decision last night. It's to be Marseilles, and we leave by month's end." Then she heaved a moment and said, "Tristan, how will you ever find us?"

"I found you here in the Loire Valley, did I not? Trust me, I will be able to learn your whereabouts." Then he nudged his horse in the ribs and made his way to the road. Had he turned around he would have seen Mala standing there wringing her hands, but he was already too heartsick to look back, and knew that if he did, he might never return to Italy.

CHAPTER EIGHTEEN

THE MOORS

After several days of travel Tristan crossed into the province of Burgundy and finally made the rise leading up to the Cluny Monastery. As he entered the gates, he encountered a bustle of activity going on within the complex, and saw that an entire caravan of foreign-constructed carriages and wagons had filled the stable area and had even spilled out into the main yard.

Then he heard a familiar voice calling to him. "Tristan! Where have you been, lad?" It was Abbot Hugh, and he look flustered.

"Are the Moors here already?" Tristan asked, already guessing the answer.

"Yes, two days ago. I wanted to begin negotiations yesterday, but Cardinal Odo's order was to have you open the session due to your knowledge of Arabic and your experience negotiating with Lord Abdul Azim and the Seljuq Turks on behalf of Pope Gregory several years ago. Praise Heaven you have arrived! We were beginning to panic."

"I thought they were not to arrive for another day yet."

"They came early for some reason! Caught us off guard."

"Oh, yes, I should have guessed," said Tristan, privately chastising himself for overstaying at Mala's camp. "It is a diplomatic maneuver the Arabs use from time to time, to catch the enemy off guard and gain an edge during negotiations. No need to worry, Abbot, we will stall for three or four days more before beginning the talks, to *repay* their courtesy."

"What?"

"Yes, to regain the advantage, to let them know they are in *our* house, therefore *we* determine the schedule, not them."

"Ah, clever lad! Yes, thank Heaven you've arrived."

The formal negotiations between the Gregorian Catholic Church and the Moors of North Africa, then, were opened by Tristan posing as Lucien Broussard, Papal representative, and began three days later than had been originally scheduled, much to the irritation of the Moors. Despite this initial displeasure, the Moors quickly developed respect and admiration for this Lucien Broussard; he was respectful, engaging, and possessed an impressive knowledge of their culture. More importantly, he spoke their language and possessed a sense of humor, dry as it was. Tristan, therefore, as Lucien Broussard, was able to establish a working rapport with the Moors, which they found refreshing. During most negotiations with Christians, they had found westerners to be arrogant and condescending.

Tristan was uniquely qualified to conduct these talks with the Moors, due primarily to a combination of his own in-depth research while a student at Cluny, his years of learning Arab and Persian tongues, and his experience negotiating with the Seljuq Turks several years earlier. In fact he was one of the few Churchmen who actually possessed a reasonable grasp of the Muslim world as it really was. Western Europe as a whole at this time viewed the Muslims as a united race of dark people who, like heathen locusts, were encroaching on Christendom from every front. Western Europe also referred to all of these people, regardless of origin or habitat, as Saracens. Tristan was well aware of the vast historical and demographic differences between the actual Saracens as opposed to the Moors and the Turks. He also knew that even within each of these three distinct groups, the rivalry and infighting was so fierce that achieving unity against the West was next to impossible. And unlike his counterparts, Tristan recognized that the Muslims were not a primitive race of idolaters, but an eclectic collection of various cultures who had embraced the teachings of Mohammed. However much he privately admired their cultures and advanced technology, he did also consider them a threat to Christendom, and feared that one day they might unite and make a move against the European continent and Christianity.

At issue during these particular negotiations was the city of Tunis where the current Mohammedan ruler had taken to capturing Christians, who were fairly populous in the region, and enslaving them for financial gain. Cardinals Odo and Desiderius had half-heartedly rattled the threat of potential war if the situation in Tunis did not improve, but the Moors had ignored these threats. They knew that the Gregorians were still at war with Heinrich who controlled Rome and also that the Gregorians had been unable to select a Pope in over a year. Having learned that the Gregorians had retaken Rome and would soon be selecting a Pope, the Moors had agreed to convene with Abbot Hugh in Cluny for negotiations.

Tristan's mission, therefore, was to convince the Moors that the war against Heinrich had turned back in favor of the Holy See and that upon the selection of a Pope, a union of Italian militias from Rome, Pisa, and Genoa would quickly sail against Tunis. This he did convincingly.

"Under the banner of Saint Peter, these armies will quickly overrun your shores as the first act of our new Pope though the Holy See would much prefer a *peaceful* settlement," he declared. "We have no desire to commence a new war, only to save our fellow Christians from enslavement, the new Pope will have no other choice. Peace or war, it is in *your* hands, my friends . . . not ours."

This created a stir amongst the Moors because, as in all political situations as this, certain individuals benefit from war, while others lose. Though victory in war is the quickest way to fill one's treasury, war is also the greatest risk to those who are content with what they already have, and many of the Moorish diplomats attending the negotiations were living a life of peaceful prosperity.

Tristan's instructions had also directed him to feed specific information to the Moors, some of which was either false or magnified in scope. This information included Mathilda's recent progress against the Germans in northern Italy as well as the number of Italian city-state militias available to the Holy See. It also included intimating to the Tunis delegation the huge amount of wealth under the control of the Benedictine Brotherhood which possessed vast estates in France, Spain, and Italy, and also enjoyed great support from the monarchs and powerbrokers of these same countries. And finally, Tristan was to wave the specter of Duke Robert Guiscard and the Normans of Lower Italy in their faces because Guiscard was known to them for conquering Sicily and certain other Muslim domains of southern Italy in previous years.

Of course, Duke Guiscard was dead and his sons Roger Borsa and Bohemud had never indicated the slightest interest in sending troops to Tunis. "Ah, the sons of Duke Guiscard are even more rabid warriors than was the old Duke himself," Tristan warned, "and would love to seize North Africa to add to their Norman domains!"

His mission, then, was one of puffery, deception, and confusion, which he shuffled out with an extraordinary mix of finesse and sophistication for one so young. Abbott Hugh was himself one of the most experienced and respected diplomats of the continent; his expertise revolved around European diplomacy, not dealing with the Muslims. And as he watched Tristan manipulate the ebb and flow of discussions as they dragged on for days, and as the days dragged on for weeks, his admiration grew.

Tristan's instructions had also directed him to do one other thing . . . grow a beard and mustache prior to his return to Rome. This he did not accomplish quite as successfully. To the amusement of the Moors, Tristan's youthful face and tender skin developed an initial stubble which was blond and fuzzy. It gradually turned into a beard that was quite meager in comparison to their own thick, dark beards. Nevertheless, Tristan made light of this with daily remarks of self-deprecation which only further endeared him to the visitors.

By month's end the talks were finalized and the Moors packed their wagons and set out for the coast. Absolutely nothing had actually been settled during their stay in Cluny, but Abbot Hugh and Tristan were well satisfied with the outcome. In reality, Cardinal Odo had not expected a breakthrough, nor had he expected the Moors to free all Christian slaves in Tunis as requested. What he did expect was that the Moors would return to North Africa with a newfound respect for the power of the Holy See, a respect that had been in decline over the past five years. This intent was yet another one of his intricate intrigues. In the back of his mind, when the moment was right, Odo did fully intend to attack Tunis. This negotiation session, then, was to notify the Moors that the Holy See possessed troops, wealth, and will, and would therefore be a formidable enemy in the future.

"Come, *Lucien Broussard*," Abbott Hugh laughed after the Moors had left.

"Our tailors have nearly completed your military uniform and they await you for a final fitting. Then you shall become Captain Stephane Broussard of the Burgundian Guard!"

CHAPTER NINETEEN

CHAOS OF ROME, EASTER OF 1086

If ever there existed a city that was damned by the dual scourges of war and political chaos in the history of continental Europe, that city was Rome during the last two decades of the Eleventh Century. Beginning in 1081, Rome came under siege by King Heinrich of Germany as a result of the Investiture Wars against Pope Gregory VII. This lengthy siege was unsuccessful yet exacted a steep toll on the city of Rome, causing death, starvation, disruption of commerce, and division of the city into two hostile camps: those who supported reform and Pope Gregory, and those who opposed reform and sided with King Heinrich.

This political division within the city population was only to become more acrimonious and violent with each passing year as King Heinrich twice more attacked and laid siege to Rome, finally conquering it and besieging Pope Gregory within the walls of the Castel Sant'Angelo in 1084. With the advance of Duke Robert Guiscard from Lower Italy to rescue Pope Gregory, Heinrich and Guibert temporarily abandoned Rome and fled north. Their supporters immediately organized protests against Duke Robert Guiscard as he triumphantly marched into the city. Infuriated by this, the short-fused Guiscard retaliated by unleashing his Norman troops and Saracen allies upon the entire population. In an act of pure barbarity, his troops then savagely proceeded to slaughter, rape, pillage, and burn, leaving Rome in ruins within a matter of days. Enraged, the population of Rome turned against Pope Gregory, forcing him to abandon the city in shame and leave for self-exile in Lower Italy, which in turn allowed the anti-pope Clement III to return to Rome and reclaim the Vatican.

Pope Gregory died shortly thereafter, thus creating the Papal vacancy that was now in question. Many Gregorian papists continued to insist that Desiderius become Pope because Pope Gregory's final request as he lay dying was that Desiderius succeed him as Pope. Further complicating this already exacerbating situation was the fact that Cardinal Desiderius adamantly refused the position.

Therefore, since the Church had now gone a full year without a Pope and the anti-pope had been driven from Rome by the Gregorian faction of the populace, the College of Cardinals felt it critical to call an assembly of the Gregorian alliance to meet in Rome to elect a new Pope. This conclave was scheduled for Easter of 1086, and drew all top echelon Gregorian clerics as well as the consuls of Rome, German Saxon princes who had rebelled against and were still fighting against King Heinrich in their homeland, high Italian nobility who supported the Gregorian movement, and several supportive warlords, most notably Duke

Roger Borsa of Lower Italy. Even though Cardinal Desiderius had refused to ascend to the papal throne, he was nonetheless summoned to this assembly for purposes of counsel and discussion. The only great champion of Gregorian politics absent was la Gran Contessa Mathilda who was still cornered to the north fighting the Germans in Tuscany.

The significance of this assembly was monumental and attracted great attention throughout Italy. It would greatly impact the political pendulum of the current Church schism between King Heinrich and the Gregorian Vatican. Because of this, Spain, France, and England also had great interest in this gathering even though they were not actively participating in the war against King Heinrich.

As dignitaries began to arrive in Rome the eve of this meeting, Romans gathered by the thousands, eager to view these celebrities of the Church and aristocracy. And they certainly were not disappointed when these men of high office and family name strode through the Vatican gates. It was as if someone had called a gathering of royal and religious peacocks. Clerics appeared in rich, flowing vestments of rare fabrics that shimmered in the sun, and around their necks hung heavy, elegantly crafted crucifixes made of gold or silver, encrusted with huge gems of every color. Their fingers hung heavy with thick, bejeweled rings, and their heads were adorned with highly decorated miters or bishops caps, also garnished with a glut of rare stones.

The nobles were equally impressive, wearing long, flowing tunics of rich fabric cinched at the waist with decorative belts and swords gleaming with rubies, diamonds, and emeralds. Over these tunics they had slung fur-collared mantles of royal purple, blue, red, or silver clasped at the shoulder with massive broaches of onyx or topaz. The warlords arrived in gleaming hauberks and helmets. And to add dash to his arrival, Duke Borsa had himself announced by a flourish of trumpets and the jangle of heavily-armed escorts marching in file with gonfalons streaming at the point of their stiffly raised lances.

For the thousands of poor who filled the streets of Rome to watch, this spectacle was the finest form of entertainment they had witnessed in years. And though one would be tempted to believe that these unfortunate mongrels of filth and starvation would resent such a display, the opposite was true. The lower classes stood gazing in wide-eyed wonder, clucking and applauding. They threw flowers at these men's feet and cried out the names of the lords and clerics they recognized as though these men were heroes who had championed their cause in life, though in reality most had done exactly the opposite.

Finally this ostentatious parade wound down and the three hundred attendees settled into the Vatican for a series of meetings and discussions that included Mathilda's war to the north, the increasing militarism of the Muslims in North Africa, Spain, and the Balkans, and the intentions of the anti-pope to once again reclaim Rome and the Vatican. Finally, satisfied that these topics had been adequately settled, attention turned to the primary focus of the gathering, the election of the new Pope.

Much was immediately said about Pope Gregory's final request that Cardinal Desiderius succeed him after his death, and as well, much was said about the fact that Gregory had also mentioned Cardinal-Bishop Odo de Lagery as his second choice. Consequently, the hall quickly fell into two camps, those who wished to see Cardinal-Abbot Desiderius ascend to the papacy, and those who supported Cardinal-Bishop Odo de Lagery.

Cardinal Odo sat at the head of the assembly on the left side of the meeting hall with Tristan, who had arrived in Rome one week earlier. As previously instructed, Tristan had grown a beard and mustache while in Cluny. Then, leaving there, he had donned a Burgundian military uniform and angled a black bandage about his head and left eye. The disguise was so effective that when he arrived at the Vatican, Odo himself did not even initially recognize his young liege. And now, as Tristan sat beside Odo in the Hall, his military garb easily blended him with the many other men-at-arms in attendance.

Cardinal Desiderius sat next to Cardinal Odo, surrounded by a retinue of his Benedictine monks from Monte Cassino. The two auspicious cardinals had shared a profound friendship over the years, and had long supported each other's position on nearly every Church matter that had surfaced over the decades. Tristan was aware of this, and he also had cultivated a strong relationship with the Cardinal from Monte Cassino. As he gazed at Desiderius' entourage of Benedictines monks, he nudged Odo.

"What is this, Cardinal? His monks are positioned like bulls surrounding the calf."

"Protection," whispered Odo. "Desiderius trusts neither the Cardinals nor the nobles. He would not have even attended except for the fact he was promised an advisory role only."

"Then, you are to be Pope?"

"Perhaps. Hopefully, Desiderius will still yet step into the breach. He has much support, including mine."

Discussion was both formal and civil as the conclave opened that first day, then passions began to rise and tempers began to flare. Each man in attendance was, within his respective realm, accustomed to being obeyed, feared, or revered. However, within this house of peacocks he enjoyed no such deference, which only escalated tensions and rivalries. Consequently, within a matter of days the assembly became hopelessly bogged down in ego, semantics, and inability to come to terms. As often happens when such a thing occurs among the powerful, the slow torment of ineffectiveness coupled with not getting one's way became too much for many of the attendees.

In frustration, the assembly adjourned for several days with the understanding that members would reconvene to make a final determination a few days later on May 23rd at the deaconry of Saint Lucy. It was Odo de Lagery who opened this final assembly. Blessing all in attendance, he led them in prayer, then issued a brief welcome.

"Today, with the Lord's guidance, we shall finally complete the business that has remained unsettled for one full year . . . the matter of Pope Gregory's succession. Specifically, from the midst of the College of Cardinals, we shall elect our new Pope. And though only the Cardinals will vote on this issue, we continue to value the counsel of you nobles, generals, governors, and consuls who have so valiantly stood by Gregorian philosophy. You have courageously stood your ground against King Heinrich and his usurping false pope, Guibert of Ravenna, who now calls himself Pope Clement III." At the utterance of this name a ripple of dissension began to circulate about the room. Odo raised his palm to the assembly and moved it in the form of a cross. Raising his voice, he proclaimed, "In the name of our Lord and Savior, our Almighty God in Heaven, I declare this final session open for discussion!"

Despite the fact that there was great expectancy in the air, talk was hesitant and spotty at first, some still weary from the previous days of discussion, others waiting to see which direction the rhetoric would flow. It seemed those who were willing to speak first felt it necessary to voice comments against the anti-pope and the German king rather than state their views on who should be elected Pope. Within half an hour, discussion began to flow more freely and attendees began to whisper back and forth, passing secret embassies amongst themselves and forming pacts. Soon the speeches began to gather heat.

"I recommend that we immediately vote for Cardinal Abbot Desiderius of Monte Cassino and bring this convocation quickly to an amenable end!" exclaimed Bishop Giovanni of Tivoli. "Our dear Desiderius is the epitome of God's servant leadership upon this earth, virtuous and humble, pious and devout!"

"Here! Here!" cried many within the assembly. "Desiderius upon the Holy Throne!"

"But Cardinal Desiderius has declined the papal throne!" objected the Archbishop of Venice from the rear of the hall. I therefore propose the name of Cardinal Odo de Lagery who has courageously conducted the business of our Holy Church even during the anti-pope's occupancy of the Vatican!"

"Here, here!" cried a chorus of Odo's supporters, not as numerous, but equally vocal.

Then another cardinal took to his feet. "We must respect the wish of our departed Father, Pope Gregory. As an inspiring servant of God, Desiderius deserves our nod! Let us, therefore, elect Desiderius with all haste!"

"Desiderius is blessed with the Holy Spirit, and bathed in its light!" proclaimed another.

"Yes, yes, Desiderius!" cried others. "'Tis the will of God!"

"Do they not understand that Desiderius has steadfastly refused the position?" Tristan whispered to Odo.

"Hope springs eternal, lad," replied Odo. "Even I hope that Desiderius may yet be swayed."

Tristan dropped his forehead into his palm and shook his head, appalled that the simplicity of this situation had become so enmeshed. *Even though Odo has not sought the Papacy,* he thought, *nor would he leave the Church hanging in the balance as had Desiderius.*

As more support continued to pour in for Desiderius and Odo from the two opposing factions, Desiderius quietly sat and listened to these many effusions of praise about himself with a faint smile; a smile that did not convey satisfaction, only apprehension. Unable to remain silent any longer, he finally stood and called a halt to the proceedings.

"I am deeply honored, Brothers and friends in Christ," he sighed heavily, "As I have previously announced to all Italy, I shall not don the red cope. It is not God's will that beckons me to the Papal throne, but your will that attempts to drag me there. You summoned me here under the guise of providing counsel only. I fear that your summons was disingenuous, which is disappointing. I tell you, I stand firm in my refusal! There are many amongst you here, many within the College of Cardinals who are qualified to lead our Church such as my dear colleague, Cardinal-Bishop Odo de Lagery, who has been equally praised by this assembly. As for me, I shall remain at my beloved Monte Cassino in Lower Italy and continue my work in the Lord's name."

The assembly sat in silence for several moments, some content to hear this endorsement of Odo de Lagery, some exchanging looks of disappointment, while others appeared to become angry. Duke Roger Borsa, who was sitting in the rear of the deaconry with his knights, cursed aloud at the words of Desiderius, then glared at him with contempt. Comment then began to circulate throughout the deaconry as those pushing for Desiderius looked at each other as if to ask, *What now?* But then these comments evolved into loud objections, some voices becoming sullen and disrespectful.

"You owe it to the Church that raised you up, Desiderius!" one of the cardinals bristled, taking to his feet and directing a shaking finger at Desiderius as he huddled down amongst his monks.

"Indeed!" shouted another, even more angry than the first. This Cardinal then also stood. "You owe it to *God,* Desiderius!" he shouted, raising his hand to the ceiling, looking all about the chamber as certain clerics and dignitaries one after another nodded or shouted out in agreement.

"The mood turns ugly!" exclaimed Cardinal Odo, rising to defend Desiderius who sat nearby. "The good Cardinal Desiderius has been a faithful shepherd these many long years. He has nurtured Norman support in Lower Italy, he has turned Monte Cassino into a gleaming representation of virtue and devotion to our Lord, and he has brought gifts and endowments beyond compare to the Benedictine Brotherhood and Mother Church itself. He has done all that could be expected of a follower of Christ, more than any of us here in this assembly. He does not deserve such a lashing as he now takes here amongst his own Brothers!"

A murmur arose. Then someone cried out anonymously from the crowd. "Here, here! Of course you support his refusal, so *you* can be Pope, Odo de Lagery!"

At this several others whistled and clapped with approval while others began to smolder with indignation at the ugly accusation. Tristan sprang to his feet and pointed at the direction of that voice, his face red with fury. "How dare you speak such vile words, you pompous ass! Stand and show yourself!"

"Tristan, *Tristan!*" Odo whispered with covered mouth. "Do not engage! You only spread the fire."

So livid he could scarcely breathe, Tristan slung himself back in his seat and crossed his arms. He had never in his entire life reacted so openly or so violently, nor never been so infuriated.

"Oh, such an insult to accuse the good Cardinal Odo of such designs!" cried Cencius jumping to his feet. Cencius was a powerful Roman consul who had worked closely with Odo since his appointment to Rome. "Odo de Lagery is a man of honor and beyond reproach! He labors daily on behalf of Rome as well as on *your* behalf! He upheld the Gregorian position even in the face of King Heinrich and the anti-pope as they ruled Rome. Shame, I say, to anyone who doubts it! We who now govern the city of Rome stand behind him. Furthermore, I propose that the College of Cardinals immediately consider electing Odo de Lagery, Cardinal Bishop of Ostia as our next Pope! Cardinal Desiderius is a saint among men, but he declines the tiara, and is within his rights to do so! And even Desiderius points to Odo de Lagery!"

One would suppose that in such an auspicious gathering as the election of a pope, the most religious, intelligent, and influential men of all Italy would conduct themselves with at least a modicum of dignity. Such animosity and ill feelings arose that the assembly turned vitriolic as incensed attendees began to shout and sling accusations at each other, while others began to push, shove, and strike out against those who held the opposite view as even cardinals, bishops, and nobles of lifelong acquaintance began exchanging blows.

"Madness!" said Desiderius, looking over at Odo. "Do you see, my friend, why I wish to remain Abbot of Monte Cassino rather than end my days in Rome?"

"Madness, indeed," Odo agreed. "What we need are level heads here, not hot heads."

The assembly reconvened that next morning, many members carrying black eyes, bruises, and bandages from the previous day's brouhaha. Again, Odo was the first to speak. "It is my sincere hope that we can come to some level of agreement today, Brothers in Christ. I pray that we remain level, and focused on the task ahead. I pray that we not allow our own views to overshadow the needs of the Church. Our time is limited. Even as we meet, the anti-pope's forces are gathering to move south against Rome, and King Heinrich supports this assault by sending additional men from Germany. We must resolve this issue quickly. We have gone without a Pope for a full year. We can no longer afford to put delay the decision. Time is of the essence."

"Thank you, Cardinal Odo," said Cencius, standing. "Yesterday I proposed that the College of Cardinals elect Cardinal-Bishop Odo de Lagery for Pope, and it caused great dissension within this assembly. Today I return with the same request. First, a question." Cencius then pointed to Cardinal Desiderius who was again protectively surrounded by his Benedictine brethren from Monte Cassino. "Cardinal Desiderius, do you before this entire assembly of the true Catholic Church still maintain your wish to remain in Lower Italy as Abbot of Monte Cassino?"

"Yes," Desiderius replied.

"And do you before this assembly renounce again any desire to pursue the true Papacy of the Roman Catholic Church?"

"Yes."

"And do you formally, therefore, support the proposed Papacy of Cardinal Odo de Lagery?"

"Yes. Yes, Consul Cencius, a thousand times yes!"

Cencius then rocked back on his heels and gazed at the crowd. "I therefore, formally, once again put forward the name of Cardinal Odo de Lagery for consideration to the College of Cardinals of Rome!"

This created a stir; nothing like that of the previous day. Discussion, though animated, remained far more civil, and attendees then began to ask questions.

"Odo de Lagery, if chosen, would you accept the Pope's tiara?" asked Giovanni Minuto, Bishop of Labico.

"I will do as the College of Cardinals instructs," replied Odo.

"And will you support Cardinal Desiderius as Pope should he change his mind during the course of this next week?" asked Pietro Igneo, Bishop of Albano.

"Yes, of course."

Heads began to nod in agreement, and it appeared that the deadlock might unknot itself.

The elderly Uberto Belmonte, Archbishop of Palestrina, stood. Despite the silken smile that slipped onto his face, it was evident to all that his deep-set eyes held purpose. He had never taken to Odo de Lagery since his appointment to Rome, most probably because Odo was a Frenchman and not Italian. Furthermore, he had resented Odo's close relationship with Pope Gregory, a position he had once himself enjoyed. "Cardinal-Bishop Odo de Lagery," Belmonte said testily, placing emphasis on the word *Bishop*, "are you aware that the *translation* of a bishop is contrary to ecclesiastical law?"

This induced a sudden silence among most of the clerics. Unsure about what had been said or what it meant, the nobles and warlords leaned forward with puzzled looks.

"Eh?" mumbled Duke Borsa, regaining interest in the proceedings. Then he nudged the cardinal seated beside him. "What goes on here?"

The cardinal, a pawn of Borsa, smiled. "Good news, Duke, that's what."

"What the hell just happened?" whispered Cencius to another consul who sat beside him."

"I'm not sure," said the man.

Then a rash of whispers concerning ecclesiastical law began to circulate amongst the clerics. Odo pressed forward, bringing side-talk to a halt. "Yes, I am aware of that, Archbishop Belmonte," said Odo calmly. "The law introduced by previous Vatican leadership may also be suspended by current Vatican leadership. In times of duress such as we face today, with the Church under assault by usurpers, I do not believe this to be a major issue. Ecclesiastical laws have been changed or suspended in the past. We stand today in peril, and even our deceased Father, Blessed Pope Gregory, would expect us to take appropriate action. Especially with Guibert of Ravenna plotting another attack on Rome and the Vatican. Again, I do not believe the issue of ecclesiastical law to be a major issue."

"Ah, I do believe this to be a major issue!" insisted Archbishop Belmonte, his eyes traveling about the room looking for consensus, especially amongst the elderly clerics who traditionally opposed tampering with ecclesiastical law. He found agreement, not in massive numbers, but just enough to throw the entire assembly back into confusion, which was unfortunate because during the night Cencius' proposal of placing Cardinal Odo forward had gained enough adherents to elevate Odo de Lagery onto the papal throne. Now Uberto Belmonte's words had flung the entire issue back into chaos as fighting began to erupt once again. Men argued, many beginning to scuffle and trade blows again, while others either fled or stormed out of the assembly in fear, disgust, or anger.

Tristan looked about the deaconry, dismayed that men of such high stature could engage in such mayhem, especially the high clerics. "*These* are the men who guide the souls of others?" he said with disgust.

Cardinal Odo also shrugged with disgust, then motioned for Tristan to follow him as he stood to leave the deaconry. "God would not approve of such shameful conduct," he said as he and Tristan carefully threaded their way through the struggling masses of clerics and noblemen.

Cencius, too, was making his way out of the chamber. Seeing Desiderius, he shook his head and asked, "Did my resolution to consider Odo de Lagery not make sense, Cardinal?"

"Yes," Desiderius replied, "perfect sense."

"These fools!" Cencius snorted. "Richest, most powerful bastards on the continent, yet too damned stupid to elect a Pope even with the wolves at the door! This entire convocation has been a great piece of nonsense!"

No one was more furious than Duke Roger Borsa. He had been watching the proceedings for over a week now, believing that in the end Desiderius would somehow weaken when confronted by the hue and cry of so many churchmen pleading with him to accept the papacy.

"Goddammit, I should have known better!" he muttered, angrily summoning his armed escort. He huddled them together, pointed to the door, and whispered something to them. They looked at him with questioning eyes though they dared not object, then quickly made for the door.

Borsa then spotted Archbishop Belmonte, made his way to the old religious, and whispered something into his ear. Cardinal Belmonte, furious with Borsa's words, could scarcely restrain an exclamation of horror and glanced at Borsa as though the Norman warlord had lost his mind. His eyes fell to the floor, as if drawn there by thought. "Si! Una buona idea!" he cried, as though some key had turned and a latch had tumbled open. He turned then, and hurriedly gathered up nine or ten of his supportive colleagues before they could leave the deaconry.

The Duke watched with satisfaction as Belmonte spoke to them. The cluster of clerics at first appeared alarmed, then like Cardinal Belmonte, came alive with agreement.

"Goddammit!" Borsa growled, his face swollen with arrogance, "To hell with these weak-kneed bastards of the Church! We'll take care of this business *my* way now."

CHAPTER TWENTY

HIS HOLINESS . . . THE NEW POPE

Cardinal Desiderius and his Benedictine escorts were barely three blocks from the Saint Lucy deaconry when behind them they heard the clatter of hooves approaching their position. Turning, they saw an armed contingent of Normans galloping their direction. Thinking that it was merely Duke Borsa's men hurrying back to their quarters for the evening, Desiderius and his monks stepped aside to let them pass. Reaching them, the Normans quickly dismounted and assaulted all in the party except the Cardinal, beating them with their fists and the flats of their swords.

"What goes on here!" shouted Desiderius, dismayed. "Stop, I say! I'll report you to Duke Borsa!"

This caused the Norman captain to laugh. "Ha!" he cried, "'Tis the Duke who sent us, Cardinal!" Then the man signaled two of his men and they quickly grabbed Desiderius and threw him belly down onto a horse, binding his neck and shoulders, running the rope beneath the horse's belly, then binding his feet so he was hog-tied astride the saddle.

"What are you doing?" Desiderius protested. "Where are you taking me?"

"To church!" the captain exclaimed, again breaking into laughter. "The Church of Saint Lucy around the corner to be exact!" Then he issued another signal and the Normans mounted their horses and began a moderate canter down the street, leaving the monks they had assaulted in a heap upon the pavement.

From his position of captivity, Desiderius could hear voices gathering in the street behind them, but could not see that this sudden accumulation was following, nor that it was made up of many clerics and nobles who had been within the deaconry of Saint Lucy. Shortly the horse came to a halt in front of Saint Lucy Cathedral, and Desiderius was untied and pulled from the horse. Next the Normans dragged him into the cathedral where before the altar stood Duke Borsa with crossed arms, Cardinal Belmonte, and forty or fifty clerics and noblemen from the convocation. Desiderius was then thrown into a chair that had been placed upon the altar and held down by a Norman knight on each side of him, and one who stood behind, holding him firmly by the neck and shoulders.

Cardinal Odo and Tristan were passing the Saint Lucy Cathedral at the same time as Desiderius was being dragged within. "What is this mob?" Tristan asked, alarmed.

"It's Desiderius!" cried Odo, sensing what was occurring. "He's under assault! Quick, to his aid!"

The crowd was so thick that Tristan and Odo could barely push their way through the entrance to the church, and once inside, there was no hope of breaking through the agitated crowd.

"What is this?" Desiderius cried from the altar chair. "What goes on here, Borsa? And Belmonte, surely you are not part of this?"

But he was. The old bishop signaled to a huddle of cardinals standing in the sacristy doorway, and one of them came forward with an armload of garments. Bishop Belmonte then stood before the struggling Desiderius, issued a blessing, and instructed the knights to force the red cope upon him. Next, as they pushed the pope's tiara onto Desiderius' head, Bishop Belmonte proclaimed, "In nomine Patris, et Filii et Spiritus Sancti, in God's name and with God's blessing, we crown you Pope Victor III!"

"Impossible!" shrieked Desiderius, nearly fainting with rage. "You cannot do this! The College of Cardinals cannot force the tiara upon an unwilling servant! This is ungodly, I tell you! It will not hold!"

Still struggling to break through the mob, Tristan and Odo could see and hear what was happening. "My God!" cried Tristan. "This cannot be!"

But it was done. And though it had been this very group of clerics who had stood proclaiming ecclesiastical law to prevent Odo de Lagery from ascending to the papal throne, they had just one hour later committed an even more grievous violation and thrown ecclesiastical law to the winds.

As he was released, the red-faced Desiderius stood glaring at all around him, so mortified and shocked that he was struck dumb. He was then inclined to pull the red cope and tiara from his body and throw them to the floor, but knowing these were sacred emblems of the papacy, he did not dare. So he stumbled about for several moments, as one lost. As he did this, each time he drew near to another, that individual quickly knelt and bowed, saying, "Your Holiness!"

This cannot be happening! thought Desiderius, dizzy with confusion. *They have shoved the tiara upon my head. In God's eyes this is not legitimate. Therefore, I still am not the Pope!*

Within the eyes and minds of all those present within the Cathedral of Saint Lucy at that moment, Desiderius was indeed the Pope. And these witnesses immediately ran forward to spread the word throughout Rome, and except for the supporters of the anti-pope, others who heard the announcement also determined that the Cardinal from Monte Cassino was indeed the new and legitimate Pope, though they knew nothing of the details.

"Hail, Desiderius of Monte Cassino! Hail Pope Victor III!" the Gregorian Catholics chanted, marching joyously and celebrating all afternoon by the tens of thousands in the streets, and then by torchlight all through the night. "God has blessed us with a living saint! Glory to God!"

And so it was that on May 24th of the Year of Our Lord 1086, in the midst of schism and bloody spiritual war, and after enduring a full year without leadership in the Vatican, the followers of the true Catholic Church finally had a Pope. And though the means by which this occurred may now seem utterly preposterous, it was little questioned at the time. After all, it was done and approved of by the College of Cardinals, the bishops and archbishops, the consuls of Rome, and the great nobles of Italy. *Surely,* thought the masses, *a collection of men so great as this could not possibly be in error.*

CHAPTER TWENTY-ONE

HIS HOLINESS, POPE VICTOR III

Such an event as the selection of the new Pope was cause for celebration, to be sure, but among those who knew about and objected to the manner in which the tiara was forced upon Cardinal Desiderius' head, there was outrage. Chief among these were Desiderius' close friends and confidantes, including the Monte Cassino monks and Cardinal Odo. Steadfast supporters of Cardinal Odo were also infuriated and prepared to launch a campaign of retribution, but Cardinal Odo insisted that such talk cease immediately.

"The deed is done, and attempting to undo it would be more useless than trying to hold back the incoming tide, impossible," he said. "Oh, how I fret for my dear friend, Desiderius! He is a fragile soul."

With reticence, then, all those who objected to this criminal act by the colluding clerics and nobles resigned themselves to silence for fear of creating more confusion and division than already existed. Cardinal Odo summoned Tristan that very next day and the two of them went to the Lateran Palace of the Vatican out of concern for Desiderius.

"He looked so lost and helpless yesterday upon the altar of Saint Lucy's," said Tristan. "I have never seen him in such a state."

"Yes," Odo replied. "He has feared such collusion between certain clerics and nobles for some time now, and only came to Rome due to their solemn promises that he would only be serving in an advisory capacity."

"They lied to him!"

"Half of history is founded on lies, Tristan. This is another track in the mud."

"To think that cardinals and bishops would be so foul and deceptive. Nobles, yes, they have no conscience, but our own high clerics? With each passing day, I become more and more ashamed of our own lack of integrity! Where is God in all this?"

"It is difficult to comprehend, I know. Be careful where you tread, Tristan. Though it is easy to assign blame to the Church, never forget the alternatives. It is the Church, after all, that cares for and feeds the poor, that holds society together, that offers hope in this world of violence and depravity. Despite our own weaknesses, imagine what would occur without the shadow of the Church overseeing the continent. There would be no containment of rape, pillage, and murder at the hands of our own Christian nobles and warlords. Their fear of Hell keeps the flow of blood and abuse to a tolerable level. Without the Church, that blood would wash over the land in raging torrents."

The rawness of these words surprised Tristan. He had always known Odo to be both reasonable and practical, yet there was a cold objectivity in Odo's tone that he had not previously encountered. "It is all a trade off, then, Cardinal?" Tristan said, drawing nearer to Odo.

"Yes."

Entering the Lateran Palace they reported to the papal chambers, but found that Desiderius was locked within his quarters. "What's this?" Odo said crossly to the quartet of guards standing outside his door. "Is our own Pope now being held hostage?"

"No, Cardinal," one of the guards replied with a shrug, "'tis the Pope himself who locks the doors. He refuses to see anyone. This morning he even refused Duke Borsa and Bishop Belmonte!"

"Of course he would," Odo said. "Do you not know what happened yesterday because of those two?"

"No, Cardinal, only that the good Cardinal Desiderius had been elected as our new pontiff, Pope Victor III. And we've been instructed to see after his safety. He's sealed himself within his quarters and refuses all communication!"

"I see." Odo then knocked upon the door. "Desiderius, Odo here. Can you hear me?"

No reply.

Odo raised his voice and pounded harder. "Desiderius, it is me, Odo, and I have Tristan with me! Please, open the door. We mean you no harm!"

At this, the shuffle of footsteps could be heard approaching the door. "Are y-you *alone*?" came a voice, weak and thready. "Just you and the lad?"

"Yes. Now please, let us in. We are concerned about you."

The lock fell out of place and the door sprung ajar slightly as Desiderius peered out into the hallway. "Quickly, come in," he then said, ushering Odo and Tristan within, then closing and locking the door behind them.

Odo immediately knelt. "Your Holiness!" he said, grasping at Desiderius' ring, only to have his hand rebuffed by Desiderius who appeared to be suffering from a crippling despair.

He was a shivering shadow of disquiet. "Oh, to be the victim of such corrosive behavior!" he grumbled thickly with complaint, his voice unsteady like that of a drunken man. "Dark and corrupt forces have conspired to place me in this position to fix things," he then bridled, "but the Church's problems are far more massive than my own humble capabilities!"

Tristan, so appalled by the sight of Desiderius' condition, had forgotten to kneel. Clumsily falling to his knees, he echoed Odo's greeting. "Your Holiness!" he blurted.

"Get up! Get up, both of you!" Desiderius wailed. "I am no Pope! The fact that these twisted powerbrokers are my masters is evidence of that!"

Odo stood, and grasped Desiderius by the arm. "A good servant controls the master," he said, attempting to sooth the old Cardinal. "God will stand by you, Desi . . . *Pope Victor*," he continued, quickly correcting himself.

Desiderius gazed at Odo with an embittered look of absolute defeat as Odo, in turn, looked upon his old friend with empathy. They were quiet for a moment then, and Tristan felt in this silent exchange the heartfelt kinship that these two men had shared over decades. He also sensed Desiderius' profound loneliness and loss of hope, and an alarming realization swept through him. *He wishes to die,* Tristan thought.

Desiderius did wish to die . . . at the moment, at least. Unbeknownst to others, his entire existence had been one inexorable struggle against an overwhelming metabolistic anxiety that had frightened and controlled him since birth. This anxiety had been omnipresent throughout his entire life, but had become vastly more acute and disabling into his forties, at times attacking him with such severity that he could barely manage to function, especially in times of high stress and controversy, such as now.

History, of course, has been heavily populated with such souls, most slipping into anonymity or perdition, many even taking their own lives out of nervous exhaustion. A small fraction of these victims, extraordinary individuals such as Desiderius, have been able to succeed and even rise to the heights of leadership through a rare confluence of perseverance, survival imperative, and good fortune. Time and age conspire eventually, to erode even these blessings, and in old age the nervous exhaustion that previously decimated others of this grain begins its corrosive effect on even the most dogged survivors. Such was the very case with the aging Desiderius whose heart had taken permanently to racing too fast and whose mind had dissolved into a blithering quagmire of doom.

"I'll not survive this treachery!" he wailed, holding onto Odo's arm, his eyes seeking Odo's for salvation from this knot that had been placed about his neck. "It's going to kill me! My health will not hold and I'll descend into madness!"

Odo looked at his friend, knowing there was nothing to be done to change what had been wrought in Saint Lucy's Cathedral the previous day. "God will direct you," he said. Although sincere, these words sounded hollow even to Odo himself. Despite the lack of conviction in their tone, Odo continued. "We also will stand by you, Holiness. You will not endure this struggle alone. You have many, many friends."

But those drowning in the bottomless whirlpool of melancholia are alone, in their minds at least, so Desiderius felt no comfort.

"I am not strong, Odo, and the times require strength. Oh, such an oncoming disaster. My papacy is all going to end poorly!"

These words pricked Odo, and he envisioned Peter the Hermit who had shouted these exact words upon being dismissed from Cluny. Desiderius' statement had the same effect on Tristan, and he glanced quickly at Odo. "The Hermit," he whispered, nudging Odo with an elbow.

Odo replied only with his eyes. Then he turned to Desiderius. "Holiness, Duke Roger Borsa and the Normans have left for Lower Italy an hour ago. Though this means he will not be attending your actual consecration next week despite his own actions, I thought it might comfort you to know that he and his troops have left Rome already."

"Yes, yes!" Desiderius cried, a cynical frown creasing his face. "Undoubtedly he is too ashamed to even look me in the eyes! And what about that serpent, *Belmonte?*"

"No, Holiness, he remains. He will be arranging the consecration, and been charged by Borsa to make sure everything goes *smoothly.*"

"What! Belmonte? Could they not at least have selected you, Odo, to perform the consecration?"

"I declined, Holiness, knowing how you felt about all this. I felt it would be a personal betrayal to participate in such a thing. I pray you are not offended."

Desiderius placed his head in his palm and his voice softened. "No, Odo, you could never offend me. You have stood by my side for many years now. Your refusal was a gesture of faithfulness to an old friend." Then he heaved a bit and placed his hand on Odo's shoulder. "Oh, it could have been so simple, Odo. We both know that you are the stronger man and that you are in a better state to lead the Church out of this morass than I." Then he looked at Tristan. "Through prayer, perhaps I shall survive this travesty and even manage as Pope, do you not agree, lad?"

"Holiness," replied Tristan with a bow, "I believe that you, unlike many in our midst, are a gift from God, as is Cardinal Odo. You will, therefore, be an exemplary leader for Mother Church just as you have been for Monte Cassino. And despite what you say, I do not believe that your Papacy will end poorly."

Even as Tristan completed his statement, a cold finger touched his heart. It was the accusatory finger of shame. He had never once in his entire existence looked anyone in the face with such sincerity while uttering what he believed to be such a bold-faced lie. Indeed, in the recesses of his brain he could not subdue the damning voice of Peter the Hermit issuing his Cluny farewell from the back of his donkey. *Desiderius as Pope will end poorly,* the voice echoed over and over.

CHAPTER TWENTY-TWO

PENDULUM'S SWING

Three days later Bishop Belmonte and several members of the College of Cardinals hurried into the Vatican and came knocking on the locked door of Desiderius' quarters, imploring that he make a public appearance to the throngs of citizens who had begun gathering outside the Vatican. "The city grows restless!" cried Belmonte. "They wish to see the new Pope!"

"Be gone you foul friend!" Desiderius retorted.

"Much rejoicing in the streets has arisen since your ascendency to the Pope's throne, Holiness. The people need to see you."

"Ha, you dare call me Holiness? I did not ascend to the Papacy, Belmonte, but was flung into it, as you well know! Go away!"

At this Belmonte looked at those in his company and sighed heavily. Then, his voice growing more urgent, he turned to the door again. "There is other news, Holiness . . . which is why your presence is needed. Whereas many rejoice, our opponents have already begun conspiring against you, Holiness. As you know, Rome is a city divided. Heinrich's imperialists are forming in the streets and calling for your ouster!"

This statement was followed by silence from the other side of the door. "Conspiring against me?" Desiderius then finally exclaimed. "Ha, they conspire against the insidious actions of you and Duke Borsa! I'll not defend my selection as Pope, Belmonte!"

"But Holiness, conditions are deteriorating quickly. Will you not at least show your face to our supporters to shore them up? I fear blood is about to effuse between the two camps!"

"Ha! And that blood will stain your filthy hands, Belmonte. *You* brought this upon Rome *and* us. Let God direct the future. I'll not tamper with it as did you and Borsa!"

Belmonte sagged with this final refusal. Looking at the others, he shook his head and said, "Best we pack and prepare to flee then, things are quickly getting out of hand. With Borsa and the Normans gone from Rome, we are at the mercy of the mobs."

The Cardinals gave Belmonte a questioning look. "Could we not knock the door down and drag Desiderius out to hail our supporters like we forced the tiara upon his head?" one of them offered with a shrug.

Belmonte shook his head. "No, he's too angry and would only subvert such an effort. Besides, I've learned that the anti-pope's forces have mobilized and now approach our position. The pendulum has swung against us again."

Belmonte and his cohorts then hastened from the Vatican to begin making arrangements to leave the city. As they fled the Vatican gates they encountered Cardinal Odo and Tristan who were arriving at the head of several wagons laden with passengers and personal belongings. They, too, had been witnessing the swell of conflict within the city between the two opposing papal parties and sensed that momentum was surging in favor of the opposition. "Did you speak to Desiderius?" said Odo spotting Belmonte.

"Yes, but he rejects me."

"And well he should, Belmonte. You did him no favor."

"It was not for my gain," Belmonte snapped, "but for the gain of the Church!"

"No one believes you," Tristan said. Then his eye that was not covered by the bandage of his disguise narrowed and he rifled a finger at Belmonte. "In your fervor, you thought yourself a king-maker the other day, and trampled over ecclesiastical law even though you cited it for your own purposes only moments before! Prince of hypocrites, you are, and unworthy to wear the cloth!"

Startled, Belmonte shrank back a moment. "Who is this young ruffian that unjustly hurls such accusations against me, Odo?" he muttered.

"Easy," said Odo, grasping Tristan by the arm, surprised by this verbal assault coming from the usually levelheaded Tristan directed towards a high cleric. Then, turning to Belmonte, he said, "Did you warn the Holy Father of the mobs gathering and the fighting to come?"

"Yes," Belmonte replied, impatient to be away from the Vatican, "but as I said, he refutes me."

"Very well, then," Odo said, looking at Tristan, "it'll be up to us to get him out of the city."

Half an hour later, after much cajoling, Odo and Tristan managed to finally convince Desiderius that it was in the best interest of all that he leave Rome. They gathered several of his personal articles and papal vestments and led him out to the waiting wagons. "Quickly, into the first wagon with us, Holiness," Odo whispered as he eyed the crowd that had gathered outside the gates. "And cover your face," he added before signaling the driver to press forward, "your enemies are thick in the crowd."

The gathered mob milling outside the Vatican had by now grown to several thousand, and though many had come to see the newly appointed Pope Victor, others had come to protest the selection and lobby in favor of King Heinrich's German anti-pope, Clement. The mob, therefore, had already turned into a seething caldron of hostility and dispute. Small groups had already begun to argue, push and shove, while in other areas small gangs had formed and had begun to engage in violence. This violence had begun with the exchange of fists and feet, but then daggers and clubs began to appear from beneath tunics and blouses and blood began to flow. This, of course, only heightened the confusion, fear, and rage of the mob, and soon all outside the gates were enmeshed in a hopeless tangle of venomous fury.

"Forward!" Odo cried to the driver as they approached the Vatican's parapets. "But the people?" balked the driver. "We'll not be able to get through them!"

"Forward, I said! And quickly! We've got to get the Holy Father out of here!"

At this, the driver snapped his whip striking the haunches of the two rear oxen of his team and pressed them forward. Feeling the urgency of the whip and sensing the bedlam surrounding them, the four massive beasts plowed with single-minded compulsion into the mass of combatants before them as they blindly flailed at each other, unaware that they stood directly in the path of three approaching wagons. And the driver, now recognizing the acute peril surrounding him, began to fear more for his own life than that of those his oxen were beginning to trample underfoot. "Hoo!" he cried in terror, urging the animals forward with neither mercy nor remorse as he cracked his whip upon the hides of his team as the other wagons followed.

Tristan drew back in horror as he found himself witnessing men and women falling beneath the crushing weight of ox hooves and wagon wheels as the wagons plowed forward through the mob like the oncoming prow of a great ship, slicing the crowd into frothing, bloody halves. "My God!" he cried, looking at Odo. "Look what we are doing!"

"Would you throw the Holy Father into this sea of insanity?" Odo shouted back above the din of the mob. "They leave us no choice!"

Before Tristan could respond, a shrill voice rang out from within the mob. "It's him! Desiderius! He's the newly appointed Pope Victor, right in the first wagon there!"

Unbeknownst to those in the wagons the fleeing caravan had entered a section of the melee that was heavily populated with supporters of anti-pope Clement. And Desiderius, so terrified by the riot transpiring about him, had inadvertently exposed his face and had been recognized by a member of the imperialist gangs surrounding the wagon. "Get him!" the voice from the crowd screamed.

Many of those surrounding the wagon did not know or recognize Desiderius, but when they heard that the new Pope was among those in the first wagon, they began to assault it and all those within. "Protect Desiderius!" Odo shouted, staving off several attackers as they grappled the driver from his perch and dragged him to the ground, beating him mercilessly. Grabbing out in an instinctual reflex of survival, Odo somehow managed to grasp the falling reins and urged the oxen forward. "Tristan!" he cried, focusing on breaking the wagon free of the mob. "Quick! To the driver's seat!"

Scrambling awkwardly forward as the wagon jerked hither and yon, Tristan attained Odo's side. Then, hanging onto the backrest for life itself with one arm, he kicked out at attackers with his feet and free arm as they continued their attempts to take control of the wagon. This same struggle ensued behind him as passengers fought off assailants from all perimeters of the wagon. It was an awkward defense as most of the men behind Odo and Tristan were elderly cardinals or bishops. Nevertheless, most managed somehow to maintain their position in the wagon, also keeping Desiderius covered and within their midst.

Though Tristan, too, was utterly unaccustomed to fighting, he put forward a vicious defense of himself and Odo as man after man came after their position on the wagon seat. His adrenaline rising to bursting, a wildness came over him that he had not experienced before, and this gave rise in him a savagery that he had never imagined possible. Then, in the very midst of this madness, he abruptly felt his vision go ablur as time and motion seemed to kick into a surreal slowdown, causing his will to suddenly dissolve. Feeling the onset of hysteria, his face then drained of color and he stood there comatose, as if a great pit had opened at his feet and was about to swallow him alive. And though he could see the horror of people screaming, brutalizing each other, and being trampled by the oxen, all sound was drowned out by the foreboding toll of a great cathedral bell resonating from nowhere, one devasting knell after another. He stood there motionless then on the wagon stoop staring vacantly ahead with his one exposed eye, as though utterly oblivious that peril surrounded him from every quarter, as the deep reverberations from this thundering imaginary bell jangled his brain and chest, probing at him, consuming him.

"Tristan!" Odo cried, witnessing Tristan's demise, realizing that he had become helpless in the very face of extinction. "Tristan, protect yourself! The mob!"

Tristan heard nothing, for he was in another place, somewhere between Dijon and Cluny at a roadside spring, under the spell of an old hag that once worked for his mother and had tried to drown him as a little boy. Duxia de Falaise pointed her gnarled finger at him; no longer that helpless old woman of the road he had met months before; now a terrifying dark sorceress who had somehow now taken possession of his destiny. "*Oh, I wonder what it is that you want, Tristan de Saint-Germain*" she cackled, her eyes aglow with a deadly shine, "*and how many men shall die as you strive to seek it!*"

"I want nothing!" he tried to say. His tongue frozen, he could not utter the slightest sound, so he stood paralyzed before her brackish reach, like the trembling mouse beneath the hypnotic thrall of the serpent.

"Tristan!" Odo shouted again, spotting a huge man emerging from the crowd wielding a club of some sort. Again Tristan did not respond. Noticing a man coming at them with murder in his eyes, Odo reached out and slapped Tristan across the face, which quickly wrenched him back to the chaos of the mob.

His first vision was the big man running up alongside the wagon. In a panic, Tristan ripped at the bandage covering his eye to clear his vision, but before he could pull it from his head, the man swung out with his club, striking the left side of Tristan's ribcage. The assailant had meant to strike Tristan across the skull. Missing due to the wagon's forward movement, the blow was nevertheless delivered with such velocity that Tristan doubled over, nearly tumbling from the wagon. The man then quickly grabbed at the wagon seat and vaulted himself upward, raising the club to deliver another blow.

"He is going to kill me!" Tristan gasped in horror.

In that flash of realization, the imperative of survival reared its head with a howl of fury and Tristan unconsciously shot a hand into his boot and extracted his dagger. Without thinking, he lashed out blindly. The razored blade sliced clean through the man's throat and bisected his Adam's apple horizontally in a single sweep. Stunned, the man froze. Within the two heartbeats it took to register what had happened to him, he tried to scream, but his effort dissolved into a bubbling gurgle as blood quickly filled his throat, drowning him in his own blood.

Witnessing the flesh of the man's throat purse open like two horrendous yawning lips, then spew forward blood in a fountain-like eruption, Tristan's mouth fell agape and a cry burst from his lips as he watched the man drop flat on his back to the ground, his open, dead eyes gazing blankly up at his executioner.

"My God! I've killed a man!" Tristan wailed. Then his knees caved and he felt his already tenuous grip on consciousness slip into blackness as he collapsed onto the wagon seat.

The oxen, by now utterly enraged by the chaos occurring all about them, began to pitch their horns about, goring and flinging those in their path to the side. Bellowing with fury, they began to foam at the mouth and grow wild-eyed, losing all trace of the domesticity that had been drummed into them through yoke and weights. It was only the oxen, then, that saved those within the wagons who managed not to get pulled into the crowd . . . and as the beasts plowed forward, a swath began to clear as the imperialists on the ground began to panic and flee. Then, too, opponents of the imperialists began to assault those who were attacking the wagons and put them to rout.

Finally, after half an hour of such mayhem, Odo drove the lead wagon out of the knotted masses and toward the gates of Rome, though the oxen were still choleric with indignation and bellicosity. Looking down at Tristan who lay motionless atop the seat next to him, Odo reached down and tried to shake him awake, but Tristan did not respond.

CHAPTER TWENTY-THREE

AFTERMATH OF CHAOS

Tristan recovered consciousness shortly after the three wagons fled the gates of Rome. "Wh-what happened?" he muttered, groggily regaining his seat beside Odo who continued to drive the lead wagon forward.

"We barely made it out, only by the grace of God. And you were nearly killed."

Vaguely remembering the assault by the huge man with the club, Tristan gingerly palmed the left side of his injured ribcage, and that was when he noticed his hands were caked with dry blood and he spotted his dagger lying on the stoop of the wagon. "I think I killed a man back there," he mumbled, a tremor riffling each word.

"You did," Odo said without emotion. "He was trying to kill you. Had you not succeeded, he would have taken over the wagon and we would all be dead. God did not wish it, therefore it did not happen."

"But the man is dead. He exists no more. I took a life and . . ."

"The man earned his way, and is now burning in Hell, I imagine. The Holy Father is safe, asleep behind you, and we make for Terracina."

"So we've lost Rome yet again?"

"Yes. Rest assured, we'll be back." There was a certainty in Odo's tone as he said this, and a cold resolve in his eye. Tristan did not seek explanation nor did Odo offer it. The seesaw battle for control of Rome had been going on now for over five years, and this latest debacle would undoubtedly not be the end of it. They were silent for a while then until Odo finally said, "Back there fighting the mob you showed great courage. There was an odd moment when I saw you freeze and gaze down onto the oxen as they trampled over those who had fallen. It was as if you had left this earth. What happened?"

Tristan did not reply immediately. He himself was confused about this sudden thing that had come over him from nowhere, seizing him. The thunderous tolling of this nonexistent cathedral bell he had experienced was similar to what had befallen him years before as they had fled Rome with Pope Gregory as a result of Duke Robert Guiscard's butchery of the Roman population in 1084. A like thing had also taken place just days after that. Standing upon the heights of Monte Cassino, he had collapsed into a comatose state on his knees with hands folded. That second episode had been declared by many to be miracle because as Tristan fell to his knees and launched unconsciously into an all-night fit of prayer, nature had seen fit to unleash a phenomenally frightening display of lightning and thunder on a day the sun was shining brightly, and this display continued all through the night and did not end until the very moment Tristan regained consciousness. Tristan thought back to those two times and remembered only scraps of the details. During both incidents he had fallen into a state of unconsciousness, just as he had this last time.

"Well," Odo urged Tristan who was lost in his own thoughts. "What happened to you back there?"

"It was, I suppose, a moment of . . . lucidity," Tristan replied after a moment more of rumination.

"Lucidity? I don't follow."

"One moment I was in the midst of a raging Roman mob, and then the next I was with an old woman in France, one who has perhaps rightly accused me of pride and ambition." He had already determined it best to say nothing to Cardinal Odo about hearing imaginary cathedral bells, so he paused a moment, weighing whether he should expose his other thoughts. "I pray this does not anger you, Cardinal," he finally continued, "but as I stood upon the wagon stoop fighting for our lives, it was as though what was occurring with the mob at that moment was symbolic of the Church that I once adored yet now increasingly question."

"How is that?"

"The wagons, the Holy Father and all the high clerics in the wagons . . . trampling over the common people. Though we and the Church purport to help the people of this earth, we exact a mighty toll, and leave a dreadful wake of damage behind us despite our best efforts to do good. And that analogy, when it struck me as we were commandeering our way through the mob and crushing those who got in the way, was unsettling. It was as though everything in this life was being played out before my very eyes on a small, powerfully symbolic scale; us, the Church, the people, survival."

Tristan's words did not please Odo, nor did they anger him. "More and more you begin to wrestle with yourself, lad, and with the Church. I begin to fear that you ignore the good while focusing only on the bad, much of which is inevitable due to the power and politics of it all. As long as men exist, they will struggle."

"My mother, she said much the same about men; which is why she is content to live in a world without men behind the walls of a convent."

"A wise woman, your mother. Remember, Tristan, we who run the Church are only men when it comes down to it. And remember this also, we are better men than are our enemies. We must, therefore, prevail. Otherwise, the world drops into darkness. You have a pure heart and wish all to be well, but beware of your mind rushing to extremes, making judgments based only on fragments of sentiment and guilt. This life is a prison of sorts . . . and we'll find our freedom only in death, lad." Then Odo jerked a thumb to the back of the wagon. "Find space back there and get some rest. We have a long road ahead and I'll need you to drive the oxen soon so I, too, can get some sleep."

When they finally attained Terracina to the south where the Volscian Hills reach the coast along the Tyrrhenian Sea, the caravan of clerics was utterly exhausted. Descending from the wagon, the bedraggled Desiderius called to Odo and Tristan. "Follow me into the cathedral for I need witnesses."

Puzzled, they quickly complied, and entering the church, they followed him down the main knave and up to the altar where Desiderius stopped, genuflected, crossed himself, then stood again. Then, reaching within his tunic he withdrew the papal tiara, set it upon the altar, and loudly announced, "Lord, before you and before all the saints in Heaven, I renounce this tiara in your name, Amen!" Next he removed the papal ring from his finger. "Lord, before you and before all the saints in Heaven, I lay aside the papal insignia. I beg your mercy for the manner in which these articles were acquired and bestowed upon my person. Though I am worthy to shepherd your humble flock of Monte Cassino, I am not worthy to shepherd the entire flock of Christendom! I therefore now abandon the papacy in your name, my dear God and Savior, and will make my way back to Monte Cassino and continue my service as abbot of the monastery upon the mount."

As he finished this announcement to God at the altar, several of the clerics who had followed him into the church began to object and protest in dismay.

"You can't do this!" gasped an elderly Cardinal as the group moved in unison toward Desiderius.

"No, Holy Father, no!" wailed another, throwing himself to the floor and dissolving into a fit of weeping.

Four Monte Cassino monks quickly surrounded Desiderius, forming a ring about him, and prevented them from coming closer. "Nothing more to be said!" shouted one of the monks. "Cardinal Desiderius abandons the papacy and returns to Monte Cassino! Leave him in peace!"

"Yes, leave Desiderius in peace, Brothers!" echoed Odo. "The tiara was forced upon his head as you all know, and he was nearly killed for it by the mobs of Rome."

"But he can't abandon the office!" cried one of the bishops. "Oh, Duke Borsa, he will be furious when he hears this news!"

"Nobles and aristocrats do not select the Pope!" Odo countered. "Only the College of Cardinals possess that right, and all outside interference is prohibited by recent ecclesiastical law as well as by God's law. Forcing the tiara upon Desiderius was a criminal act of the highest degree! Duke Borsa be damned! And our false brother, Belmonte, be damned! And all the others who joined in this charade, I damn them to Hell in God's name!"

All within the church gasped at these words and immediately fell silent, including Tristan. It was the first time he or any of the others had ever heard Odo utter a word of profanity or issue a sentence of damnation. And the fact that he had included Duke Roger Borsa in this proclamation only magnified the event. Frightened and not wishing to be associated with either Desiderius' abandonment of the Papacy or Odo's frightful words, half of the clerics quickly excused themselves. Others knelt in prayer, thinking that Desiderius' action would now spell the doom of the true Church, while yet others took seats among the pews in discouragement and began to pray.

"So be it," said Odo to Desiderius. "I respect your decision though it will cause consternation throughout the continent. Desiderius, God will guide us, so do not take on a burden of guilt caused by this ordeal, my friend. It was not of your design."

Desiderius was already drowning in guilt, and as he looked at Odo with weepy eyes, he whimpered, "Forgive me, Odo, I am not strong enough to wear the tiara. My walls are thin and such chaos will kill this weak old body, and I am not yet ready to meet our Lord for I have much work to accomplish yet at Monte Cassino."

Odo nodded with empathy. "I understand, Desiderius," he whispered back. "I truly do understand."

CHAPTER TWENTY-FOUR

REFUGE

After spending the night at Terracina, Odo led the three wagons south into the safety of Lower Italy which was controlled by the Normans. "This is where I belong!" wept Desiderius at the vision of the great rise in the distance where sat the Monastery of Monte Cassino. "Indeed, I should have never left to go to Rome this past month. Things would be much simpler now and you, perhaps, would have been elected Pope. This mess, this mess!"

"Do not flagellate yourself, Desiderius," interrupted Odo. "You were *deceived* by men you trusted like Borsa and Belmonte. They produced this quagmire, not you."

Odo's affirmation did little to calm Desiderius. In his heart he knew that he had caused harm to the Gregorian cause and also lost great personal credibility among many of the faithful. Nevertheless, he also knew that he was not physically or emotionally capable of shouldering the Gregorian yoke at this crucial time. Thus trapped, Desiderius descended into a crippling state of melancholia, one so severe that he was not even able to complete the celebration of mass upon his return to Monte Cassino for over a month.

Though the Rome debacle did not affect Tristan as deeply as it did Desiderius, it still created in Tristan a restiveness that came after him during moments of solitude or in his sleep. He could not shake the image of the slain man's gruesomely bisected throat or his dead eyes staring at him from the ground. Whereas his brother, Guillaume, had developed a natural instinct for killing the enemy through his military training with Mathilda since the age of ten, Tristan was much softer and found himself delving into a realm of questioning that only imported remorse. *Did the man I killed in Rome have a wife? Did he have children who now have no father or means of support? Did God truly sanction snuffing out another man's existence, even in self-defense?*

These questions were, of course, only compounded by his memory of assisting Brother Handel in the assassination of the nun in Rome months earlier. Then, too, the shadow of the old hag, Duxia de Falaise, would rise up in his mind at the least opportune moments. And finally, thoughts of Peter the Hermit kept creeping into his mind. Years before when Tristan was a boy, the Hermit had prophesized that Tristan was "*dangerous and would one day sow the seeds of war.*" And now, in the wake of the Hermit's recent prophesy that "Desiderius' papacy would end poorly," the Hermit's legitimacy seemed more certain than before.

The end result of this mental excavation into the very core of his soul was that Tristan's thoughts began to turn more and more toward Mala. She had been slipping in and out of his existence since the age of seven when they first encountered each other as he was being escorted to the Cluny monastery to learn under the tutelage of the Black Monks. Now more than ever, he longed to have her near. The vicious arena of politics within the grand stage of Europe was grinding him to dust, it seemed, and he wished to be free of its grasp. In its place he began to imagine a more tranquil existence with Mala.

But I am a monk, he would realize, and the dream would then evaporate as quickly as it had come.

Odo, too, was initially despondent after arriving at Monte Cassino. Within two days, he immediately set about the task of devising a strategy to retake the Vatican. "All is not yet lost," he said to Tristan as they walked toward the infirmary to check on one of the elderly Cardinals who had escaped with them from Rome but fallen deathly ill since their coming south. "Remember when we had a tenuous hold on Rome this past year? The anti-pope now experiences the same thing. Don't forget, it was a mere year ago that he himself was routed from the city."

"Rome begins to sicken me, Cardinal," Tristan sighed. "Would it not make more sense to establish our own papacy in southern France where our support remains strong?"

Tickled by Tristan's suggestion, Odo burst into laughter. "Ha, a simple solution, that. If you think the citizenry of Rome is now divided, then imagine how quickly the College of Cardinals would break into opposing camps; the very suggestion of such a thing!"

Tristan knew Odo was right and was about to agree with him when a voice rang out from the gate tower. "Rider coming up the rise! Riding hard!"

This, of course, created a bit of a stir within the monastery because such a proclamation from the gate tower could only mean the arrival of important news. "Something's about," said Odo. "Word from Rome perhaps."

By the time they reached the gate it had already been opened, and sitting there astride his lathered mount in the garb of a Carthusian monk sat a familiar figure. "Ha! It's Handel!" Tristan cried.

"Handel?" said Odo, puzzled. "Muehler and I sent him to Tuscany. He's not due back for another month or so."

"Ho there, lad!" Handel shouted at Tristan. "Handsome as ever, I see!"

"And you, Handel, theatrical as ever with your dramatic entrances wherever you go!"

Despite Odo's confusion about Handel's unexpected arrival, he was pleased to see Handel. "Ah," he whispered as he and Tristan came alongside Handel's horse, "still posing as a Carthusian monk I see, eh?"

"Yes, Cardinal," Handel replied, pointing at his clothing, "this white robe of the Carthusians is a sight safer than the black robe of the Benedictines when traveling through enemy territory." Then he winked at Tristan and said, "Of course it's a bit worn and has a hole or two in the back put there by a Byzantine nun."

At this Tristan flushed, though Handel's grin conveyed levity rather than chastisement.

"I thought you to be in the north," said Odo. "What brings you back so quickly?"

"Countess Mathilda sent me, Cardinal," Handel replied. "Mathilda?" said Tristan with interest. "So you've been in Tuscany. Have you by chance encountered my brother, Guillaume?"

"Ay, of course. He sends his regards. And damnation, what a warrior he's become! You'd be proud of him, lad, as he is so proud of you."

"And the Danes?" Tristan pressed. "How do they fare?"

"Ha, wicked as ever with ax and hammer though Orla and Crowbones begin to show age. And Guthroth, an interesting character that one, comes across as thick-headed and slow, yet cleverer than a weasel." Then Handel paused a moment and shook his head. "Orla, he lost his son, Knud, against the Germans last month."

"Knud?" said Tristan.

"Yes, a sad story. At the very moment he left this earth, young Knud saved his father's life. His death has left a great gap though, I fear, in Orla, and in Crowbones also."

"Peace be with Knud, then," Tristan said, crossing himself. "And the little one, Hroc?"

"Ha, little FiveHands! He fares well though he misses his older brother dearly." Then Handel looked back at Odo. "Though the Countess has recently repelled the Germans to the north in Tuscany and continues to push them back, her resources are sorely depleted. During this past year the Germans have sacked her estates, choked off her supply lines, and cut in half her revenues from the city-states she's chartered. She therefore requests money and arms from Monte Cassino and Cluny."

"Naturally we will provide," Odo nodded. "She has long been a generous beneficiary to the Benedictine cause and an ardent defender of Gregorian principles, and at the moment is our only ray of hope on the horizon."

"Yes, I've heard the bad news about the royalists revolting and overtaking the city. You do know that the anti-pope is already now back in the Vatican, eh?"

Odo sighed. "No. I should have guessed that he would quickly capitalize upon learning that we were driven out."

"What chaos the division of Rome has created, and such a delicate balance!" Handel said. "The anti-pope and the Germans were rousted last year by half the citizenry, now the same has been done to us by the other half. Cardinal, Duke Roger Borsa could easily move north and retake the city, eh?"

"No, he refuses. Yesterday we received from him a harsh condemnation in which he delivered a blasphemous and profane diatribe accusing Desiderius of cowardice for abandoning the Papacy and accusing me of treason for proclaiming a sentence of damnation for his soul. Nevertheless, Handel, with the Roman citizenry so equally divided, the pendulum might shift direction again."

"Perhaps," nodded Handel. "And if not from the Roman populace itself, Countess Mathilda feels that if she can receive arms and finances from your quarter, then she'll finally prevail in the north against the Germans. Accomplishing this, she fully intends to then push south and take Rome itself."

"Good news that is, Handel," said Odo. "Come down off your horse then and shake the dust from your boots. Brother Muehler returns any day from Sardinia where he has been meeting with our agents from France and Germany. Once we learn his news, then we'll reset the compass and begin greasing Mathilda's wheel."

CHAPTER TWENTY-FIVE

ODO'S GAMBIT

The Abbey of Monte Cassino was established eighty miles south of Rome around the Year of Our Lord 529 by Saint Benedict of Nursia when he and a band of his adherents traveled there from Subiaco to escape the persecutions of the jealous priest, Florentius. Finding that a temple to Apollo sparsely inhabited by pagans still crowned the summit of the mountain, Benedict broke the image of Apollo, destroyed the altar, and on the site built a church dedicated to Saint John the Baptist. From this point Monte Cassino became the cradle of the Benedictine movement over the next five hundred years.

Desiderius became Abbot of Monte Cassino in the year 1058, and raised Monte Cassino to the zenith of its glory through ambitious rebuilding projects and endowments that elevated the monastery to a scale of incredible opulence and splendor. Under him the number of Benedictine monks exceeded more than two hundred in residence, and the school of copyists and miniature painters became famous throughout Christendom. Indeed, the wealth and prestige of Monte Cassino during this period was exceeded only by one other monastery throughout the entirety of Christendom, and that was the Benedictine monastery of Cluny, France where Hugh the Great of Semur served as abbot and Odo de Lagery had formerly served as Grand Prior.

Beneath the monastery of Monte Cassino, carved into the mountainous rock, existed an underground network of tunnels and chambers used for storage and aging of wine and spirits. Every monk in residence was aware of this subterranean complex. Unbeknownst to all but Abbot Desiderius, his Grand Prior, Brother Muehler, and a select group of Benedictines serving within the Office of Papal Records, a second underground network existed that was accessible only by passing through a concealed entrance that had been constructed centuries before within the private confines of the abbot's quarters. This secret underground complex now served as the storehouse for confidential information gathered from throughout Europe through Benedictine espionage efforts over the past century and a half. Monte Cassino was more secluded and more secure than Rome itself, so it served this clandestine purpose perfectly.

It was here, within the secrecy of this underground complex, when Brother Muehler returned from Sardinia that Cardinal Odo and Muehler locked themselves in seclusion for two days and nights before summoning Tristan and Handel to meet with them. Entering, Handel immediately approached Muehler and the two exchanged a warm embrace. They had grown up together in the same small Bavarian town as boys and had joined the Benedictine order together at age sixteen. Two years later they then both entered the service of Papal espionage where they had spent the past two decades. Their German background had become especially valued by the underground upon the outbreak of the Investiture War against King Heinrich.

"Your burns, Dieter," said Handel in a low voice with fraternal concern, "do they discomfort you still?"

Muehler turned his back to the others and discreetly raised his veil, showing his face to Handel. "The pain has finally dissipated, Jurgen, but the appearance of it gives even me the horrors. God has thus taught me humility." Then he dropped the veil back into place. "Come take a seat," he then said to all. "We have much ground to cover."

"Yes, the recent loss of Rome is regrettable," said Odo to Tristan and Handel. "Today we must take the first step in regaining the Vatican. Brother Muehler's meeting in Sardinia with our French and German agents was fruitful and he has returned with a wealth of information. Coincidentally, Handel, much of that information happens to fit nicely into Mathilda's request for assistance."

At this Brother Muehler leaned over and retrieved a stack of documents from the floor, set them on the table, then patted them as one would a favored dog. "Interesting developments in both countries these days, my friends," he said. "Let me begin with France. The warlords and barons of southern France continue to match or even exceed the military power and wealth of King Philippe, as does William the Bastard in Normandy . . . yet our agents report that Philippe finds himself in the enviable position of being able to swing the balance in the south as these powerful nobles continue to wage their war of attrition against each other." He then looked at Tristan. "This past season you did some work for us in the court of King Philippe . . . did your information not also confirm this?"

"Yes. Philippe threatens to join *one* side in war, then allows himself to be bought off by the other side to remain neutral. Thus he expends no resources, his troops remain at home, and he profits merely by raising the spectre of his potential involvement, while conveniently filling the coffers of his treasury."

"Exactly," said Muehler. "The southern nobles have begun to tire of Philippe's game. Furthermore, as they are loyal to our Gregorian reforms and have for the most part ceased the practice of selling religious office and appointing clerics, they much resent the fact that Philippe continues to stack gold by selling bishoprics."

"And to our benefit," interjected Odo, "the southern nobles now seek any means available to disrupt these two practices of the King. Of course, Philippe has ignored our concerns about his lack of personal morality, as well as our objections about selling religious office. There's been no dicipline mainly due to this Heinrich mess which has kept us ducking our heads. Seeing as he has raised the collective ire of the southern nobles, Muehler and I feel that it is time we make a move and strongly censure him. And to our immediate advantage, the southern nobles have pledged to support such a move through diplomatic channels. Some are even willing to threaten war if need be in order to stop his exploitation of them. And pressure such as this would in turn exacerbate King Philippe's greatest weakness, which is his fear of William the Bastard of Normandy to his north who continues to make designs on Philippe's realm. The Bastard, learning of our pact with the southern nobles, would then begin rattling the instruments of war along Philippe's northern border. Finding himself surrounded by enemies, Philippe would find it wise to heed our demands."

Handel, who had been listening intently, leaned forward and rested his elbows atop the table. "I'm well pleased to hear the nobles of southern France have agreed to cease their decimation of each other long enough for us to throttle Philippe, Cardinal Odo. So, what does this all have to do with helping Mathilda against the Germans? She is our main concern at the moment, not Philippe."

"Ah, it's circular, you see," said Odo. "Mathilda needs help from the Benedictine treasuries of Monte Cassino and Cluny, but we will also go after additional gold and arms from the southern nobles to augment her cause."

"They've never helped her before," Handel said. "Why would they help now? I fail to follow."

Tristan saw the circle, and smiled. "Cardinal, Brother Muehler, my compliments. A fine trick, this." Then he turned to Handel. "The southern nobles will ante up to support us in our effort to support Mathilda. In exchange, they wish us to place diplomatic and political pressure on King Philippe to disrupt his practice of bartering his neutrality, which hemorrhages their own treasuries as they squabble amongst each other. Furthermore it will pressure him to stop selling Church offices for profit, which also has raised their ire. And if Philippe does not heed our censure, then he will in effect isolate himself, thereby creating a *potential* military threat to himself from his neighbors in the south as well as from the Bastard to his north."

"Ha!" cried Handel. "The clouds part! A clever trick indeed."

"There is yet another piece to the puzzle," said Muehler. "Handel, while you were in Tuscany, our German agents reported that King Heinrich, though he continues to send troops south against Mathilda, has not himself returned to Italy to support the anti-pope because the Saxon princes are on the rise again."

"The Saxon princes?" said Handel. "I thought Heinrich squelched their rebellions more than four years ago."

"He had," said Odo, "but those long burning embers have continued to smolder while Heinrich has piffled away his own resources in Italy these past years. Recent news of Mathilda's success in Tuscany has encouraged them to renew their revolt. The more troops Heinrich is forced to send south to fight her, the more his own hand is weakened at home."

"And," added Muehler, "the more it encourages the Saxon princes to also assist Countess Mathilda."

Tristan and Handel exchanged a look, impressed by the intricacy of Muehler's and Odo's crafty strategy. "Well then," said Tristan, "all is not doom and despair as imagined. So, how do we place this wheel in motion?"

"To begin," said Muehler, "Handel, you shall go to Saxony and negotiate the acquisition of gold, arms, and munitions to be sent to Tuscany. And since the Saxon rebellions were originally crushed, many soldiers have been forced back into farming, of which I'm sure they have tired. Offer them a good mercenary wage and bring any willing to follow back to Tuscany to replenish Mathilda's ranks. Also, encourage the Saxon princes to rekindle a series of skirmishes in advantageous, well-scattered locations to ensure that Heinrich remains occupied in Germany and is forced to slow his deployment of troops to Italy. Cardinal Odo has prepared a packet of letters of introduction and intent, and I have prepared a list of nine particular Saxon lords to solicit." Here Muehler leaned to the floor, retrieved a satchel, and set it before Handel. "Instructions, money, passes. All right here. And when we finish here this morning, go visit Brother Vincento and his tailors to be measured. You'll be traveling as a Bavarian merchant."

"Excellent," nodded Handel, "I've grown weary of this Carthusian garb. Besides, it's got holes in the back from . . ."

"We *know*, Handel," interrupted Muehler, "put there by a Byzantine nun, right?"

Though Muehler's face was covered from the bridge of his nose to well below his chin, Handel could tell his friend was grinning beneath his veil as he spoke these words, and this made Handel snicker. "Yes indeed, my dear Muehler, put there by a Byzantine nun who now molders beneath the ground with the worms of this earth. And had it not been for young Tristan there, though his reaction time was a bit *slow*, I might be sharing space with her!"

Odo and Muehler shook their heads in agreement though both were aware that Tristan's performance during this first venture with the underground had been less than stellar. Nevertheless, in the end, the assassination was carried out successfully and Tristan had learned some hard lessons in the process. As for Tristan, who was thinking back on Handel's scalding lecture immediately after the nearly disastrous incident at the Inn of the Sparrow, he offered a weak smile . . . having determined that Handel's remark was tantamount to forgiveness for that questionable performance under fire.

"Handel, when you finish in Saxony," Muehler continued, "you shall slip south to visit our allies in Bavaria also. Cardinal Odo has some business he wishes you to conduct with Duke Welf."

Handel grinned; he and Muehler were both from Bavaria, a part of Germany that had remained loyal to the Gregorian papacy against King Heinrich. "Ah, Bavaria," he sighed, "it's been a long while since I've been home. While there I'll be sure to pass my greetings along to your people, too, Dieter."

"And Handel," said Cardinal Odo, "while spending time with Duke Welf, be sure to impress upon him how vital his resistance to Heinrich is for the Gregorian cause. And as a reward for his loyalty, he is to receive some of the armor and weaponry you secure from the Saxons. And while there, be sure to check on the well-being and health of his son."

"Little Welf, the fourteen-year-old?" said Handel, puzzled.

"Yes, I need to know his condition. No need to discuss it now, you'll find all the information in your satchel."

"And you, Tristan," said Muehler, "will return to southern France to collect gold and arms from the French nobles. It's early June so the crops are beginning to come in, and because of the short winter and the fine spring weather they've enjoyed, they're expecting banner harvests. In other words, their pockets will be jingling with coin. You will sail for Marseilles, then work Burgundy, and finish up in Dijon."

At the mention of Marseilles, Tristan's breath caught a moment, as if on a thorn. *Mala is there*, he thought, and he would see her again much sooner than he could have ever dreamed.

"Certainly," he replied to Muehler, gazing about the table silently trying to judge whether any of the other three men had noticed his reaction when Muehler said *Marseilles*. They hadn't, he guessed.

Muehler again leaned to the floor and brought up another satchel. "Tristan, certain nobles you'll be contacting will not be as enthusiastic as the others about contributing resources. Here, within your satchel, I have left instructions on how to prod them along should they not cooperate. Completing your work around Marseilles, you will caravan the cargo you gather and proceed to Cluny. I've already dispatched correspondence to Abbot Hugh so he'll be prepared to withdraw gold and silver from the Cluny Treasury Tower to boost Mathilda's military efforts. While in the area you may again take some time to visit your mother's convent and please convey to her my warmest greetings."

"I certainly will," Tristan replied. "She is forever indebted to you for getting her out of England, and you have earned a special place in her heart, Brother Muehler."

This pleased Muehler and caused him to stare down at the table in reflection. "Ah, although that England business was the most trying moment of my life . . ." he said more to himself than the others, "it was, perhaps, my finest accomplishment." Then he looked at Tristan again. "In any case, when you depart Cluny you'll then lead your caravan to Dijon and complete your gathering of funds and arms for Mathilda." As Muehler finished this statement, Tristan nodded, but a look of concern began to enter his face. "This caravan you mention," he said, his brows drawing together, "if things go as planned, I suspect it will contain great wealth. I am to travel with escort, hopefully?"

"Yes," reassured Odo, "a military escort of Burgundian Guard that you will pick up at Cluny."

"Will I not need an escort from Marseilles to Cluny?"

"We've already sent an agent north to Tuscany," Odo replied, "to instruct the Countess to send a small escort to meet you in Marseilles. We don't wish to attract too much attention as we initiate this effort, and a full military guard leaving Marseilles would do exactly that. Mathilda's small escort will get you to Cluny, then also accompany you the rest of the way along with the Burgundian Guard to Dijon. From Dijon you will have an even larger military force get you east across the Alps and then south over the Apennines into Tuscany to deliver the wagons to Mathilda. It is essential that whomever Mathilda sends to assist you be absolutely trustworthy, therefore I've requested that she send your brother, Guillaume, and your mother's former Danish Guard."

At this Tristan nearly bolted from his stool. "My brother? And the Danish Guard!" he cried, unable to conceal his joy.

"Ha!" laughed Odo, amused at Tristan's reaction. "I suspected this news would please you, Tristan. Know that in the end, Muehler and I made this choice. There is no one more trustworthy than Guillaume in Mathilda's entire camp, nor does anyone love the Countess more. And the Danish Guard, they are true unto death to your mother, to you, and to Guillaume."

"Yes," added Muehler, "it's a sound decision that will protect you as well as the interests of the Countess." Then he slid the satchel across the table to Tristan and said, "You'll sail within the week and begin your work in Marseilles alone until your brother arrives."

"Am I to report to Brother Vincento and the tailors as well?" Tristan asked.

"No, you will continue as Captain Stephane Broussard, the same military officer who appeared in Rome two weeks ago. If asked your business by observers, you'll state that you've been commissioned by unnamed sources to gather munitions. At no time do you indicate where these munitions are headed, except to the French nobles Cardinal Odo has cited in your instructions. Oh, and the papers you'll be showing these nobles identify you as a Papal Envoy operating under the immediate authority of Cardinal Odo, under the ultimate authority of Cardinal Desiderius as Pope."

At this Tristan shrugged. "But Desiderius is no longer Pope."

"Yes, perhaps so, but the faithful of France still look to him as the figurehead of the true Church so his name still carries great sway."

"I am to maintain my beard and mustache then?" said Tristan, secretly wondering what Mala would think of his appearance in Marseilles.

"Of course," replied Muehler. Then a look of displeasure swept into his eyes. "I see you still wear the military uniform you adopted when you arrived in Rome, but why are you not wearing the eye dressing you were also instructed to wear as part of your disguise?"

The question caught Tristan off guard. "Well, I haven't worn it since got to Monte Cassino. I was thinking that . . ."

"No, you weren't thinking at all," Muehler scolded, his countenance changing. "We have visitors here, pilgrims and townsmen. Who knows how many enemy eyes are watching us in our own lair? When we send agents north, they send agents south. And you never know when the eyes watching you here will turn you in somewhere else." Then he fired his hand to his veil and pulled it aside. "Look hard at this wretched sight," he said, pointing to his face. "I made that very mistake of which I warn you, and now look like a monster because I let down my guard to a young woman I mistook for a fellow traveler on my way to England."

"Yes, I understand," Tristan mumbled, his face contracting. "I wasn't thinking clearly."

"Very well then," Muehler continued, slipping the veil back into place. "No, we want you to have no association with your Cluny past, nor with your Benedictine upbringing. And we especially want no association with your Norman heritage."

"We disassociate ourselves then from Borsa and his Normans because of his anger at Desiderius for abandoning the Papacy?" asked Tristan.

"Only for the time being, Tristan," said Odo. "Right now Borsa's fury is aimed more at me than even Desiderius. He is furious that I have proclaimed a sentence of damnation upon him, which is a good thing because it means he still fears God. He will come back into the fold when his outrage simmers out. And when that happens, I will withdraw my declaration of damnation."

Tristan shook his head doubtfully. "He is hard-edged and willful. I fear his pride alone will never allow him to support you again, Cardinal."

"Agreed, his injured pride has now bloated him to bursting," said Odo, clasping his hands across the table as if in prayer. "Never forget that Pope Gregory once excommunicated his father, Duke Guiscard the Wily, for attacking Papal territories, or that the two made peace later. Oddly, it was Guiscard himself, in the end, who came to Rome and rescued Gregory from King Heinrich two years ago. If Pope Gregory made peace with the father, then I can make peace with the son. Boiling caldron that Borsa is at the moment, he hates Heinrich and still suspects that Heinrich is conspiring with Emperor Alexius and the Byzantines to invade Lower Italy from Constantinople . . . and *that* is our trump card with Borsa."

CHAPTER TWENTY-SIX

MARSEILLES

Disembarking in Marseilles, Tristan immediately made his way to the Benedictine monastery in Marseilles and exchanged greetings with the elderly and gentle Abbot LeTour who had already been advised via underground courier to make preparations for his arrival. "Instructions from Monte Cassino were somewhat secretive and vague, I fear," he said. "I've vacated the east wing of our complex as directed by Odo for your privacy, Captain. I've told our monks the area is sealed off for the next two weeks so workmen can complete some needed repairs." Then the old abbot stared down at the ground. "May God forgive me for twisting the truth," he said. Then, after crossing himself, he looked up and added, "And I believe also that we are expecting a small company of Tuscan men-at-arms to arrive here at some point?"

"Yes, hopefully by the end of the week."

"They will quarter with you in the east wing. Their rooms, as yours, are fully provisioned for their stay so there will be no need for any of you to enter other parts of the monastery or interact with anyone else here but me." He turned to leave, satisfied that he had done everything Monte Cassino had instructed, then stopped mid-step and turned about. "Oh, and Captain," he said, "I nearly forgot, I've acquired three wagons as instructed. They're in the stables next to your quarters."

"Thank you, Abbot," Tristan replied. "But a question before you leave. If one were to seek musical entertainment and merriment here in Marseilles, where would one go?"

"Hmm," LeTour nodded, scratching at his chin, "I would never wish to point one such as yourself toward the arms of temptation, but judging from that bandage that covers your eye, perhaps you have earned a moment or two of merriment. Yes, go to the Merchant's Square in the midst of town and perhaps you'll find what you seek. At times musicians gather there in this fine summer weather to entertain the merchants and the crowds they draw." Then the old abbot smiled a bit. "I've never witnessed such a thing myself, of course," he clucked. "I've heard, too, that occasionally even dancing girls from Byzantium have appeared there from time to time. Yes, you might try walking down to Merchant's Square. You'll find music there."

Tristan quickly left and began to make his way toward the heart of Marseilles. So great was his anticipation of being with Mala again, his heartbeat began to quicken with each footstep he took, and by the time he reached the Square his breathing was labored. Looking about, he found that the Square was much larger than he had expected. It was a bustling center of mercantile activity filled with covered stands and stalls that stretched nearly out of view. Between the tight rows of these merchant stands throngs of patrons milled about noisily, as well as wandering peddlers hawking their wares from packhorses and duffle sacks. Byzantines and dark Saracens shoved their jewels and brass goods at passersby, young maidens in troops of three or four scatted about with girlish silliness opening their eyes with exclamation at every novelty encountered, and food merchants cried out the names of their delicacies as the aromatic scent and smoke of roasting meats swirled about in the breeze. Tristan hurried aimlessly from one aisle to the next, certain that he would spot Mala at any moment, but his efforts went unrewarded for nearly an hour. Then he heard the faint strum of music just ahead of him. Pushing his way through the crowded stream of market goers, he ran toward the sound, finding only a single harper singing a popular chanson of the day. Slumping with disappointment, he then began to wonder whether Mala and the Romanis had changed their mind about Marseilles and had perhaps settled in Toulon as they had originally discussed.

Spotting Tristan's disappointment as he ended his song, the harper looked at Tristan and feigned a frown. "Was my song that melancholy, soldier?" he said in jest. "Perhaps a little peasant jig might bring a smile to your long face, eh?"

"No, no, it's nothing to do with your music, sir," said Tristan. "It's just that I heard your music and I thought perhaps it was some acquaintances of mine I have been seeking here in Marseilles, a traveling troupe of Romani musicians."

"*Romani*? Hmm, never heard that word before. Might you perhaps mean *Roman*?"

"No, not Roman," said Tristan, impatient to be on his way. "*Romani*. They came to France to escape the Muslim advances in Spain. There are about ten or twelve in all now, I think, and a girl who dances leads them. She . . ."

"Oh, yes, yes. There's a foreign-looking bunch that has taken to playing music near the docks," the harper said. "And the girl you speak of, an exotic little queen that one, and lithe as the flick of a whip. She dances for the sailors, dockhands, and travelers coming off the ships. Ha! And really knows how to loosen their purses!" Then he pointed over his shoulder. "You'll find them there two blocks over."

His heart afire, Tristan made for the harbor and, arriving, immediately heard music in the distance and spied a crowd gathered near the harbor gate. Rushing ahead, he shouldered his way through the knot of people that had encircled the troupe and now stood entranced by the unfamiliar sonance of Romani music, and even more by the fluid movement of the dancer who fluttered and swirled gracefully about to its exotic timbre. The girl was absolutely striking, and as she slipped from one ethereal motion to the next, her thick mane of raven tresses cascaded and streamed about her like a shimmering black veil, at times flowing in the breeze, at times masking her mysterious eyes. The artful clang and jangle of the brass zills attached to her fingers, two secured to each hand, added to the playful lack of inhibition in her dance movements, and caused the crowd to break into sporadic applause and whistling.

"Mala!" Tristan shouted.

Mala heard the ring of her name, never breaking rhythm. When she heard her name called out again, the voice amazingly sounded familiar. Continuing her dance, she gazed quickly about from one face to the other, but recognized no one.

"Mala!" Tristan shouted a third time, stepping forward into her dance space.

This precipitated into a burst of quick Romani speech breaking out amongst the musicians. Simultaneously, the largest of them bounded from his stool and rushed forward, snarling, "Get back you bastard!" It was Fernando, the man who had dragged Tristan into the Romani camp that first night along the Loire River.

"Mala, it's me!" Tristan cried as Fernando grabbed him about the throat. Abandoning caution as Fernando throttled him, Tristan then ripped the bandage from his forehead, exposing his entire face. This caused a stir amongst the onlookers who were expecting to be confronted with the horrid sight of a mutilated eye, as did Fernando. Witnessing no injury to the eye, surprise quickly rippled through the crowd, and through Fernando as well. He stepped back, maintaining his fighting stance, and gawked with confusion.

Deceived by the appearance of this young bearded soldier, yet familiar with the voice, Mala stopped dancing, craned her neck forward, and muttered, "Tristan?" Then, after another palpition of confusion, seeking beyond the facial hair and uniform, she discerned the brilliant grey of his eyes and the shine of his golden hair. "Tristan!" she cried, running into his arms, sweeping Fernando aside. "Oh, smart boy! I've been dreaming of you coming to me in Marseilles!"

Fernando then also recognized Tristan beneath the disguise, and as he slowly shuffled back to his stool, his shoulders slumped and he muttered a string of Romani profanity beneath his breath.

For the first time in his existence, Tristan embraced Mala with unabashed openness, without hesitation or reservation. Perhaps it was his long absence from monkish garb and ministerial duties blotting out the reality of his true existence that allowed this uncharacteristic collapse of reserve. His being an unknown in a strange city and dressed in the uniform of a military man, or even that he actually forgot for a moment that he had taken holy oaths and solemn vows the year before at Cluny that could possibly have made him act so uninhibitedly. Regardless, Tristan reveled in this mad moment, a moment that he had longed for since leaving Mala by the Loire, and a moment that he wished would last forever. He held her tightly, oblivious to the crowd watching, oblivious to Fernando's searing stare, and oblivious to his actual reason for being sent to Marseilles. "Oh, my God, I've missed you Mala," he whispered, lost in his own surge of emotion.

"I've missed you, too!" Mala sighed, her heaving shoulders signaling the arrival of tears.

It was the single, happiest moment of Tristan's existence, and as he continued to cling to Mala, he gazed by chance over her shoulder into the midst of her Romani troupe, wistfully envying the simplicity of their lives. Then suddenly, obliterating the magic of the moment, he shuddered with horror as icy fingers seized his heart, forcing him to release Mala and push her away. There, sitting on a stool amongst the Romani musicians next to the simmering Fernando sat an old fossil of a woman clothed in black, staring at him.

Duxia de Falaise, the old hag from the roadside spring.

CHAPTER TWENTY-SEVEN

A CHASM OPENS

"What's the matter, Tristan?" Mala said, as he pulled from her embrace. Tristan was so appalled he could not reply. Then Mala followed his eyes and briefly determined that it was Fernando who had upset him, until she saw the old woman's gaze frozen on him, and his on her.

"That old woman," he rasped, "what is she doing here with you?"

"Duxia?" she replied, puzzled by his reaction. "We found her along the road on our way to Marseilles. She was starving to death and could barely move so we . . ."

"Beware, Mala, she is trouble," he whispered with urgency, his eyes still frozen to the old woman.

"Trouble?" Mala frowned. "She's a helpless old woman, Tristan. Besides, is it not the Benedictines like yourself who care for the sick and ailing? What's gotten into you? I've never known you to shun the helpless."

"I tell you, she is no good! Make her leave your midst, Mala, before you regret it."

"I'll do no such thing. I've befriended her, and vowed that we'd take care of her. Please, Tristan, say no more about her." Then her smile returned and she pulled him in again. "I'm overjoyed! And though the money has been good today, I'll end the music and we'll return to camp outside the city."

"No, I will not remain in that woman's presence," Tristan objected.

Nevertheless, unwilling to part from Mala, he found himself in the Romani camp within the hour along with her entire troupe . . . and Duxia de Falaise, who never once spoke to him, yet followed him wherever he went with disapproving eyes. This unnerved Tristan to the point of distraction, and it was not until night when he retired into Mala's wagon that he breathed easy. And that was when, lying next to Mala, he shared with her his history of the old woman and her attempt to drown him.

Mala could scarcely believe him at first, but she knew that Tristan would never fabricate such a thing. "It's a horrid thing she tried to do, and I don't understand it. That was a previous life," she insisted, "for both of you." Then, caressing his forehead with one hand, she scratched playfully at his beard with the other. "I barely recognized you this afternoon!" she giggled. "Though the beard makes you look more manly and distinguished, I think I like your boyish look better." Then her face settled and she said, "You came looking for me by the Loire when last we saw each other, did you come looking for me this time as well?"

"Yes, of course."

"Ah, twice now then. A good sign for me." Then she pulled him close and nestled her face into his chest, but the woolen fabric of his military blouse irritated her nose. "Take your shirt off, smart boy, it offends my sensibilities."

Tristan dutifully sat up and removed it. Then, returning to his position, he gently pulled Mala's head back to his chest. The sensation this brought against his bare skin caused a sudden stir in his loins, and he thought to suppress it at first, but the feeling was so pleasing that he closed his eyes and reveled in it. Mala herself felt his arousal as she lay against him, and she, too, began to feel something rising within her blood.

But there was something confusing her about Tristan, so she sat up in the darkness and pulled at his hand. "This is twice now that I've seen you without the black robe of the Benedictines, yet a year past I attended your ordination. So tell me the truth, Tristan, have you abandoned the Benedictine order, or been excommunicated?"

"Excommunicated! No, of course not. As I told you before, I have been given a temporary dispensation from the black robe and tonsure."

"Tristan, I don't even know what that *means*, or how that's possible," she said, trying to bridle the frustration that this vague explanation of Tristan's created in her. "I've never heard of such a thing. It's not that I don't believe you. It all seems so *strange*. Each time I see you, you are less and less like a monk. Now you wear military garb, and you showed up with a bandage over your eye this afternoon, yet there is nothing wrong with your eye."

"Mala, I can neither answer nor even entertain questions such as this. All I can say for sure is that I am staying at the Benedictine monastery while here in Marseilles, and nothing more."

"The Benedictine monastery? Yes, I know where that is. Dressed as a military officer? In the Loire you were dressed as a diplomat. I just don't . . ."

"Please, Mala, no more questions. Be fair. You asked me to accept the fact that you have taken the old woman into your troupe despite my horror at finding her here. And then insisted that I come to your camp knowing that she would be here. Well, I've done as you asked, have I not? So now I ask you to make a concession for me. Accept the fact that I cannot discuss my business."

"Very well, then, for the moment at least," Mala said. Then, sighing with the realization that they were actually together again, and now cloistered within her wagon safe from the terrors and complexities of the world, she pulled away from him for a moment, discreetly shuffling about beneath the cover they shared. In the darkness, unbeknownst to Tristan, she was removing her blouse. Then he felt her nestling against his chest again, bare breasted against him. Before he could speak, or even react, she then found his hand in the darkness and moved it onto one of her breasts, cupping his fingers about her nipple. "Do you remember when I did this years ago that night upon the hill in Cluny?" she whispered.

"Yes," Tristan whispered back, his loins aflame as his fingers instinctively began to knead her flesh, which caused her nipple to draw taut. "It was the night before I left for Rome. I was thirteen or so, and you were sixteen."

"That was the saddest night of my life, Tristan." Mala said. "I had come all the way south to Cluny to be near the monastery where you were being educated. I wanted to be close to you even if I couldn't see you but once in a rare while. I never dreamed that you would be leaving France only one day after I arrived."

"I was devastated that night also, having to tell you that I was leaving for Italy that next morning."

"You were? But you never said a word."

"Ha!" Tristan cried. "Of course not! I didn't have time. You pushed me away and stormed off leaving me standing on that cold, dark hill. Do you think I wanted to tell you such terrible news? Of course not, but it was the truth, so I had to let you know. Then I came searching for you that very next morning at dawn, but your wagon was gone. They told me you had left that very night, driving your wagon through the gate like a banshee. Do you not remember? Oh, such a temper!"

Mala did not respond at first. Finally, she said, "Yes, my temper runs away with me at times, but I was angry, Tristan, and hurt. I had come such a long distance and was in such a state of happiness as I had never experienced, only to be crushed." Then her shoulders heaved with emotion, exactly as they had that very afternoon when they first saw each other. "As I told you back in the Loire, even when you left for Rome, I came back to Cluny a month later, and stayed there for three years hoping and praying that you might return. God ignored my prayers. Oh, I loved you then, smart boy, and think I've loved you since we met as children that terrible night by the Seine when your Danes slaughtered those Norsemen who kidnapped us Romani children."

"Loved me since then? I was only seven when all that happened, and you ten, Mala. I don't think it is possible for children to understand love or . . ."

"It doesn't matter what you think, because you think too much. Maybe that's why you're so damned smart, but sometimes simplemindedness is better."

Then he felt her rustle about beneath the blanket again, and it was not until she moved his hand between her legs that he realized that she had removed her skirt-wrap and was totally naked.

"Mala," he whispered, "what have you done?"

"I want you tonight, Tristan," she breathed into his ear, slipping her hand down into his trousers. "In the Loire we talked and laughed and laid side by side at night, as would two children. Tonight I wish for us to be man and woman because I never know when I'll see you again, or if I'll see you again. Yes, so if only for tonight, I want to forget our real life and the real world. I want you to share soft lover's talk with me tonight, and touch me, love me, and forget the Church."

"Mala," Tristan whispered, "I can't . . ."

"S-h-h," she breathed, placing a finger to his lips. "I've been with other men before, Tristan, but I didn't love a one of them as I love you. I suppose that you, even as a monk, may have tasted the flesh of a woman before, but I know that you love me, too. I know it's all so confusing for you because you belong to the Benedictines, but it's confusing for me also because as much as I dream of a life with you, I know it may never happen. Still, deep, deep in my heart I continue to hope and believe that you are hiding a secret from me, and that secret is that you somehow or for some reason are no longer really a monk. Oh, what joy that would bring me if it were true. Tristan, even if you *are* still a monk, I want to be your woman tonight. I love you, always have."

Then, pressing her naked body against his while kissing him deeply, she pulled him atop herself and spread her legs in a surge of tenderness. Tristan, having forgotten the world outside, silently mounted her, and abandoned all else, losing himself in the soft, rhythmic thrall of Mala's pull.

CHAPTER TWENTY-EIGHT

BROTHERS

Over the next four days and nights Tristan and Mala feasted upon each other emotionally as well as carnally. She insisted the others go into Marseilles during those four days without her while she and Tristan shared the solitude of the camp together, making up for years of unrealized feelings, feeding each other's needs and fantasies. Then, when the Romanis returned in the evening, Mala and Tristan would retire again to the privacy of her wagon where they continued their orgy of affection and pleasure.

The other Romanis, despite exchanging concerns with each other about Tristan's presence, pretended to notice nothing and went about their business as usual. Even the simmering Fernando had to settle for skulking about silently in an impotent rage, knowing that were he to say or do anything, Mala would immediately drive him from the troupe in a fury. Old Duxia, though sharing Fernando's fury, made herself scarce. She, too, realized that Mala would tolerate no dissension concerning Tristan, for the moment, at least.

As for Tristan during these four days, he became so utterly absorbed in Mala that he, for the first time in his life, abandoned all thought of the Church except for those rare occasions when he was caught alone. At these moments, he would briefly suffer convulsions of the conscience, his guilt stirring up mud where once stood conviction. He rebelled against these intrusions upon his happiness, and dismissed them, even briefly imagining himself as a permanent part of Mala's world, which he perceived as idyllic, entailing little more than freedom, music, and frolic. And though this world was utterly lacking in finery, there was an independence about it that exhilarated him; there seemed to be no responsibilities shackling her free spirit. He was mistaken, of course. Mala carried the weight of the entire Romani troupe on her shoulders. It was Mala who made the decisions, attracted spectators, and maintained order within the camp. It was Mala who contemplated and agonized over the future while the others slipped from one moment to the next. She knew that her youth and beauty were a fleeting proposition at best and did not wish to end her days helpless and destitute like her mother and the other Romani of that generation. She, therefore, did carry the yoke of responsibility for others, and was not nearly as free as Tristan imagined.

Mala possessed great depth of spirit and carried this weight with pride. Though hardened by the transiency and hardships of her youth, she was extremely generous of heart despite her tendency to ignite when provoked. These flare-ups were generally short-lived and ended in regret. It pained her to suffer, as it pained her to watch the hurt and suffering of others. And this profound sensitivity that defined her character was, perhaps, the very thing that so vaporously tied her heart to Tristan. He, too, was weighed down by this same attribute of sensitivity. And he, too, without even realizing it, had been drawn to Mala by this common bond. Beauty, personality and physical attraction are powerful and magnetic forces within the arena of human attraction, yet it is the sharing of the soul that creates depth within the hearts of men and women drawn together in life.

Whereas love, overwhelming as it may be, is itself a rather simple concept; it invariably becomes mired in complexity by periphery aspects of life such as background, career, economics, and *thinking* . . . which quickly became the case with Tristan. By the end of his third day within Mala's camp he began to grapple with the fact that he would soon have to return to the Marseilles monastery. Guillaume and the Danes were soon due to arrive and it would be time to begin negotiations with the southern nobles. Probably, too, Abbot LeTour was already wondering where Tristan had wandered off to for several days without informing him. Something else was beginning to occur to him as well. He began to think that his situation with Mala was impossible.

One cannot set aside the black robe. It is anathema. I will be damned for eternity unless I give this up and repent.

When one is exposed to extreme indoctrination at a young age, as was Tristan amongst the reformist Benedictines of Cluny at age seven, the young mind does not interpret severe teaching as indoctrination, but as the way things really are or should be. Furthermore, when confined for so long within the rigid walls of such indoctrination, it is impossible to break free of its tentacles. Tristan, therefore, could not shed the shackles of his upbringing, or slip from beneath the shadow of the man who raised him, Odo de Lagery.

Yet he said nothing to Mala about this sudden onslaught of guilt that began to devour him from within. Every time this guilt surfaced he suppressed it, chasing it off with the single-minded obsession of a wounded man defending his home from invasion. Alas, fighting guilt is like fighting a phantom: useless.

"I must report back to the monastery, Mala," he finally said on the fourth morning. "I am expecting my brother and some others to meet me in a day or two, and must be there when they arrive. I will be occupied for several days there. I have business to conduct with them, but will come see you as soon as possible."

Although Mala wanted to believe that she was the only reason Tristan had appeared in Marseilles, she already supposed that whatever secret embassies had really drawn him to Marseilles would also pull him away. "You're not leaving Marseilles yet, are you?"

"No. I'll be here another week, maybe a few days more."

"Good," she smiled, caressing his leg as he sat astride his horse. In her mind a week of being within the same city as Tristan was tantamount to an eternity.

Other than the recent encounter in the Loire Valley, they had never been in the same locale together for more than a day or two at a time.

Returning to the monastery and riding his horse into the anticipated seclusion of the east wing, Tristan was surprised to find a small retinue of armed men milling about. Within a heartbeat he recognized his brother standing by the stable entrance talking to Orla, Crowbones, and Guthroth. "Ho there, Guillaume! Lord Ox! Crowbones! Guthroth!"

Guillaume and Crowbones looked up, surprised to be addressed by name by this man in military garb they did not recognize. Recognizing the moniker "Lord Ox," Orla knew who it was despite the uniform, beard, and eye dressing. There was only one person on earth who addressed him as Lord Ox, the name Tristan had called him since birth. "Ho, there! Boy!" he cried, running to him and nearly pulling him from his mount as he tried to embrace him. Boy was the name Orla had called Tristan since birth, as did the other members of the Dane clan.

"It's B-Boy?" stuttered Guthroth.

"Who?" shrugged Guillaume, still unable to identify his brother through the disguise. Tristan pulled the dressing from his eye and Guillaume immediately saw through the beard and mustache. "Ha, Brother!" he shouted, running forward as Crowbones and Guthroth followed.

It was a joyous reunion as the men shared embraces and jovially slapped and poked at each other. Tristan had not seen his brother or the Danes since his ordination, and the very sight of them overjoyed him. "What are you doing here so soon, Guillaume!" he cried. "I wasn't expecting you yet for another day or so."

"Ha, Auntie Mathilda never dallies as you know. She sent us packing early."

"Ah, let me look at you, Brother! Holy Saints, you continue to gain stature and muscle! No wonder you are such a feared warrior. And look here at the Danes, clothed in such long tunics of rich cloth and fine shimmering hauberks! What has become of the former Norse garb?"

"Never mind *their* clothing! What about *you*, Tristan?" Guillaume declared, pointing with laughter. "What in God's name is this uniform you're wearing?" Then he tugged at Tristan's beard. "Swineshead! And what is this *fuzz* on your face!"

"And where is the black robe, Boy?" chided Orla. "Have they booted you from the order?"

"J-ja, h-have they boo-booted you from the or-der?" repeated Guthroth.

"No, no!" Tristan smiled. Then, despite the indoctrination that had been drilled into him at Monte Cassino, and since they were family he confessed, "It is a disguise. I work with the Benedictine underground."

At this the men exchanged a glance, scarcely able to grasp that Tristan, the sensitive and upright pillar of righteousness, was capable of such a thing. "The underground?" said his brother. "Like the spy, Handel?"

But before Tristan could reply a small boy peered from around Guillaume's waist. "You are a spy now, Uncle Tristan?" the boy said, his eyes wide as saucers.

Tristan was not his actual uncle, but was so tightly woven into the Dane clan that he was considered blood.

"Well now, who is this handsome little rascal?" said Tristan. "Is this little Hroc FiveHands who has grown a foot taller since I saw him last?"

"Ja, Uncle Tristan! 'Tis me, Hroc!" Hroc beamed, an elfin laugh escaping his throat. Is it true you are a spy?"

"Hush, Hroc!" said Orla, swatting his son on the hindsides. "One never asks another if he's a spy! Another such question and it's off to bed with you."

The boy studied his father a moment, not wishing to be dismissed. "Yes, Father" he bleated, his mind still running amok with suppositions about his Uncle Tristan.

"Tristan," said Guillaume, "if you do the same sort of work Handel does, that's such dangerous business."

"Ha!" laughed Tristan. "No more so than you fighting the Germans."

"We thought you to be out saving souls," said Crowbones, pointing his stub to the sky as if directing their attention to Heaven.

"Ja, Boy," nodded Orla. "I never thought you would be doing the dirty work of ruffians such as us! We were thinking you would quickly become a great bishop or cardinal."

"Or even Pope one day," added Crowbones.

"Unlikely," Tristan shrugged. "But then, we never really know how things shall end, eh? Who would have ever thought that Guillaume and I would be adopted by la Gran Contessa, or that Mother would end up a Bride of Christ, or even that you Danes would end up in Italy of all places fighting the Germans? Enough about me. The good Abbot LeTour has filled the east wing cellar with food and drink so let us drink some wine and be merry awhile!"

"What? You drink wine now?" said Guillaume, knowing that Tristan disliked spirits in any form, much preferring the cider of fruits or buttermilk. "What in thunder has come over you?"

"True, I have never been one to drink," said Tristan, looking at his brother, "but I believe that may well change this very evening."

"Eh?" said Guillaume, puzzled by both Tristan's words and his expression as he said this.

"Yes, in light of all that has happened to me lately, I need a salve at the moment . . . and a night of wine should do nicely."

CHAPTER TWENTY-NINE

WINE

The Danes were quite partial to spirits, and upon descending into the wine cellar quickly began attacking the small kegs Abbot LeTour had set out for them, ignoring at first the trestle table he had also prepared for them that was covered with boar's head, smoked fish, cheese, and cutlets. Guillaume usually drank sparingly and Tristan rarely ever consumed alcohol at all except as the blood of Christ during mass, but so delighted at being together again, the two brothers broke with habit. And as the wine flowed, so flowed conversation and frivolity. Guillaume and the Danes gave detailed accounts of the war in Tuscany, and Tristan recounted Desiderius' debacle in Rome concerning the Papacy.

"I don't understand why he would walk away from the papal throne at a time such as this," complained Guillaume. "We need a Pope desperately."

"It is a question of his health," Tristan explained. "Desiderius has a fragility about him."

"Physically you mean? I know he's old, but then so was Pope Gregory."

"No, not just physically, but his mind also."

"His mind? Do you mean he's mad?"

"No," Tristan laughed, beginning to feel the titillation of the wine. "Nothing at all like that, but he possesses a nervousness of sorts. Ha, nothing you or the Danes would understand!"

"I've been nervous before," interjected Orla.

"Ja, me too," said Crowbones. Then, laughing, he pointed his stub to his crotch. "Like when my *root* refuses to get stiff!"

"J-ja, I get nervous, t-too at t-times," added Guthroth, not wishing to be left out of the conversation.

"Ja, every time you talk!" brayed Orla, rearing his head back, guffawing at his barb.

This brought laughter to all except Guthroth, who shook his head with embarrassment. Then, when the laughter subsided, Tristan's expression changed and he looked at Orla. "Lord Ox, I want you to know that I pray often for your son, Knud. Receiving that sad news, Cardinals Odo and Desiderius offered up a special mass for him at Monte Cassino."

Of the three Danes, only Guthroth had ever consented to being baptized. Nevertheless, Odo nodded with appreciation. "Though I'm not Christian nor was Knud, please thank them for me." Then he pawed at his beard a moment and added, "I should have tended to him more . . . he was such a good lad."

"Ja," said Crowbones, "a fine, fine lad. We miss him."

"Ja!" cried Hroc who was listening from across the room. "And my big brother, Knud, died a hero. He saved our father's life!"

Tristan looked at young Hroc, swollen with pride, and nodded. "Indeed, a true hero," he said.

"Mind your business over there, Hroc, or I'll send you to bed," said Orla. "It's not your place to interrupt man-talk."

"Yes, Father," replied Hroc, fearful of being separated from the men.

"And how goes Cardinal Odo?" asked Guillaume. "Very well," said Tristan. "And was within a whisker of being selected Pope in Rome last month. Had it not been for Duke Borsa and a handful of Cardinals, he would be wearing the Pope's tiara this very moment."

"Too bad, that," Guillaume said. "I've always thought he would be an excellent Pope. You too, eh?"

"Indeed. He is both strong and wise . . . and more intelligent than all the clerics of Europe combined."

As Tristan said this, a slight slur infected his speech, which caused Orla to chortle. "Beware the wine, Boy, it'll sneak up on you!"

"Ha, I hope it does!" Tristan laughed, reaching for his goblet. Tilting it on end, he sucked at its contents with deep gulps.

"Whoa, Boy," snickered Crowbones, "this Benedictine wine is stout and it'll put you down like a lame mule if you keep that up!"

Tristan exhaled heavily, burped, and slammed the empty goblet down onto the table, nearly knocking it over. "Lord Ox," he said, changing direction, "would you by chance happen to remember a woman by the name of Duxia de Falaise?"

The mention of this name brought silence to the room as the three Danes exchanged a look, as if someone had summoned a ghost into the cellar from the distant past. "Ja . . ." Orla finally said. "A Finnish woman who was brought into the clan by your grandfather, Guntar the Mace. She raised your mother, you know, and took care of you boys until . . ." Here he broke off, as if afraid of committing a blunder, and stared into his goblet.

"Until she tried to drown me as a child?" Tristan said, completing Orla's thought.

"You know about that?" said Crowbones.

Tristan pointed to Guthroth, who had moved his stool closer at the sound of the woman's name, and said, "Yes, and that Guthroth here saved my life."

"Ja," said Orla, "he would have killed the foul bitch with his bare hands had not your mother arrived and stopped him. A strange case, that woman. We never knew what to make of her, but she held great sway over Guntar for some reason, then later over your mother. What has unearthed all this, Boy?"

"I met her a while back outside Dijon, quite by coincidence," Tristan said, the haze of wine dragging her face to mind.

"How did you know about her trying to drown you?" asked Crowbones. "All within the clan were instructed by your mother to never speak of it again."

"Duxia told me."

Guillaume, who had been listening intently, had no idea who this woman was, nor understood anything the others were talking about. "Duxia de who?" he asked.

"Duxia de Falaise," replied Crowbones. "That wasn't her real name. The real Duxia de Falaise was a member of William the Bastard's family in the Norman court. This woman we speak of liked the sound of the name and took it for her own, dropping her Finnish name which was Mielikki."

"Ja, Mielikki," said Orla. "She was named after a Finnish goddess of the wood-lands. We suspected all along that she was a sorceress since her family lived deep in the back forests. They talked to trees and animals and such, and summoned the clouds."

"Clouds?" said Tristan, taking another deep gulp of wine.

"Ay, she and her people watched their formation in the sky. Whenever the clouds began to swirl and darken on the approach of bad weather, they would break out into a strange tongue that even the other Finns did not comprehend, and commune with the clouds in loud voices and with wild motions as though casting spells upon the earth."

Tristan reflected on Orla's words a moment. "How did such a strange woman come to be a part of my grandfather's household. Did he not abhor sorcery?"

"No. You must remember that your grandfather, Guntar, and his entire branch of the family refused to abandon the old traditions as did all the other Danes of Normandy who turned to the French ways, therefore they refused Christianity though William the Bastard pressed them constantly to be baptized . . . which is why we of the Danish Guard under your grandfather stood out so sorely amongst the Normans. They mocked us, even."

"Ha," laughed Crowbones, "except when the war horns were blasted! When it came time for the axes to be sharpened, then they wanted us right next to them. Ja, of all the Danes, only your mother was baptized back then."

Tristan sat there a moment taking in all that he had just heard. Then, his tongue thick with drink, asked, "This Mielikki, or Duxia, or whatever her name is, can she see the future?"

"What?" said Guillaume, becoming convinced that Tristan was talking nonsense through the wine.

"Certain Finnish women," interjected Crowbones, "are born with the gift of prophecy . . . like Orla's and my grandmother who taught me to read bird bones as a boy."

"But *Duxia*," insisted Tristan, his alcohol consumption by now beginning to cause his upper torso to loll slightly to one side, "what about her? Could she predict the future?"

"At times she did, Boy," nodded Orla. "And it was almost frightening."

"And curses," Tristan muttered, the wine now turning everything before him into a fog. "Did she ever l-lay curses up-on our family?"

"Only once that I recall," said Crowbones, "when she was forced out of your mother's household in Saint-Germainen-Laye."

Tristan weighed this for a moment, trying to keep his head clear though it seemed the room was starting to move about. Staring ahead, he blinked slowly, like a frog blinks, then swallowed hard to suppress the sickening queeze of retching working its way up his throat. "O-h-h," he groaned.

"What, Tristan?" said Guillaume, perceiving that the subject of this woman had set his brother on edge.

"Damn," Tristan repeated, dropping his head into his palm. "Do you not see what has happened? She placed a curse upon our household, and shortly afterwards Father was executed for treason, Mother sent Guillaume and me away to Cluny and herself descended into a hellish marriage with Desmond DuLac. Then, too, all of you were nearly killed trying to escape England, and now I am in this . . . mess."

"Mess?" said Guillaume.

"Yes, my life is unraveling one fiber at a time. She told me I am a curse on the world and on humanity." Then his eyes rolled about in his sockets as the swirling in his head caused him to flop drunkenly forward onto the table and pass out.

Guillaume and the Danes stared at him then, as did Hroc who had been listening to every word spoken about the sorceress from across the room, his eyes wide with wonder. "Is Uncle Tristan drunk?" he blurted out. "Has the witch put a spell on him?"

"Hush, Hroc," said Orla. "He's just had a bit too much to drink, that's all. Now go to bed, lad."

When the boy had left the room, Crowbones looked at Guthroth and Orla and shook his head. "Duxia de Falaise. I'll be damned. I thought surely the old bitch would be dead by now, eh?"

"Ja, me too," agreed Orla. Then he looked at Guthroth. "Too damn bad Asta didn't let you finish the old bitch off when you caught her trying to drown Boy."

CHAPTER THIRTY

TRISTAN TURNS

That next morning Tristan awoke in a haze, and immediately began chastising himself for drinking so much the night before.

"Now I know why God demands moderation," he mumbled to Guillaume as he stood at the water basin. "I feel like I've been flogged and dragged through the streets."

"It was a good night," grinned Guillaume, "until the end when you began to slur your words and started talking about that Finnish woman. What an odd tale. But a question, what on earth brought her to mind last night?"

"What brought her to mind?" Tristan said, splashing water all over his face. "A twist of fate. I ran into her again three days past, right here in Marseilles."

"What? She's here?"

"Yes. Bad enough that she shows up in my sleep from time to time, but now she is right before me again. In any case, forget about her. She is not your problem."

"I'm your brother, Tristan. Any problem of yours is a problem of mine. We only had each other to cling to growing up all those years at Cluny, or have you forgotten?"

"No, of course not," said Tristan. He loved his younger brother dearly, and had since the very day he was born. "I'm sorry, that was a thoughtless thing to say."

"No injury taken. Something else you said last night has me a bit concerned. You said you were in a mess. Is there trouble of some sort?"

Tristan vaguely remembered the comment Guillaume was referring to, but did not wish to divulge any details of his recent descent into a private purgatory of his own making, not even to Guillaume. The fact that he had helped kill a nun and an innocent bystander at the Inn of the Sparrow, the man he killed during the riot in Rome, the dissolving glue of his faith, his growing obsession with Mala. No, these deep secrets had to be held close to the heart, hidden from the world. "It was the wine, Guillaume. I simply had too much to drink."

"Very well," said Guillaume, although doubt lingered. He knew his brother had always kept his emotions in check, like their mother, and hoarded secrets. There had always been a certain darkness that would fall across Tristan's brow in times of trouble, and that shadow was there now, masking something profound.

"Good to have you here in France," said Tristan, drying his face. "A stroke of fortune that we get to work together on this mission for Auntie Mathilda."

"Indeed, the very best of fortune. So when do we begin?"

"Today, Brother, today."

Adhering to the instructions provided by Cardinal Odo and Brother Muehler, Tristan began to set about the business of arranging a series of meetings with designated noblemen of the Marseilles region.

"I'll want you at my side during each of these parleys," he informed Guillaume.

"Of course. Armed or unarmed?"

"Armed, though there will be no need for weapons. These men are bloated with their own sense of self-worth and manliness so, if nothing else, the appearance of us bearing weapons will place us on more level ground."

"I know you're gathering finances and arms, but I know nothing of the details of your strategy. Am I to speak?"

"Only if questions are directed at you about Auntie Mathilda or the war against the Germans. Otherwise, your role is strictly to observe and remain at my side at all times as a representative of la Gran Contessa."

"Easily done. And the Danes?"

"They will serve much the same purpose. In all my travels I have never seen more frightening fighting men than the Danes, so their appearance and presence will be of benefit in soliciting help against the Germans."

Tristan carefully studied the information within the satchel he had received in Monte Cassino, then with Guillaume and the Danes set out from the monastery that morning with a wagon in tow to participate in the first prearranged parley outside Marseilles with a certain Lord Dufort. DuFort was young and was neither especially powerful nor respected in the region, but had inherited a good deal of wealth upon the recent passing of his father. As he was considered malleable and eager to remain within the good graces of the Church, Odo and Muehler had determined that he should be Tristan's first parley. This would afford Tristan the opportunity to become more practiced at soliciting funds before taking on the more obstinate nobles who had been placed at the end of the list.

Their strategy was on point. Lord DuFort was most gracious and accommodating, even throwing in a precious gold ring encrusted with priceless gems as a personal gift for Cardinal Odo.

"Tell the Cardinal I shall pray each morning at mass for the Countess Mathilda," DuFort said as Tristan and the Danes prepared to leave, their wagon half full of weaponry, armor, and coin.

"Well, that was easy enough," said Guillaume as they made their way back to the monastery.

"Trust me, it will become more challenging as we move forward," replied Tristan. But he was not thinking of the next parley, he was thinking of Mala; trying to figure out how he could spend time with her now that his mission was in motion. Despite the urgency of Mathilda's needs and despite the rare opportunity to see Guillaume and the Danes, somewhere in Tristan's mind this mission seemed almost a distraction in the face of his searing desire to be with Mala.

That's twisted, he thought. *What is happening to me?*

They arrived back at the monastery before dusk, and as soon as the contribution from DuFort was tallied and recorded, Tristan went to the stable, saddled up, and struck his horse at a gallop for the gate. "Where are you going?" yelled Guillaume, running after him. He had been hoping that he and Tristan might share a quiet evening of conversation without drink at the end of the day's labor.

"Into town!" Tristan responded quickly, not looking back.

"Wait, I'll go with you. I've never been to Marseilles before and . . ."

"No, I'll be right back, Guillaume!" Tristan yelled, kicking his mount and disappearing out the gate.

CHAPTER THIRTY-ONE

MIELIKKI

Within the hour Tristan had traversed Marseilles and was working his way through the dark along the western road leading away from the city. Finally he spotted the flickering light of the Romani camp through the trees south of the road. Turning in, he ambled his horse into the midst of the wagons, but found nobody there.

"Mala!" he cried, dismounting.

"She's not here," an old voice responded from the darkness.

Startled, Tristan turned and saw Duxia's outline seated on a log outside the circle of light cast by the campfire. His first inclination was to leave, but then, despite the tiny buzz of alarm pricking his brain as he looked at her, Tristan tied his horse to a wagon.

"Where is everyone?" he said.

"So, you come slinking into camp in the dark of night to consort with my girl Mala, eh?" Duxia said, her voice dripping with scorn.

"Where is Mala, Duxia?" Tristan repeated.

"She and the others are entertaining some aristocrats at a betrothal ceremony in town and won't be back until morning," she hissed. "So no, you won't be bedding her down tonight. Oh, such unbecoming behavior for a Black Monk. It seems the demons have pried their way into your brain and slipped off with your memory, Tristan de Saint-Germain. Have you forgotten your vows? I wonder what your superiors would make of such a thing, eh?"

"A monk?" Tristan replied. "You deceive yourself, old woman. I am a captain of the Burgundian Guard."

"No, it is *you* who deceives yourself. You are not a captain of anything. You are a Benedictine monk, apparently, which explains why you were in the company of Kuku Peter when first we met, though you were not wearing a monk's robe then, either. Mala started talking about you within days of finding me by the road. She told me about meeting you as a child, about dreaming of a life with you as a young girl, and about her heartbreak last year after learning of your ordination into the Brotherhood of the Black Monks. And now she believes herself to be falling in love with you, poor girl. Why you're posing as a man-of-arms, I don't know. You are a monk, this I do know. Once ordained, no one leaves the order. No one!"

"And you," said Tristan, pointing at her with disdain, "you are not Duxia de Falaise, but a sorceress from the back woods of Finland. Your true name is

Mielikki, I have learned, and you come from a family of pagans who practiced witchcraft."

At this Duxia stiffened a measure, like a hound on the leash, and her eyes flared. Then she nodded begrudgingly, pulling the black wrap that covered her head and shoulders tighter about herself. "Yes, my name was Mielikki at one time and my family practiced the black faith, but I am no sorceress, though that accusation seems to give you comfort. I left sorcery behind at the birth of your mother, and am now a woman of God, just as I have told you, the Hermit, and the world. God is within my heart and flows in my blood, monk, much more so than in yours. He communes with me."

"Ha! God communing with *you*?" Tristan laughed derisively. "You are no different than the Hermit, playing at some twisted charade to frighten others, yet you hate the man for being your twin. Such hypocrisy, it sickens me."

"Be sick, then, if it pleases you, Tristan de Saint-Germain." Then her face twisted into a root and her voice elevated as she directed a bony finger his way. "But know this, I shall do everything within my power to separate you from Mala! She is a good woman, that one, like your mother, and does not deserve to have her life poisoned by the curse that brought you onto this earth. Oh yes, you took Asta away from me, but you'll not take Mala from me!"

"So then, it is again a question of jealousy like it was with my mother when I was born, eh?" Tristan said, thinking she looked like a viper coiled there, ready to spew venom. And though he knew she was aged and frail, there was something terrifying about the dead gaze of her dark, sunken eyes. He felt a coldness touch his spine then, and determined that it was pointless to continue this serpentine dance in which they had become entangled. Mounting his horse, he said, "I have known Mala since childhood, Duxia, and you will never divide us. We share a special bond that has somehow tethered us together over the years despite distance and despite circumstance. So know this, I will be back. And I will see to it that she does not fall under *your* claw. Yes, she is a fine woman of generous heart, beautiful and full of life and you will not cast a shadow over her happiness."

"Ah no, not me," Duxia cackled. "You are the shadow, not I. Did I not ask you once before, *What is it you want and how many men shall die as you strive to seek it?* Do you now feel you must drag an innocent girl like Mala into your web also, with your other victims? You are a man of the cloth, Tristan de Saint-Germain, and a Cluniac reform monk at that. Have you forgotten that your brethren have denounced sins of the flesh, concubinage, marriage, and now demand chastity and celibacy? Ha, what a twisted thing it is for me to watch your Hell being served here on this earth. Mala is your apple of Eden, and you've already taken a bite of the forbidden fruit, thinking you'll secretly take another and another. Oh, as with Adam, the ground beneath your feet shall soon collapse and you'll be cast from your idyllic paradise among the elite clerics of the Gregorian movement, and as with Adam, you'll in the end be forced to grovel in the dirt amongst the worms and maggots of this world!" Then, her eyes still afire with hatred in the very midst of this vile diatribe, she shriveled a moment as though attacked by a tiny seizure. Her scorn seemed to dissolve as her tiny shoulders began to shake beneath her black wrap . . . and a queer look of vulnerability slipped into her eyes. "I tell you this, Tristan de Saint-Germain," she then stammered in a near whisper, "if *truly* Mala has a place in your heart, then it is best that when you leave this camp, you *never* return, for God will never allow this thing that you have begun with Mala."

CHAPTER THIRTY-TWO

GOD'S TAX

Returning to the monastery that night, Tristan could not sleep. The encounter with Duxia was more unsettling than he had at first realized, and as he tossed and turned throughout the night, he could neither deflect nor shake her final words; they'd bitten to the very bone of what he had been silently repressing since seeking out Mala in the Loire Valley.

The old bitch is right, the wrath of God will descend upon me. One day I shall be found out, and what will Cardinal Odo . . .

Although he tried to strike such thoughts from his mind as they bubbled ceaselessly to the surface, they gave him no respite until sleep finally overcame him right before the dawn sun broke over the horizon.

Half an hour later he was roused by a hand on his shoulder. "Wake up!" It was Guillaume, peering down at him with a good-humored grin. "Saints of Christ, you look like death resurrected. And what happened to you last night? I thought you said you were coming right back. I waited an hour, gave up when I found your bed empty."

"I got held up," muttered Tristan sleepily, his mind disjointed. "It w-was business I had to attend to."

"Business? You look like you were out all night!"

"No, I came back several hours after leaving; did not sleep well. This schism with King Heinrich, your war in Tuscany, Desiderius abandoning the Papacy, it must be taking a toll on me, I suppose. Enough talk, Guillaume, let me get myself gathered. I have two parleys scheduled today."

Over the next two days as Tristan met with various nobles and communicated Cardinal Odo's request for assistance, it became immediately evident to Tristan that the information within the satchel given to him by Muehler was based on a wealth of highly accurate information. This information had been gathered over the course of the previous year by a small army of Papal agents as a means of keeping an eye to the political activities of the aristocracy, a practice that the Vatican had instituted under Pope Gregory as he fought to keep the Church independent of meddling by the nobles. This information was also facilitating the effort to acquire support for Countess Mathilda. And, Tristan decided, the agents who had collected this intelligence had apparently dug into every nook and cranny. Their information directed him who to see, where to go, and even how to address this particular noble or that particular noble based on his own individual personality, foibles, and weaknesses.

This information also instructed him to meet with certain nobles in private whereas others were to be addressed in small groups. He soon saw the wisdom this differentiation. To begin, those noblemen who openly supported each other in the effort to have King Philippe censured by the Church had already met on many previous occasions and had formed informal alliances, therefore they did not object to meeting together or sharing information. Furthermore, these particular nobles opened their purses to support Cardinal Odo's effort to send aid to Mathilda, not so much for the sake of Italy, but to strengthen their own stand with the Church against King Philippe. In fact, several of these nobles were more generous than expected, often trying to out-do the others in their show of faith.

Those nobles who Tristan was instructed to meet alone, had more clandestine agendas and did not wish to disclose their intentions or share any information with others. For example, a certain Lord Valgout continued to conspire against two neighboring lords despite having twice been forced to pay for King Philippe's exploitive bartering of his neutrality. Despite his anger at Philippe, Lord Valgout still thought it possible to eventually devour his neighbors, therefore he did not wish to become entangled in any alliances with others or divulge his intentions. He also did not especially wish to turn over any of his wealth to Cardinal Odo. In the end he cooperated so as not to raise any suspicion among his future targets.

The most challenging encounter for Tristan was the case of a certain Lord Bernard Truffault of Marseilles, younger brother to the very same Lord Thierry Truffault of Dijon who had been up-ended the year before by the riotous mob incited by none other than Peter the Hermit. The younger Lord Truffault of Marseilles, it became quickly apparent, objected strongly to providing any contribution whatsoever. This was neither due to political disagreement nor dislike for either Cardinal Odo or Countess Mathilda, only because of personal avarice and a refusal to either share or part with any of his own treasure. If Bernard Truffault did not profit from an endeavor, he saw no reason to engage in it.

Consequently, Tristan's first parley with Bernard Truffault was somewhat awkward. Making matters worse was the fact that the contentious parley was interrupted several times by an attractive young woman by the name of Lady Agnes in whom Truffault appeared to have great interest. Tristan believed her at first to perhaps be Truffault's mistress. Overhearing several exchanges between the two of them, Tristan was finally able to ascertain that Lady Agnes was actually the young wife of the older Lord Thierry Truffault of Dijon, the very woman who had nearly caused the hanging of Peter the Hermit. She was purportedly visiting her brother-in-law's wife who was a cherished acquaintance from childhood, though Tristan and Guillaume quickly noticed that this wife was nowhere to be seen. Making things even more awkward was the fact that Lady Agnes' eyes constantly raked over Tristan and Guillaume even as she draped herself over her brother-in-law during her uninvited and untimely forays into the room. To Tristan's relief, Truffault did not seem to notice.

After returning to the monastery after their first unsuccessful attempt to shake loose Truffault's purse, Guillaume looked at Tristan and shook his head with disgust. "A pompous ass, that man! He reminds me of a certain high lord in the service of Auntie Mathilda . . . Commander Vincento Balducci."

"Balducci? Ah yes, I've met the man. His favorite pasttime is counting his own fat acres up in northern Italy. That and swaggering about like a lone cock in a yard full of hens. And an odd thing, though he is a high lord, he prefers to be called *Commander* Balducci rather than *Lord* Balducci. I suppose it makes him feel manlier."

"That's Balducci precisely!" laughed Guillaume. "But this Truffault, I believe him to be even worse! And bones of God, who was that woman that kept flitting in and out of the room?"

"His sister-in-law," said Tristan.

"Eh? You mean to tell me there are two Truffault's and she's married to the *other* one?"

"Yes. Interestingly, though I had never met her before, I heard mention of her in Dijon earlier this year. She apparently had a run-in with an acquaintance of mine, Peter the Hermit."

"Ah, the crazy man I've heard about who rides his ass all about France preaching hellfire and damnation?"

"Yes, and Cardinal Odo makes mention of this Lady Agnes in the instructions he assembled for me on this mission because we will be visiting the older Truffault as we end our parleys with the southern nobles in Dijon."

"Oh? Well, I hope he's not as pompous as this one. Grateful I am that we'll not be listening to any more of his tripe."

"Wrong, Guillaume," Tristan replied, shaking his head. "Truffault is one of the wealthiest lords of Marseilles, and he clings to his wealth with the fixation of a tax collector. Nevertheless, we require his contribution so we go back to see him again tomorrow."

"What? He was adamant about his refusal. Oh, he'll not budge no matter how many times you go back. A waste of time, I say."

"I must follow orders, Guillaume. Besides, my instructions forewarned me that Truffault might be a hard nut to crack, but Cardinal Odo and Muehler have also slipped a trump card in my satchel. I'll put it into play tomorrow."

That next morning Guillaume and Tristan returned to Truffault's manor, which very much irritated Truffault. He had not been expecting them to return.

"What the hell are you two doing here again," he snorted, meeting them at the gate. "Did you not understand my refusal yesterday?"

"Absolutely," said Tristan politely, "but there *is* one other matter that I neglected to bring to the table, and since it will be of great benefit to you, Lord Truffault, I felt I would be neglectful if I did not return to address it."

"Beneficial to me, you say?" said Truffault, his interest pricked.

"Indeed, Sir, very much so. I must insist that we not be interrupted as we were during our first parley."

"Certainly," Truffault nodded.

Guillaume, sitting quietly astride his horse, looked at his brother with interest, wondering what he was poking at. "Well," he whispered, "it seems you've at least cracked the door open, I'll give you that."

Soon the three of them were sitting in Truffault's parlor, and Tristan quickly opened by saying, "I realize that you declined to contribute yesterday, Lord Truffault. My return visit will afford you yet a final opportunity to give a little more thought to Cardinal Odo's request."

"What the hell?" said Truffault. "Captain, you said you came back because you forgot to address something during your first visit. Goddammit, yet now you come at me with the same shake-down as yesterday! Did you have something else to tell me or not?"

"Yes, of course. I will ask you once more to reconsider Cardinal Odo's request."

At this Truffault slammed his fist on the table and leaned testily across it. "Are you deaf, imbecile? Now get up and leave or I'll have your ass thrown out of here!"

Guillaume sat erect and placed his palm across the pommel of his sword. "You'll not be throwing anyone anywhere," he said, his eyes narrowing.

"Who the hell are you, boy!" snarled Truffault, smoldering with indignation as he glared at Guillaume. "Christ, you look like you haven't even had your first shave, so you best not forget that you are addressing a High Lord of France here!"

"I am Sir Guillaume de Saint-Germain, nephew of la Gran Contessa of Tuscany, the most wealthy and powerful Lady of the entire continent," Guillaume responded calmly. Then the corner of his mouth up-turned in mockery. "And you should refer to me as Lord Saint-Germain, Truffault, for I am a High Lord of Tuscany!" He smiled.

Tristan saw the faint tracing of blue veins beginning to rise beneath the skin of his brother's neck as he spoke these words, so he reached over, placed his palm over the back of Guillaume's hand, and slipped him a look. *Easy*, the look said. Then he turned back to Truffault and said, "Lord Truffault, you stated yesterday that you had no interest whatsoever in either Tuscany or Countess Mathilda."

"Yes. And that position has not changed since then, dammit!"

"Very well. Let me ask you once more, do you not have an interest in the Church's censure of King Philippe?"

"No, none whatsoever," Truffault lied. "I will leave such business to the Church and to the other nobles you have so skillfully fleeced this past week."

This irritated Tristan, not so much the accusation itself, but Truffault's condescending demeanor as he gazed across the table. "Very well then," Tristan replied, mentally focusing on to the instructions hidden within the satchel that lay in front of him on the table. "Then, sir, I will ask a more pointed question."

"Ask whatever you wish, and be damned as you do it," replied Truffault, the corner of his mouth curling into a sneer. *Indeed*, he began to think, *it's time that I snip this young lout's peachy beard and call my guards.*

Tristan considered Truffault's expression a moment. Curbing a spasm of anger, he calmly reached within the satchel and withdrew a document. "If you have no interest whatsoever in Italy and no interest whatsoever in censuring King Philippe, then perhaps you . . ." Here Tristan paused a moment, and a slight tremor crept into his voice; he was on the edge of doing something he had never done before.

"Then perhaps I what?" glowered Truffault, feeling triumphant, perceiving this unanticipated reticence in Tristan's tone.

But Tristan quickly gathered himself and moved closer to the table, his stool rasping across the stone floor as he leaned forward. "Perhaps then," he said in a flat tone, "you might have an interest in Lady Agnes Truffault of Dijon, your brother's wife? The very woman who interrupted us on several occasions yesterday."

The remark was so out of context and so unexpected that Truffault was caught completely off guard. "What!" he snickered derisively, thinking Tristan had lost all sense.

Guillaume, too, was caught by surprise at this sudden departure from the original topic of discussion. *What's this*? he wondered.

"Indeed," Tristan continued, his tone growing colder with each syllable. "It appears that you have recently taken a great interest in your brother's nubile young bride."

"Ridiculous!" snorted Truffault. "She is merely here to visit my wife."

Tristan slowly slid the document he had withdrawn from the satchel forward several inches across the table. "It seems you saw fit to plant your seed within her furrows last spring, my friend." Then he pointed to the document and said, "Twice in Dijon within your brother's own bedchamber, on the Lord's Day no less, and on a score of occasions outside Dijon within your brother's hunting reserve, as well as in your brother's gardens, in the wine cellar, and in the keep. Of course, these are the only trysts of yours that have been documented. We suspect there are many, many more. Oh, and I won't even venture to express how many couplings there have between the two of you here in your manor during the, uh, absence of your wife. But then, only you would know the true count. Do you not agree?"

Nothing on earth could have jangled Truffault's brain more than these words. "I . . . she and I, we . . ." he stuttered, all arrogance quickly vanishing.

Guillaume sat back, nearly as stunned as Truffault himself, but then a look of smugness appeared.

"Of course, Lord Truffault," Tristan continued, "Cardinal Odo was truly hoping he would not have to report this disappointing news to either your brother or your wife, but it now seems that your lack of cooperation in this other matter will force him to notify both of them. Oh, and also your father-in-law, the powerful Lord Gagnon from whom you received half of your domains upon marriage to his beloved daughter. We suspect that he will be furious and this news will undoubtedly . . ."

"Stop!" gasped Truffault, turning more pallid with each word Tristan uttered. "No! No need for the good Cardinal to notify anyone! Please, accept my contribution to the cause of the beloved Countess Mathilda, in the very amount Cardinal Odo suggested."

"Unfortunately," Tristan replied, shaking his head with a silken smile, "Cardinal Odo instructed me that if at first you objected, then the contribution should be doubled."

"What! That is a great piece of tripe!" Truffault cried, feeling scalded by this extortionate demand. But then he envisioned the living hell of his future life and he quickly settled back into his seat, encountering no escape. His head then fell limp onto his shoulders, and his shoulders onto his chest. "Very well, Captain" he muttered, his face turning to ash as in his mind he began to visualize the hemorrhaging of his treasury.

At this, Tristan retrieved the document he had placed upon the table, secured it within the satchel, and stood. "We thank you for your generosity, Lord Truffault." Then, quoting the very words written within his instructions, Tristan added, "And Cardinal Odo asked that I relay to you this scrap of personal counsel concerning your brother's wife . . . though it may please the Lord that you help your brother in certain things, it really *is* best to allow your brother to till and seed his own garden."

CHAPTER THIRTY-THREE

DUXIA'S TALE

That very next morning, before sunrise, an ox-man arrived at the monastery with a wagon sent by Truffault loaded with armor, weapons, and a good amount of gold and silver coin. To Tristan's surprise, sitting next to the ox-man was Lady Agnes.

"I've come to visit you, my handsome captain!" she smiled.

Tristan was certain that she would next fly into a rage due to what had come about the previous day, but after exchanging pleasantries, it became obvious to him that Truffault had told her nothing. It also quickly became obvious why she had come. She had apparently been so taken by Tristan that she wished to cultivate, among other things, a relationship with him. Reaching up to help her descend from the wagon, she deliberately fell onto him, making sure that she cradled his head within her ample cleavage while pawing at him under the pretense of helplessness. "Oh, careful, Lady Agnes!" Tristan cried with embarrassment.

From the stable Guillaume and Orla were watching this drama play itself out with amusement.

"Ah, I thought she took a liking to *me* yesterday," snickered Guillaume, "but it appears that Tristan was the target of cupid's arrow, eh?"

Finally finding her feet, Lady Agnes unclasped her hands from around Tristan's neck, then took Tristan's hand. "Perhaps you could walk me into town, Captain," she sniffed. "I never cared much for monasteries . . . too much chastity."

"Actually, I must leave shortly with my brother, my Lady, I have . . ."

"No argument," she interrupted, tightening her grip and leading him out the gate. "Just a short promenade, my dear, so we can get to know each other a bit better."

"Ho, look there," Guillaume said, poking an elbow into Orla's ribs, "the huntress stalks the game! And poor Tristan struggles to be free of the snare, but to little avail."

Reluctantly Tristan walked beside her, and though he tried to release her grip, her response was to cling onto him more tightly, frequently brushing against him or turning into him, making certain that he felt her full breasts against his arm. By the time they arrived at the square she had already whispered several innuendo's into his ear, and anyone watching the two of them stroll by would have mistaken them for lovers despite Tristan's efforts to maintain a viable distance between their bodies. And at one point she actually reached up and kissed him on the neck, thinking surely he would not resist such an open invitation. Shocked by this advance, Tristan raised both arms to push her away, but she interpreted this movement of his arms as an embrace and pulled him closer, kissing him on the mouth.

Tristan froze, unprepared for such a blatant maneuver in the midst of the market with people all about. His eyes darted about to see whether others were watching. And that is when, over her shoulder, he spotted Fernando and two of the other Romani musicians standing at the corner watching them. Horrified, Tristan grabbed her by the wrists and shook them.

"Stop, I say!" he hissed between his teeth.

As he did this, one of the musicians leaned over and whispered to Fernando, "Ha, he seemed fine with her until he saw us, now he wants her to stop, eh?"

"Indeed," smirked Fernando, "he doesn't want us to see this little mistress he has here in Marseilles while he courts Mala before our very eyes."

Knowing that they were talking about him, Tristan turned and left Lady Agnes where she stood. Indignant, she followed him back to the monastery, casting dispersions at him all along the way. Fuming, Tristan ignored every word. Upon entering the monastery gate he went to his room, locked the door, and watched through the window until finally she took a seat beside the ox-man and they left.

His first inclination was to go immediately back to the square and attempt to explain to Fernando what had actually happened, but Guillaume and the Danes knocked on his door.

"Where have you been so long with the Lady Agnes?" said Guillaume, grinning. "Come along or we'll be late for this morning's parley west of town."

Over the course of the next week Tristan became so mired in his negotiations with the nobles that it became impossible for him to return to either the Marseilles harbor or the Romani camp. The members of Mala's troupe had no idea what had brought Tristan to Marseilles, nor were they particularly interested, especially Fernando. He despised Tristan, not only because of Mala, but because Tristan's presence always made him feel coarse and lowly. Consequently he was sure to mention to Mala, in the presence of the other two musicians who had been with him, that he had seen Tristan in the arms of another woman at the square. Unbelievably, Mala seemed to make light of it.

"Ah, 'tis probably some admiring woman fawning over him just like men do when I dance!" she said. In the silence of her heart, Fernando's story cultivated concern.

Fernando found her reaction about Tristan and this other woman odd and was disappointed by it. He'd hoped that it might turn her against Tristan. Though Fernando had never managed to develop anything but a working relationship with Mala, he had always had it in mind one day to win her heart through loyalty, proximity, and devotion. Now, out-of-the-blue, he had to contend with this handsome interloper against whom he bitterly realized he had not a prayer.

Still, it is a foible of man to farm hope even within the most barren of terrain, so Fernando began to double his efforts at ingratiating himself to Mala. He remained patient and subtle in his approach, not wishing to yet expose any trace of his burning desire for Mala's romantic affection.

Duxia de Falaise also despised Tristan and thought that she was the root of his sudden absence from Mala's camp. *Perhaps he listened to what I said the other night*, she hoped. But as her concern about Tristan began to fade, she then took notice of Fernando. And though she said nothing, she quickly put a finger to his ruse and guessed his intentions. *Poor fool*, she thought, *such a thistle to think he will ever stand next to a rose, even if the monk has departed!*

As Tristan had forewarned Mala that he would be occupied for two or three days, she anticipated his absence for a short while. When he did not appear either at the harbor or in camp after five full days, she became concerned.

"Oh," she fretted to Duxia as they sat together at the harbor while the other Romani had gone to the Square, "something bad must have happened to Tristan . . . or else he would have come to me by now!"

"No, Dear," Duxia said, seeing an opening. "I know 'tis a harsh thing to say, but Mala, do you not see that he comes and goes on his own whim? Did Fernando not tell you that he was consorting about in the market with another woman?"

"Yes, but . . ."

"He's as twisted as a greenbrier vine, that one. To begin, he's a monk, is he not? I know you adore him, Mala, but he has no business leading you on so. Even though you have special sentiments for him, don't you see he strums you like a harp? Only when he wants your flesh does he appear. And handsome as he is, when he wants the flesh of another, he appears somewhere else."

"No, Duxia," objected Mala, "it's not like that. And *he's* not like that."

"Now, now, Dear," chided Duxia, her voice taking on the soothing timbre of a lullaby. "Would Duxia ever try to hurt the girl who saved her very life? No, of course not." Then she laughed a bit and said, "Though you are kind to me, you think me old and a little foolish. But I have traveled the road of broken hearts, lies, and . . ."

"Duxia," Mala interrupted, "you don't understand. Tristan loves me in a special way. He would never hurt me or lie to me."

As she said this, Duxia detected through Mala's expression a tiny crack in her certainty, so she continued. "Dear, but I *do* understand. Come now, do you think I've always been stooped and wrinkled as I appear today? No, I was once young and attractive, heavy of bosom with a lively and ample hind end. When I passed, all men stared." Cackling with reminiscence, she added, "They dreamed only of parting my thighs! Exactly as they do now when they look at you."

This made Mala smile a bit. She had become aware of her stunning appearance as a young girl and, attaining puberty, quickly learned the difference between the gaze of appreciation and the hungry stare of lust. "Did you never find love, Duxia?" she asked.

"Oh, yes," Duxia nodded, unable to disguise the sudden arrival of bitterness. "I found a love so deep and passionate that it nearly drove me mad."

"But that is not a fond look upon your face, Duxia."

"Ah, only because it was *that* love that broke me, taught me how men really are. At fourteen I fell in love with a great hulk of man, a Norman warrior of renown who was so proud of his Danish roots that he refused to lay them aside though he was a member of the Norman court. He found me in the forests of Finland during a hunting expedition, and though he held me captive and raped me through the night, there was an allure and a charm about him that deceived a foolish girl as I was. He then dragged me aboard his ship and brought me back to Normandy to become part of his household; he said I was too beautiful and breasty to leave behind. Then, too, with those great grey eyes of his ashimmer, he claimed that he *loved* me and wished me to be a part of his life, so I did not protest."

"Did you marry then, after reaching Normandy?"

"Ha! He already *had* a wife. He assigned me cooking and maid duties, but slipped into my bed many a night so he could rut about and satisfy his manly hungers, all the time still claiming he loved me more than his wife. Year after year this went on, and my love for him only grew, as did the hope that one day something terrible would happen to his wife . . . so then he could finally acknowledge me."

"So, I suppose nothing happened to his wife then."

"Oh yes, something did happen to the wife," Duxia said, her lips tightening. "And therein lies the lesson. The wife died giving birth to their baby daughter. I thought he would, after the completion of his false grieving, claim me as his wife. Instead, he put me in charge of the baby, and began sniffing about the women of the Norman court while still slipping between my legs whenever he pleased."

"But I thought he loved you, Duxia," said Mala.

"I thought he did, too, Dear. Therein stands the bitter lesson I learned about love, a lie; a simple lie that carried my hopes forward year after year after year. He never intended to have me as anything but his whore! Oh such a slap in my face, such angst and heartbreak I did endure. I pressed him to explain why he didn't keep his word, and after much evasion he finally responded that I lacked noble blood, and though I was beautiful, he could never bring me to court; that his peers and his overlord, William the Bastard, would never approve. The truth was, I was good enough for his private lust, but not good enough for his public world."

Mala shook her head with empathy, reminded of her own lowly status as a Romani entertainer. "So what did you do, Duxia?"

"Like a fool I stayed at his side, satisfying his whimsical rutting, and one day woke up only to find that I had become an older woman who'd lost her allure. Yet I faithfully kept his household and raised his daughter." Then Duxia looked at Mala and grasped her hands, caressing her fingers. "The man I so dearly loved and sacrificed my life for, his name was Guntar the Mace, famous war lord and counselor to William the Bastard of Normandy."

"Though I know well of the Bastard, I am not familiar with Guntar the Mace," said Mala.

"Ah, you're mistaken, Dear," replied Duxia, fixing her eyes onto those of Mala. "He was the grandfather of Tristan de Saint-Germain."

"What?" cried Mala, stunned.

"Yes. Though more delicate of stature, Tristan possesses Guntar's same startling grey eyes as well as his frightful intelligence. They are of the same blood."

"I have never once heard Tristan speak of his grandfather, not even as a child."

"Because Tristan never knew his grandfather, Dear. Guntar was executed by his best friend, William the Bastard, before Tristan was ever born. In a strange twist, the baby daughter I raised was Tristan's mother, Asta, a beautiful young girl of noble blood and high status. William the Bastard decided she would make a convenient bride for the Saint-Germain clan of France, thereby solidifying a treaty to strengthen his own position. So then he commanded that young Asta marry Lord Roger de Saint-Germain, a man thirty years her senior. Her father, Guntar, objected mightily, even threatening war, because his daughter was only twelve-years-of-age and not even bleeding yet. The Bastard immediately accused Guntar of treason, put his head to the ax, then promptly saw to it that the marriage be officiated, which is how the Danes and I ended up moving with Asta to Saint-Germain-en-Laye where Tristan was born."

Mala slowly shook her head, her heart cracked ajar after hearing Duxia's tale. "So then, that is how you came to enter Tristan's life." Still reeling, she gave Duxia a hard look, gazing directly into her eyes, and said, "Duxia, I know well that you and Tristan despise each other. And as shocking as I found it to believe, Tristan told me the other night that you tried to drown him as a little boy. So I must ask you, is that true?"

Without hesitation Duxia nodded yes. "I'm not proud of myself for that, nor did I even wish to do it! Mala, there are things that only we women sense. In the curse of the blood God has forced us to expel each month, God included a gift of perception that is much stronger than what he gave men; to balance the scales I suppose. And in the blood Asta expelled on the very day Tristan de Saint-Germain came into this life, I found strange black substances; pulsating lines of flesh that foretold of future tragedy for all who fell under the newborn babe's shadow. And *that* is the only reason I tried to rid the earth of him, to save others of this world!"

Mala shot Duxia a look of disapproval and shook her head. "How could you believe such things? Though I have my own suspicions about the Church, these things you are speaking of ring with the sound of paganism and superstition, Duxia, which I reject even more strongly."

"Ah, no, listen to me, Dear, the birthing of Tristan de Saint-Germain was so horrific, so terrible and ill-fated that the infant should have perished before seeing the light of day!

"The nuns present during the birth claimed that God had saved the child. I knew better. Oh, God may have in his anger at humanity allowed the infant to survive, but in the mother's blood at the very instant she expelled him, God relayed to me a warning that day. Yes, as young Mielikki I was a pagan once, but I later had the water poured over my head and was blessed into the Church long before Tristan de Saint-Germain was born. 'Twas God that painted Asta's blood black that day. I denied it at first, and struggled against his message for three years. Finally, the truth came to me one night in a dream. In that dream I walked through battlefields strewn with mountains of dead, then cities strewn with the dead, women and children gutted and slaughtered by the thousands, and as I walked, I kept seeing in my mind those grey, startling eyes that I saw while pulling the child from Asta de Saint-Germain's womb. It was *him*, the child as a man, who had piled the dead so high in my dream."

Here she closed her eyes and paused a moment, slowly passing her tongue over the crevices of her weathered lips. Then she opened her eyes again, staring at nothing. "That very next day," she whispered, "I tried to drown him, but was caught in the act."

"I am horrified by this story, Duxia," Mala said, "and find it absolutely frightening that you would ever do such a thing!"

"Yes, yes. I've told you the truth, at least. 'Tis I who would never lie to you, Mala, not Tristan de Saint-Germain. Remember, 'tis the *lie* that sets the snare. 'Tis the *lie* that should set the warning bell ringing." Then Duxia stared down into her lap as a look of humility set itself upon her face. "Ay, I well understand your horror at what I did, but I've explained the cause of it. Still, if you find the story too terrible for me to stay in your company, then I shall immediately take my leave. I would never wish to offend one as generous as you. And know this, Mala, I love you though you have only recently appeared in the trail of my long, difficult years, and I would sacrifice my life for you because of the kindness you have shown me since finding me by the roadside that day. I fear that what Guntar did to me, his grandson will do to you. You have no place in his Benedictine world, and would be an embarrassment should he ever rise to Bishop or Cardinal, which he will surely do one day."

"Oh," sighed Mala, placing her hand on Duxia's shoulder to caress it, "your story nearly breaks my heart, Duxia, and I do better understand certain things than before. Oh, but the things you feel about Tristan, they disturb me deeply. And though you seem to believe them with all your heart, I myself don't accept them. Nor do I ever wish to hear such things again, Duxia. Therefore, as long as you never speak such things to me again, I will never ask you to leave my camp. Do you understand?"

Though she bridled the slightest bit beneath her black wrap, the old woman nodded in agreement. Then, curiously, she slowly tilted her head upwards and gazed at the clouds. Pointing, she said, "Do you see that slight grey swirl there to the east, Mala? Though the sky is clear at the moment, I believe you might wish to have Fernando return early to batten down the camp and secure the wagons."

"Oh?" said Mala, looking skyward.

"Yes, Dear, a storm is approaching in the distance."

CHAPTER THIRTY-FOUR

SEEDS OF DOUBT

When the other Romani returned from the Square they milled about in conversation a while until Fernando signaled for them to gather their instruments. "Two large vessels coming in," he said pointing to the waterfront, "we'll welcome them with music. The sun's setting and they'll be in a festive mood after being shipbound for so long. Looks like it's going to be a long night, but we'll go home with the jingle of coin in our . . ."

"No, wait," interrupted Mala, pulling Fernando aside. "Duxia says a storm is coming, so I want you to take everyone back to camp. No need in us getting caught here in a downpour and getting the instruments soaked."

"What?" said Fernando, looking skyward. "There's not a cloud in the sky, Mala, and there's money to be made with those ships coming our way."

"Fernando," said Mala, in that unique tone she possessed that signaled with certainty there was no argument to be had with her. "Have you forgotten the gale we encountered two days after finding Duxia on the roadside. She warned us of an impending storm but we ignored her. Hours later we nearly lost the wagons to wind and mudslides."

"Yes, Mala," sighed Fernando, recognizing that her tone was a warning that she would next bare her fangs, which would then result in him suffering her wrath over the next two or three days. She would then, because of her soft heart, later apologize with sincerity and treat him with deference for a week. He was not of the mind to launch his own misery, so he said nothing more and motioned for the others to gather their things.

"I must remain in town awhile, Fernando," she then said, "so I'll meet the rest of you in camp later this evening."

Fernando immediately suspected that this had something to do with Tristan, who, because of his long absence, he had nearly forgotten about entirely. "I'll stay in town with you," he quickly said. "I wouldn't want you riding about at night alone and . . ."

"No. I need you to take charge of things at camp. I'll be fine."

"Mala, don't you think . . ."

"Fernando," she said, not raising her voice a single measure yet emphasizing each syllable with the directness of her eyes.

"Very well," said Fernando, slumping with defeat. "Be careful, Mala. At night the streets are full of sailors and hooligans."

Mala appreciated Fernando's concern, but was impatient for his departure as well as that of the others. She remained there by the gate watching them disappear into the crowd strolling along the waterfront, then went to her pony and mounted. *Duxia is mistaken, Tristan would never hurt me*, she started to say aloud to herself, but instead came out with, "I . . . I'll go to the monastery. Yes, to find out whether something ill has happened to him."

It was nearly dark by the time Mala reached the Benedictine monastery. Somewhat intimidated by its sanctified, fortress-like appearance at first, she slowly rode its entire length back and forth several times, thinking that fortune might, perhaps, produce her dear Tristan entering or leaving its front gate. Then, too, there was a part of her that knew she was interloping where she had never been invited. This made her wonder, if he did by chance appear, whether he would be angry. After nearly half an hour, by which time total darkness had descended upon Marseilles, fortune did not produce Tristan. Hesitating no further, she then dismounted and approached the side door adjacent to the main gate where hung a yard bell. *Hope I'm not interrupting their prayers*, she thought, as she pulled timidly one time at the bell chain.

Nothing happened, so she rang the bell two times more, much louder than the first time. She sighed then, finally hearing footsteps and glimpsing the approach of a circle of light thrown out by a lantern. A face peered from out of the darkness through the iron grate of the entrance and she heard a meek voice say, "Who goes there at this hour?"

"Pardon, sir, my name is Mala and I am seeking information about an acquaintance who is staying here at the monastery this week."

"Oh?" queried the voice.

"Yes, I seek a friend who is in Marseilles on business of some sort." Then she paused a moment, to clear her own confusion. "A military officer, or perhaps a monk by the name of Tristan de Saint-Germain."

"Well, child, are you seeking a monk or a man-at-arms? One cannot be both, you know."

"I . . . I'm not sure." She thought a moment, then pulled together more details. "He has blond hair and may go by the name of Brother Saint-Germain, or perhaps has even adopted the name of a saint. He was educated at Cluny under the patronage of the Grand Prior Odo de Lagery who later was appointed Cardinal-Bishop of Ostia near Rome. I know this makes no sense, but he's wearing the uniform of a military man though he's a monk." Finishing these words, she expected a response, although none came though the man on the other side of the massive wooden door was still in view. She waited a moment longer, and still no response was given.

"Did you hear me, sir?"

"Yes, yes, I heard you, Mademoiselle," old Abbot LeTour mumbled, by now in a panic. He had been clearly instructed through Cardinal Odo's earlier correspondence that everything involving Tristan and the men from Italy was to be shrouded in secrecy, even from the other monks in residence. And in that correspondence, Cardinal Odo had even cited the possibility of enemy spies slipping about seeking information.

"No, my child, we have no visitors here at the moment," he blurted, sounding more confused than certain.

"Sir, that's impossible," pressed Mala, herself even more confused. "Are you certain you have no guests staying here?"

"Yes, certain indeed. My name is Brother LeTour and I am the abbot of this monastery. So I would most definitely know whether there are any guests within our walls!" As he said this, he was feverishly fingering his prayer beads because lying, for him, was a grievous sin. And though he was following the orders of a superior, it was God who was frightening him now. "N-no, there are n-no guests here, God's word," he stammered. "Not a s-single one."

Finishing these words, a jagged, bluish finger of lightening broke through the billowing cloud cover that had been building since nightfall, followed by an eruption of thunder so shattering that it shook the walls of the monastery.

"Oh my God!" wailed old Abbot LeTour, certain that the Creator had flung his wrath upon his servant for lying. Terrified, as then the night sky opened and hurled a scything, torrential rain down on Marseilles, he fled back into the monastery, hastened directly to the chapel, and flung himself onto his knees sobbing for mercy and forgiveness.

Mala stood there a while in the downpour unable to fathom how it could possibly be that Tristan had never really come to the monastery as stated. And her faith in him was so unshakeable that she refused to move despite the deluge that was beginning to soak her to the bone. Eventually, it began to dawn on her that Tristan had, *indeed,* lied to her.

But why? To what purpose?

Tristan, meanwhile, was in the east wing of the monastery performing computation and documentation of the day's contributions from the Marseilles nobles with Guillaume. He had even heard the ringing of the yard bell that Mala had pulled, and at that very moment said to Guillaume, "Hmm, who would be ringing after dark?" Of course, he could not have possibly guessed that it was Mala, desperately attempting to learn his whereabouts and condition. Nor could he have possibly imagined that old Abbot LeTour, in a lying effort to protect him, had cast him to the jagged outcrop of misdirection.

In truth, Tristan was fully intending, when finished with his work, to immediately leave the monastery and head directly for the Romani camp, knowing that Mala would be disturbed about his extended absence. Unfortunately this absence had been unavoidable due to the unanticipated distances of the last parleys. Posting his final tally, he heard a mighty roll of thunder shake the monastery and heard the sky fall in as fat raindrops began to pelt the roof of the stables and the east wing. He quickly stood and went to the door, and peering out into the blinding downpour, determined that he would wait until morning to see Mala.

"We'll not be working tomorrow," he said, turning his head to Guillaume, "besides, it's the Lord's Day. We will finish our final parley Monday."

"Excellent," replied Guillaume, "the Danes and I have yet to see any of Marseilles itself."

Tristan then peered back out the doorway, thinking he heard the clatter of hooves on the pavers outside. "Wonder who got caught in this mess?" he said, half to Guillaume, half to himself. "Poor unhappy soul!"

The clatter of hooves Tristan heard was Mala turning back through the blinding rain toward the center of town. Her head bowed to keep the rain from her eyes, but also in discouragement and disbelief over what had taken place, Mala began to shiver and tremble uncontrollably astride her horse as she fought her way forward through the storm. She loved Tristan with all her soul, and had loved him since the day she laid eyes on him. And during those four days and nights in Marseilles when he had first followed her back to her camp, he had finally returned her unadulterated adoration without reservation. They had wholly surrendered themselves to each other, had shared secrets, and had made promises. And she had thought the glue of those days and nights to be so strong and so inviolable that they would stand forever. Even if Tristan were truly still a monk, Mala had agreed to follow him and love him, live an existence of sin and secrecy, anything so they could be together. Her only condition was that he never deceive her. Even if he could not expose every detail of his life, he had vowed time and time again to never *lie* to her.

This is not possible, she repeated to herself time and time again. *Tristan, what game are you at, deceiving me so? And that woman Fernando and the others saw you with in the square . . . who is she? You make time for her now and have so quickly forgotten me!*

It was not until she gained the west road leading out of Marseilles toward her camp that Duxia came to mind. *She said a storm was coming though the sky was clear today.* Then, swiping at rivulets of cold rain trickling down her face with every step forward of the horse, Mala thought about the conversation they had earlier shared by the harbor. And as she relived the old woman's tale from beginning to end, she began to see herself in the same tragic role of Duxia, and Tristan in the role of Guntar the Mace.

More than anything, as Mala struggled her way back to camp, one certain phrase that Duxia had uttered kept coming to mind, over and over, "*Mala, 'tis the lie that sets the snare. 'Tis the lie that should set the warning bell ringing.*"

CHAPTER THIRTY-FIVE

A BITTER HARVEST

The significance of coincidence is often underestimated, or not even noticed at all, yet throughout history coincidence has directed lives, changed the course of wars, and altered history itself. Unbeknownst to both Tristan and Mala, the heavy footstep of chance had now stamped its mark on their existence, forcing a shift in the ebb and flow of their already fragile relationship. Some would say that such occurrences are the result of minor mishaps, while others would claim that fate is the culprit. Yet others would insist that all is as God wills it. Regardless of the root, the harvest of such occurrences is bitter, and once pulled from the ground can never be replanted.

So filled with anticipation at finally holding Mala again, Tristan arose and slipped away from the monastery before sunrise that next morning, setting his horse at full gallop. Reaching the site of the Romani camp, he found nothing. Thinking at first that he had perhaps deceived himself about the location, he walked about in the mud for several minutes inspecting his surroundings. Then, kicking at the soaked remnants of the campfire and spying deep ruts plowing their way to the road, it finally dawned on him that Mala and the Romani had vacated the site. *Perhaps due to the storm*, he then rationalized. *Yes, seeking higher ground.*

He then mounted his horse and rode about through the woods, following a course of higher elevation. "Mala!" he shouted, certain that he would see her at any moment. An hour passed as he traveled first the high ground, then circled back and searched the opposite direction, though it made little sense. Mystified, he then remembered that members of Mala's original troupe had become involved in thievery in Paris. *Yes, perhaps Fernando or some of the others had disobeyed Mala and run afoul of the Marseilles authorities and been taken into custody*, he decided, turning his horse back toward the road.

Accepting this explanation coming out of the trees, he saw a farmer driving his cart the opposite direction. "Good morning, sir," the man said, acknowledging Tristan's military uniform, curious why a soldier would be coming out of the woods at such an early hour. "'Twas quite a storm last night. Hope you weren't caught out in it here in the woods, eh?"

"No, I was in town fortunately. Some friends of mine have been staying out here this past month or so and I am looking for them. Oddly, I cannot seem to find them anywhere and . . ."

"Ah, the foreign musicians!" the farmer interrupted. "Yes, I gave them permission to set camp on this small patch of land I call home."

"Oh?"

"Yes, a strange thing. Last night in the very midst of the storm, they appeared at my cottage, paid me two gold coins for my generosity, then disappeared in the night."

Tristan shook his head, dumbfounded, and said, "What? In such a downpour?"

"Huh, that's exactly what I thought, lad! I asked the young woman who paid me whether they couldn't wait till morning, but she was adamant about leaving Marseilles that very moment." Then he scratched at his chin a moment before continuing. "Something bad must have occurred within the camp," he then said. "She looked very distraught at the time."

"Oh?"

"Yes, she looked upset, as though someone had died, perhaps."

Tristan's stomach knotted at these words as one wild supposition after another began stirring within the silt of his own confusion. No matter what he dredged to the surface, he could not uncover any reason for her to leave so hurriedly, especially without at least sending word to the monastery.

"Did she say where they were headed?" he asked.

"Nuh," the farmer said, shaking his head, "I asked, lad, she said she had no idea. Anyway, I felt sorry for the poor thing; so young, so heavy-hearted."

"Thank you, sir," said Tristan with a tip of his hat, imagining briefly that he had already set his horse at full gallop down the road leading west from Marseilles in the hopes of catching up to Mala within a day's time. Knowing this was impossible, due to the mission for Mathilda, he slowly turned his mount east and proceeded back to Marseilles. Before returning to the monastery he went first to the harbor, and like the hope-obsessed fisherman casting his net yet one final time before going home empty-handed, he walked about calling her name over and over, refusing to believe that she had truly disappeared.

CHAPTER THIRTY-SIX

THE STRANGER

About the time Tristan was about to leave the harbor he spotted a man, unusually slight of build, his eyes covered by the broad brim of a hat, seated at the foot of a tree next to the gate. The motionless man's back leaned against the trunk, Tristan thought the man to be sleeping at first, but when he approached, he noticed that the man was watching him.

"Morning, sir," the man said with a nod. "Have you lost someone?"

"Well, yes," Tristan replied, his eyes still searching about the docks. "There were some musicians here this past week. I thought perhaps to find them this morning."

"Oh, yes, quite an interesting bunch. And that girl who dances to their tunes, captivating." Then the man tipped his brim upward a bit, only slightly exposing his eyes. "Say there, I recognize you," he said.

This caught Tristan's attention immediately for he knew nobody from Marseilles other than Abbot LeTour. "Indeed?"

"Yes, you're that fellow who stepped in the middle of the music last week. Ha, no wonder you're looking for the musicians. I saw how that dancing girl embraced you, and you her! A long lost love, eh?"

"No, only a friend."

"What struck me odd though, she did not recognize you at first," he said, pointing to Tristan's face, "until you pulled that bandage from your eye. I was expecting to see a wound the moment you did that, but to my surprise your eye looked fine! Yet, you wear it again this morning, eh?"

As the man said this, Tristan thought he detected an odd glimmer in the man's expression, though his voice portrayed nothing less than the casual curiosity of an incidental passerby who might have been in the crowd that day. "A tiny shard," said Tristan, raising a finger to his bandage, "that one can barely see. I wear the dressing because my left eye is sensitive to light."

"Can they not remove the shard, sir?"

"No."

"Too bad," the man said, smiling, but the smile lacked empathy. "Your uniform," he then continued, "Burgundian, eh?"

"Yes, I come from the Cluny region."

Then, sensing that the man was probing, Tristan turned and was about to walk away when the man added, "Ah, Cluny. Yes, I am from there also. You know, years ago there was a boy there at the monastery under the tutelage of

Grand Prior Odo de Lagery. They called the lad the Cluny Wonder because he was intelligent beyond belief. Uh, you *are* familiar with Grand Prior Odo de Lagery, eh?"

"Yes, of course. Most in France are familiar with him, especially those of us from Burgundy. Odo de Lagery is now a Cardinal of Italy, but then I suppose you know that, sir?"

"Yes, yes. And proud we are of him! As I was saying, that boy I was talking about, such a handsome lad! So striking, in fact, as to be memorable. He had a younger brother in tow from time to time who was equally handsome, perhaps even more. I would see them together at Sunday mass in the Cluny Abby with the other boys in residence."

"What has any of this to do with me?" said Tristan, a slip of impatience surfacing.

"Well, it's that you bear a remarkable resemblance to them. Might you by chance be a relative? Or perhaps, might you even be one of those brothers?"

"Ha, most assuredly not!" Tristan laughed, taking close measure of the man's appearance. "Had I received a Cluny education at the knees of the Black Monks I certainly would not be selling my services as a mercenary. I would be a nobleman's son or a cleric."

"Yes, of course," the man nodded, "only those born of high fortune are blessed with a Cluny education."

Tristan stooped a bit then, gazing straight into the man's eyes. "Sir, might you remove your hat so I can better see your face?"

"What?" the man said, swiftly sitting erect.

"Yes. Since you are from Cluny, perhaps then I might recognize you from past years, eh?"

"No, I doubt that," the man replied quickly. "I . . ."

Tristan reached out, and before the man could react, removed his hat. "Yes, much better," Tristan said, taking notice of the stranger's sudden discomfort. The man's eyes were small and dark, like those of a marten, and his eyebrows were overly thick. The pale outline of a tiny scar ran from the hairline of his right temple down to the high point of his cheekbone, and a large mole marked its end. Finally, above the man's tunic collar, his neck skin turned coarse and weltered with the disfigurement of severe burns. All of this Tristan noticed and filed in his memory within a matter of seconds. Then, returning the hat to the man's crown, he said, "Always a pleasure speaking to a fellow Burgundian, but I must be on my way."

"Same to you, sir," the man muttered, sullenly pulling his hat back down over his eyes and leaning his back once again against the trunk of the elm.

CHAPTER THIRTY-SEVEN

ON TO CLUNY

Having gone back to the monastery, Tristan gathered Guillaume and the Danes. "I am not sure," he said, "but I believe our presence is known here in Marseilles, or at least mine is. Despite my disguise, I have perhaps been recognized."

"What?" asked Guillaume. "By whom?"

"I encountered a man by the piers a short time ago. He was asking questions . . . too many questions. Said he was from Cluny." Tristan then described the little man and recounted his entire exchange with him, then finished by saying, "When I exposed his face, he appeared disturbed. From this point, as we move about, keep an eye to all about us."

Two days later the Marseilles business was completed and as Tristan led the caravan out of the monastery gate under cover of pre-dawn darkness, he thanked Abbot LeTour and said, "If anyone should show up here making inquiries about me or the others, say nothing."

"Of course," LeTour replied, having in his old mind dismissed the appearance of the young woman who rang the bell several nights before as insignificant. "Be safe and pass my greetings along to Abbot Hugh."

During the journey to Cluny, Guillaume and the Danes engaged in jovial conversation, often teasing and ridiculing each other as brothers-in-arms are apt to do, but Tristan was unusually morose.

"Something bothers you," said Guillaume on the second day of travel. "You've been distracted these last days."

"Oh, too many Italian politics circulating up here," Tristan replied, pointing to his head in an attempt to make little of the desolation that had seized him since finding the Romani camp abandoned. There was only one thing on his mind . . . Mala. He still found it impossible that she had basically vanished without a trace and without any indication of cause or whereabouts.

Upon reaching Cluny, Tristan's first action was to send out several coded dispatches to various Benedictine agents scattered amongst different regions of southern France. *Urgent: Am seeking information on a traveling Romani troupe of entertainers*, the message said. *They were ousted from Paris for thievery, moved to the Loire Valley, and most recently were spotted in Marseilles. They are of interest to our operations in Italy. If you come across their presence, send word to me at Cluny over the next two weeks, and from there, Dijon.*

Tristan then began the process of scheduling and conducting parleys within the Cluny region, an area that had always strongly supported the Benedictine order and had continued to hold close ties with Cardinal Odo despite his relocation to Italy. He also picked up a Burgundian guard of thirty knights under the command of a certain Captain Rousseau who accompanied them back and forth from each parley. The amount of munitions and income was increasing exponentially by now. Concern for the security of the wagons now outweighed concerns for discretion.

As Sunday of their first week in Cluny approached, Tristan made a suggestion to Guillaume and the Danes. "Our next parley is not far from Marcigny where Mother is cloistered with the Benedictine Sisters. A visit may well be in order, eh?"

This pleased the Danes. They had served as her personal Guard from the moment of her birth, protecting and serving her until the past year when she entered the convent and they entered the service of Countess Mathilda. Guillaume liked the idea also and nodded with approval though he had developed little relationship with his mother. He was four years old when she sent him and Tristan to the Black Monks, and had only seen her once since then. In Guillaume's mind, therefore, unlike Tristan, it was Countess Mathilda who was more like a mother to him than was Asta.

Asta was, of course, overjoyed as her sons and the Danes streamed into the convent parlor a few days later. She had seen Tristan several times over the last year, but this was her first time to see the others since Tristan's ordination. "Oh, my dear Danes!" she wept, embracing their broad shoulders and raising to the tips of her toes to kiss them each on the cheek. "And my handsome, fearless Guillaume!"

They visited then for several hours, recounting stories of years past, trading news, and reveling in each other's company. Then a bell rang out three times from another part of the convent.

"Prayers?" sighed Tristan, not wishing for this time together to end.

"Yes, Dear." She then looked longingly at the others and said, "I must take leave now and report to the chapel." As they all stood and began moving out the door, Tristan lingered. Asta, recognizing her son's troubled expression despite his efforts to appear collected, looked at him with curiosity and said, "So, have you something turning over in your mind? The look on your face tells me that I should remain here a while longer with you now that the others are gone."

"Yes, if possible," Tristan nodded. Then he took a seat next to her, taking several moments to gather his thoughts. "Mother, tell me about Mielikki, who now goes by the name Duxia de Falaise."

Nothing Tristan could have possibly said would have brought a greater look of surprise to Asta's face. "What?" she cried, her back ramrod straight.

"Yes, Mielikki. I have come across her twice in recent months. And though I know little about her, I do know that she was an intimate member of your household until she tried to drown me as a baby."

Asta shook her head. "Lord in Heaven above, who told you about that, Tristan?"

"She did, and the Danes later confirmed it."

"They were instructed after that incident to never utter her name again, and to never speak of that horrible act of trying to murder you."

"I am a man, now, Mother. There is no need for secrecy. Besides, I pressed them for information. But what I wish to know, was she insane? Or was there validity to her?"

Asta gazed into her lap, lost to this sudden unearthing of long-buried memories. "Sh-she was as close to me as any mother is to any child of her own flesh, and was with me from my birth until that horrible day she tried to drown you." Then she looked up at Tristan and said, "Validity? Yes, she had a strong wit, good sense and an iron will."

"But was she not full of superstition and pagan beliefs?"

"Yes, of course. And from time to time she would fall prey to curious notions that appeared from nowhere, such as on the day you were born. She was struck with the sudden and bizarre obsession that you were cursed, Tristan. It was all foolishness, of course. She could not, would not let it go for some reason."

"Foolishness, Mother? Are you so certain?"

The question surprised Asta. "Oh, Son, surely you do not give credence to her ravings. It is all conjecture and superstition from the old world."

"Sorcery?"

"Yes. Sorcery of the most evil thread. Any belief that would lead to the sacrifice of an innocent little child could be nothing else. But why such questions?"

"It is . . . because of my life, Mother. At times I feel that I have become a curse to others, and more recently, even to myself. I have since boyhood felt that I was born to a great destiny; that something extraordinary awaits me, but of late I fear that my destiny entails a destructiveness of sorts."

"Ah, is the assassination of the nun you told me about still haunting you, Tristan?"

"No . . . much more than that now, I fear." Then he looked at Asta, his face coloring. "I fear I have become steeped in a life of trickery and deception while wearing monk's garb. I am becoming more and more a false representation of God, and of myself. Yet I plow forward, and revel in the role of a monk even at times. Then, too, there is something else . . ."

Asta placed her forehead in her palm, not sure that she wished for Tristan to continue, but then her concern for him overrode all else. "Something else?"

"A question, Mother, a very private one that I shudder to ask of you in light of your misfortune with two husbands. Have you ever been in love?"

"Tristan! Such a question to ask your mother!" Asta objected, turning pink. She then was about to insist that he withdraw the question, but reading the imploring expression of his eyes, she shifted in her seat a moment, then placed her hands in her lap. "Yes," she said, "one time in my life I fell in love, sick in love, driven nearly to madness though the man never touched me, and I never him. It was in England. I met a handsome young gamekeeper, Jack

Forest, while married to your witless uncle, Lord Desmond DuLac." As she said this, though it was a shocking revelation of which she had never spoken since leaving England, she was neither ashamed nor regretful. "I would have run off with him and lived a life of peasant simplicity," she continued, "but he was killed in an uprising of his own instigation against my husband by none other than Orla."

"Orla?"

"Yes. Orla thought him to be the enemy. And may God never break your heart so vengefully as to have the one you love killed by the hands of another that you love as family." Then she shook her head and added, "I suppose God was punishing me for my illicit feelings for Jack Forest. It was my own fault. In a moment of weakness and as a woman buried in a miserable marriage, I faltered . . . then was damned for it. God took his life, and left me to think about it all, and suffer. To this day here in this convent I pray for the soul of my dear gamekeeper, Jack Forest."

Though Asta could not be aware of it, her words were like a dagger to Tristan's heart. He had known well all along that his love for Mala was an inappropriate betrayal of his vows and responsibilities. He had always secretly felt that God was watching him, urging him to put Mala aside and redirect his devotion back to the Church, but secret fears, when spoken aloud by another, take on new credibility. He shriveled in place.

"Tristan?" Asta asked, observing this sudden collapse.

"Well then," he said, trying to collect his composure, "I best leave you to your prayers, Mother. Thank you for your counsel, and for baring your truth."

As Tristan then stepped outside, he saw the Danes had already mounted their horses, but that Guillaume was still afoot, speaking to a short fellow who, judging by the pack he carried, was a traveler. As Tristan began to approach, their conversation ended and the man turned and began walking down the road toward the market district.

"Who was that?" said Tristan.

"Ah, a pilgrim on his way to Cluny," replied Guillaume, mounting his horse. "He happened to recognize the uniforms the Danes and I are wearing and mentioned that he, too, was from Tuscany."

"Hmm . . ." Tristan mulled, watching the man as he disappeared around a corner, thinking that he had begun moving rather briskly. "By chance, Guillaume, did he happen to start asking questions then, such as why Tuscans were here in Burgundy?"

"Not really. In fact, he supposed that we must be on leave visiting family here in France. Simply said he was far from home and that it did his heart good to see Tuscan uniforms."

"His Italian, was it fluent or could you detect an accent?"

"Fluent. Why?"

"Something about his frame I noticed, so short and slight, like the man I encountered that morning at the Marseilles harbor that was nosing about my business. Did you happen to notice a faint scar running down his cheek?"

"No, he was standing with the sun in his eyes so he kept his head bent a bit and shaded his eyes with his hand, covering them. He . . ."

Not waiting for Guillaume to finish, Tristan quickly mounted his horse and left at a gallop down the road, taking the same turn the traveler had taken.

"What's going on?" asked Orla. "Should we follow?"

"Something's up, maybe so," said Guillaume, jumping on his horse.

By the time they got halfway down the block Tristan reappeared, holding his mount to a slow canter. "Gone," he shrugged. "Just that quick, he disappeared!"

"So, what are you thinking?" said Guillaume.

"I am thinking that possibly he is one of the anti-pope's people, or Heinrich's even. I am thinking he was unusually small like the man in Marseilles. I am thinking it odd that such a man would happen to pass by here during our visit to the convent, and also recognize Tuscan uniforms. And the man in Marseilles recognized my Burgundian uniform and immediately claimed he, too, was from Burgundy; to drop my guard undoubtedly. And this man has done the same to you, Guillaume, claiming he recognized your uniform and is himself from Tuscany. Above all I am wondering, even if the sun was directly in his eyes while talking to you, why he didn't turn aside a bit rather than stand there hiding his eyes."

CHAPTER THIRTY-EIGHT

ON TO DIJON

When the Cluny parleys were completed, Tristan's immediate group and the Burgundian Guard of thirty knights under the command of Captain Rousseau turned north for Dijon. Dijon was the historical capital of the Burgundy region, and as such, its nobles were amongst the wealthiest, most powerful lords of France. The name of Odo de Lagery carried great weight here also, as did distrust and resentment for King Philippe. Consequently, by the time Tristan's mission was coming to a close, it was necessary to secure additional wagons in order to transport the accumulation of arms and wealth. Furthermore, it was in Dijon that Captain Rousseau combined his men with an additional hundred knights of Dijon for the journey across the Alps.

Tristan's final parley was with Lord Thierry Truffault, older brother of Lord Bernard Truffault of the Marseilles region. Unlike his younger brother, Lord Thierry Truffault had early on agreed to support Cardinal Odo's quest to assist Countess Mathilda. It was to be a simple trip then for Tristan to end his mission at Truffault's fiefdom. Lady Agnes Truffault, after learning that a Captain Broussard was coming to visit her husband, made herself extremely scarce. Passing through the gates of Truffault's palatial castle, Tristan heard a tremendous racket caused by someone striking iron against the iron bars of what appeared to be a corner dungeon.

"What's all that noise?" said Hroc, who was riding double with his father.

"Hush, mind your business, son," Orla said.

Just then Lord Truffault appeared. Tristan noticed that he seemed to take no heed of the bothersome clanging going on within the dungeon, so he pointed and said, "Lord Truffault, does that clamor not drive you mad?"

"Not bothersome in the least, Captain," replied Truffault, "because tomorrow morning that prisoner meets his Maker. I've been after him for some time now, and my bounty hunters finally caught him down near the coast."

"What's a bounty hunter?" said Hroc, listening with great interest.

"Silence!" said Orla, backing an elbow into Hroc's ribs.

"A bandit?" asked Tristan. Looking toward the window, he saw only a pair of raised hands furiously riffling their shackles against the bars.

"No, not exactly," said Truffault. "Come, let's settle our business for Cardinal Odo."

Tristan and Guillaume instructed the Danes and Burgundian Guard to wait in the courtyard, then followed Truffault into his keep, which also served as his treasury. But as they sat together documenting terms of agreement, Tristan and

Guillaume could not hide their distraction. Even from within the keep, the prisoner outside could be heard striking his chains against the bars.

"Ah, music to my ears," quipped Truffault with a smile. "And tomorrow, the sound of a swaying rope against that bastard's scrawny neck will be sweeter yet."

Half an hour later their business was completed. Still the noise outside, rather than abating, had only become worse. Standing there as Truffault's laborers loaded the wagon, Tristan turned to one of them and asked, "How long has this noise been going on?"

"Two days nonstop, even through the night," the man said. "We've laid wagers amongst ourselves on whether the prisoner drops of exhaustion before his execution tomorrow morning."

Then, as the workman finished his sentence, the clanging stopped and a shrill voice rang out from the window. "Christ will strike each of you within this castle dead the moment I swing from your gallows! Best that you begin your prayers now, sinners, for this time tomorrow the Angel of Death shall be copying your name in his book, and then the tongues of Hellfire shall soon thereafter be lapping at your souls!"

Recognizing the voice, Tristan stiffened and turned his head to the window.

"What is it?" said Guillaume, observing his brother's reaction.

"God in Heaven, I know that voice!" exclaimed Tristan, impulsively running across the court to the dungeon window and directing his voice toward the bars. "Peter? Is that *you* in there?"

No reply came at first, but then, "Tristan? Is that you out there?"

"Oh, in Christ's name! What have you done now?"

"What have I done now?" came the indignant reply. "Same as before, you believer of twisted tongues! Nothing! Not a blessed thing but take a stroll down the streets of Toulon until hooligans swept me up and dragged me back here to Lucifer's lair! Ha! This devil Truffault still seeks revenge from my last visit, but it's his promiscuous wife he should be hanging at dawn, not this poor innocent hermit!"

Watching Lord Truffault exit his keep at that moment, Tristan called to him, waving for him to approach. Truffault, looking puzzled, complied. "What is it, Captain Broussard?"

"This prisoner you have, are you aware he is a monk?"

"Certainly, a black-hearted, philandering monk who is not worthy to be considered Christian! He tried to violate my wife during my absence this past year, despite my generosity to him and offer of sustenance for the day. Then the crazy little bastard set a wild mob against me and my men as he escaped with his nephew! I *still* limp because of the beating I took that night!"

"Lord Truffault," Tristan said, "I insist that you release this man."

"What? Have you gone daft, man? Did you not hear what I just said?"

"Lord Truffault, this man is Peter the Hermit, a close personal acquaintance of Odo de Lagery who you respect and admire. The Cardinal will be furious to hear that you have caused his death."

"Eh? This pile of bestial defecation is a friend of the great Cardinal?" said Truffault, surprised. Then he shook his head and said, "Regardless, Cardinal Odo himself would not abide by such lechery as practiced by this stink of a creature."

"Cardinal Odo would not abide by the hanging of an innocent man," pressed Tristan, and sure as I am a Burgundian captain, then sure is this man innocent!"

"How could you know such a thing? What is this man to you, Captain?"

Careful not to mention that he had been there beside Peter the Hermit on the night of the Dijon riot, Tristan replied, "Nothing to me, Lord Truffault. As I said, the Hermit is dear, indeed, to the Cardinal."

"Yes, like a brother!" shouted Peter, who had been listening to the exchange outside the wall. "And he will surely declare a sentence of damnation upon you for hanging a man of the cloth! Ah, Truffault, you invite the wrath of Saint Michael's fiery sword by causing my end!"

"Shut up you filthy tramp!" cried Truffault, by now a bit uneasy at learning of his victim's connection to Cardinal Odo. "You'll hang in the morning sure as the sun rises!"

"Lord Truffault, at least let us sit and discuss this," urged Tristan. "Perhaps even in the presence of your wife," he then added. "She could possibly place some new perspective on this issue."

"My wife?" said Truffault. "Ha! She wants this goose strung up as much as I." He stepped back and rubbed at his chin a moment. "Out of respect for Cardinal Odo, I shall follow your request, but only on the condition that once I hang this lout, you inform the good Cardinal that I agreed to a final review of the case, eh?"

"Certainly," Tristan replied, his mind chasing about for tactics that might withdraw the Hermit from this snare.

Truffault signaled for the guards to release the prisoner and bring him out into the court, and as they dragged him along still in shackles, the Hermit gazed skyward, his hair standing on end and his bright little eyes cracked with red lines that pulsed like tiny rivers and shouted, "Angels in Heaven, strike my enemies dead, I beseech you!" Then wringing his head about like a soaked hound who'd stepped from the stream, he made a series of guttural sounds as if invoking those very angels to appear immediately beside him.

Hroc, who was seated double behind his father's horse, watched the wild-eyed Hermit in wonder, having never in his young years seen such a sight. "Father, is that man a troll?" he gasped.

"Hush!" said Orla, though he was nearly as struck by the Hermit's feral appearance as his son.

Meanwhile, it occurred to the Hermit that this military man walking beside him appeared extremely familiar. "God's bells," he whispered. "Tristan? Is that you beneath all that garb?"

The man offered no reply, not even a glance—which caused the Hermit's face to contract with suspicion.

"Damnation," Peter muttered. "What's this odd game going on here?"

Minutes later Lord Truffault and Tristan were sitting at Truffault's table with the Hermit and Lady Agnes Truffault, who was still miffed at the captain for rebuffing her advances in Marseilles. She at first refused to meet with either the Captain or the Hermit. Fearing that she might arouse suspicion if she did not agree to her husband's demand, she finally consented.

"My Lady," Tristan began, finding it difficult to look her directly in the eye, "we are here to briefly review the actions of Peter the Hermit on the day he supposedly accosted you. He did accost you, correct?"

"Certainly," she said, her eyes narrow with resentment at her husband for being dragged into such a meeting. She, also, could not comfortably look Tristan in the eye.

"Untrue!" objected Peter, crossing his arms with certainty. "I am as chaste as a cherub and have never pursued a woman's crack in my entire existence!"

"Goddammit, shut up!" cried Truffault. "I don't allow such boorish talk in the presence of Lady Agnes!"

"Yes," Lady Agnes said to Tristan, "he ripped my clothing from me and threw me onto the bed hoping to mount me. And Saints of God, had my husband not showed up miraculously, this horrible, hairy little beast would have violated me!"

"Was there not a younger man present also, this man's nephew, Innocenzo?"

"The nephew accompanied the Hermit, but was not present at the time the Hermit broke into my bedchamber," she lied.

"What about Lord Bernard Truffault, your husband's younger brother?" said Tristan.

"What?" replied Truffault and his wife with simultaneous confusion.

"Oh, pardon, I became confused a moment," said Tristan to Lord Truffault. "You see, as you and Lady Agnes both know, I visited your brother recently in Marseilles." Then his eyes shifted to Agnes Truffault and he added, "Yes, we were drinking honey mead together one night, far too much actually, and he told me quite a bit about visiting you here, Lady Agnes, oh, and also about your visits to Marseilles, my Lady. In any case, pardon my error. So, to continue, my Lady, did anything prompt this inappropriate action by the Hermit?"

"What are you suggesting?" said Truffault. "Nothing prompted this man but his own horny fever. The man is a perverted letch and my wife is young and desirable."

"Ah that's exactly what your brother said," replied Tristan with a nod.

"What?" said Truffault. "He said my wife was young and desirable?"

"No, not that part, I meant the bit about the Hermit being a perverted letch." As Tristan said this he set his eyes once more upon Lady Agnes, telegraphing a private smile her direction, as when one holds the secret of another in the midst of a crowd. This, of course, immediately set her to wondering what information her brother-in-law might have shared with the Captain. After all, her brother-in-law had a reputation for wagging his tongue when heavy with drink.

Tristan's words had infuriated Peter. "Damnation, what are you talking about!" he cried. "I've never met this man's brother in my life!" Then he leveled his eyes at Tristan and said, "You are a monk for God's sake, how can you manufacture such tripe!"

"Ah, though you don't know Lord Truffault's brother, he knows who *you* are," said Tristan, quickly firing the Hermit a look. *Don't talk*, the look pleaded, but the Hermit missed it. He was born into life with an awareness of nothing but himself.

"A monk?" said Truffault, looking at the Hermit with bewilderment. "Did you say the Captain here is a monk?"

The Hermit was about to reply when Tristan turned and struck him across the face. "Not another word, you madman!" he shouted. Stunned, Peter shook the spots from his vision, sitting there dazed. "You see," Tristan continued, "this poor fellow is not even aware of what he does or says at times, which is why Cardinal Odo has such tender pity for the poor creature. I think, therefore, that this dull-witted child of a man had no criminal intentions with your wife at all, but is touched in the brain."

"What? Dull-witted? Touched in the brain, you say?" the Hermit shouted, but Tristan raised his hand again as if to deliver another blow, forcing the Hermit to cower in his seat and hold his tongue.

"Yes," said Agnes Truffault, her tone softening, "I believe you may have a point, actually, Captain. As I now think back, this poor little derelict did not actually touch my privates, and as he was removing my clothing, probably had no idea what he was doing." Then she turned to her husband who was totally unprepared for such an about-face. "He meant no harm, my Sweet, so release this poor imbecile," she cooed, enlarging her eyes.

"What, you think *me* an imbecile!" the Hermit cried, incensed. "'Tis your husband, the imbecile, Madame! If only he knew . . .'"

Tristan realized that the Hermit insisted on unraveling yet another effort to save his hide and could bear no more. Before the Hermit could complete his sentence, Tristan jumped from his seat, grabbed the Hermit by the throat, and threw him to the ground. "No more out of you, Sir! This kind Lady has forgiven you, so we shall be on our way!" Then he picked Peter from the floor and dragged him out the door while Lord and Lady Truffault turned and looked at each other, he upon her with admiration for her charity, she upon him with relief.

As they got outside, the Hermit rattled his hand shackles, pulling Tristan's hands from his shoulders, and cried, "I've never been so humiliated in my life! How dare you suggest such things about me, and how dare you lay your hands on me!"

Tristan had every right to be angry at the Hermit, but he shook his head and said, "Peter, in light of your insistence at slipping your own head within Truffault's noose despite my constant efforts at extricating it, you should know that I have somehow managed to save your miserable life again. I am not even sure why I did such a thing!" Then he did something he had not done since last being with Mala. He laughed.

CHAPTER THIRTY-NINE

A MAN NAMED DEFARGE

As instructed, upon leaving Dijon, Tristan turned command of the caravan over to Guillaume and the Danes who were much more adept at managing the movement of troops and equipment. In all there were twenty wagons loaded to brimming with replacement arms and armor, two wagons loaded with gold, silver, coin, gems, and precious objects to be used to finance Mathilda's new offensive, and thirty-four wagons loaded with food and supplies for those making the long overland trip over the mountains to Tuscany. Captain Rousseau, in addition to his Burgunians and the hundred knights he had collected in Dijon, had also recruited another two hundred knights and five hundred footmen and archers from the Dijon area who would fight for pay beneath Mathilda's banner.

It was a massive caravan then of nearly sixty wagons and a thousand men that set out from Dijon during the last week of August, and at this point there was no way to conceal its movement. Nevertheless, with so much manpower at hand, there was little concern for security until crossing the Alps into Italy. Even upon reaching that point, Mathilda would be sending Balducci and a large force of Tuscans to meet the wagon train in the Apennines to escort it to her stronghold in Canossa.

"You've done well, Tristan," said Guillaume, as the wagon train moved out of Dijon, "especially with contributions from the nobles."

Tristan thanked his brother, but said little else. His mind was on Mala, still wondering why she had left so unexpectedly and where she might have gone. While at Cluny and Dijon he had hoped he might receive a reply from the messages he had dispatched to other Benedictine agents, but he had received nothing.

"I've never known you to show your hand, so I certainly don't expect you to tell me your secrets now, of course," Guillaume chuckled, "but I see that something still distracts you, Brother. And I've witnessed firsthand how good you are at what you do, so I hardly think that whatever bothers you has anything to do with politics or diplomacy, eh?"

"Ah, Guillaume, it is not any one thing that bothers me," he said. "It's the culmination of many, many little things." This, of course, though not entirely true, was partially true. In addition to Mala, of late he had been questioning the Church, the ethics of the Benedictine underground, and his own personal motives. "Have you never had complicated little things stack themselves in your head, Guillaume, until you fear they will eventually topple you?"

Guillaume thought a moment. "No, not really. Tristan, you've always been the thinker, not me. I live a more simple existence, content to fight like the Danes. In war, it's simple: fight or be killed."

"Ho there!" cried Orla, pulling his horse next to the brothers. "Are you talking about us, Guillaume? I heard you say "the Danes.""

"I was saying that I'm content to fight, like you Danes, whereas Tristan was born the thinker."

"Aha! Yes, thinking, it's always given me headaches! Crowbones, too. Guthroth, now there's another thinker. He says little because his tongue gets twisted, but he's always watching, always listening, and always thinking."

"I'll vouch for that," said Guillaume.

"Me too!" shouted Hroc who was sitting beside the driver in the wagon next to them and had been listening to every word. "And what about me, Father? Am I a thinker?"

"Ha! Hardly! No, you're just *nosey*, lad," Orla replied. "Now mind your business, Hroc."

Hroc was hoping, of course, that his father was going to say, "*Yes, lad, you're nearly as clever as your Uncle Tristan and Uncle Guillaume!*" Hearing his father's reply, he propped his elbows upright upon his knees and settled his chin into his palms with disappointment. Nevertheless, he was not completely unhappy. Since the death of his mother during the escape from England, life had turned for him into a grand adventure, moving here and there with the ebb and flow of battle, living out in the open, and helping maintain arms and armor for the Danish Guard. Whereas he had once been confined to the company of his mother and the other women and children in England, he had been thrown into the company of his father, the other Danes, and Sir Guillaume; men whom he worshipped and emulated. *Oh yes*, he thought as the wagon hobbled along the rocky landscape, *I'm going to be exactly like them and my brave brother, Knud.*

"So, Tristan," said Guillaume, "It's been a profitable mission. Auntie Mathilda will be very pleased to see the wagons, and you, too."

"I look forward to seeing her also," Tristan replied, still trying to dispel the image of Mala from his thoughts. "Auntie has been a great influence on our lives, especially yours. So generous of her to take you in when Cardinal Odo and I moved to Rome."

"Yes, with your intelligence and Cardinal Odo's mentorship you were assured of rising within the Church, but without Auntie Mathilda I would have had nothing after Mother abandoned us."

"Guillaume," Tristan sighed with slight irritation, "I've tried to explain to you before that Mother did not truly *abandon* us. After the execution of our father, she had two choices: either marry Uncle Desmond, or become destitute, which would have meant that you and I also would be destitute. Would it have made you happier if she had kept us so we could scrap about in the streets for crumbs like a family of beggars? Where do you think we would be now had she allowed that to happen instead of sending us to the Black Monks? And that took money, you know, which she got from Uncle DuLac. That's the only reason she married him, to spare us."

"Look," said Guillaume, "I was four years old when she sent us away and have only seen her twice since then, the second time being weeks ago as we stopped in Marcigny." As Guillaume spoke, his expression began to darken. This topic was one he and Tristan had disputed before, and it seemed that Tristan always became agitated when Guillaume spoke honestly of his feelings toward their mother, Asta. "As for you, you were seven years old and retained some fond memories of her and Saint-Germain-en-Laye. I have no memories of either. My fond memories are stored with Auntie Mathilda and I look to her as my mother, not Asta."

"Very well then, Guillaume, consider Mathilda your mother if it pleases you. Let's change the subject," Tristan sighed, not wishing to rehash this particular argument in light of the fact he was already distraught about the Mala situation.

Nor did Guillaume really wish to argue, so to shift the conversation he said, "Quite an armed escort we have behind us. So other than the difficulty of crossing the mountains, our journey should be without incident, eh?"

"Hopefully, but I am still wondering about the little man you encountered at the convent. Then, too, this wagon train is attracting attention so I am sure other eyes are upon us by now also. Sure, I expect no problems traveling through France, Heinrich would not dare stir that hornet nest while at war in Italy, but once we near the frontier and begin traveling the Via Francigena through the Alps, we could be attacked if the Germans figure out what we are doing. Even though Commander Balducci is to meet us in the Apennines, we have a long stretch in the Alps before reaching Balducci's rendezvous point."

That night after the wagon train had pitched camp, Tristan and Guillaume were speaking to Orla and Crowbones outside the command tent when they heard a stir approaching their direction. Then Guthroth appeared out of the darkness in a fury, dragging a soldier by the collar of his hauberk. "L-look h-here!" he shouted to Orla and Crowbones, flinging the man to the ground into the circle of light afforded by the campfire.

Knowing that Guthroth the Quiet rarely lost his temper, Guillaume stepped forward and asked, "Guthroth, what's happening here?"

Guthroth tried to answer, but was so angry that he could only mutter a string of unintelligible sounds. Orla, realizing who the man was, charged forward and kicked him in the side of the head, then attacked him with his fists. Within seconds Crowbones joined him. Soon the man's face became a bloody mass of gore and tissue.

"Mercy!" the man screamed. "Don't kill me!"

Surprised by this inexplicable outbreak of violence, Tristan and Guillaume attempted to restrain the two huge Danes, but they easily broke free and attacked the man again.

"Stop it! That's an order, dammit!" shouted Guillaume.

Orla and Crowbones hesitated, then backed away. Orla's hands were still balled into fists, but Crowbones pointed at the man with his lone hand, and cried, "Oh, DeFarge, you filthy bastard!"

"Who is this man," said Tristan, "and what has he done to earn such abuse?"

"What has he done?" shouted Orla, the veins of his neck protruding like purple roots. "Why nothing but cause the execution of your father, Lord Roger de Saint-Germain!"

"What?" asked Guillaume.

"Ja," said Crowbones, "this snake DeFarge was one of your father's trusted men. For a fistful of coin, he snitched to Lord Letellier and your uncle Desmond DuLac about your father's conspiracy against William the Bastard. They then informed the Bastard, which is how DuLac got his Saxon estate and Letellier got title to the Saint-Germain fiefdom, while your father was beheaded and led to all of us being exiled from France and ending up in goddamn England!"

"Ay," growled Orla, pulling his ax from his belt, "and had we never been exiled my wife would have never been killed trying to escape England, nor would my son, Knud, have lost his life in Tuscany!"

"Wait a moment!" cried Tristan, stepping in front of Orla and looking down at the blood-covered man named DeFarge. "You there, is all this true?"

"Yes!" the man bawled, not daring to lie with Orla standing a mere four feet away with ax in hand. "Mercy! It was the greatest mistake of my life and God has punished me with hard times since that fateful day!"

"What are you doing here in my camp?" said Guillaume.

"I enlisted with Captain Rousseau in Dijon to fight for Mathilda in Italy. I have not worked in months and my wife and children are starving. I . . ."

"Oh, DeFarge, life has definitely taken a turn, you worm!" Orla shouted, glaring over Tristan's shoulder. Then he pointed to Guillaume and Tristan. "Do you know who these two are, DeFarge? They're the very two little Saint-Germain boys you orphaned by turning in your master!"

"What!" cried DeFarge, shocked. Then, wiping blood and goo from his eyes, he stared up at Tristan and Guillaume, struggling to remember Lord Roger de Saint-Germain's children. "Yes, that's . . . T-r-is-tan? And that one there, must be little Guillaume," he muttered, but he had the names crossed, mistakenly thinking that the bigger of the two, Guillaume, was the older brother. Nevertheless, by remembering their names DeFarge hoped that he might have struck a soft vein in the two men. "I didn't mean to bring misfortune to you two boys! Forgive me!" Then he scrambled to his knees, clasped his palms in prayer, and shot his eyes to the stars crying, "Oh God in Heaven, my Savior, spare me I pray!"

Beholding this prayerful stance and pleading for divine intervention, Tristan shot his eyes toward Guillaume while holding a hand up to Orla. "Guillaume, I seldom ask anything of you in life, yet I now ask that you spare this man for what he did was many years ago. We both know that our father was a vermin of a man."

Guillaume looked at Tristan, then at the seething Danes, then back at Tristan, and felt torn. "Brother, this fellow DeFarge caused our family's downfall, the exile of Asta and the Danes, and even you and I being sent away. How can I possibly justify sparing him?"

"You can *justify* it in the name of God's mercy," said Tristan, "and in the name of our Aunt Mathilda, la Gran Contessa of Tuscany, that most pious and merciful saint of a woman whom you hold in your heart as your own mother. It was in the name of generosity and mercy that she adopted us years ago, Guillaume. Honor her by being merciful yourself now. We are better off now than we would have ever been even had father lived!"

Considering all that Tristan had said, DeFarge stiffened with hope. "Ay, God has countered my wrongdoing with his own mercy, thereby balancing the scales! If indeed you two were adopted by the great Countess Mathilda of Tuscany, then God has blessed you with both fortune and a bright future. Spare me, then, to repay God!"

"You'll receive no such mercy, you bastard!" snarled Orla, waving his ax back and forth. "Ha! How interesting that you destroyed the life of these two lads, only for fortune to then shine on them so brightly. Yes, Sir Guillaume here is a high noble now and will end being a great general! And our lad Tristan there, with the help of Mathilda and Cardinal Odo de Lagery, is destined to perhaps even become Pope one . . ."

"Enough, Orla," interrupted Tristan. Then he looked at his brother and said, "Please, Guillaume, allow this man to live."

Guillaume looked one more time at Orla, then nodded reluctantly. "Very well, Brother." Then he flagged Orla off and said, "This man shall leave our camp with his life, Orla."

Orla stepped forward, shoving Tristan aside. "Indeed then, DeFarge shall leave our camp with his life." Then he swept his ax downward in the blink of an eye, cleanly severing DeFarge's right hand from his wrist in one swift motion exclaiming, "But he shall also leave our camp with a reminder of what he did to all of us standing here this night!"

Guillaume fired Orla a glance of disapproval, but it did not hold for long because Guillaume understood Orla's fury. Tristan, aghast as DeFarge shrieked in agony, fell to his knees and tried to block the blood erupting from DeFarge's wound with his bare hands, but DeFarge was rolling and flopping about so wildly that his spurting blood quickly covered Tristan's eyes and face, obstructing his vision completely. Meanwhile, DeFarge somehow found his feet and fled screaming into the darkness, his wailing voice fading into the night.

"God in Heaven, Orla!" cried Tristan, swiping blood from his eyes as he stumbled about in an effort to stand. "You should not have done such a thing!"

Loyal Crowbones stepped forward, patting Orla upon the shoulders with his stub. "Nay, Boy," he said, "my brother should have done more, much more."

CHAPTER FORTY

THE ALPS

The DeFarge incident provided fodder for much discussion as Guillaume and the Danes led the wagon train into the Alps. Having been children when DeFarge's actions had set off the sequence of events leading to Roger de Saint-Germain's execution and Asta's forfeiture of the family fiefdom, Tristan and Guillaume had never become familiar with the original political intrigue that had so profoundly affected their lives.

"A pit of vipers, all of them," declared Orla, speaking of William the Bastard of Normandy, King Philippe, Roger de Saint-Germain, and a host of other French and Norman nobles. "Though they already owned everything, it was not enough to satisfy those hogs at the trough. They had to then begin devouring each other with conspiracies, intrigue, and war."

"Like the southern nobles of France," agreed Tristan, "until this recent show of compromise in an effort to censure King Philippe who has been bleeding them dry these past years."

"Ja, same breed of swine, just a different herd. Never satisfied until they possess the final crumb to add to their full pantry while others starve!"

"You know, Lord Ox, listening to all of you talking about the old days brings back memories," Tristan said. "I loved those days in Saint-Germain-en-Laye as a boy, and often wish we had never lost the manor. I wonder what things would be like had DeFarge not wrecked it all."

"Ay, those were good days, Boy, for all of us: living in peace, raising families. And though your mother hated your father, he was gone most of the time slinking about in politics and connivery. You know, some said your father would eventually destroy himself anyway because of his greed and underhandedness."

"Ah yes, I imagine you are speaking of Duxia de Falaise."

"Indeed, she foretold your father's demise, you know. Said it would come because of betrayal, even telling that it would be by ax and not by the rope or fire or battle."

"I spoke to Mother about Duxia while in Marcigny. They did truly love each other, didn't they?"

"Ja. Like mother and daughter. And when women form such bonds, the only thing that can shear them is when one develops a stronger love for someone else . . . in this case it was *you* that broke the bond. And a woman such as Duxia, when wounded, knows no bounds. She was already hurt, you know, long before you came along."

"What do you mean?"

"By your grandfather, Guntar the Mace. She was his mistress for years, though he treated her shabbily. And when Guntar's wife died in childbirth with Asta, Duxia thought her time had finally come to stand beside Guntar, but he shunned her. She remained loyal to him, and found solace in raising Asta from the cradle and loving her. Yes, Duxia liked to imagine that she, Asta, and Guntar were a family. When you were born, everything changed and Asta no longer belonged to her, she belonged to you."

"Ah, so then, it really *was* a matter of jealousy for Duxia and not really about any kind of God curse?"

Orla thought a moment. "As you know, Boy, I don't believe in your God or your holy men. They refute all sorcery and superstition but their own, which they refer to as miracles. But no, Duxia's dread of you was not entirely about jealousy. Ja, she believed you were born cursed. Oh, there was much more to her fear of you than mere jealousy. On the other hand, never forget, Boy, she was a girl from the deep woods of Finland. Yes, she may possess some strange abilities, but then she was also blind as a mole about things, you know."

"Oh?"

"Certainly, if she was really so "all knowing," she should have been able to read the clouds and see that Guntar would never marry her, eh? Even Crowbones and I knew that was never going to happen! Then, too, she should have been able to foretell that Guthroth would show up unexpectedly as she was trying to drown you, and that her failure in that attempt would lead to her exile from the manor. So you see, who really knows whether she's as all-seeing as she claims."

Intelligent as Tristan was, he had never considered this slant that Orla had proposed, which swiftly threw Duxia into a new perspective.

"Very good, Lord Ox," Tristan smiled, "I appreciate your angle on this."

As they moved further into the Alps along the Via Francigena, Guillaume increased the size of his advance scout party from five men to twenty-five men.

"When you reach the passes, especially narrow ones," he instructed them, "be sure to dismount and scour the side trails and outcrops. If an attack comes, it'll be in such terrain. We don't want to get pinned in amongst the narrows."

That is precisely what transpired two days later as the wagon train began its ascent up a treacherous stretch of rise between two steep peaks. Waiting until the middle of the train had topped the pass and was beginning its descent, German archers let loose a flurry of arrows from hidden positions atop both peaks that had been inaccessible to the scouts because the trails leading there were located on the back side of the peaks.

This deadly shower of arrows immediately dispatched nearly a hundred of Guillaume's escort and sent men scurrying beneath wagons or onto their knees forming turtlebacks by locking shields. In panic, several of the lead wagons which were on the descending side of the pass began to charge down the slope in an effort to escape, but were destroyed by Germans in wait on the decline.

"No! Hold fast! They're trying to divide our forces!" cried Guillaume, flailing his sword at the teams of lead horses as they bristled forward. "Orla! I need you! Crowbones, Guthroth!"

The Danes, despite arrows whistling all around them, quickly joined Guillaume at the head of the train and held the wagons in place. "Brake and chock the wheels, then take cover under the wagons!" shouted Orla, charging back and forth riding his horse, waving his ax about to keep any more teamsters from taking flight down the slope. "Then ready yourself for the infantry assault!"

Tristan, unseasoned in military battle, was startled by the sudden onslaught of arrows. And as he watched men fall all about him with mortal wounds, he leaped from his horse and grabbed Hroc who was still sitting upright next to the slain driver that lay crumpled in the seat with an arrow through his neck. "Hroc!" Tristan cried, grabbing the boy and diving beneath the wagon.

Trembling, his eyes wide with fright at the sight of the dead driver who he had been talking to him moments before, Hroc released a wail of terror and scrambled beneath Tristan's torso as they hit the ground. "What's happening?" wailed the boy, confused by the sudden outbreak of battle.

Guillaume and the Danes, having settled the front portion of the wagon train dismounted and also took positions beneath the wagons. "They'll be coming on foot!" Guillaume cried to Tristan who was beneath the wagon next to him. "You look the part of a soldier, Brother, but have the Benedictines taught you to handle a sword?"

"No, never, only a dagger," responded Tristan.

"Then stay put when the Germans come, a dagger will do you no good against swords, pikes, and lances. Stay low and keep an eye to Hroc, we'll do the rest!"

Tristan nodded, feeling ridiculous dressed as a mercenary with a sword at his belt that he didn't know how to use. Pulling the bandage from his eye, Tristan nevertheless then reached over and unsheathed his sword, setting it beside him. *I will not hide while the others risk their lives*, he said to himself. *I will fight.*

Having done their initial damage, the enemy by now either taken cover beneath the wagons or turtle-backed, the German archers set their bows aside and an odd silence fell over the pass. Then came the sound of cracking stone as several rockslides began to cascade down demolishing the wagon train from the heights. Having abandoned their bows, the enemy archers had begun to unleash piles of rocks they had stored to hurl and slide down onto the wagons. The smaller rocks became deadly missiles as they tumbled down the outcrops and onto the road, ricocheting with great velocity as they struck horses, men, and equipment. After them came a series of large boulders that, hitting the wagons, shattered them to splinters, killing and maiming the men who had sought shelter beneath them, as well as the horses and oxen who stood in the open. This tactic did severe damage, destroying at least a fourth of the wagons plus dispatching another good number of the French escort, but it was primarily a diversionary tactic that bought the German infantry time to work their way down from their hiding places amongst the crags and crevices onto the road. The Germans had also hidden foot troops below the road, so when their trumpet sounded, they approached en masse from above and below.

"Clever bastards!" shouted Orla, sliding out from beneath his wagon with ax in hand to meet the onslaught as hundreds of Germans appeared from nowhere. "Come on men, to the charge!"

"Stay here," Tristan said to Hroc. Then he grabbed his sword and slid out from beneath the shelter of the wagon and was quickly engulfed in a raging current of fighting, men striking here and there, moving back and forth against each other in a dance of death. In his periphery, he saw a German coming at him, sword raised, and though he instinctively raised his own sword to counter the blow he knew what was coming. It wobbled clumsily in his grip. The German immediately sensed that the man before him knew nothing about fighting, so he snarled with mockery and prepared to deliver a quick coup de grace. Just as the German's blade began its descent, Crowbones stepped in front of Tristan and buried his ax-head into the man's forehead, cleaving his skull into halves. Having only one arm and fighting without a shield, Crowbones then quickly withdrew his ax and held it out before him in a defensive crouch to protect his unshielded torso. "Dammit, Boy, get under the wagon!" he cried to Tristan, "You don't know what the shit you're doing with that sword and you're going to get killed!"

Tristan, gasping at his own narrow escape, was about to comply with Crowbones' order, but at the moment he began to back away, he saw a German running at Crowbones' blindside, his pike aimed dead at Crowbones' ribs. Unable to reach the man, and not having time even to push Crowbones aside, Tristan grasped his sword pommel tightly, then flung the sword at the German. The sword, because of the awkward manner in which Tristan released it, spun end over end like a wheel, and in a miracle of unlikely proportions, its heavy pommel violently struck the German square on the nose, crushing it flat and knocking the man out cold. Crowbones turned in the nick of time to witness this freakish display of skill, and as the man crumpled to the ground, he buried his ax in the German's chest. "Ho, there, Boy! You saved my life! Now go get your sword and use it properly if you're going to fight!"

Guillaume, Orla, and Guthroth were several wagons down at the very head of the wagon train, and as the enemy attacked them en masse, the Germans quickly discovered that they had encountered an especially vicious and deadly cadre of fighting men. Guillaume dispatched one German after another as they dropped down onto the road from the southern outcrop while Orla did the same to those on the north side of the road trying to crawl up from below. And Guthroth, the most adept of all the Danes with a sword, protected the flanks of Orla and Guillaume as Germans continued to flow forward from the road.

At the other end of the wagon train Captain Rousseau was unable to maintain the order that Guillaume and the Danes had established to the front. Many wagons had managed to turn about and retreat back down the slope, which meant that during the archers' attack many men were left in the open. Also, since

France was to their back, a number of footmen turned and began to flee down the slope, having no stomach for mountain fighting. They, too, were intercepted by Germans who had hidden in waiting positions. Nevertheless, most of the men Captain Rousseau had enlisted in Dijon were seasoned fighting men who knew their best chance of survival was to remain in place together.

After two hours of fighting, the Germans began to gather momentum at both ends of the wagon train. Their initial attack by the archers and the rockslides had worked to their advantage, as had their positioning above and below the pass. And now it became evident that despite the size of the caravan and the large number of French mercenaries, the German forces outnumbered the French.

"Form a tight phalanx! Guard each other's backs and flanks!" screamed Guillaume, running here and there rallying his scattered forces to move together. Normally the blast of a designated trumpet signal would have announced Guillaume's intention, but this combination of Burgundians and mercenaries from Dijon had never fought with Mathilda's Tuscans. Therefore, they were unfamiliar with Tuscan trumpet commands.

Somehow he managed to pull most of the remaining men at the front of the wagon train into a knot at the very top of the pass, their weapons bristling like the spiny quills of a porcupine, the French phalanx prepared for what appeared to be a final onslaught. At the other end of the train Captain Rousseau was in very much the same position. "To the death!" he cried. "These Germans will give no quarter, nor shall we!"

As the French huddled together at their respective ends of the train then, and the Germans massed at each end to attack, a strange silence engulfed the mountain pass. It was that silence that has, throughout history, fallen upon men at war who recognize that the final outcome, still in doubt, is now shortly to be determined. In the very heat of battle men have no time to think, only time to lash out with that howling, single-minded will to survive. But when the savage clash of war suddenly pauses, as now, and the troops mass for a final onslaught, men have a moment to weigh their lives . . . and consider what they will miss in death. And though one might think this pause to be a respite of sorts, it is not. Rather, it is dreadfully frightening.

And though neither the French nor the Germans were certain who would own the pass by day's end, they each knew that they would have to fight to the death. Taking prisoners was an impossible logistical proposition in the high mountains. Great trepidation rippled through the hushed ranks of both armies as they stood staring at each like two scorpions with stingers raised.

Breaking this funeral silence, a faint blast of a distant trumpet broke the air. It was unexpected, and surprised both the French and the Germans. The blast came again, followed by a timed series of follow-up notes. Focusing completely on the sound, both sides strained to make sense of the call, but neither recognized it. Then it came again, sounding closer, as though it came from the bottom of the eastern slope of the mountain.

"It's Balducci!" Guillaume shouted. "That's a Tuscan code we hear!"

A great cheer arose within Guillaume's phalanx, which was heard by the Germans as well as by Captain Rousseau's phalanx at the other end of the wagon train. Not sure why Guillaume's contingent was cheering, Rousseau's men looked at each other puzzled. "What's this? We now cheer before the slaughter?" said one of the men standing near Rousseau.

At that moment Rousseau remembered Guillaume's mention of a Tuscan escort on their way to meet them in the Apennines. "Ha! It's the Tuscans!" he cried. "They must have tired of waiting in the Apennines and moved north into the Alps! Probably anxious to get their hands on Cardinal Odo's gift to Mathida!"

And indeed that was exactly the case. That and the fact that Mathilda's spies had received word that King Heinrich had dispatched a large force toward the Alps near the French border, which made no sense unless he had learned of Cardinal Odo's plan to send munitions across the Alps to Tuscany. In any case, on hearing the French cheers and the nearing approach of the foreign trumpet code, the Germans quickly disassembled and melted away into the mountains, leaving the mountain pass to the French.

Shortly afterwards, Commander Balducci appeared at the head of a vast column of Tuscan knights and footmen. "Damnation!" he crowed, sitting erect astride his horse with a fist to his hip, as though posing for a portrait. "What in thunder has been taking you goddamn French so long!" he cried.

Balducci had long ago perfected this irritating expression he now displayed of doubting others with a supreme air of superiority, and it was this more than anything else that agitated his peers, especially Guillaume and the Danes. On this occasion, they cheered when they spied Balducci poised astride his mount in such a manner.

"Ah, Balducci," cried Guillaume, "I never in my life thought I could be happy to see you, but the very sight of you sitting stiff atop that horse warms my soul!"

CHAPTER FORTY-ONE

HAIL, TUSCANY!

Balducci pressed for an immediate departure for Tuscany, but Guillaume quickly quelled his fervor. "Nay, we'll be staying here for at least two days. We have wagons to repair and munitions to recover that have been heaved over the ledge by the rockslides." He then set about organizing the troops into work details. The first order of business was to gather the weapons, armor, and hauberks of the dead, both German and French. The stripped bodies were then thrown over the ledge; impossible to bury them within the rocky terrain of the pass. As this process began, Guillaume called to his brother. "Tristan, look here," he said, pointing to a corpse, "our little friend from the convent at Marcigny."

Though Tristan had never actually gotten a close glimpse of the man at the convent, he immediately recognized the corpse's face. "Yes, same fellow I encountered beneath the tree back at the Marseilles harbor. He must have followed us to Cluny and Marcigny, then when we departed for our work in Dijon, he must have made haste for the Alps to guide the Germans. Kick him over the ledge."

As darkness fell, Guillaume ordered the teamsters to crack open kegs of wine for the exhausted troops. "Let's celebrate the day's outcome," he declared, "and here's to the timely arrival of our savior, Commander Balducci!"

Although Balducci and his troops had never raised a sword in the battle, Balducci was more than happy to accept Guillaume's praise, and as he drank more and more wine, even began to imagine that the wagon train would have been massacred had he not come along when he did. Though it was true that the Germans were gaining some momentum at the time of his arrival, the battle was actually evenly matched and its outcome certain. Nonetheless, in the spirit of drink, Guillaume and the Danes allowed Balducci to rattle on, often egging him on then smirking at each other over his boastfulness. It was a festive mood then that overcame the men there that night as they jovially recounted their respective involvement in the fierce battle and shared tales of their close brushes with death.

It was at this point that Crowbones, full of wine, stepped into the circle, and crouching with the gesture of a storyteller about to unveil a tale of bravery and courage, took command of the conversation. "Aha!" he roared, raising his drinking horn to the night. "A mighty warrior was born this day! Our boy, Tristan, saved my life!" Then he reared his head back with a loud guffaw and slapped his knee, saying, "And in the process, invented a new manner of fighting!"

Of course, nobody knew what Crowbones was talking about but Tristan, who immediately began to retreat. "Lord Crowbones," he said, "I don't think . . ."

"Ja!" Crowbones shouted, ignoring him. "He has invented a new way of using the sword!" As he spoke Crowbones tried to maintain a look of seriousness, but was unable to maintain this expression because of involuntary outbreaks of snickering. "The rest of us mediocre warriors use the sword for hand-to-hand fighting, but our lad, Tristan, oh, not so. He uses it as a long-range weapon. Only someone as clever as him would ever think to use a mere sword as a deadly missile!" Then Crowbones broke into several comically exaggerated gestures as though launching his drinking horn at an opponent, which caused an outbreak of riotous laughter. "Oho, Tristan," Crowbones brayed, "perhaps in the morning you could provide the troops with a private lesson on your deadly technique!"

Tristan had slipped to the back of the circle, and even now after the day's battle and in the midst of this celebration, was thinking of Mala. With Crowbones' challenge and the laughter of the others, he stepped forward and smiled weakly, knowing that to defend himself would only invite more teasing and ridicule. "Of course, Lord Crowbones," he said, crouching into a comical gesture himself, "let me show all of you how it is done!" This created even more of a stir, making even Tristan himself laugh and call for more wine.

The remainder of the journey through the final lap of the Alps went without incident, as did the trek through the more benign Apennines. Finally, the wagon train approached the Qattro Castelli: Montezane, Montelucio, Montvetro and Bianell, four castles perched atop hills that guarded the approach to Mathilda's impregnable fortress of Canossa. When the wagons completed their ascent up the twisted trail into Mathilda's stronghold, she was there outside the gate awaiting them. Guillaume had already dismounted and was moving her way. She rushed toward him. "Oh, Guillaume, good to have you back home!" she cried. Then she saw Tristan and ran to him also, embracing him tightly. "Oh, nephew, Praise God! These wagons are such a welcome sight to all of us here in Tuscany!"

Tristan loved Mathilda, and though his maternal allegiance remained with his mother, Asta, he had always greatly appreciated all that Mathilda had done for Guillaume, him, and the Church.

"I hope this renews your valiant efforts against Heinrich and his false monk," Tristan smiled.

"Oh, yes! I have until now only held the Germans in check, Tristan, but with these munitions you bring I shall initiate a new offensive and move east. Then, when Handel arrives from Germany in a few months with *his* wagons, we shall also move south. Perhaps by spring we shall reclaim the Vatican!"

CHAPTER FORTY-TWO

THE STORM

On the night the Romani left Marseilles, Mala had returned to camp in the midst of the storm. Despite the raging wind and rain, she rousted all those from the shelter of their wagons. "Harness the horses!" she cried to the men in a furor. "Fernando, we're leaving Marseilles immediately!"

The others thought it a ruse of some kind at first. Noticing the fire in Mala's eyes, they quickly began preparations to depart despite their hesitancy to take on the storm. Fernando, immediately guessed that Tristan was the root of the issue. Earlier, when Mala had insisted on remaining in town while sending the others to batten down the camp, he had suspected that Mala was planning to rendez-vous with Tristan. *Something went afoul*, he now thought. *They must have fought.*

Consequently, Fernando was more than pleased to be leaving Marseilles, even in the midst of a storm. While Duxia was scurrying about with Mala hitching the horses to her wagon, he pulled her aside. "Something's happened between Mala and that Tristan character," he said.

"Eh?"

"Yes, I've seen her angry before," Fernando said, "although never quite like this. Not sure what happened in town, but it's got something to do with *him*. Perhaps he's jealous of me and said something that made her angry."

Duxia's first inclination was to laugh. Instead she replied, "Ah, probably so, Fernando. She holds you close to her heart you know, of all you do for her, and no suitor will long tolerate a competitor! I'll ride with her tonight, Fernando, and learn what's happened." Then she crawled up onto the seat of Mala's wagon, impatient to discover the cause of Mala's rash behavior. Due to the ferocity of the storm, it was not until hours later when they were well away from Marseilles that she was able to utter the first word to Mala, whose entire attention was focused on the struggle to see ahead through the blackness of night and pelting rain while trying to keep the horses on the road.

"Something has come between you and the Saint-Germain boy?" Duxia said finally.

Her eyes fixed on the darkness ahead, Mala shivered a moment. Tightening her shawl about her shoulders, she said nothing.

"Ay, Dear, though you may not wish to talk," Duxia continued, "this old woman beside you understands. I have felt such disappointment . . . and it's a crushing thing, heartbreak." Of course, Duxia had no idea what had happened in town, but Mala's quiet nod told Duxia that she had, indeed, fallen onto fertile ground. "And I won't lie to you, Dear, time will do little to make you forget such a deep wound. Nature leaves a scar so you'll always remember the hurt. Whatever you do, Mala, don't follow my path."

At this, Mala slowly shrugged, and muttered, "And what path is that, Duxia?"

"The path of self-destruction that hope brings, Girl. Hope parts the briars ahead and lures you forward onto its primrose trail, then closes all about you, trapping you in a thorny thicket of loneliness and rejection. No, the only cure for such a situation as yours is to abandon hope and make a new beginning. And that's what I failed to do with Guntar the Mace. I hoped, I wept, I prayed to no avail. Then one day I woke up old and ugly and bitter, all because I clung to hope rather than make a new beginning. I therefore pray that you don't make my mistake."

Wiping rain from her brow, Mala nodded again. "A new beginning?" she said, ready to talk. "Yes, Tristan holds no future for me, and never did, actually. I see that now. Might it have been possible to keep him? No, because of God. Tristan is, after all, a Benedictine reform monk." The immediate image of Tristan's face arose in her mind, causing her to bite her lip as the heaviness lumping in her throat then forced from her a mournful laugh. "Ha! It was a girlish fantasy." Then she fell silent again. Her voice had arrived at that stage when one ceases speaking for fear of weeping.

Mala's relentless drive forward did not end until dawn as sporadic gusts of wind continued to batter the treetops. The rain had ceased, and as Mala pulled her wagon off the road into a small clearing, the others wagons followed.

"We'll sleep here," she said to Fernando, her voice lacking all trace of emotion.

"Could you at least tell us where we're headed?" asked Fernando.

"No," said Mala.

"Well then, is there any sort of plan I can share with the others?"

"No."

Accepting his questions were useless, he said, "Very well, Mala, whatever you decide, I'll stand by you."

"Thank you, Fernando," Mala replied, studying his expression a moment with vacant eyes. Then she disappeared into the back of her wagon, fell asleep, and did not stir until late that night. Crawling from her wagon, she found all the Romani seated about a blazing fire, in discussion.

"What's going on here?" she said, yawning, still half asleep.

"They're trying to figure out your intentions," said Fernando. "As I said before, I will stand by whatever you decide, but some of the others are less certain. It would help, of course, if you could give them some specifics."

She looked at the fire a moment, then her eyes shifted from one member of the camp to another. "Have I not always provided for each of you?" she said, her displeasure evident. "And I will continue to do so."

"We were doing so well in Marseilles," said one of the other men. "The money was coming in nicely there, better than anywhere we've ever been. Leaving doesn't make any sense, Mala, and . . ."

"Who leads this troupe?" Mala interrupted, crossing her arms.

"You do," the man said, looking to the others for support, but he found none.

"Very well then, you can either trust in my leadership, or strike out on your own," Mala said matter-of-factly. Then she turned and quietly disappeared into her wagon.

The others looked at each other, several shaking their heads. "Well then," said Fernando as others grumbled, "there it is, simply put. You either stay or go. As for me, I stay."

"Yes, me also," said Duxia who was seated next to Fernando. "I've not been with you long, but long enough to see that it's Mala who draws the crowd and brings in the money. Yes, your music's fine, but it's her dancing and beauty that lures the crowd."

Knowing that Duxia was right, the grumbling ceased. The mood was such that most left the fire and retired to their wagons. "I'll stay a while longer," mumbled one of the men as he left, "but another crazy thing like leaving in the midst of a storm at midnight, and I'm gone." The woman next to him nodded, as did several others.

That next morning Mala assembled the Romani, and acting as though nothing had happened in Marseilles, said, "We are moving to Lyons."

"Lyons?" said Fernando.

"Yes, it's a large city, and being to the north and not far from the mountains, the people there have never heard music such as ours and have never encountered Romani. Their curiosity will earn us a decent living, as good as Marseilles I venture to say."

Though several of the musicians had hoped somehow that Mala might soften her stance about returning to the profitable harbor of Marseilles, Mala's reasoning seemed to placate most of the others.

"Very well, Mala," said Fernando. Then he signaled to the others and said, "break camp, we leave immediately."

It was a different Mala that left camp that morning, as the other Romani were soon to discover. The generosity and kind consideration for others that was so attractive about her and characteristic of her nature seemed to melt away by degrees. And though she returned to her dancing with a newfound fervor, she did not display the playfully flirtatious mannerisms that attracted women and men alike. Rather, her dancing became more sullen and promiscuous, aimed strictly at separating men from their purses. It also became evident that she was becoming distrustful of men, despising them unless they gave her money. And as they worked the streets of Lyons, the money fell easily precisely as Mala had promised. The foreign complexion, lively music, and colorful clothing of the Romani were novel there. Above all, the dark, exotic beauty and lithe movements of their dancing queen became the sensation of men seeking entertainment throughout the city.

The musicians were, of course, pleased at this unexpected reversal of fortune. Whereas Mala had always generated a decent living for them, their earnings now doubled, as did the size of the crowds which were completely comprised of men. These all male crowds were more boisterous than the previously mixed crowds, and were often filled with drunks uttering profanity and inappropriate comments. Their lewd behavior only seemed to fuel Mala's dancing, which in turn generated even more coin.

"Ah, we've never done better!" the musicians commented among themselves, though they increasingly found themselves in the midst of altercations between overzealous spectators filled with drink and lechery. These altercations then slowly escalated into involving the Romani themselves as they began to find it necessary to intercede as men began grabbing at Mala and trying to touch her. Fernando actually handled the bulk of such muscle work, but increasingly found himself calling for assistance from the others.

Duxia took due note of Mala's transformation and became increasingly concerned. Though she was elated, it appeared that Mala had set Tristan aside completely. She also could see that Mala's recent behavior was an unwelcome descent of sorts. And despite the old woman's bitterness about life, Duxia had actually come to care for Mala. For Duxia, Mala had at first been a generous hand that helped her one day along the side of the road. Her generosity quickly reeled Duxia in upon inviting her to join the Romani caravan despite the fact the old woman had nothing to contribute in exchange for food and shelter.

Then Mala had insisted that Duxia ride with her as they traveled, and as the days and weeks passed, Duxia found herself being inextricably drawn to her. This in turn reminded her of those happy early years with Asta in Saint-Germain-en-Laye, and Duxia felt the tug of affection pulling her whenever she looked at Mala. Then the two began sharing secrets and intimate conversation, which cemented an unspoken bond that both valued.

This bond developed naturally, then, because the human heart when it's lost something of significance, seeks to replace it. Duxia, finally accepting that she had been preyed upon by Guntar the Mace, had then lost the thing she treasured above all else: Asta. And now, it was almost as though God had miraculously recreated the beautiful Asta in another form. And for Mala who had lost her mother years before to Spain, Duxia fell easily into her shadow. She, like Mala's mother, had experienced a difficult life and reached the point of near helplessness. In a way then, though Mala could no longer do anything for her mother, she could now at least help another who reminded her of her mother.

The truth was, then, that Duxia's horror when she found out about Mala's relationship with Tristan was not so much an issue of jealousy, but an issue of profound personal concern for Mala's future. When a caring elder watches a younger loved one blindly and happily rushing over a ledge, that elder will do anything possible to avert what is perceived as inevitable disaster. And to Duxia, Tristan spelled imminent disaster for Mala, exactly as Guntar had for herself. With Mala's changed persona, Duxia sensed trouble of a different thread weaving itself before her very eyes, and felt chilled by it.

Mala sensed no such thing. What she felt was an iron resolve to strengthen herself and her position in life. Because of Tristan, she now felt preyed upon in Marseilles, and something of the wild beast developed in her as a result. And though she had felt the ground giving out beneath her feet at first as a new loneliness invaded her life, worse than the one she had imagined before, she felt it necessary to bury the memory of Tristan and let it lay dead forever. So her old dreams fell aside like wounded sparrows in the mud, and new ones took their place, the primary of which was to somehow acquire wealth at the expense of men.

"I have a short time to fill the treasury," she said coldly to Duxia one day. "I shall not remain young forever."

"Oh, Dear," Duxia warned, "the wealthy are victims of misery also. Money, though nice, does not buy happiness."

"Oh, listen to you now, Duxia," Mala remarked with raillery. "Was it not *you* who warned me of waking up one day only to discover old age and helplessness?"

"Yes, I also said you should make a new beginning, and the purpose of such a thing is to seek happiness, which I never did. You should find a man who treats you well and cares about you . . . such as Fernando."

"Fernando?" Mala said, surprised. "Ha! He has little to offer, Duxia!"

"No, I don't mean take up with Fernando, I mean find a man who treats you like Fernando, with adoration. Forego promiscuity and insist on marriage. With your looks, Dear, it would not be difficult, I assure you."

"Marry for money?" Mala laughed. "Why not *take* men's money, then be free of them altogether?"

"My Dear," said Duxia, studying Mala a moment with shrewd eyes, "marriage to the right man brings legitimacy and stability, especially to foreign women such as you and me. Yes, if you snared a nobleman," she said, pausing. "An older one," she then added.

Mala scoffed at the idea. "We are doing quite alright at the moment," she replied. "If we continue as we are, perhaps we could settle here in Lyons, open a little shop of some sort." Then she pursed her lips into that little circle that occurs when dreamers envision themselves attaining their goal. "Wouldn't that be nice, Duxia? Just you and me. No more wagons, no more uncertainty."

Duxia nodded though Mala's words spawned in her a sudden current of dread. Old Duxia was not accustomed to things working in her favor, and Mala's idea sounded far too simple. Thinking on the proposition a moment, Duxia closed her eyes to imagine such a tranquil, rooted existence in Lyons, but then her eyelids fluttered rapidly, as if enmeshed in the countless threads of a bad dream, as that elusive feeling of something bad forming itself in the future seized her.

"Oh!" she cried, her eyes popping open.

"Duxia, what is it?" said Mala, noticing the old woman's alarm.

"Nothing, Dear." Duxia replied, her temples reddening. "Nothing at all."

Mala's erotic dancing and the Romani music continued to draw heavy crowds of men at night, and Mala continued to hoard gold coins for two months in her wagon, intent on opening a small shop down in the market district of Lyons. One evening in early September as she was in the midst of an especially physical dance, she swooned, nearly collapsing to the ground. She stumbled about awkwardly for several seconds, then continued dancing, but a short while later she felt dizzy and again nearly collapsed.

"Here, here," said Duxia, running to her side and steadying her. "You're exhausted, Dear, you've been working too hard. Come sit down." Then Duxia gestured to Fernando with a chop to her neck. "We're done for the night!" she said.

That night in camp Duxia tended carefully to Mala in her wagon, but by morning Mala only felt worse. "I feel ill," she said, grasping her throat. Then she leaned over and retched. "Arhg!" she stammered. Then, blinking several times in succession, she set her head back down on her blanket and closed her eyes. "T-tell Fernando . . . I won't be . . . working tonight, Duxia. I don't feel well."

Duxia had turned cold and white as a stone. Sitting there watching Mala, she had been struck by a frightening reality, and was chasing it wildly about in her head. "Yes, Dear," she whispered, then quickly crawling out of the wagon, she stood and cast her eyes skyward. She stood there staring at the clouds, studying their formation and following their movement. Then, after a long while, she nodded to herself and scowled knowingly, as though the clouds had confirmed what she had already begun to suspect in the wagon.

"What're you doing?" said Fernando who was watching from a distance. "Another storm coming?"

"No," said Duxia, gesturing for him to approach. "Something else, Fernando, something *much* worse, a baby is on the way."

CHAPTER FORTY-THREE

HAMMER OF GOD

"You're pregnant," Duxia told Mala two days later as she lay in the wagon.

Stunned, Mala issued a moan so mournful, so distraught, that it made Duxia's blood run cold.

"N-no," she then mumbled, fighting desperately to restrain herself from weeping. "I can't be!"

"Yes. Your tryst with the Saint-Germain boy in Marseilles, it was in June when he stayed at the camp. Tell me though, have you slept with any other man since then?"

"N-no. Of course not!" snapped Mala, drowning in a sea of unfamiliar apprehensions. "A child!" she wailed. "I know nothing of children, especially raising one! My God, what do I do, Duxia?"

"You'll have the child, Dear. You'll bear the child, then raise it. 'Tis a blessed thing, motherhood. And just as you dreamed, this will be more reason to open your shop and settle here in Lyons. The road is no way to raise a child, you know that from your own upbringing, eh?" As Duxia said this, she masked her private dread of bringing the spawn of Tristan de Saint-Germain into the world. "And don't fear, Mala, I will help you with the baby."

"It's Tristan's child," Mala said with a sudden dread of her own. "You shan't try to drown it, will you?" she asked with urgency. "Swear to me, Duxia!"

"No, no, of course not," Duxia said, caressing Mala's forehead. "I won't even consider it his child, Dear, but only yours."

"But my dancing, Duxia, I don't yet have quite enough money to set up a shop!"

"You can dance a little while longer before your belly swells; perhaps long enough for you to earn your shop."

Fernando, of course, had fallen into a fury when Duxia had first shared the news with him about the pregnancy. He knew immediately that Tristan was the father. Still, he took it upon himself to continue catering to Mala's needs, which placed him in an entirely new light to Mala. For the first time in their relationship she began to actually notice and appreciate his many efforts on her behalf.

That next day she felt better and resumed her dancing, though she tamed it considerably.

This in turn gradually drew smaller crowds of men, and by October when Mala's pregnancy was well along, the crowds had dwindled to a handful of onlookers who, at the sight of Mala's belly, quickly lost interest. Envisioning their golden goose dried up, the other Romani began to grumble and complain, and soon the camp thinned to only two wagons, Mala, Duxia, and the ever faithful Fernando.

Mala had begun bartering for a small storefront in the market district with an elderly vendor who could no longer manage his fabric business, and felt certain that the three of them could settle into commerce with the other town burghers of Lyons. "Come with me, Duxia," she said one day, "and let's finalize terms on our shop today." Then, instructing Fernando to guard the wagons, she gave him an affectionate embrace, something she had never done before. "I owe you much, Fernando," she whispered.

For Fernando, this was the grandest moment of his life. He had by now settled himself with Mala having Tristan's child, but hoped that Mala might actually consent to marrying him, if nothing else, for the sake of the child. So while watching her leave camp with Duxia that morning, his heart was filled with a newfound fervor as he began envisioning a future in which he and Mala were raising *their* child, with Duxia serving as grandmother.

Lost in this reverie, he did not hear the approach of two hooligans from Lyons slipping into the campsite. The two had been watching the Romani perform in the market district since their arrival and had remarked that the entertainment troupe was hauling in quite a harvest. Then, learning that the camp had thinned to two wagons, one of which belonged to the dancing girl who generated most of the money, they determined the camp should be an easy and profitable target.

Right when they headed for Fernando, he by coincidence happened to turn about, but before he could react the two hoodlums had attacked him. And though he was larger and stronger than either of them, together they managed to overpower him. One of the intruders struck him across the skull while the other took him to the ground. Then, taking a dagger from his belt, the man who clubbed Fernando slipped his dagger into Fernando's belly. Raising up like an enraged bull, Fernando pulled the dagger from his gut with one hand, and with his other fist struck his assailant across the jaw, breaking it with a single blow.

Staggering back in blind confusion, holding his cracked jaw with both hands, the man screamed to his partner on the ground, "Kill 'im, goddammit!"

The second man quickly extracted a dagger from his sleeve, jumped to his feet, and attacked Fernando from behind, stabbing him three times in quick succession in the back. Bellowing with rage, bleeding profusely from front and the back, Fernando staggered about helplessly for a moment, then felt his knees collapse under him. The crush of the ground against his forehead was the last thing he felt.

"Is he dead?" the first man said, still struggling with his jaw.

"Yes. Dammit, I didn't want to *kill* the poor bastard!"

"To hell with 'im. Quick now, go through the wagon and let's get the hell out of here!"

The uninjured man ran to the wagon and quickly began rummaging through clothing, cooking utensils, and an assortment of vessels and containers. After several minutes of frustration he found a wooden box hidden in the front corner of the wagon beneath a pile of blankets. Grabbing it, he jumped from the wagon and waved to the first man. "Got it!" he said. "Let's go!"

It was not until hours later that Mala and Duxia returned. Finding Fernando lying motionless upon the ground, his shirt caked reddish-black with dried blood, Mala cried out in dismay and fell to the ground beside him, desperately seeking signs of life.

"Oh, my God!" she then wailed, looking up at Duxia. "H-he's dead!"

Duxia, well-attuned to the wickedness of men, immediately looked about the camp, fearing that whoever did this might still be about. Then she saw the back door to Mala's wagon standing wide open and surmised immediately what had befallen them. "We've been robbed!" she cried. "Mala, your money!"

Mala was bent over Fernando, stroking his head and body with convulsive movements, already lost in the despondency of the bereaved and swelling with regret over the fact that she had paid Fernando so little mind.

"He was so g-o-o-d to us, Duxia!" she wept.

"Indeed, he was a good fellow," said Duxia, her hands falling to her side with resignation as visions of the little shop they had left in Lyons began to dissolve. Then she dropped to a knee beside Fernando and gently patted Mala on the back. "We're lost, Dear," she said, shaking her head back and forth woefully. "They've taken the money, they've taken Fernando, it's winter and we have a child on the way. The hammer of God has struck yet again."

At that moment, as Mala's palm was still upon Fernando's chest, she felt a slight tremor. Looking down with startled eyes, she then saw his eyelids flutter, then open.

"M-Mala?" whispered Fernando, struggling to breathe.

"My God, he lives!" Mala cried. "Quickly, Duxia, water and rags! Oh, hurry, *please!*"

Moving about with urgency, they tended to Fernando as best they could there on the ground, cleansing his wounds and closing them. And though his weight and girth made it nearly impossible to move him, they first worked his belly then turned him over to nurse his back where most of the stab wounds had been inflicted. Mala then hurried toward town to seek assistance, and happening upon two men passing by, acquired their cooperation in hoisting Fernando into his wagon.

By day's end the two women sat next to each other by a meager fire as Fernando lay within his wagon in a state of semi-consciousness, alternately moaning and calling for Mala, then slipping into deep sleep. "Will he live, Duxia?" said Mala.

"Hard to tell, Dear. The wounds are severe, but Fernando is stout as a horse. He lost much blood, though."

Mala gazed into the fire then, and issued a deep sigh, her face taking on that defeated look brought on by the crushing of dreams. "The old shop owner in town," she said, making mention of the financial situation for the first time since discovering Fernando earlier that afternoon, "I best stop by in the morning and let him know that things have fallen apart. He'll be wondering where we are."

"Yes, he was expecting us back today in merely a few hours with the money. Ah, how quick God drops the hammer upon us all."

"That's the second time you mentioned such a thing today," Mala said, looking at Duxia with curiosity. "What do you mean by it?"

Duxia spat into the fire, its flames casting her in a strange and ghostly light. "When I was pagan," she began, "we always knew what to expect from our Norse gods. They were either good or evil, you could count on that. Since being baptized, I've learned that the Christian God, unlike the Norse gods, is utterly unpredictable and merciless for no reason. It's as though things are going well and you're minding your own affairs, then for simple spite, God drops His hammer, crushing you like a gnat." As she said this, the deep creases of her weathered face tightened and her eyes grew cold. "He has followed me about like a shadow, *God*, hovering over me, hammer at the ready. Every *single* time that I find a moment's peace or think I've found a future, he *drops* it on me."

Mala digested this a while. "Do you really believe such a thing, Duxia?" she said.

"Ay, and so should you, Dear. He's done *exactly* the same to you. You were fine, Fernando told me, until the Saint-Germain boy showed up from nowhere in the Loire Valley. Ha! From *nowhere*? Nay, nay, *God* sent him. Then again things were wonderful in Marseilles. Money coming in, the other Romani were happy, a beautiful city on the coast . . . then *bang*! God dropped the Saint-Germain boy into this peaceful existence and scattered us like flies. And not content with *that* flood of misery, he then filled your belly with Saint-Germain's semen and you are now with child, and then God sends thieves into our camp to crush our final dream!"

"Oh, Duxia, you can't blame God for all that has stricken us!"

"Oh, listen to you, Girl, *you* who distrusts the Church nearly as much as I. Yet no matter where we travel or where we are, you refuse to miss Sunday mass! I find it a strange covenant you've struck between your brain and your heart. Yes, I blame God for it all. If the priests and monks are to be believed, *everything* in life is caused by God. He's the root of all things, good and evil. He's all powerful. Yet there is an anger, a vengeance about Him that is undeniable and cruel." She turned, then, and gave Mala a grave look. "Though you hide it well, Mala, I see that lost, hollow expression across your brow. It's the look of deep grieving. Ah, despite it all, you still love that goddamn monk, Saint-Germain, don't you?"

Mala sat still as a stone, saying nothing.

"Yes," Duxia said, "your silence spills it all." Duxia then gazed deeper yet into the fire and spat again. "Oh, Mala, my sweet" she rasped, shuddering the tiniest bit beneath her shawl, "if you still love that boy, then God's not yet done with us, Dear. Oh no, he has even more yet in store for us both."

CHAPTER FORTY-FOUR

DEFARGE AGAIN

Duxia's prophetic words by the fire that night soon came to fruition as in mid-October winter flung its full fury onto the region and smothered Lyons with blizzards and ice storms. Although Fernando began to recover slowly, he was helpless in terms of leaving the camp to seek employment of any means. Duxia and Mala both were forced, then, to take to the streets as beggars.

They managed from time to time to secure meager donations, but were soon forced to sell one of the two horses from Fernando's team, and butcher the other. It should be noted that these horses used by the Romani and most other distance travelers at the time in Europe were of the Icelandic breed. These small, coarse-haired ponies were hardy, fertile, utilitarian, and easily kept. They also, in addition to the walk, trot, canter, and gallop of regular horses, possessed a fifth gait known as the amble which allowed them to cover great distance without tiring and was also comfortable for the rider. The Romani used their ponies to pull their wagons, and also for individual transport.

"Though we dispose of Fernando's ponies, we must keep the two from your team alive at any cost, Mala," warned Duxia, "or we lose all hope of transport when winter is over. Once the baby arrives you can resume dancing, and with Fernando we'll make a fresh start."

The horseflesh sustained them during the day, and at night they huddled in their tiny wind-blown wagons buried beneath piles of blankets, clothing, and anything else they could throw over themselves to stave off the cold. And though Mala and Fernando had become accustomed to hardship over years of Romani wandering, they had never had to endure the state of helplessness caused by her pregnancy and his injuries. It was the old crow, Duxia, then, who kept the camp afloat, scraping bark from trees to boil tea, hunting down certain evergreen foliage suitable for human digestion as well as for the remaining two horses, and showing Mala and Fernando how to hack through frozen ground in search of tubers and other edible roots.

On New Year's morning Mala came to her as she was stooped over the camp-fire, re-stoking it. "It's a New Year, Duxia, I'm going into town to attend mass. Would you like to come along?"

"No," said Duxia, blowing into the faint heat of smoking ash, "I'm done with God. I've nothing to be thankful for, nor do you. Go ahead, Dear, if it makes you feel better." Then she straightened, placing a hand to her arthritic back, and gazed at the clouds. "Another three hard months of winter or more," she said.

"The baby comes in March; the snow and ice will still be with us. The worst lies ahead and the horsemeat is coming soon to bones and hide. Say a prayer for the child, Mala, since you still seem to believe your God listens. Perhaps though He's abandoned us, He'll have mercy at least on the infant." Then she looked over at Fernando's wagon. "We've scoured the woods these past months; the only thing left is green branches and timber. We'll need to disassemble Fernando's wagon soon for firewood or freeze to death."

January was even more brutal than November and December, and the biting wind cut so deeply that the three could barely leave the wagons to set a fire for cooking. They remained in their wagons then, and because of Mala's advancing state of pregnancy and Fernando's immobility, Duxia insisted that she be the one to venture out into the freezing weather to hack raw, frozen flesh from the scant horse remains and scoop snow for their thirst. One morning as she was bent over working the horse carcass, she heard a slight noise behind her. Turning quickly, she raised her knife and cried, "What do you want!"

A man stood there, trembling, his head and neck wrapped in rags for warmth. A blanket was wrapped over his head and shoulders, but Duxia could see that the poor fellow was missing a hand. "Th-the m-meat there," the man shivered, "I h-haven't eaten in days. M-might I have a sliver of it? Th-then I'll be on my way."

Distrustful by nature, especially of men, Duxia waved her knife about a moment. "Yes, I'll share, but stranger, best not get any funny ideas. I'm old, but I can still gut a weasel!"

The man approached slowly, barely able to move one frozen foot before the other. "Th-thank you, kind ma'am," he stammered, parting the blanket pulled about his face a bit with his single hand to better see the old woman. As he peeked out at her, Duxia straightened her crooked frame and relaxed her grip on the knife. "De-DeFarge?" she gasped.

Hearing his name, the man peeled his blanket yet wider. "M-Mielikki? Duxia?" he said, equally perplexed at a face from the forgotten past. "Wh-what the hell?"

"Come sit, DeFarge, while I saw you some flesh from this thing," Duxia clucked, squatting beside the carcass. "And pray tell, what happened to your hand? War?"

"No, Orla the Dane took it," DeFarge, snorted. "You remember that big bastard from the Saint-Germain-en-Laye days, eh?" DeFarge then recounted the tale of enlisting in Dijon to go fight in Italy for Countess Mathilda.

"Ah, the wealthiest bitch of the continent," said Duxia. "God starves the two of us, DeFarge, yet piles mountains of gold upon that Tuscan whore. Where's the justice, eh?"

DeFarge nodded, watching Duxia work the horseflesh hungrily. "Uh, if I might, perhaps, I'll take *two* little slivers of that fine looking meat, Duxia."

"Yes, certainly," said Duxia, content to have encountered DeFarge.

Years before when she had been part of Asta's household, she had liked

DeFarge. He, too, had enjoyed her company at the time, and though she was older than him, had still found her attractive back then and often imagined that it would be enjoyable to explore her bush. He stared and he marveled at how she had deteriorated. Duxia was thinking the same of him as she handed him a thin cut of frozen horse.

"Such bad luck for you to run into the Danes of all damn people," Duxia said, "Why in the world are they going to Tuscany?"

"They fight for the Countess now in Italy, under the banner of Guillaume de Saint-Germain."

"What? Guillaume? The baby brother of Tristan de Saint-Germain?"

"Yes, young as he is, Guillaume's their damned commander believe it or not, and a high lord of Tuscany apparently. He and his brother were both adopted at some point by la Gran Contessa Mathilda herself, and talk among the Danes is that with her support and the backing of Cardinal Odo de Lagery, she hopes Tristan may one day don the Pope's tiara! Such damn luck, those two boys, especially after what happened to their father." Here his cheeks turned red, as he was the cause of Roger de Saint-Germain's demise. "Anyway, yes, Tristan and Guillaume are both in Tuscany, I imagine, having long ago delivered arms, munitions, and men to the Countess."

Duxia did not hear this last statement. Her mind was far aflight, suddenly grasping about for possibilities. Tristan de Saint-Germain was now related to one of the most wealthy and powerful figures of all Europe. "Are you listening to me, Duxia?" said DeFarge, giving her a nudge. "Uh, and I'll have that other slice now, maybe a little bigger than the last, eh?"

"Yes, certainly!" said Duxia, cutting faster. "And I'll cut off these ears for you to take on the road. Then it's off you go, DeFarge, understand?"

CHAPTER FORTY-FIVE

FROM HELL'S GRASP

The moment DeFarge departed, Duxia delivered several scant shavings of meat to Fernando, then scuttled quickly into the other wagon with Mala.

"Oh, dear," she cried, "startling news has fallen into my lap. We are delivered!" She then anxiously shared what she had found out about by the horse carcass.

"The great Countess Mathilda is Tristan's aunt?" said Mala, puzzled. "He never mentioned such a thing."

"Of course not. It's more proof of his deceit and trickery."

"Even so, Duxia, what does any of this have to do with *us*?"

"Oh, my Sweet, don't you see? We shall make our way immediately to Tuscany and present you to the Countess and show her your belly! If she cares a single measure for the lad, she will then quietly pay us off to avoid scandal. My God, the woman has befriended popes and high clerics all over Europe and is in league with Cardinal Odo de Lagery himself to advance your lad Tristan up the Church ladder, to the very, very top! They'll never allow him to fall, by God!"

Mala cast her eyes to her lap and slowly shook her head with uncertainty. "No, Duxia, I don't think it's a good idea. I wouldn't do such a thing to Tristan."

"Mala!" Duxia cried. "Do you not understand that we are on death's doorstep? And your child? What about your child?"

Again Mala shook her head. "No. I don't like the idea of . . ."

"My God, Girl!" Duxia exclaimed with utter exasperation. "You've got Fernando dying of wounds and starving to death in the wagon next to us after all he's done for you, you and I are hanging on by a thread with months of hard winter staring us in the face, and we shall have an infant to feed in several months, if we survive that long! There *is* no choice here. Tristan de Saint-Germain has caused our downfall so it's foolishness to worry about him at this point. And dammit, even if you do still love him, it's not about you any more either." Then she pointed to Mala's stomach. "It's about that!"

They argued a while longer, and despite Mala's reluctance, she eventually knew that Duxia was right. "Very well, but how will we ever make it to Tuscany, Duxia? Do we wait for Spring?"

"No. We won't last that long, so we leave immediately."

"What? But the snow and ice, and Fernando, and the Alps."

"Look, nothing can be worse than this hell we're enduring right here. Nothing. Besides, we've got two stout ponies. We'll load Fernando in here with the remains of the horse carcass and firewood we scrap from the other wagon and off we go. With your help, I'll get us across the Alps to Tuscany, Mala, I swear it!"

From the jaws of disaster springs hope. And as Duxia's mind began to race forward into a future graced with the mercy and coin of the renowned Countess Mathilda, she devised a resolute strategy to save the three of themselves from the certain death awaiting them as a result of the sudden lack of options hurled at them by the robbery and the harsh winter. In the face of such hardship, Duxia's hope also cultivated great risk. She knew well that crossing the Alps in winter would be no easy proposition, but the reward awaiting them at the end of that trek should they survive could undoubtedly transform their bleak future.

So it was that this unlikely community of three castaways, bound by circumstance and misfortune, set about for Tuscany in the midst of winter. And it was Duxia who, though decrepit and stooped, though shaved to the nubs by life's rasp, took the reins of leadership in advancing their tiny wagon eastward toward the Alps. Staving off discouragement, ignoring the hardships brought on by icy roads, scything wind, and the biting cold, she drove the small ponies forward day after day until finally they caught sight of the mountains towering ahead.

She stopped the wagon, then, and called to Mala and Fernando who were huddled together within the wagon trying to keep warm. "Come stick your heads out and behold the Alps!" she cried.

Shivering, Mala cracked the tiny window shutter located behind Duxia's driver position and peered out at the terrible frozen beauty of the formidable peaks standing before them. "Oh my God!" she whispered, having never seen the Alps. "How will we ever overcome such a hurdle?"

"The only way over the Alps is the Via Francigena, which you see opening before you," said Duxia. Then she spat in the snow, some of the dribble immediately freezing to her cracked lower lip. "And though few travel this road in winter, *we'll* traverse the Via Fracigena by fighting God, my Dear," she continued, drawing out her syllables with undeniable bitterness. "Yes, put away your prayer beads, Girl, for they'll do us no good. God long ago turned his back to us. Rather, let us summon *Lucifer* himself from the crags and crannies of darkness, for he is *infinitely* more merciful . . ."

Then she flicked the reins and began the ascent . . .

CHAPTER FORTY-SIX

INTO HELL'S JAW

The first weeks of travel through the Alps provided an unexpected break in the weather as the north winds died and the sun shone brightly from above. The greatest barrier then was the ice that had layered itself upon the mountainous route toward Italy. And though the sure-footed Icelandic ponies worked the road as skillfully as could be expected, the three travelers often found themselves having to assist the ponies by pushing the tiny wagon on inclines, then holding it back with ropes on the sharper declines. This, of course, was tedious work and very much impeded their progress. Mala's pregnancy and Fernando's wounds limited their strength tremendously, yet the teamwork of the hope-driven travelers coupled with the valiant efforts of the shaggy ponies inched them further and further into the Alps.

The mood became increasingly hopeful then, as Duxia, Mala, and Fernando worked their way forward. Of all circumstances in life, sharing impossible hardship and facing mutual extinction are the two most salient experiences that humans can share. The struggle to overcome such circumstances, consequently, creates endearing bonds between the survivors of such misfortune. A glue began to develop within the hearts of the three travelers as they fought the terrain, the ice, and the hunger. And even as they gnawed through their remaining horsebone to get at the marrow, a spirit of optimism ran through them, especially at the end of day when they paused and were able to discuss the day's events and progress. They especially found solace, too, in sharing imagined images of the coming spring and their future in Italy.

Things took a sudden turn. To begin, as they reached the midpoint of their Alps crossing, the weather rapidly deteriorated and the snow flurries returned. Next, the wind resumed it merciless sweep southward, howling through the passes and down into the valleys like some uncaged monster released by angry Norse gods wreaking revenge upon the people of southern Europe. Then, as they reached the very mountain pass where months earlier the Germans had ambushed the Tuscany bound wagon train, one of the ponies fell to its knees from sheer exhaustion and hunger.

"In the wagon!" cried Duxia, her shawl trailing wildly behind her as the wind nearly swept her tiny frame over the ledge.

Fernando and Mala, too, were struggling against the wind, and catching sight of the fallen pony, knew immediately that it was dead.

"We'll have to wait things out till morning!" Fernando shouted to Mala, trying to be heard above the wind. Then he pulled her up into the rear wagon door.

This was a severe mistake in judgment. They would have been far better off unhitching the dead pony then moving the wagon off the top of the pass. As the wind struck from the north, howling directly into the pass, it gained velocity. The two opposing slopes formed a funnel of sorts, forcing the wind to compress as it squeezed between the two opposing slopes, thereby creating an even more brutal wind chill than at lower or less open sites along the mountain.

Once inside the wagon, the three slumped back against the walls of the wagon, spent. "It'll be dark soon," declared Duxia, "best that we all clump in the corner, pile everything in the wagon over us, and huddle together for warmth. Snow's not going to let up all night, nor is the wind." Then she looked about the interior of the wagon. "This could well be our grave by morning."

As she said this, a searing sensation seized Mala's stomach and sides, and she doubled over in agony. "Ah-hg!" she moaned. Then she felt herself go wet. When the pain subsided, she sat there staring blankly at her ballooned belly, and felt movement. "N-no . . ." she muttered in panic, then looked helplessly at Duxia.

Duxia's brows furrowed in puzzlement. "It's too early, Mala!"

Mala shrugged with wide eyes, too frightened to speak.

"What is it?" said Fernando, not comprehending this sudden alarm of the women.

Neither woman replied at first, then Duxia shook her head and in a low voice said, "It's the baby, Fernando, who has decided to enter life early. Not due for yet another month, but it's coming tonight, right here on this God forsaken pass in the midst of a blizzard. Light the candles, Fernando. It's going to be a long night."

Within hours Mala was in full labor. Duxia sat between her legs, struggling to calm her down, but her comforting words did little to soothe Mala's agony. Nor did Duxia's efforts do anything to calm Fernando who knelt behind her, holding a candle high to provide light. He had never witnessed childbirth, and was lost to the horror of it as Mala screamed out helplessly and writhed back and forth convulsively. And watching this, for Fernando, was worse even than the beating he had taken or the agony of recovering from his stab wounds. "O-hh, o-oh . . ." he mumbled over and over as his grip on the candle trembled incessantly, causing its meager light to shift here and there against the wagon walls.

"Be still, dammit!" Duxia shouted. "The baby's about to come!" And at that moment the baby's head began to breach as Mala cried out in terror, her thighs lurching upward. Duxia grasped Mala's hips and drove them back flat onto the wagon bed, then stuffed the remnant of a pony rib into Mala's mouth, shouting, "Here, bite down on this, Dear, and squeeze, dammit!"

Struggling to the limits of her endurance, Mala squeezed every fiber of muscle she could summon, and managed over the next minutes to expel the infant. Grabbing it, Duxia held it up for examination in Fernando's quaking light. "It's a . . . boy!" she cried. Looking closer, she caught her own reflection staring back at her in the glimmer of the infant's pallid grey eyes. Shoving the infant away from her onto Mala's belly, she backed away shuddering, and issued an unintellible burst of profanity in her native Finnish tongue.

"What is it, Duxia?" cried Mala, weakly raising her head. "What's wrong?"

"Nothing." Duxia hissed, closing her eyes, her mind traveling twenty years back in time to the moment she first pulled Tristan from Asta's womb. Then she issued that long sigh of the defeated. "Oh, but history repeats itself this night and Tristan's shadow now doubles," she whispered. Then she turned to Fernando and said, "Give me your knife!"

Watching Fernando hand Duxia his knife, Mala's eyes flared and she tried to raise up, wailing, "No! Duxia, don't kill my baby! Have mercy, I beg you!"

Duxia shoved her back down. "Be still, Mala! I shan't hurt the infant! I cut his cord."

CHAPTER FORTY-SEVEN

AN ICY TOMB

Despite the shelter of the wagon as it sat stranded at the top of the pass, those inside were unable to keep warm. The wagon had been shabbily built and gusts of frigid air continued to blast through the many cracks of its thin walls and floor. Fernando lit several more candles thinking they might alleviate the sting of the freezing temperature within, but they were useless in this endeavor.

The blizzard continued only to increase in strength throughout the night and the remaining pony had frozen to death well before daybreak. The rear and north side of the wagon was completely caked in snow and ice to the roof, and it took Fernando over an hour to work the back door open. Stepping outside to look about, the first thing he saw was the two ponies, their snouts peeled back in frozen, hideous fashion as though deliberately distorted by some horrid sculptor intent on frightening anyone foolish enough to take on the Alps in winter.

Nevertheless, Fernando took in the sight with near gratitude because they had gnawed the remnants of the original horse carcass to bone fragments two days earlier and had nothing to eat. *We'll now at least have something to sustain us until Spring*, he thought. *And with a little luck, perhaps other travelers may happen by and assist us before then.*

Hours turned into days, and days turned into a week. Nobody came. The unimaginable occurred: the weather turned even more severe. Although they were able to chew on frozen horsemeat to quell their aching stomachs, their fear of starvation was soon supplanted by their fear of freezing to death. By the middle of their second week marooned on the pass, their faces began to take on a ghostly bluish tint, and even as they lay huddled in a knot beneath blankets and clothes, they were soon scarcely able to move or speak. Mala did her best to keep the baby warm, swaddling it close to her swollen breasts. Wthin days, the weak, prematurely born infant became lethargic and ceased crying even. One morning as Mala awoke from her frozen sleep, she felt the baby's cold lips frozen to her nipple. It had perished in the night. "Oh!" she stirred, heartbroken, but so numb from the cold she was but barely able to utter sound. "Oh, God! Oh . . ."

Feeling something heavy against her side, she then turned her head, and found that it was Fernando, clinging to her in a tight curl. He, too, was cold to the touch, and his eyes were frozen open in a dead but content stare. Indeed, he had frozen to death in the night also, clinging to Mala and the baby, imagining that both were now his. He died thinking he was there within the wagon with his beautiful bride Mala, and their beautiful newborn son; that the wagon was sitting not upon a pass in the Alps, but sitting in the warm plains somewhere in his homeland of sunny Spain. So despite a lifetime of wandering and hardship, despite failed years of chasing the dream of Mala's love, he died in peace, mistakenly believing that all his dreams had finally been realized.

"Ughh!" Mala sighed, unable to move. Frozen there, she shifted her eyes over to Duxia, certain that she, too, had passed in the night. The old woman shifted within the pile, and her eyes blinked open with a start. Too frozen to move any further, she sat there, and like Mala, moved only her eyes. She first saw that Mala had pulled the blankets aside, and was clinging to the dead infant. Her eyes then shifted to the dead Fernando.

The two women then gazed at each other in silent helplessness, both unable to utter even a sound. In that meeting of their eyes a communion of tenderness arose that was so heart-wrenching and profound, words were not necessary. *As I lay here dying*, their eyes said, *I love you to the ends of this earth.*

Then they both closed their eyes . . . and found sleep.

CHAPTER FORTY-EIGHT

CARDINAL ODO REBUILDS

When the wagon train reached Canossa in early September, Countess Mathilda immediately began rearming and refinancing her offensive against the Germans. Her first action was to secure a narrow land corridor all the way from Tuscany to Rome along the western coastline of Italy, which she succeeded in doing by October. And though the Germans still held the territory from Lombardy in northern Italy to Rome itself, she managed to wrestle the coastal city of Ostia from them which was adjacent to Rome. This meant that Mathilda could now freely send messengers and small troop contingents up and down the entire length of the western Italian coastline. This greatly improved her ability to communicate directly with both Desiderius and Cardinal Odo in Monte Cassino, and also gave her access to Duke Roger Borsa and his brother Bohemud who controlled Lower Italy.

Capitalizing on this newfound control of the western coastline, Odo began to travel back and forth to Canossa for purposes of conspiring with Mathilda against the Germans. Then, too, he withdrew his damnation sentence from Duke Borsa and began making diplomatic overtures to him in order to re-establish the alliance that had previously bound him to the Gregorian Papists against King Heinrich.

"We must hold together against the German king and his anti-pope," Odo warned Borsa during reconciliation talks, "for he is not only a threat to the true Church, but he still conspires with Emperor Alexius and the Byzantines in the east to invade your realm in Lower Italy." Then Odo completely surprised Borsa with his next move. "I know that I disagreed with how you forced the Pope's crown on Desiderius and that I supported his rejection of it," he declared to Borsa, "but I now vow to become your partner in trying to convince Desiderius to accept the office." Stunned by this gesture, Borsa quickly went to a knee and kissed the hem of Odo's Cardinal's robe, vowing to once again take up arms against Heinrich.

Odo did not do this so much to subvert his friend Desiderius as he did out of pure practicality. He had determined that such an arrangement was the only means of holding the Germans in check, and quickly began a series of private negotiations with his old friend.

"I will stand by your side at every moment, Desiderius," promised Odo. "And though you may feel weak or frightened, I shall be like your suit of armor. If you feel faint, I will hold you up. If you cannot speak, I will be your voice. If you cannot decide, I will be your counsel."

Desiderius was at first dumbfounded to learn that his lifelong friend had now unexpectedly changed his stance. After many long and intimate conversations, Odo's gentle and persuasive manner began to open his ear to the possibility. In Odo's favor was the fact that Desiderius was beginning to feel better than he had months earlier, and had risen considerably from the trough of depression triggered by the forced papacy.

By New Year's Day, then, all of Cardinal Odo's hard work, travel, and diplomacy began to take root. Consequently, in late January he summoned Tristan to a meeting with Mathilda in Canossa. Tristan, upon his and Guillaume's delivery of the wagon train to Countess Mathilda, had been assigned by Odo to serve as his private courier and spokesperson in absentia.

"Shed the disguises," Odo had told him in October, "for we shall soon aggressively mobilize our new strategy. Your sole role now shall be as one of my public diplomatic legates."

"What about the underground?" asked Tristan, stunned by Odo's announcement.

"In your past. You shall now, along with me, *direct* the underground. I never intended to let you remain there for long, just long enough to get a taste of the danger and significance of the underground's efforts. Oh no, you are far too intelligent and valuable to risk getting killed in the mere acquisition and exchange of information. We need you to plot strategy."

"And Muehler, will he not object to me being his superior?"

"No. He well understands your potential and is in agreement with my decision. This past year you have proven yourself in the court of King Philippe, in the Cluny negotiations with Abbot Hugh and the Moors, and in your extraordinary success with the nobles of southern France."

Tristan was both humbled and overjoyed by this sudden elevation of his status, and knew that it would immediately cast him to the forefront of Gregorian politics. In that secret compartment of his heart that lay hidden from the world, the memory of Mala still nagged at him. He had never reconciled with her sudden disappearance from Marseilles and even now still continued to send inquiries to Benedictine agents throughout France seeking the whereabouts of her traveling Romani troupe.

Of course, he had no idea that Mala had set out to cross the Alps one month earlier during the same month of January, 1087, when he joined Odo and Mathilda in Tuscany. And certainly he had no idea whatsoever that Mala was pregnant with his child, nor that she, the child, Duxia, and Fernando were freezing to death in that high mountain pass of the Via Francigena on the very day that he rode his horse up the twisted road to the Canossa fortress. Instead, he imagined that she was happily dancing somewhere in southern France, having decided for some sudden and inexplicable reason that he had been little more than a passing fancy. *After all, she could have any man she wanted on this earth*, he thought. *I am a monk.*

This supposition had crushed him to the point of illness for months, and cultivated in his conscience a nascent and unspoken resentment over the fact that he had been directed since his boyhood days at Cluny into the Benedictine fold. And though Tristan conducted his public business with utmost professionalism, there fell upon him a sudden isolation in life that was devastating. And though this devastation had gutted Tristan for nearly six months, it went unnoticed by all except Guillaume and the Danes who, in their clannishness, only spoke of it amongst themselves. By the beginning of the New Year, he had finally managed to put Mala behind him. And though her memory remained, it seemed a hurtful and shadowy thing; a once intense inferno now reduced to ash.

The only thing on his mind then, as he met in Canossa with Odo, Mathilda, General Padule, and Guillaume that first day of February, was the information he was bringing from his recent mission in Lower Italy.

"Duke Borsa has committed to move his troops north on Rome in early March, barely a month from now," he said to the others, "but only if Cardinal Desiderius accepts the Papacy. Of course, I was not sure what to tell Borsa on that issue, Cardinal Odo."

"Desiderius has finally relented, to me in private before I left Monte Cassino to come here," said Odo. "You here at this very table are the first to hear the news, and you need to keep it confidential until we actually mobilize the troops. I do not wish to do anything that might alert the anti-pope." Then he looked at Mathilda and General Padule. "Can your army be ready to march south out of Tuscany in a month?"

"Yes . . . if need be," replied Padule.

"Hmm . . . is that hesitancy I detect, General?" said Odo.

It was Mathilda who answered. "No," she said, "it's just that we would feel more confident after word from Handel. He should be arriving from Germany any time now. In any case, we've sent Commander Balducci to escort him in from the Apennines as we did when Tristan and Guillaume returned from France. If fortune serves us well, in addition to more money and arms from the Saxon princes, Handel will be bringing in a contingent of Saxon mercenaries."

"I knew Handel's trip would be longer than my trip to France," said Tristan. "I returned in October and here it is the New Year already. What is taking him so long in Germany, Cardinal Odo?"

"In addition to gathering munitions and money as you did in France," Odo replied, "Handel was tasked with kindling a fire under the Saxons. He has been stirring dissension and revolt against Heinrich to ensure that Heinrich remains in Germany when we make our move against Rome. According to our couriers, he has been doing an excellent job. I assure you, he is on his way back now and will arrive on time to meet Balducci in the mountains."

"But he's moving his train through the Alps in winter," said Guillaume, showing doubt.

"Ha," Odo laughed, "Handel is from Bavaria and is more adept on ice than an alpine snow hare, even when dragging a full caravan behind him!" Then, bowing his head, Odo crossed himself, clasped his hands, and said, "My Brothers and my dear Sister Mathilda in Christ, we have much to look forward to and much to be thankful for, so let us pray. In nomine Patris et Filii et Spiritus Sancti . . . Lord Father in Heaven, guide our hands as we move against Satan's false emissary who now sits in the Vatican under the protection of our enemy, King Heinrich, a sinful excommunicate of your true Church and usurper of your servants' authority here on earth. In your name we pray, Amen!"

CHAPTER FORTY-NINE

A FROZEN DISCOVERY

Brother Handel was a superior winter logistician, and prior to moving his Saxon train into the Alps, he had made meticulous preparations for the crossing. Unlike the open wagons Tristan and Guillaume had employed in the warmer weather, Handel's wagons were covered, insulated, and outfitted with tiny pot-bellied, vented coal stoves for the troops' sleeping comfort at night. Certain wagons were also allocated to carry ample supplies of food, coal, and animal feed. In addition, each wagon was drawn by four large draft horses outfitted with crescent-shaped, cast-bronze horseshoes nailed to their hooves, the bottoms of which were studded for traction on ice. Handel also insisted that every man traveling with him be warmly clothed in heavy woolen winter garb, headgear, and gloves.

Moving south from Germany, he eventually intersected with the Via Francigena and took its path toward Tuscany. And though the weather was brutal, he carefully monitored the movement of the train and saw to it that both the men and the animals maintained a reasonable but not overly arduous pace.

As he led his caravan over a particularly high pass, he brought the train to a halt.

"What's that blocking the road up ahead at the top of the pass there?" he said to his lead teamster.

"Dunno," the teamster said, tightening the brake of his wagon then jumping down to chock his wheels. "Let's go see."

Handel tied his horse to the wagon and stepped ahead to inspect the blockage. "What the hell! It's a little wagon of some sort, stuck in the ice," he said. "And look at those two little ponies, frozen stiff." Then, moving to the back of the wagon, he pulled the ice hatchet from his belt and began hacking at the ice blocking the rear door.

"Hey, give me a hand," he called to the teamster, "damn thing's frozen shut."

After some effort the two men managed to pry the door free and the teamster then peered into the wagon. "Damn!" he whistled, quickly pulling his head back and looking at Handel. "Dead folks, must've got stranded up here and froze to death."

"What? Here, let me take a look," Handel said, lifting himself into the wagon. Then he saw the dead baby lying upon the woman's belly. He quickly made the sign of the cross and muttered a short prayer. "Mercy of Heaven, a baby, two women and a man," he whispered to himself, "what the hell were they thinking trying to cross the Alps in this rickety thing?"

As the words left his mouth, the blanket moved slightly and an icy hand touched his. One would think that Handel, because of the pervasive danger he endured as a hardened member of the Benedictine underground was fearless, but he was so startled by this unexpected, ghostly touch that he cried out in horror, thinking momentarily that one of the corpses was rising from the dead. Looking down upon the pallid face of the young woman before him, her eyes slowly open, and he realized that she was not dead after all, was merely trying to draw breath.

"She's alive!" he cried to the teamster, drawing her frozen hands into his in an effort to warm them. "Quick, get some sheepskins!" Then from behind him he heard another sigh. Turning, he caught sight of the old woman's ice-crusted eyelids slowly cracking open. "Another one's alive in here, too!" he cried. "Hurry!"

The teamster soon returned with an armload of furry sheepskin blankets and crawled up into the wagon. Mimicing what Handel was doing to warm the young woman, he reached for the baby and desperately began working on it until Handel shoved his hands away.

"The infant's dead!" Handel shouted, pointing at Duxia. "Tend to the old woman!"

After several minutes of rubbing the hands and faces of the two women, they buried them beneath the heavy sheepskins and Handel had the other men move them into the lead wagon and instructed them to fire up the coal stove. Half an hour later the two women began, by degrees, to show signs of recovery even though both still shivered and quaked beneath the sheepskins despite the warmth emanating from the stove. In their eyes Handel recognized that silent gaze of profound gratitude displayed by those who have been miraculously rescued from death but are yet too weak to speak.

"Heaven has spared you," he said, looking down at both of them, "so God must have a purpose for you yet."

CHAPTER FIFTY

ON TO CANOSSA

As the wagon train continued moving toward the Apennines Handel took great care in nursing Mala and Duxia. Though he could be merciless in his role as a spy and assassin he was nevertheless, in his heart of hearts, a Benedictine monk. The sight of the dead infant laying in its dying mother's embrace had torn at him, as had the realization of what these people had endured upon the pass. Offering a short prayer service, he had the bodies of Fernando and the infant covered and bound, then tied on the top of one of the wagons for transport. Normally bodies of the dead would be abandoned or cast over the ledge under such circumstances, but Handel refused to do so.

"We'll bury them properly in Canossa," he said. "Their corpses will keep atop the wagons in this cold and will be no bother to us."

Mala and Duxia were suffering from third degree frostbite, and as their wagon ambled through the mountains, they were only half aware of what was occurring around them.

The medical term for frostbite is congelation, and the effects of this condition are both dangerous and gruesome. At or below freezing temperature, blood vessels close to the skin begin to constrict and blood is shunted away from the extremities, causing the skin to become numb and develop white, red, and yellow patches. Though this constriction helps to preserve core body temperatures, this protective measure can also reduce blood flow to dangerously low levels. If freezing continues, as was Mala's and Duxias's case, the skin hardens and freezes, then blisters one or two days after freezing which results in temporarily loss of use of the area. This deeper frostbite causes purplish blisters which turn black and result in loss of feeling and nerve damage. Extreme frostbite may result in fingers and toes being amputated if the area becomes infected with gangrene, and if untreated, may cause them to simply fall off. Handel, knowing that it takes months to actually assess the true amount of damage incurred by frostbite, mixed his doctoring with prayer, hoping that neither woman would lose limb or life.

After several days, Duxia and Mala came out of their semi-conscious state and were actually able to move about and converse a bit. "My b-baby!" were the first words out of Mala's mouth. Though giving birth was a vaporous memory, she vaguely remembered holding and nursing her infant son. "Where is my child?"

"Gone," Duxia replied coldly. Though she hurt inside for Mala, she was bloated with hate for nature and for its creator, God. "Dead, Mala. Frozen to death like our ponies and like poor Fernando. Only you and I survived God's ordeal, so He can punish us more, I suppose."

At this Mala's eyes began to water. "It's not possible," she whispered, her voice dissolving into a soft sob. "Why would He *do* such a thing? What have I done to deserve such wrath at his hands?"

"Tristan de Saint-Germain, that's what," said Duxia. "He's a curse to all he touches, and just as certain as it is that we suffered, it's certain that he touched you and passed along his damnation, Mala. We should have died there, Dear, but we live, through the mercy of Lucifer."

"What?" said Mala, still crying to herself.

"Yes, Dear, as I lay dying I stared at your dead baby and dead Fernando and I prayed to Satan that he might at least deliver you and me from that frozen hell. It was my last thought before falling into the blackness. I remember that blackness now. In it I communed with Satan, and he embraced me, took me in his fold, told me that he would protect me from God's vengeance. Yes, Girl, 'tis Satan who sent these wagons our way to pull us from the pass."

This talk frightened Mala. "No more, Duxia," she said.

Duxia considered Mala with curious shining eyes a moment. "Oh, you foolish young thing. Though I love you more than life itself, you are deluded. Gain your strength, Dear, for we have work to do, you and I."

"Work? What are you talking about?"

"In that blackness as I lay freezing to death Lucifer showed me our future, Mala, and said he would help, but also said that we must earn *our* part."

"What?"

"Yes, that man Handel who saved us, he mentioned that the wagons are going to Canossa of all places."

"Canossa, is that in, Italy?"

At this Duxia cackled a bit. "Ha, it's in Tuscany my Dear, the very place we were headed to since leaving Lyons! What fortune, eh? Only Satan himself could set such a table!"

Mala's eyes opened wide, struck by this sudden information about the wagon train's destination. "Tuscany?" she said.

"Yes, these wagons are headed to the very doorstep of la Gran Contessa herself! So you see, my Sweet, the Black Prince has answered my prayers and opened the door. All we need do now is walk in."

CHAPTER FIFTY-ONE

RENDEZVOUS

Five days after discovering Mala and Duxia, Handel's train encountered Commander Balducci's camp along the Via Francigena in the Apennines.

"Hail, Handel!" Balducci shouted, riding up at a gallop. "Good to see these wagons!"

Handel gestured a greeting with his hand, but due to the beating he had received during their first encounter, he was not especially fond of the Tuscan commander. Even so, they rode together at the head of the column that next day after breaking camp and Handel managed to maintain a civil tongue, which was easy to do. Other than telling about finding the wagon frozen there, it was Balducci who did most of the talking.

"Yes, I'm having admirable success against the Germans in Tuscany at the moment," Balducci rattled on after already spending more than an hour recounting his heroics in saving Guillaume's wagon train months earlier during the German ambush. "Ah the Germans, what a dreadful, obnoxious breed of vermin, every damn one of them!"

"I beg your goddamn pardon, Balducci!" said Handel, "Have you forgotten that I myself am German and hail from Bavaria?"

"Ah, indeed," replied Balducci, too pompous to be even slightly embarrassed by his own gaffe. "I do suppose there is a sprinkle of decent Germans here and there now that I think of it."

The train paused to rest at noon, and Handel took this opportunity to check on Mala and Duxia. Balducci followed, and as he watched Handel speak to the women, tip water in their mouths, and slip slivers of cheese and smoked meat onto their tongues, the Tuscan commander was rather surprised by the care and concern Handel demonstrated.

"Did you not tell me these women must be peasants judging from the state of their wagon and horses that were stranded on the pass?" Balducci exclaimed loud enough for the women to hear. "I find it odd that you take such interest in them, especially in the middle of such an important mission." Then he pointed to the top of the wagon and said, "And dragging those two damn bodies all the way to Canossa with you surprises me also."

This irritated Handel; he knew that both women could hear every word. "I tend to these women, Balducci, because my family in Bavaria was also poor.

And to make things worse, when I was a boy my father lost both feet to frostbite after being caught in an avalanche and was then unable to provide for the family. People like you don't understand such things, do they?"

Unaccustomed to being spoken to in such a manner, Balducci reddened, but had no reply. Consequently, he was about to turn and leave when Mala raised her head slightly to get a glimpse of the man who had been addressing Handel. Whereas it is true that simple beauty can be marred by disaster or calamity, absolute beauty cannot be disguised by either. And at that moment, despite the blisters and splotch marks all over Mala's face, Balducci was instantly struck by the startling beauty of the eyes and face looking back at him. He was so affected, in fact, that he was struck dumb for a moment, then finally muttered, "U-uh, I request your pardon, my Lady, I did not mean to offend. I misspoke."

Mala neither scowled nor smiled. Her eyes fell upon Balducci's eyes, held there for several long seconds, and then her head slowly dropped back flat and she looked up at Handel. "Wh-who is that foul man?" she whispered weakly. "Tell him to go away, *please.*"

"That *foul* man is none other than Vincento Balducci," Handel replied, loud enough for Balducci to hear. "And though you would never suspect it, due to his lack of manners, he is a high lord of Tuscany."

Despite this reproach by Handel, Balducci remained in place, still peering into the wagon with the hope that the young woman might raise her head yet again. She didn't, so he then finally shrugged and left.

"He's gone," Handel said to Mala. "Please take nothing he said to heart. He's merely another aristocrat who thinks much of himself and little of others. People like us are of no interest to him. Anything he might say or think is of little interest to us, eh?"

Mala nodded in agreement. Neither she nor Handel, noticed that Duxia had taken careful measure of the brief exchange involving Balducci, nor that a keen expression was beginning to form about her eyes. She had heard the Tuscan nobleman's callous comments, but then also detected something completely different in his voice as he gazed at Mala and apologized after she raised her face to him. *A good sign,* she thought, closing her eyes, *there will be noblemen such as this all about in Tuscany, and once Mala gets well, she will start catching their eye.*

CHAPTER FIFTY-TWO

OH, DUXIA!

Handel immediately attempted to have Mala and Duxia moved into the infirmary when they got to the Canossa fortress, but it was filled to overflowing with wounded. Handel told the story of the frozen pass and Mathilda had them moved into private quarters within Huntsman's Hall, the grand complex where feasts were held and dignitaries were entertained.

"You'll be far more comfortable here," Mathilda said to the two women as they lay within large beds finely furnished with plush quilts and elegant coverings, "and enjoy much more privacy as you recover. My servants will take care of your needs and I'll have the infirmarians check on you daily."

Touched by this, Mala sat up in her bed and extended her hand to Mathilda. As Mathilda's hand met hers, Mala kissed it. "You are generous beyond Heaven itself," she said, on the verge of tears.

"Those who have much should give much," Mathilda replied. Then she looked at Handel and said, "The two bodies strapped to the wagon you mentioned, we shall hold a short service for their departed souls tomorrow morning in the cathedral. Cardinal Odo is still here so I will ask him to make arrangements. Afterwards, we will hold a burial ceremony in the cemetery."

"Ah, I didn't realize the Cardinal was here," said Handel. "What an honor it will be to have the most respected Cardinal of all Christendom give the final benediction."

"Yes, Cardinal Odo arrived two weeks ago for a strategy meeting with General Padule and me. Guillaume and Tristan were here briefly also, but Guillaume had to return to Montelucio and the Cardinal sent Tristan south to meet with the Normans."

As the Countess uttered the name "Tristan", Mala gave a start. Duxia saw this and quickly shot Mala a glance and placed a finger to her mouth. *Say nothing,* the gesture said.

"Yes," Mathilda continued, "Tristan is such a skilled diplomat for one so young. I am so proud of him, and of Guillaume as well. Such exceptional nephews, both of them." Then, as she led Handel to the door she said, "Ladies, I shall say a special prayer tonight for your swift recovery." Turning, she settled her eyes upon Mala and added, "And in the morning, my poor dear, we shall bless and bury your unfortunate child and husband."

"Thank you, Countess," interrupted Duxia. "I pray this is not asking too much, but my niece Mala and I would wish to attend the funeral services in the morning. Would that be at all possible?"

Mathilda thought a moment. "Yes, certainly. We could carry you on litters to the cathedral, then on to the gravesite."

"One final thing, Countess," Duxia added quickly. "After the funeral, would it be possible for Mala and me to have a private audience with you here in this room?"

"Yes, of course. I shall be happy to speak with you after the funeral."

"I heard you say that Cardinal Odo de Lagery is present here within the fortress, Countess. Would it be possible for him to attend also?"

Mathilda tilted her head, puzzled, then looked at Handel. "Indeed, I shall inquire," she replied. "I cannot imagine that he would object."

The moment Mathilda and Handel left the room, Duxia looked across at Mala and said, "Henceforth I am your aunt, understand?"

"But . . ."

"No buts, Mala. Being an aunt to those two boys obviously means something to the Countess, so she will understand my aunt relationship to you, which will in turn work in our favor."

"Duxia, she believes Fernando to be my husband."

"Yes, probably that man Handel assumed such a thing finding Fernando in the wagon and passed it along to her. We will clarify everything in the morning when we speak to her and the Cardinal in private."

"I'm a bit confused about this meeting you requested, Duxia. What exactly am I to say?"

"V-e-r-y little, Dear. Allow me to do the talking. I will lay everything out, and if it becomes necessary for you to speak, keep an eye to me. I'll nod one way or another. Mala, I saw how you reacted to her mention of Tristan. For God's sake, Girl, I think you still love that bastard despite all the hell he's dragged us both through! You better think long and hard during the funeral in the morning. And when they throw that frozen earth over Fernando's body, think back on all he did for you and how faithfully he stuck by you, only to freeze to death in the Alps. And when they close the earth up over your baby boy, Mala, you better think about the life he never had because that infant will be coming back to you for the rest of your existence . . . in moments of regret and in dreams. *That's* what Tristan de Saint-Germain has wrought!"

Mala sat motionless in her bed, numbly listening to Duxia, submitting to her without a word.

Duxia was not finished. "Oh, Girl, I pray you are listening to everything I'm telling you, for if you falter now, we are both lost! I am old and don't have much further to go, but you, Dear, are so young and what you do these next few days will determine the remainder of your existence! Oh, Mala, swear to me that you will do as old Duxia says!"

Without a word, Mala slowly nodded yes. As she did, a large tear began to form in one eye, then slowly began to roll down her still discolored cheek. Then the floodgates opened and she threw herself down sideways onto the bed, burying her face with an arm; it had all become too much to bear. Everything dropped upon her at once like a crushing weight: the horror of the pass, the frozen ponies, Fernando, and above all her dead baby. "Oh, God, what have you done to me!" she sobbed with abandon. "Oh, God, why have you forsaken me?"

Duxia watched this, her heart about to burst, and even she began to feel the onset of tears, then she tightened her lip and crossed her arms. "Yes, Dear, let it all out now," she said. "Rid yourself of every tear in that lost, mangled heart of yours because in the morning the well must be dry and you must be strong."

Mala soon cried herself to sleep. And as Mala had warned, the infant came to her in a dream that very night. It was a pleasant dream where Mala was sitting outside in the warmth of some southern location bouncing the beautiful baby upon her lap as the baby cooed and laughed, its bright grey eyes shimmering in the light of the sun. Tristan was there, smiling lovingly at both of them, then the dream turned, and Tristan's face turned dark and he rushed at her and the child, pulling an ax from behind his back. "Ah-hg!" she moaned, trying to drag herself and the baby from the sudden nightmare, but she could not come awake and at once Tristan was upon them. Everything turned black, and though she saw nothing, she could hear the methodical thunk of the ax into flesh and bone. Screaming aloud, she bolted upright then and came awake, bathed in sweat as her entire frame trembled and shook. The sensation of the dream was so succinct, so precise, that she thought it real at first, and it took a full minute to shake herself free of it. Then, shivering, she set her head back down and cried softly, afraid to seek sleep for fear that the nightmare would resume.

CHAPTER FIFTY-THREE

A SIN UNCOVERED

Immediately after leaving Mala and Duxia, Mathilda sought out Cardinal Odo and shared the women's gruesome experience in the Alps.

"A pity the poor child was not baptized," said Odo, crossing himself. "Yes, we shall naturally hold a service in the morning for both man and child."

The funeral service consisted of mass celebrated by Cardinal Odo who also provided a short segment of touching words about the deceased during the homily. As nobody at Canossa knew the deceased, the service was sparsely attended with only Mala, Duxia, Mathilda, Handel, Odo, Balducci, and a sprinkling of Canossa clerics present. No one was quite sure why Balducci was there, but when he found out about the service from Handel, he insisted on attending for some reason.

As promised, Mala and Duxia were carried into the cathedral on litters, and though they sat through most of the mass service grim-faced and still, they both became weepy during the homily. At the gravesite, as they began to lower the swaddled infant into the grave and cover it with earth, Mala began to shiver uncontrollably as though overcome by a seizure, and her lips began to riffle in sporadic bursts, as though she was talking to herself. Handel, who was standing beside her litter, crouched down and placed an arm about her shoulder to comfort her, but his action did nothing to stop Mala's quaking. He also failed to understand what Mala was mumbling to herself, though he could tell there was an extreme bitterness in her tone. Then, when the last shovel of earth was thrown upon the infant's grave, she fell still, as though at peace.

The litter carriers then returned Mala and Duxia to their quarters as Mathilda and Odo followed.

"So," Odo said to Mathilda, "you told me yesterday that the older woman asked to speak to you privately, then also asked for me by name to be there also?"

"Yes, it seemed a bit odd at the time, I confess. She probably wishes to thank me for assisting them and thank you for arranging the funeral service."

The moment they entered the women's room and the door was closed, the ever watchful Odo immediately perceived from the look of the old woman's face that she was about to reveal something troubling. He pulled two stools between the two beds and motioned for Mathilda to take a seat.

"The loss of a husband and child is a heart-wrenching trial of the human spirit," he said, looking at Mala, "and our prayers are with you in this moment of loss."

Mala was about to respond, but Duxia spoke first. "The man we buried, Cardinal Odo, was not her husband."

"Oh?" said Odo, looking at Mathilda who had mistakenly described the relationship the day before. "I see. He is the father of the child we buried, I assume?"

"No," said Duxia.

"Well then," said Odo, a bit confused. "A brother, perhaps?"

"No. Fernando was merely a friend. A loyal and trustworthy friend who was trying to help us get to Tuscany. We were coming to seek assistance for Mala and the child from the child's father."

"I see," said Odo. "Then Mala's husband is here in Tuscany?"

Duxia did not reply at first. After glancing at Mala a moment, she said, "Cardinal, Mala has no husband."

"The child was then . . . illegitimate?" said Mathilda.

"Yes," nodded Duxia, "the bastard son of a high person of Italy with connections in Tuscany. We have fallen on hard times and did not wish the child to suffer so we were coming to seek assistance from the father's family."

The lechery of the noble class was not only legendary in Europe at this time, but accepted in most quarters. Bastard children of the aristocracy were common and could be found in each and every province of the continent. Though a fortunate few such as William the Bastard of Normandy were able to claim a place at their father's table, the vast majority were fathered by wenches and peasant girls, therefore disclaimed and forgotten. Cardinal Odo de Lagery was a Cluniac reformist, and like most men of that Benedictine order, had declared war on immorality both within and outside the Church.

Mathilda, being a rabid supporter of the Gregorian reform movement, also shared Odo's views on immorality, so she spoke up. "It's a sad situation when a young lady such as this is exploited by the more fortunate," she said, pointing to Mala. "If we know who the father is, especially if he is in Tuscany, it is well possible that the Cardinal and I may be able to make him assist you. Even though the infant has died, it appears that you and your niece need help at the moment. So pray tell, what is the father's name?"

Once again Mala began to speak, but Duxia's eyes narrowed in on her, she remained silent. "I will mention his name in a moment," said Duxia. First a question or two to you both, if you do not object?"

Odo and Mathilda shrugged in unison. "Of course not," said Mathilda.

"Cardinal," Duxia began, "at the very heart of Benedictine reform is the issue of personal and political corruption and personal and political immorality. The Benedictines alone on this earth have taken a firm stand in favor of righteousness. I applaud you, especially since you have even determined to clean your own house, the Church. My question is, Cardinal, do you as a high cleric of the Benedictine order truly believe in your doctrine of reform? Will you stand by it at any cost?"

The integrity of men of Odo's Church credentials and stature were rarely challenged except by each other, and never from people of common birth.

Nevertheless, Odo mulled over Duxia's words a short while, then said, "An unexpected but reasonable question. The answer is yes, and yes. I believe in morality and I stand by it."

Duxia then turned to Mathilda. "As the greatest proponent on the continent of Pope Gregory VII before his death, and now as a loyal Gregorian papist, I ask you the very same two questions, my Lady."

Without hesitation Mathilda said, "Absolutely I believe in these principles, and stand by them, otherwise I would not risk war and death itself to fight my cousin, King Heinrich of Germany."

"Very well then," Duxia nodded, "I shall now name the father of the child we buried this morning." But then, oddly, she fell silent.

Mala had listened to everything Duxia had been saying, knowing that she possessed the strength and backbone of a Belgian draft horse, and knowing that she was not intimidated by anyone. Now, in the pall of Duxia's unexpected silence, Mala thought that the old woman was faltering, but she was mistaken. Duxia was not in retreat, but calculating the most effective way possible to ambush these two grand figures of Europe and throw them into chaos.

"Let me begin," she said finally, "by stating that when I mentioned the father of Mala's child was a "high person of Italy with connections in Tuscany", I was not referring to a person of "nobility." Then she fell silent again, giving Odo and Mathilda time to weigh this first surprise.

"Continue," said Mathilda with impatience, falling further and further into puzzlement.

Odo relaxed, he had decided that the two bedridden women were so poverty-stricken that a high person of Italy to them was probably merely a local knight or a political figure of minor impact.

"Yes," he said, "continue."

"This high person of Italy represents the Church," Duxia declared. "Not the church of the anti-pope and King Heinrich, but the Gregorian Church. This high person of Italy I speak of is a Benedictine."

At this, Odo and Mathilda both sat up and looked at each other simultaneously, which caused Duxia to again fall silent for the purpose of giving them time to weigh this second surprise.

Odo spoke immediately. "A Benedictine you say? Now, by that do you mean a monk, or do you mean a bishop, archbishop, or cardinal?"

"A monk."

Odo and Mathilda both felt more reassured with this response. Both knew the lower Benedictine ranks possessed a handful of errant monks. "Very well," sighed Mathilda, "give us his name and Cardinal Odo will see to it that he is brought forward and reprimanded."

"It is not a reprimand that we seek, my Lady, but assistance. An opportunity to make a new beginning."

"Yes," said Mala, speaking for the first time. "Until the pregnancy, I was self-sufficient. I had a troupe of musicians and we were doing well. When the baby came, they all abandoned us, except Fernando. I was then going to open a little shop in Lyons, but we were robbed. Then winter came and we began to starve and freeze, and our only hope was to come to Italy as my aunt has explained!"

"Very well," said Odo, "this all makes sense and I understand what brings you here. So tell me, who is the father?"

Mala fell silent and stared down at her lap, which caused Duxia to again speak up. "The father, Cardinal, is very close to you." Then she turned to Mathilda. "The father is close to you also, my Lady. He is your nephew, Tristan de Saint-Germain."

Duxia's strategy of slowly urging and prompting Odo and Mathilda to a scaffold of their own devise could not possibly have been more effective in knee-capping the two. Odo's jaw dropped in an expression of abject disbelief while Mathilda fell into an immediate rage.

"Oh! Not possible!" she cried, standing and pointing an accusatory finger at the old woman. "It is all a lie! Oh, you horrid old bitch, how could you fabricate such a monstrous story! I'll have you both dragged out of here and thrown over the cliffs of Canossa!"

More calm than Mathilda, but equally distressed by what Duxia had said, Odo stared a moment at Duxia, thinking that the old woman had done most of the talking, therefore she was the one who had hatched this shameful scheme to pick the Church's pocket. He next looked at Mala and determined that she looked more credible. Besides, her actions at the gravesite had revealed sincerity. "Young woman, is there any truth to any of this?" he said, standing over her bed.

Intimidated by the imposing symbolism of his scarlet Cardinal's robe and his frightening height, she looked over to Duxia, then meekly nodded yes. Misunderstanding this exchange of glances, Odo took it for a possible sign of collusion, and this fueled anger in him. "I am a Cardinal of Rome, young woman," he said with heat, "if you lie to me, you lie to a direct representative of God himself!" Then, moving to an adjacent table, he retrieved the leather-bound, beautifully calligraphied copy of the Bible that lay upon it. Glowering, he dropped it into Mala's lap with such anger that he broke into Latin for a moment. Then, pointing at her angrily, he said, "Swear to me on the Holy Book, young woman, and if you lie, burn forever in Hell for lying upon the words of God himself!"

Cowering, Mala placed her trembling hand upon the Bible and cried, "In the name of God, all we have said is true! I swear it! Tristan de Saint-Germain is the father of my dead child!" Then she dissolved into weeping, burying her head beneath the blanket to be away from the Cardinal.

This infuriated Duxia and she flung her own blanket aside and rose up from her bed. And slip of the woman she was, she struck Odo across the face. "Oh you pretentious bastard!" she screamed. "You are worse than the filthiest nobles alive! You preach righteousness to others, but don't mean a word of it!" Reaching onto Mala's bed, she then grabbed the Bible and hurled it at him. "Burn in Hell yourself you goddamn hypocrite!" Then, her eyes darting about the room in search of something else to throw, her eyes settled on the stools from which Odo and Mathilda were retreating. Grabbing one, she hurled it, then followed with the other.

Warrior that Mathilda was, she was not accustomed to insanity, and the savage behavior of the old woman now suddenly gone berserk caused her to grab Odo by the hand, quickly leading him out of the room and slamming the door behind them. "She's a demon!" Mathilda huffed. "I'll call the guards and have her put in chains!"

Even though they had left, Duxia continued to fume and somehow storm about the room throwing anything she could set her hands despite the frostbite injuries that had previously incapacitated her. "Oh, Heinrich of Germany, I pray that you prevail and grind these Gregorians into the dust!" she screamed. "Oh, Lucifer, Prince of Darkness, cast misfortune onto every single damned one of them until they exist no more!"

CHAPTER FIFTY-FOUR

ODO'S DILEMMA

Mathilda, though a godly woman, was fully prepared to have Mala and Duxia removed from their quarters and forced from Canossa, but Cardinal Odo restrained her from doing so. "Though I doubt their story, Mathilda, we should not cast them out into the cold, especially after what they have already endured in the Alps."

"The way that old bitch spoke to you, Cardinal, such a disgrace! And such sacrilege, throwing the Bible at you like that! Besides, we can't let them get away with such criminality."

"Best that we first step back and consider this," said Odo. "The anger I witnessed in the old woman, it was the fury of righteousness. I wonder, were she framing a web of lies, would she have been so indignant?"

"Surely you don't believe her? Or that Tristan could become embroiled in such a mess?"

"No, I will need to speak to him about this. This young woman, she seems a faint memory to me from the past for some reason. As for Tristan, though innocent, he should at least know that these women are slinging accusations in his direction. He is returning to Monte Cassino from final talks with Duke Borsa in Lower Italy in a week. I will leave in the morning and intercept him there. In the meanwhile, Mathilda, I request that you not speak of this development."

"Certainly. The two women will surely wag their tongues, don't you think?"

"No, I will speak to them this evening and let them know that I am investigating the allegations. I will also inform them that should they speak to anyone of this before I reach resolution, they shall both be imprisoned until formally charged, then severely punished."

Odo spent the next several hours wrestling over the tale provided by the two women, especially the younger one who he realized he had met at the Cluny monastery many years before as a young girl. He also examined the possibility that Tristan had indeed somehow become entangled with her, though he refused to accept it. Then, as evening fell, he went to see Mala and Duxia.

"Ah, the Cardinal returns," snapped Duxia who had returned to her bed, "undoubtedly to frighten us with more threats of eternal damnation, eh?"

"No," replied Odo calmly, "I have come to gather more information. And if your answers bear any merit whatsoever, then I shall next address Brother Tristan de Saint-Germain."

This satisfied Duxia and she pointed to Mala. "Very well then, she'll answer any questions you may have, and then you'll see that everything we've said is true."

Odo gathered one of the stools from the floor that Duxia had thrown earlier and scooted it next to Mala's bed. "Your name is Mala and you are Romani?" said Odo, taking a seat. "I seem to vaguely remember years ago meeting a beautiful Romani woman when I was Grand Prior at Cluny. She was on her way to Spain, I believe."

"Yes," said Mala, surprised that Odo remembered that occasion, "that was my mother, and we came to visit Tristan on our way south. It was me who insisted that we stop by to see him."

"Hmm, you were a child back then."

"Yes, about twelve or so, and Tristan was nine."

"What was your business with Tristan at such a young age?"

"Two years before, on his way to Cluny, the men with him rescued me and my Romani cousins from being kidnapped by Norsemen who had slipped down the Seine toward Paris. That's how I met him, Cardinal."

"I see. Still, you came all the way back to see him at Cluny two years later on the way to Spain? And you were twelve?"

"Yes, since that night I first met him, I never quit thinking of him even though I was a child. I came to Cluny yet a third time when I was about fifteen and on my own for the purpose of living there so I could be near him, but he left for Rome that very next morning with you. I was heartsick over his departure and remained in Cluny for several years hoping he might return. He didn't, until being ordained in the Benedictine order. I was in Paris by then, but came to Cluny for his ordination ceremony."

Odo digested all she had said so far, and realized that to this point, everything was true. "A strange thing, your relationship with Tristan," he said. "You were a child when you met him, then only saw him several times over a ten or twelve year period, yet you came to his ordination?"

"Yes, I was hoping perhaps that I could convince him not to become a monk, but it was far too late."

"Oh? And why did you not wish him to become a Black Monk?"

"Because I loved him and hoped we could have a life together."

"I see," said Odo, glancing over at Duxia who sat there staring at him grim-faced and certain. "Then tell me, when did you next see Tristan? After he became a monk, I mean."

"He came to me in the Loire Valley this past year. My entertainment troupe was camped along the river and he just *appeared*."

Knowing that Tristan had never been sent by either Muehler or himself to the Loire Valley, Odo's faith in Tristan only solidified upon hearing this part of Mala's tale. Yet he chose not to deny her words, thinking that by allowing her to continue, she would only further mire herself in contradictions. "Ah, the Loire Valley, a beautiful place," he said. "Tell me, what was he doing in the Loire Valley?"

"I'm not sure. He further confused me because he wasn't wearing the black robe, nor was his crown shaved in the tonsure of Benedictines as it was the night he was ordained. I was overjoyed. I thought he had left the Brotherhood perhaps, but he told me he had some kind of *dispensation* or some such thing. All I know is that he was passing through Orléans in early spring and was on his way to Paris. Then he came back to me in the Loire, but had to report to Cluny and . . ."

"Oh, I see," mumbled Odo abruptly, struggling to remain devoid of emotion. The very first tentacles of alarm had begun to slip toward him and take hold as he wondered how she could possibly know that he had been to Paris, then Cluny, that previous spring unless Tristan had informed her of such. Then too, he realized that Orléans, though south of Paris, was not entirely out of the way if one was headed to the court of King Philippe.

"Then he came to me in Marseilles in early June," Mala continued, unaware of his redness or that his attention was focusing on every word she uttered. "It was there that we slept together. Well, we slept together in the Loire Valley, too, but it was in Marseilles that we . . ." Here she blushed and paused a moment. "It was in Marseilles that I became pregnant."

Odo placed the fingertips of his right hand across his brow in an effort to betray no emotion although he was beginning to feel consumed by that sudden illness that overwhelms one when confronted with the unacceptable. Duxia spotted his faltering and clucked with satisfaction.

"There, my good Cardinal, you can see that this young woman before you is no criminal. She's done nothing except become the victim of one of your so-called reformist holy men. So now you must decide whether to take the high road or crawl into the gutter inhabited by the very worms of this world who you purport to be fighting. Since arriving in France a lifetime ago, I've heard praise upon praise for the great cleric, Odo de Lagery! We'll see whether you match your pedestal, or whether you're just another goddamned pretender."

CHAPTER FIFTY-FIVE

A COLLAPSE OF FAITH

Throughout history those who have chosen to serve God directly by wearing the collar, the robe, or the habit have possessed a different mindset than other human beings. To begin, these individuals were either born with or somehow developed an entirely different spiritual frame of reference than their counterparts. Then, despite isolation from normal society, they have devoted their entire existence to saving those who inhabit the secular world. And finally, though the Church could often prove to be a means of advancement in Medieval Europe, life for the vast majority of the religious in Europe was fundamentally an existence of sacrifice and deprivation.

In the case of Odo de Lagery who was born into the high aristocracy of France, he actually abandoned a future of wealth and privilege to follow and honor God. His intelligence, wisdom, and leadership capabilities caused him to quickly rise within the structure of French Catholicism, and also brought him notice from the Vatican and Pope Gregory VII himself. Now, as he traveled back to Monte Cassino to question Tristan de Saint-Germain, he reflected upon his own past and the myriad of circumstances that had propelled him to the top of the Church hierarchy. He also spent a great deal of time thinking about Tristan who had been sent to him as a boy of seven as the result of his father's disgrace and execution.

As Odo thought back on the young boy of seven, he could not help but smile. The child was uncommonly handsome, beautiful even, and intelligent beyond belief. Due to the army of tutor nuns under his mother's service, the boy was already fluent in multiple languages, could read and write masterfully, and was highly versed in the history of Europe and the Catholic Church. Odo, consequently, had quickly taken the young phenom under his wing and mentored him until the age of majority when he chose to join the Benedictine order.

During those years together, Tristan had become like a son to him, following him about like a shadow, clinging to him for approval and knowledge. And as time passed Tristan developed an uncommon idolatry for Odo, and Odo an uncommon bond to the boy. Then, as the boy grew, his extraordinary gifts became unexpectedly useful to the Benedictines and eventually even to Pope Gregory himself. There was no one else on this earth, then, that Cardinal Odo de Lagery loved more than young Tristan de Saint-Germain.

Yet, Odo had unexpectedly been thrown into an acute dilemma, and for the first time in their relationship, Odo began to doubt his young liege. It was with both doubt and apprehension then that Odo embraced Tristan as they met within the underground complex of Monte Cassino.

"Ah, lad," said Odo, kissing Tristan on the cheek. It felt to Odo like the kiss of Judas. Tristan was smiling with delight at being in the company of his beloved father figure, unaware of anything that had recently transpired in Canossa.

"Good news from Lower Italy!" exclaimed Tristan. "Now that he and his half brother Bohemud are assured that Cardinal Desiderius will accept the Pope's tiara, they are *both* ready to march on Rome."

"Splendid," said Odo. His expression was blank.

Knowing that his news of Borsa and Bohemud would have normally elated the Cardinal, Tristan immediately sensed the shadow covering Odo's brow.

"Ah, something must have gone awry while you were in Canossa," Tristan said, taking a seat. "Bad news with Handel's wagon train?"

"No, Handel is fine," said Odo, joining Tristan at the table. "There is something else." Odo lowered his head a measure then, leaning it into his palm. "Something concerning yourself, Tristan. Please know, I have died a thousand times within my coach as I traveled south to meet you, but now that I am here, must question you on certain accusations."

Odo said all this without looking up, his forehead still buried in his palm. This struck Tristan as he had never once over their years together seen Odo shrink or hesitate from any challenge. He knew, therefore, that something extraordinary was afloat.

"Accusations?" he said, lacing his fingers together upon the table, sitting at attention.

"Yes," replied Odo, finally looking up. "A young woman and her aunt arrived in Canossa with Handel's wagon. They were both nearly dead from the cold, having been stranded in the Alps."

"Indeed," said Tristan, unable to make any connection whatsoever between himself and Odo's words.

"Yes. And Tristan, I remember a young girl who came to visit you as a child at Cluny monastery many years ago . . ."

Nothing that Odo would have invented could have seemed more disconnected to Tristan at that moment. When Tristan had heard the word accusation, the only thing streaming through his imagination was that someone had falsely accused him of embezzling some of the resources he had recently acquired from the southern French nobles. Odo had mentioned a long forgotten visit, which made no sense.

Odo continued, his face lacking color. "That young girl and her mother who came to see you, the reason I remember them is because they were Romani, and I had heard of the Romani people at that time, but had never once encountered any of them in France. The girl's name was Mala, Tristan, was it not?"

Tristan's eyes slowly dropped to his clasped hands as he continued trying to decode Odo's narrative. Saying nothing, he nodded.

Odo moved forward. "My question to you is, Tristan, have you encountered this young woman, Mala, since your ordination into the order?"

When one is suddenly and unexpectedly confronted with the unimaginable unveiling of his own illicit actions, one quickly begins to drown in a sea of confusion. This is precisely what occurred to Tristan who one moment earlier was fine, but now was lost. Turning scarlet, he uttered a few words at first, which dissolved into incoherent mutterings. He then floundered about for some means of answering Odo's question with legitimacy without hanging himself, but found it impossible to lie to the man he loved above all other men in life. Consequently he resigned himself to saying nothing.

"Very well," Odo pressed, "since you elect silence, I will tell you what this Mala has said. She informed me that you met her near Orléans in the Loire Valley twice."

Tristan's jaw tightened and he closed his eyes.

"Then you met her again in Marseilles," Odo continued. "If this is all true, as your silence now seems to verify, not only have you violated the moral code of the Benedictine reform movement, but you have breached the secrecy vow of the Benedictine underground." Then Odo's manner of forced calm descended into agitation and he raised his voice. "Integrity, responsibility, trust of the people . . . all violated! You have acted in an unethical manner, Tristan, in the face of both the Church and God!"

Tristan had up to this point accepted all that Odo had said in silent and shameful humility, but noting these specific words of Odo's final sentence, the dam spilled forth and Tristan unexpectedly erupted.

"Oh, the Church!" he cried, jumping to his feet in anger. "How can you mention it in the same breath with integrity, responsibility, and trust of the people? The Church is no better than the people, no better than our enemies! We conspire, scheme, create war, delude the ignorant, and assassinate! Yes, yes, I am guilty as accused of being with this girl whom I love! But no more guilty of sin than every man who wears the collar, yourself included, Father!"

Hearing Tristan inadvertently call him "Father," Odo's eyes closed with remorse over the direction this heated exchange was now bound, and he felt a violent piercing occur within his heart. Nevertheless, he stood rooted with priest-like rigidity and cried, "Oh, what a nursery of false hope and aspirations is your soft, naive heart, my boy! That impenetrable head of yours continues to incline toward the insignificant while great events swirl around you. Yes, we conspire, and even assassinate. When a demonic beast blocks the sun, we must kill it in order to gain light. We must be savage if we are to save civilization, of that I am sure!"

"Oh, excellent! Such a colorful analogy, and so selfserving, Cardinal!" cried Tristan, his forehead swelling with anger. "As for me, I am no longer sure of anything. I've watched us preach virtue while not believing in it and learned there is more misery among the poor than decency among the high clergy. I've watched myself spin crafty schemes in the darkness of these very tunnels while disregarding such obstructions as the commandments or the conscience, and wondered where, oh where, did I learn such corruption! I'll tell you where, from *YOU*, and from the Gregorian Church!"

At this Odo's mouth fell open and he fell motionless witnessing the accusations written within the lines of Tristan's face.

"Oh, the great Gregorian reformists!" Tristan continued, his fury mounting. "Preaching virtue while not practicing it. Insisting on chastity and non-marriage for its clerics . . . which by the way is something invented by zealous reformists, not God! Priests and monks have always been allowed to marry until this reform movement when a small corps of men invented new laws and tricks like court magicians of some ill breed! Oh yes! I am guilty as charged of violating the magicians' new rules because I fell in love with a woman and wanted to be with her!" Tristan continued, his face turned blue by the frustrated weight of years of repressed, pent up feelings pouring so unfettered from his mouth. "Before so mighty a temptation as love for a beautiful woman, I fell! And I love her still!"

Odo moved back to the table, pressing a hand on its surface to prop himself up; Tristan's words had taken such a toll. "Stop, Tristan!" he cried. "I cannot bear to hear such things, nor even think about what has happened between you and me this day! There is one thing yet you do not know, lad." Then his tone dropped and he muttered, "This girl, Mala, she had a child."

Tristan, in his fervor, was already about to resume his verbal barrage, but this last comment stilled him, as though he had been struck across the temple with a stone. "What did you say?" he shrugged, confused.

Odo threw himself onto a stool and slung his arms onto the tabletop with discouragement. "There was a child, Tristan. Mala was pregnant and bore you a son."

Nothing could have stunned Tristan more than these very words. He stood, slightly inclined at first, then paced one direction, then the next, disbelieving what his ears.

"That's why she was coming to Tuscany," Odo continued, "to seek assistance from Mathilda upon learning she was your adopted aunt."

"What?" said Tristan, still unable to register any of this, and still unable to fathom why she had disappeared from their mutual state of elation together in Marseilles nine months earlier.

"Yes. Mala, her aunt, and a man named Fernando, out of desperation were crossing the Alps in mid-winter to seek Mathilda. A money scheme I thought at first, but now I believe they were truly seeking assistance to make a new start. In any case they got stranded on the ice and that's why the man froze to death, and that's also when Mala fell into childbirth, which according to the old aunt, was a month or so too early. Tristan, the baby also froze to death."

Tristan's grave face betrayed no emotion, but his heart had begun to palpitate well out of control. The first revelation about Mala being pregnant had taken his breath away; this final revelation shook his very soul. Knowing not what to do, he backed away a few steps and bowed with awkward deference. "I . . . I'm sorry, Cardinal Odo, I have sinned grievously," he said, dropping his chin onto his chest. "I regret everything I have done, and also everything I have said to you this day." Then his eyes began to water. "Th-this thing with Mala being with child, and this horror she has endured, I did not know."

Tristan dissolved degree by degree. Watching him struggle unsuccessfully to stifle his sudden grieving, Odo covered his eyes with a palm, unwilling to bear witness to such a descent in one he so dearly loved.

Tristan began to shiver then, and not looking up, he whispered, "Mala, is she still there in Tuscany?"

"Yes, in Canossa with her aunt."

"This aunt, is her name, by chance, Duxia de Falaise?"

"Yes, I believe so."

"I must go to Canossa, then," Tristan said, beginning to shed hot tears. "There is something I must tell you, Cardinal Odo. As I was slipping around trying to be with Mala, I felt myself a coward. I knew what I was doing went against all that you and the Black Monks stand for, and all that you together have taught me since I was a lost boy at Cluny; that cowardice left me today, just moments ago. I wish to thank you for all you have done to shape my life and raise me up. I violated your trust though you have done nothing but good for me, for the Church, and for the people. My tongue should be ripped from mouth for ever having uttered such vicious barbs. I shall never further disgrace you as long as I might breathe. As I walk from this tunnel, I forever take my leave of you, Monte Cassino, and the Benedictine Brotherhood."

Tristan then quietly left the tunnels, mounted his horse, and rode north.

CHAPTER FIFTY-SIX

THE UNEXPECTED

Mala and Duxia were by no means being held prisoner within the Canossa fortress by Countess Mathilda, yet they clearly understood that the Countess considered them to be criminals. Consequently, on the day Cardinal Odo left for Monte Cassino to confront Tristan, Mala and Duxia both decided it would be best to remain within their quarters as much as possible, thereby remaining out of Countess Mathilda's view and thoughts.

As Duxia peered out the window that morning and watched Cardinal Odo's coach depart, she said, "A good thing Cardinal Odo is a reasonable man, otherwise this bitch countess would have had us manacled to the wall of her dungeon."

"He's a decent man, I suppose," said Mala. "Learning the truth he may see to it that we receive assistance. Then we can return to Dijon, maybe do as we originally planned and open a small shop."

"The truth? Ha, you still assume then that your lad Tristan will come clean on this business? I doubt it! He'll deny everything. There's no telling what will become of us, Dear. The powerful make little problems and nobodies like us simply disappear, you know."

Mala did not reply. Despite the wall of regret and resentment for Tristan that had arisen in her heart, she still somehow felt that he would not deliberately stand in the way of her making a new beginning, especially after the child she had lost.

"Yes, that countess," Duxia continued, "if she has her way we'll be . . ." A loud rap came at the door then, interrupting her thoughts. "Who is it?" she said, drawing back, fearful that the guards had come to haul them off somewhere.

"Vincente Balducci!" came the reply. "I've come to see how the two of you are doing."

Duxia looked over at Mala, shrugged, then slowly opened the door. "Come in, my Lord," she said, bowing.

Balducci entered the room as one would enter a grand ball. Standing unusually erect, he gazed about the room as though posing for a throng of admiring peons, then settled his eyes on Mala . . . who did *not* bow.

"Yes, what can we do for you?" she said with coolness. She cared little for the nobility, thinking them rapacious and untrustworthy.

This response surprised Balducci. He was not accustomed to such cold greetings, especially from those who had nothing. Nevertheless, he allowed it to pass. He did not wish to displease the object of his visit, which was Mala herself. Despite the effects of frostbite that covered her face and limbs when he had first encountered Mala in the Alps, he had noticed even then that she was an extraordinarily eye-catching young woman. And since recovering at Canossa, that beauty had become even more evident. Quite simply, he was smitten.

"Ah, you're looking healthy again, and absolutely lovely," he smiled, his eyes assessing Mala from head to toe. Then noticing that Duxia was staring at him with suspicion, he quickly added, "both of you, my ladies!"

"Thank you, Vincente," said Mala. Right as she said this, Duxia signaled disapproval from behind Balducci and lipped the words "*Lord* Balducci."

Being called by his first name by a commoner ruffled Balducci a bit. Mala saw this, which caused her to titter. Her eyes lit with laughter and a smile filled her face.

Balducci was immediately disarmed. "I am a high lord of Tuscany," he grinned, "but yes, *you* may call me Vincente."

The officiousness with which Baldcucci said this struck Mala as comical, and she now broke into open laughter, which Balducci did not at all understand. Mala's laughter was so infectious that he found even himself snickering a bit. Duxia had taken a seat behind the two of them, and was watching Balducci with keen interest. Since first meeting Balducci she had found him to be overly inflated with self-importance and offensive, therefore she cared little for him. In asking about, Duxia quickly learned that he was both wealthy and influential. More importantly, he was still single.

Balducci's visit that morning lasted well over an hour. And though most of the conversation was centered on Balducci himself while Mala merely listened and nodded, Balducci left the conversation with a feeling of sheer exhilaration. This, of course, caused him to come back that next morning, and then the morning after that. During these encounters Duxia never left Balducci alone with Mala, per Mala's insistence. Duxia would make herself as inconspicuous as possible, and listen to every word that Balducci said. As well, she watched every facial expression he made and noted his every reaction to things that Mala said or thought.

On the tenth night after Balducci had begun these daily visits, Duxia sat upon Mala's bed and looked at her with hawkish eyes. "I talked you into crossing the Alps," she said, "in the hopes that the Countess Mathilda might provide us a new start in order to save her nephew's good name. I am so sorry, Child, for all that has arisen since my fateful advice. And even now I see my plan unraveling for the Countess has a heart of stone as far as the two of us are concerned. Tell me, Dear, what are your feelings about this Balducci?"

"Balducci?" said Mala, nestling her head onto her pillow. "A silly man, that's all."

"Ah, too bad, Mala. He is rich beyond our imagination, and single . . . and he has an eye for you, Dear."

Mala chortled at this. "He flirts, Duxia, as men did while I danced. Besides, he told me he marries this summer, some nobleman's daughter from Genoa, some little bird by the name of Marianna Bertucci; an aristocrat, of course."

"He marries only if you wish it."

"What?"

"Yes, I've been watching him closely. He does not love that woman, nor even want her. It's you he desires. There's a little fire burning in his heart and loins for you and it grows each time he visits you. You could easily stoke it higher."

"Oh, Duxia!" laughed Mala, half burying her face within her pillow to stifle herself. "You see so much when there is so little to see!"

"Laugh if you wish, but old women see what young women miss. I say a change of plans might be in order, Dear. Have you no *feelings* for Balducci?"

Mala grew still, realizing that Duxia was gazing at her with that serious expression that came right before offering counsel. "No, none whatsoever," she replied.

"No matter, then. You have heard my story of love and the unhappy outcome, and now you yourself have seen where love has landed you, so let's forget love and talk about money. If you were to marry Balducci, everything changes. Everything!"

"I am a distraction for Balducci, and a commoner, Duxia."

"I tell you, Dear, this man is on fire for you. I've been foolish for love. You've been foolish for love. We risked everything and lost. So let this man Balducci be foolish for love. Besides, he has little to risk here except marrying down. And even at that he wouldn't be the first to break with convention by taking a commoner as his wife. And God knows he doesn't need to marry to increase his wealth. He's already got everything!"

"Oh, Duxia, even you said that Guntar refused you for that very reason . . . you were a commoner."

"No, that was different. 'Twas me that loved Guntar; he only used me. This Balducci, he burns for you as I burned for Guntar and you burned for Tristan. He would be like clay in your fingers, Dear. Imagine, the world at your feet."

"Oh, Duxia, I am no whore!" Mala said, sitting up. "What you ask is horrid and malicious."

"Oh, indeed? The poor of this world whore for crumbs while kings and popes whore for crowns. The poor are castigated for whoring while kings and popes are acclaimed, yet their actions don't differ. Very well then, take your chances with the Countess Mathilda, or the Cardinal and the blessed Church! Take your chances with men who offer nothing but suffering. Yes, that's it, Dear, surrender your heart to poverty instead of using your brain for benefit!" Then Duxia angrily slipped over to her own bed and blew out the candle. She was still, then a few moments later in the darkness she said, "I'm old and don't have much longer in this life, if I'm fortunate, Dear, but you have a long road to walk yet. It hurts me to watch you follow in my footsteps."

CHAPTER FIFTY-SEVEN

GONE

Tristan's ride to Canossa was a brutal exercise in emotional disintegration where he alternately cursed his own failures and weaknesses, then cursed those of the Church. Mala was foremost on his mind during every moment of this hellish struggle, and he swore to himself that he would make up for every previous occasion when he had faltered in committing his life to her. As he pressed his horse forward he tried to picture the hardships she must have endured during her pregnancy and the ill-advised crossing of the Alps. Then, too, he tried to envision the actual birthing of the child, *his* and Mala's child, in the brutal temperatures of the high mountains . . . and it was the image of this child slowly freezing to death that haunted him above all other images. These convulsions of the conscience exhausted him as he pushed further and further north toward Mala, and he determined that the worst days of the past seemed enviable in light of the debacle he had made of his and Mala's life and the resultant uncertainty that lay ahead.

It took him a full seven days of hard riding to arrive at Canossa, and as he dashed through the gates he cried out "Mala!" in the hopes that she might be right there within the entry. He even imagined her seeing him as he galloped in, then dashing toward him in a rush of passion. She was nowhere to be seen and the only greeting he received was a curious look from the guards.

Then he saw Mathilda in the distance descending the cathedral steps, so he kicked his horse in the ribs and shouted to her, "Auntie, I seek Mala! Cardinal Odo told me everything in Monte Cassino!"

Mathilda, having no idea what had transpired between Odo and Tristan during their encounter, was still of the opinion that Tristan was innocent. "Oh, my poor nephew!" she cried, hugging him as he dismounted. "Such an undeserved travesty, these wicked accusations thrown against you. Praise Heaven, God has already settled the account for you!"

"What?" said Tristan, his eyes still wandering about the courtyard, thinking that Mala might appear at any moment.

"Yes, those two horrid women both left Canossa yesterday."

Hearing this in the wake of his arduous, desperate ride to find Mala here, Tristan's arms dropped to his side and he stared at Mathilda, deflated. "Why? Where did they go?"

"I have no idea," said Mathilda with a smile, thinking that the news would be pleasing to her nephew. "They left in a coach belonging to Vincento Balducci.

So glad was I to see them leave that I gave them each a small purse of coin and wished them well."

"What were they doing in Balducci's coach? How in God's name did they ever meet Balducci of all people?"

"He was with Handel's wagon train when they were rescued in the Alps, then he took an interest in helping them while here at Canossa."

"Balducci, taking an interest in others?"

"Yes, I know, a bit out of character," nodded Mathilda. "In any case, I imagine the two women realized that their little scheme to get rich by blackening your name had fallen apart, so they wished to be gone by the time Cardinal Odo caught up with them again. I don't blame them. Balducci offered them his coach and an escort. Like I said, most likely they are on their way back to France."

Tristan shook his head. "No, after their ordeal in the Alps they would never try to cross again until late spring or summer. They have gone somewhere else right here in Tuscany, and if not in Tuscany, somewhere near Tuscany."

"Ah, what do we care? They came, they lost their little gambit, and left. Everything is back as it was though I must confess, they did create quite a little false stir for a while."

Tristan looked at Mathilda and shook his head once again. After his cowardice of sneaking about this last year to be with Mala, and after the heart-wrenching episode back in Monte Cassino that had created an irreparable division between him and Cardinal Odo, Tristan decided that he would no longer engage in further deceit.

"No, Auntie, it was no false stir that Mala tried to create. It was true . . . all of it. And though it shames me in a thousand ways, I shall not shrink from the truth. I love Mala. I think I have loved her since childhood, but never realized it. I had no idea whatsoever that she was carrying my child. That child is dead, very much because of me I suppose, and I must now make amends."

Mathilda stood listening, struggling mightily to accept what she was being told. As a pious and militant Gregorian reformist, she found immorality to be offensive, in particular amongst men of the cloth. Human judgment, of course, can be merciless and unforgiving when assessing the sins of strangers. Unexpectedly discovering that the one sitting in judgment is *family*, an odd thing occurs . . . the rocky, jagged edges of self-righteous indignation are quickly replaced by the cushion of forgiveness. And this is what was occurring to Mathilda.

She moved closer to Tristan, taking his hands in hers, and said, "You have sinned, nephew. God created the confessional for the purpose of cleansing the soul and erasing sin. Beg God for forgiveness, give your penance, then stand and resume your life having learned from your mistakes. Yes, even many of our greatest saints found themselves awash in sin, but then found light. You have much to do yet for the Church, Tristan, as a monk."

"No, Auntie. I am done with the Black Monks. I shall confess my sins and remain faithful to God, but I am a monk no longer. There in the tunnels of

Monte Cassino before Cardinal Odo himself, I renounced my Benedictine vows."

"Tristan," Mathilda exclaimed, "you can't do such a thing! One can't walk away from the Brotherhood! You could well be excommunicated!"

"They may do as they wish, Aunt Mathilda. I am resolved to finding Mala and spending my life with her! Priests and monks throughout Europe are married and have children, and have been doing so since the days of Christ. My only misfortune was to be cast in as a child with a band of zealous Cluniac reformers who have declared that clerics should be celibate and remain unmarried. They made this law, not God."

"Oh, Tristan, such sacrilege! Please, say no more to me!"

"I know you are unmovable on such issues, dear Aunt, so I will not argue the point. I must find Mala. Pray tell, where is Guillaume now stationed?"

"I have given him command of the fortress of Montelucio that guards the approach to Canossa. You'll find the Danes there also."

"Very well," Tristan replied, mounting his horse. Then, looking back, he said, "Aunt Mathilda, know that I love and admire you to the end of my days. You are an extraordinary woman and shall remain in my heart forever. God bless. Please pray for me."

CHAPTER FIFTY-EIGHT

IN SEARCH OF MALA

Tristan rode immediately to Montelucio and gathered Guillaume and the Danes and apprised them of all that had occurred, beginning with that first night he had met Mala by the Seine as a boy.

"Ah, I'll be damned!" said Orla. "Yes, I remember that girl, and her beautiful mother."

Crowbones and Guthroth shook their head in agreement, thinking back on that night when they had ambushed and slaughtered a rogue band of Norsemen. Guillaume remembered none of this since he was four years old at that time.

Tristan then continued, describing the few occasions he and Mala had encountered each other up until his ordination, the visit in the Loire Valley, and their rendezvous in Marseilles. At this point, as he related Mala's unexplained disappearance, her pregnancy, and the crossing of the Alps, he began to falter and his voice would trail off at times as his eyes began to glisten with moisture. Finally, he finished with a long sigh and said, "I know this surprises and disappoints all of you. No one is more disgusted in me than I myself. I feel criminal for what I have done to Mala and how I have misled others."

"You are only a man," said Orla. "Each of us standing here has made grave mistakes in life."

"Ja," added Crowbones. "Besides, I've never in my life heard of such foolishness as celibacy and non-marriage! Only the most twisted of Christians could invent such an unnatural series of law!"

"J-ja, un-un-nat-ural," nodded Guthroth.

"Ja!" cried Hroc who was standing next to his father, upset at seeing his uncle Tristan in such a state of defeat.

"And you, Guillaume," said Tristan, "what are your thoughts?"

Guillaume had always held great reverence for his older brother, and had also imagined him to be infallible. Furthermore, he had always been certain that Tristan would become a great figure within the Church hierarchy. Consequently, Guillaume could not grasp the thought that Tristan would walk away from such promise because of a woman. Short of eighteen, Guillaume had never been in love nor even been infatuated with a female because of the two environments within which he had been raised: first a Benedictine monastery, then the military arena of his aunt and the Tuscan Knights. The very thought of Tristan trashing his existence because of something as frivolous as obsession over a woman appeared ludicrous to Guillaume, and he did not hold his tongue about it.

"I think you're rushing over a cliff, Brother, and advise you to halt. How this woman has managed to get her claws so deeply into your flesh is a mystery to me. By God, you barely know her!"

"I have known her my entire life, Guillaume."

"No, you met her long ago, have only seen her on a handful of occasions, and that according to your own words. This is a folly! I cannot agree to it, Tristan."

This very much disappointed Tristan. "Well then," he said with regret, I came here to ask that you and the Danes help me find Mala. She is somewhere near yet, I believe. Knowing how you feel, I'll not make the request."

"Nay, nay," said Orla, "Guillaume may be my military commander, but he does not speak for me on this, which is a family matter. I will help, Boy."

"Ja, me also," interjected Crowbones.

"Ja, and me!" cried Hroc, as Guthroth quietly nodded yes also.

"I refuse to contribute to your downfall, Tristan," said Guillaume, standing firm, "nor will I stand in the way of the Danes helping you." Then, looking at Orla, he said, "You have two weeks until we mobilize with General Padule at the fortress of Bianell. He intends for half of the army, which includes us, to move east and meet the other commanders in the recently reclaimed territory of Commander Balducci, then it's south to Rome."

"Ah, Balducci!" Orla snickered. "Yes, we'll be ready in two weeks, Guillaume. Besides, Crowbones, Guthroth and I wouldn't wish to miss the opportunity to see *that* lout in full strut! Now that he's recovered all his estates and wealth from the Germans, Balducci'll be worse than a goddamn buck in the rut season!"

"Balducci offered his coach and an escort to Mala and the old woman as their means of leaving Canossa," said Tristan. "Is it possible they're on their way to Balducci's territory?"

"Eh?" said Guillaume. "What is Balducci's interest in any of this?"

"If this Mala looks anything like her mother did," said Orla, "Balducci's interest is in *her*, I'd guess."

"Yes," Tristan nodded. "Mala is even more beautiful than was her mother."

"Well," shrugged Guillaume, "I've never taken up for Balducci. He is a man and he is single, Brother, and cannot be faulted for coming to a beautiful woman's assistance. Nevertheless, if you're going to confront Balducci, best I come along after all. He gets hot-headed, especially in front of his troops, and he had a rather large escort here at Canossa."

Pressing their horses hard toward the east, they caught up to Balducci's caravan on the third day. Spying a coach in the middle of the ambling escort, Tristan rapidly whipped his horse forward and began crying out Mala's name. It was Duxia who heard him first, and saw his approach. She looked quickly over to Mala who heard his voice also. She cut her head toward the window of the coach but Duxia who was between Mala and the window pushed her back.

"Goddammit, child!" she hissed with desperation. "Don't falter now after all you've been through! And remember that Balducci told me this morning that upon reaching his estates, he will be asking your hand in marriage!"

Mala settled back in her seat, the look of confusion was unmistakable.

Her heart yearned to see Tristan, but her head knew better. He had betrayed her, and furthermore, he was a monk. All those things they had felt between childhood and Marseilles were dispersing shadows now, and needed to be put aside forever.

Tristan halted the coach and dismounted. Then, glimpsing Mala within, he opened the door and grasped at her hands. "Mala, I've come for you!" he cried in a burst of emotion. "I've renounced my vows! Come leave with me now!"

Mala rebuffed his hands and slid further away from him into the coach. "No," she said, refusing to look at him, "get away!"

This confused Tristan. "Forgive me, Mala, I only learned a short time ago about the baby from Cardinal Odo," he pleaded. "I had no idea! I never understood why you left Marseilles without telling me. What happened? We were so happy then!"

At this, her eyes afire, Mala turned and gave him a searing glance. Then she pointed a finger and cried, "Oh, you continue to play me for the fool! Fernando and the others told me about that woman you were cavorting with in the square while I foolishly wondered where you had disappeared to, Tristan! Then, in concern, I went to the monastery looking for you only to find out that you were never there in the first place! You lied to me! You must have been staying with that other woman while slipping away to see me only when you became bored with her!"

Stunned, Tristan shook his head with confusion. "What are you talking about, Mala? I was there at the Marseilles monastery with my brother and the Danes. I knew that Fernando would probably tell you some story about that woman in the square. It wasn't as it appeared, I swear!"

They were both shouting by now, and Duxia also had begun to shout, screaming obscenities at Tristan and striking out at him in an effort to get him away from the wagon door. This, of course caught the attention of Balducci's escort as well as Balducci himself who was riding at the head of the column. He quickly turned his horse and galloped back to the coach, only to find several of his men restraining Tristan and pulling him away from the coach. This in turn angered Guillaume and the Danes, and they charged forward with weapons drawn, scattering Balducci's men who had also drawn their arms.

"Halt this madness!" cried Balducci, having no idea what had started this melee. Then, looking down at Tristan, he said, "And what the hell are *you* doing here?"

"I've come for Mala," Tristan replied, wiping blood from his lip.

"What?" asked Balducci. Then he glanced at Guillaume and the Danes. "What the hell is he talking about, Guillaume?"

Guillaume started to offer an answer, but Duxia cried out from the wagon. "Say no more! Say no more!" Balducci had no inkling of the relationship that had existed between Mala and Tristan, nor did he know that Tristan was the father of the dead infant that had been found in the wagon upon the mountain pass, and Duxia knew that further open discussion would inevitably reveal this information. "Lord Balducci," she said, pointing at Tristan, "I ask that you give me a private moment with this man."

"No, I will not speak to this old bitch!" cried Tristan. "I wish to speak only to Mala!"

"If she wished to speak to you she would have come out of the coach!" Duxia hissed. Then looking at all of the men gathered about the coach with weapons drawn, she said, "Put away your arms and answer me this one question. Is there a man here who would *force* this young woman within the coach to speak to this man if she did not wish to?"

The opposing groups looked across at each other, then shook their heads no. "She's right, Tristan," Guillaume whispered to his brother. "We can't force Mala to talk, nor can we force her come back with you. Besides, I become more confused with each passing moment . . . I thought she would want to come with you. What's going on here?"

Tristan did not reply. He was at that moment drowning in unimaginable confusion. In fact, everything about Mala since Marseilles had been puzzling, but now it had turned into a quagmire of impossible perplexity. And even though he understood Mala's mistaken concept of Lady Agnes Truffault in the square of Marseilles thanks to Fernando, he did not understand her latest accusation about him never being at the monastery. Furthermore, he had imagined that when she heard he had renounced his vows, Mala would be overjoyed. She was refuting him with a hostility he did not comprehend.

"Very well," said Balducci, looking at Guillaume and the Danes. "If the old woman's proposal is acceptable to all, then so be it. No need for bloodshed amongst allies in arms, for Christ's sake." He then held out his arm and helped Duxia descend the coach. As he did so, he peered into the coach and saw Mala weeping, her face buried in the fold of her shawl.

Duxia moved clear of the coach and all the men, then motioned for Tristan to follow. When both were a good distance from the others, Duxia pulled him near, and through her clenched teeth spoke low. "Oh, your black presence is once again about to take its toll you bastard! This man Balducci has fallen under Mala's spell and will soon offer his hand in marriage, thereby pulling her from the disaster you created for her!"

"What?" said Tristan, unprepared to hear such news.

"Yes, it's almost too good to believe. Surely you would not snatch this one opportunity to be happy and secure from her, would you? Oh, you once claimed to me that you loved her, and I in turn told you what you must do if your love was true, leave her to live her life in peace because you belong to the Church."

"No. I have renounced my vows. I will . . ."

"Ha! The Church is so deeply engrained in you that it runs in your blood. First it was your mother Asta preaching God, then the army of nuns that tutored you in Saint-Germainen-Laye, and then the Black Monks of Cluny! Oh, you may have renounced your vows in a moment of passion, but you'll take them back up when the moment passes. And it shall pass, Tristan de Saint-Germain, because I was there at your birth and know you better even than you know yourself." Then she spat on the ground and looked deep into his eyes. "Would you truly destroy Mala, this beautiful and giving soul who so very much deserves at least one measure of stability in her life instead of wandering about as a child, wandering about as a young woman? She has this single opportunity awaiting her after all her trials. Don't crush it. Don't crush her!"

Tristan looked over at Balducci, his heart palpitating wildly with equal measures of anger and sorrow. "But Balducci is so *difficult*," he muttered aloud to himself, unable to picture Mala in Balducci's grasp.

"Ha! No more so than you," cackled Duxia. "And don't fear for Mala, for she will drive the coach in this marriage, not him." Then she added, "Balducci knows nothing of you and Mala, nor that 'twas you who sired her lost baby, and he does not *need* to know. Only Mathilda and Cardinal Odo know, and in their effort to protect you, they have told no one."

Tristan palmed his forehead, unable to believe that he was caving to Duxia's counsel. "I have told my brother, and the Danes."

"God dammit!" Duxia hissed. "Make them swear to keep it close to their hearts then! And for your own sake, never speak of it again to anyone! What's done is done. The child was lost, frozen to death in the Alps . . . and there's no need to dredge up the dead!"

Tristan's face was the image of sheer defeat. And to magnify the bitterness, it all transpired before the person he most despised in life, Duxia de Falaise. "I d-don't understand any of this," he whispered. "Why did she leave Marseilles without telling me? Was it you and Fernando poisoning her against me?"

"Why? Because you lied to her, boy, about being at the monastery. Then you bedded her down while consorting with some other woman, at whose residence you were undoubtedly really staying while in Marseilles!"

Tristan lifted his gaze from the ground and looked Duxia in the eyes. Then he slowly shook his head. "No. On God's word, old woman, neither of those is true."

Duxia started to argue, but before she could utter the first word she stopped herself; something in Tristan's lost gaze told her he was not lying. Indeed, as impossible as his denial sounded, the profound depth of mourning that arose in Tristan's eyes at that moment made her believe that there was a deeper complexity to all this than anyone understood, even Mala and Tristan them-selves. Nevertheless, she set this aside, spat on the ground once more, and said, "So, what will it be, boy? Do you leave her be or shall you throw her into the fire once again?"

Saying nothing, Tristan walked away. Then signaling Guillaume and the Danes, he mounted his horse and turned away from Balducci's caravan. He set his horse at a slow canter, looking back several times, thinking perhaps to see Mala outside the coach watching him leave, at least.

She never appeared.

CHAPTER FIFTY-NINE

TRISTAN'S DESCENT

Tristan dissolved into inconsolable grief when they returned to Montelucio. Guillaume and the Danes attempted to reason with him, provide cheer, and offer counsel, but when one is drowning, the voices of others go unheard and unheeded. And in this state of melancholy and dejection, Tristan's thought process began to distort itself, which in turn caused a twisting of Tristan's view of himself and life itself. The primary effect of this was that he began to believe himself a failure in all things, which meant that he also believed that God was punishing him.

"Oh, I deserve God's wrath!" he confessed to Guillaume one night. "I slunk about breaking his laws, I destroyed a beautiful young woman I loved, and an innocent child was sacrificed . . . as if by my own two hands!"

"No," insisted Guillaume, "if anything, God has *spared* you, Brother, for greater things. What would you have accomplished in life restrained by that woman and a child? No, you were gifted by God at birth, and he intends for you to serve a greater purpose than disappearing into the ranks of the mediocre."

"Oh, such fierce faith you have in me, Guillaume, and fierce expectations. Yes, my entire life I have felt on the verge of great things. At last I have come to my senses. I realize I have felt this way only because others have thrust it upon me, forcing it down my throat since birth! First our Mother, then Cardinal Odo and the Black Monks, then our Aunt Mathilda and a host of others. I am not, apparently, what all of you believe me to be, because the weight of your expectations has crushed and destroyed me. I have failed in all things!"

"No, Brother. You are wounded, yes. And discouraged, yes. And you have failed in this one thing with a woman you should not have engaged in the first place. Get yourself to a Church, Tristan, throw yourself on the altar of forgiveness and perform your penance. Then rise and serve God."

"Oh, Guillaume, listen to yourself, you sound like Odo and Mathilda and the rest of them!" Tristan laughed with derision. "Such a strange creature you have become. 'Tis you who should have become the monk, not me. You are always so certain about the subject of God. For you there are no questions about serving God, even when slaughtering other men in His name!"

"You are correct in this, Brother," replied Guillaume calmly. "There's no confusion in my heart concerning right and wrong as taught by God."

"Oh, what about as taught by men pretending to represent God? Do you not realize that nearly all Church rules and law have been created by this man or that man, this group or that group over the centuries? Do you not see that it is all about power and who makes the rules?"

"No, it's about right and wrong, Tristan. And God gives us the ability to choose."

Tristan threw his arms in the air and cried, "Oh, where is the wine at times such as this!" Arguing theology with Guillaume was like arguing with the walls of a cathedral, the firmness of his beliefs impenetrable. This irritated Tristan at times such as this, yet he also envied Guillaume's certainty.

A week later Guillaume and the Danes mobilized with Mathilda and General Padule and moved east to meet Balducci's troops and several other Tuscan commanders for the march south on Rome. Guillaume had hoped that Tristan might accompany him on this march. He declined for two reasons: First, he did not wish to enter Balducci's realm for fear of possibly encountering Mala, an encounter that his heart could not bear. His second reason was that if the army succeeded in reclaiming Rome, Tristan knew that Cardinal Odo would be there, and this was yet another encounter his heart could not bear. Consequently, he remained behind in Montelucio with young Hroc.

Hroc had wanted to accompany his father on this march. Orla had staunchly refused. "No, Hroc, I shan't so soon lose another son to the Germans," Orla had said. "You stay behind and promise to keep an eye to Uncle Tristan for he is not in a good way."

"Yes, Father," Hroc said, setting his boyish battle dreams aside with disappointment. "One day I'm going to fight by your side, huh?"

"Yes. That day's not yet arrived, son."

Hroc was not exactly sure what his father meant at first about Uncle Tristan. Within days he began to understand. His uncle, who seldom drank, began to consume large amounts of wine and ale, often beginning early in the morning. He would then by noon begin launching into tirades about the Church and the clergy, both Gregorian and anti-Gregorian, and Hroc quickly noticed that within the first week of his father's departure the servants and cooks began to scatter when his uncle approached. Hroc, now eight years of age, did not exactly comprehend the source of his uncle's change in behavior. Daily he followed him about out of respect for his father's request. When Tristan would begin his diatribe against the Church, often in a stumbling stupor to an empty room, Hroc would sit there patiently and listen though he understood very little of what was being said. Then, when his uncle would pass out at the table or onto the floor, Hroc would send for the servants who carried him to his quarters.

After several weeks of this, Hroc determined one morning that he should speak up. He approached Tristan who was already half inebriated and said, "Uncle, this church that you talk about each day, is it the same church in which you are a monk?"

Tristan looked down at Hroc through bleary eyes and snorted. "Eh? Yes, of course. Although I am no longer a monk."

"My father says that once a boy becomes a man, he is always a man. Once a warrior, always a warrior. Once a Dane, always a Dane. Does this not hold true then with monks?"

Tristan leaned his hand against the table to prop himself up and considered the question. "No," he said, "apparently not, because I am no longer a monk."

"Uncle Guillaume says you are still a monk, and I heard Countess Mathilda say that you have not yet been defrocked, whatever that means, so you are still a monk."

"I assure you that defrocked or not, I am no longer a monk," Tristan stammered. "Why does that concern you, lad?"

"I like you being a monk. A question then, are you still a spy?"

"Uh? No. I am nothing at the moment."

"Well then, what shall you be later on, then? Father says you can't be a warrior because you don't know how to fight. So what will you be? A merchant, perhaps? After all, you can't drink wine every day and talk to yourself as you've been doing, huh?"

Since intercepting Balducci's caravan and being rejected by Mala, Tristan had listened to nothing that anyone had said in terms of counsel. They had been either scolding or preaching; he wanted none of either. As he listened to Hroc, the boy was throwing out questions, and these questions addressed an inevitable reality. *What, indeed, would I do for a living?*

Plopping himself awkwardly on a stool, Tristan gave the thought consideration. He could possibly serve as logistician to his Aunt Mathilda's vast enterprises, or even for her army. The sheer thought of serving as an accountant for the rest of his life caused him to quickly dismiss that option. He then thought of commerce as Hroc had inquired; business seemed mercenary to him, self-serving. Academia offered several possibilities; being confined to libraries and digging through manuscripts and books also held little appeal. His thoughts then returned to Mala and the dream of future reconciliation. Reaching into his pocket, he fished for the small ring of Moorish silver that she had given him as a child and examined it. It was the only memento he had of her other than memories. No, he decided, pushing the ring back into his pocket, his relationship with Mala was dead; he had killed it somehow, along with their child, though he still did not comprehend how.

Hroc had taken a seat and was staring at him now, his elbows propped upon the table and his chin nestled in his palms. Tristan looked at the boy and envied his innocence. "Oh, I wonder what shall become of you at times, Hroc," he sighed. "The world is full of traps, especially for one as young as you."

"Yes, and even for one as smart as you, eh, Uncle Tristan?" Hroc replied with a sad expression. "Everyone says you are the most intelligent man on this earth, you know, and I think they're right. Nobody is as clever as you or knows as much either."

At this Tristan sighed with disgust, at himself. "Ay, it seems I do not know as much as others think, Hroc, or I would not have lost my soul. That is what has happened to me."

"Oh?" said Hroc. "Then I'll help you find it again, Uncle Tristan."

"Ha! You will?" laughed Tristan. Orla had refused to allow his son to be baptized and the boy had little concept of the Christian soul. "Very well then, Hroc, start looking, and let me know when you find it."

CHAPTER SIXTY

BATTLE FOR THE VATICAN

During Lent of that year, 1087, Cardinal Desiderius finally yielded to his followers and took up the Pope's tiara. He and Cardinal Odo de Lagery celebrated Easter mass in Monte Cassino as Duke Roger Borsa, Bohemud, and the Normans moved north against the anti-pope Clement III in Rome. Countess Mathilda also moved a contingent of her troops south from Tuscany against Rome. Caught unprepared, Clement III and his forces fled Saint Peter's, and on May 9th Desiderius was willingly consecrated and enthroned as Pope Victor III.

It was a jubilant moment for the Gregorian papists who finally once again had their Pope in control of the Vatican. The moment was short-lived as German forces counterattacked with the support of many Roman citizens, and forced Desiderius to flee after a tenure in Saint Peter's of only eight days. By June the anti-pope once again controlled the Vatican and Desiderius escaped to Monte Cassino with the help of Mathilda and Jordan of Capua. To the joy of his followers, he did not abandon his Papacy.

Two months later in August, with much assistance from Cardinal Odo, he called the Council of Benevento where he officially excommunicated anti-pope Clement III and in the tradition of Gregorian reformists, condemned lay investiture, thereby banning royals from making clerical appointments. The anti-pope had already been excommunicated by Pope Gregory, of course, and lay investiture had already been condemned by him also. Being the new Gregorian Pope, it was considered important that the new Pope repeat both actions for the sake of continuity. Of new significance was his action of proclaiming a crusade against the Saracens of North Africa who continued to persecute and enslave Christians of their region. Though Muslims and Christians had clashed for centuries, this was the first time war against the Saracens was officially documented in terms of a united Christian crusade against Islam. The term crusade had been loosely thrown about by various European power brokers over previous decades. Until the Council of Benevento, earlier wars between Arabs and Europeans had been framed more as struggles between two military powers fighting over the conquest of territory. The Council phrased this particular struggle in terms of race and religion.

Three days into the Council, Desiderius fell ill. "I don't feel well," he complained to Odo as he took to his bed. "I should retire to Monte Cassino."

"Holiness, we need you here to finish this business with North Africa."

Desiderius lifted his tired eyes to Odo and said, "Ah, you have always been much better than I at organizing and inspiring others, which is why you should have been Pope from the very beginning. This illness that has seized me, it is what I have feared all along my friend. I sense my end approaches."

"No, no, Desiderius, it is the pressure of recent affairs, purely your old enemy, anxiety, come to visit you again. It will pass."

Desiderius looked at Odo fondly, and reached for his hand. "Oh, Odo, ever the optimist," he whispered. "Always marching forward, never afraid, never daunted. A man knows his own body, dear friend, and I tell you, my end is near. What I fear most, Odo, is the chaos I leave behind. We've lost Rome yet again, and when I die, we shall once again be forced to begin the tedious process of selecting a new Pope which will create fresh battles for power and bitterness."

"No, Desiderius, you will be fine I tell you. Yes, retire to Monte Cassino and I will be your voice here at Benevento."

"Good, good," said Desiderius, closing his weary eyes. "Odo, you have always been my faithful friend . . ."

That next day the Papal entourage departed for Monte Cassino and the Council of Benevento resumed without him. Within a week a courier from Monte Cassino arrived and made an announcement to the assembly. "It is with great regret that I inform you that the health of his Holiness, Pope Victor III, has seriously deteriorated. His physicians believe he shall expire within days and the monks of Monte Cassino are preparing to administer the sacrament of Extreme Unction. It is also my duty to inform you that his Holiness has appointed Cardinal Oderisius, Grand Prior of Monte Cassino, to the position of succeeding him as Abbot of Monte Cassino Monastery. His Holiness further advances the name of Cardinal Odo de Lagery, and proposes that he be considered for election as the next Pope of the true Church!"

A great stir arose within the hall as the courier completed his announcement. Attendees were shocked to hear this unexpected news of their Pope's approaching death, and no one was more stunned than Odo himself. Desiderius' appointment of Cardinal-Prior Oderisius as his successor in the position of Abbot of Monte Cassino was not surprising as moving from Grand Prior of a monastery to Abbot was a traditional transition. Attendees were not prepared to hear that Desiderius had already put forth the name of a successor Pope. And though many within the assembly had always assumed that Cardinal Odo would one day be Pope, they had thought this eventuality to be far off in the future. There were also those in the assembly who opposed Odo de Lagery, and there were yet others within the assembly who smelled an opportunity to hatch a power sweep of their own.

This development, as Desiderius himself had predicted, quickly gave rise to a new ripple of chaos amongst the Gregorian faithful, which erupted a few days later on September 16th when the death of Pope Victor III, previously known as the beloved Cardinal-Abbot Desiderius of Monte Cassino, was announced. Only four months earlier the Gregorians had captured Rome and finally consecrated their Pope within the walls of Saint Peter. Now, the anti-pope possessed Rome once more and Pope Victor III lay in his grave. The Gregorian movement, therefore, was thrown back into the very state of confusion of the years following the death of Pope Gregory VII.

"Ah, the chaos never ends!" cried Cardinal Odo to Duke Borsa and Mathilda after the burial of Desiderius. "And I should be flogged for pressing my friend Desiderius into accepting the Pope's tiara. It killed him! And never was there a more faithful servant of God than dear Desiderius. Oh, the good souls we sacrifice in the name of the Church! And once again we are a ship without a rudder."

"Cardinal," said Borsa, "all know that Desiderius proclaimed that you should follow him as Pope. And though I opposed your appointment previously in favor of Desiderius, know that I shall now support you. I'll even raise arms if need be."

"Ah, no," said Mathilda, looking even more glum than Odo, "it's not done that way, Borsa! For God's sake, did you not learn your lesson forcing the Papacy on Desiderius the first time?"

"Exactly," said Odo. "The Pope must be selected properly. Not by arms but by the College of Cardinals."

"Then let's gather them and be on with it, I say!" Borsa snorted.

"They are scattered all over Europe," sighed Odo. "It will take months to convene the College, then the *haggling* begins."

"A waste of time," declared Borsa. "Desiderius proclaimed your name so let it be done." Then Borsa paused and gave Odo a curious look. "Unless, of course you intend to resist as Desiderius did! Is that it, Cardinal?"

Odo shook his head. "No, if I am chosen, I shall accept. It must come ethically. There is a process and a procedure. Though Desiderius advanced my name, there are other aspirants, good ones. My point here is that once again we have no leadership and establishing that leadership shall take time. Meanwhile, the anti-pope solidifies his hold on the Vatican and the Saracens continue to run amok in North Africa."

"You must hold things together again, Odo," said Mathilda, going to his side and grasping his hands, "exactly as you have been doing all along."

Odo exhaled heavily and closed his eyes. "Oh, Mathilda, my dear Mathilda, I thought it was over and that we had finally won taking Rome this past spring. How could I have ever guessed that we would suffer such a setback so quickly?" Then he released her hands and turned about. "This never ending seesaw is taking its toll on me I fear, Mathilda."

A knock came at the door then, and a Benedictine courier appeared. "I have a message for Cardinal Odo," he said, holding out a letter sealed in black wax.

"Thank you," said Odo, knowing the black seal indicated grave news. He tore the letter open, read a few lines, then turned pale and sighed heavily. "Lord in Heaven, William the Bastard of Normandy is dead, a week ago."

Borsa and Mathilda looked at Odo, dumbfounded. William the Bastard was one of the great figures of Europe and this sudden news of his death was a shock to all in the room. Mathilda shook her head and looked at Borsa who, although his Norman branch of the family no longer had political ties in Normandy, still had relations there. "There will be chaos in Normandy as his sons fight over William's holdings and his vassal barons smell opportunity."

"Yes," said Borsa, "there'll be uprisings."

"Yet more chaos on the continent now," Odo shrugged, a look of defeat creasing his face. "The last thing we need."

Mathilda looked at Odo with empathy, then motioned for Borsa to leave.

"Give me a moment with Odo," she whispered. Borsa nodded, and when he closed the door behind him, Mathilda then went to Odo and placed her hand upon his shoulder. "You've not been well these past months, Cardinal. I see it in your eyes and in your movement. The energetic, unstoppable man I know and adore has become *vacant*, I fear."

"Ah, it is exhaustion and frustration."

"Perhaps, my dear Cardinal, it is something else, also."

"Oh?"

"Yes. Tristan."

"Eh?"

"Ah, don't play ignorant with me, Odo, I'm a woman and see through the false veil of mighty men such as yourself. You haven't spoken his name one time during my presence in Rome, nor at Benevento, nor here at Monte Cassino. I see you thinking of him, or should I say grieving for your loss of him?"

"You may as well plunge a dagger into my heart as speak of him to me, Mathilda," replied Odo with a tinge of bitterness. "Yes, I think of him, worry about him, miss him. He was like a son to me."

"Was? No, I think he still is."

"He has not sent me a single correspondence since storming out of Monte Cassino. No news, no greeting, nothing."

"How many letters and inquiries have *you* sent to Montelucio, Odo?"

"None, of course, you know that. It was he who left, he who renounced his vows!"

"A strange thing, Odo, that was nearly half a year ago, yet I've never once heard another clergyman speak of Tristan renouncing his vows. I suspect that's because you've told no one. Yes, I think you've been holding that information in confidence so he won't be defrocked . . . in the hopes that he might come to his senses?"

Odo bristled at this, but it did nothing to dissuade Mathilda, and this finally forced a tiny concession out of Odo. "You women, though the frail gender, think yourselves far superior in matters of both the head and the heart, don't you, Mathilda?"

"Of course, because we are, but never refer to me as the frail gender, for there is nothing frail about me, Cardinal."

"Oh, indeed," Odo smiled, "you are manly! All you lack is the beard and the swagger. Very well then, since you are going to tell me anyway, how is Tristan doing up in Montelucio?"

"Not well, I fear. Guillaume tells me he has taken to bouts of drink, and that he's lost all direction in life. He mopes about doing nothing. Oh, such a waste of God-given talent and ability to go wasted; talent and ability that you honed to perfection by the way."

"Bah!" Odo snorted, dismissing Mathilda's comment with a flap of his hand. "He accused me of making him *corrupt*, Mathilda. You should have heard his ugly accusations."

"Oh, the anger of a young man . . . which should be evident to an older man. The two of you acting like pouty schoolboys, each refusing to acknowledge the other. Go to Montelucio, Odo, and reel him back in before it's too late, for *both* of you. You are the father, you wield the power. And Odo, *you* are the Church. Can you truly preach charity and forgiveness to the world, yet deny it to one so close to your heart?"

CHAPTER SIXTY-ONE

MONTELUCIO

Although Tristan was not expecting Cardinal Odo's arrival in early November at Montelucio, the Cardinal had notified Guillaume of this visit well in advance. "You have a visitor, Tristan," said Guillaume when notified by the guards that Cardinal Odo's entourage of carriages was making the rise to the fortress.

"Oh?" Tristan muttered. "Tell them to go away."

It was late afternoon and Tristan had had nothing to drink. He had not risen that particular day until after noon, and had been drinking heavily the night before. He was feeling shaky, haggard looking, and not in the mood for company.

"Tell him yourself, Brother," said Guillaume.

"*Him?*"

"Yes, an old acquaintance of yours, Cardinal Odo de Lagery."

"What!" Tristan shuddered. "What is he doing here?"

"He's come to see you according to the letter he sent last month."

"And you said nothing to me of it?" Tristan objected.

"No, because you would have most likely fled. In any case, he's here now and you shall address him, Tristan."

"N-no, I do not wish to see him." Then Tristan looked himself up and down and passed a hand over his unshaven face of several days. "Especially not like this," he said.

"Oh, yes, Brother, you shall see him. And I warn you, if you make a move for the door, I'll throttle you a good one and tie you back onto your stool. Oh, it'll be good for the Cardinal to see the fine state you've descended into this past year."

Tristan glanced at the door then back at his brother, and decided it was futile to challenge Guillaume who was a head taller and far stouter than himself. Then the door opened and the tall figure of Odo de Lagery filled the entrance, his scarlet Cardinal's robe ablaze. Tristan quickly buried his face in his palms.

"Good morning, Cardinal Odo," said Guillaume, offering a bow. Then he left the room.

Odo stood there and stared at Tristan a while, barely able to believe his unkempt appearance. "Well," he said finally, "I see you have been enjoying the hospitality of your brother's wine cellar, Tristan."

Tristan did not wish to look up. Eventually, he peered through his fingers at Odo. Then with resignation, he removed his hands from his face and sighed heavily. "I am s-sorry to have you see me like this, Cardinal," he stammered. "If I had known you were coming, I would have cleaned up."

"Or left the premises, more likely, eh?"

"Yes, very likely."

"Well, I am glad I caught you, then. I have missed you. Please know that I did not come to criticize or accuse. I came to see how you were doing. I heard that you still grieve for the young Romani woman and the loss of the child, your son. Know that I have prayed daily for that infant, as I have for you."

"Thank you, Cardinal Odo," Tristan said, feeling awkward. "I fear your prayers have done little good, for me at least."

"Oh? Prayers do not always bring about instant results you know. Perhaps they have done more good than you imagine. I have prayed for myself also, because of some of the things you said to me back in Monte Cassino before coming north to seek Mala."

Tristan stiffened at this. "I should never have said such things to you, Cardinal," he said. "I have chastised myself a thousand times over for those harsh words. I was angry and confused." Then he shook his head. "I am still angry and confused . . . about Mala, about myself, about what happened in Marseilles, about why Mala . . ." Here he stopped and threw his hands to the air. "None of that matters now. I am filled with sorrow and cannot seem to free myself of it."

"Have you prayed, Tristan?"

"No, Cardinal, to be perfectly honest I have not."

"Your anger has kept prayer at a distance, son, and I understand that, believe it or not. Tell me, have you given up on God then, or is your anger directed at the Church and its rules?"

"I have never given up on God. I love God, and worship God. He is the center of all things. Yes, I suppose that I possess a certain anger at the Church. I fail to understand some of our actions."

"Our actions?" said Odo with interest. "You said *our* actions, Tristan. Does that indicate that you still feel yourself a part of us?"

"I was just talking. No, I renounced my vows in your presence, you know that."

"I heard what you said down in Monte Cassino, Tristan, but even now am not sure you meant what you said, because rage can be like a sweeping tide, washing aside all in its path in one clean sweep. Even the great saints have been guilty of rage, or grief, or fear. Saint Peter himself thrice denied Christ in the garden, but found salvation in contrition and penance. You have renounced your vows, Tristan, but only to me, and I have made no motion as yet to release you. Thus the purpose of my visit. I thought perhaps that you might wish to reconsider."

Tristan looked up at Odo. "I am not worthy to wear the black robe, Cardinal. I have sinned, and in my selfishness, hurt others."

"You are worthy, son," said Odo, moving closer and standing over Tristan as he sat on his stool. Then he reached his hand out and spread his fingers over the top of Tristan's head. "We need you, Tristan. The Church needs you, and I need you. We have lost Rome once again, Desiderius has died and we have no Pope, the

Normans are back to fighting amongst each other, the Saracens continue to take advantage in North Africa. Yes, we engage in intrigue, the immorality of politics, and at times even corruption. I have told you time and again, without our efforts darkness falls upon the land. It is the kings and nobles who have twisted us and forced us to sully our hands with devious tactics. There is no other way to block them than by using their own filthy tactics against them. To do otherwise means we are lost, which then means civilization sinks back into the morass where nobles plunder the land at will, ravage the populace, pick the clergy, and turn this garden that God has given us into a landscape of horror. Stand up then, and join our effort once more, lad. Above all, forgive yourself. Yes, forgive yourself Tristan, because you have sunk into a state of self-punishment."

This last statement went to the very core of Tristan's heart; it was so precise. And the precision of these words forced tears to slowly begin streaming down Tristan's unshaven cheeks as he realized that his confusion was as much about himself as it was about the Church. His descent into drunkenness and filth was indeed self-punishment because he had not been able to reconcile himself with either Mala's suffering or the death of their child. He began to weep then, and fell to his knees holding onto Cardinal Odo's robe. "But God, will *He* ever forgive me over the child?" he sobbed.

"God forgives all, Tristan. Through contrition, God forgives all."

CHAPTER SIXTY-TWO

PENANCE AND REDEMPTION

Tristan offered his confession to Cardinal Odo within the cathedral of Montelucio, and then Cardinal Odo issued his penance, which was threefold. First, Tristan was to be confined for thirty days, unshackled, in the Montelucio dungeon. Odo's intent was to deprive Tristan of access to wine and spirits for a full month to force a cleansing of the bloodstream. Next, Tristan was ordered to flagellate himself as recommended by canon law under the Decree of Gratian and the Decretals of Gregory IX. In this particular case, Odo prescribed that Tristan would pass ten blows of the scourge over his right shoulder and ten blows over his left shoulder each morning after rising and each night before retiring, ten representing God's commandments. Thirty days of such flagellation was an extreme penance. Odo's intent was neither retribution nor cruelty. He knew that Tristan had buried himself beneath a crushing weight of guilt and that the only way to counter this guilt would be for Tristan to bleed it out by suffering great pain himself, thereby mitigating his own misdeeds. And finally, Tristan was ordered to strip naked and spend ten hours each of the thirty days upon his knees in prayer, the state of nakedness representing humility, and the hours of prayer representing complete submission to God.

Odo also insisted that Tristan complete this penance with neither witness nor supervision. "When you have completed this trial of suffering and sacrifice," he told Tristan, "your sins and transgressions shall be forgiven and you shall once again regain the stature of Black Monk. Should you fail to complete each and every measure of this penance on your own honor, then be damned in the eyes of God for the rest of your days."

On the first morning of Tristan's penance, Guillaume happened to be giving feeding instructions to the jailer, a man named Antonelli, as Tristan arose and began administering his first scourging. With each pass of the scourge he groaned in agony, which forced Guillaume to wince each time the leather thongs stung his brother's back. *Why does he not go easy on himself?* Guillaume wondered, knowing that such flagellation would increasingly exact a heavier toll with each passing day. Soon he realized that after each strike of the scourge, Tristan was whispering to himself, "Forgive me, Mala! Forgive me, my son!" Guillaume then understood that Tristan's grief over what he had done was so profound that he felt the need to balance the scales for Mala and the lost child. Hurting himself to the limits of human endurance, then, would be the catharsis by which he hoped to find forgiveness.

So distressed was Guillaume that he told the jailer, "I need to keep an eye to my brother so disregard what I've just told you. It shall be me who brings him water and bread each afternoon."

And so Guillaume began the daily regimen of doing so in order to check on Tristan, though he never once spoke to him, afraid of disturbing his prayer. Guillaume gazed at Tristan kneeling upon the stone floor of the cell each day, his back bared and bloodied. His concern grew and he considered going to Cardinal Odo to plead for mercy, but he realized that such action would anger Tristan so he remained silent.

For those of altruistic heart, the destruction of others is unconscionable. For Tristan, then, what he had done to Mala and his own child had begun causing in him an inner collapse from the very moment Odo had told him of her ordeal in the Alps. This collapse had intensified after learning that Mala had departed Canossa, then intensified yet more from being rejected by her enroute to Balducci's territories. Crushing defeats of this magnitude are unbearable to any human, especially so to those of sensitive constitution such as Tristan. Each day spent in solitude praying and reflecting during his penance was, without the benefit of wine to blot out his thoughts, far more horrid to Tristan than the ten passes of the scourge he administered to himself each morning and night. The state of listlessness that had been brought on by alcohol during the past half year had at least numbed his senses to the point of lethargy. The clarity he began to feel brought everything back into acute focus, and this sharpening of his wits soon caused him to wish for his own death.

Dreams of the conscious form have driven man forward since the dawn of time, luring him to risk limb and life in the quest for prosperity, conquest, freedom, and a better future. The fact that dreams, for humans, create this infinite wellspring of hope is indeed what separates man from beast. Yet even more fascinating than dreams of the conscious form are those dreams of the subconscious form that come during sleep. These vaporish, ethereal visitors slip upon man during his most helpless state, and they communicate through mystifying images and symbolism, rarely illuminating their actual message. Because of this, men have attempted to decode their meaning down through millennia, certain that they somehow hold the key to the future. This attempt to interpret the significance of dreams becomes especially urgent during times of trauma and stress, such as before battle or within the wake of personal tragedy.

In his weakened state of mind Tristan began to experience a strange series of dreams by the third week of his penance, and each morning upon rising he sought desperately to find meaning in what he had envisioned during his sleep. The first dream involved Mala and Duxia de Falaise standing before a blistering bonfire as Duxia was casting about the moon and stars seeking a curse to place upon him. In this dream Mala and Duxia were not speaking French, but communicating with each other in a frightening, guttural tongue of unearthly origins. Then, when Duxia had finished communing with the celestial bodies of the night sky, she handed a small doll resembling Tristan to Mala who began submerging the doll into a bucket of water. She held it there, as drowning it, then finally withdrew it and held it up to the moon, a look of ecstasy consuming her face.

This dream was so vivid that it caused him to awake with a jolt and a cry, so cold with sweat that it took him a good while to realize that it was only a dream. This same nightmare occurred for several consecutive nights, and caused Tristan to struggle over its meaning. *Mala now wishes me dead like Duxia does*, he shivered morning after morning, brokenhearted.

After four consecutive nights of this horror, he began to fear sleep. He was so spent by then that he was forced to lay his weary head upon the straw palette of his cell despite his fear of encountering the two women yet again during the night. On the fifth night as Tristan dropped into a restive slumber, the women did not appear as he had feared. In their place came new visitors, rampaging Saracens swarming like locusts over the landscape of Italy, Germany, Spain, France and Italy by the hundreds of thousands, burning Christian churches as they swept forward, and torturing and murdering all Christians who refused to convert to Islam. This dream frightened him even more than the first, and even though he thrashed for hours in the straw trying to dispel the nightmare, he was unable to wrench himself free of the nightmare's grasp until dawn when the glare of sunlight began peering through the bars of the dungeon window. Even as he came awake and relief swept through him, he still imagined the rattling of Saracen instruments of war and the clatter of their hooves rumbling across the continent of Europe. Blinking, he shook his head and rubbed at his eyes. Although only fragments of the nightmare remained and the grizzly details had faded, the ugly mood of the nightmare clung to him throughout the day.

During his prayer vigil he spent a great deal of time reflecting on the Moors he had negotiated with in Cluny earlier that year over the issue of enslaving Christians of North Africa. He also thought about the Seljuq Turks he had met in Rome years before while serving as interpreter for Pope Gregory VII. As with many Europeans Tristan felt that Islam presented a future threat to Christianity in the Holy Land, in Africa, in southern Spain, and other distant locations. In this dream, the Saracens were actually invading the west itself and eradicating Christianity. The dream revisited him that next night, which caused his prayers of the next day to focus entirely on Europe's salvation from the encroachment of Islam. This dream also gave rise in him a deep suspicion that in time, something must be done to halt the aggression of the Islamists, and with time this suspicion would only grow.

It was the final series of dreams that disturbed him the most. During the final days of his penance, he began to experiences a series of dreams in which no Catholic Church existed whatsoever. In these nightmares he witnessed the nobility ravaging the land, setting towns afire, violating women and children, and butchering the innocent. And in the jumbled confusion so characteristic of dreams, the faces of many of the nobles wreaking this merciless havoc included allies of the Gregorian party itself such as the Normans and the Tuscans.

In these dreams he also encountered two endless hordes of people wandering the land, one suffering of starvation while the other suffered of disease and infirmity, while nobles stood idly by mocking them. The contemptuous nobility offered no assistance to these dispossessed masses, which Tristan found astounding. Worse yet, no Church existed to offer either respite or services, no monasteries existed to offer food to the poor or treatment to the ill, and no clergy existed to offer salvation in the next life. This world of his dreams was, in other words, a living Hell on earth in which no guiding morale force existed to hold the nobility in check or to offer comfort, direction, hope or education to the masses. This nightmare haunted him for several nights, and soon proved to be so disturbing to him that he began to reassess his previous criticisms of the dark, crafty policies of the Benedictine underground.

Meanwhile, the daily scourging took a vicious toll on his back, and as one week rolled into the next, Tristan's strength began to deteriorate such that he could barely maintain consciousness by the time his penance neared its end. Furthermore, the skin of his kneecaps had grown raw nearly to the bone from ten hours of daily contact against the stone floor of the cell. Spiritually, the hellish punishment Tristan endured during his penance served to redirect his priorities, which in turn caused him to reassess his thoughts about the contributions of the Church to civilization and to mankind.

On the very last morning of his penance, Tristan could barely stand. Teetering about on his feet like a drunk, he slowly passed the scourge over his shoulder and struck himself, barely able to hold onto the handle. Even as the tips of the scourge flicked his back, he felt nothing because his entire back, though blistered and cracked, had lost all feeling days earlier. His lids half closed, and only half aware of his surroundings, Tristan then fell to his knees and began his prayers. And that was when the thundering toll of a great cathedral bell rumbled its first knell in the back of his head, spawning in him a familiar current of dread. He closed his eyes in terror and threw his hands to his ears to cover his splitting eardrums, and when he opened his eyes again, his field of vision turned into a constellation of bright specks flickering about the room. The first knell was followed by a second, and a third, each causing Tristan's heart to shudder and his ribs to vibrate with its deep, reverberating resonance.

"God in Heaven, what's happening? The walls are coming down!" Tristan cried out, not knowing that the monstrous bell existed only in his head as it had on the previous occasions he had been seized by its thrall. Then, clasping his hands in prayer, he fell into a catatonic state and froze in position, leaving his cell and the fortress of Montelucio far behind him.

As this was taking place, Guillaume happened to be just outside the cell, talking to Antonelli, who was telling him that Tristan had been muttering strange things over the past week about 'a woman and a baby.'

"His ravings are a mishmash that makes no sense," Antonelli was saying. "It seems that this woman he keeps talking about disppeared for some reason, and the child he reaves about died. It's as if he blames himself for it all."

Antonelli had just finished this report when Guillaume heard Tristan's cry.

He opened the door, ran to his brother's side and knelt next to Tristan. Seeing that Tristan was in some strange state of unconsciousness, Guillaume shouted to Antonelli to get Cardinal Odo and the Danes. "Hurry!" he cried, "I need help here!"

Within minutes Cardinal Odo burst into the cell, followed by the Danes. "What is it, Guillaume? What is happening here?"

Guillaume was on his knees shaking Tristan by the shoulders. His brother was showing no signs of life though his eyes were wide open and he was clearly breathing. Comprehending, Odo pulled Guillaume away from Tristan and said, "Let him be, Guillaume. He is now as he was more than a year ago upon the summit of Monte Cassino when the blue sky broke into thunder, and lightning lit the clear night sky until dawn of the next morning, do you not remember?"

"Yes," Guillaume replied, shaking his head with concern, "but I don't understand it!"

"Nor do I," said Odo, "I only know that . . ."

"What the hell's the matter with Boy?" interrupted Orla seeing Tristan. "Swineshead! Is he dead?" Then he glared at Odo and shouted, "Look what you've done to him! Are you happy now? Oh, such unreasonable punishment you administered to him!"

"Be calm, Orla," said Odo. "I have seen this happen to Tristan several times before: upon the summit of Monte Cassino, as we fled Rome with Pope Gregory VII, and as we fled Rome again with Desiderius after being caught by the mob. And when he is seized like this by whatever force it is that controls him, he returns to us hours later, as though nothing had ever happened. Pope Gregory VII, witnessing this happen to Tristan atop Monte Cassino, and watching the unnatural outbreak of thunder and lightning on a clear day as Tristan entered this transcendental state, declared it a miracle. In the end, Pope Gregory determined that God was, somehow, communing with Tristan. Perhaps that is what is occurring now."

"What?" asked Crowbones. "I've never heard such tripe! He's obviously under some spell, probably cast by that bitch Mielikki!"

"Indeed," agreed Orla.

"In-d-deed!" nodded Guthroth.

"No," Guillaume said. "The Cardinal is right. I was there when this happened at Monte Cassino. He'll be fine, I think. His penance is done, so let's carry him to his quarters and get him in bed."

The Danes quickly gathered up Tristan who was naked, and placing their arms beneath his knees, litter-carried him to his quarters.

"By damn," snorted Crowbones, "Boy's knees are as bloody and ravaged as his goddamn back! Damn that Cardinal!"

"Ja," said Crowbones, guiding the others as they pried Tristan's limbs apart and set him belly-down on the bed, "only Christians would treat their own in such a manner." Then he turned and nudged Hroc who was standing behind him. "Get me some more rags, boy, to clean up this gore on his back."

Hroc did not move or even respond. He stood there staring at Tristan's back, horrified by the deep, puss-filled lines cutting through his uncle's flesh and the crusty black ridges of dried blood that followed their course. "Is h-he going to live?" Hroc stammered, tears beginning to flood his cheeks.

"Yes, Hroc, he'll live if you get me the damn rags!" barked Orla, seething over the condition of Tristan's back. "You'd think someone as smart as Boy here wouldn't make such a goddamn mess of his own back! Bones of God, he didn't have to beat himself so damn hard."

Tristan regained consciousness one day later. Then for the next week he lay shirtless and prostrate while Guillaume daily administered salve and herbs to his injuries. And though Guillaume was a seasoned warrior who thought nothing of slashing an enemy to ribbons, watching his brother suffer in such a manner disturbed him immensely. He made every effort he could muster to soothe Tristan's injuries as well as his lingering grief. "Know that I suffer along with you, Brother," he told Tristan one morning as he lay there, "and I pray that Cardinal Odo's harsh penance has not broken you."

"No," Tristan replied, his cheek resting upon his arm, "I feel my strength returning, physically and spiritually. And I vow to God that I shall never allow wine to touch my lips again save during mass, and I shall never weaken again to the temptation of the flesh."

Guillaume then noticed that as his brother lay there saying this, he was holding a small object within his fingers. "What have you there?" he asked.

"A silver ring," Tristan sighed. "Given to me when I was a boy by . . . a young Romani girl."

"Mala?"

"Yes."

This concerned Guillaume. "So tell me then, have you not set her aside?"

Tristan did not reply at first, but after some reflection he finally said, "During my penance I determined that I would forever leave deceit behind, so I must confess that Mala will forever be in my heart, Guillaume. I shall love her until the day I pass. Even though I return to the Brotherhood and know that I must remain celibate and chaste, it is not a sin for even a monk to love and treasure another within the confines of his own heart. To answer your question, yes, I have set her aside, but I will never forget her. Can you understand that?"

Guillaume was about to reply, but at that moment the door opened and Cardinal Odo entered with Countess Mathilda and two other monks. He was carrying a black robe and the monks were carrying shaving instruments. "Ah, you're looking much better, Tristan!" Odo smiled. "I have a gift for you." He then extended his arms, holding the robe by the shoulders for display. "The last time you wore the black robe was the first month after your ordination. Since then it has been one disguise after another with the underground, but from this moment forward you shall dress as a Benedictine. So sit up now, lad, so Brothers Antonio and Marcus can shave your crown into a proper Benedictine tonsure."

Tristan slowly rose and sat upon the edge of his bed as the monks began to clip the sides of his head and shave the center of his crown. This seemed to please Tristan and he offered a weak smile. "Ah," he said, "I feel more monkish already." Then, glancing at his brother, he said, "Guillaume, how does my head look?"

"Terrible," Guillaume frowned.

"And you, Aunt Mathilda?" Tristan chortled. "What do *you* think?"

"Wonderful!" she beamed.

"Yes, wonderful indeed," said Odo. Then, reaching into the billowing sleeve of his Cardinal's robe, he extracted an ornate, beautifully engraved gold medallion attached to a heavy gold chain, and slipped it over Tristan's head.

The gold felt heavy and cold against Tristan's bare skin. "What is this, Cardinal?" he said.

"This, my boy, is the medallion worn to identify Official Papal Envoys, of which there are only twenty in this entire world . . . you now being one of them."

Stunned, Tristan tried to speak, but quickly found himself fumbling for words.

"We have no Pope at the moment, of course," Odo shrugged, smiling, "but we must continue to carry on papal business regardless." Then Odo slipped his hand into a hidden pocket of his robe and withdrew a large gold ring. "This is your envoy seal. Oh, and I nearly forgot, I shall expect you in Monte Cassino within three weeks on New Year's Day for your induction ceremony and blessing into the Papal Envoy Service."

Tristan stared at Odo, speechless. As Odo looked back, their eyes shared a silent but profound communion of affection that reached back over the years, encompassing their entire existence together as prodigy and mentor. Mathilda observed this communion, so touched by it that she placed her fingers to her lips. "Amen!" she whispered, looking over at Guillaume with a smile.

CHAPTER SIXTY-THREE

THE POLITICS OF GOD

Thus it was that Tristan de Saint-Germain took on new fervor as Cardinal Odo de Lagery allowed him to recoup his designation as a Black Monk. Spurred on by his arduous act of contrition and his deep sorrow over the suffering inflicted upon Mala and the baby, Tristan resumed his service to the Church with a different resolve than he had the day of his ordination. The dreams during his penance in the cell had also affected him, especially the two concerning the abuse of the nobility and the threat of the Saracens, and created in him a new fever to hold both of those elements in check.

On New Year's Day of 1088 Tristan's entry into the service of Papal Diplomacy was formalized and celebrated as part of the Monte Cassino mass welcoming the New Year.

"May God direct this young soldier of Christ always," declared Cardinal Odo as the ceremony ended, "and may he become a pillar of righteousness against the forces of evil and the rising tide of earthly sin!"

The mass was then followed by a feast attended by throngs of pilgrims, high clerics, and aristocrats. It was Odo who organized this feast, and it was also Odo who now oversaw Papal diplomacy in the vacuum created by the death of Desiderius. Odo had already taken on a cumbersome load of responsibilities since the death of Pope Gregory, and this load increased even more as a result of Desiderius' passing. Odo continued to supervise the Benedictine underground as well, and also began to fill other roles left vacant by a number of deceased Cardinals and other papal officers who had become too elderly to carry on their duties. The result of this, of course, was that Cardinal Odo's influence within the Gregorian power structure began to eclipse all other clerics. Even other aspirants to the papacy recognized that they would garner few votes during the upcoming papal election in the face of Odo's formidable shadow.

Anxious to settle the issue of the vacant Papacy, the Gregorians issued a summons to as many bishops of their party as possible to attend a meeting at Terracina in March to appoint a new Pope; Terracina being chosen because Rome was still under the hand of the despised anti-pope, Clement III. This assembly was looked upon with great anticipation as Pope Victor III had been deceased for six months, which meant that the Gregorian faction had now gone half a year without a Pope. Most attendees had already concluded by this time that there was only one viable candidate to lead them, Cardinal Odo de Lagery.

Consequently, as the meeting opened, Cardinal Abbot Oderisius of Monte

Cassino immediately took the floor and declared, "Just as our blessed Holy Father Victor III, known to us as the beloved Desiderius, proposed that his faithful friend Cardinal Odo de Lagery succeed him as Pope, I also therefore nominate and vote for Cardinal Odo as the rightful heir to the Pope's throne! What say you, Brothers in Christ?"

Tristan was seated beside Odo as Cardinal Oderisius made this announcement, and listening, gazed about the gallery to weigh the assembly's mood. Many of the clerics began to whistle and applaud with appreciation as Odo's name was proclaimed. In the far corner a small circle of clerics remained silent, among them Cardinal Belmonte, the very man who with Duke Roger Borsa, had forced the tiara upon the unwilling Desiderius. Tristan nudged Odo then, and whispered. "Look there, it is the dour Belmonte again."

Odo nodded and in a low voice replied, "Yes, he has been stirring discontent, I hear."

Several other bishops and cardinals took the floor and also voiced support for Odo, most notably Giovanni Minuto, Bishop of Labico. "Never has there been a more devoted follower of Pope Gregory VII's policies of reform than Cardinal-Bishop Odo de Lagery of Ostia!" he declared. "He is a faithful servant of the Lord, of the Church, and of the people. He is the glue that has held us together in the face of the wicked Heinrich and his false monk, Clement III! Furthermore, Cardinal Odo was the right hand and intimate friend of Pope Victor during his unfortunately short reign as our Father. Let us immediately elect our blessed brother, Odo de Lagery, to now lead the faithful!"

This brought another round of whistles and applause. When the stir died down, Cardinal Belmonte stood. "Most of what Bishop Minuto claims is true, I must agree," Belmonte proclaimed, gazing about the room with a restrained smile, "but I must cry foul at his so-called close ties to our dear deceased Holy Father, Pope Victor! The truth is, Odo de Lagery opposed the original election of Desiderius because Odo de Lagery had hoped to become Pope himself!"

This caused a ripple of grumbling within the gallery until Bishop Bruno of Segni jumped to his feet and pointed angrily at Belmonte. "Indeed he *did* oppose that, but so did I and many others. That travesty was no *election*, Belmonte! The tiara was *forced* upon poor Desiderius by you, Duke Borsa, and others. It was out of loyalty to Desiderius that Odo opposed that *trumped-up* first appointment of Desiderius to the papacy. Most of us here recognize that entire episode as a pure abomination. And never forget, 'twas Odo who actually convinced Desiderius to accept the cope in the end!"

"Loyalty, you say?" cried Belmonte. "Ha, and I say it was a strategy of self-advancement! Also, don't forget that after convincing Desiderius to abandon the papacy that first time, Odo de Lagery then declared a sentence of damnation upon our greatest ally, Duke Borsa of Lower Italy!"

This infuriated Tristan who quickly looked at Odo and said, "Oh, foul words, you never tried to convince Desiderius to abandon the cope, he simply never wanted to wear it! And you have since lifted the declaration of damnation from Borsa. Oh, if you refuse to defend yourself against Belmonte's twisted rhetoric, then I shall seize the floor!"

"Shh . . . there is no need," answered Odo. "Belmonte only makes a fool of himself, thereby fortifying my position, not weakening it. Best to let others speak while I remain free of the fray. Say nothing, Tristan. Only listen."

Belmonte lodged another dubious charge or two, but was quickly and violently contradicted by a good number of other more reputable clerics, and eventually driven from the gallery by shouts and threats of violence.

"Bah!" he cried with exasperation as he fled the assembly with his handful of followers.

And thus, on March 12, 1088, Cardinal-Bishop Odo de Lagery of Ostia was unanimously elected Pope at Terracina, Italy. And as he donned the Pope's tiara and the red cope under the name of Pope Urban II with Tristan standing beside him, his first act was to exhort the princes and bishops who had been loyal to the Gregorian cause in the fight against King Heinrich.

"Oh, you faithful, know that I declare my intention to follow the policy and example of my great predecessor, Pope Gregory VII," he proclaimed. "All that he rejected, I reject, what he condemned I condemn, what he loved I embrace, what he considered as Catholic, I confirm!"

CHAPTER SIXTY-FOUR

POPE URBAN II

The former Cardinal-Bishop of Ostia Odo de Lagery, under the name of Pope Urban II, was now Pope to the Gregorian party and all of Europe to the west of Germany and Italy, and certain sections of Germany and Italy. As he ascended to the papacy in March of 1088 he inherited an extremely battered Gregorian Church that had been engaged in a costly war of eight years against King Heinrich of Germany who had crowned himself as Holy Roman Emperor. This bitter war had created deep divisions within Germany between Heinrich's royalists and the rebellious Saxon princes as well as in Italy between nobles and the clergy.

Worsening matters was the fact that the Normans of Lower Italy, staunch supporters of the Gregorian party, had broken into civil war between Bohemud and Roger Borsa, which meant that the Normans were too occupied fighting themselves to help in the effort against Heinrich and anti-pope Clement. In addition la Gran Contessa Mathilda of Tuscany, who was the other staunch military supporter of the Gregorian party, had lost much of the momentum she had recently gained against the Germans and was in retreat again in northern and central Italy.

Assessing his situation one week after his consecration, Odo called Tristan to his temporary office in Terracina. "We are in disarray," Odo said, "and have been for years now."

"Yes, Holiness," Tristan replied with a bow, still finding it somewhat difficult to fathom that his mentor and father figure was now the Holy Father of the true Church.

"Holiness?" shrugged Odo. "Ah, I suppose I shall have to become accustomed to the title, as well as to my new name, Pope Urban II. Coming from you, it sounds a bit odd."

"Yes, Holiness," Tristan replied, a slight smile creasing the corner of his mouth, "it is a bit odd to me also. I had a difficult time calling you Cardinal Odo after years of calling you Prior Odo at Cluny. It will take me some time to adjust."

"Very well then, let us not make things difficult for either of us. From this moment, in private, you are to call me "Odo"."

"Pardon, Holiness?"

"Yes. I am now one of the most powerful men on the continent, if not the world. I fear that such lofty heights could spoil a man into thinking himself greater than he is. I need at least one person in this life to keep me grounded. That will be you, Tristan."

Tristan backed away and shook his head. "Oh, Cardinal . . . I mean, Holiness, I could never refer to you by your first name!"

"It is not a request, Tristan, but a command. And we shall not discuss it further. I feel absolutely ridiculous when you call me Holiness, especially when we are alone. In public, of course, address me by the appropriate title, but not alone such as this, for the sake of my own humility."

"I beg you, Cardin . . ."

"No!" Odo interrupted. "Now go on, say my name. You will not turn to stone, Tristan."

Tristan stood mute for nearly a full minute, turning redder by the second. Finally he stammered, "Yes, O . . . do."

"Come now, you can do better than that."

"Y-yes, Odo."

"Excellent. Now that we have that out of the way, come sit and share your thoughts on our current situation, which is dire, unfortunately. I have formed some ideas on how to move forward, but would like to hear your thoughts on the matter also. By the way, that Papal Envoy medallion you are wearing, give it back to me, and the ring also."

"Pardon?" said Tristan, disappointment washing over his face.

"Yes, I need to replace it with this," said Odo, reaching over and opening the small wooden box that sat upon the table. He withdrew another medallion, larger, its outer edge encrusted with precious emeralds and rubies. Handing it to Tristan, Odo said, "Read the inscription."

Tristan examined it a moment, then looked at Odo, dumbfounded. "It reads Private Secretary to Pope Urban II, with all due authority."

"Yes, you are no longer a Papal Envoy, but my First Counsel. Oh, and here is your new insignia ring."

Tristan's face dropped. "I . . ."

"I told you many years ago that as I rise within the Church, you too shall rise. Do you not remember?"

"Yes, but I never thought that you would . . ."

"Become Pope?" laughed Odo. "Nor did I, even though others suggested the possibility from time to time."

Tristan reflected a moment and nodded. "Yes, Peter the Hermit for one. It is frightening to think how many things have transpired as he prophesized. The papacy of Cardinal Desiderius did indeed go poorly with him rejecting the tiara at first, then dying so soon after finally accepting it. Precisely as the Hermit predicted, you have become Pope. It makes me wonder where he is and what he is thinking now."

"Hopefully he remains far away in France! And hopefully he never comes to Italy!"

"Indeed. Still, it makes one wonder." Tristan then removed his Papal Envoy medallion and replaced it with the new one. "I am truly honored."

"There is a reason for the appointment, Tristan. Actually, a multitude of reasons. To begin, you have a heart for the people and for justice. You are also undoubtedly the most intelligent human to ever come out of Cluny which is in itself the very beacon of academia and wellspring of the greatest minds of the continent. Then, too, your extraordinary grasp of languages is phenomenal, far beyond anyone within our ranks. Also, you are perceptive and read people as well as anyone I have ever encountered, and because of that you have a natural knack for effective diplomacy. And lastly, you are as close to being my blood as anyone on this earth, and I need someone close to me that I can trust. And with what I am about to set into motion, I am in desperate need all of those qualities."

Here Tristan sighed and looked into Odo's eyes. "Yes, *trust*," he said in a low voice. "Spare not my feelings and tell me, from your heart and as my father in this life, have you truly forgiven me for my transgressions, and do you truly trust me?"

"Indeed, Tristan, with my very life. I was angry, and disappointed in you. Then I remembered my father becoming infuriated at me when I entered the Brotherhood. He wished me to follow in his steps as an aristocrat, a warlord, and his heir. Yes, I hope that one day you might take my path, but you are not me, so you will forge your own path, and undoubtedly stumble a time or two along the way as I did when young. As I bear my heart to you, I do have one concern, and that is your hesitancy at times about tactics. This has been an area of disagreement between us before and you have strongly voiced your concerns and objections, so I need to ask for my own peace of mind. In order to save the Church and advance the general good, can you be strong and resolute as we take on the enemy, turning their own ruthlessness against them? Because if you cannot, then we are doomed to fail."

Tristan looked down at his new medallion and rolled it about between his fingers as he remembered the dreams that had invaded his cell night after night during his penance. He still carried them about with him, and the concern they had caused him then had not abated a single measure. He thought for a moment that now might be an appropriate time to share these dreams, but then set that idea aside. Instead, he said, "Yes, to save the Church and to advance the general good, I can now stand firm, Father, even in the face of questionable tactics. I can do this because it has finally become clear to me that in the end, the Church must prevail. Its collapse, as you have taught me my entire life, invites darkness to descend upon the world. The Church represents man's moral compass on this earth, and without it, man is lost here as well in the next life."

CHAPTER SIXTY-FIVE

ODO'S WHEEL

During that next week within the monastery at Terracina, Odo carefully reviewed his objectives for the beginning of his papacy as Urban II with Tristan. No one else was allowed in chambers during these private meetings, and at night the chambers were locked and guarded in order to secure documents and maps. For Tristan this experience was an eye-opening, heady entry into the very lair of Gregorian intrigue, but the most difficult aspect of the entire week was getting used to calling Odo by his first name. He felt uncomfortable and squirmed doing so those first several days, but after a time it came easier to him.

"We will gradually share my strategy with others as it unfolds, Tristan," declared Odo. "Until then, we shall keep everything close at hand so as not to give away our position."

"You mentioned the other day that your first step was to gain at least a foothold in Rome again," said Tristan. "I did not question it then, yet I must ask. Our Norman allies of Lower Italy are at war with each other again. Furthermore, Mathilda is in retreat to the north and once again seeks refuge in the mountains. Without assistance from either quarter, how do you propose to enter Rome?"

"Yes, unfortunate developments with our allies, not unsurmountable. To begin, I hope to mediate a settlement between Borsa and Bohemud as quickly as possible and acquire their assistance again. I leave soon for a secret meeting with Borsa in Troina, Sicily within the month. Later I will meet with Bohemud."

"What stick will you use to force an end to their feud?"

"Heinrich. Muehler has recently sent news that the German king is conspiring anew. He is making attempts to talk Emperor Alexius of Constantinople into invading Lower Italy. The fact that Borsa and Bohemud are now fighting provides an opportune time for Alexius to launch an invasion from Constantinople if he wishes. The only thing holding him back is pressure coming from the Turks to the east, but Borsa and Bohemud are not privy to that information. Therefore, by frightening the two brothers with Heinrich's overtures to Alexius, I should be able to talk Borsa and Bohemud into quelling their bad blood long enough to make a truce desirable, otherwise both of them risk losing Lower Italy to the Byzantines."

"Ah, an excellent motivation, that!"

"Now, as to this crusade Desiderius declared against the Moors in North Africa at the Council of Benevento," Odo continued, "against my advice he placed General Bertucci at the head of this campaign, and I am receiving reports that he is making ill progress."

"Bernard Bertucci? The Duke of Genoa?" said Tristan, immediately thinking of Mala. "Was it not his daughter that Balducci was to wed before his unexpected marriage to . . ." Here he paused abruptly.

Odo sensed this, and quickly continued in an effort to spare him. "Bertucci is a grizzled veteran of many campaigns here in Italy as well as in Greece against the Byzantines, but he has never fought the Muslims. Furthermore, he is a bit of an old crank and believes in the hammer over diplomacy. Your expertise on the Saracens, Turks, and Moors, I believe, would be of benefit to his efforts in Tunis. Also, I hear that squabbling has broken out amongst his own troops so I need you to settle things down."

"The army consists of Gregorian Romans, Pisans, Genoese, and Amalfitans if I am not mistaken," said Tristan. Then he shook his head. "Due to the intense competition for commerce these city-states despise each other, so I imagine this hatred has carried over to the various militias. I may have a time of it, Odo."

"If anyone can negotiate peace amongst that bunch, it would be you, lad. Also, while there, I need you to ensure that our expeditionary force is properly representing the banner of Saint Peter, no rape, pillaging, and the like. And remember, old Bertucci can be an ass, so deal with him carefully."

"I understand."

"When you get back, you shall then go to northern Italy and meet secretly with Conrad, the fourteen-year-old son of King Heinrich."

"Ah, you send me directly into the lion's den, then?"

"No, not really. Prince Conrad is not to be confused with his father in any sense. He was appointed Duke of Lower Lorraine and Margrave of Turin at age two, then last May was made King of Germany in Aachen, his father Heinrich retaining the title of Holy Roman Emperor. As a child, Conrad was placed under the care of Archbishop Tedald of Milan and remained in Italy most of his years, therefore is not close to his father. Your visit to Conrad will be protected under the guise of respectfully delivering my Papal condolences to the boy for the loss of his mother three months ago. Neither Heinrich himself nor Archbishop Tedald will object to that."

Tristan looked at Odo carefully, then asked, "What is the *real* intent of my visit?"

At this Odo chuckled a bit. "Oh, you begin to anticipate my motives, eh? The fact is, our German agents have sent word that Conrad privately complains about his father's war offending God. Having been raised in a religious environment, the boy is far more devout than his father imagines. Consequently, I need you to go measure the width of this little rift between father and son. Furthermore, though his mother has recently passed away, Conrad is displeased that his father has so quickly forgotten her and is already courting other women. As time goes by, we may actually be able to create a divide between the two."

"I understand."

"And finally, while in Germany, I want you to visit our Bavarian ally, Duke Welf and his son of the same name. As you know, the Bavarians have long been staunch Gregorians. And even though Duke Welf was awarded the ducal dignity of Bavaria by King Heinrich in 1070, Welf turned against Heinrich when Heinrich declared war against Pope Gregory and began this accursed Investiture War."

"And what is my objective in Bavaria?"

"To discuss marriage of the younger Welf."

"Eh?" said Tristan. "If I recall, the younger Welf is fifteen or so, is he not?"

"Yes, indubitably old enough to soon be wed. The truth is, I actually began conducting preliminary correspondence with Duke Welf the Elder concerning his son's marriage before gaining the papacy through our agent Handel who is himself from Bavaria. After collecting arms and money from the Saxon princes, I commissioned him to stop by Bavaria to check on the condition of Duke Welf's son. What I didn't mention that day to you was my reason for having Muehler check on the boy."

"Yes, I remember now," said Tristan, recalling the day he and Handel had received their instructions from Odo and Muehler concerning the wagon trains.

"As for your role in Bavaria, I need you to formalize the arrangements and set forth the conditions and expectations surrounding young Welf's marriage."

"I see," said Tristan with sudden interest. "The Welfs are extremely wealthy and powerful, so pray tell, who is to be the fortunate bride? She must certainly be someone of substantial note, I would imagine."

Odo nodded slowly. "Yes, of course. Actually, young Welf is the fortunate one, his future bride's wealth far exceeds that of his own family."

"What? The Welf family fortune is immense," Tristan said with surprise. "I must know then, who *is* this young German woman for whom I shall be making betrothal arrangements?"

"Not German. She is a Medici."

"Ah, Italian. Come now, what is her name?"

"Her name, lad, is Mathilda Medici, Countess and Princess of Tuscany, your adoptive aunt."

Tristan's jaw dropped. After a moment, he laughed aloud, thinking it a joke. "Oh, ho! Seldom do you jest, but that was a good one, Odo!" Then he reared his head back and laughed more. "Oh, you led me into that snare with such *guile!*" he roared with hilarity. "Ha! Young Welf is a boy, and at least twenty-six years or so younger than Auntie Mathilda who is forty-two!"

Odo did not join in Tristan's laughter. He stood there calmly watching Tristan's outburst of amusement for a while, then placed his hand on Tristan's and said, "I do not jest. This marriage is to strengthen our position against Heinrich. Both parties benefit. Mathilda guarantees her alliance with Bavaria, and the Welfs solidify their position against Heinrich along their southern borders. There is no bond stronger than marriage in terms of guaranteeing alliances."

"But . . ."

"Do not concern yourself with all this at the moment for you have other things to do first," said Odo. He knew beforehand, of course, that Tristan would become unraveled when he found out about this marriage, and was not surprised by the shock consuming Tristan's face that was robbing him of his capacity to speak. "And Tristan," he said with reassurance, "just as you will make a fine diplomat in Africa, you shall make a fine matchmaker in Bavaria."

CHAPTER SIXTY-SIX

MALA

The effect of beauty on even the most stone-hearted of men is similar to that of the sea wearing down the hard edged cliffs of a rocky shore. The effect of absolute, stunning beauty magnifies this effect tenfold, and the effect is more like that of a raging storm erupting against the face of this rock, carving out deep chasms and rapidly disassembling its foundation. And such was the effect that Mala was having on Vincento Balducci.

Balducci had always thought himself entitled, due to his doting mother who fussed and circled about him during his childhood as would some nervous manor maid, terrified that the master might show the least sign of displeasure. As a result of this rearing Balducci learned to treat women with disdain and had developed into a seasoned misogynist by early adolescence. Women, of course, immediately sensed this, and generally demonstrated subservience to him as a means of avoiding his sneering attention.

It was with difficulty then that Balducci interacted with la Gran Contessa Mathilda who was vastly more wealthy and powerful than himself. Mathilda had little patience for either Balducci's behavior or his inflated sense of self, and either dismissed him as one would dismiss a spoiled child or struck back with the bluntness of a well-placed bludgeon to the head. This confused him at times, but as with all bullies, he retreated in the face of such superior arms. Unbeknownst to Balducci at the time he fell beneath Mala's spell, like Mathilda, Mala was also the type of woman who could strike back. And with the wise and bitter Duxia de Falaise at her side for counsel, the two would form a female juggernaut the likes of which Balducci had never encountered beneath his own roof.

The first clue that Balducci was helpless in the thrall of Mala's beauty was the rapidity with which he flung himself at her, proposing marriage only six weeks after meeting her at the Alpine pass despite her humble origins and lack of dowry. Next was the fact that he had already promised himself in marriage a year earlier to one Lady Marianna Bertucci, daughter of Duke Bernard Bertucci, a powerful figure of Genoa. Breaking off this engagement insulted the entire Bertucci clan, which was widespread in both north and central Italy, and caused the raising of many eyebrows within aristocratic circles. "God forbid," the whispers went, "Balducci favors this whorish dancing girl over the Bertucci family and fortune!" Of course, they knew little about Mala other than she had been an entertainer, was a commoner, and that she was foreign and of dark complexion. Many quickly assumed that she must be Saracen, therefore immediately shunned her. And the final clue to Balducci's weakness for Mala was the fact that, despite her gender, he treated her with unprecedented courtesy and deference. She was so alluring that he did not wish her to be displeased with him.

The wedding of Lord Vincento Balducci to Mala the Romani, which took place shortly after his arrival back to his reclaimed territories, turned out to be a rather awkward affair. Balducci sent out invitations to all the grand aristocrats, political figures, and high clerics of the Gregorian camp who resided in central and northern Italy. And to showcase his lovely bride and celebrate his marriage, he spared no expense in preparing an ostentatious ceremony. This was followed by a fabulous feast catered by servants flittering about serving wine, fruit, and delicate sweets piled high upon exquisitely engraved copper and silver platters. Additional servants moved about offering roasted pheasant, heron, crane, and goose while the groom's table had four roasted hogs exquisitely splayed, carved, and dressed. Despite the wondrous setting that Balducci had so fussily orchestrated and his high level of anticipation, attendance was sparse. The thin crowd consisted primarily of Balducci's immediate family, his vassals, and a smattering of neighboring nobles, minus many wives who had refused to attend because of Balducci's flagrant insult to the family of the rejected Marianna Bertucci of Genoa. Of course, these women did not hold Marianna herself in especially high regard, thinking her homely and dull. The fact that Balducci married a commoner was to them, insufferable. Countess Mathilda did not attend the wedding, nor did General Padule, Guillaume, the Danes, Odo de Lagery, any of the high clergy, nor politicians of note, nor anyone even distantly related to the Bertucci clan.

It is a quirk of human nature that the insensitive are themselves doubly wounded by slight, but as Balducci gazed about the bare wedding hall, he was wounded by this shunning of so many he had thought to be friends and close acquaintances. This disappointment soon gave rise to a simmering resentment as he pulled his manor master to the side halfway through the reception.

"Compile a list of every damned person who chose not to make an appearance on this grand occasion of my wedding," he barked bitterly.

Compounding this already stilted atmosphere was the fact that Balducci's own mother and sisters made it evident at every turn that they did not approve of the Romani bride, nor did they approve of her strange and elderly cohort who, despite the occasion, was wearing her habitual black garb accompanied by a black shawl draped over her head and shoulders. "So gauche," Balducci's sisters, Celia and Cosima, complained, "the old nag could have at least put on some jewelry and decent clothing!"

"And the very looks of that old bitch tells me that Vincento's new wife comes from poor peasant stock," cried Lady Alda, Balducci's mother, fanning herself with her hand. "The old mule is the girl's aunt, for God's sake, which means that Vincento's bride herself will resemble the old hag in a few years! Such coarse features, these *peasants*."

Balducci overheard this and became furious. "Show some goddamn consideration!" he cried, flinging his goblet of wine at the three. "If not for my wife and her aunt, then at least for me, damn you!"

A hush fell upon the wedding hall as Balducci's outburst elevated, causing his mother and sisters to flee the room in tears. Mala quickly pulled him by the arm and led him away. "Calm down, Vincento, don't make a fool of yourself in front of your guests," she said, vowing secretly to blister the catty threesome at a later time.

Duxia had not left Mala's side at any point during the reception and was trailing her even as she said this to Balducci. "Let it pass, Dear," she whispered, recognizing that inflamed look that had swept into Mala's eyes despite her effort to hide her anger. "Smile, Dear, and be gracious despite the arrows flung our direction. Do nothing you'll regret later!"

Mala looked back at Duxia and gestured with a slight nod. Then she looked at Balducci with her large almond eyes and began to stroke his arms and his shoulders, soothing him. These movements and Mala's intimate touching quickly made him forget the snubbing of friends and relatives, and he became impatient to be away from the wedding hall. "Let me call this fiasco to an end," he urged, "and let's retire to the wedding chamber, Mala. You have held me at bay long enough, and my body burns for you!"

Although he had attempted every ploy imaginable to lure Mala into his bed upon the arrival of his caravan back to his territories, Mala had steadfastly refused him. "Not until I wear your wedding ring, Vincento," she would reply, rebuffing his advances. This, of course, only served to further stoke Balducci's fire, as Duxia had predicted.

"Yes, very well," Mala replied softly, looking over at Duxia who was nodding the slightest bit.

Balducci then declared the feast ended, and with great brouhaha before the other men in attendance, he announced loudly that he and his bride would be *retiring* to the wedding bed. His face rosy with wine, he then marched her back and forth before these men with great pride, knowing that each and every one of them envied him at that moment more than any man on earth. As for Mala, she played her part well during this promenade as an approving Duxia watched on, and strutted sensuously before her admirers with the svelte, sweeping movements of the lithe dancer she was. For Balducci, seeing his peers ogle his ravishing wife was the banner moment of the night.

Bursting with anticipation, Balducci then swept Mala from the floor into his arms and fairly ran up the stairs to the wedding suite where, upon closing the door, Mala then slowly and skillfully satisfied Balducci's ardent advances until he was utterly sated. Then, in the morning as they awoke, she repeated her actions of the night before, as Duxia had instructed. From that moment on, also as Duxia had predicted, Balducci abandoned all previous ties to family and friends and belonged solely to Mala.

CHAPTER SIXTY-SEVEN

THE MARRIAGE

Balducci was so captivated by Mala's allure that he immediately began to shower her with gifts, compliments, and kindness . . . to which she gave only slight acknowledgment.

"Be more appreciative," Duxia would suggest, having decided that Balducci's happiness was now the foundation upon which their future rested. "He adores you unashamedly as did poor Fernando, can't you see that?"

Mala found it difficult to be demonstrative. The vivacity she had possessed since birth had withered that stormy night she had led her Romani troupe out of Marseilles, then completely dissipated with the nightmare of the Alps crossing. Fortunately, for Balducci's sake, her temper had also slackened, so she unwittingly slipped into a more suitable frame of mind in terms of appearances befitting a nobleman's wife. She developed a calm, dignified demeanor that seemed to erase all trace of her common roots. She also took a sudden interest in learning Italian and proved to be an extremely adept learner. Adding Italian to her native Romani tongue, her fluency in French, and her basic knowledge of Moorish Arabic from her childhood days in Spain, made her quartolingual, which was no insignificant feat for anyone of the day, especially a woman. This only fueled her hunger for knowledge and soon led her to enlist a corps of private tutors for the purpose of teaching her to read and write in both Italian and French.

All of this pleased Balducci, of course, as it did Duxia. "A fine thing this," Duxia would cluck. "You're establishing an independence that will serve you well one day, Dear."

Balducci's primary immediate concern, as with most men recently wed, was Mala's performance in the bedchamber. And though it could not be said that Mala actually loved her husband, Balducci would have never guessed such a thing based on what he perceived as their many nights of unadulterated passion during their first weeks of marriage. He felt the pleasure to be mutual, of course, and further felt that his romantic prowess had placed a firm bridle upon his young wife. He was mistaken, since these nights had in fact only served to heighten Mala's control over *him*. And though she did everything he could possibly desire in the privacy of their bedchamber, it was also there that she managed to let him know that she possessed a firm resolve of her own and could quickly flush into a torrent of retaliation if ever humiliated or mistreated.

"I must as your wife confess to you that I am a wanted woman in Normandy, Vincento," she told him on their fifth night together. "There is still a bounty on my head there for killing the son of a certain Duke LeBrun."

"What!" said Balducci, startled and intrigued in equal measure by this sudden revelation.

"Yes, he tried to rape my mother and when she resisted he cut her face to ribbons. I came upon them as this happened, quickly withdrew my dagger and plunged it into his heart."

"You used to carry a dagger?" said Balducci, appearing amused.

"Vin-cen-to," she said without changing expression, emphasizing the syllables of his name like she had done before when dominating Fernando, "I still do." Then she slipped her hand beneath the pillow and withdrew a dagger. "I keep this with me at all times in case I am ever threatened with harm by a man, *any* man. Remember that, Vincento. I shall require respect from you at all times."

He looked at her, dumbfounded. When surprise finally fell aside, he raised up to voice objection to her concealing a dagger within their bed. As he surveyed her dark, stern eyes, they told him it would be useless. So he said nothing.

Despite his complete adoration of Mala, there was one thing about her that did displease Balducci, and that was Duxia. It seemed that other than in the privacy of their bedchamber, the old woman was omnipresent. Of further irritation to him was Duxia's incessant habit of whispering into Mala's ear. Whenever this occurred, Mala would listen intently to whatever the old woman was saying, then would invariably nod yes . . . which indicated to Balducci that Duxia was constantly giving Mala counsel and Mala was accepting it. This was not so much an issue of jealousy for Balducci as it was an issue of concern. He did not like the idea that his wife so heavily depended on and seemed to heed the words of this mysterious old wretch. Furthermore, he often felt that Duxia was making derogatory comments to Mala about him, which was intolerable.

He could not have been more wrong. Duxia's whispering was actually her effort to mollify Mala by tirelessly reminding her of the lean days. In reality then, it was Duxia who served as much of the glue holding this marriage together; not because Duxia cared the least bit for Balducci, but out of concern for Mala who had by now become the only light in what she saw as her own final years.

Balducci voiced his displeasure about Duxia to Mala on several occasions, but his objections were met with immediate displeasure of her own.

"Vincento," she replied with a frigidity that stopped Balducci mid-sentence, "If you cannot tolerate Duxia, then she and I will pack our belongings and leave Italy *together*. Otherwise, there's no point in discussing the matter." Then she would turn on her heels and walk off.

This response was so swift and so inflexible that it confused Balducci, leaving him feeling dissected, much as when the Countess Mathilda would cut him off at the knees. Again, there was such fierce resolve in Mala's expression whenever he broached the subject of Duxia that he realized there would be no bartering over the presence of the old woman in the household, so he decided to leave well enough alone.

Thus began the marriage of Mala to Vincento Balducci. And as it could not be said that Mala loved her new husband, nor was she disinclined toward him since he treated her well and provided things she had never imagined within reach. Her feeling toward him then was not unlike her feeling toward the deceased Fernando other than the fact that she shared her bed with Balducci. Even this was not entirely unpalatable to Mala. There were times when wrapped within her new husband's lustful embrace that images of Tristan would arise from nowhere. When this occurred she would at first experience sudden pangs of heartbreak and reminiscence, but then the shadowy memory of the Alps and her lost infant would overcome her and Tristan's face would melt from her thoughts.

In truth then, Mala who was once anchored as the vibrant leader of her own Romani entertainment troupe had now become a wandering soul. She was neither happy nor unhappy, and her previous self had somehow evolved into a new persona. Of course, she did not miss the hunger or the uncertainty of the poor days, but she also did not especially indulge in or appreciate the sudden comforts that wealth now afforded her. And independent as she had once been, she allowed herself to be directed more by Duxia than by her own drive because, in truth, she had little drive left within herself.

This lack of emotion in Mala concerned Duxia. She had hoped that Balducci and his wealth would bring happiness to Mala. It soon became evident to Duxia that the probability of such a simple outcome occurring was slight indeed. Consequently, she then decided the next best thing would be for Mala to at least preserve Balducci's pride in public and keep him satisfied in private.

"*Oh, be wise,*" Duxia would whisper in her ear daily, along with a dozen other bits of advice geared solely toward sustaining Balducci's happiness. "*Bow to him in public, and own him in private, my Sweet, with your eyes, your breasts, and your thighs.*"

As time ensued, the greatest ally of this marriage proved to be the fact that Balducci, as commander of an army serving beneath the banner of Countess Mathilda, was gone much of the time. And though Balducci obsessed over his beautiful bride during these absences, Mala was quite content having the run of his estates without him. In the end then, it could be said that Balducci considered himself happily married while Mala considered herself married. Their marriage, then, was not dissimilar to many aristocratic marriages of the day where one partner was engaged in the relationship while the other remained ambivalent.

CHAPTER SIXTY-EIGHT

THE SERVANTS

In the households of the wealthy, the masters give small consideration to the needs, wants, or dreams of the servants. It is the servants of the two, then, who more closely follow and scrutinize the actions of the other. From this they learn to decipher the code of gestures, posture, and facial expressions displayed by their superiors. A good servant, then, can read the master like a book, and at times even anticipate what the master is thinking. The manor servants of Balducci's household were of this caliber. Balducci, due to his haughty nature, was easily read by his servants; predictably demanding and scornful of others. Balducci's mother, Lady Alda, and his sisters, Celia and Cosima, were also haughty, but to a lesser degree. This and the fact that they existed in a constant state of rivalry, often forming ever changing alliances of two against the one, made them a shade more difficult to read than Lord Balducci. Nevertheless, the servants of the household had become quite adept at manipulating this triangle of aristo-cratic females while simultaneously dodging the crossfire of their bickering. The pecking order of the house, therefore, was Balducci first, and the mother second, unless Celia and Cosima had happened to form an alliance against Lady Alda which would cause Lady Alda to wither with distress and temporarily shrink from prominence.

The entrance of Mala and Duxia, threw the servants into a state of confu-sion. They had at first expected the new wife to slip into the family hierarchy beneath Lady Alda. It soon became evident that Mala refused to defer to the manor matriarch. This meant that Lady Mala had unseated the mother and was now in second position, which caused a stir that lasted for months. Lady Alda felt Mala to be inferior, as did Celia and Cosima.

Duxia caused even more chaos for the servants who had at first expected that the old woman would take her place at the very bottom of the family chain. Soon they began to realize that Lady Mala and her aunt were tightly bound in a formi-dable alliance of their own, one that did not change from week to week or month to month . . . which meant that old Duxia had also dislodged Lady Alda, as well as the two sisters. Then the unthinkable occurred. With time the servants grad-ually began to perceive that it was Lady Mala, with the guidance and counsel of old Duxia, who actually appeared to be directing Lord Balducci.

Further complicating this situation was the fact that, unlike the four Balduccis, Mala was nearly impossible to read. To begin, she was neither haughty nor scornful to the help, therefore dissimilar to all aristocrats they had previously experienced. Furthermore, Lady Mala said very little to anyone except her aunt and displayed little emotion, which kept them guessing the state of their service and wondering whether she was pleased or displeased with them. And finally, they were so confounded by the fact that Lady Mala could manage to drive Lord Balducci with the simple movement of her brow that they became somewhat fearful of her though she never once threatened or mistreated them. They also became fearful of old Duxia, who said little to them but developed the habit of daily watching their every move with hawkish attention, as though probing for misdeeds.

Change, like a stone thrown into a pond forces ripples across the surface, the arrival of Mala and Duxia caused great speculation and chatter among the servants of the Balducci manor. This chatter was, of course, exchanged with visiting coachmen who would then pass along what they had heard to the servants of their own respective estates, and occasionally to the masters themselves. Consequently, Lady Mala and Duxia became favorite subjects of discussion within the staid existence of the manor servants throughout Tuscany since they were new arrivals. More interestingly, the two possessed unusual backgrounds . . . in other words, they were foreigners and, like the servants, were commoners. Mala and Duxia, then, served as living examples of peasant fantasies come true for many of these people, especially the women.

Embellishment is a required ingredient in the exchange of stories if one is to entertain others, so many of the female servants began to romanticize Duxia's and Mala's existence. "Ah, the old bitty is a sorceress and holds unnatural sway over the beautiful Lady Mala," claimed one woman. "Yes, and I heard that Lady Mala was once an exotic dancer in the court of a great Saracen emperor," reported another. "No," another disagreed, "can you not see that she is no commoner at all by the way she carries herself? Indeed, she was born a Saracen princess. She was kidnapped by the Norse, somehow escaped and was working her way back east to Arabia when she was caught in the Alps!"

Each new presumption spread by this servant gossip about Mala was more preposterous than the previous. One common thread that was agreed by all: "There is a strange sadness that lingers over Lady Mala. She spends hours each day sitting in the orchard staring at nothing, lost in reflection. If she truly loved Balducci, she would not drown herself in such solitude. We women recognize that mournful gaze; there must either be a lost or an unrequited love somewhere in her mysterious history."

CHAPTER SIXTY-NINE

DUXIA'S WEB

One day during Balducci's first absence from the manor, Mala happened upon Duxia as she was carrying several items to her room. "What have you there, Duxia?" she said.

"A gold goblet and two silver candlesticks," Duxia replied, looking about to ensure that no one was listening. Then she gathered the items closer to her bosom and covered them with her shawl.

Mala had noticed that the items were a tad tarnished, and laughed. "Oh, Duxia, we have servants now! There's no need for you to shine the metal ware."

"Oh, nay," Duxia, replied in a low voice, "I have no intention of shining them. I'm hoarding them beneath my bed, Dear."

"What?" asked Mala.

"Yes, each week I collect an article or two and slip them into the saddlebags I have concealed beneath my bed."

"Duxia! You are stealing?"

Duxia nodded. "Yes, of course, only for your future. Just as you tumbled unexpectedly into abject poverty, then tumbled into sudden wealth, you may yet again lose everything in the blink of an eye! Such is the hammer of God, so I will continue to gather precious articles from this manor. If we're ever driven from this place, you will at least have a start."

"Duxia, I insist that you put everything you've taken back in place. Besides, I hardly think you need to worry about me. Rather, it is me who worries about you. You've endured such hardship and heartbreak over the years that I want you to finally be happy."

This touched the old woman. Cradling the items in her possession over to one arm and reaching out with the other, she raised a hand out and squeezed Mala's hand. Then her head quavered in that involuntary bobble of the elderly as her eyes began to moisten.

"Oh, Mala, that means everything to this old wretch," she whispered. "And that is all I wish for you, Dear, yet I fear you have not yet shaken the memory of Tristan de Saint-Germain from your soul."

Mala was not expecting to hear Tristan's name; the very sound of which gave her a start. She'd not heard it spoken by another since arriving within Balducci's territories. She began to mumble a reply but then fell silent.

"Ah, you see," said Duxia, disheartened, "you can't even bear to hear his name without sinking. That breaks my heart. You are in such a good place now, yet don't see it. Beautiful as you are, if you don't give more of yourself to Balducci I fear he may eventually tire of you. Yes, my entire life has been a struggle, and a losing one at that. With what I've come to see in you and with all that we've suffered through together, I've come to love you as I once loved the Lady Asta many years ago before being driven from her household. And as I look back over my years of misery and begging, I vow that I'll never allow you to squander your one lifetime on this earth as I have mine. Therefore, don't force me to replace these things I collect. They're baubles to Balducci. While it's true that you may never need them, the other is also true. Trust the instincts of an old defeated woman, my Dear, I beg you."

The supplication within Duxia's expression at that moment struck Mala to the soul, and she could not summon the will to deny her old friend's effort to help.

"Very well then," said Mala, gently kissing Duxia upon the forehead. Then she looked at Duxia and smiled. "We are a pitiful pair, we two, eh?"

"Yes, I suppose," Duxia whimpered, as tiny tears began to roll down the crests of her cheekbones, "but we have each other at least. I was certain that I was destined to die alone on some unfamiliar road to nowhere, but you took me in and have given me reason to live, my Dearest." Then she dried her eyes and shuffled into her room, content that she was doing what was best for Mala.

The hoarding of precious household goods was one part of Duxia's overall strategy to fulfill Mala's needs. She had from the very beginning upon meeting Balducci at Countess Mathilda's Canossa fortress done everything possible to draw his attention toward Mala, and these efforts had succeeded beyond expectation. Then, securing an engagement and marriage, Duxia had then dedicated herself to keeping Mala in line with Balducci's aspirations. Clever as she was, Duxia also soon perceived that he appeared to resent her for some reason. Rather than allow this to continue, she decided to take matters into her own hands and approached him in private one day.

"My Lord Balducci," she said with a bow, "it seems that I have displeased you in some way, and that troubles me to the point of desolation. What may I do to correct any misdeeds I may have unwittingly committed?"

Balducci sneered at Duxia a moment, surprised at being confronted so directly. Nevertheless, since Mala had so bluntly dismissed his concerns about the old woman, he decided to jump on this opportunity to unleash his resentment. "Quite simply," he snapped, "I tire of you being constantly in our presence. You're like a goddamn shadow!"

"I see," nodded Duxia, showing no offense.

"Furthermore, dammit, I don't approve of the way you're constantly whispering things to my wife about me."

Duxia reflected on this comment a moment, then said, "Lord Balducci, please know that when I whisper to my niece in your presence, it is only to make her aware of your wishes and needs."

"Huh?" said Balducci.

"Yes, my Lord, for you see, Mala is in a new environment and is not familiar with the etiquette of aristocracy. I on the other hand was once closely attached to a noble family in France and try to keep her apprised of your expectations without embarrassing her or yourself. So you see, it is never *you* that I whisper about, merely about maintaining the dignity of your household." Then she drew nearer. "Let's be honest. There are many here in Italy who don't approve of my dear Mala, and mock her common roots. I am primarily protecting her and also defending your own interests."

This had never occurred to Balducci, and as he listened to Duxia last comments, he begrudgingly shook his head in agreement. "Yes . . . she has received a chilly reception from certain quarters though she does not deserve it."

Sensing at once that she had probed into an area of sensitivity, Duxia then decided to strike against Balducci's mother and sisters. "The Lady Alda and your sisters, Celia and Cosima," said Duxia with gentleness, "I fear they too *disapprove* of Mala."

Balducci said nothing at first; the look in his eyes confirmed Duxia's claim. Then Balducci's brows drew together and he said, "Nevertheless, they had best keep such things to themselves. They've not been impolite to her during my absence, have they?"

"They have said nothing, my Lord, but silence speaks volumes, does it not? They shun her, and my poor niece grows so lonely here in your absence with only me to comfort her; though she would never distress you with such a confession."

Mala, of course, had no interest whatsoever in the company of Lady Alda or the two sisters, and found them to be affective and pretentious. Balducci was not aware of this, so he immediately fell into Duxia's web.

"Dammit," he exclaimed, "to think my poor wife is being mistreated by my own flesh and blood! Hunh! I will tend to that matter myself, then."

"Thank you, my Lord."

Balducci looked down at the stooped Duxia and seemed to regard her in a different light. "You may call me Lord *Vincento*," he said without smiling. "After all, we are family of sorts, I suppose."

At this Duxia bowed and took her leave. *Lord Vincento indeed,* she thought, satisfied that she had driven yet another wedge on behalf of Mala between Balducci and his bitchy relations. *Yes, and I must allow Balducci more privacy with Mala it seems.*

CHAPTER SEVENTY

NORTH AFRICA

Although Tristan possessed a hoard of expertise on Islam, the Arab and Persian tongues, and the ethnic origins of various Arab and Turkish races through in depth study and research, his only direct dealings with Muslims had taken place in the diplomatic arenas of Rome and Cluny. Ifriqiya was an entirely different environment, and as his ship left the Gulf of Tunis, worked its way through the Lake of Tunis, and docked at the port of Halq al Wadi, Tristan could barely rein in his own excitement. This was his first landing upon the soil of a non-western culture.

He was greeted by Duke-General Bertucci upon disembarking, and as Bertucci's coach moved through the city of Tunis, Tristan gazed about in wonder, immediately struck by the vibrant colors of clothing and décor, the new smells and unrecognizable foods of the marketplace, and the exotic atmosphere of the streets and architecture.

"So striking, all this!" he exclaimed to Bertucci.

"Bah," snorted Bertucci, "dirty and foul, I say, and full of foreigners!"

Tristan considered the remark, noting its xenophobic tenor as well as the contempt in Bertucci's eyes as he watched the native Muslims milling about in the streets as the general's escort meandered its way through the narrow streets toward the Italian stronghold at the edge of the city.

"Tell me about your troops," Tristan then said, "you have four different militias within your force so I wonder how they fare together?"

"They're fine when the Saracens come at them," grunted Bertucci, "but the dumb bastards fight amongst themselves constantly in camp, the Romans against the Genoese, the Pisans against the Amalfitans. Already had over a hundred flogged, have another forty or so shackled in the tower, and had to execute two Amafatins last week for murdering a Pisan."

"I see," said Tristan. "And how fares the campaign itself, General?"

Bertucci shook his head. "Tougher than I imagined. I figured we'd arrive, rout the goddamn Saracens, free the Christians, then pile back in our ships and sail back to Italy, but the Saracens have us bogged down at the moment."

"Actually, these are not Saracens you are fighting, General, they are Moors, a compilation of Berber tribes. The Saracens come from the lands of Arabia, not Africa."

"What the hell's the difference?" Bertucci snapped. "They're all dark and they're all Muslim, so they're Saracens."

Wishing to neither offend the general nor launch into an intellectual dispute, Tristan said, "Very well, they are Saracens. In any case, I dare say that you expected them to be primitive and backward," said Tristan.

"Well, yes."

"That is a western misconception, I fear. These people are as advanced as we are, if not more so, and their leadership is extremely sophisticated in terms of education, art, and warfare."

Bertucci scowled a moment, then acknowledged Tristan's comment with, "Well, by damn, I must admit they're pretty good with the sword, too, I'll give you that."

After arriving at the expeditionary stronghold, Bertucci gave Tristan a lengthy briefing on the army's activities since landing in Tunis. When he had finished, Tristan praised the general's efforts, unsuccessful though they were, then asked, "So how many alliances have you formed with the outlying or dissident tribes of the region, General Bertucci?"

"*Alliances*? What the hell are you talking about? Christ, we're here to defeat these goddamn people, not to make friends. It's Christianity against Islam for God's sake, as stated by Pope Victor himself before he died! Has Odo de Lagery forgotten that since becoming Pope Urban? This invasion of Tunis is a crusade against the heathens!"

"Yes, of course," said Tristan politely, understanding why Odo had opposed placing Bertucci in charge of the invasion of Tunis. "Pope Urban is well aware of that. The truth is, he helped engineer this expedition. Allow me to ask you something, General, with all due respect, are you familiar with the old proverb, 'The enemy of my enemy is my friend'?"

"Yes, of course. What's your point? We're talking about Saracens here, not Christians."

"Certainly. You must remember that Duke Robert Guiscard the Wily conquered Saracen Sicily and retook Lower Italy from the Saracens many years ago only by forming alliances with dissident Saracens. He used bribery and the promise of revenge, and would have never prevailed without their assistance, and you are in the same position now . . . you will not succeed here in Tunis unless you recruit Saracen *allies*. Look, General, the population of Ifrqiya is deeply diverse and tribal, rife with blood feuds, animosities, and vendettas. You are having enough problems getting your own four militias to cooperate, are you not? Magnify that by ten, then, when speaking about the North Africans you are fighting and you will quickly see that you have a huge advantage here."

"What do you mean?"

"Just as we are suffering from the religious schism between the Gregorians and the King of Germany, these people are divided spiritually into Sunni and Shiite, and much blood has effused between the two. On top of that you have Bedouins, Berbers, the Shia Fatimid Caliphate who still tries to rule from Cairo, the Zirids who once were Shiite but are now Sunni, the Maghribi, the Tuareg, and the Banu Hilal from Arabia who were unleashed upon this land by the Fatimid Calipahate in retaliation for the Zirid break away from Cairo. They are all mixed here together in one boiling caldron, and regardless of who rules, there is festering discontent beneath the surface. You must mobilize this discontent here in Ifriqiya and turn it to your advantage, General."

Bertucci looked at Tristan as though he was speaking a foreign tongue, confused by all the tribes and sects Tristan had quoted. He was impressed, and somehow began to sense that this young sprout standing before him was going to be an asset. "Where the hell did you learn so much about the Saracens, in Rome?" he asked, as the slightest trace of a smile began to break the corner of his mouth.

"No, mostly in Cluny where I studied their language, culture, politics, and religion as a boy."

"As a boy?" whistled Fazio. "Christ, you don't look to be much more than a boy now!"

Tristan smiled at this comment and said, "Ah, the journeys I have traveled in my short years, General. At age fourteen I also served as interpreter for Pope Gregory when he summoned the Seljuq Turks to Rome concerning abuse of Christian pilgrims in the Holy Land. I learned a great deal from the leader of the Turkish envoy who came from Baghdad, a certain Lord Abdul Azim. And last year I assisted Abbot Hugh in Cluny as he was negotiating with these very same North Africans that you are now fighting. We threatened war if they did not stop enslaving Christians here in Tunis, and I will tell you that their delegation was split hearing this. Half opposed war and seemed concerned at the prospect of a Papal invasion while the other half seemed ambivalent. While here, I will try to locate those who agreed that the enslaving of Christians should stop. Mind you, their reason was not moral, merely economic. They feared that war would jeopardize their prosperity and that conquering Papal armies would lead to the confiscation of their property and riches. And as you know, General, the smell of *money* is a great motivation."

"So, you actually think we as invading Christians can *divide* these people?"

"Most certainly. One other thing, we as Christian invaders have declared this campaign as a crusade against Islam, but these North Africans look at our presence as more of a political dispute than as a war over religion . . . which is another advantage for you. If truly they saw it as a war of religion, race, and culture, they would quickly unify and we would be lost. This is a good time to carry on this fight, because one day Islam *will* unite. And woe be unto the West when the Moors, the Saracens, and the Turks come together beneath a single banner. It could well signal the death of Christianity, and I fear that time approaches."

"Impossible!" sniffed Bertucci. Pondering what he had heard, Tristan's words began to make a bit of sense. "Well then," he said finally, "perhaps it's a good move our new Pope has made, sailing you my way. Now, I do have several citizens of Tunis here, Christians of course, who I've placed under pay as interpreters and guides. I'll place them at your immediate disposal and they can provide you the lay of the land. With their help and your knowledge of the heathens, then perhaps we can begin to fashion some of these alliances you mentioned." Bertucci then began to leave, but turned and said, "By the way, those five chests we unloaded at the dock, my men were bitching that they were heavy as hell. What're they holding?"

"Did you not smell it, General?"

"Smell it? Smell what?"

"Gold and silver from Pope Urban, General. He has sent half his treasury to help you form and buy alliances."

CHAPTER SEVENTY-ONE

MERCHANT OF GOD

Over the next week Tristan managed to develop an amicable relationship with crusty old Bertucci. The general, thoroughly impressed with Tristan's startling, humble display of intelligence, quickly learned to trust Pope Urban's young envoy, and saw that his unusual familiarity with the Moors and their culture was going to manifest itself well in battle. And though Tristan was not familiar with war strategy itself, he was a master at manipulation of diplomacy and placing his finger on the pulse of the local populace. Accordingly then, he soon smelled an opportunity in weakening the current regime.

Bertucci's original challenge had been the fact that this campaign did not replicate the battle scheme of flanking movements and cavalry charges over open ground that he had built a career upon. The Tunis campaign involved brief skirmishes outside the city, ambushes within the narrow streets of Tunis itself, and the use of deception and miscues by the Moors by disguising soldiers as locals rather than outfitting them in identifiable military garb. Success, then, depended heavily in acquiring intelligence about the city and its demographics, an area in which Tristan had become well-versed while working within the Benedictine underground.

Combining this information with the generous outlay of bribes and future promises, Tristan began to undermine the local regime. Furthermore, Tristan advised Bertucci to integrate his four militias in order to create a more cohesive expeditionary force, thereby decreasing the division that had been escalating due to their continued separation into distinct city-state militias.

As General Bertucci began to see the effects of Tristan's efforts, he began to feel that nascent affection for him that often develops in older men who happen upon a young male liege whose company they enjoy. This eventually led to General Bertucci sharing stories of his past and news of his family in Genoa. "Yes, my poor daughter, Marianna," he said one night to Tristan in a moment of wine and homesickness, "she's still brokenhearted over that goddamn Balducci of Tuscany."

"*Vincento* Balducci?"

"Yes, he had promised marriage to my Marianna, then suddenly ran off with some little whore he met on the road."

This comment angered Tristan. He took a moment to reflect, then calmly said, "General, I met the young woman you speak of in France, on several occasions actually. She is no whore."

"What?" Bertucci bristled. "I was told she was a damned street dancer. Of course she's a whore!"

"You are incorrect, General, and so is anyone who makes such a claim. Dancing was her trade, yes, but amongst the Romani, dancing is a time-honored profession. The truth is, she was simply born of common roots and did not have the good fortune to be born of a noble house."

"Good fortune?" said Bertucci, feeling slighted. "Ha, I'll have you know that I have worked hard for everything I possess!"

"Indeed," Tristan replied, standing firm, "you had a good start from your father, and his father before him. You were not destined at birth to remain poor. God was generous to you, more so than he was to this Romani girl who has been maligned by the idle gossip of aristocrats who know nothing of crawling through life on their knees."

Tristan expected the old general to snap back at this charge, instead Bertucci shook his head and grinned. "Ah, I forgot for a moment that you are a monk, lad. Of course you incline toward the poor, such as they are. You undoubtedly sprang from such roots yourself, eh?"

Tristan shook his head. "No, my brother and I were born into French nobility. Politics dashed our future and we were sent to a monastery. Fortune snatched us up again and I was taken in by Grand Prior Odo de Lagery."

"Odo de Lagery? The new Pope?" said Bertucci, surprised.

"Yes, and my brother and I were also then adopted by the Countess Mathilda of Tuscany. She is our aunt."

The mention of Odo de Lagery had impressed Bertucci. Deciphering the connection with the great Mathilda, he sat back and nodded with approval. "Well now," he exclaimed, "here, here!" Then he raised his goblet, perceiving Tristan from a different angle. "You are a nobleman, then," he smiled, "even though you wear the black robe and tonsure. In any case I was talking about my poor daughter, Marianna. As I was about to say, bad enough that goddamned Balducci humiliated her and insulted our family name. The worst of it is that Marianna can't seem to get over Balducci, jackass that he is!"

"A pity," mused Tristan. On the contrary, it was Mala he was envisioning married to Balducci. The picture offended him greatly.

"Indeed, there's justice in this world. I hear that Balducci jumps about like a lapdog for his new bride. She apparently isn't that keen on him, though."

"Oh?" said Tristan, his curiosity pricked.

"Yes, my relations in Tuscany claim that as my Marianna pines for Balducci, Balducci's wife pines for another. She apparently carries that vacant look about her that is only brought on by the loss of a lover or spouse."

"*What?*"

"Yes, undoubtedly she has never recovered from the loss of her first husband."

"First husband?" said Tristan, confused.

"Yes, he froze to death in the Alps along with their baby. Balducci has mentioned to others that the death of her husband was such a blow that she still mourns him on occasion. Of course, come to think of it, she undoubtedly also mourns for the infant she lost."

"Yes, undoubtedly so," Tristan replied, knowing that Bertucci was mistakenly speaking of the unfortunate Fernando, and also that Mala had neither married nor loved Fernando.

"Are you ill, lad?" said Bertucci, noticing that Tristan's face had turned ashen.

"No, I am fine," Tristan mumbled, his mind sinking.

That night as he tried to find sleep he did grow ill, overcome with worry, anxiety, and a sudden compelling need to see Mala again. And as he tossed from side to side, he became increasingly wracked with confusion over Bertucci's report of Mala's melancholia. *Is it possible that it is me she thinks of?* he wondered anxiously. Dismissing the thought, he convinced himself that any desolation that lingered in her heart was because of the baby. *Still, perhaps she does think of me, just as I think of her.* Quickly he would admonish himself, realizing that they had both moved on; they had so severely damaged each other. This only unearthed in him again the great mystery of why she had so abruptly and without explanation bolted from Marseilles two years earlier.

The conversation with Bertucci the night before so unsettled Tristan that from the very next morning until his departure from Tunis six weeks later, every time he saw the smooth caramel skin and dark eyes of a young Moorish woman, he could not help but think of Mala. Even though this afforded him an odd sort of comfort, it also distressed him. Prior to coming to Tunis he had been certain that his newfound fervor for the Church had set Mala behind him.

Finally, satisfied that his work in Tunis was complete, Tristan boarded a papal vessel and sailed for the northwestern coast of Italy, taking to land in Genoa where a papal coach and escort awaited him. From there the caravan proceeded to the northwestern section of the Po Valley between the rivers Ticino and Adda into the first reliefs of the Alps until they arrived at the court of young King Conrad, who was king of Germany only in name; it was his father who retained all power through his self-crowning as Holy Roman Emperor.

"Excellency, I have come to pass along to you personally the sincere condolences of Pope Urban II on the loss of your beloved mother," said Tristan meeting Conrad. "Pope Urban would have come himself but the regretful conditions of war existing between the Gregorian Papacy and your father prohibits such a journey."

"Yes, of course," replied Conrad, who seemed genuinely touched that the new Pope would think to send a special delegation such as this despite the ongoing war. "I have long admired Cardinal Odo de Lagery, so upon your return to southern Italy please convey my congratulations on his rise to the Gregorian Papacy as Pope Urban II."

As Conrad said this, Tristan took close note of Conrad's expression, and found there no trace of false courtesy. Nor could he detect any hint of deception during the exchange of gifts and the elaborate feast that followed. Instead, he found that Conrad demonstrated a peculiar combination of courtly maturity one moment, then would lapse into boyishness that seemed incongruent with his behavior moments before. Tristan found this amusing. When Conrad displayed such lapses, Archbishop Tedald would scowl and Conrad would immediately slip back into sophistication. Tristan also noted that Archbishop Tedald kept an extremely close eye on Tristan and others in the visiting Papal delegation, and never left the boy in their company without being present himself. This, of course, only served to increase Tristan's caution.

In a stroke of fortune, the Archbishop was called into the city on the third day of Tristan's visit, which afforded Tristan a full afternoon of private visitation with Conrad.

"Excellency," Tristan said as they strolled through the royal gardens alone, "it is so unfortunate that this war continues to drag on with no end in sight, and that so many lives continue to be lost. Please know that Pope Urban begins each day in prayer that the bloodshed and division will soon end. If I may humbly ask, what are your thoughts on this subject?"

Tristan expected that Conrad would reflect on this question then offer some vague, rehearsed reply, but without hesitation Conrad replied, "I well understand my father's position of trying to protect the sovereignty of his empire in Germany and northern Italy, Brother Tristan, I fear at times that he fails to remember that there is a far greater power than the royal throne of earthly kings. I pray often that my father regains his memory before passing on to the next world."

Surprised, Tristan followed with, "I see, surely you have not told him that, Your Excellency, after all he claims the crown of Holy Roman Emperor."

"I tried to broach the subject once. He went into a fury, of course. He is a hard man, my father, and thinks me soft. I never brought it up again. Still, I pray for him."

"If I dare, might I ask your thoughts on Clement III who we Gregorians refer to as the anti-pope?"

"Ah, yes, the former Archbishop Gilbert of Ravenna," said Conrad. "A man of God to be certain." Then he paused and stared at the ground thoughtfully. "He was not elected by the College of Cardinals. He was appointed by my father, who is not himself what I consider a *pious* man. And I find it somewhat contradictory that an unpious man would be the one to appoint a Pope, who is God's direct representative on this earth. And you, Brother Tristan, do you not find this contradictory?"

"I have pondered the question," said Tristan, careful not to tread too heavily. "In truth, it never occurred to me that you had thought such things also, Highness. Which makes me wonder how Archbishop Tedald deals with your independence of thought."

"Oh, Tebald was also appointed by my father, so he of course remains loyal to him. Tedald has been very good to me, but I have begun to worry him a bit of late." Conrad then grinned, more to himself than to Tristan, and said, "When I was little, his word was law, as though God himself were speaking to me. He accuses me lately of attaining that rebellious stage. I've been asking questions about what happened after Canossa. You were there. When my father performed penance in the ice and snow for three days begging Pope Gregory to withdraw his sentence of excommunication? Then too, I often ask him about the Gregorian movement and the Benedictine reform movement. It makes him uncomfortable. I think he, like certain other of my father's appointed clerics, struggles with his conscience."

"Oh? In what sense?"

"He struggles between the political and the spiritual. Unlike the Gregorians who have absolutely no question about their righteous position, my father's appointees sometimes sink into bouts of uncertainty. They have gladly accepted my father's temporal reward of high clerical office, yet wonder whether they in fact might not be punished in the next life. It must be a terrifying inner struggle. If I were a member of the clergy, I would far prefer the solid ground beneath my feet enjoyed by the Gregorians like yourself . . . in terms of Heaven and eternity, I mean."

As Tristan listened, he envied the simplicity with which the young king viewed things. He also admired the boy's honesty and sincerity, and Tristan quickly found himself taking a liking to him. The rest of the afternoon passed quickly then as they exchanged stories of their families, their travels, and their interests. In particular they enjoyed discussing their mutual upbringing by men of faith, Conrad having been raised by Archbishop Tedald within the confines of a bishopric and Tristan having been raised by Cardinal Odo within the confines of a monastery.

Tristan had several more engaging talks with Conrad during his final two days there; restricting the conversation to non-political topics due to the hovering Archbishop Tedald. Tristan was well-satisfied that he had already learned what Odo wished to know about the young German royal, and was content to discuss one insignificant thing after another in the presence of the domineering Archbishop.

Tristan's delegation then traveled north to Germany, where upon arriving in Bavaria it was warmly welcomed by Duke Welf the Elder who immediately sent the servants scurrying to prepare a feast. Then, proud as a peacock, he introduced his fifteen-year-old son, Welf the Younger. "Ah, have you ever seen such a fine looking young stallion!" the senior Welf exclaimed to Tristan, his red face ashine with pride. "Oh, if only Odo could see this fine young man face to face!" Then he bowed. "Ahem . . . a thousand pardons . . . I meant to say if only *Pope Urban* could see this fine young man face-to-face."

The boy looked exactly like an adolescent version of his father, who positively was not what one would consider handsome. Nevertheless, Tristan bowed, praised the boy's appearance profusely, as well as the father's, and said, "Duke Welf, what a joyous occasion this."

"Oh, joyous indeed!" cried the Duke, nearly stumbling over his own feet, which was Tristan's first clue that the man was inebriated. "Ha! Ha! And to think that my son is soon to be promised to one of the grandest ladies of all Europe! Who would have ever thought it?"

The Duke then insisted on giving Tristan and his delegation a tour of his beautiful manor, and during this tour fell flat upon his face twice and once upon his back despite a herd of servants following him about for the distinct purpose of catching him. He moved about so quickly, breaking into different directions and spastic movements, that their efforts were fruitless. Picking himself from the ground, he would then lurch about a moment or so, angrily scold the servants for allowing him to fall, then charge off mid-sentence to show off another feature of his fine home.

When the feast was prepared, dinner was equally chaotic because of the good Duke. Through all, it was the younger Welf at the opposite end of the long table who caught Tristan's attention. Sitting unnaturally erect, the boy conducted himself as though holding court, and spoke to others as though they were children at his feet, using gestures so demonstrative that he appeared absurd. Obviously, decided Tristan, this boy lacks the humility and sincerity of Conrad. As Tristan continued to observe the younger Welf, he could see that he treated the servants miserably, often calling one aside for a scolding, making sure that everyone saw that he was in full command. And this brought to mind his Aunt Mathilda. From the very moment Odo had informed him of this unlikely match between a woman in her forties and a boy not yet out of his teens, he could not stomach such a pairing. After meeting the boy, the possibility of such a marriage seemed even more impossible, especially involving Mathilda, who he imagined would not tolerate such boorishness for a moment. Then, for some reason, the act of consummating this marriage struck him, which of course forced him to blench. In disgust, he quickly chased the image away.

Duke Welf did not awake until noon of the next day, and when he appeared, he was lethargic and pale. Nevertheless, he sent for Tristan and his son and insisted that the three sit privately in his study to begin the discussion about marriage.

"Oh, I apologize for yesterday," groaned the Duke, "too much wine, too much excitement. Let's begin. First, know that my son and I are extremely honored by the prospect of this marriage." Then he looked over at Welf the Younger and said, "Aren't we, boy?"

"Yes, Father."

"Next," the Duke continued, "Please know that we will do whatever is required and whatever is expected." Then he looked over at his son again. "Won't we, boy?"

"Yes, Father."

"Of course," the Duke then said, "there are some specific expectations that my son and I have also, right, boy?"

"Yes, Father."

Thus the conversation began, and thus they continued throughout that preliminary meeting, with Duke Welf doing most of the talking, and Welf the Younger nodding dutifully and saying, "Yes, Father."

The next day was reserved for recreation, which involved the Welfs inviting Tristan and his delegation to a boar hunt. Tristan did not hunt, but out of courtesy attended the affair with his entire delegation. Like he was the night of the feast, Welf the Younger was pretentious in posture and conduct, and was especially rude to the stable hands. At one point he kicked one of them for failing to cup his hands properly while Welf the Younger stepped into them to mount his horse.

"Imbecile!" young Welf cried. "Get out of my sight!"

The next day was reserved for the second round of talks about marriage, the day of recreation having served as a time for both parties to absorb what had been discussed during the preliminary meeting. This was a common negotiation practice in certain high households, especially when the order of business involved lifelong impact such as marriage.

"So, Brother Tristan," Duke Welf began, "let's get down to some details today now that we've managed to hammer out some general agreements. My first specific concern, then, is the actual consummation of this marriage."

Not expecting such a statement, Tristan proceeded carefully. "I see. In what sense, Duke Welf?"

"In what sense? Ah, there's only one sense when one talks of consummation, Brother." Then he pointed to his crotch and added, "You know, I'm talking about poking the old pole into the old crack, for Christ's sake!" At this Welf the Younger snickered, which in turn also made his father snicker.

"Yes," said Tristan, "I understand what consummation means, Duke, but in what sense is this a concern?"

"The great Mathilda Medici in earlier years married her humpbacked stepbrother, Godfrey the Hunchback, Duke of Lorraine, did she not?"

"Yes," Tristan replied. "They later separated. Her husband went to Heinrich's side, and Mathilda went to Pope Gregory's side. And as you know, the Humpback later died."

"Yes, when they first separated, he received none of her vast lands in Italy as he should have. Then, too, reports circulated that the marriage was never consummated and an un-consummated marriage in an invalid marriage."

"The marriage *was* consummated. Mathilda gave birth to a child, but the child died during its first year."

"There were rumors that the hunchback did not father the child, and they're believable. Who in hell would lay with a goddamn hunchback, anyway? I wouldn't, would you?"

Tristan did not reply.

"Well, I don't think Mathilda would either!" the Duke huffed. "I have a point I'm trying to make, Brother Tristan. How many times has the Church declared a marriage nullified years afterward on grounds that the marriage was never consummated?"

"A good number of times. What is the point you're trying to make here, Duke Welf?"

"My point is that I want witnesses documenting that this marriage is consummated so that at no time can the Church or anyone else come back later and declare the marriage nullified for political reasons."

"Witnesses? Do you mean in the wedding chamber itself, upon the *wedding bed*?"

"Yes. When young Welf sticks his staff into Mathilda's little honey pot, I want witnesses present."

Tristan shook his head, offended by such talk. "I refuse to address such a thing without Countess Mathilda's explicit consent."

"You don't *need* her consent, Brother Tristan. Does that medallion you wear not signify that you speak for Pope Urban II himself? He is in favor of this marriage, you know, and wishes it to happen! Mathilda did whatever Pope Gregory told her to do, she will do whatever Pope Urban tells her to do."

"No, I stand my ground, Duke Welf. Tell me, you voice concerns about rumors and innuendos concerning la Gran Mathilda's first marriage that I find difficult to swallow. So what drives this grave concern about consummation?"

"Property, that's what," said the Duke. "Mathilda owns more land than anyone in nearly all of Europe, and as her husband, Welf the Younger must have a guarantee that he is the valid heir. He is much younger than Mathilda, and should she die first, the land and property should all go to *him*."

Welf the Younger had been sitting there listening to this conversation and had said nothing, but now he spoke. "Yes, Brother Tristan, the land and property should go to me."

"What?" said Tristan, his temples turning scarlet. "The two of you already lay Mathilda in her grave?"

"No, of course not," snapped Duke Welf. "I merely speak of *precautions* for the future, you know, should anything occur to the Contessa. In addition to a guarantee of consummation by having witnesses present, we would also like a guarantee of inheritance to Mathilda's property in the event of her death . . . you know, in writing . . . a formal contract." Then he looked at Welf the Younger. "Wouldn't we, son?"

"Yes, Father."

Again Tristan balked. "In marriage, the right of inheritance is *understood*," he said.

"I have never been one for spoken agreements or understood agreements. I much prefer a written contract, and so does my son. *Don't* you, Son?"

"Yes, Father."

"Well, Duke Welf," Tristan said, "despite this medallion I wear, I cannot in good conscience make promises without consulting the party I represent, which is la Gran Contessa Mathilda."

"No," Duke Welf insisted, "you represent Pope Urban II, and it was Odo de Lagery who first approached me about the marriage of my son to Mathilda. He wants this bargain sealed, I tell you."

Tristan reached about his neck and pulled the medallion from his neck. "There now," he said calmly, "I no longer represent Pope Urban II, at the moment at least. And I shall not place the medallion about my neck again until I leave your territories . . . then I shall once again represent the Pope."

Duke Welf pointed a finger at Tristan, his voice elevating. "The moment I leave this table, I shall commission my fastest courier to Italy to report this insolence to the Pope, young man!" Then he stood and stormed out of the room.

Welf the Younger, left alone with Tristan, gawked in the direction his father had taken. Then he looked over at Tristan and began to say something, but it caught in his throat and he sat there stupidly, his mouth agape.

Tristan looked at the boy with contempt, then placed the medallion back about his neck. "I regret this did not go better," he said. "This is a job better left to Pope Urban and Countess Mathilda themselves. I have no stomach for it!"

CHAPTER SEVENTY-TWO

RETURN TO ITALY

It was July by the time Tristan rejoined Odo in Terracina. "I suppose you have received word from Duke Welf of Bavaria that our negotiations did not go well," said Tristan to Odo entering the privacy of his office.

"Indeed, an angry letter blistering your name arrived two days ahead of you. And the Duke provided such colorful descriptions of your character."

"Please know that I . . ."

"No, no," said Odo with a flap of his hand. "Go easy on yourself. The truth is, the Duke is difficult and demanding, so I expected as much." Then he smiled. "I also recently received word from old Bettucci in Tunis, and it appears you worked wonders there. Apparently with the alliances you set up and the bribes you shelled out, our expeditionary force is nearing a negotiated settlement. Good work, Tristan, the enslaving of Christians there nears an end. Pray tell, what about King Heinrich's son?"

"A fine character that boy-king, Conrad, right at the point of discovering his own mind. Despite the fact that Archbishop Tedald is in Heinrich's camp and keeps a watchful eye on Conrad, the archbishop must have incidentally taught him too well about God. Conrad doubts the validity of his father's actions, and I sense this disapproval will only grow with time."

"Ah, excellent," clucked Odo.

"And what about Borsa in Sicily? Does he see the wisdom of stopping this blood feud with his half brother, Bohemud?"

"Well, let me just say that he is *thinking* about it. Last week he agreed to send envoys to Bohemud's people to inquire about the possibility of declaring a temporary truce until such time as the threat from Emperor Alexius and the Byzantines dissipates. And I, of course, have already offered to mediate if Bohemud finds such a truce amenable."

"Well," said Tristan, "it appears that things are coming together, except your proposed marriage between Mathilda and Welf the Younger. I hate to sound defeatist, but this entire marriage business concerning my aunt is beyond my capabilities. I am not pleased about it, and the thought of her marrying that little lout offends me to no end. I leave it entirely to you and Aunt Mathilda. Explain to me, how do you plan to deal with the Duke's demands about witnessing and documenting the consummation of the marriage and guaranteeing to Welf the Younger the right of inheritance?"

Odo did not respond immediately. After a minute he placed his hand to his forehead and said, "There is a slight possibility that I can resolve the consummation issue. It is not uncommon to show proof of things on the wedding night, such as the groom's family demanding to see the virgin bride's blood upon the sheets that next morning."

"Ha, easily and frequently solved with a pot of sheep's blood," said Tristan.

"Yes, deception is used at times, but in the end the witnesses are satisfied, even if they have been deceived. You know very well, Tristan, sometimes people *wish* to be deceived, so let me think on that."

"What about the other demand?"

"Ah, we have a slight problem there," said Odo, shaking his head. "As you know Pope Gregory and Mathilda were extremely close, so close, in fact, that rumors circulated in certain quarters. In any case, Pope Gregory counseled Mathilda into signing all of her property and wealth over to the Church upon her death. This document was recorded, stamped with his seal and hers, and remains in safekeeping, within the tunnels of Monte Cassino. The only other witnesses to the signing of this contract were Desiderius and Abbot Hugh of Cluny, so nobody else on this earth knows about it except Abbot Hugh, me and Muehler who are privy to the secrets of Monte Cassino, and now yourself, as my First Counsel."

Tristan's mouth fell open and he looked at Odo in stunned silence. The Papal estates, the Benedictine holdings, and lands held by the various monasteries and churches were already incredibly immense; Mathilda's property dwarfed any single Church property tenfold.

"God in Heaven," he whistled, "I never would have imagined that she had signed all her possessions over to the Church, nor would anyone else!"

"Yes, an unimaginable gesture on her part. So you see, Duke Welf's second demand is totally impossible."

"Then so is the marriage, is it not?"

"Oh no. Let me think on it a while, Tristan. And as I said before, some people prefer to be deceived than to be denied."

CHAPTER SEVENTY-THREE

ODO ATTACKS ROME

Pope Urban managed to negotiate a truce between the half-brother princes, Borsa and Bohemud of Lower Italy, and with limited assistance from these Norman allies made his first entry into Rome in November of 1088, eight months after his election as Pope. This entry was inauspicious since Pope Urban was not afforded adequate troops to dislodge anti-pope Clement who continued to control most of the city. Consequently, Urban was forced to take refuge on the Island of Saint Bartholomew. Clement, likewise, was unable to rout Urban from the island since he also lacked an adequate troop force.

From his heavily fortified position on the island, Urban immediately launched a fiery verbal attack on the enemies of Gregorian Catholics throughout Europe.

"Know that I excommunicate Archbishop Guibert of Ravenna, known to us as the anti-pope Clement III and declare him a beast sprung out from earth to wage war against the Saints of God! I also excommunicate Heinrich of Germany who professes to be the Holy Roman Emperor, as did once my predecessor and dear friend, Pope Victor III, and as did twice his predecessor, Pope Gregory VII!"

Clement retorted by calling for a synod within Saint Peter's Basilica before which he demanded that Pope Urban appear to answer for crimes against God and humanity. This war of words eventually culminated in a vicious and desperate three day battle in which Clement was driven from the city and Pope Urban finally took possession of Saint Peter's.

"Praise God, Odo!" Tristan cried as he and Pope Urban marched in triumph through the Vatican gates into the Lateran Palace surrounded by Norman troops. "Final victory at last!"

"Nay, far from it," Odo replied, keeping a careful eye to the crowd that had amassed. "Victory for the moment, yes, but the city population remains split and could turn on us at any moment. You were here yourself and witnessed how they turned on Gregory and Desiderius both, and never forget that they have also twice turned on the anti-pope. Rome has been embroiled in this war for over five years now and has learned that survival depends on bending with the wind, between us and Heinrich, whoever possesses momentum possesses Rome, but only until the pendulum swings again."

"Ah, you are more flexible than was Pope Gregory, stronger than Desiderius, and unlike Clement you are the legitimate Pope. You will know how to manage the population and still the discontent."

"Perhaps. Never forget that the shadow of King Heinrich looms large to the north in Germany. When he finds out about Clement's defeat he will double his efforts against Mathilda, which is why we must hasten this marriage between Mathilda and Welf the Younger in order to fortify her position and solidify our alliances. Should Heinrich ever gain the upper hand against Mathilda, then he will surely march south against us again. And if these fickle Romans feel the threat of Heinrich's hammer, they will quickly switch sides again in order to avoid destruction of the city."

"Then we will be vigilant," Tristan replied, "and continue with the building of bridges to keep Heinrich in check. We are beginning to make inroads in Lombardy within the communes of Milan, Cremona, Lodi, and Piacenza by turning some of Heinrich's former allies against him. As you said, this marriage between Mathilda and young Welf will be yet another check against Heinrich, and the Normans to the south will never abandon us. I believe we can hold Rome."

Once settled into the Vatican, Odo immediately set about the task of doubling diplomacy efforts in order to consolidate support against King Heinrich. Tristan was instrumental in carrying out these efforts, and soon found himself shuttling month after month to Saxony, Bavaria, Tuscany, Lombardy, and Lower Italy. He became so buried in these diplomatic missions that he found himself thinking of Mala only during the rare moments of inactivity that Odo's missions now afforded. Yet, when these occasions arose, they managed to send him plummeting into periods of introspection and regret as he relived memories of being with Mala in the Loire Valley and Marseilles. This in turn, oddly, made him miss the anonymity of his earlier work within the Benedictine underground, for he had become an extremely public figure recognized within the important political circles of France, Italy, and Germany.

He enjoyed this work and felt that he was making a more significant impact in the restoration of Gregorian Catholicism than he had during his days with the Benedictine underground. His earlier work with the underground served him well in this new capacity; much of the diplomacy he became involved in dealt with secrecy and intrigue. Because of this, he continued to work closely with Muehler within the tunnels of Monte Cassino and also continued to encounter Handel throughout Italy and Germany.

CHAPTER SEVENTY-FOUR

ODO'S STRATEGY

As the year 1089 dawned, then, Pope Urban II and the Gregorian Catholics controlled Rome and felt confident that they had sufficiently stirred adequate discontent and rebellion in Germany to keep King Heinrich from attacking Rome again. To cement this newfound security, Odo immediately began to finalize arrangements for Countess Mathilda's marriage to Welf the Younger of Bavaria who had now turned eighteen.

"No mention must ever be made about Mathilda making the Church heir to her property," he told Tristan. "No matter what is asked or said about the topic, our response to the Bavarians shall be to insist and agree that the right of heirship is an *understood* aspect of marriage within the Church, which is by no means untrue . . . under normal circumstances. Mathilda and I have already devised our strategy."

"What about Duke Welf's insistence on a contract in writing on the issue?"

"He cannot force Mathilda to do such a thing, especially with me as Pope in agreement with Mathilda. Remember that this marriage is as militarily strategic and beneficial to Bavaria as it is to Tuscany and to us. Mathilda and I together shall outweigh his insistence on a contract."

"And on the consummation of this marriage before witnesses, how do we handle that? Surely Aunt Mathilda's modesty and dignity would never allow such a thing."

"Absolutely not. I have Muehler working on that down in Monte Cassino. You'll be seeing him within the month and he'll set forth his plan.

"I still find it difficult to believe that Aunt Mathilda is about to wed a boy of eighteen," said Tristan, "and such a distasteful young welp! I wish I could say I looked forward to the wedding, but Welf the Younger is so offensive. Nevertheless, I shall mask my disapproval for Aunt Mathilda's sake."

At this Odo frowned and shook his head. "No need for you to worry about the wedding, Tristan. You will not be attending."

"Oh?" said Tristan, surprised though not overly disappointed. He had disapproved of the marriage since first hearing of it.

"After you leave Muehler in Monte Cassino, I am sending you back to North Africa to check with General Bertucci and our crusade against our Moslem antagonists. He is in poor spirits, I fear. His wife and daughter both contracted the pox and died two months ago. He came back to Genoa for the funeral, but it nearly broke him. They say it was the loss of the daughter, Marianna that crippled him most."

"Marianna?" said Tristan. "Was she not the one who was once engaged to Lord Balducci?"

"Yes, they were to be married until . . ." Here Odo stopped, wishing to spare Tristan the mention of Balducci's scandalous marriage to the Romani girl. "Bertucci has returned to North Africa. I need you to convey my condolences and also to see that he remains focused on the crusade. Otherwise, I shall replace him."

"Yes, certainly."

"Then, when you leave Africa, you will proceed to the court of King Philippe in Paris, then to Normandy, and then to England. I would go myself, but I dare not leave Italy under the current circumstances so I place this burden on you. You are to represent my office as the new Pontiff's First Counsel and translate my positions on both political and spiritual affairs. Unfortunately, reports indicate that King Philippe of France continues to sell important Church offices to the highest bidder. Then too, rumors are beginning to surface that he seeks excuses to divorce his wife of many years, Queen Bertha, because she has become fat. He apparently openly ridicules her, and does so in the presence of the entire court. And though there has existed little affection between the two since the onset of their marriage, it is Bertha who is the faithful ally of the Church. We need to protect her."

"And what is your wish in Normandy?"

"Since the death of William the Bastard, succession wars have broken out in both of his domains, Normandy and England. The violence there is becoming intolerable, and civilians are being caught in the crossfire. We need to sue for peace . . . for the good of the innocent."

"The Bastard left Normandy to his eldest son, Robert, did he not?" asked Tristan.

"Yes, and he left England to his second surviving son, William II. The two sons are not fighting each other, but putting down rebellions and invasions in their respective realms that have been precipitated by the death of their father. England is especially of concern because of William II, the new king. He harbors resentment against the Gregorian cause because Pope Gregory accused his father, the Bastard, of being too violent and butchering the innocent."

"Yes, he *was* too violent and *did* butcher the innocent."

"Indeed, the very thing a man *does* is the very thing he does not wish to be accused of. There is another issue in England. Archbishop Lanfranc of Canterbury recently died and the obvious candidate for replacement is our own Abbot Anselm of Bec in Normandy, but the new English king has refused to fill the office."

"Abbot Anselm? The famous scholar who has attracted the finest academics from all over Europe to the Abbey of Bec while serving there as prior?"

"Yes, the same. He remains in Normandy and has not been allowed to enter England. Meet with him before leaving Normandy and learn more details on what is occurring across the Channel. Listen to him carefully, Tristan, and heed any personal advice he offers."

"Personal advice?" said Tristan, puzzled.

"Yes. Our agents report that not only are we losing ground in England, but many of our abbeys have been raided and much of our property has been confiscated. Though I am hoping that you may be able to approach the new king, Abbot Anselm is closer to the fray and may advise you to avoid England."

"I understand."

"Go then, and be my voice, my eyes, and ears. Though Heinrich and anti-pope Clement keep us occupied here in Italy, it is crucial that we maintain our moral and spiritual authority to the west. Clement has been sending delegations there in hopes of gaining legitimacy for his own papacy, but has been ignored thus far in most quarters. We must keep it that way."

"Yes, I agree," Tristan replied, "and it will be my honor to represent you."

CHAPTER SEVENTY-FIVE

MUEHLER SPEAKS

One week after meeting with Odo, Tristan was within the tunnels of Monte Cassino following Muehler into a chamber with which Tristan was unfamiliar.

"What is this place?" he asked, looking about as five or six monks worked and moved about the length of several long tables whose surfaces were stacked with vials, containers, herbs and minerals. An acrid smell permeated the room, as did wisps of smoke and pungent fumes.

"This is our alchemy chamber," replied Muehler, "and these are our chemists and physicians." Muehler then approached the eldest of the monks working the tables. "So, Brother Marco, how goes our little project?"

"We're finished, I think," nodded the old monk, holding up a small vile filled with a dark liquid.

"You've worked up the proper dosage, then?" asked Muehler. "Damnation, we don't wish to kill the boy, only incapacitate him."

"Yes, we've been testing the dosage for a week now, and after killing off half a dozen sheep and tempering the solution, we've tested it on several of our laborers. If your information about Welf the Younger is correct, then this dosage I hold should do the trick, Brother Muehler."

Tristan listened with interest, although his knowledge of alchemy and potions was limited. "So what have you come up with, Brother Marco?"

Marco held the vile up to the candlelight. "During the wedding feast of la Gran Contessa, one of our agents shall slip this liquid into Welf the Younger's wine. It's the juice of the belladonna berry mixed with sugar and thinner."

"Belladonna berry?"

"Indeed, its uses were known to the ancient Greeks who named it Atropos, and later called it the Mandragora of Theophrastus. It is poisonous, but when the proper dose is administered it can actually cause a sedative action that brings about relaxation of the smooth muscles of the body . . . or also physical and mental exhaustion, possible hallucinations, and a general paralysis of the body."

Tristan shook his head with concern. "Poisonous? God in Heaven, Muehler, this is taking on the sound of a dangerous gamble."

"I trust Brother Marco's work," said Muehler. "We've given him Welf the Younger's exact size and weight, and he assures me he's calculated the proper dose to get the desired results."

"The desired results? How is all this going to satisfy the Bavarians' demand concerning the consummation of Welf and Mathilda's marriage in the presence of witnesses?"

Muehler looked at Tristan a moment, and though his veil concealed most of his face, his eyes betrayed a flicker of merriment as he stuck his index finger forward in a rigid position. Then he slowly curled it downward into a flaccid position. "We intend to render the boy impotent by the time he crawls between Mathilda's thighs," he said. "Yes, and he'll discover his stump is limp as liver. When he fails to produce the slightest erection, out of sheer mortification, it will be young Welf who rids the room of witnesses, not Mathilda."

This plan sounded far-fetched to Tristan. Nevertheless, he nodded. "Very clever, Muehler, I hope we don't end up *killing* the boy and starting up yet a new war."

"Ah, *that* I leave to our good Brother Marco, and to God, of course," said Muehler, crossing himself. "In any case we'll find out within the month, eh, Marco?"

"I'm not worried," said the old monk. Then he snickered a bit. "I must confess, Brother Muehler," he said sheepishly, "I've tried this dosage out on myself, and it works. Indeed, made my old man-root shrivel like a grub!"

"Eh?" said Muehler, a glimmer of humor filling his eyes. "You old devil, Marco, I wouldn't think at your age your old stump would ever get stiff in the first place!"

At this the old man broke into laughter, braying like a schoolboy. "Aha Muehler!" he cried with merriment. "What the hell would you know about my goddamn stump anyway? Hell, it still gets as stiff as a broom handle!"

The other monks broke into laughter, not so much over what old Brother Julien had said, but because of the comical manner in which he had said it.

"Ah, enough! Enough, you old goat!" guffawed Muehler, causing his veil to move in and out at the mouth with each inhalation and exhalation of laughter. This delighted Tristan. He had never before seen Muehler laugh. "Ay!" Muehler continued, still laughing, "Your stump could get stiff as a broom handle only if the handle was made of a grape vine perhaps!"

This caused another outburst of snickering among the other monks, and caused them to begin trading snide remarks about each other's male anatomy while touting the largesse of their own. Then, their outbreak of adolescent joviality finally quenched, Muehler led Tristan back to his private office and the two took a seat.

"Some rather interesting news from Germany has been coming our way," said Muehler, having shed all trace of humor. "It seems the memory of King Heinrich's recently deceased wife has already slipped his mind. Though he now approaches the age of forty, he chases a young girl of eighteen. Eupraxia of Kiev, the daughter of Vsevolod I, Prince of Kiev and the Rus."

"What?" said Tristan. "I thought she cloistered herself in a Convent of Quedlinburg after the death of her first husband, Henry the Long, two years ago."

"Ay, so impressed was Heinrich by her demure beauty, he now plans to marry her in Cologne, and she plans to take the name Adelheid upon her coronation as queen."

"Does Prince Conrad know this? I was told that he disapproved of his father courting other women so soon after the death of his first wife, but I never heard anything of an upcoming marriage. And I recently visited Conrad to deliver Pope Urban's condolences on the passing of his mother."

"Conrad knows now, but probably was not aware of this business during your visit. He is not pleased, needless to say. Of greater concern to us is a possible alliance now between King Heinrich and the Rus. I've already sent a delegation to Kiev to open negotiations with the Rus."

"Ahhh, this marriage will solidify the Rus with Heinrich, as Mathilda's marriage to Welf the Younger will solidify our own alliances," said Tristan, with utmost concern. "What chance will our delegation have in Kiev?"

"There's a crack in the door, a certain concern so to speak that we hope to capitalize on. It seems that King Heinrich has also recently taken an interest in the Nicolaitan sect, and we intend to share this information with Kiev."

"The Nicolaitan sect? Oh, surely not King Heinrich? They are fornicators who share their wives and women and engage in orgies. Their founder claimed centuries ago that "unless one copulates every day, he cannot have eternal life!" And what of the black mass they are said to practice?"

"Yes, interesting isn't it?" said Muehler, putting his hand to his veil. "It's hoped, of course, that Kiev will be surprised and offended by such reports. In any case, I'll handle the Kiev issue and Mathilda's wedding while you travel to Africa, France, and England. That work is critical, and we all count on you to anchor our position to the west." Then he grew still and gazed silently at Tristan a moment.

"What is it, Brother Muehler?" said Tristan, feeling Muehler's eyes probing at him.

"I was thinking about how far you've come these past several years;" said Muehler, "how you've changed and matured. I want you to know that I am proud of you, lad. *Very* proud of you."

Tristan was not prepared for such praise from the calloused Muehler. "I . . . may not be all that you suppose me to be, Brother Muehler," Tristan said with humility.

"Oh," Muehler chortled through his veil, "I know more about you than you suppose. I know there's a softness in you that objects at times to our tactics, and an integrity about you that becomes confounded at times due to things we must do to keep the Church independent and strong. Yet you've made peace, it seems, with these things, and become our strongest soldier. I know there's an uncertainty within your heart that never rests, and a longing for things that can never be. I know you're a dreamer. Yes, I know about the Romani girl and the child, but I think I understand it also."

Absorbing this last statement, the pink coloring that had been creeping up Tristan's neck deepened. "I . . . I am imperfect, Brother," he stammered. "I . . ."

"We're all imperfect, Tristan," interrupted Muehler. "There's something I want you to know before you make this grand diplomatic sweep to Africa, France, and England. You are not alone on this earth. I've gone through much of what you have endured: the confusion, the uncertainty, even sins of the flesh, and yes, perhaps even love. Through this turmoil and fog, in the end I still wear this black robe of the Benedictines, and the older I grow, the more certain I am that I've chosen the right path. The purpose of my existence is still what I thought it was as a young monk, and that is to save others, and raise them up."

"Yes, Brother Muehler, I find myself moving in that direction."

"The thing I wanted you to know, Tristan. Several years ago Odo de Lagery was caught in the seesaw of Church schism, war, and the turmoil of the world stage. In the midst of that grand chaos he stepped back and commissioned me to find a way to help your mother escape England, her intolerable marriage, and the misery of her separation from you and your younger brother. So as you wrestle with the evils of Church politics, never forget who Odo de Lagery really is beneath that papal cope, and what he truly stands for here upon this earth. And as you do this, never forget who I am, or who you are, or what *we* stand for in this life or that our mortal existence is limited to only a short span here on earth, which means our opportunities to fight evil are equally limited. We can't afford to squander these opportunities, then, even if it means crossing a line here or there."

Then Muehler crossed himself, stood, and walked away, leaving Tristan alone in the tunnel. Tristan remained there for a while, weighing Muehler's words, trying to guess his intent at sharing such private thoughts. And then, finally, though Muehler was gone, Tristan tipped his head and said aloud, "Thank you, Brother Muehler . . . from my heart, thank you."

CHAPTER SEVENTY-SIX

A GREGORIAN GATHERING

The wedding of Countess Mathilda Medici to Welf the Younger of Bavaria was one of the magnificent affairs of the age. Despite the continuing war that plagued central and northern Italy, aristocrats and high clergy attended from all over Europe. King Heinrich, despite five bitter years of war against his first cousin Mathilda, had shared a close relationship with her during childhood and had never forgotten that she had pleaded his case with Pope Gregory at Canossa in 1077 upon his first excommunication. Accordingly, Heinrich saw fit to order a lull along the war front for one month as visitors from France, Italy, Germany, Sicily, and Spain flocked to Tuscany in royal coaches accompanied by long caravans of servants and attendants.

The Canossa fortress could house most of the visiting nobility and clergy, but could not possibly accommodate all the teamsters and servants who accompanied them. Consequently, the high clergy, including Pope Urbans's delegation, remained at Canossa while the nobility and their entourages were housed according to rank among the Qattro Castelli of Montezane, Montuetro, Bianell, and Montelucio that guarded the approach to Canossa. Mathilda had requested that Guillaume and the Danes quarter Duke Welf and Welf the Younger as well as their entire entourage from Bavaria at the fortress of Monteluccio. Though Guillaume, like Tristan, was appalled by this marriage of his aunt to Welf the Younger, Guillaume complied with Mathilda's wishes and opened his fortress to the Bavarians. Within a matter of two days, Guillaume and the Danes began to develop a dislike for both of the Welfs.

"Bones of God," complained Orla, "I'm not sure who's worse, the father or the son!"

"Ja," agreed Crowbones, "the father drinks like a fish and has taught the son to do the same! Both seem to think highly of themselves and others as inferiors, especially us. If that lad treats me like a houseboy once more, I'll stick a boot up his little Bavarian ass!"

"J-ja," chimed in Guthroth, "h-he needs a b-boot up his ass!"

"Ah no, no," responded Guillaume, "we must accommodate Auntie Mathilda for these two weeks, then it'll be done and the old man will return to Bavaria."

"Ja, what about the sprout?" snorted Orla. "He'll be remaining in Tuscany, but if he starts ordering me around, I'll crack his skull."

Guillaume gave no reply. He himself was unsure how Welf the Younger was going to fit into things in Tuscany. Nevertheless, he did all he could do to make the Bavarians feel welcome. Further complicating Guillaume's situation was the fact that Mathilda had also assigned Commander Balducci and his entourage to stay at Montelucio. Balducci had initially refused to attend the wedding as Mathilda had not attended his wedding, but after some thought he changed his mind, thinking this to be an opportune time to parade his young wife before many of those who had disapproved of his marriage. *Indeed, a perfect opportunity to arouse jealousy amongst those bitches who have been shunning her,* he decided.

He had hoped to leave his mother and two sisters behind, but after much heaving and sobbing, the three women managed to get Balducci to relent and he allowed them to travel with Mala, Duxia and himself, which meant Balducci's entire trip to Canossa was steeped in the bitter, self-imposed silence of two opposing female camps, each eyeing the other with resentment and suspicion. Then, upon being welcomed by Guillaume at Montelucio, further irritating Balducci was the fact that both of his sisters immediately began to fawn all over Guillaume with absurdly affective behavior though he was nearly twenty years their junior. Of course, he thought little of the fact that he himself was nearly twenty years older than his own young wife.

"Goddammit," he muttered to Duxia, "Celia and Cosima are embarrassing all hell out of me over Guillaume, and the damn Danes over there are loving every minute of it. They'll be mocking my family for the next year now!"

"To hell with the Danes, they are dust in your shadow, my Lord," Duxia replied, unable to mask her own bitterness at them from their earlier years together at Saint-Germain-en-Laye.

Balducci knew nothing of this previous relationship, of course, and he appreciated Duxia's response. *You know, I've really taken a liking to this old woman,* he thought to himself as he led the women away with Guillaume to their quarters.

Mala had lingered behind in the coach gathering her things. As she descended the coach she immediately recognized the three Danes, although she had only seen them once before in her life as a child of ten when they had rescued her and her young Romani cousins from raiding Norsemen who had kidnapped them along the Seine River beyond Saint-Germain-en-Laye.

"Oh, Heavens," she said, putting a hand to her mouth, "I remember you." The Danes looked at her, struck by her statement as well as by her appearance. Before they could speak, she approached them and smiled. "I am Mala," she said. "I was little more than a child when you saw me last. Do you remember me?"

It was an awkward moment for the Danes as they did remember, albeit more recently they had faulted her for Tristan's recent demise. But as she spoke to them, smiling and thanking them for their heroism so many years before, their previous conceptions of her began to melt away.

"Ja, lass," said Orla, "I remember that day. Most of all I seem to remember your beautiful mother. God's spine, you look just like her!"

There was a pleasant exchange of small talk then. When she began to say something else, Mala noticed a young boy standing to the side staring at her, as though hypnotized. It was Hroc. He was so taken by Mala's appearance that he could not keep his eyes from following every gesture she made.

"Hey, FiveHands!" Orla shouted, catching sight of his son's impolite stare. "Have some manners there, boy!"

Mala smiled at Hroc and went to him then, giving him an affectionate hug. "Such a handsome little man!" she said, making a fuss over him. As she said this, Guillaume returned from taking the others to their quarters, and as he approached, Mala's breath caught. She stood there speechless for several seconds, so struck by his resemblance to Tristan that she could barely breathe. Never having met Guillaume before, though Tristan had spoken of him on occasion, the familial resemblance was so startling that she knew immediately who this was.

"Guillaume?" she whispered.

Guillaume had never met Mala either, but he also knew immediately who this dark, young woman was, the woman who had broken his brother, and was now the wife of Vincento Balducci.

"Yes, Guillaume," he said, extending a hand while trying to force a smile.

At that very moment Mala wanted to take him in her arms and lose herself in his embrace. It was as though Tristan himself was standing before her after all this time, after all this suffering and heartbreak. Her lips trembled a moment then, and she had to steady herself as she reached out to extend her hand in exchange. She offered a gentle shake, then quickly withdrew it.

"I nearly mistook you for your brother," she said. "Word is he's abroad and will not be attending your aunt's wedding?"

"True, he won't be here," replied Guillaume. Then he reached for her bags and said, "I've already situated the others of your party, so come along, I'll show you where you'll be staying these next two weeks."

As she and Guillaume left, Orla looked at his brother and shook his head. "Swine's head," he muttered, "I can see now why Tristan lost his head. That girl is the most beautiful creature I've ever seen walk the face of this earth!"

"Ja," nodded Crowbones, "and beauty such as that is trouble."

"J-ja," mumbled Guthroth, "ev-ever-l-lasting trouble."

CHAPTER SEVENTY-SEVEN

THE WEDDING

The wedding ceremony itself was preceded by two weeks of gaiety and special events hosted primarily at Canossa. During the day the men were occupied with hunting excursions, equestrian and weapons competitions, and frequent bouts of drinking and braggadocio. The ladies, meanwhile, engaged in gossip, talk of fashion, and polite parlor games. Countess Mathilda, of course, spent her time with the men. Mala and Duxia attempted to mingle with the other women at Canossa during the first three days, but the chilly reception they received led them to remain at Montelucio except for certain formal evening dinners for which Balducci insisted their presence. These dinners usually involved music and dancing afterwards, and it was on the dance floor that Balducci found his greatest pleasure, sweeping Mala here and there within his arms, arousing the jealousy of the other women and the envy of the men. In particular, he enjoyed the lively peasant dances which allowed all to see Mala's slender form wispily weaving one graceful motion into the next as she glided effortlessly across the floor.

This, in turn, led him to insist that Mala join the musicians Mathilda had commissioned to entertain the guests. "On the night of the wedding feast don your Romani garb, Mala, your flowing skirt, your veil, bracelets, and zills, and entertain these folks!" he cried, his face red with drink. "This dull crowd had never seen dancing such as yours and they'll enjoy it!"

Mala objected immediately, but as Duxia listened, she discreetly motioned to Balducci. *I'll take care of it*, the gesture said. Balducci winked back at her, thinking again that old Duxia was a welcome addition to his household.

Duxia pulled Mala aside when they got back to Montelucio and whispered, "Mala, dance as your husband requests for it means a great deal to him. And he is correct, these people are dull with wealth and propriety. Show them how a Romani woman dances, Mala, and fling your grace in the faces of these sour-faced bitches."

Duke Welf the Elder quickly became a nuisance at Montelucio. At home in Bavaria, he generally became intoxicated each day by mid-afternoon and his boisterous behavior became the bane of servants at Monteluccio and Canossa alike, especially the females. Welf the Younger mirrored his father's behavior when at Monteluccio, but whenever at Canossa and in the presence of either Pope Urban or his bride to be, he appeared to fall into an uncharacteristic state of humility.

It was Guthroth who noticed this first, and pointed it out to Orla, who grunted, "Ha, if only Mathilda knew what a little shit the boy really is! He's an ass here at Monteluccio with us, then acts like a choirboy at Canossa with her!"

On the day of the marriage ceremony, the Canossa Cathedral of Saint Nicholas was filled to overflowing with high nobility and clergy. Many of the men wore fur-lined mantles, cloaks of vermeil, and boots made of soft chervil while others wore their finest military garb and stood there glimmering in polished hauberks and armor. The women wore rich fabrics, fine linen, and sendal, and crowned their heads with fashionable conical hats of the day draped with wispy tails trailing behind that fell onto the shoulders. The highest clergy wore their scarlet cardinals' finery with bejeweled medallions that rivaled the gems worn by the wealthiest of lords, while the archbishops and bishops wore vestments that bested the most beautiful worn by any woman present. It was, in other words, a show of wealth where groups and individuals were on full display, and intended to place their best face forward for others to see.

The wedding took place during a high mass which was celebrated by Pope Urban himself who also delivered the homily and administered the sacrament of communion to all attendees. After communion Pope Urban then performed the holy rite of matrimony and joined Mathilda Medici of Tuscany with Welf the Younger of Bavaria in marriage.

As the service concluded, the Pope held Mathilda's hand to Welf's hand and declared, "I bless this marriage in the name of God our Father and Savior, Amen!" As he said this, he felt Welf's cold hand trembling beneath his own and Mathilda's. "Are you ill, my son?" Odo whispered, having already noticed that young Welf had appeared as pallid as the deceased throughout the entire marriage ceremony.

"N-no . . ." stammered Welf, though he was quaking with terror. Though he had been treated with deference since birth, the youngster had begun to suffer humility and fright from the moment he arrived in Tuscany and fallen beneath the intimidating shadow of Countess Mathilda. He felt small in life, and inadequate. And from the moment Mathilda first addressed him, he knew that she would be the master in this marriage, for she was an adult, a powerful princess, and a general . . . and he could already detect in her glances that she took him for a child. He had not anticipated such a thing, and the thought of his father soon leaving him in Tuscany was now filling him with apprehension.

"Welf," whispered Mathilda, barely moving her lips, "gather your senses immediately for we are about to walk down the nave of Saint Nicholas Cathedral as husband and wife . . . do not look pitiful before my generals and commanders."

This was not a request, but a command, and it forced Welf to close his eyes to summon courage. Then, as a scolded child would follow his mother's instructions, he stood erect and turned to walk down the nave as Mathilda led. "Yes, Dear," he said awkwardly. These words sounded foolish to him and made him feel ridiculous, as though he was a silly child trying to play the role of an adult.

"Yes, *Countess*," he then said, wondering how this had all come about in the first place. Then he glanced to the side and saw his father, Duke Welf the Elder, standing there watching him walk the nave, his chest swollen to bursting. *Oh, Father, what have you done to me*, he thought, *and what shall become of me when you return to Bavaria next week?*

All then proceeded from the cathedral to Huntsman's Lodge which was the grand hall at Canossa for entertaining guests. One side of its walls was hung with hundreds of boar heads, stag heads, ram heads, antler collections, and bear and wolf skins while the other was hung with an impressive collection of military weapons. The hall's décor was entirely male oriented, yet for the special occasion of this wedding it had been heavily decorated with fine fabrics, tapestries, flowers, and ribbons. As soon as guests began arriving, an army of servants began to bustle about carrying forth platter after platter of roasted boar, mutton, calf, and smoked fish. This was complemented by endless rows of trestle tables stacked with exquisite selections of squab, lark, quail, pheasant, crane, and goose. Wine, ale, and mead flowed freely while musicians gently played soft and melodious tunes that filled the void of the vast hall yet did not overplay conversation. Over a thousand guests mingled politely in the hall as Mathilda and Welf the Younger stood at its far end with Pope Urban, General Padule, and Duke Welf greeting guests and accepting lavish wedding gifts.

"Such wealth," Duxia whispered to Mala with disgust, "as half the world outside starves and scrapes about for crumbs . . . and the Church is right in the middle of this all."

"Indeed," said Mala, "I thought Vincento was wealthy, but such wealth as this I never imagined, Duxia." Then she spotted Guillaume and the Danes across the hall and said, "Come along, let's visit our Montelucio hosts, at least they'll talk to us."

"Nay, the Danes despise me and I them. Dear, you go along and enjoy yourself for I know this has not been a pleasant trip for you."

Mala spent the next hour in friendly conversation with Guillaume and the Danes, and though she was sorely tempted to inquire about Tristan's whereabouts and well-being, she determined it best to remain silent about him, just as they had remained silent about him since her arrival at Monteluccio. A bell was rung then, and General Padule walked to the center of the hall accompanied by the musicians who had previously been playing chamber music in a corner of the Hall. Several of them had changed instruments before following General Padule, and it was evident that a livelier style of music was about to ensue. "On behalf of Countess Mathilda and her new husband, Welf the Younger," announced General Padule, "I am proud to announce that the newly married couple will now retire to their wedding chamber for the evening. For your entertainment this evening they have provided the floor for dancing until dawn!"

This precipitated a loud round of applause that echoed from one end of the hall to the other as guests cleared the center of the hall for the dozens of costumed entertainers who appeared from nowhere and took positions next to Padule. Then, as Mathilda and Welf neared the door followed by four monks, a din arose within the hall as the visiting Bavarians began to whistle and howl, knowing that shortly young Welf would be planting his semen between Mathilda's thighs, thereby sealing this most important of marriages.

Sensing that some of the comments and gestures they were making were lewd in nature, Guillaume became incensed and raised his fist at the Bavarians, shouting at them until Orla slipped beside him, reached up, and lowered Guillaume's arm.

"Let it pass, Guillaume," he said, "it's a grand moment for the Bavarians and they are simply trying to encourage the poor lad. If I were his age, I'd be shitting my pants at the thought of crawling into bed with the mighty Mathilda. And they say he has to do this thing tonight with those four monks following them out the door watching on as witnesses!"

And indeed, the four monks following Mathilda and Welf out of the hall immediately then accompanied the newly-wed couple directly to the wedding chamber. It had been agreed in advance, in order to satisfy Duke Welf the Elder's demands that two Benedictine monks of Mathilda's choice and two Benedictines of Duke Welf's choice would serve as witnesses to the consummation of the marriage. At Pope Urban's insistence the condition was imposed that all four monks must be unquestionably pure of heart and chaste of body. Duke Welf selected two young Benedictines fresh from completing their novitiate in his own territories of Bavaria. Mathilda selected a certain Brother Justin who was an elderly Benedictine in her service at Canossa. Her second choice was none other than Brother Jurgen Handel of the Benedictine underground.

As instructed by Pope Urban and Muehler, toward the end of the wedding feast Handel had discreetly slipped the Monte Cassino belladonna formula into Welf's wine. Precisely as planned, the effects of that formula quickly began to take effect. As Mathilda and Welf mounted the steps to the wedding chamber, Welf twice stumbled and once had to stop to gain his bearings.

"I d-don't feel so well," he muttered, holding onto Mathilda's arm as the two young Bavarian monks steadied him from behind.

"Ah, 'tis only the wine, Welf," Mathilda said with assurance. "You drank like a true German this night, my husband."

"Y-yes, but I don't usually feel like this when I drink, C-Countess," he replied, feeling more disoriented with each step upward.

When they reached the bedchamber, Handel bolted the door and pointed to the chairs that had been arranged along both sides of the bed, two on each side. "Be seated, Brothers," he said, "and let's be done with our task as quickly as possible so as to afford this couple the privacy they deserve."

Mathilda then disappeared into an adjoining room, and when she returned she was wearing a thin, elegantly embroidered sendal gown that covered her from neck to ankles. She then crawled up on the bed and lay flat on her back, making sure that her gown extended all the way to her toes. The two Bavarian monks, seated beside each other on the far side of the bed, looked at each other momentarily, and one of them asked timidly, "Brother Handel, is Countess Mathilda not going to remove her gown?"

"What?" Handel crowed indignantly. "Surely you do not suppose that the Countess is to lay there butt-naked in the presence of four men who are not her husband! In the name of the Almighty, we are Benedictines, not a herd of primitive pagans!"

The young monk shrugged a bit with confusion, then said, "But how are we to document consummation if she is *clothed*?"

"Oh, Lord above," Handel snorted, "have neither of you Bavarians ever attended a consummation rite before?"

They shook their heads no.

"And you, Brother Justin?" Handel asked

"Yes, of course I have," Brother Justin replied, just as he had been instructed days earlier.

"And so," Handel continued, with evident agitation, "I suppose neither of you two lads has actually witnessed or experienced . . . *copulation*?"

At this the faces of both monks colored. "Of course not!" one of them objected. "'Twas the condition of the Pope, was it not, that all four of us witnesses be pure of heart and chaste of body?"

"Yes, agreed," Handel replied quickly. "There are Church manuscripts that give description and pictorial representations of sexual intercourse for the benefit of academic instruction to clergymen. Hmm . . . it appears that neither of you have yet been exposed to them. Very well then, allow me to explain how copulation is performed." Instead of continuing on the topic, Handel glanced over at Welf who was standing behind the two Bavarian monks in an apparent stupor, his eyes heavy-lidded and his head drooping onto his chest. "Lord Welf, are you with us?" he said.

Welf, his mind blearier even than his eyes, gave no reply so Handel motioned to the Bavarian monks and said, "Best help him undress. He appears a bit *confounded* at the moment."

The monks stared at Welf, then stood and began to undress him. "Do we remove all of his clothing, Brother Handel, or do we leave him with his trousers?"

"Good God, one cannot copulate through his own trousers!" Handel snorted. "Take it all off so we can see his staff. After all, it's the *man's* work that interests us tonight, not the woman's, eh?"

"Uh, yes, of course," the monks mumbled, having little idea whatsoever how to proceed or what to expect. When Welf had been stripped, they then led him to the bedside. When Welf crawled onto the bed, he immediately fell on his belly and closed his eyes, which only further confused the Bavarians. Flustered, they looked over at Handel and asked, "What now, Brother Handel?"

"Well, well," said Handel, feigning disappointment, "it is actually *Welf* who is supposed to be doing something, not us. It seems he prefers sleep. Such an insult to the Countess and to all of Italy. Don't you agree Brother Justin?"

"Oh, an insult beyond belief," replied Brother Justin sourly. "Absolutely intolerable!"

This mortified the Bavarians, and as they exchanged a glance of dread, one of them said, "Help us then, Brother Handel, what are we to do?"

Handel stood and examined the naked and unconscious Welf. "Hmm . . . perhaps you could lift him up and place him atop the Countess. Then she will lift her gown, spread her legs, and accept his duty."

The monks quickly complied, but laying Welf atop the Countess, who had not said one word since entering the bedchamber, Welf began to snore loudly. This further befuddled the two young monks, and they began to wring their hands with frustration. Finally, after staring at Welf's bare buttocks for nearly a full minute, one of them reached down and pulled the sheet over Mathilda and Welf.

"What are you doing?" said Handel.

"I, uh, think we can do this without actually having to see or watch their privates, can't we, Brother Handel?"

"Well, this is a bit irregular, but yes, if that's what you think, I suppose we can proceed in that manner."

Mathilda reached her hands beneath her waist, and after a bit of a struggle due to Welf's dead weight laying upon her, managed to raise her gown to her stomach.

Witnessing this movement of her hands beneath the sheet, Handel looked at the Bavarians and said, "Well, she's ready, lads, so the passageway is clear. Time for Welf to get busy."

All four of the monks stared at Mathilda and Welf then. Of course, nothing happened. Welf was dead to the world and snoring even louder than before.

"Oh, this is not going well," sighed one of the Bavarians. "Duke Welf will not be pleased at all. He will be furious!"

"Ho!" objected Handel. "The good Duke may well be furious at his son, or at the two of you, but he best not raise complaint with me or Brother Justin. Oh no, none of this is *our* doing! And what about the dear Countess? She has graciously agreed to this documentation nonsense insisted by Duke Welf, but now she lays there humiliated and offended. I suggest you try to wake the boy. And if he doesn't come alive, then I suggest you reach down and start lifting him up and down, up and down, up and down."

"What?" cried the Bavarians.

"Yes, you know, make his body go up and down, up and down . . . that is the way of copulation, I believe, is it not, Brother Justin?"

"I wouldn't know for sure, of course," replied Brother Justin, "but I do believe your description approximates what I saw in the Church manuscripts many years ago."

"Well then, better get to it, lads," snapped Handel, "after all, Welf is *your* responsibility, not ours! I'd hate to report to the Pope and to Duke Welf that the two of you failed to see this thing through tonight. The future of Bavaria and Tuscany lies in the balance of your inaction, you know."

At this one of the Bavarians went to the other side of the bed, then the two reached down, grasped Welf at the waist, and began pumping him up and down upon Mathilda's torso. Within a minute both monks' breathing was labored. "Brother Handel, how long must we do this?" said one of them, completely winded.

"Well, knowing very little about copulation other than that of farm animals and what I came across in the records, I'm not quite sure. Perhaps you should ask the Countess, she was married once in years past."

The monks looked at her, and conveying to them a look of absolute aversion, she spoke for the first time since entering the room. "It is done," she said.

The two monks, perspiring heavily, dropped their hold on Welf and immediately moved toward the door, which was still bolted. "Hold on there!" cried Handel, "You must sign this document along with Brother Justin and myself before you leave. And due to the high sensitivity of this evening's business, I suggest you not speak of this affair other than to say it was *done,* don't you both agree?"

"Yes, certainly, certainly," the two Bavarians said in unison, anxious to be gone from the bedchamber, and anxious, as well, to return to Bavaria.

CHAPTER SEVENTY-EIGHT

MALA AND GUILLAUME

The departure of Countess Mathilda and Welf the Younger from Huntsman's Hall signaled the conclusion of formalities for the evening. This departure was also accompanied by the departure of Pope Urban, the cardinals, archbishops, and bishops. They knew well that the level of gaiety amongst the guests was about to escalate, and clergymen had learned that it was often best not to bear witness to such frivolity since it, at times, got out of hand. And such was the very case on this night.

After General Padule's announcement about the commencement of professional entertainment, the wine began to flow in rivers as red-faced guests laughed uproariously at jesters, gawked at jugglers and magicians, and elevated the volume of their own banter. Promiscuity also began to surface in certain quarters as nobles who had come without their wives began to seek overnight female companionship with stray females, and even many whose wives were present began to do the same.

The mood continued to elevate as inhibitions fell to the wayside for nearly two hours more. Then the music came to an abrupt halt and Vicento Balducci strolled to the middle of the floor, clearing all aside bar the musicians. "I have a surprise for you this evening my friends," he declared. Then his eyes narrowed and slowly raked across the hall as he added, "Yes, and even for those of you who are *no longer* my friends. My wife shall perform for you a Romani dance. Please note that I said *Romani*, not Saracen. I point this out because apparently many of you, it seems, have determined that my wife is Saracen, though she is not. In speaking to the fine musicians here this evening I learned that they are not familiar with Romani music itself, yet are familiar with certain strains of Byzantine music which bear a distant similarity, according to my lovely wife, Mala."

As Balducci spoke, several of the older women, including his own mother, began to exchange glances of disapproval, roll their eyes, or turn away. Balducci's speech had aroused a keen interest amongst the men and younger women within the hall. All were aware of Mala's extraordinary beauty and were ever so curious about her dancing. Although none had never witnessed it, they knew that dancing had been a part of her mysterious history.

As the crowd gathered in a large circle about Balducci and the musicians, Balducci gave a signal and the musicians broke into a loud and lively strand of Byzantine music. From the back of the hall the crowd then began to part as Mala moved through them, each step accentuated with exaggerated, graceful movements that made her thin, flowing gown cling to her long legs in one motion, then swirl outward in waves with the next. Attaining the open center of the hall, she then began to cavort about in large circles, offering ethereal movement of her arms, sweeping them left, then right, then over her head and about her long, elegant neck. As she did this her head and neck communed in a sensual combination of abrupt then graceful motions that mimicked the movement made by swans as they glide across the waterways in nature's display of poise and dignity in its purest form.

In her dance, Mala's dark eyes flashed here and there, often settling on individuals in such a manner that those watching thought she was focusing and dancing only for them. This, of course, served to ignite the fantasies and libidos of the men watching on, and also added fire to the enthusiasm of the younger women who smiled and clucked with approval. The dance lasted only seven minutes, but during that brief time all who watched stood in wonder, completely absorbed in Mala, her costume, the hypnotic jingle-jangle of her zills, and the ebb and flow of her limbs, skirt, and billowing embroidered sleeves. Even those who had turned away began to rejoin the crowd, unable to resist the applause, whistles, and exclamations of approval that began to swell in waves from the captivated spectators. Then, when Mala was finished, she quickly vanished from the center of hall and was not seen again that evening though many clamored for more of her and more of her dancing. Of all those watching, it was Balducci and Duxia who were the most exultant about her performance. And though their rationales were quite different, perhaps, they both sensed a triumph of sorts for Mala, as well as for themselves.

Another thing began to occur, also. As often happens after the excitement of a stunning performance, since the appreciative spectators could not get next to Mala who had become the object of their adulation, they then sought those nearest to it, which were in this case Balducci and Duxia. Men thronged Balducci, slapping him upon the back and congratulating him in the wake of Mala's dance, and several of the younger women even approached old Duxia, overflowing with praise and questions.

Mala left the hall determined to leave the wedding celebration at that very moment and gathered her coach driver. As she was getting into her coach, Guillaume appeared. "Such an artful performance, Mala!" he declared. "Pray tell, why did you leave? Where are you going? They're clamoring for you in the hall."

"Oh, Guillaume," Mala said, surprised to see him. "I'm returning to Montelucio."

"Mathilda has pitched tents and provided overnight accommodations for her guests this evening. Montelucio is nearly half a night's ride."

"Perhaps so, but I've had enough of this place, and these people. They disgust me."

"I see," said Guillaume, as a glimmer of disappointment crossed his eyes and then he shrugged. "Actually, I've grown weary of this affair myself, especially these bawdy Bavarians. Would you object if I accompanied you then?"

"No, of course not," smiled Mala, pleased by Guillaume's unexpected offer. "I would enjoy the company. In fact, it's been a rather lonely visit here these past weeks, actually. Vincento has been off hunting and socializing and others have chosen to ignore me. Yes, come along then, Guillaume, I would very much enjoy having someone to share conversation with on the long ride back."

As the coach began working its way down the steep approach to Canossa, Mala and Guillaume exchanged polite conversation about their respective difficulties during the two weeks preceding Mathilda's wedding, and soon found themselves sharing laughter over the antics of Duke Welf, Welf the Younger, and others.

"Ah, I thought many times that I was on the verge of cuffing my rude Bavarian guests," said Guillaume, "but that would have offended my aunt Mathilda, and I would sooner die than do such a thing."

"It's evident that the two of you share a great affection. As for me, I fear she holds me in low regard."

As she said this, Mala's tone was edged with both regret and bitterness, which brought a sudden end to the levity which both had been enjoying since leaving the feast. Guillaume reflected on her statement a moment, then said, "Yes, you must understand, she is Tristan's aunt also, and it's only out of concern for him that she rejects you. I must confess, I myself took the same position after finding out about what happened between the two of you. Since making your acquaintance these past days, I bear you no ill will, nor do the Danes. What transpired between you and my brother was unfortunate."

Mala did not reply immediately. "Unfortunate in most ways, yes, but also fortunate in others, I suppose."

"Eh? I see little in your suffering or Tristan's that offers the least trace of good fortune."

Mala considered these words thoughtfully before replying, then said, "Well then, I suppose you have never been in love then, Guillaume?"

Guillaume shook his head. "I know nothing of such things. Indeed, I barely even know any women other than my aunt, and she is more manly than feminine. Besides, I took an oath of chastity and celibacy two years ago, at the knees of Cardinal Odo de Lagery himself before he became Pope."

"What?" said Mala, appalled. "Guillaume, that makes no sense. How old are you now?"

"I'm about to reach my twenty-first year."

"Oh, Guillaume! Who on this earth talked you into such foolishness? Odo de Lagery?"

"No. It was my own decision. I'm a soldier of Christ and have vowed to worship and fight for the true Church and God, my Savior and Creator."

Mala shook her head. "How ridiculous is life! Your brother is a monk yet he did not remain chaste, and you are not a monk, yet you take a vow of chastity! For you to take such vows is nearly as sad as Tristan taking the vows of monasticism. Oh, Guillaume, do you not see what these people have done to you and your brother?"

"Done to me and Tristan?" said Guillaume, perplexed. "They've done nothing less than help the two of us. Cardinal Odo brought Tristan up from nothing, and Aunt Mathilda did the same for me."

"Oh, no Guillaume, they've done more than that, they've turned you into *themselves*. They've filled you with their own beliefs, extreme beliefs, Guillaume, both you and Tristan! That's why you're so much alike now."

Guillaume shook his head. "Though I love my brother dearly, I am a different person than him, Mala. And know this, I didn't approve of his fall from grace because of you, though I understand it, especially since meeting you and experiencing the goodness of your heart, as well as your frightening beauty. Nevertheless, he shouldn't have weakened. His being a monk, his moral collapse was a sin against God. And God made him suffer."

Mala laughed at this, lacking all trace of humor. "God made him suffer? Oh, you're mistaken yet again, Guillaume. It was me who suffered, not Tristan. It was me who lost a child in the Alps, not him. Tristan is the root of my suffering. No, he has suffered little because of me."

"Oh, not true," insisted Guillaume. "Had you been there to witness his penance, you wouldn't say such a thing."

"His penance?"

"Yes. Being told of your ordeal in the Alps and learning of the child you bore him, he refuted his Benedictine vows before Cardinal Odo de Lagery himself. Then, after you rejected him as he found you traveling to Balducci's territories, he fell into a trough of grief and sorrow. He took to drinking, cursing, blaming others, and questioning the Church even. Then Cardinal Odo Pope appeared after a time and forgave him on the condition that he perform an excruciating penance of thirty days within a dungeon cell praying and flagellating himself."

Mala's eyes narrowed as she took in these words and she whispered, more to herself than to Guillaume, "I never knew of this."

"And when he had completed his punishment, he was bloodied and bowed, he couldn't even stand or walk. I stood by the cell those many days of his penance, and heard him cry out in despair and sorrow over you and the lost child. He hurt himself to the point of near death to atone for what he had wrought. To this day, Mala, he doesn't understand why you abandoned him in Marseilles without warning."

Mala had lost herself in the images Guillaume was describing, and was touched to the point of tears, but with his last statement, her expression flared with indignity. "So, Tristan continues to play innocent and you for the fool like he did me in Marseilles. The truth is, Guillaume, he lied to me, deceived me, and betrayed me while I foolishly fell for his ruse in Marseilles."

"Eh?" said Guillaume, baffled. "What do you mean by such a thing? He told me that his time in Marseilles with you was the happiest moment of his entire life, that you mysteriously vanished without even offering the slightest explanation."

"No explanation was needed, for Tristan knew well what he did to me in Marseilles," retorted Mala, feeling her anger rise. "Either you are defending him to the grave because he is your brother, or you are as gullible as I was! Tristan lied to me about where he was staying in Marseilles, then deceived me with that other woman he was spending time with in Marseilles as well. Don't deny such a thing because he told me you were in Marseilles at that time, unless of course, he was lying about that as well."

"Indeed, I *was* in Marseilles *with* Tristan," said Guillaume, more confused than ever. "And the Danes were there with me. We were staying at the Benedictine monastery with Tristan while in Marseilles."

Such a fabrication brought Mala nearly to the point of outrage. "Not true!" she cried, convinced that Guillaume was in collusion with his brother. "I went there myself and spoke to the abbot of that monastery, a certain Abbot LeTour. He said there were no soldiers staying there at the monastery, and knew nothing of a Tristan de Saint-Germain. He said there were no guests whatsoever staying at the monastery and that he had no idea what I was talking about!"

Guillaume sat back in his seat, trying to recollect details of the mission in Marseilles. "I was there with the Danes, Mala, at the Benedictine monastery of Abbot LeTour," he insisted, "and so was Tristan. We were on a clandestine mission to collect money and arms for Mathilda's fight against King Heinrich. If the old abbot told you such a thing, it was because he was under orders by Odo de Lagery to conceal our presence so as not to attract attention from Heinrich's spies. Tristan was working for the Benedictine underground at the time. Did you not know he was a spy in those days?"

"What?" said Mala, her breathing coming to an abrupt halt.

"Yes, right after his ordination he joined the Benedictine underground. He posed as this and that, which is why he never wore monk's garb nor had his hair cut in the Benedictine tonsure. He was forced to live a life of disguises."

Mala's hand went to her breast as she remembered Tristan's vague responses concerning a temporary dispensation that allowed him to wear layman's clothing rather than the black robe of the Benedictines. Even though she felt the ground crumbling beneath her feet, a part of her insisted that he had still betrayed her. "But he and that woman in Marseilles that my friends saw; the two of them were embracing and kissing right there in the street! Surely if you were in Marseilles with him you know who of which woman I'm speaking of!"

"Woman?" said Guillaume. "There was no woman in Marseilles." After a few moments of reflection he recalled the morning that Lady Agnes Truffault had appeared at the monastery to deliver a wagon load of arms and money. "Ah, wait!

Yes, there was a certain Agnes Truffault who came to the monastery one day. A promiscuous little bitch whose husband lived in Dijon. She was visiting her husband's brother in Marseilles, consorting with him, apparently. She happened to take a liking to Tristan immediately, and threw herself at him openly, hanging all about him. It was a source of embarrassment to him."

"Embarrassment?" said Mala, her voice declining into weak and thready syllables.

"Yes, we only saw her twice, once at her brother-in-law's manor where we first met her, then one time later as she and a teamster delivered a wagon to the monastery."

"Tristan only saw her twice then?" said Mala, sensing that she was on the edge of internal collapse. "He was not staying with her throughout his stay in Marseilles?"

"Definitely not. He was with me every night. On the morning she came to the monastery, as she was out of sight of her brother-in-law, she immediately began to paw at Tristan and cling to him as though they were lovers. She insisted that he accompany her into town that morning, and as they left the monastery I could see Tristan attempting to stave off her advances. I'm not certain what your friends thought they saw going on between my brother and that woman, but I assure you, Lady Agnes Truffault was the only one making advances, certainly not Tristan. He thought her repulsive."

At this, Mala fell silent, and her chest began to break into sporadic heaves that began to arrest her breathing. "Ooh . . ." she finally sighed, her eyes falling shut and her hands beginning to tremble. "O-oh!"

"What is it, Mala?" said Guillaume, grasping her shoulders to hold her up. She withered in his grasp and soon fell into a heap across his knees, breaking into inconsolable sobs. He could feel her quaking in his lap as one taken by seizures. Nothing he could say or do did anything to abate her sudden and inexplicable grief. This continued for nearly an hour and Guillaume sat there motionless, cradling Mala with his arms and hands until finally, the sobs dissolved into whimpers. When the whimpers finally ceased, he looked down at her tear-stained face. She had fallen asleep.

CHAPTER SEVENTY-NINE

MALA'S DEMISE

Finding herself so rudely jolted from her unshakable but erroneous assumption about Tristan's activities in Marseilles, several things began to occur to Mala, much as they would to anyone experiencing such a drastic reversal of information. To begin, on the coach ride back to the Balducci manor after the wedding and for several days following, Mala became steeped in a ceaseless struggle of disbelief and denial which caused her wrestle back and forth with what she had previously believed and what Guillaume had revealed.

Then, as this passed and she finally accepted the truth of matters, she began to assail her lack of faith in Tristan and her own greatest weakness, her temper. It was her temper that had sent her into a fury that last night in Marseilles. And it had swept her into an overreaction so complete that she had disregarded the violent storm raging about her that night and had also endangered all those in her company at the time. Furthermore it had caused her to tear the troupe away from its most prosperous engagement ever into eventual dissolution, and had also led to the horror of the Alps. Above all, it had smashed into hopeless fragments the enduring, boundless love that had begun to blossom into full array between her and Tristan.

After several days of castigating herself for not controlling her emotions in Marseilles, she then began to examine what had led her to make the rash decision to storm out of Marseilles and away from Tristan. This blame quickly fell onto the dead Fernando and Duxia. *Ah, but they led me by the bridle into my own inner storm,* she concluded. So bitter she became that one day she grabbed the unsuspecting Duxia aside and gave her a sound verbal thrashing.

"Oh, you were wrong about Tristan in Marseilles!" she cried at the old woman who was completely unprepared to experience such wrath from Mala. "You and Fernando led me to believe one foul thing after another about Tristan, and none of it was true! I learned the truth from Guillaume in Canossa two weeks ago, and now I shudder every time I think of my own foolishness the night we left Marseilles, a foolishness fed by both you and Fernando!"

Mala's anger was so inflamed that old Duxia could scarcely listen without fear that Mala would next attack her, then drag her about the manor as one might drag a prisoner about the streets for public humiliation. Finally Duxia summoned the wherewithal to grab Mala by the shoulders and cry, "Stop this foolishness! Even if Fernando and I were wrong, even if we misled you, the boy was still a monk! And even if there was no mistress in Marseilles, the Church was his mistress, and still is!"

This forced Mala to pause her rampage, only briefly. "He was going to leave the Church, Duxia, for me! He refuted his vows! He was coming for me, but you kept him from me when he caught up to Balducci's caravan on the way to his manor! Oh, Duxia, I thought you loved me! No, you have only led me into desolation! You know I don't love Vincento, I love Tristan and always have!"

At this an expression of horror washed over Duxia's face and she sprang forward, violently clapping one hand over Mala's mouth and holding the back of her head with the other. "Oh, hush!" she hissed in a high whisper. "Never say such a thing aloud in this household, Dear! Oh, Vincento's mother and sisters would love to hear such words. How quickly do you think they could get to Vincento's ear, eh?"

Duxia's action so startled Mala that she froze in place a moment. Then, removing the old woman's grip, she sagged a bit, knowing that Duxia was right. "I'm sorry. It's that I'm so confused and distraught," said Mala, tears beginning to form in the wells of her eyes. "No, it's not your fault Duxia, it's mine. 'Twas me the fool."

"In the end, perhaps not," said Duxia, becoming distraught herself at seeing Mala in such a state. "As I said, Tristan de Saint-Germain still belongs to the Church, maybe more so even than before, for he directly represents the Pope. I know your heart is broken, Dear, and it's been for some time now. Even before this new information you learned in Canossa, I could see in your carriage and manner that you walk about without that drive that once possessed you when you collected this old carcass from the roadside."

"I've become lost, Duxia. I no longer know who I am or what I am. When I danced that night at the wedding, for one brief moment I became the old Mala, alive and on fire as in earlier days. When I finished dancing and realized it was but a fleeting illusion, it saddened me to the point of fleeing Canossa that very night. I miss those days, Duxia! Oh how I miss them!"

"Ay," nodded Duxia, "be careful for you are in a good place now, Mala. Think about where you are, also think about where Tristan is at the moment. I care nothing for the young man, but just as I warned him not to destroy you, I now warn you, if you pursue this obsession with him, it might well destroy him along with yourself. The two of you are as moths attracted to the flame. We know what the flame does to the ever fragile wing of the moth. I beg you, step back and consider all things. Vincento has been good to you, Mala, and adores you above all else in his life."

"Yes, I know," sighed Mala. "I wish that I loved him, I do, but . . ." She did not finish the sentence. Instead, she shook her head and walked away.

Duxia spent the next several days doing everything possible to cater to Mala in an effort to raise her spirits, but Mala's distress only deepened and she refused to say another word to Duxia about Tristan. Despite Mala's best efforts to mask her troubled heart, this newfound melancholia of hers did not go unnoticed by others of the household. Though the servants had suspected a touch of despair in Mala's countenance from the very start, this despair now seemed more pronounced and more profound, and they often exchanged thoughts on this development in hushed whispers and private huddles amongst themselves.

It was Vincento Balducci who was affected the most by Mala's descent. He noticed a change in Mala immediately following Mathilda and Welf's wedding. It was nothing he could place a finger on, but he sensed that little about the manor or its surroundings appeared to satisfy her anymore. His first reaction was to bury her in gifts, jewelry, and gestures of affection. Each maneuver he attempted seemed not to enliven her, but served only to increase her brooding.

His next reaction was to seek information from Duxia, whom he had finally come to trust and respect. The old woman claimed ignorance of any distress or unhappiness that Mala might be experiencing, and further insisted that Mala had never been more content in her life. This, of course, only confused and frustrated Balducci, which in turn led him to eventually confront Mala directly one night as they lay within the privacy of their bedchamber. "Something ails you, Mala," he said. "Is it something my mother or sisters have done?"

"No, Vincento."

"Me, then . . . have I done something that has offended you? If so, I wish to apologize."

"No, Vincento."

"Well, something's damn sure raised your ire, and I'd like to know what it is. I'm leaving in one week to resume the fight against the Germans and won't be back for quite some time. I'd like to know what the hell's going on. So are you going to tell me or not!"

"No, Vincento."

These brief, spiritless replies only further reinforced Balducci's certainty that something was about with Mala, and for the first time since their marriage, he became cross.

"Listen to yourself," he snapped, "it's as if I'm talking to the dead! And you've rebuffed me in this very bed ever since the Canossa trip. I'm your husband, goddammit, and deserve better than this. Something is pulling at you, and I want an answer. Now!"

"Vincento," replied Mala coldly, turning on her side toward him, "I don't like your tone." Then she raised up on an elbow propping her head in one palm, incidentally sliding the other hand beneath her pillow, and stared at him a moment.

Balducci saw her hand slide beneath the pillow, mistook this as her reaching for the dagger that she had kept there since their marriage, and this angered him. "Oh, so now you threaten me with your blade!" he shouted.

Mala had had no intention whatsoever of reaching for her dagger, and upon hearing her husband's charge, withdrew her hand immediately. "Vincento," she said calmly, "you are acting the imbecile."

"Imbecile?" cried Balducci. "What? How dare you address me in such a manner! Goddammit, I'm a high lord of Tuscany and commander of the Tuscan Knights!" Then he jumped from the bed and began a tirade that lasted over a full minute. When he was finished his face was scarlet and the veins of his neck pulsed in high relief, and he stood there a moment glaring at her in the candle-light. Then he cast a finger at her and cried, "Oh, it's that goddamned Saint-Germain bastard isn't it!"

Mala shrank back at the mention of this name, certain that the unbelievable had occurred . . . Duxia had betrayed her.

"Oh yes," Balducci continued, "that's it! I should have known! Indeed, I should have slit his throat the very moment I learned about your whorish antics with him!"

Shocked, Mala fell limp, unable even to find words to defend herself.

"Oh, yes," Balducci blathered, spittle flying from his mouth with every word, "I know all about Guillaume riding back with you in the coach after your little dance in Canossa! No, I trusted you and I trusted him! Oh, what a goddamn fool am I!"

The look of shock then disappeared from Mala's face and she broke into laughter, which Balducci somehow mistook for verification of his accusation. "Vincento!" cried Mala, her voice full of mockery. "Yes, you are truly a fool! Guillaume de Saint-Germain innocently accompanied me back to Monteluccio that night, as any chivalrous gentleman might do, and nothing happened between us buth conversation!"

"I don't believe you, Mala! You're lying! He's a handsome lad, I grant you, and he seduced you that night, either that or 'twas you that seduced him!"

"Vincento! Stop this foolishness now, I say, before you regret it!"

Balducci took this as another threat. Furious, he charged the bed and reached out to grab Mala by the head, but as his fingers filled with her hair, he felt a sharp blade poking at his throat right beneath his chin. Stunned, falling back to the floor, he shot a hand to his neck and felt the warm smear of blood oozing between his fingers. It was not a deep wound, only enough to cut him and cause him to cry out. Then, before he could rise or even collect his senses, Mala flung herself upon his chest, straddling it, and held the blade to his neck again. "Vincento," she hissed, *"never* attack me again, or it will be your end. I told you once before, I shall never tolerate what my mother endured at the hands of a man!"

Balducci eased his head and throat back and stared up at her, his eyes wide with disbelief. "Y-yes," he gasped, "I understand."

Mala then stood and wiped her blade across her gown, leaving a bloodstain as its point slid across the fabric. "I shall sleep in Duxia's room tonight, Vincento, so don't come looking for me. And because of your wild accusations and your attempted attack on me, I shall sleep in Duxia's room from this night until your departure in one week. And from there, when you return, we shall sort this out, do you understand?"

CHAPTER EIGHTY

TRISTAN'S TRAVELS

Sailing into Tunis with four other monks and a heavily armed papal escort, Tristan's delegation reported immediately to General Bertucci at the Christian stronghold outside the city. Although the general was already well into his years, he appeared ten years older than when Tristan saw him last.

"Oh, Tristan, lad," the general proclaimed sadly greeting him, "some tragic developments for me since you were last here!"

"Yes, I have heard," Tristan replied, noticing that the general had been drinking heavily. His expression was glazed and his eyes ran red with tiny rivers that pulsed within his sockets. "Indeed, I share your grief and have prayed continuously for your departed wife and daughter since learning of their tragic end. And know that Pope Urban has sent me here to convey his personal condolences also."

"Ah, how could God cast such misfortune upon me in my late years?" the general moaned. "For I've been his good soldier my entire life!"

"His mysteries are beyond our grasp, General. I am certain that your wife and daughter sit beside the Creator this very moment and are shining their grace down upon you as we speak."

Coming from the Pope's First Counsel, these words consoled Bertucci, as did Tristan's very presence. "I've been back from Italy for nearly three months now, but my heart is still in Genoa, I fear," he said, taking another deep drink of wine from his goblet.

"Beware the drink, General," Tristan said with sincerity. "I have followed that path once myself, and though it dulled the senses for a moment, it nearly led me to perdition."

"Now I'm alone and wonder what purpose I have left on this earth. Every morning as I rise I curse that goddamned Balducci for breaking my daughter's heart. Oh, my poor Marianna. Even as she gasped her final breath she was asking about that sorry bastard!"

"General, your clan is large and spread throughout central Italy, is it not?"

"Yes, siblings, nephews, nieces, but no heir. My great hope was to deliver a grand dowry for my daughter's wedding day and live to see the birth of grandchildren. Now the sole trace of my lineage has passed from this earth. I stand alone despite my clan, and their only interest in me now will be who inherits my wealth." At this he shook his head ruefully and lifted his goblet to his mouth.

"You do not stand alone, General, and there remains purpose to your life. The Church stands with you, recognizing your valor and your contributions and sorely needs you to continue to carry its banner for the cause of all Christians who are being abused and enslaved here in North Africa. Pope Urban does not wish to overburden you. He wishes to know whether your heart is too heavy to continue the fight, or whether you wish to retire to Genoa."

"Retire to Genoa?" said Bertucci. "In which sense does he apply that word? Does he mean retire as in returning to Genoa, or does he mean retire as in turning in my sword and sitting out my days upon my death nest?"

"What he means," replied Tristan, perceiving Bertucci's sudden rash of sensitivity, "is, what do you think is best for you?"

"I've never retreated and I've never not finished what I've begun!" cried Bertucci, emotion filling his cheeks with more color than had the wine. "Besides, there's little left for me in Genoa any more. No, I'll remain here until we collar the last of these goddamned Islamic heathens. Before I left to bury my wife and daughter in Genoa, our troops were making impressive strides, thanks to the guidance and strategies you suggested your first trip."

"And since your return?"

"We've *still* got them on the run, and furthermore, we're about to install a new regime here in Tunis. The money you brought from the Pope has bought us many friends here, and as you said, there's a thirst for vengeance amongst these different tribes and clans. Give me another several months and *then* I'll return retire to Genoa carrying a victory banner!"

"Ah, you possess the heart of a lion."

Bertucci appreciated this comment, and his temperament softened as quickly as it had flared. He refilled his goblet, took another drink, then said, "In the morning I'll introduce you to our new Saracen allies and show you the gains we've made since your last visit. I think you'll be impressed."

By the end of the next day, Tristan was pleased to see that Bertucci had not exaggerated his claims of the previous night. The Italian expeditionary force, with the assistance of multiple rebellious Islamic factions, had placed the enemy on the defensive. Furthermore, Tristan learned that upon final completion of this campaign, the assisting Islamic factions had vowed to stop the enslavement of Christians and respect their right to freely worship in the name of Gregorian Catholicism. Content that circumstances in Tunis were better than originally reported, Tristan remained one week more, primarily for the purpose of providing conversation and company to General Bertucci, as well as offering him spiritual and heartfelt solace on the loss of his deceased spouse and daughter. Bertucci greatly appreciated this time spent together, and on the day of Tristan's departure, he begged Tristan to stay yet a few more days. "I don't know what it is about you, lad, but you do this old heart of mine much good!"

* * *

Two and a half weeks later Tristan's delegation arrived at the court of King Philippe in Paris where, showing his medallion and documents, Tristan was immediately ushered into the inner sanctum and presented to King Philippe and Queen Bertha. They recognized neither his face nor his name the first time they set eyes upon him. Then the queen, spotting his extraordinarily clear grey eyes, raised both hands in the air and exclaimed. "Oh, it's Ambassador Lucien Broussard, Philippe!"

Taking a second look, the king acknowledged the face. Immediately suspicion clouded his countenance and he said, "Yes, Ambassador Broussard, but what then is this *Tristan de Saint-Germain* business here on your documents, sir, and why are you dressed and have your head shaved as a Benedictine?"

"I have been ordained into the order," replied Tristan, not specifying that his ordination had actually occurred well before his initial visit to their court, "and adopted a new name."

Queen Bertha then issued a hearty congratulations and a warm welcome. The king's greeting was less cordial. "I see," he said, "so you have become a monk. Poor soul, I pity you. Last time, when you appeared here as papal ambassador, I could tolerate you at least because you were a normal man, not a reform-minded fanatic." Then he issued a regal glance of disdain and complained, "So, I see that Rome has decided 'tis time to check up on me again, eh? Christ, you would think finally having a French Pope instead of those tiresome Italians would lighten the climate a bit, but Odo de Lagery is as prudish as the Italians, more so perhaps!"

"Never mind that lout," whispered Bertha to Tristan afterwards, "for he only gets worse with each passing year. Right this minute he digs for a legal means to divorce me, hoping to eventually sequester me in some distant, long forgotten manor at the edges of his realm."

"Oh, my Lady, how can that be?" said Tristan, noticing that Queen Bertha had indeed gained a good amount of weight since his first visit to court several years earlier . . . though it appeared to him that King Philippe himself had put on twice the amount of weight Bertha had gained since that visit. "Especially in light of the fact that you have provided him not only an heir to the throne of France in the form of your son Louis, but four children more."

"Indeed, you would think that would count for something," sniffed Bertha, "but he finds me more repulsive with each pound I gain, and announces his disgust to the world. Oh, if only you knew the public humiliation I now suffer from the tip of that venomous tongue of his!"

"Has he not looked in the mirror?" said Tristan, incapable of comprehending such hypocrisy. "He is far, far larger than yourself."

"Mirror?" twittered Bertha, putting a hand to Tristan's arm and drawing him closer. "Of course he looks in the mirror, day and night . . . *admiring himself*. He does not see a fat oaf, but only the comely king of France! Let us not speak of weight, for it has become a sensitive subject to me of late."

"Certainly, my Lady, I shall speak of it no more," Tristan responded, bowing respectfully. "Please know that Pope Urban shall never stand for your husband divorcing you."

"Oh, who would have thought that our own Odo de Lagery would one day become Pope," sighed Bertha. "We are so proud of him here in France. And no, I shall never lose faith as long as he wears the cope. He is a valiant man of God who continues to stand upon the principles of our deceased, saintly Pope Gregory."

After two days in court, Tristan sought out Brother Augustine who was still posing as a layman and court calligrapher under the name of Stephane LeBeau.

"Aha, lad," the old monk winked laying eyes on Tristan, "you have quickly risen through the ranks, eh? Good for you! And glad I am that Odo has finally sent someone to my little corner again, for King Philippe has become more flagrant than ever about selling Church office. And I've continued documenting it all."

"Thank you, Brother Augustine. Laboring here year after year in secrecy and solitude, you are salt of the earth and the bedrock of the Benedictine Brotherhood. Tell me, what is this divorce talk that Philippe has been circulating? And to what end would a divorce serve the king? He knows divorce is anathema to the Church."

"Anathema, yes, or so we claim. Philippe isn't blind. He looks about and sees a divorce granted *here* by the Church, then a marriage annulled *there* by the Church." Then Augustine closed his eyes and issued that gleeful little snicker of those who comprehend the ridiculous. "Ha," he said impishly, "divorce is always anathema unless, of course the Church decrees it as acceptable! So our good King Philippe is somehow trying to finagle a means of acquiring a Church sanctioned divorce from Bertha so he can continue to spray his semen wherever he pleases!"

"But," said Tristan, confused, "he does that anyway and doesn't seem to care what others think."

"Ah, but he's the King, and king's don't like to be criticized, or censured. Fortunately, he still fears excommunication and the red-hot fires of hell! That's the only thing keeping him in check at the moment."

Tristan nodded at Augustine's simple, realistic approach to the actions and misdeeds of others, including Mother Church itself. "I see. How is he going about this scheme?"

"Easily. As you know, he's sold many a bishopric and archbishopric to questionable characters within his realm, eh? So what stand do you suppose these Church whores who have purchased office from Philippe will take? He's already gathered the signatures of a good many of them supporting his wish for a divorce. In our favor is the fact that the legitimate clerics still outnumber the hooligans who milk their parishes to the bone. With each passing year our numbers dwindle and his grow. It's only a matter of time, my young friend, and he'll make a move."

"Perhaps so, but Pope Urban shall never approve of such a thing, and he is the final word."

Augustine looked at Tristan, his bright little eyes filling with mockery. "Aha! Odo de Lagery would not be the first Pope to be pressured into doing the unthinkable because of circumstances or the petitioning of others, eh? Are you not the same lad who, upon me telling you that Pope Gregory knew of Philippe's lechery and selling of Church offices yet did nothing, raised your voice in criticism of the great Gregory? Ah yes, that was you, wasn't it, lad? And my reply was that Pope Gregory did nothing because he couldn't afford to raise the ire of King Philippe due to the continuing war against Heinrich. Ah, and that war still rages, doesn't it?"

Tristan nodded. "Yes, but Odo de Lagery is not Pope Gregory."

"Indeed," Augustine winked, "Odo is far more flexible than was the iron-willed Gregory. Odo is the wiser of the two and a consummate politician. So we'll see how this future battle with Philippe shapes up when Philippe finally decides to fire the first volley of arrows, eh? And feel free to pass along everything I've said to Odo, for he knows me well, and I've never told him a lie, only how I see things."

Augustine's comments about Odo being a consummate and judicious politician were on the mark, and Tristan appreciated Augustine's line of reasoning.

"Brother Augustine, have you any advice then to pass along to him?"

Augustine laughed. "Ha! I don't offer advice, especially to men more intelligent than myself. I only report observations and perceptions of what occurs before my very eyes. Don't worry, lad, Odo de Lagery will make the best call for the Church, and he might even gamble with a cast of the die if he's feeling fortunate. Oh yes, Odo de Lagery is full of surprises at times."

"Indeed he is," said Tristan. Then he closed one eye at Augustine, mimicking the wink that the old monk so often issued himself, and said, "And you, too, are full of surprises yourself, Brother Augustine."

Tristan remained in court for several days more, spending much of that time reassuring Queen Bertha that Pope Urban would do everything possible to support her position as the legitimate Queen of France. He also consulted with the legitimate clergymen of Paris concerning Bertha's fears and acquired from them firm promises that they would line up behind Pope Urban should the issue of divorce actually become a reality. In addition, he also dropped both veiled and direct threats of retribution from Pope Urban himself amongst those clergymen of Paris who had purchased their positions from King Philippe and voiced support of his inquiries for a possible future divorce.

After leaving Paris, Tristan led his delegation northwest into Normandy and found there a war ravaged region that rivaled that of north and central Italy itself in terms of destruction and ruination. This was due to the death of

William the Bastard, later known as William the Conqueror, in September of 1088. During his final years the Bastard had already begun encountering a series of difficulties in his domain of Normandy and England which included the death of his wife, rebellions supported and encouraged by King Philippe of France, feuding with his own half brother, rebellions in Maine, and threatened invasions of England from Denmark. Prior to his death William the Bastard named his eldest son, Robert, as heir to Normandy and his second surviving son, William, as heir to England. Upon the Bastard's death, previously loyal Norman nobles as well as rebellious Normans and traditional enemies saw an opportunity to seize lands and disassemble the Bastard's empire.

Although Tristan and his papal delegation were respectfully received nearly everywhere they traveled in Normandy, he was unable to make the least headway in making peace in the region as Odo had hoped. Tristan was successful in securing promises from all quarters; they would continue to recognize the Gregorian party as the true Church and Pope Urban II as the legitimate pontiff. While in Normandy and its neighboring areas, Tristan also made contact with Abbot Anselm, the Abbot of Bec. Abbot Anselm was already a noted champion of scholasticism and a strong voice within Normandy for Church independence from royals and nobles alike. He had been involved in several disputes with William the Bastard while he was alive, professing loyalty to the Gregorian cause, and was now engaged in similar disputes with the Bastard's successor sons, Robert of Normandy and William of England.

"We applaud you for your courage," said Tristan meeting Abbot Anselm. "And due to the recent death of Archbishop Lanfranc of Canterbury in England, we expected you to be the obvious choice as the new Archbishop of Canterbury. Why have you not taken the office?"

"The Bastard left England to his second son, William II," said Anselm, "and now William has seized the possessions and revenue of Canterbury for himself. Furthermore, as King of England, William II has refused to refill the position of Archbishop of Canterbury. And as you know, he also refuses to recognize Pope Urban II because of his father's previous disputes with Pope Gregory. William II despises the Gregorian party. Nevertheless, we are thankful at least that he also does not recognize the anti-pope Clement!"

"So, he believes himself above the Church?"

"Yes, he has a bit of his father in him," chuckled Abbot Anselm, "and so does Robert who has inherited Normandy."

"Both places are under siege at the moment."

"Yes, which is why William absconded with Canterbury's wealth, to finance his wars. The same may well happen here in Normandy with the older brother, Robert."

Tristan shrugged and said, "Odo told me Normandy and England were in a mess, but I did not expect circumstances to be this bad. I am to sail to England after Normandy to open negotiations with King William II, but the prospects look bleak."

Anselm shook his head. "I advise that you not go at all," he said. "The climate there is bad for Gregorians at the moment. Your presence would only inflame the new king, and that would do more harm at the moment than good. I know Odo well and he trusts my judgment. I will send word to him that I counseled you to stay out of England for the good of the Gregorian cause . . . unless of course you wish to become a martyr."

"No, I will do as you suggest, Abbot. Besides, Odo has already advised that I follow your recommendations."

In light of the fact that Tristan determined not to go to England, he directed his delegation and armed escort east across France toward the port of Marseilles and instructed them to sail back to Italy while he remained for several days in the Cluny area. He spent some time there visiting with Abbot Hugh, former teacher-monks, and his former classmate Scule, the Benedictine dwarf, but his primary intent was to visit his mother at the Marcigny convent.

Meeting each other within the convent's visitors' parlor, they exchanged a warm embrace. "Oh, Tristan," Asta exclaimed, "it's been over two years since I saw you last. You look so manly and mature."

"I'm twenty-four now, Mother, have traveled the continent, and have seen more than I ever wished to see." Then he settled his eyes upon her a moment. At age thirtyseven, she was as beautiful as ever. For the first time in his life the realization that she had borne him into this life short of her thirteenth year struck him. He had never given it much thought before, but at this particular moment the thought disturbed him for some reason.

"What is it, Tristan," said Asta, recognizing that hesitant look of thoughtfulness his brows subtly issued when something was on his mind.

"I was just thinking," he said. "Your forced marriage to my father when you were a child must have been a horror, finding yourself in his embrace at night."

"It was," she replied slowly, thinking back. "As was finding myself in his brother's embrace after the execution of your father in Rouen, shortly after sending you and Guillaume off to the monastery. Life has left me few choices, and men have directed my entire life until I arrived here at Marcigny. What prompts such a subject?"

One of the mysteries of the human condition is the capacity of mothers to both draw out and soothe in their offspring the secret angst their children bury deep in the backwash of their conscience, keeping it hidden from others until at some point, the secret must finally be unearthed lest it unleash itself in the form of self destruction. And at this very moment, Tristan felt that unique attribute of motherly trust pulling at him. He rubbed his eyes with a thumb and index finger, pinching them together a moment, then looked at his mother, clearing his throat. Though his expression was calm, his stomach was knotted from trying to suppress the sudden palpitations of the heart that had begun seconds before, realizing that he had to, finally, release the shame that had been crippling him since learning about Mala's ordeal in the Alps.

"I have had some things occur to me since our last meeting," he said slowly, drawing out each word, "and have spoken to no one about them in depth. Yet I feel compelled to tell you, perhaps to ease my own guilt."

"Guilt?" said Asta, covering her eyes with an outstretched palm, feeling her heart wither a tiny measure. Tristan was one who had always had difficulty sharing secrets, so she sensed the approach of something profound, something that once released, could never be retracted. Nevertheless, she moved forward.

"In your first visit," she said thoughtfully, "you confessed that you had assisted in the assassination of a Byzantine nun and that an innocent man lost his life during the effort. Then, when I saw you last, you said that you feared that you had become steeped in illicit trickery and deceit while advancing the Church. These are severe experiences that cause one to examine the conscience. Yes, life often forces the unimaginable upon us, Tristan. I know that whatever you have done that now hounds you, it was not deliberate, for you were born with a gentle heart."

Tristan sat back and exhaled heavily. "Mother, you told me that you fell in love once with a young gamekeeper while married to Uncle Desmond in England. And you said to me, because you faltered by falling in love with the gamekeeper while married to another, God punished you by taking his life. Well, I believe God has done the same to me."

"Tristan, you speak in riddles. I don't understand."

Tristan exhaled again, then moved forward in his seat and took his mother's hand. "I fell in love with a girl years ago when I was a young boy. I did not realize that at the time, of course, because I was so young and children have no grasp of such things, but it actually happened. The realization only came to me recently, only several years back. And though I was a monk, bound by vow to the Church, I pursued this girl. Not out of lust, Mother, but truly out of love. As a result of this coupling, she had a child, *my* child."

Asta's hand went to her mouth as a single broken gasp caught in her throat. She quickly fought to subdue it, knowing that Tristan was watching her reaction carefully. "Ah, I see," she then whispered. "Where is this child, Tristan?"

Tristan began to answer, but twice balked. "Dead," he finally said, "frozen to death while his mother was trying to cross the Alps to get assistance. I faltered in sin, Mother, and God has thus punished me by taking the infant."

Asta gazed into her son's eyes and gently tightened her grip on Tristan's hands. "Oh, Tristan, dear sweet son. I know your heart bleeds over this, and eats away at you day and night, night and day, for there is nothing in this life more sorrowful than the loss of a child. I know because I felt such pain surrendering you and Guillaume to the Black Monks after the execution of your father when you both were so young." Then large tears formed within the wells of her eyes and she said nothing more; the grief she felt for her son allowed her no words. She sat there in silence, shuddering.

This, in turn, prompted tears to begin streaming down Tristan's cheeks. He had blamed himself, accused the Church, turned to drink, and bloodied himself during his penance to atone for what had passed, but this was the first he had shed a tear throughout the entire ordeal. "That Finnish woman, Mielikki," he wept softly, "she was right. I was damned at birth and bring nothing but horror upon others. I caused the death of my own child, and destroyed the life of the woman I loved."

"Oh, Tristan, son," Asta whispered through a heaving sob that nearly burst her heart, "you were not cursed at birth. You unfortunately had a moment of weakness. It was the loneliness that befell you when I sent you away, the same loneliness that overcame me when my father was executed and I was forced to marry Roger de Saint-Germain. Strong as we are, we two, we both grew weak and were unable to stave off temptation in the face of that pervasive, life-killing loneliness that was thrust upon us by life and circumstance. You are the Pope's First Counsel now, Tristan, and everything you do in the service of God will atone for that single momentary collapse. And though this thing with this woman you met culminated in the death of your child, a horror that I know drives your God-filled heart mad, it was not your fault!"

Tristan shivered as she spoke, comforted by her words yet still buried by the weight of his own perceptions.

"Th-thank you, Mother," he whispered, rising.

"You aren't leaving so soon, are you Tristan?" said Asta, wiping tears from her eyes.

"Yes, I must go now," he said, the wells of his eyes swollen red with sorrow. "I have held this inside myself, unspoken for so long, and now that the dam has broken, I can bear no more." He then gave his mother a firm embrace and quietly departed. Had he turned, he would have witnessed his mother tearfully withdrawing her prayer beads and falling to her knees, beseeching her Creator and Savior to help her son somehow find forgiveness within his own lost soul.

CHAPTER EIGHTY-ONE

THE WAR IN ITALY RESUMES

Within two weeks of the conclusion of Mathilda and Welf's wedding ceremony, the war in northern and central Italy resumed with a vengeance. During the lull declared by King Heinrich, the German King had secretly released thousands of troops south across the Alps and filtered them into the Apennines to reinforce the troops who were already there. The Tuscans were unaware of this maneuver, and when Mathilda's armies moved into battle, they were immediately repulsed and sent reeling into retreat.

"That bastard tricked us!" cried General Padule to Balducci as German cavalry swarmed them from hidden positions upon the slopes during the first battle. "Sound the retreat!"

"Indeed," shouted Balducci, "we took Heinrich for a gentleman in declaring the lull, but it was all a ruse!"

"I'll get word to Mathilda to make back for Canossa, Balducci, but I need you to hold the Germans back while we try to throw together an organized retreat!"

Balducci quickly signaled his bugler. Though wounded, an arrow poking from his left shoulder, the bugler hoisted his trumpet to his lips with his right arm and painfully blew the general retreat. Then, gathering his breath, he issued a second, more complicated trumpet code. Hearkening to the general retreat called, Tuscan footmen and archers kept their face to the enemy but hastily began a process of backstepping as they fought. Designated troop phalanxes retreated fifty yards or so while being covered by other phalanxes, then the covering phalanxes would reverse roles, thereby creating an orderly retreat.

The second bugle call was a signal to the Tuscan cavalry that they should move forward on both flanks then wedge themselves between the retreating Tuscan infantry and the oncoming German infantry, thereby providing both time and protection for their own footmen. Translating this code, Guillaume, the Danes, and several Tuscan horse units charged forward from their position on the left flank while Balducci and others charged forward from the right flank.

Before either group could attain their position, the Tuscan infantry retreat began to falter under the strain of the massive German onslaught. "Our lines are collapsing!" shouted Guillaume, whipping his mount forward.

"Ja, they're about to break!" Orla cried, ax raised. "Quick, into the fray!"

Indeed, as the two Tuscan cavalry flanks arrived in position, panic spread like wildfire amongst the Tuscan footmen and all semblance of order vanished. "Run!" cried several of the infantry captains. Within seconds, the already fragmenting phalanxes fell apart entirely and men began to turn their backs to the enemy and flee. The clutter of dead soldiers and horses, arms strewn about the ground, and the wounded wandering about in a fog, prevented open flight. With their backs turned to the enemy, the fleeing Tuscan footmen were now easy prey for the advancing Germans, who then smelled slaughter.

"Goddammit!" screamed Balducci to his horsemen, sensing the massacre that was about to begin. "Follow me, men! Into the German front!"

This was, of course, tantamount to suicide. Since leaving home, the burning memory of his feud with Mala had created in Balducci a brooding fury that was unquenchable. Although he had shared none of this with anyone, those who encountered him knew that he was not the same man they had previously known. Whereas it is true that he had always been difficult, conceited, and egotistical, there was now something about him that had not been a previous part of his make-up.

This dark metamorphosis that had arisen in Balducci was being felt by the unfortunate Germans within his path as he cut a bloody swath into their midst, swinging his sword from one side of his horse to the other, striking out blindly at whatever came at him. Then, too, Balducci continued to kick his horse's flanks, causing it to raise up angrily on hind feet and strike out with heavy hooves, smashing the skulls and limbs of all who stood within reach. Balducci's bold actions stirred inspiration amongst those following him, and spurred them also to drive their horses into the German front, which quickly began to evolve into a bloodbath as both Germans and Tuscans began to fall aside by scores.

Coming in from the other direction, Guillaume and the Danes had similarly charged headlong into the German front, and similarly inspired the Tuscans behind them to do the same. As the bloodbath deepened, German cavalry began to arrive and close in behind both Tuscan flanks. "We're surrounded!" shouted Crowbones, swinging his ax in savage arcs with his lone arm at the German footmen below him.

"Ay!" cried Guillaume, pointing to his left. "Time to break out!"

Orla, Crowbones and Guthroth simultaneously turned their horses in the direction Guillaume had pointed and spurred them onward, harnessing their massive weight to run over and crush oncoming Germans with the surge forward. "We're nearly there!" shouted Guillaume, as he caught sight of a clearing in the near distance. The precise moment the Germans gave way, it happened that Guillaume glanced behind him. At that very moment, he saw Balducci's horse raise up on hindquarters as five or six German footmen surrounded him and began dragging him onto the ground.

"Ho! Balducci's down!" Guillaume cried to the others, turning his horse back toward the downed Tuscan commander.

As the Germans got Balducci to the ground, they swarmed him, striking him with sword, morning star and dagger. He managed to cover himself at first with his shield for a few moments, but that was quickly pulled from him and the Germans began their butchery. One raised his sword over his head, and in one mighty descent of steel, nearly severed Balducci's leg at the thigh. Another, aiming his sword at Balducci's heart, missed, and drove the sword instead through Balducci's shoulder. Yet a third was striking at his helmet with a morning star while another was trying to poke his dagger between the collar of Balducci's hauberk and the bottom of his helmet.

"Arhg!" Balducci moaned, feeling the searing entrance of each blade and point. Then, his eyes closing, and his mind fading due to the loss of blood, he cried out, "Ma-Mala!"

As he did this, Guillaume and Guthroth arrived and threw themselves all over the Germans. The Germans put up a stiff resistance, but then Orla and Crowbones arrived and sealed their doom. "Get him on my horse!" Guillaume cried, grabbing at the back of Balducci's neck and shoulders.

"Nay, he's dead!" shouted Orla, as he and Crowbones jumped upon their mounts. "And look there, more Germans coming! Let's be off, quick!"

Guthroth went to his knees, grabbing Balducci, and threw him across Guillaume's horse. "Th-there!" Guthroth cried, looking at Guillaume. "N-now go!"

Guillaume managed to mount as a horde of Germans surged into the pack of fleeing Danes, trying to pull them from their horses. Guthroth was the only one left afoot, but from that position was actually better able to fend of the attackers than those struggling to remain mounted. Grabbing his reins at the very moment one of the Germans broke through, Guthroth decapitated the man, then flung himself upon his horse and drove it forward into the Germans who were still trying to pull the others to the ground. With extraordinary skill and guile, Guthroth quickly maneuvered his horse forward, backward, and sideways as a battering ram, knocking Germans to their feet and sending them flying hither and yon. Then, with the area cleared, he glanced at the others and cried, "L-let's g-go!"

Putting their mounts at a full gallop, they pressed them to the limit and retreated into a tree line where Tuscan archers had set up and had finally managed to slow the enemy advance. Guillaume pulled Balducci from the horse and lay him out on the ground, cradling Balducci's head in his lap. "Get water, Guthroth! He's still breathing!" shouted Guillaume.

Guthroth took off at a run while Orla and Crowbones joined Guillaume. "He's done," said Orla, seeing that Balducci's leg was hanging on only by a single band of mangled muscle and his hauberk was riddled with holes from which blood oozed in pulsating spurts.

"Ja," agreed Crowbones, "poor bastard doesn't have much longer. Damnation, I've never seen him fight as hard as today, like a goddamn madman!"

Guthroth returned with a water vessel and doused Balducci's face to loosen the crusted and blackened blood stains, then rubbed at them to clean his face a bit. This revived the unconscious Balducci and he slowly opened his eyes, confused, as though coming from far away. He tried to speak, but could not manage words. Then, after gazing at his perforated torso, his eyes caught sight of his mutilated leg.

"M-my G-God," he gasped, his eyes flaring wide.

"Don't look, Balducci," urged Guillaume in a gentle voice, turning Balducci's head away. "It'll do you no good."

Balducci looked up at Guillaume and in a labored and raspy voice muttered, "Y-you c-came back for me and dragged me off the f-field. Wh-why?"

"I saw you go down. We're brothers-in-arms. You'd have done the same for me."

Balducci tried to shake his head in disagreement, only managing a slight crook of the neck. "No," he said in a whisper, his strength quickly ebbing. "You are a b-better man than me, Saint-Germain." He gasped then, struggling to take in air, and his arm shook involuntarily. Then gazing up at Guillaume with a blank stare, he said, "T-tell me just one th-thing, S-Saint-Germain . . ."

"Yes, Balducci, what is it?" said Guillaume, knowing time was short.

"Th-that night you rode back to Monteluccio with my w-wife . . . was she unfaithful to me? Did the two of y-you . . ."

Guillaume looked at Balducci, confused at first, then glanced up at the three Danes surrounding him, then looked back at Balducci. "No," he said, "your wife was not unfaithful to you. Nothing passed between the two of us, only conversation, Balducci, I swear it."

Balducci did not reply at first. Instead his eyes carefully searched every feature of Guillaume's face for the slightest trace of deceit. They found none. Then the faint shadow of a smile slipped into Balducci's fading expression as he closed his eyes. "Oh . . . it appears that I f-falsely accused her. I was a fool, Guillaume . . . but then, everyone has . . . always thought me a fool, eh. . . ?"

"Easy there, Balducci. Rest a moment," replied Guillaume, motioning Guthroth to administer water to Balducci's dry, cracked lips. Then, for the very first time since their contentious acquaintance, he called Balducci by his first name. "Oh, Vincento, I regret that you would even think such a thing of her, or of me. Though you and I have had our differences, I would never betray you in such a manner. Besides, although the two of us have had our differences, I . . ."

"Guillaume," said Orla, shaking him about the shoulders, "you're speaking to the dead, lad."

Looking down, Guillaume saw that Balducci had turned his head aside and quit breathing. "In nomine patris et fili et spiritus santi," said Guillaume, crossing himself, "In the name of God I commend thee." Then he lay Balducci's head down the ground and stood. "He fought so valiantly today, like a hero, and doesn't deserve to be left here for the crows. Guthroth, have the porters make arrangements for his body to be taken back with us as we retreat to Canossa . . . and see to it that word is sent to both Mala and his mother."

CHAPTER EIGHTY-TWO

AGAIN, THE PENDULUM

The German advance continued over the next week and Mathilda's forces were sent reeling backward while suffering yet two more defeats in their attempts to reach the refuge of the mountains, the Qattro Castilli, and Canossa.

"Heinrich continues to pour troops into Italy all of a sudden," said General Padule as he and Mathilda met with the Tuscan commanders. Then he looked over at Welf the Younger who had accompanied them on the campaign though he had been of little use in battle. "And where the hell are our German allies and why aren't they holding him at bay to the north?"

"The Saxons are beating a retreat in Germany also, as is my father in Bavaria." Welf replied. "I don't know what . . ."

"The tides of war have shifted in Heinrich's favor," interceded Mathilda, seeing Padule's displeasure with Welf. "He can't maintain such momentum, his finances and manpower are not infinite, after all. Now that we're tucked into the refuge of the mountains we'll regroup and send out the call for reinforcements." Then she looked over at Guillaume and said, "Difficult as he could be at times and such as he was, the death of Balducci is a severe loss. Guillaume, I appoint you as commander in his place. Take charge of his troops immediately." Two years earlier such a pronouncement would have raised objections among the Tuscan commanders, but Guillaume's proven spirit of fearlessness coupled with the current predicament led the Tuscan commanders to congratulate him for this sudden promotion in the field. Balducci's body was carefully wrapped in linen and transported back to his manor by a small contingent of his own men-at-arms.

Learning of her son's death, Lady Alda Balducci ran out to the wagon carrying his body and fell upon his corpse in a state of hysteria. After half an hour of such unabated howling and sobbing, she had to be carried off to her chambers by the servants. The two sisters, Celia and Cosima, were struck with grief also, but their tears were short-lived.

As they stood by the wagon staring at their brother's corpse, Celia said aloud, "We shall mourn the death of Vincento, Cosima, but we shall also celebrate the eviction of that Romani whore and the old hag from this estate and from our lives." Mala turned, her eyes afire. Without uttering a word, she threw herself upon Celia and began pummeling her in the face with both fists. This merciless and unexpected assault lasted for over a full minute before the two stunned wagon teamsters could intercede, by which time Celia's nose was broken, her cheeks split, and her face a bloody mess.

Cosima, more stunned even than the teamsters, stood there in shock watching and was no help whatsoever to her sister. Duxia, on the other hand, appeared well satisfied with Mala's actions as both teamsters struggled mightily to control the vicious movement of her elbows, legs, and fists. The teamsters had thought they would easily subdue Mala, but had no idea that they were dealing with a woman who had endured the impossible and whose tolerance had erupted into seething fury.

"I'll kill you, you goddamn bitch!" Mala screamed, her eyes afire. "I'll kill both of you bitches and your mother, too! I'm weary of your sharp tongues and hatefulness!" Finally, ceasing her fight to ward off the grip of two teamsters, Mala settled on her own and looked down at Celia who was being collected from the ground by the servants. Dazed, her nose was mashed flat and bent to the side, her face and dress were splattered in blood, and tufts of hair were missing from her scalp. "Oh, my God!" she snuffled helplessly, having never experienced violence in any form throughout her entire pampered existence. "Oh, my dear God!"

Mala, her nostrils still aflare, looked over at Duxia and shrugged. "Pack your things," she said, "they'll have us out of here before the suns sets."

Duxia did not appear concerned. Instead she smiled and gave Mala a brief embrace. "Did that feel good, Dear?"

"Yes," huffed Mala, collecting her breath. "But it was costly, I fear. With Vincento gone, all three of them will be coming after us, Duxia, and we'll be lucky if we don't end up in shackles."

"Ha, I don't believe so!" cackled Duxia.

Mala recognized that cackle. It only came along once in a rare while when Duxia had pulled off a coup.

"Ah, the gold and silver you've been hiding beneath your bed," said Mala. "I thought you silly at the time, but you knew what you were doing, eh?"

"Ah no, Dear!" laughed Duxia. "Something far better than that, as you shall soon learn."

Ancient Roman law was the bedrock upon which medieval law was built. And though Roman law had faded into obscurity over the century following the decline of the Roman Empire, jurists in Pavia and Bolgna rekindled a revival of Roman law toward the end of the Eleventh Century. With canon law, this revived Roman law formed the common medieval law of Western Europe, the *ius commune,* which provided medieval jurists with a sophisticated model for contracts, rules of procedure, family law, and testaments.

Over the days following Mala's assault on Celia, the three Balducci women confidently united in an attempt to strip Mala and Duxia of all claims to the Balducci family name, property, wealth, and possessions. To their unadulterated dismay, they soon learned that Vincento Balducci had issued and documented a contract that awarded Mala a full two thirds of his possessions in the event of his death. Furthermore, it had been Duxia who had convinced him to do such a thing. "You know, my Lord," she had warned him time and again, "if anything should happen to you, your mother and sisters will immediately commence to contemptuously abuse your wife." So enamored of Mala was he that he decided that he should follow Duxia's recommendation. Even after their argument during his last week at the manor, he deigned not to change the contract he had secretly put into place because he desperately hoped that he and Mala would make amends upon his return.

And so it was that Lady Alda, Celia, and Cosima were removed from the main Balducci manor and relegated to a smaller manor far away while Mala found herself in the position of an extremely wealthy widow. Much to the delight of the manor servants and staff, the mood at the manor elevated considerably with Mala's takeover, and even their suspicions of Duxia began to wane as the ever present bitterness inherent to her character seemed to decline due to the recent turn of events.

The greatest change arose in Mala herself. Free of a husband, free of the three Balducci women, she rediscovered her independence and literally began to revel in her newfound freedom. The fire returned to her eyes, which gave rise to her attacking one project after another such as renovation of the manor, reassignment of duties of the household, and investing in several city state construction ventures. She also began to make more trips into town, traveled to neighboring provinces, and even began inviting her many new acquaintances to the manor as overnight and weekend guests. As the wife of Vincento Balducci she had been spurned as a scandalous commoner and foreigner, but now she was seen in a different light because it was *she* who actually owned property and wealth. Furthermore, it quickly began to appear that she was untapping in herself a previously unknown ability to make money and invest in successful financial ventures.

All of this delighted old Duxia whose greatest pleasure in life became watching this sudden resurrection of Mala's once dead spirit. And though Duxia's status had been elevated as had Mala's, she was content to remain in the background in her humble black garb, quietly counseling Mala and guarding her interests with the keen eye of a faithful guard dog.

CHAPTER EIGHTY-THREE

THE DARK TIME

As Pope Urban II, Odo de Lagery's diplomatic finesse far surpassed the timidity of Desiderius as Pope Victor III as well as the inflexibility of the great Pope Gregory. He also kept a close eye to the pulse of the Roman population, and after being in possession of Rome for nearly a year without rebellion or incident, he decided it was finally safe to leave the city in the hands of able assistants while he traveled to conduct a series of synods with the bishops of southern Italy. His primary interest was to solidify support from them on his continued push to implement Gregorian reform.

Accordingly, in the autumn of 1089 while Tristan was conducting his diplomatic missions to the west, he met with seventy bishops in the city of Melphi which was located in south central Italy. While there he successfully promulgated decrees against the sale of Church office and the marriage of clergymen. He also managed to negotiate a lasting peace between Roger Borsa and Bohemud, the feuding Norman half brothers who had previously only agreed to a temporary truce, and acquired formal alliances with them both. Feeling extremely successful with the completion of these important endeavors, Odo then directed his papal entourage back north for Rome.

Inexplicably, due to the Germans' sudden and continuing success against Mathilda to the north, the fickle citizens of Rome sensed an ultimate and final victory for King Heinrich and the anti-pope after years of Investiture War. Fearing retribution and a possible sacking of the city from Heinrich, the population opened the gates of Rome to the anti-pope during Pope Urban's absence and invited Clement to resume his papacy within the Vatican.

This was a terrible blow to Gregorian Catholics, and in particular to Pope Urban who had been so convinced that he had finally stabilized the political climate of Rome.

"Ah, I have grossly miscalculated," he confided to his entourage as they attempted to force their way within the city. "We should have never left the city."

Their arrival was met with resistance, and though Pope Urban was able to approach the walls of the Vatican on Christmas day and anathematize anti-pope Clement who was celebrating mass within Saint Peter's Cathedral, Pope Urban and his followers were soon forced from the city.

As they headed south then for Lower Italy and the protection of the Normans, Odo shook his head in discouragement and cried, "After all these years of war and bloodletting, has it really come to this? Is it possible that

God would favor kings over his own humble and faithful servants here on earth?"

And thus began a three year period of uncertainty during which Pope Urban II was compelled to wander the roads of southern Italy in exile. And though Odo was hailed wherever he appeared in Lower Italy and managed to hold councils, organize synods, and improve the overall character of ecclesiastical discipline, it was a desolate time for him. This desolation drove him into prayer, and it was not unusual for him to pray without interruption for days at a time. Exile also redirected him, causing him to spend more time with the poor and dispossessed, and built in him a greater appreciation of the humble masses who had little in this life. He became less political for a time, and more pious.

Odo's exile was a difficult time for Tristan also. He continued to directly represent Pope Urban on diplomatic missions to France, Spain, Sicily, North Africa, Saxony, and Bavaria. More importantly, he even managed to make inroads into England with the resentful King William II, and facilitate the entry of Abbot Anselm into England where he was finally appointed the Archbishop of Canterbury as had been hoped years earlier. Tristan also continued to work closely with Brother Muehler and the Benedictine underground out of Monte Cassino, and frequently met Handel during his ventures here and there. Through this entire period there was a pervasive and unspoken loneliness that followed him about, like some lingering shadow that refused to dissipate, even in the light of important work amongst the most important figures of the continent. Much of this loneliness was still rooted in the memory of Mala, as well as in a profound regret over the child she bore him that he had never seen. Indeed, each time he visited Canossa, he would spend hours praying over the grave of the lost infant.

Another part of Tristan's lingering despondency, he supposed, was himself. Although he had attained the heights in terms of career, prestige, and recognition, there existed a dark void within his soul. It was the result of two things, he decided: his uncertainty about his true relationship with God and his lack of personal fulfillment. *Everything considered,* he thought, *I am still alone in this life . . . and have not met my true destiny.*

As Tristan and Odo continued to work their way through this bleak period, each passing year saw new victories for Heinrich in Germany against both the Saxons and Bavarians. The same was occurring in Italy as each time Mathilda's war weary troops ventured out from the shelter of Canossa and the Qattro Castelli, they were sent reeling backwards in one bloody defeat after another. By the third year of this demise Guillaume had attained the age of twenty-four and had become a hardened, battle scarred veteran of war, and had risen to third in command of Mathilda's army, outranked only by General Padule and Welf the Younger.

"The years are catching up to me," Padule confessed to Guillaume after yet another exhausting retreat into the mountains. "I can't hold up to much more of this, you'll have to take over soon. I only pray that we have an army left by then."

"What about Welf. His rank is higher than mine."

"No matter, that," Padule sighed, spent. "Besides, Mathilda awarded him the rank only as a gesture of courtesy. After all, he's her husband, such as he is. She no more trusts him to lead troops into battle than she would her chambermaid."

Orla, Crowbones and Guthroth had also collected more wounds and scars. They, too, were seasoned veterans of battle, but they were no longer youngsters. By 1092 they had been embroiled in non-stop, hand-to-hand combat for seven years, and it was evident in their war-weary faces. "Will there ever be a resolution to this bloody mess?" complained Orla. "Bones of God, these people call themselves Christians, then happily butcher each other for a decade, and still there's no end in sight."

"Oh, the end is in sight," replied Crowbones, "especially if we don't win a battle soon."

"J-ja," frowned Guthroth.

Hroc was now nearly fourteen, and whereas others were war weary, he was still itching to enter the fray. Unlike his older brother Knud who had been smaller in stature, Hroc had grown taller than Guthroth and his upper torso had swollen in girth to nearly the size of his father and his uncle Crowbones. In fact, the Tuscans fondly referred to him as "Goliath". While Guillaume and the Danes were in the field fighting, Hroc practiced ceaselessly with sword, ax, and pike. He had also become impressive on the back of a horse, and could wheel his mount about as a battering ram nearly as effectively as Guthroth, who was unsurpassed in using his horse as a weapon and was passing along this skill to Hroc between battles.

"I'm grown and ready, Father!" Hroc would cry each time Orla appeared back in the mountain refuge, but Orla steadily denied his son's request with, "You're young yet, FiveHands. Don't be in such a hurry to join the dead."

"But I'm ready, Father, and as big as any Tuscan within the ranks!"

"Bah, your *head* is bigger perhaps!"

"I'm strong, too," Hroc insisted, "and know what I'm doing with both sword and ax, just like you."

"Nay, you only think you do, son. You've never had a man come at you with blood in his eyes, intent on putting you down. Your time will come, boy. Each time I think of you going to war, I can't dispel the image of your poor brother, Knud, lying there butchered on that field. Besides, this war is nearly done, no need in being the last one killed, especially in defeat."

It was a dark time, then, for Mathilda, Guillaume, the Danes, and Gregorians throughout Italy. There was one person who prospered greatly during this period . . . Mala. Having become acquainted with several of the local politicians of neighboring city-states shortly after Balducci's death, she became privy to information concerning city expansions and major building projects. These politicians were always looking for investment capital, of course, and this melded perfectly into Mala's strategy of investing her wealth as opposed to sitting on it.

As the war itself was being fought in the countryside and in the mountains and was being funded by the royals, nobles, and the Church, the city-states themselves continued to grow as a result of bristling trade amongst themselves and from abroad. Mala's investments, therefore, immediately began to provide handsome returns. Furthermore, she drove hard bargains and made soliciting politicians from the various city-states compete for her capital.

This prompted her to take gambles despite Duxia's advice to the contrary. Having become adept at manipulating finances in Tuscany, and calculating that the overseas trade was on the rise, she determined that she could do even better in a large seaport environment. Accordingly, she placed her Tuscany manor and vast farmlands under lease and moved to the bustling port of Genoa. Continuing the entrepreneurial practices she had established in Tuscany, she soon discovered that her gambles were, in fact, not gambles at all. The Genoans eagerly sought her support in construction endeavors, as well as in trading ventures to Spain, North Africa, Byzantium, and the Middle East. Within three years she was one of the wealthiest financiers in Genoa, and became a highly celebrated presence within the community. The Genoese, the vast majority being commoners themselves involved in trade, the crafts, shipping, and solicitation, respected Mala's business acumen and held her common background up as a model rather than something to be looked sneered at.

"Oh, these people are so different than the nobles!" exclaimed Duxia. "And you have their hearts, Mala. Who would have ever imagined that you would rise to such a level? And to think that your greatest dream was once to own a little shop. Now you own entire sections of town!"

During her second year in Genoa she happened to encounter an elderly gentleman during a ship's auction. The white-haired man kept bidding against her on the purchase of a fine French trading vessel, *La Reine*, that was only two years old and had been making voyages back and forth to North Africa. Mala had every intention of owning that ship by the end of the day, but it seemed that the elderly gentleman's pockets were as deep as her own. Curious, she took a seat beside him and introduced herself, hoping he might back off his bids. After some initial competitive banter, the two then somehow became engaged in more personal conversation, and found themselves taking a liking to each other.

"Ah, you are a lovely young thing, my dear," the gentleman said, "and so uncommonly clever about trade. Are you married, by chance?"

Mala laughed at this, thinking the old man would next propose. "No, Sir, I was married once, but my husband was killed in the war against Heinrich."

"Oh, poor thing, you must be lonely then?"

Mala laughed again. "Certainly not! And if you are attempting to seduce me, Sir, my only interest at the moment is the purchase of *La Reine* sitting along the pier there!"

"Ah, a shame that, for if you were seeking a husband, I would fall on my knees this very moment and beg you to be my wife!"

Mala wasn't certain, but she thought she perceived a tone of jest in this statement, which prompted her to return the favor. "Oh, so you mock me, now, eh?" she chided.

"I'm serious my dear. Look at me! I'm not a young man and don't have much longer to go. And I'm alone in life. I wouldn't be a bad catch for a young woman like you and I have more money than I could ever spend in my remaining years."

"Ha! I have my own money!" Mala laughed. "But I like you, Sir."

"Yea, and I like you." Then he scratched at the slight stubble gracing his chin and reflected a moment. *It saddens me that I'll probably never encounter this striking woman again*, he thought. Then his eyes brightened as an idea popped-up. "My dear," he said, "why don't we purchase this ship together and be done with this bidding war?"

"Together?" said Mala.

"Yes, certainly. We can share the cost, the risk, and the profits. A joint venture."

"Indeed," replied Mala. Without thinking a moment more, she said, "I accept!"

The old man passed his hand in the air and the auctioneer closed off the bids. "Sold!" he cried, "To the white-haired gentleman sitting on the front row!"

"Well, it appears we have a ship, eh?" said Mala, delighted.

"Yes," said the white-haired man, handing Mala a slip of paper. "Here are the directions to my estate outside Genoa, and if you'll bring your representative by in the morning, I'll have the contract drawn up and we'll figure out what to do with this beautiful vessel." Then he stood, with the help of his cane, and turned to leave.

"But, Sir," said Mala, "I don't even know your name!"

"Oh, indeed," he replied clumsily, nearly tripping as he turned about. "I am Duke Bernard Bertucci. Many here in Genoa call me the "General", though I am retired since the recent crusade in North Africa. I would like you to call me Bernard."

That next morning Mala and her financial agent appeared at the Bertucci estate. "Oh, how extravagant!" she commented as the coach entered the gate and moved along the impeccably landscaped approach that wound its way to his castle.

"Indeed," replied the agent, a man named Salvetti, "Duke Bertucci is the wealthiest man in Genoa and comes from old money. I'm surprised of his interest in a joint venture for he's not known for either sharing or collaboration with others."

"He likes my appearance," said Mala matter-of-factly. Her stunning beauty had not waned a single measure though she had attained her thirtieth year, and had in fact taken on a new, even more striking elegance since taking on both emotional and financial independence.

Moments later, Mala and Salvetti were seated at a table with Bertucci and three of his financial handlers who scurried about him pointing out details of the lengthy contract they had drawn up.

"Enough!" Bertucci cried. "This is a simple enough affair. I clearly wish to enter into a fifty-fifty agreement with this young lady."

"May I review the document," said Salvetti, his tone all business. Then, without waiting for a response, he reached over, pulled the contract into his grip, and began examining it.

"You know," said Bertucci, lost in Mala's eyes, "I gave you my name yesterday, but did not think to get yours. So what's . . ."

"I am Mala," she interrupted.

He waited a moment, expecting more, but she said nothing. "Have you no last name, my dear?"

"I am a widow, Sir. When my husband died unexpectedly in battle three years ago, I decided to abandon his name and go by my birth name, which is Mala. My husband's name, to satisfy your apparent curiosity, was Lord Vincento Balducci."

A blow to the temple could not have unsettled the old man more than these words. "Balducci!" he cried, nearly choking on his own words. "My God! Y-you are that Romani girl he married? The dancing girl?"

"Yes, I am," said Mala, surprised. There was no apology in her voice. "You look as though you swallowed a bird! So tell me, what is any of that to you?"

Bertucci was shaking by now, and his face red with reaction. "Oh, that bastard Balducci, he was betrothed to my daughter, Marianna until *you* came along!"

"I see," said Mala, showing no emotion. "Please know that I may have "come along" as you so aptly put it, but I did not pursue Vincento, he pursued me. Nor did I suggest marriage because I denied his insistence to wed three times before finally consenting." Then she signaled to Salvetti and stood. "Very well, Duke Bertucci, I can see that this joint venture you suggested is not going to come together then. Salvetti, call the coachman and we'll be on our way."

"Yes, certainly," Salvetti replied.

"And Duke Bertucci," Mala continued, her tone now turning cross, "I regret any inconvenience my marriage to Vincento may have caused your family. I will tell you this, so very good as Vincento was to me, he was no prize in the way he treated others. I therefore estimate that your daughter would have been miserable in the end, and if you were any judge of character at all you would already know this! Furthermore, don't *ever* blame me for your daughter's failed engagement because I have been ostracized, humiliated, and scorned by others like you in the past. Sir, those days are dead! I'll no longer tolerate such talk from you so-called *nobles*, who are no nobler than my own herd of mules and jackasses back at my estates of Tuscany, and you are welcome to convey my thoughts to your daughter also!"

At the mention of his daughter, Bertucci's face dropped. "Sh-she's dead," said Bertucci in a low, subdued voice. "She . . . died shortly after Balducci called off the wedding."

These words and Bertucci's expression filled Mala with remorse over the verbal lashing she had delivered to the old man. "I . . . I'm sorry, Sir, to hear that. I apologize for my words. It's just that . . ."

"Yes, yes, I know," grunted Bertucci with a flap of his hand, "I heard all the talk about you . . . and even engaged in it myself, without ever meeting you." Then he looked up at her and said, "Your beauty struck me yesterday at the auction, to the point of absurdity for an old man like me. You interested me, and I was thinking that after the auction I would never see you again . . . and I didn't want that."

"Goodness, Duke Bertucci, what are you saying?" said Mala as Bertucci's three financial handlers looked on, mouths ajar, their full attention focused on the Duke.

"What I'm saying, young lady is that I would like to do business with you. Oh, I'm not so foolish as to think one as young and lovely as yourself would ever take up with an old badger like myself, but we could do some business together, multiply our wealth, and be friends at least, eh?"

Mala looked at old Bertucci's pleading eyes and settled her hands on either side of her hips as a smile began to form.

"Well," she replied, "I *was* hoping to strike up a partnership to launch several overseas ventures with someone here in Genoa who has as much money as myself and you might do nicely in that regard, Duke Bertucci."

"Ah, wonderful!" replied Bertucci, his posture loosening. "And please, call me Bernard."

CHAPTER EIGHTY-FOUR

WINDS OF FATE

That hope can spring eternal even at the darkest hour is a curious but enduring trait unique to mankind. And this reliance on hope is so deeply engrained in the human mindset that even against all odds and under the most impossible of circumstances, it draws men forward, often straight to the precipice of folly and over its edge into self-destruction.

Occasionally, even in the face of inevitable annihilation, hope can also blossom into the wellspring of miracles, turning the impossible into the possible. Of course, the odds of a miracle overturning inevitable defeat are often fueled by the folly of the enemy himself . . . which in this case was King Heinrich.

Having finally arrived at simultaneously quelling the Saxon revolts, containing Bavarian resistance, defeating Mathilda, and regaining the support of the Roman populace who had called anti-pope Clement back to Rome, Heinrich did what any good egomaniac would do . . . toss caution, common sense, and character to the wind. Finding himself finally in a favorable position, he thought himself invincible, smarter than the opposition, and holier than the Church. In other words, he thought himself bigger than the world.

That emperors would devise a proposition as preposterous as "divine right" in the first place is understandable. It benefits them by cloaking their authority in Godly legitimacy. That people would accept this preposterous concept in an age of ignorance, superstition, and powerlessness among common man is even somewhat understandable. That an emperor would actually believe such a self-serving contrivance is more difficult to comprehend. Heinrich appears to have fallen into the same snare of self-aggrandizement as other emperors through the ages who swallowed their own theory that their right to rule was a divine status awarded by God himself.

Accordingly, throughout the years 1092 and 1093, rather than deliver the coup de grace to his enemies, he allowed himself to become involved with distractions within his court, many of which involved his own abusive conduct and licentiousness. His involvement with the Nicolaitan sect grew to the point of debauchery and culminated in the outrage of his young wife, the former Eupraxia of Kiev who had upon her coronation adopted the name of Queen Adelheid.

It was Handel who conveyed this information to Tristan one night during a rendezvous within the Benedictine monastery of Cremona while Tristan was completing a secret diplomatic mission in Lombardy.

"Ay, said Handel, "strange rumors abound in Verona. We have an agent planted there in the midst of Queen Adelheid's court and he's managed to get close to her."

"Verona?" said Tristan, puzzled. "What is she doing here in Italy?"

"Heinrich apparently forced her to accompany him south from Germany as he leads his army against Mathilda in this final assault. It seems he didn't trust leaving her behind in Germany for fear that she might flee back to her family in Kiev."

"What?"

"Yes, it sounds strange," nodded Handel, "but something's gone afoul within Heinrich's marriage as well as within his court. Now that Heinrich has dragged her to Italy and she can't make her way back to Kiev, she has indicated that she wishes to cross over to Mathilda in Canossa."

This news stunned Tristan, as Handel knew it would. "Heaven be praised," Tristan finally said, realizing the potential implications of such a development.

"Yes," continued Handel, "our Verona contact has secretly arranged to facilitate her flight now that Heinrich is about to leave Verona to lead the German attack against the Qattro Castelli and Canossa. She and a small entourage of her trusted Rus will make their escape in three weeks' time. One other thing, Tristan, after you report this news about Adelheid to the Holy Father, you need to return north and visit Conrad."

"King Heinrich's son?"

"Yes. I spoke to him last week and he wishes to speak with you."

"About what, Handel?"

"He wasn't specific; only that you needed to come to his court in the Po Valley at your very earliest convenience."

After his meeting with Handel, Tristan hastily completed the remainder of his business in Cremona, traveled to the port of Genoa, then sailed south to Lower Italy where he reported the news about Queen Adelheid's imminent defection to Pope Urban who was temporarily situated in Salerno.

"When news of Queen Adelheid's flight from Heinrich becomes public," he told Odo, "there will be many repercussions, all of which shall be in our favor. I advise that you meet her when you arrive in Canossa."

"Yes, certainly," replied Odo, reflecting on this unexpected turn of events. "I'll dispatch a message to Mathilda immediately and leave Salerno within the week."

"Travel must be by ship to Genoa then overland east to Canossa, Odo. The Germans have us blocked coast to coast along the routes south of Rome and also control much of the north except the regions surrounding Canossa. If Heinrich's upcoming assault succeeds, we will lose that, I fear."

"Yes, and that will spell our end," said Odo. "Will you be accompanying me to Canossa, then?"

Tristan shook his head no. "While meeting with Handel, he also informed me that Conrad wishes to speak to me in private as soon as possible."

"Oh?"

"Yes. Not sure what Conrad wants, but Handel sounded as though it was pressing. I best make my way to the Po Valley then while you tend to Queen Adeleid in Canossa."

Ten days later Odo was greeted by Mathilda, General Padule, and Guillaume at Canossa.

"So good to see you, Holy Father, in these dark times," said Mathilda as she bowed, then gave him an embrace.

"How are you progressing on your defensive preparations?" asked Odo, observing the swarming activity of the fortress.

"We're doing the best we can," replied Padule. Then, pointing to Guillaume, he said, "Thank God for Guillaume's cavalry sorties. He's managed to keep the Germans off our backs while we stock arms and fortify the Qattro Castelli. Heinrich'll have a difficult time working his way through them getting here to Canossa, but our troops are exhausted and morale is low. I'm not sure we can hold. We've suffered high casualties and are low on manpower while Heinrich continues to bring troops in from Germany now that he's put down the Saxons and Bavarians. Had he attacked us at any point these last few months, his banner would already be flying over these very ramparts!"

"We'll hold, General," said Guillaume with a look of certainty. "Outnumbered as we are, the Germans'll be fighting uphill and will have to make it through four fortresses before taking Canossa itself, and we're well supplied. Yes, we'll hold."

Mathilda looked at Guillaume, and though her expression was far less certain, she managed a smile. "Oh, the confidence of youth," she sighed, slapping him across the shoulder with affection. "If only I had a hundred like you and the Danes, Guillaume."

Three days later a rider scurried up the approach to Canossa. It was Handel. "The German queen's half a day behind me, riding hard," he said dismounting. "She'll be here by nightfall."

As dusk fell over the mountains, Odo and Mathilda positioned themselves at the gate, and two hours later Queen Adelheid's small entourage of three coaches and twenty Rus guards struggled up the sharp incline to the Canossa fortress.

Minutes later, as the German queen stepped from her coach, Mathilda cried, "What is this, Adelheid! How is it you flee your husband?"

"Heinrich forced me to accompany him on this last military campaign and has had me sequestered against my will in Verona all this time," Adelheid said, visibly distraught. "Oh, such a horrible beast he has become!" Realizing Odo's presence, she threw herself prostrate and cried, "Oh, Holy Father! Pope Urban, I must confess my sins, sins forced upon me by my wicked husband!"

"My dear Adelheid," said Odo, "fleeing this marriage is no sin. 'Tis Heinrich who needs to confess his trespasses, sinning so with this war against the Church."

"No, I have hungered for confession for two years now," Adelheid replied, wringing her hands. "Heinrich's priests have done me no good for they are all in league with him! They condone all that he says and does. Truly, God has vacated Heinrich's realm and left there a dark scum of unholiness. I must be divorced of him!"

"Be calm, Adelheid," said Odo, placing his palm upon her head. "I shall absolve you of this marriage, for Heinrich is an excommunicate. In the eyes of the Church your marriage to him was therefore never sanctified. We shall call together a council, charge Heinrich with wrongdoing, and have your marriage annulled! Rise then, I pronounce you free of this marriage until such time as formal proceedings are completed."

Adelheid remained down. "Oh, the sins I have been forced to commit!" she wailed. "Sexual trysts, orgies with hundreds of others running about naked, fornicating openly! And m-me forced to surrender myself to other men, and even women! Oh, Holy Father, I beg that God forgives me for there was nothing I could do! I was helpless!"

Odo's eyes flared listening to these charges and he stepped back, exchanging a glance with Mathilda who whispered, "God in heaven, Odo!" Then she moved closer and reached for Adelheid's hands as the young queen wept, her face buried in her palms. Tilting her head with concern, Mathilda whispered, "What is this you are saying, Adelheid?"

"The Nicolaitan sect!" Adelheid sobbed. "Heinrich has become steeped in it and has embraced their promiscuous rituals with the fire of an enraptured convert. His orgies are staged during the celebration of mass, the *black* mass!"

"The black mass?" said Mathilda, placing a hand to her lips in horror. She looked over at Odo, but he appeared too disturbed to find words, so her eyes fell back upon the German queen. "Oh, my poor dear," she mumbled, "my poor, poor Adelheid."

Odo crossed himself, then leaned down and began consoling Adelheid with a blessing followed by soothing words of comfort. Then he raised her up and slowly led her across the courtyard toward the cathedral where, shoving open the massive doors, he led her into one of the confessionals located at the rear of the edifice and began to hear her confession.

God help her, thought Mathilda, standing alone, *can there possibly be merit to these charges she makes against Heinrich?* Then she thought back on Adelheid's history. Before her coronation as Queen of Germany, Adelheid was Eupraxia of Kiev, a prayerful and devout Catholic of the purest strain. And after the death of her first husband, young Eupraxia had taken up residence in the convent of Quedlinburg where she was pursuing a life of prayer until Heinrich found her there. "Indeed," Mathilda then whispered to herself, "a woman such as this would not fabricate such horrendous charges unless they were . . . true."

CHAPTER EIGHTY-FIVE

SEEDS OF HOPE

Confident that Mathilda's army was depleted, outnumbered, and ready to collapse, Heinrich finally launched a major offensive against her final stronghold in the mountains one month after his wife's flight to Canossa.

"This is it," said Guillaume to Orla, his face grim, as they watched the massive German army move into the valleys that led to the first of the Qattro Castelli. "We either hold this time, or surrender."

"Ja, it's come down to this battle, and it's not looking good for us," replied Orla. Then he looked over at Guthroth and Crowbones. "Brother Crowbones, watch your arm this day and don't lose it . . . otherwise I'll be stuck feeding you like a damn baby for the rest of your years!"

"God's spine!" Crowbones grinned back, waving his stub defiantly. "Worry about your own goddamn arms! I rolled my bird bones last night and things look good for me, but not so good for you!"

"And wh-what about m-me?" stammered Guthroth. "Wh-what did the b-bones say?"

"Aw shit, Guthroth, they said you'll be dead by dusk, skewered with a pike."

"R-reall-y?" said Guthroth, his face filling with dismay.

"No, you dumbass!" laughed Crowbones. "Stick close to me anyway, Guthroth."

An hour later the Germans led with a probing maneuver carried out by two hundred light cavalrymen only halfarmored, for speed. They scoured the valley in four separate groups suspecting that the Tuscans had concealed themselves along the heavily wooded rises and ridges ahead. Hoping to draw them out, the German horsemen boldly advanced up the mountain trails, offering themselves as bait with the intention of speeding away once the Tuscans revealed their positions. General Padule foresaw this tactic and had given strict orders to hold until Heinrich's main force began advancing through the narrow pass that separated the Tuscan army and the main German force.

"We'll attack them as they're halfway through the pass, thereby splitting up their front and rear lines in the bottleneck. Then we'll only have to fight the leading half while the rear guard gets stuck to the rear."

As the main German force approached the pass, rather than marching through as expected, it abruptly halted.

"What the hell's going on down there?" said Orla, straining to see down the mountainside and through to the far end of the pass.

"Hmm . . ." mulled Crowbones, "it appears they're milling about or something, trying to decide whether to enter or not. I'm not sure what . . ."

Before Crowbones could finish, a German bugle blasted below and hundreds of German knights began to drive their horses forward through the pass at full gallop as thousands of footmen followed behind at a dead run.

"Dammit!" Guillaume cried. "They guessed our attack strategy and are rushing through the bottleneck so as not to get divided!" Then he swung his horse about and cried to his bugler, "Quick, sound the charge or we're lost!"

Being the only Tuscan unit that was positioned to clearly see what was happening in the pass, Guillaume's trumpet signal at first confounded General Padule who was concealed across the valley on the opposite ridge lying in wait to unleash a flanking movement when the Germans were halfway through the pass. "What's this?" cried Padule, who wasn't expecting to hear Guillaume's signal so soon. "What the hell's going on here?" Nevertheless, trusting Guillaume's instincts, he led a thousand horsemen thundering out of the trees and down the slopes into the line of Germans streaming through the gorge.

Padule's cavalry arrived at the valley floor minutes after Guillaume's did, and due only to Guillaume's swift reaction, half of the German army was held up in the pass as originally planned. And as the Tuscan cavalry's pincer movement came at the Germans from opposing flanks, Mathilda then moved her main force forward into position to hold the valley. Her archers formed and began blindly firing arrows by the thousands into the pass where the Germans were trying to break through. This caused temporary pandemonium amongst those caught in the pass and they tried to surge forward to escape the barrage, but their own front lines which were under attack from Guillaume's and Padule's flanking movement were blocking their progress. Anticipating the bottleneck strategy taking shape, Mathilda then sent half of her main cavalry and footmen into the fray while holding the other half in reserve.

The fighting was ferocious, with both Germans and Italians knowing that this battle could finally bring an end to ten long and bloody years of war. Men on both sides strained heroically to decimate the enemy standing before them, hacking, slicing, and hammering their way forward with the single mindedness of men within grasp of a long sought prize. Men on horseback attacked each other and ran over enemy footmen while the footmen grappled with each other and pulled knights from their mounts, attacking them with daggers, pikes, morning stars, and hammers.

The German advance through the pass came to a standstill as volley after volley of arrows took their toll and the number of dead quickly began to mount. Many of the German troops who had not yet entered the pass, witnessing the slaughter of those within the pass at the hands of the Tuscan archers, became hesitant about advancing while those in the pass struggled feverishly to climb over their own dead and break through their own advance guard.

Guillaume and the Danes worked as a pack to keep from being singled out and pulled off their mounts, remaining together in a tight formation while slashing out with sword and ax, driving their horses over all who approached them. As he fought, Guillaume looked to the pass and saw that the Germans had finally begun to clear away dead men and horses and were managing to stream forward. "To the pass!" he cried, signaling the Danes and Tuscan knights nearby to follow. Within seconds fifty knights drove headlong into the oncoming German foot soldiers, obliterating the first three ranks as they fell beneath the thundering shock of horseflesh. More Germans came, as did more Tuscans, until the opening of the pass had evolved into a tangled knot of humanity struggling against itself as men on horseback and foot, bathed in sweat, struggled to survive their own orgy of blood and steel.

"They're falling back!" Guillaume screamed, sensing that the German surge was beginning to wane and pull little by little back into the mouth of the pass. At that very moment a terrified, riderless horse on his flank reared up, then pitched headlong into Guillaume's horse, knocking Guillaume to the ground. Both horses then raised up in combat, attacking each other with hooves, neck swings, and teeth, burying Guillaume in a murderous mash of bestial fury. Guillaume instinctively curled into a fetal position, hoping his armor would protect him, but then his helmet was knocked free of his head, and feeling a sudden blow to his forehead, he blacked out. Crowbones saw this, but having only one arm and being under assault by a German horseman himself, he cried out to Guthroth and Orla. "Guillaume's down! Guillaume's down!"

But they were warding off a swarm of enemy footmen also, and could not break free to help Guillaume. "Goddamn it, he's lost!" screamed Orla hoarsely.

A large Tuscan knight who had followed Guillaume into the pass, despite being surrounded by oncoming footmen, quickly dismounted, gathered the unconscious Guillaume from the ground, and flung him across his horse. Easily flinging himself into the saddle despite the weight of his armor, he reined his angry horse skillfully to and fro, backward and forward, as a battering ram, crushing Germans and scattering them like a flock of crows. His way cleared, the knight gestured to the Danes, then turned his horse toward the Tuscan rear and took off at a full gallop to carry Guillaume to safety.

The savage battle continued for yet another hour as Germans fought desperately to stop the Italian advance into the pass, but as the Italians continued to progress, Germans at the back end of the pass began to sense that momentum had shifted against them. Panic then began to spread, and despite efforts by their officers to herd them back into position, footmen in the rear positions began to flee the pass.

"We've broken them!" cried Orla! "Forward!"

Tuscan horses swept forward, taking possession of the pass, meeting stiff resistance as they came through to the other side. Though many Germans had fled the field, the Germans had vastly outnumbered the Italians from the onset, and were now equal in number to the enemy. Momentum in battle stirs both courage and confidence, and as the Italians pressed forward, they began to smell victory.

An hour later, it was over. The German army fled, and though it would have behooved Mathilda's forces to chase them down and slaughter as many as they could, the exhausted Italians were utterly spent.

"Swine's head . . ." muttered Odo to Guthroth and Crowbones as they walked the valley floor, piled high with dead. "We've lost half our army today."

"Ja, we've finally checked the Germans," said Crowbones. "Though they've pushed us about for the past two years, they now know it's a heavy toll breaking through to Canossa."

"Ay, maybe so. Regardless, we can't survive another such attack even if we carry the day again. Our ranks are depleted."

Crowbones nodded, then said, "Orla, did you see Guillaume go down?"

"Yes, and I saw a Tuscan sweep in and retrieve him. I couldn't tell whether Guillaume was alive or not."

"L-look th-there," said Guthroth, pointing across the pass to an approaching horseman. "The knight th-that saved Guillaume . . . he'll b-be able to t-tell us."

Glancing up, Orla and Crowbones recognized the approaching knight's horse and armor from earlier in the battle. "Good work today, knight! And what about Guillaume? Does he live?" As he approached, the knight did not reply. "Hey there, you *Tuscan*," Orla said as the man slowly rode his horse into their midst, "did you not hear me?"

The knight nodded, then slowly removed his helmet. "Yes, I heard you, but I am no Tuscan, Father." The three Danes gawked, too stunned to reply. "And yes," said Hroc, "Lord Guillaume lives."

CHAPTER EIGHTY-SIX

OH, CONRAD!

As Odo made his way to Canossa to greet Queen Adelheid, Tristan struck further north to meet Conrad. "Ah, Excellency," he said, kneeling before the German royal and kissing his ring, "I barely recognize you." And indeed, all trace of boyishness had vanished in Conrad since Tristan's last visit, and he had taken on the robust features of a confident young man entering his prime. "And imagine my delight when I learned from Handel of your request that I come with all speed to your court here in the Po Valley."

"It has been on my mind for some time now, actually," replied Conrad. "Come," he said, turning and stepping off at a brisk pace, "I wish to speak to you alone."

Tristan followed him into a private chamber, still somewhat uncertain about the purpose of his visit. He then noticed that Conrad, closing the door, carefully secured the lock. Furthermore, Tristan thought it unusual that the hawkish Archbishop Tedald was nowhere to be seen, and this prompted Tristan to inquire about him.

"I did not see Archbishop Tedald when I arrived. Is he away?"

"Yes," said Conrad, "permanently."

"Pardon?"

"I came to the conclusion some time ago that Tedald, despite all that he has done for me since childhood, is no longer looking out for my interests, nor my heavenly salvation, Brother Tristan. He was once a devout cleric, but politics have overcome his piety, unfortunately, and I have dismissed him."

"I see," said Tristan, surprised. "Excellency, did your father not object to this?"

"Ah, my father," sighed Conrad. "Well, you see, I have likewise dismissed my father."

"What?"

"Yes, when you last visited years ago I spoke to you of my objections to his behavior. Despite my prayers, he has not improved which brings me to the purpose of our visit. In several days I shall formally denounce my father."

If Tristan had been surprised by Conrad's first remarks, this final comment sent him into a state of shock. "I see . . ." he stammered, though he did not comprehend a thing.

"I suppose you know by now," Conrad continued, "that my father's wife, Adelheid, has gone over to Mathilda's camp?"

"Yes."

"She had spoken to me of that possibility several times this past year, and I pledged my full support should she actually decide to do such a thing due to my father's growing depravity and attraction to sin. The horrors he has forced her to endure are unconscionable in the eyes of decent men, and more importantly, in the eyes of God. Are you aware of what I am speaking of, Brother Tristan?"

"No, Excellency, I am not privy to any information other than her actual flight from Verona. I know nothing of her motivation to leave your father, but please know that Pope Urban has gone to meet her at Canossa."

"Well then, I am certain that the Holy Father shall inform you of the details soon enough. In any case, I wish to corroborate all charges she shall soon file against my father . . . for they are true. It is my hope that Pope Urban sees fit to grant her a divorce, and please know that I therefore offer myself as a witness to her claims during the formal proceedings that shall surely arise. More importantly, please notify la Gran Contessa Mathilda that I intend to declare war against my father, marching against Milan within the week."

"Milan? But that is the site of your father's court in Italy and the German royalist seat of power and author."

"Yes, of course," interrupted Conrad, "which is why I shall seize possession of it. I was given the titular crown of Italy some years ago by my father, but have been king only in name. I intend to be a king of Italy *in fact*. Many of my father's troops are absent from Milan due to the offensive against Canossa, so now is the time to strike. Furthermore, I have been in communication with the Lombard League and have received their pledge of support as well as command of their militias."

"The Lombard League? All members?"

"Yes . . . Milan, Lodi, Piacenza, and Cremona. They, despite long years of allegiance to my father, have grown weary of his abuses of the city-states. I know la Gran Contessa Mathilda has been carrying on this fight alone for years here in Italy, but tell her that she now has new allies, and that we intend to help her drive my father from Italy for good."

"Yes, certainly," Tristan replied, flushing with the realization that heavenly intervention had somehow delivered the Gregorian cause on the very eve of their own capitulation. "I have prayed for such a turn of events," he said, as though talking to himself, "and that you would find the courage to stand up to your father."

"Yes, I have prayed on the matter also," said Conrad. "Now let us pray we can win."

CHAPTER EIGHTY-SEVEN

A TURN, VISITORS, AN INVITATION

Tristan made south for Canossa, after leaving Conrad's court, to relay to Mathilda and Odo the startling news of Conrad's and the Lombard League's declaration of war against King Heinrich.

"Oh, God has swung the pendulum back in our direction!" proclaimed Odo, jubilant in the retelling of this report.

"Indeed, and to think that two weeks ago I was fretting over the loss of young Welf," mused Mathilda, a slight smile creasing her face.

"The loss of Welf?" said Tristan. "Has he been slain in battle?"

"No, nephew," said Mathilda, "he and his father have gone over to Heinrich."

"What?" cried Tristan.

"Uh, yes, Tristan," said Odo, "because of a little misunderstanding concerning . . . inheritance. It seems Welf was incessantly pressing Mathilda about specifics concerning his rights to her territories and possessions upon her passing, he being so much younger and all."

"Indeed," sniffed Mathilda, "day and night, night and day. In a moment of disgust, I informed him of my previous secret agreement and contract with the deceased Pope Gregory. In revealing that all my lands shall go to the Church upon my death, except what I have reserved for you and Guillaume, he flew into an adolescent rage, packed his things, and made quickly for Bavaria. Then two days ago, a courier delivered a Bavarian declaration of war against me, informing me that the two Welfs have formed an alliance with Heinrich, who is now dangling Tuscany as a reward to them as an enticement to my defeat."

"Aha," said Odo, beaming, "your news from Conrad more than balances the scales. Conrad and the Lombard League far, far surpass the strength and value of Bavaria. So it appears that the only *defeat* in question is that of Heinrich!"

Tristan shook his head. "How quickly the sands have shifted," he said. "Tell, Aunt Mathilda, what about your marriage? After all, Welf the Younger is still your husband, is he not?"

"Not for long," interrupted Odo. "Mathilda has recorded in writing that on the night of their wedding, Welf the Younger failed to have an erection and consequently failed to consummate the marriage. Furthermore, Brother Handel of Monte Cassino and Brother Justin of Canossa have documented that neither of them witnessed penetration of Mathilda by Welf the Younger, and that he immediately passed-out after crawling into the wedding bed. All of which, according to both lay and ecclesiastic law, lays the groundwork for annulment of this ill-fated marriage."

That night in Canossa as he lay in bed, Tristan reflected on the strange chain of events that had so quickly befallen King Heinrich. *He deserves it*, Tristan thought. *He is wicked, ungodly, underhanded, and abusive. Not only the Lombard League, but even his own wife and son have turned on him! No wonder, then, that God has abandoned him.*

The more he weighed and measured the sequence of events that had unfolded over the past years, the more he realized his own underhandedness, and that of the Gregorians, including Odo, Muehler, Handel, and Mathilda. This shamed him a bit despite the fact that the ghost voices of Odo and Muehler kept echoing about ". . . the ruthless violence of the enemy and the darkness they would cast upon the earth should they ever gain the upper hand." It was a restless night then, for Tristan, and even as he spiraled down into a black, bottomless sleep, the push and pull of right and wrong continued to eat at him as one visitor after another slipped, uninvited, into his dreams. First there came the murdered Byzantine nun at the Inn of the Sparrow, followed by the Byzantine nobleman who had appeared at her door. Each of their faces were bloodied, and he could hear them moaning and see them pointing at him with accusatory fingers, calling his name to someone above . . . *God?*

Then came Brother Domingo and Brother LeDoux of Dijon, murdered not by Tristan and the Gregorians, but by the Germans and Byzantines. And after their shadows dissipated, there came the man Tristan stabbed as he, Desiderius, and Odo were fleeing the mob in Rome. His face, too, was scarlet with blood, and as he stumbled about as a man half dead, he cursed Tristan for turning his wife into a widow and his children into orphans. Then Tristan heard the heaving and bellowing of oxen, crushing people beneath the massive weight of their stampeding bulk and bursting their bodies with the sharp and merciless hammering of their hooves. Next, as the oxen faded into blackness, Tristan found himself standing in the middle of a battlefield strewn with the dead, thousands and thousands of them, being feasted as carion by crows and picked over by looters and camp ghouls.

This too faded after some time, and a peacefulness descended then . . . until he heard the distant clatter of pony hooves upon ice. Then he felt the air grow cold as a blizzard blew in from the north and icy snow began to bury the ponies and the wagon they drew behind them at the top of a frozen pass high in the Alps. And though he could not see in the wagon, he heard coming from within the wail of a newborn infant, and the tearful sobs of . . . *Mala?*

And finally, before he shivered himself awake at dawn, it was Peter the Hermit and Duxia de Falaise who appeared. They were laughing like old friends, and pointing at Tristan. "Ah," cried the Hermit, "*I told that boy he was dangerous, that he would plant the seeds of war!*" "*Yee-hee-hee!*" cackled Duxia in reply, "*and I told him he was cursed at birth and even asked him what it is he wanted, and how many would die as he strived to seek it!*"

Starting up on a single elbow, Tristan moaned, not knowing for a moment whether he was awake or caught back in his nightmare. After wringing the dream from his head, he exhaled deeply and sat up. The ugliness and guilt of the dream lingered a moment, until he chased it away with several more shakes of the head and a roll of the shoulders. *God help me,* he thought, running his palms over his forehead and through his hair, *it was all so real.*

Even as he dressed and went about his business that morning, he could not completely expel images from his nightmare, nor the faint ghost voices that called out within his subconscious.

"What is it, Tristan?" said Odo at one point. "You seem distracted this afternoon. Or perhaps you are not feeling well?"

"No, no . . . I am fine," Tristan lied. "Just weary after all my travels."

"Well, perhaps I should forego telling you about the message that came to me this morning by courier, asking to have you stop by Genoa within the week."

"Genoa?"

"Yes, from the old war horse himself, Duke-General Bertucci. Apparently you made quite an impression on him in North Africa. Somehow he heard you had been passing in and out of Genoa this past year, yet have never stopped in to visit him. He would like to see you."

Tristan thought back on Tunis. "Yes, yes, Bertucci. Different as we were, we managed to strike up a rather odd friendship during my two visits there. He has set the sword aside, has he not?"

"Yes, and in retirement is enjoying his wealth immensely I hear, though he is alone now. You know, Tristan, you do indeed look weary. I have pressed you month after month, year after year. Why not go to Genoa and visit Bertucci? And take some time for yourself before I send you to Constantinople."

"Constantinople?" said Tristan, puzzled. "The Byzantines have been our enemies for years."

"Ah, yes, as we have learned, today's enemies may well be tomorrow's friends. 'Tis the way of politics, n'est-ce pas? Emperor Alexius Comnenus has asked that I go to Constantinople for a secret embassy, but I dare not leave Italy in the midst of current developments, especially now that I hope to march against Rome and the anti-pope. Nor can Alexius leave Constantinople, apparently, because of incessant Saracen incursions against his empire from the east."

"What of the alliance Alexius has held with Heinrich throughout the Investiture War? Besides, we have never trusted the Byzantines since their schism from Rome decades ago."

"I have no idea what Alexius would want with me at this point. Perhaps he has already heard of Heinrich's defeat at Canossa, or of Adelheid's and Conrad's defection to Mathilda. Who knows? In any case, Tristan, this is a very sensitive and confidential embassy. I would like you to take Handel with you. Go to

Genoa first; enjoy the coast, the salty air, and the sunshine. Then, in two weeks, meet Handel in Monte Cassino. Muehler will have your documents, finances, and travel arrangements prepared."

CHAPTER EIGHTY-EIGHT

GENOA

Genoa was a thriving and independent Italian city-state and one of the great Maritime Republics which also included Venice, Pisa, and Amalphi. Nominally it fell under the authority of the Holy Roman Emperor, King Heinrich, and was governed by the Bishop of Genoa who served as president of the city. True power was wielded by a number of consuls elected annually by popular assembly. Duke-General Bertuccci now sat at the head of this body, and was greatly responsible for much of Genoa's prosperity through his heavy support and involvement in overseas trade, shipbuilding, and banking. Genoa was also heavily involved in the slave trade, and its powerful navy practically held control over the entire Tyrrhenian Sea, including Sardinia, Corsica, and Nice.

The old general's face was bright with laughter and delight as he met Tristan at the port of Genoa. He nearly knocked him over as he reached out to embrace and greet him.

"Oh, lad, what a sight for sore old eyes!" he cried. "And one of my favorite people in this entire world!"

Tristan was not expecting such an enthusiastic welcome, and was immediately struck by the new life that had been blown into Bertucci's once luffing sails. "You look so much younger, General," Tristan commented, "since I last saw you in Tunis."

"Oh, that was a dreary time for me, lad. God has seen fit to give me new direction." Then he laughed and added, "Yes, and he's given me a scent for money, which has become my latest passion!" Bertucci then loaded Tristan into his sumptuous coach and immediately launched off on a tour of Genoa's shipyards, manufacturing area, banking district, and mercantile center.

"My partner and I have prospered beyond belief these past years," he crowed. "I thought I had a nose for business, but my partner is the real genius, not me. She could turn a pile of donkey shit into a mound of gold, you know!"

"*She*," said Tristan. "Your partner is a woman?"

"Yes, and *such* a woman, lad. Here in Genoa they call her la Gran Signorina. You'll meet her this evening. In fact, we shall be passing the next few days at her estate as she hosts our anniversary celebration. It will be a time of gaiety and frolic for all the high politicians and merchants of the region are spending three days there."

"Anniversary?" said Tristan. "General . . . have you married since Tunis?"

Bertucci laughed. "Oh, not at all, lad! We happily celebrate the third year of our partnership. Last year the event was held at my estate, but this year my partner is hosting. I must tell you, what an estate she has built along the waterfront! 'Tis the envy of every nobleman along the coast."

It was early evening before Bertucci directed his driver to the estate of la Gran Signorina. As they arrived at the gates of the enormous estate, they were met by a brigade of twenty guards who were lined up in formation along both sides of the entrance. Then, as he gazed down the massive, head-high stone wall that began at the gate and ran down both sides of the gate until out of view, he noticed more guards stationed every hundred feet or so apart.

"A veritable fortress, this place," Tristan said.

"Yes, la Gran Signorina believes in security. Besides, she holds more wealth here than half the banks of Genoa combined."

As the coach then proceeded into the heart of the estate, a palatial mansion came into view, and though Tristan was well traveled and had been exposed to many of the finest palaces of Europe, he was awe struck by the opulence of landscaping, architecture, and statuary before him.

The coachman eased the carriage into the circular, granite-paved entry among the many other coaches that had already arrived or were arriving at that same moment, and Bertucci then led Tristan up a majestic, artfully constructed flight of marble stairs that led into the vast mansion itself. The grand foyer and entry area was filled with guests exchanging greetings and engaged in lively chatter, and as Tristan walked further into the house, it opened into an enormous banquet hall surrounded by a second story walk-about from which people could view the proceedings going on below in the main hall. This elevated viewing area ran the entire perimeter of the chamber, and was accented by a great set of marble stairs, highly polished, that gave access to the walk-about. And along the length of these stairs, along both sides, stonefaced military guards stood at attention facing outward.

Then, as Tristan was about to comment on the majesty of the banquet hall, a man appeared at the head of the stairs as a quartet of trumpeters issued a riffle of introductory notes to gain the crowd's attention. "Ladies and gentlemen, visitors and guests!" the man cried, "it is my distinct pleasure to introduce you to your host for this evening and the next three days of celebrating the prosperity of Genoa . . . la Gran Signorina of Genoa!"

A hush fell over the crowd as the trumpets then heralded the appearance of la Gran Signorina as she appeared at the top of the stairs, accompanied by an old woman dressed in black at her side, her head and shoulders covered by a plain black wrap.

"Ah, my lovely business partner," whispered Bertucci, pointing at the top of the stairs.

Recognizing la Gran Signorina and the woman at her side, Tristan was seized by an attack of heart palpitations that nearly took him to the floor as his body fell limp and his face grew pallid. A thousand emotions seized him then, one flooding over the other until he was unable to stand. Feeling himself dissolving, he grabbed at Bertucci's shoulder while trying to grasp his arm for support and cried out. Before the sound vacated his throat even, everything turned black as his knees collapsed and he felt himself go down in a heap, his skull crashing against the marble floor.

"Tristan!" cried Bertucci, awkwardly reaching out in an unsuccessful effort to break Tristan's fall.

CHAPTER EIGHTY-NINE

LA GRAN SIGNORINA

Tristan felt himself fall into an ethereal state as he sensed himself being lifted and moved about as voices flittered in and out, intermittently exchanging suggestions and counsel. Then, he felt himself being laid on something soft, a bed he supposed, and all grew quiet.

After a time the ceiling above and the insides of his addled brain ceased swirling, and as he tried to clear his head, he heard an ancient voice hiss, "You don't belong here! Oh, what curse has brought you here to Genoa!"

Gaining his elbows, he raised up, and in the dim candlelight of a strange room, he saw Duxia de Falaise glaring down at him from the side of the bed. Thinking himself in a dream, he shook his head trying to awaken himself, but quickly discovered that he was already awake. "D-Dux-ia?" he muttered, confused.

"Such depravity, so brazenly appearing here in Mala's new world after all you've done!" the old woman rasped, her teeth clenched with hatred. "Have you come to spread your misery upon her as you have all others you've touched? Oh, I . . ."

The door opened and Tristan heard the approach of quiet footfalls as Duxia fell silent and another voice said. "Duxia, I don't wish you to be here. Go and tend to the guests, and do not approach him again during his stay."

Tristan recognized the voice though it was hushed, as Duxia looked down at him one last time, her eyes brimming with resentment. Then, silently, she left the room, closing the door behind her.

The person who had entered the room took a seat at the edge of the bed. "Tristan, can you hear me? It's Mala."

"Mala," he replied, unable to find other words.

"Such a commotion you caused in the banquet hall. You ruined my grand entrance." Her voice was not cross, and he sensed in her gaze an attempt at humor. "Imagine my surprise descending the stairs and learning it was *you* who had collapsed to floor." Then she smiled. "I see that I still have quite an effect on you."

Tristan attempted to return the smile, but the effort failed. "Yes," he said. Then, gathering his senses, he looked at her and sighed. "You are as beautiful as ever; *more* beautiful than ever."

Mala reached down and slowly passed her palm over Tristan's forehead. "You look very different in your church garb and your tonsure. The last time I saw you like this was your ordination in Cluny. Though your eyes remain as piercing as ever, I think I liked the look you carried in the Loire Valley and at Marseilles far better."

"*Mar . . . seilles*," said Tristan, slipping back to a simpler time. Then his forehead furrowed as he realized that Marseilles had not been a simpler time at all . . . indeed, it marked the beginning of the downfall.

Witnessing his sudden exchange of expression, Mala took his hands in hers, guessing his thoughts. "Marseilles was the greatest moment of my life, Tristan, but I shattered it in a moment of misguided distrust, thinking you had betrayed me with another woman."

"What?"

"Do you not remember being with a woman in the marketplace of Marseilles, and seeing Fernando and several of my musicians there? They saw the two of you in an embrace and led me to believe that you had been carrying on with her throughout your stay there, at the same time you were visiting me."

Tristan tried to recall the incident; his memory was cloudy, then the face of Agnes Truffault fell into place and he said. "Oh, yes, but Mala, it was not as it appear . . ."

"I know. Now I know, and understand. Your brother explained it me a long time ago in Canossa." Then her voice faltered a measure as she continued. "I must confess, I've carried the shame of my misjudgment in Marseilles within me for three years now."

Tristan absorbed these words a moment, then slowly shook his head as his eyes closed. "Ah, you say the word "shame". It is me who has lived in shame these past years; you, the child you bore and lost in the Alps, my deceit in slipping here and there to see you though I was a monk. I have tried desperately to make amends these last years by turning the remainder of my life into a living act of contrition by worshipping God and restoring the true Church to Rome and the Vatican. Your memory slips into my mind when I least suspect it and undoes all that I have sought to rebuild."

Mala squeezed his fingers. "You did nothing wrong, Tristan, except fall in love with me, just like I fell in love with you. We were children when we met, I know, but God placed us in each other's path twenty years ago, and brought us together at various and odd times. There must have been a purpose to it, don't you think?"

"Or a curse, perhaps, as Duxia claims," Tristan said, shaking his head.

"Never mind Duxia," Mala said. "I love her beyond words. She has shared my misfortunes and done her best to advance me all these years. I also know about her misguided feelings about you since the day of your birth. Superstition drove her life in those days, and still does to an extent. She will bother you no longer while here at my estate." Then she smiled. "General Bertucci has mentioned you a time or two since my acquaintance with him, but I had no idea he had invited you to visit him here in Genoa."

"Yes, we were together in Tunis on occasion. How on earth did you two chance to come together?"

"Over business," Mala said. "And over time we've become very close friends. I never had a father as you know, and he has begun to fill that role. I adore him, and he adores me." Then she withdrew her hands and stood. "We have much to discuss and sort through," she said. "I have over five hundred guests awaiting downstairs and must tend to them. Rest here tonight, Tristan, and we shall take back up in the morning."

CHAPTER NINETY

NEW LIFE . . . OLD QUANDARY

"Oho!" shouted Bertucci that next morning as Tristan appeared in the meandering gardens. "Feeling better, I hope?"

"Yes, quite," Tristan replied. "Not sure what overtook me last evening."

"No matter, you look better today, I'd say. Come along, Mala is out on the lawn involved in a bocce tournament. I've told her about our adventures in North Africa so she wishes to be introduced to you."

This told Tristan that Bertucci knew nothing of Tristan's and Mala's prior relationship, which was just as well, he decided. As they traveled through the length of the gardens they saw endless groups of merchants, seamen, town burghers and politicians engaged in table games, cards, and conversation. It was not the elite gathering he had become accustomed to within the palaces of royals and popes, but these people seemed to be natural in their ease and comfort with each other and also seemed to be lost in the frolic of the moment rather than focused on etiquette and posing. Watching this, it occurred to Tristan he himself had never taken time to enjoy such simple pursuits. Indeed, he had never been afforded the opportunity.

As they caught sight of Mala on the other side of the vast lawn, she had apparently successfully rolled her boule against the jack and was holding her arms high in the air, squealing amidst the throes of victory as onlookers applauded and her opponents moaned with feigned discouragement.

"Is she not absolutely stunning?" said Bertucci with a smile. "She has brought such joy into my life since my return from Tunis."

Remembering that Bertucci once cursed Vincento Balducci and the woman he married in favor of his own daughter, Marianna, Tristan marveled at the quirk of such a turn in life. That particular quirk paled in comparison to the turn that Mala herself had taken.

"You know," Bertucci continued, "Mala feeds the poor of Genoa and heavily supports the monasteries also as they tend to the ill."

"Oh?"

"Yes, she shares her wealth . . . far more than I, I hate to confess. And as you look about, you see the wealthy as well as the working folk here enjoying her grounds for this celebration. Many of these townsmen and sailors work for her or are involved in our joint ventures. She has a generous heart, that one."

Sensing their approach, Mala stepped forward as Bertucci bowed and kissed the back of her hand. She then curtsied as he introduced Tristan, and the smile that she issued should have told Bertucci that something profound had once existed between the two young people he so adored, but he missed it entirely.

The three spent the remainder of the afternoon together, with Mala hooked on Bertucci's arm much of the time. By evening he wished to spend time talking up a business transaction with some new arrivals, so he excused himself. As soon as he left, Mala immediately reached over and looped her arm within Tristan's and continued to walk. She felt a slight hesitancy in Tristan's step as she did this, and saw that he was gazing about nervously. This caused her to twitter a bit, and she chastised him with a jerk of her arm.

"Be calm, Tristan, I often hold onto my business associates and friends like Bertucci, as well as the monks of Genoa whom I frequent. No one will think it odd," she snickered a little, "but you, of course!"

"I'm not accustomed to such a casual atmosphere," Tristan objected defensively. He loosened his grip and looked at her as they walked. "I never thought I would see you again, Mala," he said in a hushed voice.

"Nor did I think to see you either," Mala replied. "As I told you last night, God threw us together once long ago, and continues to do so." Then, lowering her eyes and her voice, she said, "I love you still, smart boy."

Taken by surprise, Tristan stammered a moment, but before he could actually utter anything intelligible, Mala released her hold on him and ran to greet a woman who was hailing her a few steps away.

Stuck there confused and alone, he looked about quickly to see whether others had been watching them or had sensed anything out of place by the way he and Mala had been strolling together arm in arm. Tristan glanced across the lawn to the steps of the mansion, and there stood Duxia, glaring at him from the distance. She had been scrutinizing them closely, apparently, and despite the distance Tristan could feel the full brunt of her beady eyes. She stared at him a moment longer, her fists planted on her hips, then turned and disappeared.

Festivities continued for two more days. On the last night of the anniversary gathering, Bertucci appeared to Tristan and Mala with unexpected news. "I must leave Genoa first thing in the morning, lad. I apologize profusely for I had intended to spend the entire week taking you about the city, but I learned last night that I've had two of my ships go down off the coast of Corsica! It's a mess and I'm needed there as soon as possible."

Tristan masked his disappointment saying, "Absolutely, General, I understand. I will depart Genoa for Monte Cassino three days earlier than planned. It will be no bother."

Mala's face had also dropped in the unveiling of Bertucci's dilemma. Recovering, she quickly took Bertucci by the arm and said, "Oh, Bernard, such bad news! Your friend Tristan is welcome to stay here for a few days longer. Besides, I've taken a liking to him. He's so full of stories about the Pope's affairs and Heinrich's recent calamities here in Italy."

"Yes, a wonderful idea!" Bertucci beamed. "Tristan, do you object to such a proposal?"

"Absolutely not," Tristan replied quickly.

And so it was that Bertucci departed Mala's property at the same moment that Mala's guests took their leave. And when the estate was vacated by that next afternoon, Mala and Tristan found themselves alone, except for the guards surrounding the estate . . . and old Duxia, who slipped about in the shadows, mumbling to herself in Finnish and conjuring ways to distance Tristan from her beloved Mala.

The sudden privacy of the empty estate was awkward at first for Tristan, though Mala seemed to revel in it. She continued to hold onto his arm whenever they walked within the gardens or the long length of seashore that ran along the endless southern boundary of her property. Tristan could not help but feel a tug of guilt pulling at him as she began to hold onto him more closely as the afternoon faded to dusk. By late evening Tristan found himself abandoning any resistance to her touch, and even began to hunger for it.

They dined alone that night and stayed up until the wee hours of morning discussing memories of their early encounters, trading thoughts on the politics of the day, and even touching on their respective trials as a result of their previous relationship. This was a sensitive subject, and each at various moments during this exchange would break with emotion at certain points, causing them to embrace each other from time to time with tender regret. Finally, no longer able to bear the unearthing of such sorrow, they took their leave from each other at dawn and found their ways to their separate bed chambers. Shortly after removing his monk's robe, Tristan heard someone pacing about outside his room. Slipping to the door, he silently cracked it open, thinking perhaps to see Mala, only to discover that it was Duxia walking the hallway, mumbling to herself and moving her hands about in strange motions as though casting spells around Tristan's room.

CHAPTER NINETY-ONE

TEMPTATION'S CALL

Having been up all night with Mala, Tristan did not rise that next day until nearly dusk. A soft rain had begun to fall earlier that afternoon, and by the time Tristan dressed and left his room, it had turned to a downpour.

"Mala?" he cried, making his way down the marble stairs to search for her. He heard a noise in the distance, outside the banquet hall toward the covered outdoor patio that graced the inner courtyard of Mala's house. He couldn't quite identify the sound he heard. Approaching the doorway to the patio, it grew in timbre and pace, becoming familiar to him.

Standing there at the threshold of the patio, he looked out into the covered area at Mala, dressed in her vibrant Romani dancing skirt of old, lost in her own movement, swaying high, low, and around, her eyes closed, lost in her dancing and in another world and time. The jingle-jangle of the zills fastened to her fingers accented the rhythm of the rain pattering the tile roof of the patio, and as he watched her lithe movements, a look of near rapture possessed her face. Her eyes still closed, she launched into a slow sweep as her arms and hands undulated with extreme grace, telling stories with each set of motions, one after another. She was in a trance of her own devise, he decided, and that trance was in turn entrancing him.

Abruptly she stopped and the zills on her fingers stilled as she opened her eyes, then drew back, startled. "Oh!" she cried, her cheeks filling with color. Then she laughed as her embarrassment subsided. "I thought I was alone."

"Ah, it's only me, Mala. I did not imagine that you danced anymore."

"I pull out my zills from time to time, in the solitude of days such as this. There's a sadness in the rain that seems to draw out the old days, you know? It was raining the night I left you in Marseilles, storming terribly actually. Every time it rains now, which is frequent here in Genoa, I can't help thinking of that night, and you."

"You come to me also," Tristan sighed, "in my moments of loneliness. There's something I meant to ask you last night and never quite got there. That day I caught up to your caravan as you were following Balducci to his territories, why would you not speak to me, or even acknowledge me? A word from you, a moment of sanity, might have changed everything for us."

"Oh, Tristan, poor Tristan. It would have changed nothing. I was too bitter at the time. I had just buried the baby and Fernando, my body was full of sores from frostbite, I had lost all faith in Mathilda and your Cardinal, whatever his name was at the time."

"Odo," said Tristan. "Cardinal Odo de Lagery, who is the Holy Father Pope Urban II. Beyond that, he is the man who raised me, taught me everything I know, and provided me a future."

"Yes, I have heard that he is now the Gregorian Pope. Do you believe he gave you a future?" said Mala with an unexpected measure of doubt. "Has it ever occurred to you, Tristan, that you were a little boy of seven when you fell into the hands of the Black Monks, and that the Benedictines used you when they discovered your phenomenal intelligence and academic abilities?" Then she approached and stood immediately in front of him, wrapping her arms about his neck. "Put your arms around me, smart boy," she then whispered.

He felt the full press of her swelling breasts against his chest, as well as her pressing, half exposed belly and everything below it. This caused an uncontrolable stirring in him, yet his hands did not move from his side.

"Here, I'll help you then," said Mala, taking his hands and forcing them about her bare waist, "since you continue to worry about things. I have even sent Duxia into town for the night, so we are utterly alone."

As his hands felt the soft, bare skin of her waistline and she continued to press her breasts against him, he felt a sudden swelling between his thighs.

Mala felt his swelling also, and tittered in his ear, "There now, let nature do its work, smart boy, and stop thinking so much." Then she pressed her lips against his and kissed him deeply, her tongue slipping hungrily about in search of response. Tristan was frozen in place, lost within her promiscuous embrace. Mala moved her head back a little and looked at him a moment, then kissed him again. Once again feeling no reaction, she left her mouth upon his, reached to her shoulders and slipped her blouse down to her waist. Then, standing there bare from the waist up, she took Tristan's hands and pulled them upward, opening his palms and laying them flat upon her ample breasts. Covering his hands with hers, she then gently moved his hands about so that they were plying her breasts, and his fingers were grazing back and forth over her erect nipples.

"I want you tonight, Tristan."

"I . . . Mala . . . I . . ."

"I don't ask you to leave the Church." Mala whispered, clinging to him. "And I don't ask for marriage, nor promises. All I ask is that you make love to me tonight and tell me how much you love me, Tristan; how much you miss me and need me. We are alone here and completely free of the world's prying eyes."

Tristan dropped his hands from Mala's waist and backed away a step. "I cannot do this, Mala. I *do* love you. *Desperately.* There is an emptiness in me that only you can fill. It's always been that way since we first met, but I cannot do this, not *now.*"

Mala released her hold on him. "It's Odo de Lagery, isn't it?" she said, a storm of emotion brewing in her eyes. "Even locked away in this hidden world of mine, far from his eyes, ears, and reach, you can't shake free of him can you, Tristan?"

Then she raised the top of her blouse, covering herself, and turned away. "That man that you adore so much, why can't you place things in perspective about your relationship with him? He didn't give you a future, but *denied* you a future, by raising you up in his own image within the confines of Cluny Monastery in the company of reform minded fanatics! You never had a chance, Tristan, don't you see that! As intelligent as you are, are you *really* so blind to the reality of what has been done to you?"

Tristan looked at her, drawing from the only instincts he knew. "I am a monk, Mala, and a Gregorian. I know that Genoa operates under the name of King Heinrich of Germany, Mala. Have you really turned against us and taken Heinrich's part?"

"Oh, Tristan," she sighed with frustration, "I'm not talking politics here. I'm talking about you as a little boy, and what the Black Monks have put in your head. Besides, Genoa is independent and operates under its own name. Heinrich has no authority here despite these so-called territorial maps the Gregorians and Heinrich draw up in their damnable game of chess that has blighted the land." Then her frustration began to evolve into anger. "And Tristan, you know well that Heinrich has neither influence nor presence here. The Gregorians have been freely using the port of Genoa throughout this war!" she retorted. "And many here like General Bertucci openly support the Gregorian party! Oh, how *dare* you accuse me of making a political stand simply because I charge your precious Odo de Lagery with exploiting you since childhood!"

"I am a Benedictine by choice, Mala, by my own free will," insisted Tristan.

"Oh, just as I was a poor Romani dancer by choice, I suppose, eh? Dammit, Tristan, open your eyes! You are what you are because of Odo de Lagery, and he never allowed you to be anything else."

"Not true . . . my brother Guillaume, he did not choose to become a Black Monk. Of his own free will he became a man-of-arms!"

"Tristan," Mala cried, losing herself in exasperation, "Odo de Lagery and the Black monks *ignored* Guillaume at Cluny. He was not raised to manhood by Odo de Lagery like you, but left Cluny and was raised by your aunt Mathilda. Even at that he too has become a fanatic Gregorian at *her* hands. There is far more to life out there than the Investiture War and the Church, Tristan!"

Disputes can shatter the most intimate of moments. Disputes that combine family, politics, and religion in one basket wreak absolute havoc upon them. This is precisely what was occurring between Mala and Tristan with each word uttered. Angry, disillusioned, wounded beyond imagination, Mala stormed from the patio and disappeared inside. As Tristan listened to her dissipating footsteps, he too was angry and hurt, and blamed Mala's tirade solely on her temper.

That night in bed he wrestled for hours over Mala's words, especially the accusations slung at Odo de Lagery. And though he made an honest effort to at least think about her accusations, he refused to accept that either the Black Monks or

Odo de Lagery had done anything but look out for his best interests as a child under their stewardship.

That next morning when Mala arose, she sorely regretted the heated exchange that had ensued the night before and went straight to Tristan's room. When she got there, Duxia was standing within the doorway.

"Duxia, when did you return from town?" said Mala

"I was worried about you being here alone with the monk and decided I best get back here by dawn."

"I instructed you not to bother him. Why are you here by his room?"

"Oh, I'm humbly changing out the linens," Duxia clucked. "I'm not bothering him. He's gone."

"Gone?" said Mala, her heart dropping into the very pit of her stomach.

"Yes, according to the guards your monk asked for a coach and left in the middle of the night."

CHAPTER NINETY-TWO

CONSTANTINOPLE

Though Tristan's sudden departure from Genoa was of his own volition, it was both hurtful and confusing. He had wanted more than anything that night to take her in his arms, return her affection, and lose himself in her warm embrace. Something deep within himself had forbidden such action, something that even he did not understand. It may have been his conscience, it may have been his long climb back within the graces of the Church, and it may have even been the shadow of Odo de Lagery looming somewhere in the back of his mind. Regardless, as his ship sailed toward Lower Italy and he then crossed east from the coast to Monte Cassino, he could think of nothing else but Mala. With each day he admonished himself more, though on the night he had found her dancing within the patio, he had fought temptation and resisted her advances. Now he was asking himself why, and could not come up with any answers that did not fall directly in line with Mala's accusations on that night.

I am a fool see-sawing back and forth with these hopeless emotions that possess me about Mala, he thought. *I loved her no less in Genoa than I had in the Loire Valley and at Marseilles, yet I failed to act there in the secrecy of her inner court-yard, even though she made no demands and had no expectations. Will God never give me rest? Is this, indeed, my curse in life, or my trial?*

He then tried to justify his stand on that last night in Genoa by recallling such things as integrity, his Benedictine vows, and his fidelity to Odo, but the more he stood pondering these precepts, the more Mala's words pierced his defenses. This confused him more. At Monte Cassino, Muehler and Handel fortunately turned his attention to Constantinople.

"It'll only be the two of you, traveling incognito as Merchants from Genoa," said Muehler to Handel and Tristan. "Your contact there is a member of the Byzantine court, a commercial liaison officer working for Alexius by the name of Fantinus."

"Looking like a merchant will be easy enough for Handel," said Tristan pointing at his own hair, "but my tonsure will give me away as a monk."

"You'll wear a hat at all times until you arrive at Alexius' court," said Muehler.

"Aha," mused Handel, looking at Tristan, "looks like you're back to the old days of disguises, eh, lad?"

"Indeed," said Tristan. Then he looked at Muehler. "Since Emperor Alexius does not wish Heinrich to know we are coming, the German-Byzantine alliance must still be in place. Are we to expect treachery, then?"

"No. Alexius has heard that Heinrich's now on the run, that Mathilda's taken back all of her lost territories in Tuscany and central Italy, and that Conrad has declared himself King of Italy and is in possession of nearly all of Lombardy and much of the rest of northern Italy. Nevertheless, Alexius also knows that Heinrich has rebounded more than once, so by keeping this embassy secret, he's hedging his bets. In any case, we wish to re-open channels of communication with the Byzantines. This is an ideal opportunity. Obviously Alexius *wants* something from us."

"I'll tell you what that bastard wants," said Handel, "help against the Saracens. They've already overrun Asia Minor and are now pressing against the western frontiers of the Byzantine Empire. God knows, Pope Urban has neither money nor troops to spare, especially for the Byzantines. This damn war against Heinrich has nearly driven him to ruin."

"You're correct, my friend," Muehler replied, gazing at Handel over his veil, "so neither of you will make commitments of any kind. Also, Handel, don't allow your hatred of the Byzantines to foil this embassy. Listen to what Alexius has to say and we'll sort it all out when your return. Perhaps by that time we'll have driven Heinrich back to Germany for good, and the Holy Father will be on more solid ground." Then he handed Tristan a satchel. "Here are your documents, letters of introduction, and finances. The tailors have completed several fittings of merchant garb for you both. You'll leave in two days for Taranto in the south, and from there cross the Ionian Sea into the Mediterranean and then into Constantinople."

Tristan was a boy when he first met Handel, and was intrigued by him the moment he learned Handel was a papal spy. Tristan held him in even higher esteem now, knowing that he was the most highly regarded Benedictine agent within the underground. The long voyage to Constantinople, then, was pleasurable in Handel's company as he reeled off story after story about both his past and recent exploits. Tristan was curious about one aspect of Handel's character, so as they sat deckside gazing out at the sea one day, Tristan asked him, "Handel, how many people would you say you have killed during your time with the underground?"

"Twenty-five or thirty through assassination," Handel replied matter-of-factly. "I've lost exact count, but that's a close number I imagine. Then probably another nine or ten incidentally, you know, like the Byzantine who showed up in the nun's room at the Inn of the Sparrow."

"You do not seem the least bothered by such a thing whereas I cannot bear to even think of killing anyone, though I *have* a time or two. Does your conscience never bother you on this matter?"

"My conscience? Hell no! I kill for the Church, lad, not for pleasure. There is a Godly purpose to my actions, violent as they may be."

"Yes, but are you so certain that God condones killing, even on his own behalf?"

"He led the Hebrews out of Egypt and into the Promised Land, did he not? How many tens of thousands of the enemy were slaughtered by his Chosen People, at his own direction? Let me ask you a question. How many men do you suppose your brother, Guillaume has killed? And your fierce kinsmen, the Danes? Don't be fixated on *my* small numbers. Then, too, there is face-to-face killing, and there is indirect killing through politics, intrigue, diplomacy, alliances. And that, lad, is *your* specialty. Whether you acknowledge it or not, your hands have filled graveyard after graveyard with dead soldiers as well as civilians who got caught in the middle. Oh no, you are far more efficient at decimating the population than old Handel here! You don't like the smell and sight of blood at your table, lad, because it offends your sensibilities, yet you don't think anything of feasting on the butcher's handiwork afterwards in the form of roasted lamb and hog."

This remark cut Tristan with the precision of a razor, and though Handel's words disturbed him, Tristan knew there was certain merit to them, ugly as they were. "There is still a difference," he said to Handel, shaking his head. "Thrusting a dagger into a man's heart is one thing, intrigue is quite another."

"If it helps you sleep at night, then so be it, there's a difference. But the difference exists only to *you*, not to the dead. Their fate is the same regardless, whether by way of assassin or some diplomat's scheme. Let's talk of more pleasant things, my head's not as complex as yours, fortunately, and such talk overburdens my small brain."

As their vessel finally approached Constantinople, a city famed for its massive defenses, Handel and Tristan were both immediately overwhelmed at the sheer size and beauty of the vast city as it unfolded before them. Built on seven hills as well as on the Golden Horn and the Sea of Marmara, its impregnable walls enclosed magnificent palaces, cathedrals, domes, and spires that extended from one edge of the horizon to the other, then as far back up the hills as the eye could see until finally disappearing in the distance. Originally founded as a Greek colony under the name of Byzantium in the 7th century BC, it later took the name of Constantinople under Roman emperor Constantine who moved the capital of the Roman Empire there in 330 AD. The site was especially strategic militarily and commercially since it lay astride the land route from Europe to Asia and the seaway from the Black Sea to the Mediterranean, possessing in the Golden Horn a superb and spacious harbor.

"By God!" cried Handel gazing beyond the seven hills and the massive double walls enclosing the city, "I've never witnessed such splendor!"

"Nor I," Tristan answered. "Such architectural masterpieces! Rome and Paris are but pastoral communes in comparison, and poorly outfitted at that!"

Disembarking, Handel and Tristan spent three full days moving about the city, circulating within the harbor, visiting marketplaces, scouting shipyards, and walking the arcaded avenues and squares. Their purpose in this was to generate conversation with various elements of the citizenry in order to put a finger to the political pulse of the general population before actually meeting with the Byzantine emperor. "Such damned wealth and opulence," commented Handel with suspicion, "strange that the Emperor should want anything from us."

On the fourth morning they then reported to the palace of Emperor Alexius Comnenus under the guise of shipping business from Genoa, and after exchanging code words with a commercial liaison officer by the name of Marcus Fantinus, they were led into the inner sanctum of the palace and presented to the Emperor who sat alone with a single advisor upon his gilded throne. That advisor was Patriach Nicholas III, holy pontiff of the Greek Orthodox Church.

"I welcome our good Gregorian friends!" exclaimed Emperor Alexius with great fanfare as Handel and Tristan bowed, then dropped to their knees in deference to the emperor.

Patriarch Nicholas said nothing, but only stared vacantly at the two visitors. as if displeased.

"Good friends we are now, eh?" whispered Handel, gritting his teeth. "How many of my Benedictine friends have his agents killed these past years?"

Formal introductions were made, gifts were exchanged, and Alexius then launched into the purpose of his request for dialogue with Pope Urban. "I have been embattled here in Constantinople since taking the crown. First, bitter wars against your allies, the vicious Duke Robert Guiscard and his Normans of Lower Italy. Then disturbances in Thrace against the heretical sects of the Bogomils and Paulicians, followed by raids by the Pechenegs who made league with Tzachas, brother-in-law to the Sultan of Rum. All of these threats I have managed to counter, but I am fighting the Cumans in the Balkans while at the same time the Saracens are moving west across my borders and eyeing Constantinople."

"When you say the Saracens, Majesty," said Tristan, "you refer to the Seljuq Turks, do you not?"

"Yes, the most foul and violent breed of Islamists to ever populate the earth. These vermin originated among the Hsiung-nu tribes on the northern edge of the Gobi Desert and the Altai Mountains in Asia, but after a time moved west off the steppes of Central Asia."

"Yes," said Tristan, "it happens that I am familiar with the Seljuqs through a certain Lord Abdul Azim whom I met while assisting during negotiations with Pope Gregory in 1079."

"You met Abdul Azim in 1079?" sniffed Patriarch Nicholas, a look of doubt slipping across his face. "Judging from your youthful appearance, Brother Saint-Germain, you couldn't have been but a boy at that time, and you claim that you were *assisting* in the Pope's negotiations?"

"I was fourteen at the time, Holiness. I possessed a good deal of knowledge about the Arab and Persian tongue and culture and was able to assist Pope Gregory and the Cardinals of Rome despite my youth. Anyway, as I was saying, I am familiar with the Seljuqs. A century ago they adopted Islam and established themselves around Bukara in Transoxania under their khan, Seljuq. Then one branch moved into India while the other struck west and entered the military service of the Abbasid caliphs of Baghdad, the spiritual leaders of Islam at the time. The Turkish horsemen, known as gazis, eventually turned against the Abbasids and occupied Baghdad in 1055 under their leader, Tugrul Bey. From there they began to make incursions into Anatolia, Armenia, and eventually your territories."

Alexius sat back and placed his hands in his lap, impressed. Handel was also impressed by Tristan's recitation of Seljuq history, and it reminded him why Tristan had as a boy so quickly come to the attention of the Black Monks of Cluny.

"Knowing what you know, then," said Alexius, "you well understand my concerns. I seek assistance against these Muslim locusts before they march in full array against Constantinople itself."

Tristan nodded and said, "Certainly, Majesty and we in Italy have ourselves led a recent expedition against a certain faction of Muslims in North Africa."

Then Handel spoke. "Sire, with all due respect, I must inquire . . . in light of the contentious past relationship between the Gregorians and the Byzantines, have you also requested assistance from King Heinrich of Germany?"

"Yes, I have sent embassies in the past to Germany for the purpose of probing his sentiments on the issue. The truth is, we feel that Heinrich is finished in Italy, and he never had France, Spain, or England who have from the very start of the Investiture War steadfastly refused to recognize Heinrich's anti-pope. Therefore, I see Pope Urban as the sole spiritual light in the West."

"You are correct, Majesty," said Tristan. "We, too, feel that Heinrich's days in Italy are coming to an end."

"Majesty," said Handel, "again, with all due respect, I must inquire in the interests of our Holy Father, Pope Urban, to what advantage would he provide assistance to the Byzantine Empire in light of the long-established schism between Roman Catholics and Byzantine Catholics of the Eastern Rite?"

Alexius reflected on the question, then smiled. "Ah, Brother Handel, you do not waste your arrows, do you? Let me propose a simple concept. Divided as Byzantium and the West may be, we are both still Christians, albeit now Roman Catholic and Eastern Greek Orthodox. The Muslims are all dark heathens, whether from Africa, Asia, or the Middle East, and will not be content until they have forced their heathen faith upon the entire world by sword and fire. And I assure you, if they overrun my realm, they will then look further west to Italy and France, and beyond."

"The Spaniards have checked the Moorish advances in Spain," replied Handel, "and are reconquering much of the Iberian Peninsula as we speak. Furthermore, as Brother Saint-Germain mentioned, we have recently completed a successful crusade against the Moors of North Africa who were kidnapping Christians for their thriving slave trade. The Saracens have not enjoyed success against us to the west as they have here in Asia Minor and Eastern Europe." Then he looked at Tristan and said, "We don't fear them in Italy as Byzantium fears them here, do we, Brother Saint-Germanin?" Tristan's eyes narrowed as he glanced back at Handel.

You are doing exactly as Muehler instructed you not to do, the glance said. Turning back to the emperor, Tristan said, "Majesty, I have found that the Saracens are not actually this monolithic, unified race that we so often describe within Christian circles, but more akin to a loose confederation of feuding races and tribes who spend most of their time attacking each other. I have long thought, therefore, that an attack against them before they unify would be a strategic necessity. The very thing you propose may, indeed, be the moment of which I speak. Also, I must agree that the Seljuq Turks are the most aggressive, dangerous, and populous of these races."

"But the Turks are *your* neighbors, Majesty, not Italy's," interjected Handel. "Pope Urban has no quarrel with them."

"Strange talk from a Benedictine monk, Brother Handel," sniped Patriarch Nicholas.

"Yes," agreed Alexius, displeasure seeping into his voice. "But then I would not expect a monk to embrace the military view, so let me focus on the spiritual aspect of this dilemma. Let us consider that Jerusalem and the Holy Land have been under the foot of the Saracens for many years now, which in itself is an assault on Christianity and should be considered anathema by any good Christian. Worse yet, the Seljuqs are abusing, murdering, and raping western pilgrims along the route to Jerusalem. The Abbasids, when in power, at least respected the right of Christian pilgrims to travel back and forth to the Holy Land in safety, but these goddamn Seljuq's are a different breed."

Though Alexius had not raised his voice while making this last statement, the entry of profanity into his otherwise dignified manner signaled to Tristan that the emperor's demeanor was elevating.

"We hear everything you are saying," said Tristan with a respectful bow, "and vow to you that we shall convey it to Pope Urban in a precise and unbiased manner. As for my cohort, Brother Handel, he merely carries out his solemn duty, which is to question and analyze all that is proposed to our Holy Father, the Pope. No good servant would do otherwise."

"Certainly, I cannot argue with that, Brother Saint-Germain," said Alexius, his frown still settled with Handel who stood there unrepentant. "There are several things I ask that you and Brother Handel do while here in Constantinople."

"Anything you request, Majesty."

"First, I ask that you meet with my generals and review with them the recent activities of the Seljuqs. I then ask that you speak to our bishops and archbishops who, unlike yours in faraway Italy, now feel the heat of Islam's approach. And finally, I ask that you visit the infirmary and hospice of the Church of Hagia Sophia. You will find there a good number of pilgrims who, while in the Holy Land, fell victim to Seljuq handiwork, Brother Saint-Germain. These followers of Christ respectfully wished to make a pilgrimage to the Holy Land and walk the paths taken by their Lord and Savior, Jesus Christ, but encountered the intolerance of Muslim fanatics. Then, when you have completed these three things, I will then ask you a final time before returning to Italy whether we should surrender access to the very cradle of Christianity, or must we as Christians form an alliance and hold back the bloody tide of Islam?"

CHAPTER NINETY-THREE

HAGIA SOPHIA

That next morning a corps of Byzantine generals accompanied Tristan and Handel to the Military Palace where they were taken into a large meeting hall and given a brief history of Saracen involvement and conflict with the Byzantine Empire beginning with the Abbasid Dynasty of Arabia and ending with the current situation against the incursive Seljuq Turks. Listening as the generals took turns describing various campaigns and showing lost ground upon the huge maps pinned along the wall, Tristan was appalled by the actual amount of territory that had either been conquered by the Turks or ceded to them by the Byzantines.

"Coming out of the Asian steppes," he commented, "they have moved across half a continent!"

"Indeed," one of the generals replied, "and they have no intention of stopping."

Even Handel was surprised at the amount of land mass the Seljuqs had acquired, and said, "I must confess, these Seljuqs have been on the move these past decades and have easily swept all opponents aside."

"They are ferocious men-at-arms," the general said, "and far more sophisticated in weaponry, war machinery, and tactics than you would expect."

By the end of the day the generals had completed their briefing, and over the next five days Tristan and Handel were taken on a full tour of defenses for Constantinople and several surrounding cities. In addition they were shown a full array of hand weapons and war machinery captured from the Turks, and also afforded the opportunity to speak to a number of Seljuk prisoners.

Finishing their time with the Byzantine generals, Tristan and Handel were then directed to the antechambers of Hagia Sophia Cathedral where they conferenced with Patriarch Nicholas and nine of his bishops. "The Seljuqs are a plague throughout the continent," began Nicholas. "They lack the religious tolerance and diplomatic skills of their predecessors, the Abbasid Dynasty, with whom we had little quarrel."

"A question," said Tristan, "do you feel that the primary interest of the Seljuqs is military or is it conversion of others to Islam?"

"They make no differentiation," the Patriarch replied. "They carry the Koran in one hand, the sword in the other."

"As devil's advocate only," Tristan said carefully, "we Christians carried the cross in one hand and the sword in the other during the Germanic and Scandinavian conversion wars. Wherein lies the difference?"

"I am aware of the history of Christianity within the continent of Europe, Brother Saint-Germain," Patriarch Nicholas replied sourly, "and your point is well taken. However, there is a vast difference in that the Saracens, *all* Saracens, are heathens. We, on the other hand, worship the one true God. It is a question of darkness and light, ignorance and enlightenment."

"Of course it is," said Handel, "but I also have a question. As clerics of the Eastern Rite, do you Byzantine clerics addressing us not find it at all odd that your emperor would seek assistance from Pope Urban after supporting King Heinrich and the Germans throughout these past ten years of war in Italy?"

Tristan placed his hand upon Handel's wrist and shook his head. "Handel, please do not instigate."

"No, it is a fair question," said Patriarch Nicholas, "and I shall answer it. Yes, it could be considered odd if one prefers the Turks to rule Byzantium, but I don't think you in Italy would want such a thing. Yes, it could be considered odd if you believe that Islam should prevail over Christianity. I don't think you believe such a thing. And yes, it could be considered odd if you believe the differences between Roman Catholicism and the Byzantine Rite are too great to create common cause against a heathen race of non-believers."

Handel nodded, trying to force a smile. "Framed in such a manner," he replied. "Alexius' request does make at least a little more sense to me, Patriarch Nicholas."

Their discussions continued for two more days as the Byzantine bishops provided their individual and particular views on the Seljuq threat while Tristan and Handel riddled them with questions. These sessions were extremely informative, overall, and upon completion the Patriarch said, "Now follow me to our hospice and you will have the opportunity to speak to some of our unfortunate pilgrims who have actually dealt with the Seljuqs more directly. The monks of Hagia Sophia have taken it upon themselves to provide shelter and care for these unfortunate souls."

The hospice was comprised of a number of outbuildings and courtyards located adjacent to the cathedral itself. Entering the first courtyard, Tristan found a number of invalids sitting and laying about, some missing an arm or a leg, others missing both arms or both legs. As he proceeded, a circle of children gathered from nowhere, like a flock of sparrows, surrounding him. They were laughing and scampering about as all young children do, but as Tristan's eyes found them, he noticed that each child possessed a deformity of one form or another. One, who was being dragged about by a friend, appeared to have had his eyes plucked from their sockets. Two others were missing both hands, while yet another's entire face and body was covered in the rough, wrinkled distortion of burn scars, as though he had been scalded by boiling water or oil. The sight of the adults as he had entered had disturbed Tristan, but seeing these injuries to the children sickened him to the very core of his heart, and he felt unsteady upon his feet.

"My God, Patriarch Nicholas," he whispered so the children would not hear, "what is this horror?"

"The Turks."

"But *children?*"

"Men, women, children, it makes no difference to them. Which is why we seek your Pope's assistance. Though Rome and Constantinople have been in opposite camps these past decades, it now becomes a matter of Christian against Muslim, right against wrong. You have yet to enter the actual infirmary where the true horrors await, pilgrims confined to beds for the rest of their lives, or near death. Come along and listen to what the wounded themselves have to say about the Seljuqs."

CHAPTER NINETY-FOUR

THE LATERAN PALACE

The flight of Queen Adelheid from Verona, Mathilda's defeat of Heinrich near Canossa, and the unexpected alliance of Conrad with Mathilda reversed the political landscape for Pope Urban II and Gregorian Catholics, who months earlier had been standing at the edge of collapse. Sensing opportunity, upon Tristan and Handel's departure to Constantinople, Pope Urban immediately marched on Rome in hopes of quickly ousting anti-pope Clement. Clement's partisans tenaciously defended and held on to the strong parts of the city, knowing that neither Mathilda nor Conrad could yet spare troops to assist Urban's effort to take over Rome. Many Romans also thought Heinrich's defeat at Canossa to be a temporary setback for the German king, and were convinced that his army would quickly rebound as he had so frequently in the past.

Consequently, a strange period followed where Pope Urban took up residence in Rome within a fortress near the Palatine Hill belonging to the ever faithful Frangipani family. Despite the fact that Odo was now at least back in Rome, the ensuing period proved to be the most piteous of his papacy. Years of war and managing the papacy in exile had utterly depleted his finances, and had also incurred a huge amount of debt through borrowing to reinforce Gregorian allies in the fight against Heinrich. Consequently, he was forced to depend on the charity of others. Help arrived in the form of donations from various sources, most notably the French Abbot Gregory of Vendome, and Pope Urban managed to somehow keep his papacy afloat during these meager days in Rome.

This state of limbo continued month after month with both pope and anti-pope both residing within Rome under an uneasy peace. As the year 1094 dawned, a most unusual and unexpected thing occurred: The Governor of Rome, deciding that Heinrich would soon lose his hold on Italy completely, offered to surrender the Lateran Palace to Pope Urban on payment of a large sum of money. The Lateran Palace had originally been given to the Catholic Church as a gift by Constantine, the first Christian Roman emperor. In the year 324 it was dedicated by Pope Sylvester who declared it to be "Domus Dei" . . . "The House of God." The Papal Throne was placed within its interior, thus marking it as the Cathedral of Rome, and from that time on it also served as the residence of the Pope.

This offer by the Roman governor to oust the anti-pope from the Lateran Palace for money was tantamount to a huge bribe in exchange for handing Rome over to Pope Urban. In essence, it made far more sense than conducting another protracted military battle within Rome for the papacy. Lacking funds, Urban was forced yet again to seek charity if he wished to complete the proposed trans-action. Again Abbot Gregory of Vendome was among the first to come forward, selling his monastery's possessions in order to further Urban's cause. This alone did not provide enough revenue to satisfy the greedy Roman governor.

Word of the Pope's plight also reached the citizens of Genoa. Few appeared to show much interest in Urban's dilemma except for one individual in particular, the single wealthiest citizen of the city. Thus it was that la Gran Signorina sailed to Rome in the company of an old woman dressed in black and a financial repre-sentative by the name of Salvetti.

Several days later, gaining admittance into the Frangipane fortress, la Gran Signorina was given a private audience with Pope Urban.

"Ah, Signorina," said Odo, "such a pleasure to finally meet you after our exchange of correspondence this past month. And how can I ever thank you for your kind offer of assistance?" Then, looking at her curiously, he added, "I must confess, I expected someone much older."

"After a series of difficult trials, God decided to finally show me some kind-ness," she replied, her demeanor dark. "He graced me with wealth upon the death of my husband, and then also when I moved to Genoa led me into an extremely profitable partnership with an old acquaintance of yours, Duke Bernard Bertucci."

"Ah, Bertucci!" said Odo. "Yes, I had hoped that he might step forward in this time of need."

"Step forward? Oh, no, he is little interested in your predicament at the moment. I am here on my own, Holiness. God has seen fit to fill my purse after my earlier years of scratching scraps from the tables of others, I have deter-mined that I shall now return that gesture by helping you bribe your way into the Lateran Palace."

Struck by the baldness of her words and the manner in which she delivered them, Odo nodded without smiling. "For the good of the true Church," he said.

"No, not for the good of the true Church, nor even for your own benefit for that matter, Holiness." Then she gave Odo an odd look and tilted her head a bit. "You don't remember me, do you?"

Odo started to reply, then hesitated, running through his memory. "No," he finally said.

"I met you as a child once at Cluny while you were serving as Grand Prior," she said, her dark eyes piercing him. "I found you to be frightening. Then I met you again six years ago at Canossa after nearly freezing to death crossing the Alps. You frightened me also at that time."

The mention of nearly freezing in the Alps, Odo remembered her, but made no gesture of acknowledgment. Instead, he slid back in his seat a bit and put a hand to the side of his temple, recalling the details of that long forgotten encounter. Then nodding, he returned his hand to his lap as she continued.

"I came seeking assistance for my infant, an old woman, and a man named Fernando," she said, "but my baby and Fernando froze to death before reaching

Canossa; they are both buried there. I stated my case to you and Countess Mathilda, but doubting my intentions, you shunned me, as did the Countess. You know, as I look back, it would have taken so little for either of you to pull me from hopelessness and despair, but I never saw you after our conversation, and the Countess would have nothing to do with me until Vincento Balducci took me from her fortress."

Odo's neck began to show a slight trace of color as he shifted in his chair. "Your arrival at Canossa was a shock to us, Gran Signorina, and . . ."

"My name is Mala," she interrupted. "Please call me Mala, I am no more of a great Signorina than yourself. I am a poor Romani girl who once danced for a living."

"Very well, as you wish. I was saying, we were not prepared to hear such preposterous news as you delivered that day in Canossa. The reason you did not see me again is because I did as I said I would, I went immediately to Monte Cassino in search of the father of your child, who you claimed was Tristan de Saint-Germain."

"And?"

"I learned that you were telling the truth, much to my dismay. Tristan made no denial. Know this, he never knew that you were with child when he last saw you. Learning of the baby and its fate, he renounced his Benedictine vows before storming out of Monte Cassino in search of you. I was told later that he found you, but that you refused him. Now I am curious. You came here offering assistance in this business over the Lateran Palace, yet you stated you are not doing it for me, nor even for God. Why then are you considering such a thing?"

"For Tristan de Saint-Germain," she said without hesitation. "You see, though I both see and acknowledge the sheer futility of my feelings, I still love him more than life itself. I have loved him since we first met, though we were very young. I would never expect you to understand that; I myself don't even comprehend the possibility of such a thing, nor does Tristan. I have suffered in his absence nearly my entire life, and I suffer still.

"And though I've resented your pull on him since childhood, I know that you have been a guiding light in his life and that he loves you as a father. Therefore, I shall help you secure the Lateran Palace and Rome only because of my undying devotion to Tristan. I made a horrible misjudgment about Tristan years ago in Marseilles; I listened to others rather than rely on my own faith in him. That misjudgment cost me all hope of happiness, the life of my child, the life of my faithful friend Fernando, and gave rise to endless confusion and misery for the man I love above all else on this earth. As I was once told, the merciless hammer of God fell upon me though I did nothing more than love a man who loved me.

"And though this man was a monk, it was only by chance that he had fallen in as a child with reformist Benedictines such as yourself at the Cluny monastery after being abandoned by his mother. For centuries and centuries monks and priests have married and had children, and even now in much of Europe they still do. My misfortune and Tristan's misfortune is not God's law, but *Gregorian* law, which is a fabrication invented by overzealous men of recent history, such as yourself, who are so blinded by their own vision of God that they forbid love, or marriage, or family for the very servants of God, the clergy, even though God never made such demands on his own twelve apostles. Though men such as you insist that Tristan's time with me was illicit and sinful, it was the most joyful time of my life; the *only* joyful time of my life.

"I realize that due to this, he has chosen to return to the Church. It is all he knows . . . that is all you taught him. And he will remain faithful to that Church now, I suppose, though in his heart he knows the rest of his days will be tainted with regret and loneliness . . . and so will mine." Saying this, the firm resolve she had shown fell away as a single tear began to stream over her cheekbone and slowly work its way down her face to the corner of her mouth.

This touched Odo, as had her expression of love for Tristan. "In light of what you feel and what you believe," he said, his voice subdued, "it would be disingenuous of me to accept your offer of assistance, Signorina. Therefore I cannot possibly . . ."

"No, my gift stands, and you shall remain forever silent about its source," said Mala, standing to leave. "What I have shared with you today has been like a killing poison that I've harbored in my heart for six years now. By speaking my peace to you, I've finally shed the venom. With what has been given by others, my sizeable contribution will put you, after all these years, upon the Papal throne. And Holiness, you shall accept my gift if for no other reason, than an acknowledgment of what you have done to a small boy of seven who was placed in your care at the Benedictine monastery of Cluny many years ago." Then she paused a moment, and stared deep within Odo's eyes. "I ran into him recently by chance in Genoa," she said, with a touch of bitterness. "I tried to take him back from you, but he recalled his childhood. He was a boy when he came to you, and he never had a chance to be anything else but a reflection of yourself, a Benedictine monk out to stamp his own vision upon the world. I hope you are happy. Remember this, if the opportunity ever arises, and he slips from your grasp, I shall not hesitate to claim him again for my own." Mala turned then, and quietly left the room.

CHAPTER NINETY-FIVE

A DISCUSSION FOR HISTORY

As they sailed back to Italy, Tristan and Handel shared hour upon hour of discussion and dispute concerning their visit to Constantinople.

"I say no to Alexius," said Handel time and time again. "He supported Heinrich for years, his agents killed off our people, and he sent nearly half a million gold pieces to bribe Heinrich into attacking Rome simply to get Duke Guiscard and the Normans off his back when they invaded Byzantium. He doesn't deserve consideration in this matter!"

"Yes, did you not see the plight of those pilgrims at the infirmary and hospice of Hagia Sophia, Handel? Christians *must* have open access to the Holy Land and the city of Jerusalem without being molested, tortured, and killed."

"I have seen a hundred infirmaries, and Hagia Sophia is no different. It's full of the injured and the maimed. We have similar places throughout Italy, Germany, France filled with wounded from the wars against the Saracens in Spain and North Africa, and our own wounded in Italy from fighting Heinrich."

"There is a great difference, Handel, between the war-wounded and those who are killed and tortured for worshipping God. It is a matter of those *choosing* to fight as opposed to the innocent."

"Oh, so you suppose that the dead soldiers now moldering in their graves *chose* their profession? Ha, the knights and nobles perhaps, but what about the poor archers and footmen who are poorly armed and slain by the thousands and tens of thousands? No, they fight to provide a few morsels of bread to their families while the nobles fight over vast estates, territories, and loot."

"Handel, the children we saw at Hagia Sopia, did they not sear your very heart?"

"Oh, do *not* suppose that we lack mutilated children in our very own infirmaries and hospices of Italy, *innocently* caught in the tussle of war."

"You are correct to an extent, Handel, yet you still ignore the primary issue here, the sanctity of the Holy Land. It is the birthright of Christians to visit and follow the very steps of Jesus Christ within the Holy Land while he was upon this earth. Also, did you not pay attention to the Byzantine generals as they showed their maps and the vast loss of territory in Asia Minor and the Balkans? I respect the Arabs and the Turks far more than most westerners, as you well know, but my eyes have been opened on this trip, Handel. I am beginning to see for the first time an immediate threat to Christianity and our very way of life. It behooves us to do something here, Handel."

These conversations wrangled on day after day. The end result was typical of all political discussions, and that was that each man only entrenched himself deeper in his own philosophy.

As they landed in Naples, they were pleased to learn that King Heinrich was in full retreat in northern Italy, and equally pleased to hear that Pope Urban had recently taken possession of the Lateran Palace and Saint Peter's Basilica. From Naples they went by coach to Monte Cassino to report to Muehler, and were further surprised to learn that Muehler was going to accompany them to Rome as they relayed information acquired in Constantinople to the Pope. Since his ordeal and escape from England years before, Muehler had always refused to leave the sheltered confines of Monte Cassino Monastery. He did not wish to go out into public; even hiding his disfigured face behind the cover of his omnipresent veil.

When they arrived at the Lateran Palace, Odo was surrounded by at least a dozen ministers, Cardinals, and bureaucrats, all buzzing about trying to shoulder their way before the Pope. Greeting Muehler, Handel and Tristan, Odo immediately cleared the room and placed guards at the door.

"So many things going on all at once, it is dizzying," he said. "This business with Adelheid's divorce, Conrad's claim to the crown of Italy, our reclaiming of the Vatican, and now this mess in France."

"France?" said Tristan, as they took positions about the table. "Pray tell! Bad news?"

"Bad news, indeed," said Odo. "It seems the good King Philippe has taken his wandering erection a step further now, and fallen in love of all things."

"Eh?" said Handel. "In love? Was he not content dipping his wick everywhere he pleased? Now it has to be in *love*?"

"Yes, apparently so," said Odo. "He was smitten by Bertrade of Montfort, evidently, and lost his mind. He has *married* her."

"Bertrade of Montfort?" said Tristan, stunned. "Is she not the wife of Count Fulk of Anjou? What about Queen Bertha?"

"Yes, unfortunately, the French king has married a *married* woman, and we are trying to figure out how to handle this awkward business."

"'Tis a simple matter," said Tristan. "Bigamy is against the laws of both man and God. Philippe has long flouted his power by selling religious offices, acting with incessant promiscuity, and selling alliances as bribes. He is a disgrace. How is it that any cleric upon this earth would sanction such a marriage?"

"Easily," mused Muehler. "He's sold countless bishoprics and archbishoprics throughout his realm to the highest bidder. I dare say they were standing in line to accommodate Philippe."

"Exactly," said Odo. "Enough about Philippe, what about the bigger issue, Byzantium?"

As Tristan and Handel began to describe their visit to Constantinople and the request of Emperor Alexius, Odo and Muehler listened intently, frequently asking questions and exchanging thoughts. And as these four men conversed, they knew that the issue under discussion possessed significant implications, but they could never have guessed at that early juncture how monumental this discussion was, or that the impact of their words that day would leave its mark on history for centuries to come. Great events throughout history have often taken seed from such innocuous beginnings, and what begins as a simple conversation between men can unsuspectingly evolve into a watershed moment for the entire human race. And this is exactly what was occurring within the private meeting office of the Lateran Palace on this particular day.

Tristan and Handel conveyed their opposing positions on Emperor Alexius' request as Odo and Muehler picked each man's position apart. Tristan, being exponentially more eloquent and analytical than Muehler, carried the day and managed to convince both Muehler and Odo that a Muslim threat did, indeed, exist, and that this threat was growing. What especially impressed Muehler and Odo was the fact that Tristan was unmovable in his stance that Christian pilgrims were being molested by the Seljuq Turks, and that this abuse would worsen unless military action was taken in the form of a crusade, such as had been previously carried out in Tunis against the Moors.

Handel was equally vehement about avoiding entanglement in Alexius' conflict with the Turks, and felt that the Byzantines should be left to their own fate. "The Saracens, whether they be Moors, Arabians, or Turks, would not dare attack continental Europe again," he insisted, referring to their defeat by Charles Martel in the year 732 at Tours. "We are far, far too powerful!"

"They continue to fight in Spain despite the Reconquista," responded Tristan. "And never forget, they once controlled Sicily and Lower Italy until the Normans came, and now push west against Byzantium. It seems I have always said that the Saracens are a loose confederation of Islamists, what we must fear most is the possibility of them uniting one day. And I warn you, that time approaches. Best that we make a move before time becomes our enemy."

"The more I listen to you, Tristan, the more I agree," said Muehler. "The Holy Father has no money for such a venture, nor troops. Only because of the generosity of others did we manage to even get him here within the Lateran Palace. No, the cupboards are bare, I fear."

"He needs neither money nor troops," said Tristan.

This so confounded the other three that silence fell amidst the room as they exchanged looks, then stared simultaneously at Tristan.

"What the hell does that mean?" said Handel. "Analyzing your initial objections about Pope Urban getting involved in the Saracen incursions into Byzantium," said Tristan, "Alexius then resorted to making an issue about Christians retaking the Holy Land, but he has no interest in that, actually. Fundamentally, what he *really* wants is western mercenaries to throw against the Turks who are invading his borders." Then he looked at Odo and said, "Europe is full of dispossessed second sons of nobility, adventurers, and mercenaries. All you have to do is be the voice that *raises* this Christian army. With your voice, they will appear by the thousands, by the tens of thousands. The Papacy need not provide troops or money. Let the nobles and the knights finance their own venture into the East. But as they advance against the Turks, let them continue on to the Holy Land and reclaim it in the name of Christianity. In the process, they can claim Islamic territory, castles, and wealth, which is abundant to the east."

"Such a war as this," said Muehler, shaking his head with concern, "is well beyond the scope of what we undertook with our Italian expeditionary force in Tunis. Indeed, it is even beyond the scope of what is currently going on in Spain against the Moors, or even beyond the scope of our war against Heinrich here in Italy. We are talking about mobilizing an entire continent against another continent, an entire race against another race. There's never been such a war. It would be . . . devastating."

"If only you and Muehler could have been in Constantinople," Tristan said, looking at Odo in earnest. "If only you could have seen the military maps, spoken to the high clerics, or walked the hospice of the Hagia Sophia. Then you would . . ."

"Handel," interrupted Muehler, "you were there in Constantinople with Tristan, yet you don't share his passion over reinforcing Alexius. Why?"

"I agree with Tristan in that what we saw there was disturbing. Muehler, you said it best a moment ago. A war of this magnitude would be *devastating*. I've worked this bloody damned Investiture War for ten years now, and have had my fill. I've too often walked among the dead strewn about like cordwood, one atop the other, in the aftermath of battle, and *that* bothers me. I've also seen villages and towns set afire by the enemy, as well as by our own troops, and when towns burn, people burn. I've seen fields and crops laid to waste and ground salted, and when this occurs, starvation follows. I've seen the hordes of refugees freezing and starving along the roadside in winter, the elderly, women and children, and was able to do nothing to help. I'm sick of war, and a war such as Alexius proposes will be a butchering such as man has never witnessed before, nor endured. This may all sound odd coming from an assassin such as myself, but I am still, after all, a man of God." Then Handel fell silent.

The others fell silent also, momentarily losing themselves in personal reflection over Handel's words. Finally, Muehler looked over at Handel and said, "Thank you, Jurgen, your thoughts are sincerely appreciated." Then he turned to Tristan, who appeared touched by what Handel had said, and asked, "And how do you respond to these profound words by Handel."

"I cannot and will not dispute the ugliness of war, especially in the wake of Handel's sincere and heartfelt description of it," Tristan replied. "I more than anyone in this room have expressed concerns about violence and assassination within our own Benedictine operations. History is replete with great men and great institutions who failed to take decisive action at seminal moments, and who also ended up disappearing into the fog of history. There has never been a greater institution upon this earth than Christianity, and though I do not believe it is yet under direct assault, the moment is not far off. Failure to act now while the Turks, Moors, and Saracens are still disaggregated could well prove to be fatal. This is exactly what I told Duke-General Bertucci in North Africa, and having been to Byzantium, I feel even more strongly that Islamic power is on the rise and that eventually a great leader will appear in their midst and call for unification against the West.

"My concern is not for Emperor Alexius, but for the survival of Christianity itself, the right of common men to worship and follow their faith without fear of persecution. I ask you this, if the Turks take Byzantium, why would they stop at Constantinople? No invading horde has *ever* halted their advance in the face of success, only halted upon being repelled. Indeed, once Constantinople falls, the doors to the rest of the continent stand wide open."

CHAPTER NINETY-SIX

THE RISE OF URBAN II

After Pope Urban took possession of the Lateran Palace through his payment to the Governor of Rome, anti-pope Clement III retreated to the Castle Sant'Angelo on the right bank of the Tiber River. This massive, cylindrical edifice, which was originally the tomb of the Roman Emperor Hadrian, had been converted into a military fortress in 401 AD and sat adjacent to the Vatican itself. Many Gregorians insisted that Pope Urban oust the anti-pope from this stronghold, but realizing that Clement still had many supporters in Rome, Pope Urban decided to leave him there rather than risk rioting and revolt. As Urban expected, without support from Heinrich, Clement's authority and influence soon began to wane as Urban's, on the other hand, began to rise.

Noticing that King Heinrich's position in Italy was quickly weakening, Odo hastened to northern Italy to hold a council at Piacenza in the interest of peace and reform. His first order of business was to formalize the case of Queen Adelheid of Germany who had earlier fled to Mathilda's camp at Canossa, and make settlement on her accusations concerning the horrid sexual and spiritual misconduct of her husband. Her case was heard by the Pope and his high clerics with King Heinrich not being present, of course, nor even sending representatives or correspondence to defend himself. Consequently, Queen Adelheid was publicly declared innocent and absolved from any censure.

The next order of business was the case of King Philippe of France who had repudiated his wife, Queen Bertha, and married the younger Bertrade who was still legally married to Count Fulk of Anjou. Several French bishops had recognized this union. One bold cleric, the Archbishop of Lyons, had mustered the courage to excommunicate King Philippe for adultery and bigamy. Odo summoned both King Philippe and the Archbishop of Lyons to attend the Piacenza Council, but both failed to appear. Nevertheless, Odo and his hierarchy heard the evidence of the case, and in their final judgment, King Philippe was given a respite of sorts when the council decreed that they would give the French king time to reconsider his actions, remove Bertrade, and take back as his queen his legitimate wife, Bertha of Holland. The hapless Archbishop of Lyons was summarily suspended from office.

This absolutely incensed Tristan. "God in Heaven, Odo!" he complained bitterly in private. "You suspend the one honest man in France while catering to an adulterer and bigamist who openly steals the wife of another."

Odo shook his head and said, "Yes, this *adulterer* as you describe him happens to be the king of France, and having finally run Heinrich out of Italy, we do not wish to start yet another conflagration. Besides, I did not come to this decision alone. The council determined this outcome by vote. They felt that given some time, Philippe will see the error of his ways."

"What about the Archbishop of Lyons? Why in Heaven's name was he not given respite as well?"

"A show of deference to the king," replied Odo.

"Oh, deference to the king, even in the face of mortal sin!" cried Tristan, infuriated.

"Your altruism is overriding your common sense, Tristan," said Odo. "The Papacy is a spiritual office, granted, but you fail to understand that it is equally a political office, and politics require compromises at times, distasteful as they may be. I am not pleased with this decision. Think about it, we have graciously given Philippe a second chance to reconsider his position."

"I am less concerned about Philippe than I am about the Archbishop of Lyons," insisted Tristan. "Oh, you have disappointed me, Odo."

"It is not the first time, I suspect, Tristan, nor shall it be the last. You display the impatience of youth. This matter is not over yet, and in the end the good Archbishop of Lyons could yet be reinstated. Do not abandon me over this business with Philippe, for tomorrow we face a much more serious matter."

"Yes, I know, the delegation sent by Emperor Alexius from Constantinople," said Tristan, shedding his exasperation a bit. "Which direction will the Cardinals and Archbishops sway?"

"Only time will tell."

Tristan nodded, then set his gaze directly upon Odo. "And would you go against them, Odo, if their stand opposes what we believe must be done?"

"It is a sensitive time, Tristan, so at the moment I could not say. My papacy is gaining its feet after six years of war and chaos, and it would not be wise to charge again into the fire so quickly. As things suddenly and unexpectedly fell into place for us these past six months, we could just as easily knock them back out of kilter, eh?"

"Yes, Odo . . . very easily," Tristan replied, trying to shove his discontent over the impurity of politics aside.

That next morning in Piacenza the air was filled with expectation as Patriarch Nicholas III and his delegation from Constantinople came before the Council. Word had already spread throughout Italy about the alleged plight of Byzantium, and as during the unfolding of any volatile debate, there were people on both sides of the aisle.

Nicholas delivered an impassioned plea on behalf of Byzantium as cardinals, archbishops, and bishops huddled together in their seats throughout his delivery, exchanging comments and thoughts. Nicholas' early remarks provided a brief political backdrop to the conflict between the Seljuq Turks and the

Byzantines. Then Nicholas moved into Catholic theology, taking great care not to touch so much the differences of the Roman Catholic Rite and the Eastern Catholic Rite as to emphasize the commonalities. "Oh, the gulf between Rome and Constantinople is but a matter of semantics!" proclaimed Nicholas. "In the end we are all Catholics . . . we are all Christians . . . we are all faithful followers of Christ . . . and the Saracens are infidels!"

Grasping that the nodding and gesturing of the audience swung in his favor with this statement, Nicholas then launched into an emotional tirade about the plight of Christian pilgrims suffering at the hands of merciless Seljuq Turks. Providing horrific descriptions of torture, maiming, and delimbing, his voice rose and fell, then rose again and fell again, with the consummate skill of a master storyteller as listeners sat on the edge of their seats, some even dissolving into quiet tears while others broke into open sobbing.

Handel was sitting next to Odo and Tristan as Nicholas wove his tales, and after some time of listening to the Patriarch, Handel looked at Tristan with disgust. "Oh, he so greatly exaggerates the number of injured you and I encountered at the Hagia Sophia hospice!" he grumbled. "He's worse than a merchant of false relics!"

"Silence!" hissed Tristan, throwing an elbow to Handel's ribs. "He is fighting for the very life blood of Byzantium, Handel, and possibly the future of Christianity. Do you not see the significance of this moment?" Then, after glancing at Odo who was so deeply engrossed in the Patriarch's speech that he appeared entranced, Tristan looked out over the crowd and determined that there would be little dispute over assisting the Byzantines by the end of the day.

Within the hour, as Patriarch Nicholas surrendered the floor, disagreement did arise from certain quarters. The financial minds of Italy's Catholic hierarchy dissented on the grounds of financial shortfalls already being suffered by their bishoprics as well as by the Vatican itself. Also, many of the older clerics who throughout their lives had viewed Byzantium as the false Catholic model, could not bring themselves to the point of joining hands with Constantinople. Patriarch Nicholas had set the younger clerics afire, and they made their enthusiasm known by calling down, shouting, and rudely whistling at the naysayers. And though the warmongering noblemen and knights present were not allowed to vote on the ecclesiastical affairs of the Council of Piacenza, they too loudly voiced their support of Patriarch Nicholas' plea for help against the Turks, and some of them even began to issue threats and jostle about those who questioned the stance.

It was decided by the end of the Council of Piacenza, then, that Pope Urban would go forth across the continent of Europe to perform the greatest mission in the history of the Catholic Church since the days of the apostles themselves. He would sound the trumpet and raise a hue and cry to the valiant nobles and knights of Western Christianity to enlist their support and their arms in a blessed crusade against Islam, and inspire them to march east to reclaim the Holy Land and the sacred city of Jerusalem.

In addition the Pope would send scores of couriers, legates, and orators to spread this message throughout Italy, Germany, England, and especially France where it was decided that the Pope should focus his greatest efforts.

"Travel northern Italy for me, Tristan," Odo said afterwards, "and spread our message with all your heart. Then, cross the Alps and pave my way in France. Let them know I am coming. Let them heed the trumpet call of Christianity. I will meet you there in Clermont, France then, in November, where I shall call the greatest ecclesiastical synod in the history of France. And while there, I shall also settle this matter of King Philippe and his bigamist marriage to Bertrade de Montfort if he continues to refute his rightful wife, Bertha of Holland."

CHAPTER NINETY-SEVEN

RETURN TO GENOA

Thus the great period of Christian oration within Western Europe began as the most persuasive and inspirational speakers that the Church could pluck from within their midst were unleashed upon the continent, spreading messages of fear, horror, and Christian destiny amongst the masses. And it mattered little to the spellbound crowds of Europe that nearly none of these messengers had ever been near the Holy Land, nor Byzantium for that matter. Nor did it matter that these harbingers of war were poorly educated about Saracens, Moors, Turks, the Koran, or the tenants of Islam itself. What mattered to the listeners was the lurid images these speakers conjured in their tales of Seljuq horror, and that Saracens were dark, foreign, and ungodly.

The talk of a holy crusade against the Saracen quickly spread with the inflammatory rage of wildfire throughout Italy and France, then extended south to Spain and west to England, even preceding at times the actual arrival of legates and messengers of the Church. As noblemen gathered at social functions, religious feast days, and formal events, the only topic of interest was the impending destruction of Byzantium at the hands of the Saracens unless knights from the west boldly made the arduous journey eastward to pull their fellow Christians from the fire. These conversations also centered on the fabulous wealth of those lands to the east, and the possibility of taking them over as prizes for doing the Lord's labor. The heathen enemy was termed as the *Saracens*, and no differentiation was made between the Moors, the Turks, or the actual Saracens who had fallen to the sword of the Seljuk Turks decades earlier. And indeed, this imaginary war began to fire the hearts and souls of every man in the west, even the dispossessed peasants and the poor who envisioned themselves dropping their farm chores and charging to war with spades and pitchforks in hand to take back the Holy Land in the name of Christendom.

Tristan quickly became one of most arousing of the Pope's messengers. He was by his very nature generally calm, rationale, and disciplined in presentation, which is why he had become such an extraordinary diplomat over time. Not even knowing from where this inner fire originated, he came alive with the Holy Spirit and delivered one impassioned speech after another throughout northern Italy, arousing enthusiastic masses of listeners and gaining their rabid support for a war against the Saracens. Beginning far to the east in Trieste, he moved westward to Venice, then to Verona, from there to Milan, south to Turin, and finally to Genoa where his mission in Italy would end and he would then travel to France to prepare the way for Pope Urban's tour of southern France and eventual Council of Clermont.

As the furor in Italy grew over the Saracen threat, Duke-General Bertucci found himself becoming the object of military adoration in Genoa for reasons of his earlier successes against the Moors in North Africa. To his delight, he began to enjoy the revival of his exploits in Tunis as citizens related and exaggerated tales of Bertucci's exploits there though they generally knew nothing whatsoever of the campaign. Nevertheless, the old general had *beaten the Saracens,* and was held up as a shining example of what the western knight could do against the heathens. Many even insisted that the octogenarian come out of retirement and lead Italian forces to the Holy Land. These miscreants, of course, had no knowledge of Tristan de Saint-Germain's involvement in the crusade of Tunis, nor that without his help Bertucci would have bungled the entire effort. Bertucci knew, so he was quite happy to greet and welcome Tristan upon his arrival at the gates of Genoa. "Ah, lad," he cried, "such happy days that have befallen Christianity! And with you at Pope Urban's helm, we shall put these Saracens in their place!"

Mala and Duxia had come along also with Bertucci to greet Tristan. Mala embraced him, lingering there a moment, then looked up into his face and smiled.

"Tristan, you look more handsome than I've ever seen," she whispered, "and your eyes are so bright with purpose. You are content, then, that your Odo de Lagery has taken over Rome and ousted the anti-pope from the Vatican?"

"Yes," Tristan replied, his expression illuminating in Mala's presence again, despite their last argument. The fact that she had shown up with Bertucci told him that she had put their vitriolic exchange aside, and now wished to see him again. "The generosity of others bought his entry into the Lateran Palace, and since then Pope Urban has only risen!"

"So I've heard," Mala replied dryly. "Excellent, I am happy that your vision for Odo de Lagery has finally come to pass."

During this exchange, Duxia stood to the side, staring at Tristan in his monk's garb with complete disdain. And though her mouth and lips were moving about in little spasms as though she was about to speak at any moment, she held her tongue; to do otherwise would have invited a tongue lashing from Mala.

After a brief exchange of conversation outside the gates of the city, Tristan had his coach follow the others to Bertucci's estate where it was agreed that Tristan would spend the week there while in town addressing the throngs of eager Genoans who had already received word of his spellbinding oratory skills. It was also determined that Mala would coordinate Tristan's transportation from one speaking venue to the next, and as Bertucci was enjoying his own notoriety within his home city, the old general would actually introduce Tristan to the people of Genoa at each engagement.

"You've already become somewhat of a legend here in Genoa," grinned Bertucci "They've been awaiting you with great anticipation!"

"Yes," said Mala, "and it is with such pride that I hear your name bandied about the streets, Tristan. They say you are the very heartbeat of Pope Urban himself, and that you will follow in his footsteps as Holy Father of the Roman Catholic Church one day."

"Oh, let us hope not," Tristan replied with humility. "I have no wish to carry the crosses he bears. I very much lack that hard edge that is required to effectively wear the tiara and red cope."

That next morning notices were posted throughout Genoa identifying times and locations for Tristan's speaking engagements during his week at Genoa, and one day later he began. Speaking from wagon beds, within market places, squares, and cathedrals, people thronged by the hundreds at first, then by the thousands to hear and see this celebrated First Counsel of the Pope who had become so lauded. "He was called the Wonder of Cluny when but seven years old!" people in the know related to others. "Ay, and he stood upon the ramparts as a child with Pope Gregory himself as King Heinrich did his penance in the snow and ice of Canossa so long ago!" said others. "Yes, and even as a boy he served as papal ambassador to Pope Gregory and his successor, our blessed Desiderius! Indeed, God himself has sent this young saint down to us to warn of the impending Saracen threat!"

Tristan's speeches drew such increasing numbers that by midweek those engagements that had been scheduled within cathedrals were forced to move outside. Mala accompanied him each day, as did Bertucci and the ever silent Duxia, whose sullen eyes seemed to darken even more with each passing day. Mala and Tristan also spent much time together in the evening, sharing conversation, dinner, and laughter. And though they shared many an intimate moment and touch, they both knew that their love for each other would now remain in check, regardless of the irresistible pull at their hearts. It was a wonderful week for both of them as each basked in the warm, comforting company of the other.

Duxia kept her distance as instructed by Mala, but at the moment Tristan finished delivering his final speech in Genoa, she caught him alone as Mala and Bertucci departed in search of the coach. "Oh, you slithering serpent of foul intent!" she hissed. "My prophecy appears to be slipping up behind you right onto your very shoulders, eh, Saint-Germain?"

With all that had transpired over recent years, Tristan had long since managed to set his trepidations over Duxia aside. As her dark eyes raked over his features, he gave her little consideration. "So, old hag, you continue to skulk about, like those filthy insects creeping about in the dark, feeding on the decayed underbelly of things rotting in the night. Peter the Hermit was right about you, you are a bitter, poisonous spider who sees no good on this earth, and wishes no good for its people. What is this nonsense you spew about your prophecy?"

"Oh, long ago in your mother's blood I foresaw your destiny the moment your bright, evil eyes popped forth from her womb and cast their deadly shine towards this old woman. You were born with the curse of death, destruction, and doom for others. And even as you so eloquently spoke within the market square today, I saw you luring others to their grave with such silken finesse, like the Judas goat leading his own flock to slaughter, tinkling his little bell to make them follow all the way to their destination, only to fall prey to the ax."

Tristan sneered and shook his head. "So colorful, your analogies, Duxia . . . or should I say *Mielikki*, Finnish sorceress of the deep northern wood? Yes, you are a sorceress just as Peter the Hermit charges, and I pray each day that Mala will one day be free of your witch's grasp."

"Don't speak to me of Mala, Saint-Germain, for she's mine. I love her and she loves me. You could have had her once, but you threw her away, destroyed her, like you're doing now to these people all over Italy who you summon to war."

"You know nothing of this matter with Byzantiun," said Tristan, his neck reddening at the juncture of his neck and monk's cowl.

"I know enough to see that you preach war, Saint-Germain, a war beyond all other wars we've ever seen on this blighted earth. I know that you cast one portion of the world against another, one breed of man against another, and one faith against the other . . . and I know that this earth doesn't contain enough graveyards to hold such infinite piles of the dead as shall arise in the aftermath of such a war as you preach!" Then she started to turn and walk away, but she hesitated and gave Tristan a final look. "I will ask it one final time, and then you shall hear it from me no more . . . what is it you want, boy, and how many men must die as you strive to seek it?"

CHAPTER NINETY-EIGHT

FAREWELL

On his final evening in Genoa, Tristan dined with Bertucci and Mala at Bertucci's estate. "Such a passionate speaker you are!" crowed Bertucci. The recent attention he had been receiving and all the talk of war had him in high spirits. "By God, I nearly thought the people this afternoon were going to run home, gather their arms and start marching this very night to the Holy Land! Dammit, were I not so decrepit, I'd lead them! Truly, lad, I've never seen people so riled up in my life!"

"It is easy, I suppose," Tristan replied with a smile, "to show courage from the curb of your home when the war is a continent away, eh, General?" Tristan, too, was in high spirits after his speaking engagement, and just now descending from that euphoria that seizes one after being hailed by an appreciative audience.

Mala was not as enthused as the two men, and as she quietly ate, she offered little to the conversation despite frequent prompting by both Tristan and Bertucci. Finally, when she had completed her meal, she stood and said, "It's been a long day, a long week actually, so I'll take my leave."

"So soon?" said Tristan, visibly disappointed. "I leave for France in the morning, Mala, and will not be back to Genoa for quite some time."

Mala looked at him sadly, and nodded, then said, "You may accompany me home in my coach, Tristan, if Bernard doesn't mind, and when we arrive there, my coachman will bring you back. I would enjoy that. Bernard, do you object?"

"Of course not!" Bertucci replied. "It has indeed been a long week and I was trying to figure out how to politely excuse myself so I might retire for the evening."

As Tristan and Mala entered her coach, a soft rain began to fall. "Ah, the rain again," Mala sighed. "It seems that every time we part, the rain comes. First in Marseilles, then the last time you were at my house." She looked at him, then, and lowered her eyes. "I hope you're not still angry at me about all that."

"No," said Tristan, barely able to see her in the dim light of late dusk. "I have kicked myself a thousand times for leaving in the middle of the night as I did. It was childish."

"I said some harsh things to you that night, about Odo de Lagery and the Black Monks. You know, Tristan, I don't wish to anger you, but I meant every word I said, and to this day believe everything I told you. I didn't mean it to be hurtful."

"Perhaps so, but . . ."

"No, no, no, we aren't going to dig it all up again, Tristan. I've been distraught all day, and we're not going to make each other cross on your last night here."

"I noticed that you didn't appear happy this morning, and that you've been silent most of the day."

"Undoubtedly, because of you. I've always felt like this when I know you're about to leave. And this time, with this business in Byzantium and the Holy Land, God only knows when you'll return, or even if you will return." Then she put her hand to her forehead and sighed. "Every time you leave, Tristan, it's as though I know I'll never see you again . . . and my heart can scarcely bear such a burden."

Tristan, sitting across from her, shuffled in his seat a moment. "I know," he then said.

"You know?" she said.

"Yes, the same thing occurs to me. Every time I look at you, Mala, I wonder what turn we might have made years ago. Every time we have to say goodbye, I know that I shall miss you dearly and sorrow crushes me with its weight of defeat. And when you are gone, I think of you constantly."

Mala moved across the coach and took a seat beside Tristan, grasping his arm. "If what you say is true, then tell me how you kept your distance that night on the patio as I was dancing? I was prepared to give myself to you—no conditions, no expectations—just you and me alone in the privacy of my estate." Then she placed his arm around her shoulders and slid her chin beneath his. "We are alone again, Tristan, in this coach. The curtains are closed and the world sees nothing." Then she reached up and kissed him on the mouth, a long passionate kiss like the ones she had given him in Marseilles as they hungrily shared their bodies night after night.

Tristan did not pull away, but returned the kiss, and held onto her tightly, as though she might slip from his grasp at any moment. He kissed her several times, each kiss becoming more urgent than the last. Then, slowly, he withdrew, and Mala saw him cross himself in the dim light of a passing street lantern.

Confused, she returned her chin beneath his and said, "So now you pray again?" Her tone was more saucy than angry. "Very well then, I shall be content to have you hold me close until the coach reaches its destination. Can you at least give me *that*?"

"Of course," said Tristan. "I need to feel your touch, Mala, and I need to know that your heart is mine."

Acknowledging this, she pulled the coach curtain aside and yelled to the driver, "Don't go immediately home. Make the long loop of the harbor and the town square five times!"

"Yes, Signorina!" the driver replied.

Mala then nestled back into Tristan's embrace. "So, you do love me then, smart boy?" she said.

"Yes," Tristan replied, "more than you could ever understand, I fear, or grasp. And though I shall not take your flesh as other men take the flesh of their women, I love you, Mala, beyond life itself. There is one thing, if I have learned nothing else, we never know what the future holds. Perhaps one day things will . . ."

Here he stopped, and though Mala would have liked him to finish, there really was no need; in her mind, she knew what he was going to say. "Yes, perhaps one day . . ." she echoed.

CHAPTER NINETY-NINE

A GATHERING IN FRANCE

Leaving Genoa, Tristan and a small delegation traversed the Alps and moved into central and southern France, spreading word of the impending crusade against the Saracens and the approaching arrival of Pope Urban II from Rome. Odo de Lagery had been well known throughout France since his days as Grand Prior at Cluny. Crossing the Alps, he enjoyed a wildly receptive welcome from his native Frenchmen. He made public speeches within a number of large cities, and arrived in Clermont, France on November 15th, where he was joined by his First Counsel, Tristan de Saint-Germain. This meeting had been highly publicized throughout France, and was promoted as a hugely significant synod where Pope Urban would lay out his full ecclesiastical agenda to the people of the province of Auverge.

Word of a call to arms against the Saracens had filtered across the Alps from Italy well in advance of Tristan's delegation to France, but the work of Tristan and his delegation as they spread from one province to another ensured that all France was aware that this and other important topics would be broached by Pope Urban at the Council of Clermont, including the situation with King Philippe's illegal marriage to Bertrade of Montfort. Just as in Italy, it was the topic of the Saracens that fueled the imagination of the public. Tristan and his fellow legates, therefore, had little problem arousing the crowds.

Of all those speaking on behalf of Pope Urban, none could match the fervor of that master of oratory, Peter the Hermit of Amiens, who decided on his own that he would represent the Pope's cause against Islam. Embracing Urban's call to arms, he rode tirelessly from city to city astride his small donkey, preaching his personal vision of what Christians should do in the face of this heathen threat from the East, which to him was for everyone to abandon life in France and march immediately to the Holy Land. Everywhere he appeared he spread hatred for the Saracens and love for Christianity, often inciting violent riots that careened out of control. As there were no Saracens in France for Peter's mobs to abuse, they often transferred their anger over the Saracens onto the Jews of France for some reason, burning down their homes and shops and driving them from town. Undeterred by such misguided reactions from his followers, the Hermit ardently continued to preach against Islam. "Oh, abandon your farms, abandon your cities and your crafts in the name of the Lord!" he would cry entering every new city. "Take to the roads, march eastward to the Holy Land and defeat the Saracen in the name of God!" And incredibly, as he slowly made his way to Clermont for the purpose of listening to Pope Urban speak on the topic of this holy crusade, hundreds of peasants began to abandon their farms and villages and take to the road behind him. By the time the Hermit gained Clermont, a rabble of over a thousand impoverished men, women, and children followed in his wake.

Countess Mathilda and General Padule had also crossed the Alps to attend the Council of Clermont, as did Guillaume and the Danes.

"Such a gathering I have never seen!" proclaimed Orla as they maneuvered the crowded roads of Clermont now choked with wagons, coaches, military contingents, caravans, people of foot, on horseback and mule, all coming to see and hear Pope Urban II of Rome, the Holy Father of Christianity.

"Ja, Father! 'Tis like a grand circus watching all these people!" cried Hroc, who found great entertainment watching the steady flow of humanity clogging the road ahead. He had also noticed the extraordinary number of pretty young French girls lining the road and his eyes were following one as he said this.

"Ho, there, Hroc!" cried Orla, "What are you staring at, boy?"

Turning red, Hroc quickly took his gaze off the girl he had been eyeing ahead of him on foot, and gave his father a toothy grin. "Nothing!" he said, sheepishly.

"He's looking at that little French pastry to his side!" snorted Crowbones, loud enough for the girl to hear.

The girl looked at Crowbones a moment, then looked over at Hroc who was purple with embarrassment and pretending that he had done nothing. The girl smiled and waved her hand in a friendly arc of greeting, which in turn quickly brought a smile to Hroc's face.

"Ho!" bellowed Orla, "FiveHands is growing up, Crowbones!"

"J-ja," stammered Guthroth, not wishing to be left out of the banter. "F-FiveHands has a w-woman!"

As the date of the Council approached, the availability of overnight accommodations within Clermont quickly disappeared and tent cities began to appear around the entire perimeter of Clermont itself. Many of the aristocrats, foreseeing such a development, came prepared and began to set up extravagant camps outside the city walls. They also, of course, instructed their guards to keep the less fortunate a good distance away. The town burghers, craftsmen, and merchants, consequently, were forced to set their tents and campsites further beyond the city walls. These people in turn were offended by the rabble that Peter the Hermit had brought to Clermont, and forced them to find shelter in the surrounding woods as they had no tents and were poorly provisioned, which caused many of them to beg and steal.

The actual Council of Clermont began on November 19th and was to extend until November 29th. In convoking this meeting of three hundred high clerics from all over France, Urban urged the three hundred bishops and abbots he summoned to bring with them the prominent lords of their provinces, thus turning this council into a mixed synod of ecclesiastics and laymen of the Catholic Church.

Although one of the major issues to be discussed was Pope Urban's call to arms against the Saracens on behalf of Byzantium and the Holy Land, there were many other topics to be discussed, the first of which was the administration and enforcement of Benedictine reform, whose origin was rooted in the Black Monks of Cluny Monastery in Burgundy, France, the very monastery where Tristan and Guillaume had been sent as young boys by their mother Asta in 1073. It must be remembered that clerical concubinage, promiscuity, and marriage were still widespread throughout much of Europe at this time, especially among non-Benedictine orders of monks and priests. The discussion on the topic of celibacy and chastity for clergymen, therefore, often grew heated. Embracing the rigid reforms laid out by Pope Gregory after his ascendency to the Papacy in 1073, Pope Urban refused to veer from the path of Gregory's stringent reforms, and demanded that all Catholic clergymen adhere to these reforms.

The next issue to be settled was the matter of King Philippe who had repudiated his wife, Queen Bertha of Holland, for being too fat, and in 1092 had married Bertrade of Montfort despite the fact that she was already married to Count Fulk of Anjou. King Philippe had been excommunicated by the Archbishop Hugh of Lyons in 1094 for adultery and bigamy, but Pope Urban had temporarily rescinded that excommunication at the Council of Piacenza, and subsequently suspended Archbishop Hugh of Lyons from office. As the Council of Clermont neared, King Philippe had still refused to take back his rightful wife, and remained married to Bertrade of Montfort. Taking a bold stand at Clermont, Pope Urban reversed his earlier judgment and proclaimed the formal excommunication of the French King, which greatly pleased Tristan and restored in him much faith in both Odo de Lagery and the Gregorian Church itself. It must be remembered that Philippe, although the King of France, was neither the most wealthy nor the most powerful aristocrat in France, nor did he possess most of the actual geographic landspace of France. His opponents in both the Church and among the French aristocracy, therefore, were well pleased by Pope Urban's excommunication of the errant king, especially the southern nobles. Pope Urban did stipulate that King Philippe's excommunication would be withdrawn if Philippe would denounce his illegal marriage and return to his lawful wife, Queen Bertha.

It was not until November 28th, the next to the last day of the Council of Clermont, that Pope Urban was scheduled to address the issue of the Saracens, Byzantium, and reclamation of the Holy Land for Christianity. This, of course, was the subject that had most captured the imagination of those who had traveled to listen to the Pope, especially the nobles and the knights. Furthermore, this was the only portion of the Council of Clermont that had been declared open to the public. It was originally scheduled to take place within the grand Romanesque cathedral of Clermont, but the crowds had swollen to such proportions that the session had to be moved to an open field outside the city gates.

As preparations were being made to hastily construct an outdoor pavilion for the Pope in the meadow to the east of the city gates, Tristan and Guillaume made their way toward the masses that were already gathering there.

"Never seen a crowd this big and so charged with anticipation," said Guillaume, "or so unified in spirit."

"All of Europe is uniting," said Tristan, "which is difficult to comprehend in light of all the bloodshed, feuding, the Investiture War, the in-fighting within England, Normandy, and Flanders." Then, gazing at a small rise in the distance overlooking the pavilion area, he pointed to it. "Look there, Guillaume, knights wearing opposing heraldry standing side by side. Who would have ever thought to see such a sight?"

As they continued walking, they soon came about a large mass of human rabble gathered to the west of the speaking pavilion. Appalled at the condition of these people, Tristan began to converse with several of them in an effort to inquire about their origin. "We've followed the Hermit of Amiens here from all over France," came the reply.

"The Hermit of Amiens?" said Tristan. "*Peter the Hermit*?"

"Yes, he told us that we must . . ."

"Ho there, lad!" a loud voice interrupted, as a short, squatty man appeared from within the knot of paupers, wearing simple hair shirt and trousers, no shoes, his hair disheveled as though he had been living in the wild. It was the Hermit. "God's bells! Everything's unfolding as I foretold," he cried, his eyes glazed, his hands raised high above his head. Then he tilted his head as his eyes grew wide and he pointed skyward. "Oh, you who have doubted me these years! Now do you admit that the Lord speaks to me directly? I prophesized that Odo de Lagery would wear the Pope's crown years ago. God told me so. I told you that things would go poorly if Desiderius became the Pope, and how dearly did the Church pay! And even you, Tristan de Saint-Germain, I told you when you were a young boy that you'd sow the seeds of war one day, and that day has arrived! 'Tis *you* who went to Constantinople. 'Tis you who came back and spread the word, just as a man sows the spring seed! 'Tis you who turned the Pope's ear and laid the groundwork for this great mobilization of Christian soldiers that shall soon go to the Holy Land. *So,* Tristan de Saint-Germain, what do you say now about old Peter the Hermit, eh?"

Tristan considered Peter's words a moment while Guillaume peered at the Hermit, repulsed. "Is this not the strange little fellow that we encountered at Lord Truffault's manor years ago?" whispered Guillaume to Tristan.

Tristan had already begun to answer the Hermit. "As always with you, Peter," he said, "there was enough truth in what you prophesized to startle and confuse. I am still not as convinced about your own divinity as you are. Tell me, what in God's creation is this mass of people you have assembled here? They appear hungry, ill clothed, and destitute."

"The army of God, boy! Nearly a thousand, and by the time this crusade launches, it will be fifty thousand, or a hundred thousand!"

"Army?" said Guillaume, shaking his head in disbelief. "Surely you jest, either that or you've gone mad. No, this is no army."

"Indeed," agreed Tristan. "These people can scarcely care for themselves let alone travel across the continent and face the Turks!"

"Oh, the inspiration of God will drive them forward and sustain them, as will prayer, and they shall overcome the heathen horde and retake the Holy Land!"

"God in Heaven," Tristan whispered, pulling the Hermit aside as those around them were intently listening to every word being said, "have you lost your mind? This crusade is a military venture, not a pilgrimage! These people can't fight . . . they'll only get in the way."

"No! No!" the Hermit shouted, moving Tristan aside with a sweep of the hand. "This is no day for naysaying! I'll not listen to such talk, especially from you who have doubted me for so many years, even in the face of truth after truth that has come about just as prophesized!" Then the Hermit walked away, talking to the sky with gestures of his head and hands."

Guillaume and Tristan regarded each a moment, then beheld the pitiful gathering of dispossessed people before them. "Surely these people understand that he's basically leading them to slaughter?" shrugged Guillaume.

Before Tristan could answer, a young boy of about eleven who was listening tugged at Guillaume's arm. "No," he said, "you are wrong, Sir, for God speaks to the Hermit directly, and has told him that we shall prevail."

CHAPTER ONE HUNDRED

THE CRY TO ARMS

As Pope Urban and his hosting entourage of French archbishops arrived at the pavilion, the crowd fell still, knowing that what they were about to witness would be a monumental moment for the entirety of Christendom. And as Pope Urban began to speak, nary a single person moved, nor even whispered.

"Oh, race of Franks from across the mountains," he began with immediate passion, "race chosen and beloved by God as shines forth in your very many works set apart from all nations by the situation of your country, as well as by your Catholic faith and the honor of your Holy Church! To you our discourse is and for you our exhortation is intended! We wish you to know what a grievous cause has led us to your country, what peril is threatening you and all the faithful.

"From the confines of Jerusalem and Constantinople, a horrible tale has gone forth, namely that a race from the kingdom of the Persians, an accursed race, a race utterly alienated from God has invaded the lands of those Christians and has depopulated them by the sword, pillage, and fire. They destroy the altars, after having defiled them with their uncleanness. They circumcise the Christians, and the blood of the circumcision they either spread across the altars or pour into the vases of the baptismal font. When they wish to torture people by a base death, they perforate their navels, and dragging forth the extremity of the intestines, bind it to a stake . . . and what shall I say of the abominable rape of women? To speak of it is worse than to be silent!

"Let the deeds of your ancestors move you and incite your minds to manly achievement, glory and greatness of your kings who have destroyed the kingdoms of the pagans. Travel the road to the Holy Sepulchre, wrest that land from the wicked race, and subject it to yourselves accordingly; undertake this journey to the remission of your sins, with the assurance of the imperishable glory of the Kingdom of Heaven!"

When Pope Urban had said these things and many other things exhorting Christians to take up the sword against the Saracens, he ended by proclaiming, "Dieu le veut! God wills it!"

The massive crowd, so utterly inflamed by his descriptions of Saracen torture and the defiling of Christian icons, surged forward and as one body echoed his call, "Dieu le veut! God wills it!" And as this deafening cry reverberated up and down the open meadow, ten thousand knights raised their banners and struck their shields with their swords, creating such a clamor that the ground shook and the pavilion on which Pope Urban stood began to quake.

CONCLUSION

And thus, on November 28th in the Year of Our Lord 1095 at Clermont, France, began the Holy Crusades, a bloody and merciless war of slaughter and intolerance that was to extend over the next two hundred years; the repercussions of which are still felt even now, a thousand years later.

The question is often posed: Is man inherently good, or is man inherently evil? The truth is, the character of man is not static, it is ever-changing and responds to time, circumstance, and environment, and is therefore continually crossing and recrossing the boundaries of right and wrong. In other words, the raging currents of forces far beyond man's control are incessantly twisting and pulling at man's character, and men alternate between withering and holding strong, regardless of level of courage, integrity, or altruism. So even good men with good intentions can unwittingly fall by the wayside, as evidenced by the many diverse characters within this story.

To illuminate these characters and the fate-filled impact of the Council of Clermont, let us begin with Odo de Lagery. As Pope Urban II, he was to go down in history as the catalyst of the Holy Crusades and as one of the greatest pontiffs in the entire history of the Roman Catholic Church. As for la Gran Contessa Mathilda, great supporter of the Gregorian papacies, following King Heinrich's complete withdrawal from Italy in 1097, she recovered all of her territories and reigned uncontested as the *Grande Dame* of Italian politics until her death in 1115 of gout. Her death signaled the end of an era in Italian politics and marked the rise of the new era of city-states in northern Italy. Interestingly, her tomb was removed from Tuscany in the seventeenth century and moved to the Vatican where it now lies in Saint Peter's Basilica.

Losing his struggle in Italy, King Heinrich IV denounced his son, Conrad, as heir and named in his place the younger son, Heinrich V. Conrad slipped into political insignificance and died in Florence in 1101 at the young age of twenty-seven. King Heinrich IV's younger son also rebelled against his father and in 1104 defeated him and had him imprisoned in the castle of Bockelheim where he was obliged to swear that he had unjustly persecuted Pope Gregory VII and illegally named Clement III as the Pope. The fifty-six-year-old king escaped in 1106, raised an army against his son and defeated him at Lorraine in March of that same year, and died six months later. His son, Heinrich V, succeeded him despite having been defeated in Lorraine, and he also made peace with la Gran Contessa Mathilda in Italy, showing her every sign of dignity and respect.

Pope Urban named French Bishop Adhémar of Le Puy as the actual leader of the First Crusade instead of selecting any of the celebrated nobles or military figures who sought this position since the Pope considered this venture to be, first and foremost, a spiritual venture, not a military venture. He selected Tristan de Saint-Germain as his personal legate for this crusade, whose responsibility it was to document the details of the advance eastward and the war itself. Post war, whether successful or unsuccessful, Tristan was then to provide a full account of the entire expedition to the Vatican. Odo also expected to appoint Tristan to the position of archbishop despite his young age, then shortly thereafter advance him into the College of Cardinals where in the future he could eventually position himself for election to the papacy itself.

Guillaume and the Danes, with the blessing of la Gran Contessa, decided that they would accompany Tristan on the Holy Crusade. Orla, Crowbones, Guthroth, and Hroc all sailed east to Constantinople, then rode and fought their way overland with the French Crusaders toward the Holy Land, but they would never actually reach Jerusalem.

Faith, it seems, held an entirely different destiny for each of these valiant warriors . . . as would soon be prophesized by the desiccated bones of a long dead raven hanging aoubt the neck of Crossbones within a tiny leather pouch.

Duxia de Falaise died one week after the Council of Clermont, and on her deathbed in Genoa, with her final breath, she pleaded for Mala to vow that she would free herself once and for all from the pull of Tristan de Saint-Germain. As much as Mala loved the irascible old Duxia, she refused to lie to her, even as she lay dying. Two months later, Mala discovered the route to be taken by the French Crusaders and anticipated arrival in Constantinople. She boarded a ship for Constantinople and purchased a palace there. *I will be here when Tristan arrives in the spring to make final preparations for the final march east,* she had decided, *far from the reach of Odo de Lagery and the Benedictines . . . and we shall see whether God has purposely thrown Tristan and I together since childhood into this impossible knot of unrequited love, or whether he means for us to overcome together the rigid, intolerable barriers of Gregorian reform.*

Tristan and Guillaume, despite full intentions of marching east with the great massing armies of Christian cursaders heeding Pope Urban's call, would become entangled instead in the most bizarre war expedition of all recorded history—The Peasants's Cursade . . . a murderous and suicidal march led by Peter the Hermit across the continent of Europe into Turkish territory to reclaim the Holy Land.

But, as concerns the arduous struggle of Tristan, Mala, Guillaume and the Danes to reach Jerusalem, the Christian crusaders, the Seljuq Turks, and the horrific bloodletting unleased by Christians and Muslims alike as the First Holy Crusade begins to unfold . . . that is an entirely different story called *A Horde of Fools.*

ABOUT THE AUTHOR

Robert E. Hirsch was born in Pusan, Korea, in 1949. In 1953, Hirsch's mother sent him to the United States to live with his biological father due to Korea's harsh wartime conditions. He spent the next thirteen years as a military dependent, traveling all over America and passing three years in France, where he attended school at a French lycée.

Hirsch graduated from Cameron University in Lawton, Oklahoma, and began teaching French and social studies. He retired in 2012 after forty years, having served during his career as a teacher, principal, and superintendent. Hirsch has lived with his wife, Melissa, in Ocean Springs, Mississippi, along the Gulf Coast, since 1980.

THE DARK AGES SAGA OF TRISTAN DE SAINT-GERMAIN

FROM OPEN ROAD MEDIA

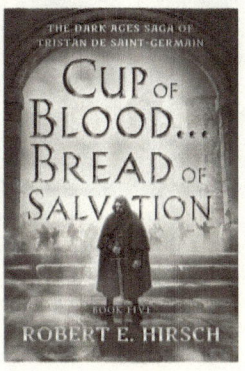

OPEN ROAD

INTEGRATED MEDIA

Find a full list of our authors and titles at www.openroadmedia.com

FOLLOW US
@OpenRoadMedia